1984: British Pop's Dividing Year

David Elliott

Dedicated to Liz, Alyssa and Naomi

First published in the UK by York House Books
© David Elliott 2020

A CIP catalogue record for this book is available from the British Library.
ISBN: 9781527272187
Cover designed by Wolfgang Fenchel
www.davidelliott.org

Printed and bound, a mile from the author's home, by SRP.
Printed on 400gsm Respecta Satin (cover) and 120gsm Inspira (text), PEFC certified as coming from a sustainable source. All waste paper is collected from their factory and recycled.

The tune had been haunting London for weeks past. It was one of countless similar songs published for the benefit of the proles by a sub-section of the Music Department. The words of these songs were composed without any human intervention whatever on an instrument known as a versificator. But the woman sang so tunefully as to turn the dreadful rubbish into an almost pleasant sound.

George Orwell *Nineteen Eighty-Four*

Contents

Preface

I was of that lucky generation whose late teens and college days coincided with punk and post-punk. I devoured the weekly music papers and at college did what many music-obsessives fired up by punk's DIY ethos did: started a fanzine, ran a cassette label and formed a group. My niche was electronic music, ranging from krautrock to industrial, but in that captivating 80s dawn was also in thrall to post-punk and new pop.

In 1984 I moved to London. It felt like a new beginning. January ushered in the 20th anniversary of Top Of The Pops, the Beeb banned 'Relax', Madonna made her UK television debut at the Hacienda and Einstürzende Neubauten and friends attempted to drill through the stage of the ICA. In the broader media world, Apple introduced the Macintosh personal computer, Sky launched Britain's first cable TV station and George Orwell started appearing in shop windows across the land. It looked like it was going to be an interesting year.

I started freelancing for Sounds – album and live reviews, the occasional feature. I felt incredibly lucky, getting into gigs for free, seeing Simple Minds and Test Dept one week, Cocteau Twins and Nick Cave the next, and coming home with an armful of albums from the weekly visits to the paper's office which at the time was above Covent Garden tube station. It was exciting living in London in 1984: ZTT's year of fun, the Frankie Say T-shirts, going to warehouse parties. But it was also a year of tension: the miners' strike, record levels of unemployment, the Troubles in Northern Ireland, the Brighton bombing, the Libyan Embassy siege in St James's Square, and a sense that something (more than just my innocence) was coming to an end.

A few years later the day job took over and much later, at the end of the 90s, I moved to Tokyo. It was there that the year started gnawing away at me. It slowly became a 'thing', compiling mixtapes, sharing them with friends. Then, around about the year I left Japan, three books came out in quick succession: Ian Glasper's *Burning Britain, UK Punk 1980-1984*, Simon Reynolds' *Rip It Up and Start Again: Post Punk 1978-1984* and Martin Lilleker's *Beats Working For A Living: Sheffield Popular Music 1973-1984*. Their end-of-an-era titles seemed to confirm my suspicions that the year was somehow 'important', but still it remained just a personal interest. Then in 2012, Graham Smith's *We Can Be Heroes, Clubland 1976-1984* was published. I think that's what did it. What was it about 1984? A couple of years later I started researching and then writing this book in parallel with my day job which for most of the time has been overseas, which gave me a helpful external perspective.

One of the pleasurable things about popular music is reading and talking about it. You can try and be objective but before you know it, sooner or later, subjectivity puts a spanner in the works. I could spend hours waxing lyrical about David Sylvian's

1

Brilliant Trees, The Blue Nile's debut album and Cocteau Twins' *Treasure,* while a friend cannot understand why I've never really embraced The Smiths or The Jesus and Mary Chain, or why I prefer Les Disques du Crépuscule to the records of Creation. So, of course subjectivity has played its part in the writing of this book, which is less about a Top 10 that looks like this:

> Frankie Goes To Hollywood, *Welcome to the Pleasuredome,* Wham! *Make It Big,* Sade *Diamond Life,* Howard Jones *Human's Lib*, Madonna *Like A Virgin,* Prince *Purple Rain,* Bruce Springsteen *Born in the USA*, Nik Kershaw *The Riddle,* Thompson Twins *Into the Gap*, The Smiths *The Smiths*

and more one that looks like this:

> David Sylvian *Brilliant Trees,* Cocteau Twins *Treasure,* U2 *The Unforgettable Fire,* Depeche Mode *Some Great Reward*, Nick Cave *From Her to Eternity,* This Mortal Coil *It'll End in Tears,* Echo & The Bunnymen *Ocean Rain,* The Blue Nile *A Walk Across the Rooftops,* Bill Nelson *Trial by Intimacy,* Coil *Scatology*

although there's room for both.

A word about the word 'pop'. I'm using it in the broadest sense of popular music, including rock. I thought long and hard about using 'popular music' or 'rock and pop' in the book's title but it was a bit of a mouthful. Suffice it to say, the book covers everything from Top Of The Pops regulars to Nurse With Wound. Which brings me on to genres. One of the things I wanted to do was cover the artists who usually get left out of 80s appraisals. So, alongside the usual suspects – the ones who appeared on *Now That's What I Call Music* compilations at the time and *Best of the 80s* box sets since – are artists as diverse as Shriekback and The Shillelagh Sisters. I also wanted to deal with bands which weren't post-punk or post-punk influenced (although so many were). So the jazz revival gets a chapter, as does heavy metal, and British soul and reggae share another. The more experimental, 'industrial' acts (these days often termed 'England's Hidden Reverse') are grouped together, as are the difficult to pigeon-hole artists who were neither old nor new wave, from Kate Bush and Bill Nelson to David Sylvian and Brian Eno. It was clear almost from the start that Scotland deserved its own chapter and, in consequence, also the Irish and Welsh scenes. Folk is touched upon in various chapters, but as a mainstream force it was largely AWOL in the 80s – certainly in comparison with the crossover appeal it had enjoyed in the previous decade and its 'revival' in more recent years.

This is a book about the cusp between one era and another, in Britain. There *are,* however, a couple of chapters on America, the two scenes having such a symbiotic relationship – the Second British Invasion going one way, hip-hop and dance culture the other – although at 17 pages it is almost an insult. Also, I couldn't resist a highly selective summary of Australian, mainland European and Japanese links to the UK scene.

Other 'year' books – Jon Savage's *1966* and David Hepworth's *1971*, for example, both of which came out as I was writing this – adopt a month-by-month approach, but I've gone for genres interspersed with chapters on music videos, sleeve design, music on radio and television (crucial in an era before Spotify and YouTube), pop's important interplay with politics, the equally pivotal role of technology (especially the shift from analogue to digital), the influential music press, and record labels – and not *just* the cool independent ones, but also the role of the majors and the sometimes blurred distinction between the two. There's the ever-present danger of duplication. Simple Minds are covered more in the Make It Big chapter and rather less in the one about Scotland; music's response to the Troubles in Northern Ireland is dealt with in both Chapters 6 and 10; and where to put Queen? Oh, don't tempt me.

If this has resulted in a book that is 'listy', bordering on OCD absoluteness, then it was a conscious decision. There's a good chance you'll find your favourites in here, whether it's ABC or Anhrefn, David Bowie or Dennis Bovell, Culture Club or Cardiacs.

*****

Thanks go to the following for reading various drafts, permission to use pictures or extended quotes, fresh quotes specific to the book, publishing advice, and general encouragement: Kenneth Ansell, Neil Arthur, Stuart Bailie, Tom Bromley, Elvera Butler, Cortina Butler, Iain Campbell, Thomas Dolby, John Doran at The Quietus, Eugene Doyen, Sam Dutton, Andy Earl, Mark Ellen, Rudi Esch, Terry Farley, Yuka Fujii, Philip Hoare, Andrew Hulme, Andrew Jackson, David Johnson, David Laurie, Stephen Lowe, John Massouri, Mick Mercer, Martin Newell, James Nice, Rickard Osterlund, Jules Peters, Michael Pollard, Simon Reynolds, John Robb, Bernard Rose, Greg Selby, Graham Stanton, David Stubbs, Brett Sullivan, Gee Vaucher, Laurence Verfaillie, John Waters, Don Watson and Paul Woods. Particular thanks go to Simon Pound for rectifying a whole series of formatting glitches near the end and to Wolfgang Fenchel for his excellent cover design and advice throughout. Apologies for any omissions.

The book is dedicated with love and gratitude to Liz who arrived in my life just as the 80s finished and shares a love of much of its music (though maybe not Nurse With Wound); and to our daughters Alyssa and Naomi who not only tolerate fairly constant Spotify playlists from yesteryear but have made sure I keep up with the present.

Introduction

The 80s continue to be reviewed, reissued, reassessed and occasionally reviled. Since the new millennium there has been a constant flow of revival tours and festivals; innumerable compilations of the known and unknown; a wave of new bands who sound like their 80s antecedents, using analogue synths or copycat plug-ins; new, niche magazines like Classic Pop; and of course the vinyl revival shows no sign of abating.

Much of the attention tends to focus on the early part of the decade, when post-punk and new pop was at its height, or the very end, as dance and rave took over. Its mid-period is remembered by some as being a bit naff: Band/Live Aid, gated drums, the early hi-NRG hit factory sound of Stock Aitken Waterman, *Absolute Beginners*, Bowie's Glass Spider tour, soft rock, terrible fashion, worse haircuts. And it's true, 1985 and 1986 were probably guilty as charged. But it was also a time when everything was in flux. 1984 was the whole of the 80s rolled into one year. It was British popular music's great divide: the end of synthpop and 'artifice' and the re-introduction of guitars and 'authenticity'; the passing of the baton from post-punk to indie; the shift from analogue to digital; the last British invasion of the US charts; and with Band Aid, the beginning of popular music's obsession with global causes; the beginning of the end of vinyl and the end of the beginning of CDs (although nowadays, incredibly, it seems to be increasingly the other way round).

Arguably – literally – it was British rock and pop's most politicized year, responding to the miners' strike, the Troubles in Northern Ireland and record unemployment, alongside the wider global divisions of capitalism versus socialism, and the cold war. Rock and pop also played a significant role in renewed efforts to tighten the screws on Apartheid South Africa, and of course there was pop's compassionate and unprecedented response to the famine in Ethiopia. At the heart of the division was Margaret Thatcher. Following victory in the Falklands in 1982 and a landslide election the following year, 1984 was the year she exerted her authority. You either embraced her view of an entrepreneurial, capitalist future or opposed it. Very few musicians openly supported her policies, and those who did were mercilessly lampooned by the left-wing music press. It was tempting to see new pop as right wing or at least agnostic, and post-punk as lefties, but the reality was a lot more complicated.

As was whether the fictional *Nineteen Eighty-Four* might project itself onto the real 1984. There were some similarities – not least the threat of nuclear armageddon, the increasing number of CCTV cameras appearing on Britain's streets, and the Orwellian ad which Ridley Scott shot to launch Apple's Macintosh home computer. But in the end it was Orwell's own haunted face, rather than Big Brother's, that gazed from reprints, bookshop windows and television documentaries. There were also two feature film interpretations: Michael Radford's *1984* and Terry Gilliam's (initially named) *1984½*. Both were filmed during the year, although the former's autumn premiere forced Gilliam to retitle his *Brazil* for release the following year. Both also featured major pop artists: Eurythmics and Kate Bush respectively (although Bush's recording of the theme song was not, in the end, used[1]).

By 1984 pop was 30 years old and 'mature', even if – when watching Top Of The Pops – it still seemed (somehow reassuringly) *im*mature. As it aged, it created, borrowed and stole so that by the early 80s it was an art-form that was extraordinarily rich and influential. Other art-forms made their own leaps and bounds too but – fashion aside – none, in Britain at least, had such a direct, symbiotic relationship with youth. By the early 80s popular music was a hybrid of rock, soul, blues, folk, ska, reggae, punk, metal, prog, jazz, funk, disco, hip-hop and even the avant-garde. Not in a single song (as far as I know, it has never been tried!), but across the artists and bands that had, year-on-year, been added to pop's pantheon.

By the mid-80s, thanks to punk's DIY creed, there were hundreds – nay, thousands – of groups and solo artists plying their trade across the country (500 are mentioned in this book alone). Not just pub or bedroom bands, but releasing records, making videos, touring internationally, being written about in the music press and forging 'careers'. This was very different from the 60s or most of the 70s when, if you wanted to be in a band, it was assumed you had to be a proficient musician and pay your dues. Then, releasing a record was a mysterious process which many performing bands didn't understand or were even party to. There were hardly any independent labels and there was no culture of doing it yourself. Punk changed that. At the same time, pop and rock embraced new technology, and lyrically it revelled in politics. 1984 was probably the last year when you could find such diversity in the charts. For the rest of the 80s and 90s it became, if not middle-aged, then risk averse, dance-oriented and more alike[2].

Up to the mid-80s, pop music had almost single-handedly defined pop culture. Britain's youth obsessed about records, had a choice of seven weekly music papers[3] and stayed in on Thursday and Friday evenings for Top Of The Pops and The Tube. Thereafter it had competition. The internet and social media were still some way off, but music programmes started to be replaced by 'yoof' programmes (ushered in, on BBC at least, by Janet Street Porter); videos (bought and rented) opened up home entertainment; and basic computer games and a nascent computer culture were making in-roads into the nation's consciousness[4].

The introduction of music videos was hugely influential. As Mark Ellen told me: 'That was the key change. Up until then groups had hits by playing live and building an audience big enough to buy enough of their singles to earn them a place on Top Of The Pops. When videos arrived, they didn't have to be able to perform them onstage, merely mime them on film, just look colourful and interesting, and thus a whole new species of pop group flooded the market.'[5] But it was difficult to do well in pop if you weren't a pretty face. In rock you could get away with it, but not in pop. To pop's young, fickle audience, it mattered whether your image was more Michael than Joe Jackson.

Alongside the new peacock culture was a slightly misplaced new patriotism which grew in intensity in the early 80s. Each event, however, came with a paradox: the launch of the Mini Metro in 1980, 'a British car to beat the world' promoted by a we-shall-fight-them-on-the-beaches ad – despite the fact that it was much less iconographic than the Mini it was designed to replace and the British car industry was in steady decline; the pomp and splendour of the Royal Wedding – despite its ill-matched bride and groom and the riots that raged in a number of cities that summer; Liverpool's footballing dominance in Europe – despite English hooliganism which was also at its peak; the Oscar-winning *Chariots of Fire* and *Gandhi* – despite the fact that the British film industry was actually in crisis; a trade surplus in 1980 and '81 – despite the daily lists of redundancies on the news, somberly read out as if they were wartime casualties; and of course the victory in the Falklands War in 1982, the patriotic moment to top them all – despite the moral ambiguities of that particular adventure. Much of the sentiment was actually about looking back to the more certain times of Empire and dreaming spires – 'reactionary chic' as Peter York put it.

Pop's new-found optimism, however, was not misplaced. This was its self-assured, 'imperial' phase: the brightening of new wave with synths and strings, fretless bass, funk and fun, and the Second British 'Invasion' of America. It was confident and glamorous. It even attracted royal patronage (Princess Diana was a Duran Duran fan). And yet, for all the make-up, hair, shoulder pads and general frivolity, pop was no longer so naive. It became ambitious and much more business-like, echoing Time magazine's more general naming of 1984 as 'The Year of the Yuppie'[6]. Earlier, Heaven 17 had started appearing in suits and ties in front of boardroom tables: 'The new partnership that's opening doors all over the world'. It was ironic (just) and not new – PiL had even called themselves a limited company back in 1978, donned suits for the cover of their first album and talked of records being just one aspect of activity – but now bands started actually reading their recording contracts and setting up merchandising and publishing companies almost before they played a gig. Even Bowie, tired of being in the (relatively) impecunious vanguard, got serious and suited for the massively successful Serious Moonlight tour in 1983.

Critics pointed to the mid-80s as being the high point of postmodernism. Except no-one could agree what postmodernism meant, much less when it began or ended. Was it ironic pastiche? Sampling from the past? The opposite of high, elitist arts, therefore low, inclusive arts? In music it was hard to define. You could say that *all* popular music was/is postmodern, especially that which plunders (samples) the past, which most does. Modernism was beyond style, but for postmodernism style was everything. Indeed style, in 1984, became something people preferred to buy rather than create. At the top end, Yohji Yamamoto and Comme Des Garcons arrived on London's South

Molton Street, while on the High Street George Davies was made Chief Executive of NEXT offering stylish clothes to wear in Habitat dining rooms. But perhaps the biggest lifestyle change was the introduction of café culture, starting in London but soon to take hold throughout the country, as noted by Richard Elms. 'All we'd known was dodgy old boozers and crappy caffs and suddenly in 1984 we had this. The Soho Brasserie was ultra-cool in the laid-back continental style, and it was aimed not at fat businessmen but at bright young things. […] Nick Logan conspiring with Tony Parsons, Peter York lunching with Julie Burchill. […I]t wasn't like we were in London. It was like we were in some bourgeois, comfortable European city. […] It was the start of something'[7]. Also in Soho, work started on transforming an old Italian restaurant into The Groucho Club. Food, generally, underwent a revolution. Sandwiches were transformed from stale, white Mothers-Pride-and-paste affairs which curled up at the edges to multigrain brown stuffed with coronation chicken and rocket. We became the kiwi fruit generation. We started buying bottled water instead of drinking it free from a tap. What we ate became a lifestyle choice as much as a nutritional one.

Narcissistic new pop – termed new romanticism – may have peaked in 1982 but two years later there was still a definite romance in pop. It just got more grandiose. Songs were embellished with lush strings (real and electronic), arrangements filled out, productions became bigger. And, if you'll forgive the pun, the 12-inch ruled[8]. Extended and remixed versions of singles became *de rigeur*, usually collected with a couple of extra non-album tracks. The single could then be kept in the charts with yet more remixes. Singles were the big thing in Britain in 1984 with six of them being million-sellers, the first time that had ever happened. (The rest of the decade saw only one song, Jennifer Rush's 'The Power of Love' in 1985, hit the million mark).[9]

Fashion too remained opulent, filling the style magazines which were now aimed at men as much as women. Vivienne Westwood had gone from ripped and torn to lustrous and upmarket. Men – well, *some* men, gay and hetero – became sensitive, metrosexuals bearing their souls. Actually, it wasn't so much romantic, more glamorously asexual. These 'haircuts', as they were known in the US, made up the majority of the so-called Second British Invasion which reached its peak in 1984. In January, Boy George and Annie Lennox made the front cover of Newsweek, its headline 'Britain Rocks – Again', but it might as well have been 'Which One's the Boy'? A year later, in January 1985, Life magazine's lead story was 'Gender Benders: The Year of Living Androgynously'.

Indeed, androgyny in both rock and pop was probably at its peak. Boy George was cuddly, sexless and harmless, someone even your parents wouldn't mind, although his agenda was more about encouraging mainstream Britain to accept effeminate men rather than overtly championing homosexuality. Marilyn was prettier than George but less talented. Annie Lennox toyed with the suits and short hair, even dressing up as Elvis Presley at the Grammy Awards. Pete Burns was in your face weird-sexy. Even the aptly-named Queen – who'd arrived in the glammed-up early 70s but then retreated into, on the face of it, hairy, hetero rock – upped the camp quotient in the

7

video of 'I Want To Break Free'.

Women's place in mid-80s rock and pop was much the same as in other industries – subjugated. Punk and new wave had empowered some female artists (Siouxsie Sioux, Poly Styrene, Lene Lovich, Toyah Wilcox, Hazel O'Connor, Chrissie Hynde) and the mini-scene of ramshackle post-punk girl-groups. But new pop and the video age, with its emphasis on image, was actually a backward step for women. Some used it to their advantage: Annie Lennox and Kate Bush made videos on their own terms (both, interestingly, acting out male characters in 'Who's That Girl?' and 'Cloudbusting'); Siouxsie and Sade projected themselves as icy cool and untouchable; others like Alison Moyet and Bonnie Tyler simply got on with the music, putting up with video as a necessary requirement. Girl groups were few and far between[10]. Four of them – The Belle Stars, Dolly Mixture, The Raincoats and Belle and the Devotions – all split in 1984, leaving the field wide open for, if not Dawn Chorus and the Blue Tits (a trio formed that year by Carol Vorderman, Liz Kershaw and Lindsay Forrest, the first two going on to become major TV and radio presenters) then Bananarama who would become the most successful all-female group ever, in terms of global charting singles[11]. On the one hand they had shifted from ditsy chancers to nobody's fools, but on the other would move from charmingly casual to Stock Aitken Waterman marionettes. In 1984 they were still beguilingly rough around the edges, and everywhere, including part of Band Aid. In the US that year it was all very different: Madonna and Cyndi Lauper, Laura Branigan and Jennifer Rush all projected strong images of womanhood, particularly in the videos; as did American girl groups like The Go-Gos (on their way out) and The Bangles (on their way in). And of course the powerful posse of Tina Turner and Chaka Khan (both enjoying re-launched careers), Deniece Williams, The Pointer Sisters and a debut single by Whitney Houston ensured that it wasn't just white women taking control. By contrast, the year saw very few black female singers making waves on this side of the Atlantic.

Inventive, alternative singles still populated the charts. There were hit songs about sado-masochism, swimming horses, caterpillars and a character from a 1920s German expressionist film[12], another borrowed from a 1970 Chilean political campaign sung half in English, half in Spanish[13]; The Smiths released two songs referencing child abuse, and there were two gloriously catchy Fairlight-drenched songs about heroin, by the same artist, within a few months of each other[14]. Punk svengali Malcolm McLaren turned to opera, The Fall teamed up with dancer Michael Clark, and David Sylvian went from pop pin-up to auteur. Half the charts seemed to be politically oriented. Bronski Beat's 'Smalltown Boy' was arguably the most important song of 1984, if not the 80s, in bringing LGBT issues to the fore, and although AIDS was not directly referenced in songs, pop played its part in bringing it into the public consciousness.

There was no one 'big thing'. Punk, disco, new romanticism and ska were over; post-punk was about to give way to indie; there were jazz and psychedelia revivals; even a short-lived craze for psychobilly and cowpunk. White pop appropriation of black music was widespread, while to a lesser extent black music (especially hip-hop) was starting to plunder heavy white rock. Genres like underground and progressive rock, which had split from pop in the late 60s and early 70s to become album-oriented, returned to the singles charts, most rather unsuccessfully, although Yes and Genesis found a whole new audience this way.

1984 was the year when recording and consuming music started the move from analogue to digital, and the beginnings of a shift from vinyl to compact discs. The first CD had gone on sale in Japan in 1982 but it wasn't until Bruce Springsteen's *Born in the USA* became the first CD album to be manufactured in the US in September 1984 and Dire Straits' *Brothers in Arms* sold its first million in early 1985 that pop embraced the format. It was a slow, quiet revolution, and would take until 1993 for CD sales to surpass those of vinyl or cassettes. What the CD failed to address, however, was the whole issue of portability, a factor which extended the life of the humble cassette until the new millennium and the introduction of the iPod.

In parallel, the tools that made and recorded the sounds were also switching to digital. Analogue synthesizers made way for digital versions, drum-machines and samplers. Samplers were key for they ushered in a new era in which singers, songwriters and instrumentalists could be usurped by producers and DJs. Producers like Trevor Horn and Steve Lillywhite ruled the roost, while the year also saw Stock Aitken Waterman set up their Hit Factory. Concert technology also progressed in leaps and bounds with giant sets and screens starting to become central to the arena rock experience[15].

Arenas were about to become the venue of choice for many bands. In truth, sheds like Wembley Arena, Earls Court and the NEC in Birmingham had been hosting the biggest bands since the 70s, but the 80s saw the beginning of medium-sized ones skipping the more traditional Odeons and Gaumonts and focusing on the bigger venues in fewer cities. Financially it made more sense, even if the atmosphere was often lacking, the acoustics questionable and the fans had to travel further. And for those who were serious about cracking America, arenas were mandatory. The term 'arena rock' came to define a genre of music, embracing bands like U2 and Simple Minds but also the radio-friendly heavy metal and 'epic' soft rock of scores of American bands. It was about anthemic riffs, power ballads and strident choruses, about writing music specifically for huge audiences.

Central to arena rock was the guitar. For a while its supremacy had been under threat from the synth-heavy Second British Invasion. But as 1984 progressed, many American bands favoured regression, a reinstatement of the guitar to its rightful position as rock's foremost instrument. It symbolized authenticity, a return to America's proud rock heritage. There was a backlash in Britain too. Synthpop acts were fast becoming endangered species, with Morrissey and Alan McGee quick to put the boot in and usher in the guitar-fronted indie era. And yet, for all the talk of 'authenticity', of returning to rock's roots, most mainstream pop and rock would be utterly transformed by technology, the guitars and drums augmented or usurped by Yamaha DX7s and Fairlights, to create a homogenous, radio-and-arena-friendly sonic whole.

Of course there was a lot of rubbish too: Black Lace, Roland Rat, Jo Fagin, Shakey, Steve Wright; 70 stars like Alvin Stardust, Sweet and Slade trying to remain relevant; gimmick-hits by Neil and Toy Dolls; tedious soft rock by the likes of Chicago, Toto and Foreigner; and (pointlessly) bracketed song titles seemed to go into overdrive. As Giles Smith wrote in *Lost in Music*: 'When people complain that the charts are full of crap, they forget one crucial thing: that even when they were brilliant, the charts were full of crap. Crap is what the charts are made to be full of.'[16] But the charts are important, and always have been. They are the barometer of popular taste and ultimately anyone making a pop record will want to get it into the fabled top whatever. There is no other art form, apart from books and films to a much lesser extent, where charts play such an important role in measuring 'success' – particularly of singles. Their influence was huge from the 60s to the 90s, but into the new millennium they rather lost their meaning, especially when Top Of The Pops ceased to be. Reading these lines now, and regardless of your age, who's #1 in the charts this week?

So, let's look at this fascinating year. A year Paul Morley described as 'one made up of beauty, yearning, strangeness and an implicit promise of fantastic adventure... [a year] that is not often considered in the usual histories of the decade, but in the middle – or at the edge – of all the excess...'[17]

Chapter 1: Make It Big
From new pop to arena rock

If we stay in small clubs, we'll develop small minds, and then we'll start making small music. [1]
Bono, U2

It was a pivotal year. Everything rotated around 1984 in the 80s. Quite a changing point, I think culturally as well [...], everything was larger than life. [2]
Jon Moss, Culture Club

Pretentious? I should jolly well think so. [3]
Nick Rhodes, Duran Duran

After punk came new wave and post-punk. The former popularized punk's three-minute salvos, softened their edges and made them radio-friendly; the latter retained punk's angst while at the same time experimenting with structure and instrumentation. It wasn't as black and white as that, and indeed both still shared a certain monochromatic sensibility – not least in fashion: the cheap black suits, skinny ties and long overcoats. Then, around 1980, new wave fragmented into synthpop and the dandyish new romantic scene, influenced by Berlin-era Bowie (and a European aesthetic generally), Roxy Music and synthesizers, which in turn quickly became new pop[4].

For the most part, post-punk thought fairly small, recording in cramped studios on independent labels, while new pop was more ambitious with big productions in big studios on big labels with big budgets. Simple Minds' *New Gold Dream 81-82-83-84* typified new pop *and* nailed the dates, but other examples were Human League's *Dare,* Japan's *Tin Drum,* ABC's *Lexicon of Love,* Duran Duran's *Rio.* The rise of the 12-inch single was also important. Although originally meant for DJs, the larger format was perfect for the wide-screen ambition of new pop, and by 1984 accounted for nearly a third of all singles sales. Cracking America also required artists to think and sound scaled-up, reflected in album titles: *Make It Big* and *Arena.* Even Echo & The Bunnymen, who were somewhere between post-punk and new pop, got in on the act with *Ocean Rain.* But for sheer brazenness, Yello's *You Gotta Say Yes to Another Excess* couldn't be bettered.

Of the many groups who might claim the year as theirs, pride of place must surely go to Frankie Goes to Hollywood. They existed before and after, but it centred absolutely on one hyped-up, action-packed, roller-coaster of a year. The five lads from Liverpool – two gay frontmen, three straight musicians – had arrived via a plethora of short-lived, post-punk bands, one of them – Big In Japan – big enough to have fostered not only Holly Johnson but also Budgie, Bill Drummond, David Balfe and Ian Broudie, key figures all, despite only recording seven songs.

11

Like many of the cast of 1984, William Johnson had been a Bowie-boy and then a punk. The Holly moniker came from sex-change Warhol starlet Holly Woodlawn, as name-checked in Lou Reed's 'Walk on the Wild Side'. Aside from being in bands, he'd also released two unnoticed solo singles, 'Yankee Rose' and 'Hobo Joe'. After the demise of Big In Japan, Johnson joined forces with brothers Mark and Jed O'Toole (the latter soon to be replaced by Brian Nash) and Peter Gill and they became Frankie Goes To Hollywood, named after a Sinatra headline in the New Yorker. A little later, Paul Rutherford joined on backing vocals and dancing (aping, coincidentally or not, Human League's enrolling of Joanne Catherall and Susanne Sulley and, unbeknownst to most people at the time, Happy Mondays' drafting of Bez). It was this gay/straight line-up that provided a certain tension.

From the very start, Frankie courted controversy, gigging and partying in their black S&M fetishware in select northern clubs. Finally they were invited to record four songs for a Peel Session in October 1982 and perform another song, 'Relax', in an empty Liverpool State Ballroom for broadcast on Channel 4's The Tube. We were now into early 1983 and they still hadn't made a record. But nor had they gone unnoticed. Trevor Horn had seen them on The Tube and thought they might be right for a new label, ZTT, he was setting up. Apparently it took some convincing of his A&R partner, Paul Morley, but before long they were signed up and ushered into Sarm West studio in London.

'Relax' had innuendo in spades but it was still a fairly basic club number and might have remained so in any other producer's hands. What Horn did was turn it into a thumping, grinding slab of aural sex. However, it still took nearly three months to slowly make its way up the charts, and it wasn't until 5 January 1984, when they performed it on Top Of The Pops, that it rose from #35 to #6. Only then did Radio One's Mike Read suddenly notice the sleeve and lyrics, declare the record obscene and decide not to play it any more. The rest of the BBC followed suit (and for the record, Smash Hits refused to publish the lyrics). Of course it went straight to number one and stayed there for five weeks.

As 'Relax' eventually slipped out of the charts, out came their second single at the end of May – and so began the summer of Frankie. 'Two Tribes' was on the one hand a straight-forward anti-war song, on the other a ringside seat to witness the showdown. If 'Relax' was big-production, 'Two Tribes' was gargantuan. It had everything: a walloping beat, orchestral explosions, sirens, government nuclear warning advice, a video featuring Reagan and Chernenko lookalikes wrestling in a ring, and endless 12-inch remixes (the only format that could possibly do it justice), all of which kept it at the top of the charts for nine consecutive weeks, with 'Relax' surging back up to #2 to keep it company.

With the Cold War at its height, the timing was spot on. Many people genuinely thought a Third World War was imminent. The threat might have put people off buying 'Two Tribes', but not so. Anti-war songs are often sombre, cerebral affairs but

'Two Tribes' was exhilarating and physical. And the point about Frankie was that they were scallywags. You knew that they were basically just having a laugh. As was Ronald Reagan on 11 August ('Two Tribes'' last day at #1) when he jokingly announced in a radio soundcheck: 'My fellow Americans, I'm pleased to tell you today that I've signed legislation that will outlaw Russia forever. We begin bombing in five minutes.' It wasn't real, and nor was *Threads*, a BBC docudrama broadcast a month later, about the likely effects of a nuclear attack on northern England, but it just went to show how real many people thought the possibility was.

On a lighter note, there were the Frankie Say T-shirts. Come summer they were everywhere. The idea wasn't new: fashion designer Katherine Hamnett had created the sloganeering line of big black letters on white T-shirts the previous year, and famously wore one which screamed '58% Don't Want Pershing' when she met Margaret Thatcher at a Downing Street reception in February 1984. And in Wham!'s 'Wake Me Up Before You Go-Go' video, 'Choose Life' was emblazoned on crisp white Ts, showing off tanned torsos. Paul Morley simply appropriated the idea as a piece of Frankie PR and before you could say Relax Don't Do It, they were everywhere. Frankie Say War, Hide Yourself; Frankie Say Arm The Unemployed; Frankie Say Relax is a Four Letter Word. It's estimated that about three quarters of them were pirated by the East End rag trade.

And then there was the album, a thing of pure unadulterated indulgence. Amongst Morley's interminable, mad-as-a-hatter sleeve notes, most of which had nothing to do with the band or the music, was an imagined chat between Frankie and ZTT: 'Hey, Zang. Yes, Frankie? Let's make it a double. It'll be a pleasure'. But it wasn't. Frankie were essentially a singles band, albeit ones that rejoiced in the 12-inch form and endless remixes. *Welcome to the Pleasure Dome* comprised both singles and their B-sides, two more singles-to-come (one of which was the title track which tried hard to fill up all of side one), three cover versions and a few other bits and bobs. 'A single LP stretched over four sides' was how Smash Hits put it. Still, it included a mail-order form via which you could order a plethora of Frankie merchandise, such as Jean Genet Boxer Shorts, Virginia Woolf Vests and Edith Sitwell Bags, just in time for Christmas.

For all of Frankie's vague socialist roots and radical lyrics, the PR machinations were becoming positively Thatcherite, designed to fleece the fans: myriad versions of the same song, make it a double, the silly merchandise. The band always seemed to be smirking, as if they were in cahoots with the con or, more likely, they couldn't believe their luck. And who *were* the fans? Were they girls, guys, gays? The traditional pop fan fancies their idols or has some close connection with the lyrics or thinks their music is good to dance to. Frankie undoubtedly had admirers in all three areas, but ultimately they may have been regarded simply as a good laugh. Like Slade perhaps.

There was a third #1 single in December, the surprisingly beautiful 'The Power of Love' ("The only good song I've written", opined Johnson[5]) but as the clock struck midnight at the end of the year, the fun and magic disappeared in a puff of hyperbole.

Early in 1985, the album's title track was announced as "the fourth no.1 single", even before it was released. When it only made #2 (itself astonishing given that everyone already had it), the game was up. There were squabbles with ZTT and within the band, a surprisingly good UK tour, a not very good second album and it was all over by early 1987. In the accounts of Frankie you're more likely to read the names of Horn and Morley than the names of the band members. They were peddled like a traditional 60s band with a one-sided contract and not much say in how they were marketed. But it was a wild and rollicking adventure and certainly without Horn they wouldn't have sounded half as good and probably wouldn't have made the charts. It's a familiar story. A struggling band, unwise to (and usually uninterested in) the small print, seduced by the allure of fame and fortune.

Give 'em enough rope. Paul Rutherford and George Michael get nautical.

Meanwhile in north-west London, school friends George Michael and Andrew Ridgley had formed Wham! in 1982 and, like Frankie Goes To Hollywood, the pair signed a similarly 'iffy' contract with an independent label, Innervision. Their rise was fast and it was clear that Michael, particularly, had real talent. With their first four singles all going Top 10, their advance of £500 each and royalties of just 8 per cent of UK albums and singles (and even worse for those sold in the US)[6] looked as bad as it was. What's more, Innervision had signed an equally 'iffy' licensing deal with CBS, so both label and band were screwed. It took fabled manager Simon Napier-Bell to extricate Wham! from the mess and by March 1984 they were on CBS's Epic subsidiary on a far higher royalty rate and, in theory, ready to reap the dividends.

The matey, slightly political 'soul boy, dole boy' image offered by earlier singles 'Young Guns', 'Wham Rap!' and 'Bad Boys', had given way to the lighter, breezier confection of 1983's 'Club Tropicana'. But it was the following summer's chart-toppers which ushered in world domination. 'Wake Me Up Before You Go-Go' and Michael's debut solo release, 'Careless Whisper', established Wham! as a world-beating pop act and Michael as a precociously talented songwriter. 'Wake Me Up' may have borrowed extensively from Motown, but there was no denying that it was impeccably constructed, a guilty pleasure, a perfect piece of pop. Even arch aesthete Peter Saville, who designed the cover, was seduced. 'Careless Whisper' was the counter-balance. It was actually a much earlier composition but cannily held over until just the right moment. It has the poise and sophistication of a songsmith twice Michael's age (he turned 21 that summer), featured *that* sax solo[7] and one could almost imagine Bryan Ferry singing it. It promptly went to #1 in about 25 countries.

Autumn saw a return to Wham! with another single, 'Freedom', the *Make It Big* album (which, like Frankie's double, was full of singles and the rest filler), before rounding off the year with the double A-side 'Everything She Wants' / 'Last Christmas' – the latter painfully, deliciously twee, but trumped by that *other* Christmas single. Nevertheless, it could be argued that 1984 was as much Wham!'s year as Frankie's. It certainly established George Michael as a star. It was also a year in which Napier-Bell went to Beijing umpteen times to discuss arrangements for an international promo caper to top them all: the first western pop group to play in China, which duly took place in April the following year[8]. And soon after that they split up.

Wham! were not the only north London white soul boys with big pop ambitions. Spandau Ballet – brilliantly named, but perhaps better suited to another band – had their origins in the new romantic movement. But by 1983 they had traded in their dandy threads and funky European-sounding singles like 'To Cut a Long Story Short' and 'Chant No.1', for pastel suits and the smoother blue-eyed soul of singles 'True' and 'Gold' which reached #1 and #2 respectively. In 1984 the group was resting on its laurels, releasing their fourth album *Parade* at the end of May, followed by four Top 20 singles. It is customary to poo-poo Spandau. Yes, any edges had been softened by the time of *True*, and *Parade* was more of the same: a bit bland, a bit 1985. But first single 'Only When You Leave' was decent, and 'Highly Strung' wasn't exactly offensive.

Band rivalry has always been an essential ingredient of pop. The Beatles and The Stones, Bowie and Bolan, Oasis and Blur. Stoked (OK, made up) by the tabloids and band managers, but not exactly discouraged by the labels and the artists themselves, it was all a bit of fun. 1984 was no different. Ian McCulloch went on and on about how Echo & The Bunnymen were the greatest band in the world and *so* much better than U2 (to no avail); Morrissey's ego made Mac's look like Mother Theresa's; Lydon carped, Boy George bitched…. It was all good copy. The competition between Spandau Ballet and Duran Duran was a perfect example of the fairly friendly feud, taken to the logical conclusion of 'fighting it out' on TV's Pop Quiz at the very end of the year, which Duran won – a metaphor not lost on the great British public.

Duran Duran joined Frankie and Wham! in claiming 1984 as their own, despite the absence of a new studio album, which they made up for by milking their five-month long *Sing Blue Silver* world tour. Fed up with being regarded as a pretty-boy, MTV band, the year saw Duran projected as a rocking live band. The Nile Rodgers-remixed 'The Reflex' (possibly a song about masturbation, but an April #1 nevertheless on both sides of the Atlantic) came with a live promo featuring an audience *so* heated up that they had to be cooled down with a wave of water emanating from the stage. The bit when the animated 'tsunami' actually hits the panting, perspiring girls at the front – basically someone throwing a small bucket of water over them – inadvertently gives *Spinal Tap* a run for its money. But the song will mostly be remembered for its whining "Why-yi-yi-yi-yi-yi don't you use it / bruise it / don't lose it" refrain. The milking continued with a documentary film and book (both called *Sing Blue Silver*), a concert video and underwhelming live album (both called *Arena*), a made-for-TV version of the concert video (*As the Lights Go Down*); and a video EP, *Dancing on the Valentine*. The money was flowing in (merchandise alone made them millionaires many times over), but it was also flowing out thanks to the drugs, private jets, colossal hotel bills and, when they weren't on the road, fancy homes.

And then there was 'The Wild Boys'. It is now almost impossible to separate this song from its accompanying Russell Mulcahy-directed video – surely, at the time, the last word in pop visual excess. Filmed in Pinewood Studios, it was inspired by William Burroughs' 1971 novel, *The Wild Boys: A Book of the Dead*, though in the end looked like very expensive outtakes of *Mad Max 2*. (For a fuller description, see Chapter 4). It hardly mattered what the song itself was like, but 'bombastic' would be about right.

Whereas Spandau were beginning to look smart and almost conventional, Duran had become progressively unreal: the hair, the clothes, the make-up – all of which were very much in evidence when both Roger Taylor and Nick Rhodes got married that year, upstaging the hapless brides. Rhodes took polaroids of TV set interference in his hotel suites which resulted in an exhibition at the end of the year at London's Hamilton Gallery (where David Sylvian, whom Rhodes admired, if not idolised, had presented his own exhibition of figurative polaroids in the summer). Self-indulgence and excess reigned supreme. In March the Duran juggernaut rolled into New York to play two sell-out nights at Madison Square Gardens. In his book, *In the Pleasure Groove*, bassist John Taylor describes feeling like a 'A MASTER OF THE UNIVERSE' (his caps)[9], a term Tom Wolfe would use to describe Sherman McCoy, the anti-hero of his first novel *Bonfire of the Vanities* which began serialization in Rolling Stone – a music paper, interestingly – in July. One of the quintessential novels of the 80s, it was published in full three years later[10]. Ronald Reagan's landslide second term victory in November 1984 – echoing Thatcher's the year before – had ushered in a mid-80s wave of largely unfettered capitalism and nouveau-riche excess. McCoy, along with the Gordon Gecko character in the 1987 film *Wall Street,* became figureheads of the greed-is-good possibilities of making big, big bucks and the trappings that went with it, even if both got their come-uppance (the Stock Market too, on Black Monday in October 1987). As for Duran, guilty of excess if not hit-and-run or insider-training, the tears would come sooner, in 1985, the band splitting into two groups, Arcadia and

Power Station. They did re-group, however, and against all the odds managed to make it into the 90s and are still going even now.

*****

Meanwhile, back in the mundane midlands from which Duran had come, King were typical of the new, mid-80s groups who fell between Duran and Spandau. Formed by Paul King in Coventry in 1983 from the ashes of ska band Reluctant Stereotypes, their debut single 'Love and Pride' (April 1984) was a confident, ambitious start. However, it took a re-release nine months later to make it chart (impressively, at #2), by which time there was already an album, *Steps in Time*. Coming across like Tony Hadley and the child-catcher in *Chitty Chitty Bang Bang*, loud suits with spray-painted DMs, it looked likely that King would be chart mainstays, but second album 'Bitter Sweet' sounded like so much else and they split in 1986.

If Frankie were glam-punk, Wham! and Spandau London-soul, and Duran synth-funk, then Culture Club were a mix of soul and reggae. Or at least, that's how it began. George O'Dowd had been a new romantic, presiding over the cloakroom at Blitz (where he picked up his Boy George name) and living in Fitzrovia's squats[11]. Before long he was approached by Malcolm McLaren to join Bow Wow Wow but it didn't work out and soon he formed his own band with drummer Jon Moss, bassist Mikey Craig and guitarist Roy Hay. The group went through various names – In Praise Of Lemmings, Sex Gang Children, Caravan Club, Can't Wait Club – until finally settling on Culture Club. Boy George's connections and spectacular looks alone were probably enough to get them a record deal, but it turned out that he could sing. Really well.

By their third single, 'Do You Really Want To Hurt Me?', Culture Club were stars. Albums *Kissing To Be Clever* and *Colour By Numbers* both went Top 5 and 'Karma Chameleon' became the UK's biggest-selling single of 1983. The following year started well enough with 'Karma Chameleon' occupying #1 in the US charts for three consecutive weeks while 'Miss Me Blind' and 'It's A Miracle' (also from *Colour By Numbers*) both hit #4 in the UK. They were also becoming huge in Japan, a fact reflected in their sleeves, videos and of course Boy George apparel (he had worn kimonos at Blitz). But the constant touring, internal disagreements, drugs and Boy George's over-exposure in the media was beginning to have an effect. Autumn saw the release of 'The War Song', the earnest lyrics of which advised us that 'War is stupid' ('War is naughty' parodied Spitting Image) and in a video directed by – who else? – Russell Mulcahy we were treated to Boy George leading hundreds of kids in skeleton suits down Shad Thames with the band bringing up the rear perched upon a tank. There was even a Pink Floyd link: the wailing 'Great Gig in the Sky'-type vocals near the end were sung by Clare Torry, who did the honours on *Dark Side of the Moon*. It still made #2. The album that followed, *Waking Up With The House On Fire*, was mediocre even by their own admission. Thereafter Boy George fell from grace, his drug addiction and the band's in-fighting providing the backdrop to a long, painful death rattle. They would manage one more album before splitting up in 1987,

17

although, like so many bands in this book, the new century, and the 80s revival in particular, has seen them get back together on numerous occasions.

*****

Away from pure pop, but just as popular, U2 were looking for a new, bigger sound. They'd gone about as far as they could with Steve Lillywhite and his productions for *Boy, October* and *War*, in turns youthful, spiritual and heroic; now they wanted to be Important. And arty. They'd spent some time courting Brian Eno who was naturally cautious. Taking Bowie and Talking Heads into new directions was one thing, but what could he bring to U2? Were they open to the kind of change that Eno was renowned for? Of course, Bono's skills of persuasion won out and thus began an on-off collaboration that lasted for years and has been a major factor in the U2 success story. Part of the deal was to bring in Daniel Lanois with whom Eno had been working on ambient music for much of the early 80s. Lanois's job was the traditional producer's job of setting things up while Eno adopted a more strategic, conceptual role. U2 must have felt something significant was in the offing as during the recording they brought in a film crew to capture the process[12], this back in the days when 'making of' videos were still in their infancy. Sessions started off in Slane Castle in County Meath before moving back to Windmill Studios in Dublin.

So what was different about *The Unforgettable Fire*? Whereas before the group had always rejected the idea of recording songs that couldn't be replicated live, they now embraced the technical possibilities of the studio. Listen to the huge wash of infinite guitar, strings and Fairlight that makes the title track, for example, so much more than just guitar-bass-drums. Recording in a castle ballroom was also a statement of intent, as Bono said in the accompanying making-of documentary, "The sound of this room suits our music". Big music. There were also big themes, allowing people to think that this was more than just pop music. And not, as with 'Sunday Bloody Sunday' on the *War* album, limited to local issues. Bono now concerned himself with big American themes: Martin Luther King (not one, but two tracks), Elvis Presley and the 4th of July. And in a break in recording that summer, he emphasized his major league status by joining Bob Dylan at the latter's Slane Castle concert on a version of 'Blowin in the Wind' – with new words reflecting the Troubles. Big was better. 'If we stay in small clubs, we'll develop small minds, and then we'll start making small music'[13].

The big sound and themes were one thing – OK, two – but the other was Bono's mouth. Like Boy George he was instantly quotable and opinionated, though he was also thoughtful (bordering on preachy) rather than bitchy. This annoyed some people, including Ian McCulloch of Echo & The Bunnymen. But it was jealousy on the latter's part. In 1984, U2 were more together as a band, they had better management, a better label, bigger ambitions and a sound that was clearly designed to appeal to America. The 'spat' made good press but it was one-sided. Bono simply didn't need to come down to that level; he, the band and their manager, Paul McGuinness, had more important things on their collective mind. First single 'Pride (In The Name Of Love)' was a UK #3 hit, but could only manage #33 in the US. It would take another three years for them to top the charts there.

Bono, The Edge and Eno take advantage of Slane Castle's spacious surroundings.

Bono's stagecraft – the hovering over the stage monitors, the reaching out to the back row – was modelled on Jim Kerr's of Simple Minds, and *The Unforgettable Fire* was part-influenced by the ecstatic ambience of *New Gold Dream*. In turn, trying to keep up, Simple Minds bigged up their sound and sense of self-importance. Not lyrically – that would come with 'Belfast Child' and 'Sun City' – but in terms of sound and intent. Originally edgy and experimental, then, riding the new pop wave, seeing themselves as synth-drenched European romantics, the group re-invented themselves as stadium rockers before even playing in them. 'Waterfront', a single released at the tail end of 1983, was a portent of things to come. It was epic, if not in terms of what it said (nothing much), then in terms of its beefed up, throbbing sound. Produced by Steve Lillywhite (whom U2 had 'dropped', perhaps because they heard this and didn't want to go down that route, though they could have so easily), the single was followed in February 1984 by an album of equally grand proportions, again if not in subject matter then in production values, especially the drums which clattered like pots and pans dumped in the knave of Glasgow Cathedral. Both sleeves heralded (literally, they looked like coats of arms) something important. It was also a return to rock. From the "1,2,3,4" count-in to second single 'Up On The Catwalk', it was clear Simple Minds now saw themselves as a rock, not a pop, group.

Yet for all the posturing, *Sparkle in the Rain* is a fairly thrilling almost live-sounding record, their last great album? The strutting 'Book of Brilliant Things' is the closest

19

they get to *New Gold Dream*; third single 'Speed Your Love To Me' hurtles along at 100mph before twice shifting gear and key and upping the intensity even more. An abbreviated cover of Lou Reed's 'Street Hassle' (thankfully half the length of the original 11 minutes) is a fairly pointless inclusion, as is the closing wordless 'Shake Off the Ghosts' (the last instrumental they ever recorded?). The group were seemingly always on tour, playing bigger and bigger venues and yet in May somehow Jim Kerr found time to marry Chrissie Hynde. The rest of the 80s saw them become one of the biggest groups in the world, writing earnest, arena-arresting anthems such as 'Belfast Child' and 'Mandela Day'. Kerr was no Bono though, and couldn't quite carry off the rock star as political evangelist character that the Irishman inhabited so naturally.

Having metamorphosed from the orthodoxy of The Tourists into the unconventionality of Eurythmics, the new incarnation hit the big time in 1983 with two albums, *Sweet Dreams (Are Made of This)* and *Touch*, plus a string of successful singles in between: a re-release of the sinister 'Love is a Stranger', a mournful 'Who's That Girl', both with gender-bending videos, and an upbeat calypso-style 'Right By Your Side'. It was a brilliant, and brilliantly timed, suite of new pop combining the new synth sound and Annie Lennox's soul-influenced vocals. 'Here Comes the Rain Again' was a deliciously melancholic opening to 1984, perfectly suited to a British January, and at the Grammys the following month Lennox flummoxed the audience by appearing in male garb looking like Elvis Presley. They seemed to be at the vanguard, but were about to regress from quirky, pervy, interesting synthpop to, if not The Tourists, then 'authentic' rock with black backing singers, brass sections and the return of loud guitars.

But not before *Touch Dance*, which was a problem of a different kind. The idea of remixing old tracks into longer, new ones was not new, but *Touch Dance* was a cynical RCA cash-in on the success of its parent album that even the band disowned. "Couldn't stand it", said Stewart. "Never listened to it", echoed Lennox. "Nothing to do with us" chorused both[14]. The second problem was the music for a film adaptation of George Orwell's *1984*. It was Virgin Films' first feature and they wanted a big-name pop soundtrack, commissioning Eurythmics in place of director Michael Radford's original idea of Dominic Muldowney's more traditional score. Orwell's estate also wanted Muldowney, Stewart and Lennox had no idea what was going on and an almighty row ensued. In the end the film came out with bits of both, and the album with just Eurythmics' contribution. Along with this, Annie Lennox was splitting up with her husband of just six months, German Hare Krishna devotee Rahda Raman. Nevertheless, in January 1985 they booked a studio in Paris and in basically just a week came up with the more rock and soul oriented *Be Yourself Tonight* complete with Stevie Wonder, Aretha Franklin, a gospel choir and lots of guitar. Compared to *Sweet Dreams* of just two years earlier, it might have been a different group.

ABC had stuck a retro-looking guitar on the cover of their October 1983 single 'That Was Then But This Is Now', and *struck* many more on the sophomore album, *Beauty Stab,* which followed a month later. From the expansively orchestrated *Lexicon of Love* to the riff-heavy *Beauty Stab* was seen by many as a backward step. The one exception was the gorgeous sax-and-handclap 'S.O.S.' released as a single at the beginning of 1984 which seemed to signal a new direction, its video symbolically dropping both a guitar and Steve Singleton's sax into the deep end of a swimming pool. What happened next was that Singleton left, reducing ABC to just Martin Fry and Mark White, who in turn recruited two new non-playing members, Fiona Russell Powell – who'd been a teenage friend of the group and had just started writing for The Face – and bald, diminutive, Corbusier-bespectacled American photographer David Yarritu. Neither actually did anything other than look sexy and cute in ABC's next 'look'. It wasn't the look of love. Instead, Fry and White went for a cartoon image based on the The Archies' 'Sugar Sugar' and Jackson 5's TV series, both hits as the 60s turned into the 70s. It was a bizarre move, made incongruous by first single 'How To Be A Millionaire''s anti-consumerist lyrics and animated video of them drowning in luxury goods. The single scraped into the Top 50. An album, *How To Be A Zillionaire* (the price had gone up), followed early the next year, though it had to wait until the autumn after Martin Fry had beaten Hodgkinson's Disease, a rare form of skin cancer. It was a return to form.

  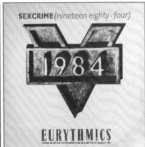

Simple Minds, Tears For Fears and Eurythmics would do 'big' better than most.

Like Eurythmics, Tears For Fears moved from quirky synthpop to multi-instrumental poprock. However, whereas the former's style was reverting to their soul roots, Tears For Fears managed to steer a course between a number of styles, gaining new audiences as they moved forward. It took until August for the first results to appear – a single, the raucous, garrulous 'Mother's Talk' – but it was 'Shout', released at the end of November, that pushed the group back into the public eye: a slow, almost plodding song, with a rhythm appropriated from Talking Heads, and a crescendo of drums, Fairlight counter melody and a chorus that stayed in your mind forever. Many a journalist was quick to connect its content to the primal therapy sessions Orzabal had talked about having, but in reality it was more of a generic protest song. Nevertheless, psychotherapy references were all over the album which followed, *Songs From the Big Chair*, including the title which referred to the 1976 American TV mini-series, *Sybil*, about a woman with multiple personality disorders whose only place of comfort was her analyst's big chair.

The album was recorded throughout 1984 but released in the first weeks of the new year. For such a big-sounding production, it was remarkable that the recording took place not in a top London studio but in the house of Ian Stanley, the band's keyboard player. Producer Chris Hughes simply brought in a recording console and they worked at their leisure. They loosened up and 'got real'. 'Rock & roll was a dirty word to us before which is ludicrous', opined Orzabal. 'This [album] has got a very basic excitement in it that was lacking in our earlier work'[15]. There were only eight songs but they were longer and stronger. The lyrically serious yet musically upbeat 'Everybody Wants to Rule the World' (originally 'Everybody Wants to Go to War') would be the third single and signature tune; 'Head Over Heels' was a rhapsodic love song; slowing the pace down; 'I Believe' was originally written for Robert Wyatt and would appear as a single late in 1985[16]; 'Broken' is all wailing guitars, drums and a piano that sounds like peeling bells; and finally 'Listen', a song which somehow combines prog and world music complete with Spanish mantra and extraordinary sound effects. It was also the album and the year in which the group became less of a duo and more of a Roland Orzabal vehicle. (The scale of Tears For Fears' operation had a knock-on effect on fellow Bristolians The Escape who supported them in 1983 and were also signed to Phonogram; after a final single 'Russian Lady', mainmen Nicky Holland and Alan Griffiths jacked in their group and joined Tears For Fears' touring band, alongside Will Gregory who, much later, would form Goldfrapp).

One would have been hard-pressed to predict that the singer of 1978 novelty single 'Toast' by Streetband or the early 80s horn-heavy Q-Tips would become platinum-selling solo act Paul Young by the middle of the decade. But swapping the rough-edged band for a sophisticated production based around lush keyboards and Pino Palladino's in-demand fretless bass, and then dressing him in an Anthony Price leather suit, transformed him from journeyman pub rock to the real thing seemingly overnight (even if the million-seller *No Parlez* was recorded on the Old Kent Road). 'Wherever I Lay My Hat' and 'Come Back and Stay' were huge hits in 1983, and a re-release of 'Love of the Common People' sat near the top of the charts as the new year began. Essentially an R&B singer, releasing a cover of Joy Divisions' 'Love Will Tear Us Apart' was not a wise move (it didn't even chart, much to the relief of post-punks everywhere), but it was quickly put to rights with two more Top 10 singles and the opening lines of Band Aid's 'Do They Know It's Christmas'. Young was always a slightly awkward pop star, not on stage where he was in his element, but in front of camera or doing the PR rounds. The fact that he made it big simply with his voice was unusual and refreshing.

As did Alison Moyet. Her brief but brilliant stint as one half of synthpop duo Yazoo with Vince Clarke prepared her for a solo career which would focus on her voice and not what she looked like. Calling her debut album *Alf*, released in the autumn of 1984, was another way she tried to downplay her femininity. Not that it was actually an issue. People instantly 'got' her voice: big and powerful, and the production by Jolley & Swain was perfect for the times. Three singles, 'Love Resurrection', 'All Cried Out' and 'Invisible', were all over the charts in the second half of the year and the album topped them. Young and Moyet may have shared big, soulful voices (and would duet at Live Aid the following year) but they were different in that Young was essentially a covers guy while Moyet did originals. The rest of the 80s saw continued success for both of them, although from then on they become somewhat marginal figures until the 80s revival tours.

If Moyet made big soul-pop music, the husky-voiced Bonnie Tyler made big *rock-pop* music. Her Jim Steinman-penned and -produced 'Total Eclipse of the Heart' in 1983 was about as overblown as it got, although 1984's 'Holding Out for a Hero' gave it a run for its money. Its video showed her standing on the edge of the Grand Canyon so everyone got the scale thing. It also featured in *Footloose* that year and has been the obvious choice for movie denouement scenes on both sides of the Atlantic ever since, including *Shrek*. Not many people were making this style of music in the UK: her songs had a very US sound, her styling looked American, like she was from Dallas. Tyler was going for the US market big-time, a sound that was a cross-between Rod Stewart and Meat Loaf.

Having spent the entire 70s as probably the most influential artist in popular music, David Bowie could be forgiven for resting on his laurels as the new decade dawned. Only he didn't: 1980's *Scary Monsters (and Super Creeps)* and singles 'Ashes To Ashes' and 'Fashion' maintained his high standards, a strident step into the 80s. Bowie then took a step back from music, waiting for his management deal with Tony DeFries to expire. Instead, he returned to acting, on the stage (an extraordinary performance as *The Elephant Man* on Broadway), on the small screen (Bertolt Brecht's *Baal* for the BBC) and on the big screen (a vampire in Tony Scott's *The Hunger* and a prisoner of war in Nagisa Oshima's *Merry Christmas Mr Lawrence*). He was also planning his next move: a career in the mainstream, or fairly near to it. As 1982 drew to a close, and in a clean break with the past, he brought in producer Nile Rodgers, hired a whole new band and in a lucrative deal moved from RCA to EMI America. *Let's Dance* was big, accessible (the title alone pointed the way) and Bowie had his hits. It also had a knock-on effect on his back catalogue. At one point in the summer of 1983 he had 10 albums in the UK Top 100. It was the year he became a superstar. Bowie was no longer alternative, he was 'normal', albeit (paradoxically) 'superstar-normal'. He re-emphasized his heterosexuality, worked out, got a tan and forbade drinks and drugs on the huge Serious Moonlight tour which ran from May to December. A concert video was released, and there should have been a live album too – it even got to the stage of being mixed by Bob Clearmountain – but for some reason it didn't come out. As 1983 turned into 1984, Bowie found himself back in the studio, under pressure from EMI for a *Let's Dance 2*, exhausted and totally unprepared.

What followed was *Tonight*, the first bad album of Bowie's career. Perversely, instead of bringing in Nile Rodgers again, he chose an inexperienced producer, Derek Bramble, formerly bass guitarist with Heatwave, backed up by an experienced engineer, Hugh Padgham, who had worked with Phil Collins and The Police amongst others. This set-up was strange, but the songs were the real problem. Three of them were Iggy Pop compositions, two were Bowie/Pop co-writes; there was a dreadful version of The Beach Boys' 'God Only Knows' and a passable interpretation of a Lieber & Stiller song from 1962. Which left only two songs penned solely by Bowie – 'Blue Jean' and 'Loving the Alien' – which perhaps not coincidentally were the best on the album. As with *Let's Dance,* Bowie didn't play any instruments, but even his singing was called into question by Bramble who insisted on countless retakes – frustrating for an artist who was famed for nailing things first time. Even the sleeve was weak, heavily indebted to the work of Gilbert and George. Hugh Padgham – who in the end took over from Bramble – summed it up, wishing he'd had the conviction to be more critical. "But it is difficult. Who am I to say to Mr David Bowie that his songs suck?!"[17] Later, even Bowie himself disowned the album and indeed the few years that followed: "I wasn't really interested and I let everyone tell me what to do. I let people arrange my songs. I let photographers choose stylists who brought along what they thought were great, trendy clothes. And I really couldn't be bothered […] A wave of total indifference came over me"[18].

The other big star of the 70s, Elton John, had seen his career dip as that decade made way for the 80s, with four successive albums failing to reach the Top 10. 1983's *Too Low For Zero,* however, saw him reunited (full-time) with lyricist Bernie Taupin and original band, prompting not only a Top 10 album but also two huge singles, 'I Guess That Why They Call It The Blues' and 'I'm Still Standing'. A third, 'Kiss the Bride' was remarkable only in that it unintentionally announced Elton John's engagement to Renate Blauel the London-based, German assistant engineer who'd been working on the album. Their marriage on Valentine's Day 1984 – in Sydney, whilst on tour – took everyone by surprise, not least because it was common knowledge John was gay. "You may still be standing", his old mucker Rod Stewart's wedding telegram famously read, "but we're all on the fucking floor!" The Sun's headline was even more pithy: "Good On Yer, Poofter". The marriage would last four years, compromised not just by his sexuality but by his constant touring, recording, partying, drug-taking and chairmanship of Watford FC[19]. The two worked together on the aptly named *Breaking Hearts* which reached #2 and yielded two more hit singles in 'Sad Songs (Say So Much)' and 'Passengers', both of which featured expensive, glossy videos with obligatory street dancers.

Aside from reuniting with Taupin and the band, and his reputation as a great performer, the thing that was key to Elton John (and of course a whole pantheon of other artists) in the mid-80s was video. Director of choice was Russell Mulcahy who played it camp with Arlene Philips-choreographed dancers (bodypainted in 'I'm Still Standing', fedora-hatted in 'Sad Songs'), and when Mulcahy wasn't available Simon Milne's direction of 'Passengers' was pretty much 'I'm Still Standing 2'. John also found a composing style that was conducive to the era. He started writing on the synthesizer rather than the piano and entered an MOR zone of safety which just about carried his audience with him, especially in America.

In terms of Big, you couldn't get much bigger than The Beatles. Following their break-up, they had entered a strange 70s limbo. Back then, the rock heritage industry didn't really exist and in any case there was enough coming out of them individually to avert the need for wistful 60s reverie. Lennon's assassination in 1980, however, changed all that. It meant that, ten years on, the possibility of the four getting back together again, however slight that was, was *really* over and that, paradoxically, the group could now be revived as a product. The autumn of 1982 kick-started a 20th anniversary flurry of re-releases of their earliest singles which continued through the mid-80s. In 1984 a section of New York's Central Park was ceremoniously renamed Strawberry Fields; Yoko Ono and son Sean visited Liverpool, donating $90,000 to a children's home on the site of the original Strawberry Field; the Cavern Club re-opened for business; the ghost of Lennon was reportedly seen in another club, the Jacaranda; and *Milk and Honey*, the follow-up to Lennon and Ono's *Double Fantasy*, finally came out that year too. But in terms of new music the onus was on Paul McCartney (George Harrison having been happily distracted by his new role as an executive producer at Handmade Films while Ringo Starr was narrating Thomas the Tank Engine on the small screen). It was not a great year for Macca, despite two hit singles. 'No More Lonely Nights' was a deserved #2, but 'We All Stand Together' – from a Rupert the Bear animation, co-credited as Paul McCartney and the Frog Chorus (Smash Hits interviewed three of the frogs) – was laughable at #3. Even more risible, however, was the vanity project par excellence, *Give My Regards to Broad Street*, McCartney's attempt to write, produce and star in a film. As one critic wrote: It was "about as close as you can get to a non-movie, and the parts that do try something are the worst"[20].

Another big MOR star of the mid-80s, Phil Collins, really could act (as a child he'd played the Artful Dodger in the London stage production of *Oliver!* and in 1988 he'd make a decent fist of playing the lead role in an otherwise bad movie, *Buster*), but for now he was content to monopolise the pop charts. 1984 saw Collins finish a Genesis tour, release the maudlin 'Against All Odds' (a US #1 and UK #2), produce albums by Philip Bailey and Eric Clapton, drum for Band Aid, record his third solo album, *No Jacket Required* (released in January 1985) which would top the UK charts either side of the Atlantic, and get married. Collins had become a workaholic hit-machine, summing up the wishy-washy reaches of the charts. 'Sussudio' was a personal favourite of the Patrick Bateman character in Brett Easton Ellis' *American Psycho,* having deemed 1970s Genesis as "Too artsy, too intellectual". Respectively, nine and seven years on from *The Lamb Lies Down on Broadway* and (the genuinely innovative) *Moroccan Roll,* Collins was now moving in very different circles.

In the end, making it big meant both a big sound and commercial success. And there were few better examples of that than Bryan Ferry's 1984-recorded (1985 released) *Boys and Girls*. Its sound was certainly big, but in truth it was the *width* that grabbed you, its guitars (played by David Gilmour, Nile Rodgers and others) and richly textured keyboards multi-tracked almost ad infinitum. Thanks to inspired mixing by Bob Clearmountain, it still sounds amazing 30-odd years later even if the actual writing was perhaps average, the overall effect the aural equivalent of a seductive coffee table book. It was Ferry's first and (probably) last #1 UK album. Also playing on the album was Mark Knopfler, whose own band was already reaching millions. Formed in 1977, yet the antithesis of punk, Dire Straits were the quintessential pub rock turned arena band, Britain's middle-of-the-road, less muscular version of the Boss, complete with bandana. No new studio album in 1984, but *Alchemy Live* hit #3 and they would start recording *Brothers in Arms* before the year was out.

Of all the bands with widescreen ambitions, U2 and Simple Minds would nail it better than most, embracing the big themes, studios, productions and arenas, and kept going through thick and thin. Others would focus on certain elements of the above: Depeche Mode, for example, became a huge band in terms of sonic ambition and the more leftfield millions they reached, rather than for adopting political issues. But most of the other bands in this chapter split up before the decade was out, either permanently (in the case of Frankie and Wham!) or temporarily (everyone else).

Chapter 2: Absolute
Synthpop broadens its palette

A golden age of pop music had started in England. It began with the Human League and ended with Frankie Goes To Hollywood. Brits were using lots of synthesizers and electronics, and people in the American music scene were very suspicious of us.[1]
Tom Bailey, Thompson Twins

We thought we were avant-garde, but we were the future of pop.[2]
Andy McCluskey, OMD

I said I bet that you look good on the dance floor
Dancing to electro-pop like a robot from 1984
From 1984!
Arctic Monkeys 'I Bet You Look Good on the Dancefloor'

Punk had given license to teenagers to form bands whether they could play or not, but it still meant learning at least a few chords, tuning a guitar and carting around a drum kit. And it was still basically the same instrumental line-up as rock had started out with. Buying a monophonic synthesizer (no chords to learn) and a drum-machine (a bunch of buttons and dials in a box) was an attractive alternative. The radical simplicity of punk transferred well to the stark simplicity of synthpop, and the synth was something new.

Well fairly. As a musical instrument, the synthesizer goes back to the 60s. But at the time they were large, complicated, unreliable and expensive machines used by only a few musicians and producers. Its use in pop could arguably be dated back to three records in 1972: the #1 hit 'Son of My Father' by Chicory Tip – co-written by a young Giorgio Moroder and featuring the Mini-Moog as lead instrument (played by Chris Thomas, house engineer at Air Studios, who would later go on to produce the Sex Pistols amongst others); the novelty instrumental 'Popcorn' by American covers band Hot Butter which reached #5; and the first Roxy Music album which featured the VCS3 'played' by Brian Eno, though not really as a lead instrument, rather as a way of treating the sounds made by the other musicians. Prog-rock groups like Yes, Pink Floyd and ELP also featured heavy use of synths.

But by the mid-to-late 70s it was Germany that influenced the way electronic music was being integrated into pop. It wasn't particularly the 'kosmische' music of Tangerine Dream and Klaus Schulze, or the quieter electronic vignettes of Cluster, or even the propulsive semi-electronic beat of Neu!, although they would all play their part. The biggest electro-influences on mainstream pop were Kraftwerk and the Italian-born, Munich-based Giorgio Moroder. Kraftwerk had had a surprise hit in 1975 with a 3-minute version of their 23-minute long 'Autobahn', and their first concerts in Britain in September 1975 and October 1976 had a profound effect on many young men with aspirations of forming bands, even before punk – Orchestral Manoeuvres in the Dark (OMD) amongst them. But it was *Trans-Europe Express* (1977) and *Man Machine* (1978) that showed how electronic music could be accessible and – crucially – danceable.

Moroder, meanwhile, was working with Donna Summer. His production and her orgasmic vocals had resulted in the disco hit of 'Love to Love You Baby' (1975), but it was the totally electronic 'I Feel Love' (1977) which was the game-changer. Whereas 'Autobahn' had condensed a long album track to 3:27 minutes, Moroder went the other way, stretching a song of equally limited lyrical content into nearly six minutes of relentless electro-throb[3]. Its impact was as dramatic as Kraftwerk's, as remembered by David Bowie while recording *Low* in Berlin:

> *One day... Eno came running in and said, 'I have heard the sound of the future.'*
> *... He puts on 'I Feel Love' by Donna Summer ... He said, 'This is it, look no*
> *further. This single is going to change the sound of club music for the next fifteen*
> *years.' Which was more or less right.*[4]

There were other influences: Sylvester's 'You Make Me Feel (Mighty Real)' (1978), produced by Patrick Cowley; the bright technopop of Yellow Magic Orchestra from Japan (where most of the new synthesizers like Roland, Korg and Yamaha were being made); and, probably subliminally at this stage, the classically-influenced Jean-Michel Jarre and Vangelis, and the ambient music of Eno (often mimicked by others as 'arty' B-side instrumentals[5]). These were all on the radar of the post-punk bands who had been inspired by punk but were less interested in its limited 'garage rock' musical construction, and saw synths and drum-machines as the future. As Stuart Moxham of Young Marble Giants said, 'It was a really interesting time technologically. We were into Eno and Can and Kraftwerk. There was a lot of sexiness in getting away from conventional instruments'[6].

The sound of the first wave of British synth bands was largely simplistic, experimental and bleak, partly because they were not musically proficient, partly they were still influenced by punk's nihilism – both used as advantages. Cabaret Voltaire, Throbbing Gristle and The Normal were good examples. Others like The Human League, Ultravox and OMD were more melodic, more interested in crafting electronic pop songs. However, it was Gary Numan – initially as part of Tubeway Army, then solo – who perfected the formula with 'Are 'Friends' Electric' and 'Cars' (both 1979, both #1 hits).

As the 70s turned into the 80s, more and more synthpop groups began to make inroads into the charts: Depeche Mode, Soft Cell, Buggles, M, Blancmange, A Flock Of Seagulls, China Crisis, Yazoo, Thomas Dolby, Visage and so on. Some, like Japan and Simple Minds, took a leaf out of Tubeway Army's book by abandoning their previous guitar-driven pop/rock and going for, respectively, a more Oriental or Euro synthetic approach. Others like Duran Duran, Spandau Ballet and ABC, used synths as lush embellishment to a hybrid style that owed less to punk and more to funk (especially Chic). They also became associated with the new romantic movement that sprang out of The Blitz and Barbarella's club scenes in London and Birmingham.

Although some audiences were overtly hostile to synthpop, notably in America, it achieved an appeal among those alienated from the dominant heterosexuality of mainstream rock culture, particularly among gay and female audiences. In a way, it was the 80s version of punk, but more forward-looking and colourful.

Arctic Monkeys got it wrong when they sang about 'dancing to electro-pop like a robot from 1984'. Robots were passé by then. Kraftwerk had moved on from man machines to cyclists, Gary Numan had switched from electrical alien to Norse warrior and the faintly ludicrous Tik & Tok jerkily bowed out that year too. By 1984, synthpop was no longer really a genre, not in the same way that it had been used in the early 80s. Then it had referred to the *exclusively* synthetic, often quite stark electronic pop of Numan, Depeche Mode, Human League, Soft Cell and others. In those early days, most synthpop groups weren't that interested in exploiting the full range of sounds that their synths were (sometimes) capable of. It was more a question of choosing sounds that definitely couldn't have been made by traditional rock instruments backed by simple but danceable drum-machine or sequencer beats – its 'monophonic innocence' era. But over time, it became less stark, artificial and futuristic, and more warm, sophisticated and symphonic, as the string settings of polyphonic keyboards began to fill out the canvas, and drum machines (like the Linn) began to sound like real drums. In 1981 *Dare* had boasted "Only synthesizers were used on this album." On *Hysteria* no such claims were made, partly because they'd said it before, but also because guitars had sneaked in.

*****

Human League were the most synthpop of them all. One of a number of bands formed in Sheffield in the immediate post-punk years (along with ABC, Cabaret Voltaire, Clock DVA, Artery, Graph and – odd ones out – Def Leppard), the group had started off as a quirky electronic quartet comprising computer programmers Martyn Ware and Ian Craig Marsh, ex-hospital porter Philip Oakey on vocals and art student Adrian Wright who projected slides. Their first two Virgin albums were brilliantly odd: pop, but somehow not of this world. They wanted to be pop but they wanted to be experimental too.

It came to a head in 1980 with Ware and Marsh being ousted from the group they created, setting up the British Electric Foundation (BEF) and soon afterwards Heaven 17, while Oakey and Wright carried on with the League. With concert commitments looming, the latter quickly hired keyboard player Ian Burden from fellow synth band Graph, together with two schoolgirls, Joanne Catherall and Susanne Sulley, as dancers and backing singers, famously chanced upon in Sheffield's Crazy Daisy Nightclub. It was an unlikely and inspired move. Tour completed, ex-Rezillos guitarist Jo Callis was added (although not initially to play guitar) and off they went to record *Dare* with producer Martin Rushent. After its massive success, and the ground-breaking remix album, *Love and Dancing* a year later, the pressure from Virgin for a follow-up was enormous. Two singles, 'Mirror Man' and '(Keep Feeling) Fascination', had filled the gap admirably enough, but the album took what was then an eternity.

By 1984, they had exhausted three producers – Rushent, Hugh Padgham and Chris Thomas (as well as Air Studio's tape op, Renate Blauel, who took time off to marry Elton John) – and people were beginning to wonder whether the group was dead and buried. But finally, in April, a long-awaited single appeared. 'The Lebanon' was an odd affair: a guitar-heavy 'political' song about 1982's Sabra and Shatila massacre in Beirut, with naive, if well-intentioned, lyrics. The faux live video attempted to portray the previously fey, lightweight synth pop band as a rock group with conscience. Somehow it worked.

The album, though, was a bit of a letdown. Titled *Hysteria* (alluding to the pressures of the previous year or so, rather than the fake euphoria of the audience in the above video), it looked good – with its glossy, bold, big-lettered gatefold sleeve – but sounded tired. There were, however, at least three more decent tracks, 'Life On Your Own', 'Louise', and 'Don't You Know I Want You', the first two of which duly came out as singles later in the year.

Released in June at the beginning of a sizzling summer dominated by Frankie and 'Careless Whispers', 'Life On Your Own''s opening lines, 'Winter is approaching, there's snow upon the ground' had a jarring effect, and the video featuring Oakey as 'the last man on Earth' wandering through a post-apocalyptic London, was similarly against the grain, although it tied in with the cold war theme of 'Two Tribes'. That said, it was more typical Human League, electronic to the core, but peaked at #16. 'Louise', which followed, went three places higher but was even more downbeat, or at least poignant. A sequel of sorts to 'Don't You Want Me', it featured the same characters three years on. Oakey bumps into his old flame and the result is a genuinely affecting moment of understated real life. On Top Of The Pops, a clearly sympathetic John Peel told the great British public: 'That's the Human League and 'Louise' – one of their best songs I think. I mean, I know you don't care what I think, but I thought I'd tell you anyway.'

Human League, Heaven 17 and OMD: now simply pop groups rather than synthpop groups.

In the midst of all this melancholia, Oakey had teamed up with his idol, Giorgio Moroder, to release 'Together in Electric Dreams' - an upbeat song from the film

Electric Dreams, directed by Steve Barron (who'd previously directed three Human League videos). It was a huge success, eclipsing the band's own current efforts.

So, what to make of Human League in 1984? Clearly *Hysteria* didn't measure up to *Dare*, and it didn't help that they didn't tour it[7], but it still sold around a million copies and received surprisingly good reviews ('Human League have delivered. It's more than you and I dared hope' trumpeted Melody Maker[8], although NME were predictably unimpressed). There'd be another long gap before their next album *Crash* (1986), which yielded the brilliant 'Human', and ever longer gaps after that, but at time of writing they're still going, still centred around Oakey and 'the girls'.

Meanwhile, the band that had spun away from the Human League, had similar expectations to live up to. Ware and Marsh set themselves up as a production team, British Electric Foundation (BEF), *and* formed a band, Heaven 17, and in singer Glenn Gregory they found the perfect replacement for Oakey. Their debut album, *Penthouse and Pavement* was released in the same year as *Dare* but without the same impact. Ironically, the electronic boffin half of the League had chosen a funkier, some might say more conventional route, than Oakey and Wright.

With the acquisition of a Fairlight, this changed, and their second album, *The Luxury Gap* (1983), brought back a more sophisticated, synthetic sound and gave them minor hits in 'Crushed by the Wheels of Industry' and 'Let Me Go', and a huge one in 'Temptation'. But which direction next? In the end, 1984's archly titled *How Men Are*, tried for all things at once: heavy use of Fairlight, funky rhythms, brass (the Phoenix Horns, borrowed from Earth Wind and Fire), a trio of female singers collectively known as Afrodiziak, even an orchestra. The result was a kind of prog-pop: clever, sophisticated, confident, but ultimately a bit soulless, despite the attempt at bringing soul in. Lyrically, they kept to their self-imposed ban on using the word 'love' but the words they did use were curiously unengaging. Two singles, 'Sunset Now' and 'This is Mine', failed to make a big impression on the charts. One track, however, '...And That's No Lie', saved the album from being drab. A 10-minute opus, it has everything: an opening minute of eerie Fairlight ambience, a catchy finger-picking guitar melody, a piano solo from Nick Plytas, a whiff of orchestra and ending with everything stripped out except the backing vocals – an acapella denouement. The 'Close to the Edge' of pop, it was released as a truncated single in early 1985 with all the best bits taken out.

Parallel to the recording of *How Men Are*, the three had played an important part in rejuvenating Tina Turner's career. Gregory had already duetted with her on the #6 hit 'Let's Stay Together' at the end of 1983, while Ware and Marsh, as the resuscitated BEF production team, produced chunks[9] of her five million-selling *Private Dancer* album, which ended up being entirely recorded in Britain.

If Human League and Heaven 17 hadn't *quite* got it right in 1984, then nor had OMD. Their 1981 album *Architecture and Morality* had spawned three hit singles (all of which went Top 5) but they had followed it up with the quirky, austere *Dazzle Ships*, whose two singles, 'Genetic Engineering' and 'Telegraph', bombed. Would they continue being experimental, or return to the pop fold? They chose the latter route, but with just enough edge and darkness to remain interesting. Peter Saville's sleeve seemed to echo this, the lustrously coloured flowers emanating from a fathomless black. The album started where *Dazzle Ships* had left off with a brooding Tijuana-brass infected instrumental, reassuringly followed by a song about electricity ('Tesla Girls'). And then there were the lyrics, some of which were as bleak as anything written by Ian Curtis. Who would have thought lines like "I'm going to break every bone in your body, that perfect little body that's been so close to mine" ('White Trash') were OMD's? Nonetheless, much to Virgin's relief, there was plenty on the album that – if you overlooked the lyrics – could brighten up the airwaves, including *two* electro-calypso songs, 'All Wrapped Up' and 'Locomotion'. The latter was the first single, reaching a very respectable #5 in April. The charming 'Talking Loud and Clear,' with its harp-like arpeggio and synthetic brass-and-oboe counter-melodies, peaked at #11 in June. Two more were squeezed from the album but they failed to make the Top 20. Nonetheless, OMD had definitely returned to the pop fold, though rather lost what had made them special in the process. In time, they cracked America, but America cracked them.

No-one could accuse Howard Jones of morbidness. Arriving seemingly from nowhere, Jones's debut single, 'New Song', went straight to #3. In a way, he was typical of the optimism of new pop, bright and breezy with the haircut and clothes to match. But he was actually older than most of his peers. As an 18-year-old he'd been in a prog-rock band, studied piano at the Royal Northern College of Music, discovered the synthesizer in 1979 and spent the early 80s gigging around High Wycombe with a bald mime artist called Jed Holie who 'interpreted' his songs on stage. However, it wasn't until a Kid Jensen session and a support slot with China Crisis that things began to come together. A deal was struck with WEA (after he'd nearly signed to Stiff Records, as unlikely a pairing as one could imagine[10]), and the result was 'New Song', with its jaunty synth melody and lyrics about challenging preconceived ideas and saying goodbye to long-standing fears. Self-help hogwash or enlightened mantra, the public bought into it and the only way was up for Jones.

1984 was his year. 'What Is Love?' reached #2 in January, 'Hide and Seek' #12 in March; a debut album, *Human's Lib*, went to #1 in April, a fourth single from the album, 'Pearl in the Shell', peaked at #7 in May, he toured with Eurythmics in July, and a new song, 'Like to Get to Know You Well', made #4 in August. And like Lennox and Stewart, a remix album hit the racks before the year was out. Jones was much maligned by music journalists at the time. The 'faux positive' lyrics, the hair, the clothes. It's a fair cop on the last two – though frankly everyone looked silly in the mid-80s – but Jones's interest in self-help was genuine, stemming from his Buddhist faith. (He was, and still is, a member of the Soka Gakkai International sect). 'What is Love?' seemed like a genuinely good question to ask, even if he didn't provide the answers. That said, 'Like to Get to Know You Well' was genuinely irritating[11] and by 1985 he was playing arenas, working with Phil Collins, wearing ever-more suspect clothes and his hair was out of control.

Along with Jones, Nik Kershaw, is often seen as the whipping boy of mid-80s pop. In a way, he didn't fit in. He may have had the ambition of new pop but he lacked its vogueish swank; he was never 'fashionable'. Nor was he a typical synthpop artist, his main instrument being guitar. He was awkward in front of camera, short (five feet four), sported a terrible mullet, wore fingerless gloves, hated the business – the classic reluctant pop star. Like Jones, Kershaw had been in a prog-ish group, Fusion, but landed a manager (Mickey Modern, who managed Nine Below Zero) and a label (MCA). 1984 was as much his year as Jones's. Two albums, *Human Racing* and *The Riddle*, released in March and November, hit #4 and #3 respectively, while five singles all went Top 20. In fact, he spent more weeks in the singles chart that year than any other solo act. However, commercial success was one thing, critical plaudits another. 'Competent but relentlessly dull synthesised meanderings of no importance to anyone but Mr Kershaw himself (and even *he* doesn't sound that interested)' was the very NME-like verdict on his debut album, except that it was written by Smash Hits, whose back-handed compliment of his second – 'a commendable offering from the thinking man's Limahl'[12] – was almost worse. Playing his two albums now, it's not so much that they were *bad* as *bland* – characterized by a soulless, clinically clean mid-Atlantic faux-funky sound that was creeping into mid-80s production values. The 70s might have been a better decade for him. The aforementioned Limahl, incidentally, had been sacked from the came-from-nowhere, cringingly named Kajagoogoo, a synthpop band who shared muso similarities with Level 42 but effectively had their 15 minutes of fame in 1983 with 'Too Shy'. Both kept up appearances in 1984 – Limahl getting one over his former bandmates when 'The NeverEnding Story' (#4) trumped Kajagoogoo's 'The Lion's Mouth' (#25) in the early part of the year – but they were effectively history by the second half of the decade.

Thomas Dolby was also a rather reluctant pop star but he was quirky, full of energy (Kershaw always seemed so lackadaisical) and used his boffin image to winning effect. He didn't have a mullet to worry about either. Dolby's thoroughly mature debut, *The Golden Age of Wireless* (1982) and 'She Blinded Me With Science' (#6 in the US singles charts) had hinted at a decent, sophisticated solo synth career, but he surprised everyone with the variety of his 1984 output. 'Hyperactive!', released in January, was exactly that: an ebullient mix of hi-tech rhythms, Fairlight doubling as-flute and trombone, and a frantic duet with Adele Bertei[13] over the top. A suitably bonkers video with every trick in the book made sure it was constantly on TV. It went Top 20. The album *The Flat Earth* followed a month later. On the one hand it was like a Fairlight demonstration record (check out the subdued African sounding rhythm of the title track and 'Mulu The Rain Forest'), but also what a *band* could do, for the album – and the tour that followed in May – was very much a group effort. Dolby expanded on the group ethic:

I played in bands well before I started doing my one-man-show thing with my synths. [...] When I went solo, I was interested in exploring an all-electronic sound, yes; but I also used the synths as a way to simulate a broader instrumental palette. I was eager to write for brass sections, choirs, orchestras. And my songs were the kind you could sit down and plonk out at the piano – they had chord sequences, intros, verses and choruses and middle eights. So what I did was always distinctly different from the DIY electronic ethic, where you sort of celebrate letting machines be machines, with all their quirks. When you program synths or computers to play music, the individual elements obey your commands (hopefully!) and they have no knowledge of each other, whereas when musicians get together in a room, they are responding in real time, to their own ear canals and fingertips, and to the sound waves bounding around the room. So 'band' music has an organic quality that electronic music will never have – at least until there's AI involved. Still, as a skilled programmer and producer you can chip away at the notes and sounds, smooth the rough edges, and overcome the inherent dumbness of electronics, blending and sculpting them into something more human. If that's what you want, of course.[14]

Perhaps the most surprising track was a cover of Dan Hicks' 'I Scare Myself'. Originally a mildly frenetic gypsy-ish song, Dolby slowed it to a languid metronomic beat, fretless bass, piano, plaintive brass and Dolby's wistful voice. The fact that it was released as a single and sneaked into the Top 50 was a surprise bonus. A third single, the more upbeat 'Dissidents', came out in the summer but by then Dolby had effectively had his turn in the pop spotlight. The rest of the year kept him busy with a remix project called Dolby's Cube and producing the second Prefab Sprout album but his next album wouldn't appear until four years later. Bored with the music industry, it was somehow not too surprising when, in the 90s, he became a tech entrepreneur in Silicon Valley.

If Howard Jones's support to China Crisis in May 1983 had set him on his way to stardom, then the main act had continued to develop in less dramatic fashion. Gary Daly and Eddie Lundon had been in various post-punk bands around Liverpool but it took them until 1982 to form China Crisis and record their first single, 'African and White', for Liverpool independent label, Inevitable. They were then picked up by Virgin, releasing the absurdly titled *Difficult Shapes & Passive Rhythms - Some People Think It's Fun to Entertain* album later that year, followed by another mouthful, *Working With Fire and Steel (Possible Pop Songs Volume Two)*, in late 1983. At this stage, China Crisis could still be described as a synthpop band. Certainly 'Wishful Thinking', which went Top 10 in January 1984, was a gorgeously electro-lush piece of melancholic pop balladry punctuated by synthetic strings and oboe. Thereafter China Crisis began to sound more and more like a pop version of Steely Dan, culminating in said group's Walter Becker producing their next album, 1985's overlooked *Flaunt the Imperfection*. One of the things that stopped China Crisis slipping into saccharinity was their lyrics. It was difficult to decide whether they were purposefully surreal or just an incomprehensible stream of jibberish. Consider this from 'Hanna Hanna', their second single in 1984: 'Tape record her and telephone / Conversations in pyramids alone / Why should I stop to think what they're about.' Quite. Or maybe they were deep all along: 'Papua' was about hydrogen bomb tests in the Pacific. Another distinguishing mark was their beautiful, sad instrumentals, largely confined to B-sides.

Operating in the same, synth-based, sensitive-souls neck of the woods were two more Liverpool groups. The Lotus Eaters' 1983 debut single, 'The First Picture of You', had been a hit before they'd even played a gig. A decent album, *No Sense of Sin*, and a couple more singles followed in 1984 but they struggled to maintain the impetus and split the following year. Likewise, Care released a trio of polite singles in 1983 and 1984, 'Whatever Possessed You', being the standout, before they too split (guitarist Ian Broudie forming the Lightning Seeds). This sort of touchy-feely, metro-man synthpop – other practitioners included Fiction Factory, Fiat Lux and Virgin Dance – went down better with Smash Hits rather than NME readers, but there was a beguiling melancholy and anti-machismo about the best of them.

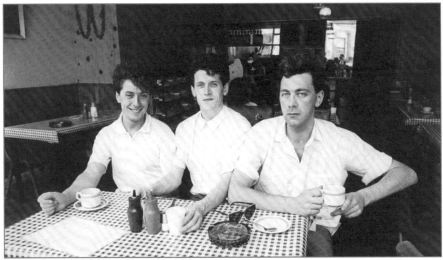

For one photo only, The Blue Nile are The White Nile.

Beauty and sadness were The Blue Nile to a tee. Paul Buchanon, Robert Bell and Paul Joseph Moore had met at Glasgow University, releasing a little-known single ('I Love This Life') in 1981, before painstakingly recording an album in a tiny studio east of Edinburgh. Calum Malcolm, the engineer, had connections with the hi-end hi-fi manufacturer Linn Products[15] which resulted in the company offering to release the album on their own Linn Records, set up especially for them. Released in April 1984, *A Walk Across the Rooftops* was a revelation. 'Synthpop' barely described them. It's true that drum machines and synthesizers punctuated the sound and tracks like 'From Rags to Riches' and 'Heatwave' (both of which sound like they could have been recorded with Ryuichi Sakamoto) had a very electronic feel, but others – particularly 'Easter Parade' and the title track – felt very organic, the string settings extremely 'real'. What really characterizes this wonderful album, though, are Buchanon's fragile, aching, weathered, soaring, soulful vocals and the music's seemingly contradictory minimal lushness – there is not a single wasted note on the album. Its indisputable highlight, though, is 'Tinseltown in the Rain', possibly the best song in this book. When Buchanon sings "I know now, love was so exciting" he sounds exactly like Frank Sinatra – and you could imagine him covering it. It was released as a single but astonishingly only made #87, a clear case of either an incompetent marketing department or the public not knowing what was good for it. Possibly both. For what it's worth, it was Annie Lennox's favourite song of the year[16]. 'Stay' was also a single but peaked ten places lower. That The Blue Nile spent five years recording (or not recording) their next album, the equally sublime *Hats,* and another seven years followed before their third, was indicative of their infuriating under-achievement, and of course sealed their romantic artists status.

Apart from Midge Ure, Ultravox weren't Scottish, but in many ways the whole (new) romantic synth scene started with 'Vienna', their solemn 1980 elegy to middle Europe. From then on they had hit after hit, far surpassing the John Foxx-fronted exclamation mark version in terms of popular if not critical acclaim. The music press never warmed to Mk2. They were considered cold, pompous and melodramatic – terms which could just as well have applied to the Mk1 version – and by 1984, celebrating ten years of existence in some guise or other, they were backed into a corner. *Lament* does what it says on the tin. From the funereal Peter Saville sleeve (which wasn't just black, it was 2-tone black), the album was eight tracks of unmitigated gloom. The U2-sounding 'One Small Day' sounds uplifting but was about battling depression; 'Dancing With Tears In My Eyes' described an impending nuclear power plant meltdown; the title track ("In stillness, in sorrow, returns that softly sighing lament") was obviously not much fun; and 'Heart of the Country' was just plain miserable. And they were all singles! That said, it was kind of exquisite, a beauty in sadness. There was variety too, with at least half of the album showcasing a more guitar-driven sound. But it couldn't be denied: it was a bit of a downer.

In a concerted attempt to take themselves less seriously, October saw them release yet another single, the non-album 'Love's Great Adventure', a kind of boys' own / Indiana Jones-style caper with (in the video) much winking of eyes and the fairly amusing moment when the music stops for Ure to catch his breath. In fact, Ultravox would have the last laugh as Chrysalis chose the moment to release the million-selling *The Collection.* In addition, Ure was just about to immerse himself in Band Aid. In contrast, John Foxx had a very quiet year, in between albums, one passable, the other weak, after which he temporarily withdrew from music and reverted to his earlier career as a graphic designer.

No-one could accuse Neil Arthur and Stephen Luscombe, Blancmange's odd couple, of being humourless. First there was the name, then the homage to the cat-fixated artist Louis Wain on the sleeve of their debut album, and I couldn't imagine Midge Ure singing "God ain't in the lampshade, I think we're safe." On the face of it, they were a typical synth duo: Neil & Stephen, Vince & Alf, Marc & Dave... Certainly synthesizers and drum-machines were the basis of their pop and their music had an appeal in both the charts and in the clubs ('Living on the Ceiling' was a dance floor hit in 1982). But there was much more to them than that. Firstly, they'd been part of the late 70s experimental electronic scene, and before that Stephen Luscombe (as an 18-year-old) had played on Brian Eno's *Taking Tiger Mountain (By Strategy)* as a member of the Portsmouth Sinfonia. Their 'otherness' could also be seen in their love of Indian music.

1984 saw them at their peak. The infectious 'Don't Tell Me', with its wonderfully cheap video of Arthur and Luscombe larking about in Valencia, hit #8 in April. It ushered in their second album, *Mange Tout*, which was to become their most successful. Included were 1983's 'Blind Vision' and 'That's Love, That It Is' singles, and more of the same really. One surprise was a cover of ABBA's 'The Day Before You Came', released as a single in July. ABBA had split up just two years earlier and were at the time unfashionable; moreover, their original version had only reached #26 in the UK charts[17]. It didn't even have a chorus. But Blancmange made it their own, particularly on the 12-inch which turned it into an 8-minute raga, allowing tablas and santour and a peculiar Tijuana-style trumpet solo free rein. Arthur's delivery of what is an extraordinary lyric (an inventive take on boy meets girl taken from the viewpoint of the dull, predictable, commuter-belt life of one of them - very Reginald Perrin - before the actual, never-to-be-described encounter) captures the mixture of retrospective anticipation, romance and even dread, perfectly.

The Indian groove was taken a step further with a single, 'Ave Maria', by Stephen Luscombe's West India Company side project featuring Hindi movie voiceover star Asha Bhosle, regular percussionist Pandit Dinesh, and Vince Clarke. It wasn't the first time Indian instrumentation had been married to a Western synthbeat – two years earlier, Monsoon's beguiling 'Ever So Lonely' had been a surprise hit – but 'Ave Maria' took the genre a stage further, combining the Christian Hail Mary with a Hindi salutation to Ganesh. Needless to say, it didn't chart although one would be hard-pressed to find a better dancefloor track that year. Blancmange managed one more album, 1985's *Believe You Me*, but Stewart Levine, better known for working with soul artists, was the wrong choice as producer. That and the commercial expectations of a major label (London). They split the following year.

Vince Clarke had had huge success with Alison Moyet in Yazoo, releasing two albums in as many years. But by 1983 they were drifting apart, with Moyet going off to achieve solo AOR stardom (see previous chapter) and Clarke forming one-hit-wonders The Assembly with engineer-of-choice Eric Radcliffe[18]. 1984 was an in-between year for the restless Clarke, as he pondered his next move, which would turn out to be Erasure. But one thing he did continue with was his fledgling label Reset Records which he'd started the year before and which mostly revolved around his old Basildon mate Robert Marlow. Despite the Clarke electro-glitter, the songs didn't measure up. 'Claudette', released in 1984, was the third of Marlow's four efforts but none charted and the planned album *The Peter Pan Effect* was shelved[19].

Meanwhile, Vince Clarke's first group, Depeche Mode, were on a role. Although Clarke had been their principal songsmith, new recruit Alan Wilder helped guide them from weightless synthpop to a more sophisticated sound. The release of *Construction Time Again*, featuring lyrics about the environment, capitalism and nuclear war, was set to the sounds of in-vogue sampled urban detritus. 1984 was the year they became stars, while at the same time going dark and kinky. From the cricket gear of their first PR photos, to awkward new romantic threads, the group had finally discovered black – and it suited them (their fifth album would be called *Black Celebration*). But it wasn't the butch, leather look of bikers, if was more feminine and in the case of Gore, bordering on submissive. Weird but safe.

In January the group had returned to Berlin's Hansa Studios, where they'd mixed *Construction Time Again,* to start work on their fourth album. One of the earliest tracks was the Alan Wilder-penned 'In Your Memory', a cruel-sounding slice of factory floor electronica that never made it onto the album but backed the first of the year's three singles. Even Depeche Mode must have been surprised by the international success of the A-side. With the sampled scrapyard now sounding a bit hackneyed, lyrics that were naive at best, naff at worst, and a video that showed the boys messing around on HMS Belfast, 'People are People' could have been an embarrassment. Instead it went to #4 in the UK and Top 20 in most of Europe, including six weeks at #1 in West Germany where it was used as the theme for German TV's coverage of the 1984 Olympics.

Work on the album continued until August whereupon a second single, 'Master and Servant', was released to a bemused public. Overtly BDSM, it could have followed the same fate as 'Relax' but somehow Auntie Beeb let it pass and the kids on Top Of The Pops got down to lyrics like 'You treat me like a dog, get me down on my knees' and 'This play between the sheets, with you on top and me underneath'. It would have seemed more subversive if Gahan and co hadn't still looked like boys.

Finally, the album, *Some Great Reward*, arrived. The musings on capitalism and the environment were replaced by sexual politics, religion and adultery, set to 'industrial' rhythms and infectious melodies. Opener 'Something To Do' married boredom and grey skies with oil-stained dresses and leather boots. 'Lie To Me', with its irresistible rhythm, was about an adulterous relationship ('So lie to me, but do it with sincerity'). There was even a piano-backed ballad, 'Somebody', in which Martin Gore took over on vocals. To get that 'vulnerable' feel, he sang it starkers in the studio. The accompanying ambient street sounds gave it a creepy feeling. But it was 'Blasphemous Rumours' which ruffled feathers. It opens with one teenager's failed suicide attempt and concludes with another finding Jesus Christ before being run over by a car. In between Gahan accuses God of having a sick sense of humour. Not exactly singles material, but that's what it ended up being, coupled with 'Somebody' as a double A-side, giving the radio playlisters a choice: miserable/anti-religious or just plain miserable. Amazingly, it still went Top 20 in the UK. The album cover – newlyweds belittled in a West Midlands steelworks – reinforced the alluring gloom.
Depeche Mode spent the remainder of the year touring the UK and rest of Europe before moving on to the States in 1985 where they were fast becoming a major act, if still alternative. It was this alternativeness that was their strength. They were moving away from pop but weren't rock. They used synthesizers but in a beefed-up, architectural way. They looked cool in black, goths liked them and their lugubrious lyrics appealed to disaffected teenagers (male and female in equal measure),

particularly, for some reason, in central Europe. A decade later they were a proper rock band, America in the bag, with Gore on guitar, Gahan on heroin, Fletcher increasingly sidelined, Wilder gone, real drums, and grainy back and white videos by Anton Corbijn.

Depeche Mode discovered black in 1984 and never looked back. Scritti Politti admire each other in the Gentleman's Room of the National Liberal Club, London.

If Depeche Mode had gone from pure synthpop to a more alternative rock style with socio-political leanings, then there were two bands who went exactly the opposite way. At the beginning of the 80s, Scritti Politti and Thompson Twins were struggling, earnest post-punkers living in squats (in London's Camden and Clapham respectively), with ever-shifting line-ups. But by 1983 they'd both transformed themselves into trios of slick synthpop, though with rather different influences.

In truth Scritti Politti's conversion was not overnight, and the pop signs were apparent on their *Songs To Remember* album in 1982, but it was frontman Green Gartside's discovery of black music and specifically hip-hop, that prompted a dramatic change of direction. Green disbanded the original Scritti line-up, moved from Rough Trade to Virgin and from London to New York, hooked up with American musicians David Gamson and Fred Maher, frequented the clubs, locked themselves into several expensive studios and beavered away on a new concept. The release of 'Wood Beez (Pray Like Aretha Franklin)' in March 1984 was a revelation. Never had Fairlights and Synclaviers sounded so soulful. Sure, it namedropped the queen of soul, but it came with an arty sleeve and a bewildering video featuring a pyjama-clad band performing on a giant bed, with beekeepers, fencing, Black Power salutes, and Michael Clark prancing around in the background. The only thing missing was Miss Respect herself (although Eurythmics would fix that a year later). 'Absolute' was even more clubby, reinforced by a video that somehow turned a Midsummer Night's Dream set into a Manhattan night club. The perfect mix of black and white clubbers disappeared to the loo, not to snort coke, but to put Absolute drops into their eyes, while Green looked androgynous in an excruciatingly naff shellac tracksuit. A third single, 'Hypnotize', stuck to the formula, and finally the album, *Cupid & Psyche 85* was released in January and two more singles would be squeezed from it in April and June of that year. It all boded so well. Scritti had created a kind of state-of-the-art synth-funk perfection, weirdly feminized – the voice, the hair, the inner sleeve photo of Green gazing at himself in a five star bathroom, flanked rather homo-erotically by Gamson and Maher – but Gartside struggled to better it (was he grooming or grooving?), or at least take it into a new direction. It took him three years to issue the largely disappointing *Provision*, and a further 11 years for the one after that.

Thompson Twins, meanwhile, had moved on from their frenetic post-punk pop. After their 1982 album *Set*, they slimmed down to an impeccable gender/racial balance of ex-music teacher Tom Bailey, Kiwi percussionist Alannah Currie and ex-actor and roadie, Joe Leeway. Synths were embraced and guitars shown the door. 1983's *Quick Step and Side Kick* got them on their way, but it was 1984's *Into the Gap* that made them stars on both sides of the Atlantic. Singles 'Hold Me Now', 'Doctor! Doctor!', 'You Take Me Up' and 'Sisters of Mercy' could be heard everywhere, equal part catchy and irritating. The videos showed them getting progressively more draped in designer clothes and pearls. But were they happy? A full-length video of a concert in California, *Into the Gap Live*, was illuminating, if not for the concert particularly, then for the ten-minute quasi-documentary preamble which indicated that they were *not* having a good time. It seemed a strange confession to include on a retail video (one of the first of its type). Given the moping, many hoped they might call it a day, but they soldiered on into 90s irrelevance and a dozen greatest hits compilations.

Gary Numan *had*, famously, called it a day – at least in terms of touring – back in 1981, although inevitably he was back on stage within a year. The fall of Numan from po-faced synth supremo to po-faced jobbing rocker was epic. In truth it had been on the slide for some time. *Dance* (1981) and *I Assassin* (1982) were brave moves away from a totally electronic sound, thanks in part to heavy use of fretless bass played by Japan's Mick Karn on the former and Pino Palladino on the latter, but his queasy, quasi, gangster look lost him fans who preferred him as an alien. He then hired Bill Nelson to produce *Warriors* (1983), bleached his hair (his own, not Nelson's, although come to think of it, both went peroxide that year) and tried a tough guy Mad Max look. It wasn't convincing, Nelson took his name off the sleeve and more fans departed. By the end of the year he'd left Beggars Banquet and set up his own label, Numa Records, a gutsy move at the time. But despite *another* change of image – white clothes and blue hair – 1984's *Berserker* didn't even make the Top 40. To rub salt into the wound, Beggars chose to issue a retrospective album of *demo* recordings from 1978, *The Plan*, which outperformed new Numan on Numa. The decline continued for the rest of the 80s and into the 90s. You had to feel for him.

Tarred with the same brush were A Flock Of Seagulls, loathed and loved in unequal measure, even if most of the ridicule seemed to be targeted at frontman Mike Score's haircut rather than the music. As with Gary Numan, there was a connection with Bill Nelson who'd produced their first single, 1981's '(It's Not Me) Talking', which they followed with a trio of hit singles the next year. By 1984 they were supporting The Police on tour but/and were out of vogue, at least in Britain. They'd stopped wearing make-up, Score had adopted a mullet and they looked more like plumbers than popstars. But 'The More You Live the More You Love' and album *The Story of a*

Young Heart still went Top 30 in the summer. Like Billy Idol, The Psychedelic Furs, Modern English and others, the band moved to the States but struggled to adapt and split soon afterwards.

*****

Some of the most intriguing synthpop fare in 1984 didn't quite make it. Yorkshire band Fiat Lux were typical of the synthpop bands who came out of the new romantic scene. Again there was a Bill Nelson connection: their first single produced by him, released on his Cocteau label and the band included his brother Ian. That release led to a deal with Polydor and a couple of singles, 'Secrets' and 'Photography', which sounded like China Crisis meets Japan, all wistful synth lines, melancholic marimba and yearning sax. Unfortunately, the other tracks on their debut 1984 mini-album, *Hired History*, weren't as good and they split the following year. Annabel Lamb is best remembered for her cover of 'Riders on the Storm' (#27 in 1983), but her sophomore album, *The Flame,* was pop with synths rather than synthpop. Lamb's often disquieting lyrics and deep voice (sometimes tough, sometimes tender, similar to Anna Domino's, if that's not too obscure a comparison) were showcased in a lucid production, peppered with some of the best fretless bass the year had to offer. If the reggae-ish single 'So Lucky in Bed' ('so unlucky in love') doesn't quite work, it didn't spoil an otherwise assured album. But she'd effectively had her 15 minutes of fame.

Midlands band B-Movie had been on the same Some Bizzare compilation Depeche Mode had debuted on. Three singles followed soon after (one of which, 'Nowhere Girl', did reasonably well in countries like Italy), but for some reason an album wasn't forthcoming, and by 1983 even the singles had dried up. Which made it all the more surprising when the Jellybean Benitez-produced, 'A Letter from Afar', suddenly appeared on Sire in January 1984. It was very Factory, similar to, but actually a lot better than, Section 25's 'From A Hilltop' which it preceded by two months. An album, *Forever Running*, followed but it disappeared into a black hole. And that was effectively that. Emanating from the Royal College of Music in London, Kissing The Pink released consistently innovative singles like 'Big Man Restless' (1983), 'Radio On' and 'The Other Side of Heaven' (both 1984) but struggled to break through. Shortening their name to KTP and going dancey didn't help.

Another Pink group working in skewed synthpop were Pink Military (1978-81) who became Pink Industry (1981-87). Fronted by former Big In Japan's Jayne Casey, they were described at the time (by Trouser Press) as 'Siouxsie Sioux fronting [the other] Japan'. That may have been over-flattering but their sound was downtempo unusual, laden with atmosphere despite the scant electronic instrumentation. Two laudable albums were released in 1983 and another in 1985 but they petered out a short while afterwards. Dalek I Love You had also been part of the late 70s / early 80s Liverpool scene, exchanging members with OMD and The Teardrop Explodes. Their eponymous late 1983 album was probably better known for its fabulous cover (a beautifully shot, colour-saturated photo of a model masquerading as a horror-struck actress in a 50s sci-fi film) than the music inside and their last vinyl outing would be a track on the aptly titled Liverpool synth compilation *Small Hits & Near Misses* in 1984. On the other hand, Black (aka Colin Vearncombe), also from Liverpool, was in slow ascendancy. After a couple of indie singles, by 1984 he was on WEA and onto his third, the gorgeously mournful 'Hey Presto' and a reworking of his second, 'More Than The Sun' which Marc Almond would have been proud of. It all boded well but they failed to chart and he was dropped. WEA's loss was A&M's gain as he had his moment in the spotlight with single and album *Wonderful Life* three years later.

Possibly the most intriguing of all was Scottish musician Thomas Leer. He'd been in the thick of the early experimental, electronic singles scene in 1978 with 'Private Plane', followed in the early 80s by a small number of excellent releases on Cherry Red. By 1983 it was clear he had the ambition, talent and actually the looks to become a bona fide pop star – if he wanted it. So he left Cherry Red for Arista, bought himself a Fairlight and set about crafting a smoother, chart-friendly sound. First up in the summer of 1984 was the plush, vaguely oriental-sounding 'International'[20]. Its beguiling melody was offset by lyrics about a drug trafficker ("Came in on Flight 83, making a drop here for the company; Seems to be travelling light, a secret compartment holds the Chinese white [...] Carrying it across the world and selling it to boys and girls") which Arista presumably either didn't clock or turned a blind eye to. Not to be outdone, the follow-up single, 'No.1', had a similarly oriental B-side titled – wait for it – 'Chasing the Dragon', which opened with the strike of a match. Neither advocated drug-taking of course, but it was still outré. A rather too smooth album, *The Scale of Ten*, with strings by Anne Dudley, followed the next year, but none, er, scored. Leer went on to form Act with ex-Propaganda Claudia Brücken but chart success remained elusive and Leer promptly disappeared for a decade or so. His career, so promising up to 1984, is one of the decade's great 'might-have-beens'.

A phrase that has also been applied to Stephen Duffy, who had the misfortune of co-founding and then leaving Duran Duran before they were famous. Nonetheless, adopting the alias Tin Tin, he had an eventual hit – it was released three times between 1982-85 – with the single 'Kiss Me'. September 1984's single, 'She Makes Me Quiver', was as arch as his eyebrows, but failed to keep the momentum going, and another Hergé-monickered side-project, the electro-ish Dr Calculus, did neither him nor his collaborator Roger Freeman of Pigbag any favours.

One group that was in the process of shedding its synthpop skin and becoming more rock *and* at the same time more experimental, was Talk Talk. Following the early days of supporting fellow double-namers Duran Duran (including sharing a producer and label), the group were becoming increasingly jaded with the pop world. *It's My Life* was the first of two transitional albums between the two worlds, and the first to employ Tim Freese-Greene as producer. He would produce all subsequent releases, also becoming a band member, although chose not to join them on stage. Transitional it may have been, but the group were steering a fascinating course between accessibility and investigation. And while the album sold averagely in the UK (peaking at #35), as did the three singles it spurned, they were becoming huge in mainland Europe, especially live.

The tension between playing the game and experimentation was evident in videos for the three singles, all directed by Tim Pope who encouraged their wilful contrariness. On 'It's My Life' (released in January), a glum, raincoated Mark Hollis filmed at London Zoo can't even be bothered to lip-synch; on 'Such A Shame' (April), a woolly-hatted Hollis gives an exaggerated, uncomfortable, piss-taking performance in which he looks uncannily like actor Tim Roth; and on 'Dum Dum Girl' (July), the group perform without instruments in a field in Bedfordshire, peppered with ironic laddish banter. 'We're very much against the grain at the moment', Hollis told Melody Maker in March. 'What we're doing on the new album is [...] to give everything a lot more room to develop'. This sense of space would become more and more of a feature, continuing with the critical and commercial success of *Colour of Spring* in 1986, after which the spaces took over and their last two albums, were exercises in minimalism. So much so that after *Laughing Stock*, there was very little more to be said, so they split up, Hollis leaving music pretty much altogether.

As most synthpop groups changed to become simply groups that used synths and other instruments, two new groups arrived on the scene who would continue to carry the synthpop torch. Bronski Beat didn't last long but the impact of singles 'Smalltown Boy', 'Why?' and 'It Ain't Necessarily So', plus album *Age of Consent*, all released in the second half of 1984, was considerable, if not musically then politically. For a start, all three members were openly gay and their songs reflected this. The combination of outspokenness with bright, danceable tunes, together with an image that normalized gay culture (their utterly functional clothes and haircuts were the antithesis of new pop's narcissism) made them appealing to a wide, working class audience. Unfortunately, tensions in the band resulted in singer Jimmy Somerville leaving in 1985 and although Bronski Beat carried on in some form or other they were a shadow of their former selves.

The new face of synthpop: Bronski Beat and Pet Shop Boys: one short-lived, the other illustriously long.

The other group that carried the torch into the second half of the 80s and well, well beyond were of course Pet Shop Boys. Another in a long line of synth duos, Neil Tennant (Assistant Editor at Smash Hits) and Chris Lowe (fledgling architect) had started making music in 1981, but it wasn't until two years later when Tennant was on a Smash Hits assignment in New York (interviewing The Police as it happened) that things started to come together. While there he arranged to have lunch with hi-NRG producer Bobby Orlando, gave him a demo tape and they ended up recording around a dozen tracks together. The first result was 'West End Girls' which appeared on Orlando's own Bob Cat label in April 1984, licensed to UK Epic. Heavy on the cowbells and handclaps, it was a minor club hit in the US but did nothing in Britain. Compared with the 1985 Stephen Hague re-recording, the original sounds quite weedy, but it was a start. And was it disco or rap or New Order or what? The B-side, simply called 'Pet Shop Boys', was more experimental, essentially an instrumental. A second single 'One More Chance' followed in June, which spread the word round a bit more but was an import-only luxury. Bobby O also advised the duo on image, saying that they should look staid, and look like guilty Catholics. And that's exactly how they've looked ever since.

In September Pet Shop Boys made their debut live performance at the Fridge in Brixton, attended by half of Smash Hits. Tennant's position at the magazine gave the group insider knowledge on how to play the industry game, but he never used its pages to promote the group. 'The Pet Shop Boys are only ever mentioned in Smash Hits when I go on holiday, and our record was never reviewed there because I said I didn't want it to be'.[21] The duo deftly bridged the gap between early 80s synthpop and electro and the influx of late 80s dance music. More than that, they would become one of the most successful, resilient acts of the late 20th and early 21st centuries, reinventing themselves (through working with zeitgeist producers, occasional guest vocalists and a keen eye for image and fashion) just enough to keep them fresh with every single – 60 and counting. Their intelligent, very English lyrics would mix catty Wildean wit with often overlooked keen social commentary. They also ushered in a more savvy approach to working with and in the record industry acting as role models for artists who might otherwise have simply signed on the dotted line and never mind the small print. Their influence is incalculable.

Where Pet Shop Boys got it right, most synthpop groups in 1984 got it wrong. Of the old guard, Visage bowed out with the limp 'Love Glove' single and *Beat Boy* album. Torch Song promised much, and with a young William Orbit at the controls, the production of debut album *Wish Thing* was assuredly techy and sophisticated, but it lacked decent songs. The naffly named Savage Progress, featuring former Roxy Music bassist Rik Kenton and Thompson Twins drummer Andrew Edge, released a decent debut album, *Celebration*, and three equally decent singles, but called it a day by the end of the year. Even Brilliant, who could boast former Killing Joke bassist, Martin Glover (better known as Youth), Jimmy Cauty (later to join Bill Drummond in the KLF), Ben Watkins (aka Juno Reactor) and a fine singer in June Montana, couldn't make it work. Managed by David Balfe, their 1984 single 'Soul Murder' was the first ever release on his newly-formed Food label, but when that flopped they lurched from synthpop to funk before, in an act of desperation, drafting in Stock Aitken Waterman to produce their only album, *Kiss the Lips of Life*. It was the kiss of death.

The plight of synthpop label Survival Records was also indicative of the times. Stuck in a 1981 timewarp, nobody wanted groups like Play, Thirteen At Midnight and former robotic mime and Gary Numan support act Tik & Tok anymore, although all three hung on in there until 1985. So, true to their name, the label switched the game plan to heavy rockers The Quireboys (via EMI) and later the Celtic band Capercaillie (initially through BMG).

There were scores of other synthpop outfits with product released in 1984 who barely lasted the year let alone the decade[22]. Many have been rediscovered via compilations like Cherry Red's *Electrical Language: British Synth Pop 78-84*. Some have even reformed and continued recording. They all sounded a bit like Ricky Gervais's band, Seona Dancing, who chose the year to split up after 1983's two inadvertently hilariously portentous singles which, knowing Gervais as we do now, sound like the Spinal Tap of synthpop.

Chapter 3: Restless Albion
Inter-city post-punk in England's dreaming

The rain falls hard on a humdrum town.
The Smiths 'William, It Was Really Nothing'

If 1984 was the point when post-punk was officially 'over', it was unfortunate that it was just then that we released our first album.[1]
Tracey Thorn

Memorable but not-quite-essential-to-buy stuff that fills out a contemporary record collection and turns it into a cultural library.[2]
Julian Cope

Punk may have been year zero in many respects – culturally, politically, lyrically, sartorially – but musically it was still guitar, bass, drums. For the most part, the music that immediately developed out of it – new wave and post-punk – continued with the same instrumental line-up. To grossly over-generalise, new wave was the more 'commercial', radio-friendly but still quirky continuation of punk, while post-punk described the less commercial, earnest, often gloomy groups. New wave bands were generally willing to play the game, post-punkers were more subversive. New wave bands tended to play conventional instruments, perhaps with a smattering of keyboards and brass, whereas some post-punk bands (not all) experimented with the synthesizer and drum-machine. Of course, it was never that simple. Was Siouxsie and the Banshees' radio-friendly debut single 'Hong Kong Garden' post-punk? Was the John Foxx-era Ultravox! a new wave band? How could Throbbing Gristle be post-punk if they hadn't been punk in the first place? And in any case, they were better known as 'industrial', a whole other genre.

In any case, by 1980 new wave as a genre was over[3] as it splintered into 2-tone, a mod revival, synthpop and new romanticism, which then became new pop. Post-punk, meanwhile, had gone through its intense, innovative first phase (from 'The Public Image' and 'Warm Leatherette' to *154* and the death of Ian Curtis) before settling into a fairly grim, grey groove populated by the likes of Echo & The Bunnymen, Gang Of Four, The Fall and a host of others. As the early 80s progressed, there was further diversification as some responded to the electronic dance music coming out of the New York clubs (New Order, A Certain Ratio, Cabaret Voltaire), others went goth (Bauhaus, The Cure, Siouxsie and the Banshees) and still others switched from post-punk to new pop (Simple Minds, Scritti Politti, Thompson Twins).

This chapter is about those who kept largely to the straight and narrow of guitar, bass, drums through the transitional year of 1984, as post-punk 'ended' and indie 'began'[4]. A few were ambitious and canny enough to craft a sound that would hit the charts, but the majority were disaffected young men and (some) women who'd been inspired by punk, angered by Thatcher's first few years in office and didn't particularly feel the urge to break away from a style and stance they felt comfortable with. The scene was politically charged and strongly regional (the north a post-punk bastion), somewhat fatalistic while at the same time trying to make a decent fist of life, and metaphorically played out in a rain-sodden post-industrial landscape. It was a breeding ground for Peel Session bands. It was the opposite of new pop. What follows doesn't attempt to cover everyone – there were literally hundreds of bands – and many are dealt with in other chapters, but it does indicate the quantity, quality and variety of bands that made up this particular scene. As John Robb of The Membranes wrote:

> *The mid-Eighties post-post-post punk scene was a diverse collection of bands who were joined together by wild nights in a never-ending series of gigs in venues up and down the UK, aided by reportage in fanzines and radio play from John Peel.[...] Some of the bands went on to mainstream success, some of them were rounded up and placed awkwardly in the middle of the NME's C86 cassette which arrived a couple of years after things got going, some of them faded away and some of them have become seminal influences*[5].

Robb was talking about the noisier, thrashier end of post-punk but there was plenty of subtlety too. And rather than 'some', *most* faded away. One of the strange things about the slew of bands who'd formed in the aftermath of punk was how so many of them split at the turn of the next decade and then, seemingly *en masse*, reformed in the new millennium. It was as if the 90s was some kind of hibernation period: the end of reacting against something (miners' strike, Apartheid, Thatcher, Poll Tax) and the beginning of a more hedonistic period which they somehow didn't fit into. Most of the 80s post-punk bands failed to adapt to the ensuing dance scene – exceptions being groups like The Beloved, Underworld and The Shamen – pushing them into solo, session or production work, or careers outside the music business. Not even britpop or grunge served as coattails on which their forebears could tag a ride.

If the 'end' of post-punk was not understandably its highpoint, it was nevertheless an important year serving up a dozen or so classic albums, each very different: Echo & The Bunnymen's *Ocean Rain*, U2's *The Unforgettable Fire*, Cocteau Twins' *Treasure*, This Mortal Coil's *It'll End in Tears*, Nick Cave's debut, The Psychedelic Furs' *Mirror Moves*, *The Wonderful and Frightening World of The Fall*, Shriekback's *Jam Science*, XTC's *The Big Express*, Siouxsie and the Banshees' *Hyaena*, The Cure's *The Top*, The Smiths' debut, etc. By any yardstick, most of the above were critically and commercially successful. But there were plenty of post-punk bands who, despite being lauded in the music press and with sizeable followings, struggled commercially; the bands who get omitted from 80s histories but for whom 1984 was a significant year for themselves, for their fans and for influencing the next generation of music-makers, as evidenced by the young audiences attending their reunion concerts in the new millennium. Hardly any of the bands which follow made it much beyond the turn of the new decade, at least in their first incarnation, but here follows an inter-city tour of England, by Ford Transit or creaky British Rail train, of the great and the good, the known and the unknown, who together made up the tail-end but still potent mid-80s British post-punk scene.

*****

Let's start in Hull, UK City of Culture in 2017 but in 1984 a pretty run-down place, struggling to come to terms with its declining port. In post-punk circles, Hull is forever associated with Everything But The Girl and The Housemartins, formed there in 1982 and 1983 respectively, but was also responsible for siring Sade's band, Roland Gift of Fine Young Cannibals and, going further back, Mick Ronson and (pre-Throbbing Gristle) COUM Transmissions. Other post-punk bands included Red Guitars, Luddites, International Rescue and the 'kooky' Indians In Moscow, all of whom featured on The Tube's Hull special in December 1983. Red Guitars had been filmed performing their anti-IT minor hit 'Good Technology' in a car breakers yard, and the following year saw them continue with protest songs like 'Marimba Jive' (anti-apartheid) and 'Steeltown' (anti-government: 'It doesn't matter how I vote, the same confederacy of fools get in'), the former a wonderful – if marimba-less – jit-style concoction. A debut album, *Slow To Fade*, followed but they somehow managed to disintegrate the following year, spawning The Planet Wilson, who also failed to make it into the 90s.

Not included in the programme, Nyam Nyam were onto their second single, 'Fate/Hate', produced by Peter Hook for Factory Benelux, which did well enough for them to 'upgrade' to Situation Two, who released their sole album *Hope of Heaven*. Hook remained in touch, the following reminiscence highlighting the prosaic, comradely life of a typical post-punk band (comparison of cars notwithstanding):

> *New Order were recording Low Life in the daytime, so Hooky drove over [...] in his Audi Quattro at midnight, crossed the Pennines in about 45 minutes, with their Emulator and Prophet 5 so we could overdub all the keyboards in one night. Then he drove back to work on his own album. It was all quick, maybe 10 evenings for all the recording and mixing. [...] Then at five am, we'd push my girlfriend Sarah's Morris Marina off in the snow to start it – I had to get it back at six so she could get to work on a local pig farm.*[6]

If the music was sweepingly melancholic, the lyrics were pointedly bleak, describing, if rather obliquely, the austerity and violence of early 80s Hull. 'If this were to sell in huge quantities, pop music would never be the same again. Sadly it won't, and it will', was the accurate verdict of Melody Maker[7]. They split a year later, frontman Paul Trynka going on to become Reviews Editor of Mojo and author of books about The Stones, Bowie and Iggy Pop. Opening too late (October 1984) for inclusion in The Tube special was the now semi-legendary Adelphi Club run by Paul Jackson, based in a tatty terrace house which nevertheless would later host early gigs by the likes of Pulp, The Stone Roses, Oasis and Radiohead. Continuing the theme, *Warped Houses* was the 1984 debut (cassette) album by the brilliantly-named Punctured Tough Guy. Splitting up to mass indifference the following year, its guitarist David McSharry met

Steve Cobby on a night bus, the destination of which would be the eventual formation of Fila Brazillia.

Just up the road in York, The Redskins combined a nod to Motown with hardcore left-wing post-punk. Fronted by NME scribe Chris 'X Moore' Dean, they were heavy on anti-Thatcher polemic and in 1984 had the perfect soapbox on which to vent it. But although singles like 'Keep On Keepin' On!' were unashamedly jaunty and Jam-ish, Dean's lyrics were weighed down by Marxist cliché. They split in 1986. Whether it was due to Thatcher's then impregnable position or musical differences is a moot point. The city was also home to Red Rhino Records, distribution and shop, run by Tony K (so-called because no-one could ever pronounce his Polish surname, Kostrzewa), the label releasing just shy of a hundred titles in its roughly ten-year history, including Killing Jokey wannabes 1919 from Bradford and Pulp's first album. Its distribution wing played an even more important role, connecting the whole of the north's post-punk scene.

Twenty-five miles down the road in Leeds, the Gang of Four were by now the gang of three. The limp funk of 1983's *Hard* and an equally unconvincing live album, *At the Palace*, the year after gave post-punk a bad name. They split mid-year though perhaps it would have been kinder on their legacy had it been a couple of years earlier. Formed at the same time and of a similar Marxist bent (Leeds was a haven for lefty students), The Mekons had been the first signings to Bob Last's Fast Product. They had been largely dormant during the early 80s but were spurred back into action thanks to the folk-collectivist spirit brought on by the miners' strike. With the addition of steel guitar, harmonica and fiddle, they became alt-country, performing miners' benefits and recording their first album for five years, *Fear and Whiskey*, released the following year. Their guitarist Jon Langford was actually in two bands, having formed The Three Johns (with Johns Hyatt and Brennan) during the former band's earlier hiatus. 1984 saw the release of their debut album *Atom Drum Bop*, bearing the slogan 'Rock'n'Roll Versus Thaatchiism' [sic], and the stomping 'Do the Square Thing' single which comfortably made the NME writers' end-of-year Top 50. Like The Redskins and The Mekons, you could find them playing miners' benefits up and down the country. Some of Leeds' gothness rubbed off on them, and there were similarities (especially the central role of drum-machine) with another Leeds band, Red Lorry Yellow Lorry, whose 'Hollow Eyes' single that year, complete with Joy Division growly bass and metronomic drums, put them on the map – although both bands would split at the turn of the decade.

Also getting going were The Wedding Present (formed from the ashes of the short-lived Lost Pandas and releasing their debut single in 1985) and Age of Chance. The former would be vanguards of the indie movement, the latter a blueprint for a slightly different, club-influenced take on the genre. 'In Leeds at the time the goth-type stuff was massive and we didn't want to sound like that. […] All of us had been informed by punk and especially the post-punk stuff. […] Cabaret Voltaire, Suicide or Fad Gadget, who was living in Leeds at the time'[8]. Age of Chance would turn out to be the second-half-of-the-80s' cool chancers, into manifestos, graphic design and multicoloured cycle tops, while their post-modern demolition of Prince's 'Kiss' was a key moment in the development of indie dance.

*****

The cover of *Made In Sheffield*, a film by Eve Wood made much later, in 2001, shows a guitar being hurled from the top of a typically grim, grey Sheffield tower block, and for a few post-punk years that was effectively the city's calling card: the futuristic world of the Human League and Heaven 17, and to a lesser extent Cabaret Voltaire and ABC (neither of whom were really synthpop *or* futuristic). But by 1984 the guitars were creeping back in: Cabaret Voltaire and ABC had always featured them, in the former's case unconventionally, in the latter's unapologetically (the cover of their 'That Was Then But This Is Now' single was totally dominated by one); Heaven 17 were increasingly using funky guitar chops; and the Human League's long-awaited single 'The Lebanon' was plastered with a guitar riff that would have done Def Leppard proud. Or Comsat Angels, who flew Sheffield's guitar-driven post-punk flag but after three decent but unsuccessful albums on Polydor, in 1984 found themselves on the ill-fitting Jive label who wanted them to be a pop band. It didn't work out, although their one earlier hit, 'Independence Day', got a makeover which scraped the charts. Artery similarly struggled to find an audience and after their 1984 album *The Second Coming*, and a couple of singles, they split the following year. (They got a third coming thanks to Jarvis Cocker's Meltdown festival in 2007 at London's Royal Festival Hall).

The strongest coterie of Sheffield's mid-80s post-punk bands was built around Cabaret Voltaire and fellow travellers Clock DVA, The Box, Hula and Chakk. Cabaret Voltaire were ten years into their strange trajectory which had taken them from avant-garde attic doodlings and scratchy paranoid post-punk on Rough Trade to fairly sophisticated if resolutely edgy synth-funk on Some Bizzare/Virgin, starting with the excellent *The Crackdown*. In January 1984 they were on the cover of Sounds and gearing up for a possible major breakthrough. It was a long wait though, interspersed with producing the very Cabs-sounding one-off single 'Shake It Right' by Six Sed Red (featuring Soft Cell affiliate Cindy Ecstasy and early B-Movie member Rick Holliday) and a collaboration with Paul Haig. Finally, in October, the thrilling single 'Sensoria' boded well, but the album that followed, *Micro-Phonies*, sounded thinner and a tad predictable compared with its predecessor. The band would keep striving to combine the alternative with the accessible for another ten years, including a house-fixated spell with EMI at the turn of the decade, but by the early 90s had reverted to instrumental electronica around the same time as IDM and Warp Records had caught up with them.

Clock DVA were cut from the same cloth, experimenting with electronics and tape loops and falling under the 'industrial' tag, having released an early cassette album on Throbbing Gristle's label of the same name. But after the critically acclaimed vinyl debut, *Thirst*, frontman Adi Newton decided he wanted to go in a funk direction, sacked the rest of the band and released the major label *Advantage*. This didn't work out either so he ended up returning to his experimental roots in 1984 by forming the ultra-conceptual The Anti-Group, while guitarist John Carruthers joined Siouxsie and the Banshees. Meanwhile, the members of Clock DVA's original line-up formed The Box, described variously as no wave, skronk and 'like The Fire Engines', releasing a couple of albums, including 1984's *Great Moments in Big Slam* and the single 'Muscle In' before splitting the following year.

In the shadows: Sheffield's Cabaret Voltaire and new kids on the (industrial) block, Pulp.

The most interesting – and complementary – takes on industrial funk, however, were by Hula and Chakk, both formed in 1982 and both hitting their stride two years later. Hula's *Murmur* album and 'Fever Car' single sounded like *Red Mecca*-era Cabs, dance music for claustrophobic cellars, and they would get even better until 1988 when the Red Rhino label and distributor went bust. Chakk were similar, possibly even better, but burned brightly and *got* burned when signing to a major. Debut single 'Out Of The Flesh', brilliantly produced at the Cabs' Western Works and released on Doublevision, was ferocious white funk. MCA stepped in, sensed hits, gave them a massive advance – enough to set up a studio, FON[9], to rival Western Works – and the rest is your typical major-doesn't-understand-gets-second-thoughts-and-drops-band history. Manager Dave Taylor reflected that Chakk could have been the Chilli Peppers meets the Prodigy, in 1984. After splitting, both Chakk and FON members (notably Mark Bryden who would form Moloko, but also engineer Rob Gordon) would go on to help shape Sheffield's next generation: purveyors of bleep'n'bass and IDM, and of course Warp.

There were countless others: In The Nursery, identical twins Klive and Nigel Humberstone, who started off in vaguely 'industrial' territory but have since carved out a successful (if largely ignored in the UK) niche in scoring new music for classic silent films; Bass Tone Trap, whose only album *Trapping*, released in 1984, was as much free-jazz as post-punk; Dig Vis Drill, described by Martin Lilleker in his excellent compendium of Sheffield bands, *Beats Working for a Living*, as 'started out with a dozen great songs [and] by time the band split up sometime in the late Eighties [...] still only had 12 songs - the same ones, only longer'[10]; the heinously overlooked UV Pop; as well as They Must Be Russians, Mau Maus, Vendino Pact etc. The list is long.

A 40-mile drive west across the Peak District prompts a comparative link between one more Sheffield band and their Manchester equivalent. For sheer dogged determination, it was hard to beat Pulp and James, two bands formed at the beginning of the decade but who spent almost all of it in relative obscurity. Both had released debut records in 1983 (*It* mini-album and 'Jimone' single respectively) and the following year saw them gigging quite regularly, in Pulp's case largely locally[11], in James's more extensively, including supporting The Smiths. Pulp's guitarist Russell Senior felt it was then that they arrived at the Pulp sound, the songs written through a collaborative process but with Crocker taking over on vocals[12]. Nevertheless, it would take the baggy embrace of Madchester to put James on the map, and Britpop to make stars of Pulp.

*****

Manchester in 1984 could rightly – and if you were Tony Wilson, *incessantly* – claim to rival London as the country's most exciting music scene, and not just because of New Order, Factory and The Smiths (all dealt with in Chapter 15). The city's punk pedigree had been established with The Sex Pistols' two Free Trade Hall concerts in 1976, inspiring and galvanising a group of young musicians who had been waiting for something to come along and shake things up. Buzzcocks, Slaughter and the Dogs, The Fall and Warsaw formed as a response. Magazine and Joy Division led the way in post-punk, closely followed by a wave of other 'Factory bands'. Maverick movers and shakers like Richard Boon, Tosh Ryan, Tony Wilson, Rob Gretton and Alan Erasmus began to patch it all together, making it up as they went along. Writers like Paul Morley, Jon Savage, John Robb, Mick Middles, Dave Haslam and photographer Kevin Cummins had documented it all in fanzines like *In The City, Modern Drugs,*[13] *Rox* and *Debris*. By 1984, Joy Division, Buzzcocks and Magazine were already history but the Manchester scene was still thriving, if coming to the end of its post-punk phase – marked, for instance, by the closure of Cargo Studios where so many of its chief exponents had recorded[14] – and at an interesting crossroads.

The Fall were at the top of their game, thanks in part to new guitarist, Brix Salenger, who'd recently become Brix Smith. The American brought not only a more accessible sound but also a new look. 'You're not going on stage dressed like that', was surely an utterance made by wife to husband in the early days of their relationship. Amazingly, November 1983 was the first time they'd performed on national TV – on The Tube, at the insistence of number one fan John Peel – and the following year they were on a roll, touring their *Perverted By Language* album, releasing three singles (including the fabulous 'C.R.E.E.P.', Mark's slurred magic realist monotonal drawl offset by Brix's sunny west coast harmonies), another album, *The Wonderful and Frightening World of The Fall*, and the start of a collaboration with dancer Michael Clark. Clark had just left the Royal Ballet to set up his own company, one of their first performances being to dance to The Fall's 'Lay of the Land' on the Whistle Test that autumn, Clark in fetching (or perhaps cheeky would be the right word) arse-baring strides.[15] Mr and Mrs Smith even featured, 'interviewing' Clark, in the mock-documentary, *Hail the New Puritans*, directed by Charles Atlas and eventually released in 1986[16]. They would collaborate again on the highly amusing *I Am Curious, Orange* at Edinburgh Festival in 1988. Even their sleeves looked half decent. Perhaps it was love, but in any case, the second half of the 80s would see the band arguably at their peak, the 90s a Brix-less blur of drink, drugs, infighting and below-par records, but astonishingly they kept going, outlasted their champion, Peel, attained national heritage status, until Smith departed for the great bar in the sky in 2018.

Newly-weds: The Fall's Mark E and Brix Smith. Hulme: squats for many Manc musicians and artists.

The revolving door of The Fall's line-up had, in 1983, deposited Marc Riley on Manchester's pavements, whereupon he quickly picked himself up, dusted himself down and formed his own band, The Creepers, and (with Jim Khambatta) a label, In-Tape, the former releasing three singles and two albums on the latter, all in 1984. It wasn't a million miles from The Fall's sound – rough, edgy, urgent – but it served them well for four years. Riley went on to a career in radio, co-presenting with Mark Radcliffe the long-running Hit the North (ironically named after a song by Riley's former employers) on BBC Radio One. Also ex-Fall, Martin Bramah, Una Baines and Rick Goldstraw had formed Blue Orchids back in 1979, but were always an on/off band and by the mid-80s were off. Rougher, edgier and more urgent than either were Big Flame. Their 'Sink' single in that year was a minor masterpiece of concise art punk with guitars that sounded like scratching an itch, and its video a terrific low-budget version of rotoscoping; but, exhausted physically and musically, they never made it beyond 1986. Linked to Big Flame were A Witness who released their debut EP, the wonderfully named *Loudhailer Songs*, at the end of the year. Both bands were on Ron Johnson Records who would contribute five tracks to the NME's indie-defining *C86* compilation. On splitting up at the end of the decade, guitarist Keith Curtis went on to play with The Membranes who'd been around since punk and who in 1984 had just relocated to Manchester from Blackpool. After a few early 80s singles and a debut album, they released the semi-infamous punk-thrash single, 'Spike Milligan's Tape Recorder' (which nearly ended up being the unlikely first release on Alan McGee's Creation), became Single of the Week in four music papers[17] and reached #6 in John Peel's Festive 50.

Many of Manchester's post-punkers lived in Hulme Crescents, the failed urban housing experiment just south of the city centre. It was where Factory effectively started, at the Russell Club, and the Hacienda and university were a short walk away. In 1984 Manchester City Council stopped collecting rents and simply abandoned it. If you didn't mind a bit of dystopian discomfort, it was perfect for cash-strapped artists and musicians. The area became home to A Certain Ratio, Section 25, The Passage, a young Ian Brown and many others. 'A three-bedroomed flat had a thousand square feet of vacant space to do what you wanted with. [...] The amount of space was fantastic. It created freedom. There were reggae bands, punk and ska bands, jazz bands, loads of bands because of this'[18]. Typical, indeed formed there, were The Birthday Party-influenced Inca Babies who released a string of angry singles and albums in the mid-80s. Surroundings begat the band.

Contrary to popular opinion there were venues other than the Hacienda. The Free Trade Hall (famous not only for the Pistols but also Bob Dylan and the famous 'Judas!' shout in 1966), The Apollo, Manchester University on Oxford Road (where the BBC's ORS was presented), the Poly, and a host of live music venues doubling up as nightclubs like Band On The Wall, The Boardwalk, The Gallery, Legend, Manhattan, The Ritz, Berlin, and International 1 & 2. The Hacienda was an incredible space, but its colour-coded, cavernous interior, designed by Ben Kelly, was better suited to the acid house and rave scene of the late 80s rather than post-punk.

Following the dissolution of The Buzzcocks and Magazine in the very early 80s, their two frontmen had gone solo with initially some degree of success, but both had relatively quiet 1984s: Pete Shelley's 'Never Again' single flopped, while Howard Devoto contributed to This Mortal Coil's *It'll End in Tears*. Meanwhile, Linder Sterling, the common thread between them (she'd designed sleeves for both bands and had dated Devoto), also struggled, choosing that year to dissolve her group Ludus following an aborted recording session in Brussels. Another band to split around this time were The Frantic Elevators fronted by Mick Hucknall. They'd been underachievers, but one of their handful of singles, 'Holding Back the Years', would be re-recorded by Hucknall and his new band of musicians, called variously World Service, Dancing Dead, Red and then Simply Red, and the rest is (blue-eyed, red-haired soul) history.

Formed in the north of Manchester 1981, The Chameleons were a great band who slipped between the cracks. Sounding like Psychedelic Furs fronted by Julian Cope with Stephen Morris on drums, the production quality (initially by the band with Colin Richardson) was leagues ahead of most post-punk groups. Their strange label history took them from a debut single on Epic to two albums on the independent Scottish label, Statik, and then to Geffen, all in just four years. 1984 saw them at an in-between albums peak, touring mostly in Europe – they were huge in Spain. Why didn't they become big in Britain? Was it the ghastly artwork? It would be difficult to blame their manager, whose untimely death in 1987 affected them so badly, they promptly split up.

The early-to-mid 80s also saw the first stirrings of the city's *next* generation of alternative bands, although by the time they fully surfaced it would be as part of

Madchester and Britpop, five and ten years off respectively. The Stone Roses had been around in various guises since 1979, first as The Patrol, then Waterfront, before settling on their more familiar name at the beginning of 1984. Singer Ian Brown and guitarist John Squire had been school-friends and there had been various other mates drifting in and out, but when Alan 'Reni' Wren joined on drums in May, they were halfway to finding their lolloping groove. They played their first gig on 23 October, supporting Pete Townshend at an anti-heroin concert at the Moonlight Club in London[19] and a single produced by Martin Hannett followed the next year. At this stage they could have been the perfect band for Creation with their Byrds-influenced melodies but the pieces of the jigsaw still weren't in place. It was only when Gary 'Mani' Mounfield joined on bass in 1986, and when indie and dance collided at the end of the decade, that the Roses *really* arrived.

The Happy Mondays were also demoing around the same time (in fact had been doing so since 1981 under different band names), played their first gig at the GPO Club in Blackpool and in 1985 entered Mike Pickering's Battle Of The Bands competition at The Hacienda, coming last. Pickering urged Factory to sign them anyway, and their first single was released later that year. But like the Roses, they'd have to wait. As would Inspiral Carpets, who'd also formed in the early 80s[20]. After the rapid form-record-and-release of punk, it was strange how these three Manchester bands – and James to an extent – took so long to gestate and 'make it'. (Meanwhile, Liam and Noel Gallagher were 11 and 16 respectively[21] and Oasis just a dream).

*****

There was no equivalent[22] of Tony Wilson extolling the virtues of neighbouring Liverpool, but its music spoke for itself. Liverpool's role in the birth of British popular music doesn't need repeating, except perhaps to say that for 51 of the 60 weeks between April 1963 and May 1964, there was a Merseybeat record at #1. Its international outlook and scally sense of itself contributed to a music scene that was the equal of Manchester's, 'a proud, boastful Celtic city where the lads dream big and talk big'[23]. Its late 70s / early 80s scene was almost as fast-moving, incestuous and successful. Synthpop vied with post-punk, Eric's provided the stage[24] and Zoo, Probe and Inevitable the record labels[25]. This variety meant that Liverpool – or, to be strictly accurate, Merseyside – was as much new pop as post-punk. If Manchester was dour, Liverpool was happy-go-lucky and unembarrassed about wanting to have hits and be famous. However, as with most British cities around this time, unemployment in the city was at an all-time high (double the national average at 27%) and its population had declined from around 900,000 in 1951 to half that in 1986[26].

That said, 1984 was a good year to be a Scouser. Liverpool won the League for the third year in a row, and Everton the FA Cup (when that still meant something). As we have seen, Frankie Goes To Hollywood topped the charts, with Dead Or Alive just behind them, and although overtly electronic groups like A Flock Of Seagulls, Dalek I Love You and Pink Industry were by now defunct or on the wane, the synth-inflected OMD, China Crisis and The Lotus Eaters were still riding high. As an aside, synthpop was never really embraced by Liverpudlians, even if these bands were often more innovative than the more accepted guitar bands.

One such guitar-wielding would-be star was Pete Wylie, who had come through the city's labyrinthian network of late 70s new wave bands, having spent seemingly a month in each, before forming Wah!. Wylie always thought big and had a mouth with which to tell everybody about it – in song, in interviews, in the pub. After a #3 hit with 'The Story of the Blues', Wylie signed to WEA, was dropped, reconfigured the band, signed to Beggars Banquet and returned in 1984 as The Mighty Wah! with an album, *A Word to the Wise Guy*, and another hit single 'Come Back' – John Peel's single of the year. And you can see why. Peel and Wylie were ardent Liverpool FC supporters, and there was something of the Kop in lyrics like 'A small belief can mean you'll never walk alone' and the urgent, stirring emotion of Wylie's voice. At the end of its promo video, he is seen relaxing with a bottle of champagne having 'made it'. Tongue in cheek it certainly was, but for all of Peel's championing and Wylie's talking and scheming, post-1984 success was to be elusive.

Aspiration was Echo & The Bunnymen to a tee, and in 1984 they were at their striving, passionate peak. *Ocean Rain* is forever held up as the group's masterpiece, even by themselves (*especially* by themselves[27]), and it was certainly their last great album. Bill Drummond, their manager, encouraged the band to get a more natural sound: brush sticks, double bass, acoustic guitar. It is above all a romantic album, drenched in strings recorded in Davout Studios in the east end of Paris and full of gibberish words like 'Blind sailors, imprisoned jailers' or the frankly bewildering quatrain, 'C-c-c-cucumber, C-c-c-cabbage, C-c-c-cauliflower, men on Mars'. Three singles, 'The Killing Moon', 'Silver' and 'Seven Seas' graced the charts (all Top 30) and mouthy, perfectly-lipped-and-coiffed Ian McCulloch released a decent cover of Kurt Weill's 'September Song', as extravagantly orchestrated as *Ocean Rain*.

In May, Drummond organized something called Crystal Day, inviting fans to join the band in a 12-hour happening, a Magical Mystery Tour if you will. Beginning with food at the group's favourite café, Brian's Diner, it took in a choir recital in the Anglican Cathedral, a banana fight on the Mersey ferry, a mass bicycle ride, and finished with a concert in St George's Hall, much of which was filmed by The Tube. It was bonkers, very Drummond and very Liverpool. But there were frictions within the band and with their record company and ultimately the album proved a difficult act to follow. A compilation followed in 1985, a proper follow-up, simply titled *Echo & The Bunnymen*, two years later (you always know a band's in trouble when they resort to releasing self-titled albums well into their careers… except in the case of that other Liverpool group, The Beatles), McCulloch quit in 1988, drummer Pete de Freitas was killed in a motorbike accident the following year and the band dissolved in the early 90s.

In the early 80s, the Bunnymen's main local competitors were The Teardrop Explodes fronted by Julian Cope, but in a contrariness that would mark his whole career he started to take an anti-pop stance, allowed the group to disintegrate, became obsessed

'The Killing Moon', first single from Echo & The Bunnymen's *Ocean Rain*. You could find it and many others in Probe on Liverpool's Button Street, home also of label Probe Plus, both run by Geoff Smith (sitting on steps).

with drugs and psychedelia, and 'went off on one' (see Chapter 17). The Teardrops' place was taken by The Icicle Works who had enjoyed some chart success with 'Love is a Wonderful Colour' in 1983. An impressive eponymous debut album did moderately well on release in March 1984, and the re-release of an earlier single, '(Birds Fly) A Whisper to a Scream', should have clinched it, but for some reason the single failed to make the Top 50. The equally fine, 'Hollow Horse', did even worse. They soldiered on before the predictable split at the end of the decade. Of course this happened to countless bands, but it seemed particularly hard on one that was loved by the critics and wrote such accessible songs. Two other bands who seemed equally poised to make a breakthrough were The Room (formed 1979) and Pale Fountains (1980). The former had started off, like most Liverpool bands, on the more melodic side of post-punk, but their fine third album, *In Evil Hour*, produced by John Punter and Television's Tom Verlaine, and including the catchy 'New Dreams for Old' single, inexplicably flopped in 1984 and they disbanded the following year. Likewise, the Pale Fountains who moved at great expense from Operation Twilight to Virgin. Debut album *Pacific Street,* released in February 1984, was a bit of Prefab Sprout, a bit of Lloyd Cole and a bit of Everything But The Girl, complete with trumpet and bossa nova beats, but its zigzaggy nature frustrated rather than pleased. A second album followed in 1985 but they split soon after.

There were scores of other groups, a number of which ended up on two 1984 Liverpool compilations, *Small Hits and Near Misses* and *A Secret Liverpool*. The former, released by Inevitable, home to the earliest releases by Wah!, China Crisis and Dead Or Alive, also included the only song recorded by Margi Clarke (aka Margox) who starred in the Liverpool film *Letter To Brezhnev*, released the following year[28]); the latter, on Davies Records, included the first recorded track by The La's –

the curiously titled 'I Don't Like Hanging'. Much much later, Cherry Red released a 5CD box set of some 100 Liverpool bands of the era, but not even that included Crikey It's the Comptons! and The Jactars, both formed in 1984, and about whom, incredibly, a whole book was written by Sara Cohen[29].

One group who saved their best for later were It's Immaterial. In 1984 they were ploughing a lonely furrow of guitar-driven post-punk, the bizarrely named 'A Gigantic Raft (in the Philippines)' sinking to Mariana Trench-like depths[30]. Within a year, however, they were writing more refined songs which somehow managed to be both commercial *and* alternative, adding sophisticated, increasingly electronic instrumentation, a production that major label bands would have killed for and a sense of space in which John Campbell's companionable voice and lyrics were allowed to breathe. In two years' time they would release one of the defining road songs of the 80s, 'Driving Away From Home', which took the listener along the M62 to Manchester and beyond. An album, the excellent *Life's Hard and Then You Die*, and two more stonking singles followed but they couldn't maintain the momentum and by 1990 after a patchy second album, *Song*, they drove off into the sunset.

The second half of the 80s saw Liverpool in a bad place with most of the above groups split or dormant and a succession of tragedies (Hatton, Heysel, Hillsborough[31]) hanging over it. True, jangly groups like The La's, The Farm, The Lightning Seeds and The Christians would attempt to provide light relief, and Cream would usher in hedonistic club culture, but it was difficult to argue the case that, band-wise, the city had rather had its day.

******

In 'Driving Away From Home', Campbell had suggested dropping in on Newcastle, a city with a rock and pop heritage which included Sting, Bryan Ferry, Mark Knopfler and Neil Tennant. It was also, of course, home to The Tube – essential viewing across the nation on Friday early evenings. Newcastle's post-punk scene revolved around Kitchenware Records and a coterie of bands who weren't so much post-punk as leftfield pop. Prefab Sprout (see Chapter 17) and The Kane Gang enjoyed chart success in 1984, the latter's 'The Closest Thing to Heaven' hitting #12 in the charts, while others just missed out. Martin Stephenson and the Daintees' debut single, the airy cajun-style 'Roll On Summertime', should have been a hit, and Hurrah!'s 'Who'd Have Thought' might have been.

There was a decent live circuit with City Hall presenting major bands – and St James's Park hosting Bob Dylan on 5 July – alongside smaller venues like M's and Broken Doll, and The Riverside would open the following year. But for many, including Simon McKay, editor of Eccentric Sleeve Notes fanzine, it was on the turn: "[By 1985] the real 80s had arrived. Separateness was no longer celebrated. The aim was to appeal to as many people as possible and generate large quantities of money"[32]. No-one told The Crawling Chaos, an oddball Tyneside group who'd somehow had a single on Factory in 1980, were then 'demoted' to Factory Benelux for a stupendously nonsensical album, and by 1984 found themselves self-releasing *The Big C* which turned out to be relatively 'normal', if unfashionable anti-post-punk.

*****

Birmingham and Coventry's post-punk scene was heavily influenced by black music and its large multiracial population, much more so than in most other conurbations. 'You had people of different races forced to work together, and then forced to stand together in the dole queue', remembers Dave Wakeling of The Beat[33]. The integration enabled reggae, soul, jazz and funk to inform new bands like UB40, Dexys Midnight Runners, Pigbag, Swans Way and even Duran Duran. But it was ska that had the biggest influence. Exactly paralleling post-punk, the so-called 2-tone bands like The Specials, The Beat and The Selecter brought both substance and fun to the pop charts. The substance was in 2-tone's political outlook, the fun in its boisterous music. However, the early 80s saw the three bands in question shed original members and by 1984 only The Specials – re-named The Special AKA – remained.

In between, there had been Fun Boy Three, formed by Terry Hall, Neville Staples and Lynval Golding after they'd left The Specials. Strangely, despite a string of great singles and two fine albums, it was a short-lived affair. Hall chose instead to form a more 60s Caucasian pop-influenced group, The Colour Field, reinforced by his choice of accompanying musicians, ex-Swinging Cats members Toby Lyons and Karl Shale. In January 1984 they declared their intent with a fine, vaguely menacing, eponymous debut single, followed by the eloquently bitter 'Take', and 'Thinking Of You' which sounded a bit like Bacharach and David's 'Do You Know The Way To San Jose' and just missed the Top 10. *Virgins and Philistines* arrived early the following year – an overlooked album, Hall's doleful voice offset by classy, cool, upbeat arrangements. Staples and Golding, meanwhile, had formed Sunday Best which stayed closer to their West Indian roots. They were joined by former Selecter singer Pauline Black, but their one single, 'Pirates on the Airwaves', was dire. As was, somewhat surprisingly, The Colour Field's synth-heavy, directionless second album later in the decade. So true to form, the restless Hall split them up and went onto something else.

The demise of The Beat had also resulted in the formation of two new groups in 1984: General Public and Fine Young Cannibals. The former were generally considered to be 'the most likely to', co-singers Dave Wakeling and Ranking Roger setting their sights on a kind of post-punk, post-ska supergroup, drafting in Mick Jones of The Clash, Horace Panter from The Specials, and Mickey Billingham and Andy Growcott from Dexys. Jones left early on, but still featured on debut album *All the Rage* which steered a fairly safe, pop-by-numbers path through the lower reaches of the charts, though they had some success in America. The Beat's other half, guitarist Andy Cox and bassist David Steele formed Fine Young Cannibals, drafting in singer Roland Gift, and debuting with their 1984-recorded single 'Johnny Come Home'. Its clipped, chart-friendly sound of ska guitar and piano, jazz trumpet and crisp drums together with Roland Gift's magnetic frontman presence prefaced a hugely successful string of bigger-production hits in the second half of the 80s.

However, the West Midlands wasn't just about post-ska. As far as straight, guitar-driven post-punk was concerned, after The Cravats and The Au Pairs had split in 1983, it was left to a new generation of bands to take on the Birmingham baton. The Very Things had risen from the ashes of the Cravats and were originally going to be called BushesScreamWhileMyDaddyPrunes but to everyone's relief it became the title of their second, 'breakthrough' single and debut album, both released in the summer of 1984. They were a strange group: dada-esque and sci-fi gothic, but despite their theatricality (frontman The Shend would turn actor in the 90s) and having two songs in Peel's Festive 50 that year, the band never made it into the real charts. The Nightingales also started life as another group, The Prefects – 17-year-old wannabe punks who'd hung out with The Ramones and played on The Clash's *White Riot* tour. Despite the initial thrill, it was not a happy experience. Disillusioned with punk, they became wilful and awkward, changed their name, released edgy records on numerous labels and recorded endless Peel sessions. *The Crunch EP* was their only release in 1984 and they would split by the end of the decade, but like so many others would reappear in the new millennium, including collaborating with Faust of all people. Nightingales may have been a misnomer, but Napalm Death were, and still are, purveyors of music that is entirely in-keeping with their name. Formed in 1981 in the village of Meriden somewhere between Birmingham and Coventry, 1984 saw their first music committed to vinyl, 'The Crucifixion of Possessions' on the Crass Records compilation *Bullshit Detector Volume 3*, after which they went through untold line-up changes, were championed by John Peel and, for those interested in trivia, went on to become the seventh best-selling death metal band in the US[34].

*****

Returning to less raucous sounds and moving east a bit, Nottingham was home to the underrated C Cat Trance whose 1984 'Dreams of Leaving' single (alongside much of their work in fact) was post-punk with a world music groove, anticipating 90s acts like Transglobal Underground and Loop Guru. However, it's likely that their vaguely Arabic visual identity and ethnic instruments painted them into a corner. Leicester, on the other hand, had one of the country's quirkiest scenes including In Embrace, The Deep Freeze Mice, Yeah Yeah Noh and The Cardiacs (see Chapter 17).

Just down the road in Northampton, The Jazz Butcher not unsurprisingly had the scene largely to themselves, that year releasing four singles and an album, *A Scandal in Bohemia* on Glass Records – crisp, driving songs all. Frontman Pat Fish loved the dumbness of pop: single 'Marnie' was about a girlfriend who wanted to keep a lion in her room, 'Zombie Love' was like Jonathan Richman meets The Monochrome Set, while their cover of the former's 'Roadrunner' was also a minor hit that year. They were also terrific live. Just for the record Jason Pierce and Pete Kember were just getting going with Spacemen 3 in Rugby, recording a 1984 cassette called *For All The Fucked Up Children Of This World We Give You Spacemen 3*. It barely announced them to Rugby, let alone the world[35], but Pat Fish heard it and recommended them to Glass, and the second half of the 80s saw them pioneer a very particular brand of minimalist, droning psychedelia, otherwise known as shoegaze[36].

Bristol's long history of multiculturalism fuelled a vibrant reggae, dub, soul, funk and jazz scene which in turn influenced its post-punk bands, notably The Pop Group, Rip Rig + Panic, Maximum Joy, Glaxo Babies and Electric Guitars. When hip-hop arrived in the early 80s, neighbourhoods like St Pauls became alive with bass-heavy sound-systems, rappers and graffiti artists. One such crew was The Wild Bunch[37] (see Chapter 7) who in turn mutated into Massive Attack who in turn inspired the whole trip-hop scene of the early-to-mid 90s. Of course there was more mainstream stuff: Peter Gabriel and synthpop bands like Tears For Fears and Naked Eyes in Bath, and synthjazzers Startled Insects in Bristol itself. But it was the dubby-edgy combination of Jamaican sound-systems and US hip-hop culture that defined the black and white Bristol sound.

Like with other cities, some bands followed the well-trodden path to London. Goths Specimen did so, and so too did Mark Stewart after The Pop Group split in 1981. Stewart made a bee-line for the loose collective of musicians who orbited around Adrian Sherwood's On-U Sound label, putting together his own group, the Maffia, and releasing two albums, *Learning to Cope with Cowardice* and *As the Veneer of Democracy Starts To Fade*[38], either side of 1984, both examples of post-punk at its most disturbed, discordant and distorted. It was like randomly tuning into Bristol pirate station Savage Yet Tender but holding the dial on the interference rather than the station. Another Bristol musician, Gary Clail, would follow in Stewart's footsteps, working with both On-U Sound and US sympaticos Tackhead.

Bristol's post-punk scene included a sizeable real-punk contingent based around Bekki Bondage and The Vice Squad, more mainstream bands like The Escape, whose 1984 'Russian Lady' single (a spy caper complete with video shot in West Berlin) was their last, and The Brilliant Corners who had released their first three singles that year which were all vaguely rockabilly before cashing in on the C86 indie movement. But best known were The Blue Aeroplanes who began life as The Art Objects in the early 80s before changing names and releasing debut album *Bop Art* in 1984. This was more conventional guitar-driven post-punk territory and would serve them well throughout the 80s and beyond. They even had a dancer like Bez.

London of course had its fair share of post-punk bands, both those that were formed in the capital or moved there later. Some are dealt with elsewhere in this book because of their crossover into other genres while one particular band, Wire, who virtually created post-punk, were in the last year of their five-year hiatus so don't figure at all. On the same quality level, Matt Johnson's The The had a relatively quiet year following 1983's never-bettered *Soul Mining*, still a template for what post-punk could achieve, with its diverse instrumentation and motley musicians (Orange Juice's Zeke Manyika, Thomas Leer, Jim Thirlwell and Jools Holland amongst others). Indeed, it would take him until 1986 to release the more conventional if more gloomy *Infected*. Formed in south London in 1979, The Sound shared the usual post-punk milestones. Small label beginnings, sign to a major, major loses interest when the hits don't come, major drops band, band struggles on for a while, band splits. Fronted by the talented but troubled Adrian Borland, the group had been signed to WEA subdivision Korova and there were similarities with label-mates Echo & The Bunnymen, but commercial success proved elusive, not helped by a pointedly 'difficult' third album in 1982. However, the *Shock of Daylight* mini-album released in April 1984 and the recording of a full one, *Heads and Hearts* in November for the independent Statik label was a triumphant return to accessibility. Sadly, success continued to elude them, they split up in 1988, and Borland committed suicide a decade later.

Formed in Ealing in 1979, Furniture had released a single and EP in the early 80s which both sank without trace, but 1984 saw them up their game with the weirdly drum-patterned, jazz-tinged 'Dancing the Hard Bargain', as odd a single that didn't grace the charts that year. It caught the attention of Stiff Records who by the end of the year put out another oddity. 'I Love Your Shoes' was both pervy and funny, its accompanying video pitching frontman Tim Whelan with hundreds of high-heels, presumably pooled from the bands' girlfriends and thrift stores. Stiff kept the faith and a year and a half later they would secure their 'one hit wonder' moniker with 'Brilliant Mind'. Whelan and drummer Hamilton Lee were also members of fellow Ealing band The Transmitters which in the early 90s mutated into Transglobal Underground.

Spear of Destiny produced their best album in 1984, although masterpiece might be pushing it. Formed from the remnants of Theatre of Hate, the band set about crafting a more chart-friendly direction. Debut album *Grapes of Wrath* set out their stall in 1983, but the brash, stomping 'Prisoner of Love' single (January 1984) and ensuing *One Eyed Jacks* album nailed the sound. To truly embrace Spear of Destiny, you had to love Kirk Brandon's voice which split those that were listening right down the middle. Even a song as obviously strong as 'Prisoner of Love' is compromised by a voice that wobbles and strains so much that you think Brandon will self-combust[39].

While The Sound staggered, The Psychedelic Furs swaggered.

The Psychedelic Furs were moving away from post-punk having relocated from London to New York in 1982 looking for a more radio-friendly sound. They found it in Todd Rundgren, producer of their third album, *Forever Now*, but switched to Brit producer Keith Forsey, who was enjoying writing success in the US with Billy Idol and mainstream fodder like *Flashdance*. Forsey, originally a drummer, had got into electronics and neatly slipped into providing the Furs with a slick rhythmic pulse. The first fruits of the collaboration, the gloriously uplifting 'Heaven', boded well, reaching #29 in the UK charts in March, and two months later their fourth album, *Mirror Moves*, looked like it would appeal to the same people who'd just bought *Ocean Rain* or *The Top*. But ultimately the new slickness of the Furs' sound somehow failed to translate back on this side of the Atlantic. Two more decent singles, 'The Ghost in You' and 'Heartbeat', followed but neither made a big impression on the charts. It would take a re-recording of an older song, 'Pretty in Pink', included on the soundtrack of the same name, for them to 'break' America in 1986. They split five years later, however, before reforming again in the new millennium – a trend followed by many.

Sounding not unlike the Furs, Immaculate Fools formed in 1984 releasing their first two singles before the year was out. Despite Sounds describing an early gig as 'It must have been the same to have seen the Sex Pistols first gig […] they are going to be massive'[40], they weren't. Nor were two south London bands, The Lucy Show and A Bigger Splash, both signed to A&M. The former were conceived by two Canadian ex-pats in 1984, releasing the very Cure-ish 'Electric Dreams' and supporting R.E.M.'s UK tour in November. Three albums followed but they split in 1988. The latter had put out a couple of singles on tiny labels before signing with A&M and enticing its biggest star, Sting, to produce 'I Don't Believe a Word', a new version of their first single. It failed to make it a hit and they too split soon afterwards. Obscure and short-lived was one thing, obscure and lasting four decades was something else. Breathless's first two singles, 'Waterland' and 'Ageless', both released in 1984, were very 4AD, and indeed singer Dominic Appleton appeared on the second and third This Mortal Coil albums, though the label never signed them up. At time of writing they're still going, with seven albums to their name, all released on their own label.

The Blow Monkeys had been knocking around London for three years with just one indie single to their name, but by 1984 they'd managed to secure a deal with RCA and out came a debut album *Limping for a Generation* and four more singles. Despite their Morrissey-meets-Weller broad appeal and frontman Dr Robert's fine cheekbones, none charted, but RCA kept faith and they were rewarded with a couple of hits in 1986 and 1987, which in turn prompted a more sophisticated, dance-oriented sound, a collaboration with Curtis Mayfield and, ultimately, a lost muse, splitting in 1990. The Passion Puppets were formed in Camden and supported both Paul Young and The Psychedelic Furs in 1984, which perhaps explained why they sounded caught between pop and post-punk. Wacky videos for singles 'Like Dust' and 'Beyond the Pale' were ill-conceived, possibly an attempt by their label, Stiff, to present them as a harder-edged Madness (also from Camden). In any case, none of it worked and they split before the year was out. The Woodentops were much more convincing, their 1984 Smiths-ish debut single, 'Plenty', on Rough Trade (packaged in the first of many distinctive sleeves by artist Panni Bharti) being named Single of the Week in Melody

Maker by none other than Morrissey himself.

*****

The Woodentops and The Smiths weren't really post-punk, they were indie. Of course, at that precise time, they weren't labelled either – and the demarcating year, 1984 (some might argue 1985), was identified later. It was difficult to pinpoint the difference. Certainly, the Creation bands represented a shift from angsty JoyDiv-inspired music and lefty lyrics to a more 60s sound and apolitical stance – although The Smiths *were* political. It was a slow process though, and the bands were still largely pale white youths, studiously dressed-down, avoided clichéd pop lyrics and frowned on posturing. Goth wasn't indie because goth *was* about posturing (clothes, make-up, hair and sounding portentous – which isn't a criticism: done well it was appealing and dramatic). Orange Juice were the perfect indie-before-indie band: bookish boys with guitars, casual but clever.

In any case, there was a shift. 'If 1984 was the point when post-punk was officially 'over', wrote Tracey Thorn of Everything But The Girl, 'it was unfortunate that it was just then that we released our first album. We were in the uncomfortable position of being products of an era and a musical movement that was winding down before we got our chance to make ourselves heard, and for most of the rest of the 1980s nothing would really fill that void left after punk and post-punk disappeared into the ether'[41]. It's interesting that Thorn doesn't mention indie.

Indie wasn't just a style though. It also meant independent of the majors: small, low-budget labels with separate distribution channels which, although lacking the marketing clout of the majors, 'understood' its artists and were music fans first, business people second. In the second half of the decade the 'indie' question would provoke confusion, even raging arguments.

As stated earlier, not many post-punk bands formed in the late 70s or early 80s were active in the 90s. But perhaps the prize for shortest-lived band in this book goes to The Sid Presley Experience who managed to both form and split in 1984 before becoming The Godfathers. They left behind a single, 'Public Enemy Number One', which seemed to sum up both the thrill and end of post-punk. Opening with a cop shouting 'The place is surrounded – come out with your hands up', and the inevitable, fuck-you punky retort, 'You'll have to come and get me!', the track careers off into a frantic, guitar-driven romp across London's rooftops, accompanied by police sirens and automatic gunfire. Post-punk was dead. Long live indie.

Chapter 4: Close to the Edit
Pop, video and MTV

The 80s was a great decade for treading new ground. [...] It was kismet, a time that will never happen again.[1]
Steve Barron, director

No-one knew what they were doing, including me.[2]
Russell Mulcahy, director

I don't think music videos have to make sense. They only have to be really cool-looking.[3]
Nick Rhodes, Duran Duran

Videos were very European at first. Then things started to get less Euro and more big-titted and American.[4]
David Holmes, MTV

In 1984, music videos were everywhere like never before. For a record label they were now the chief way to market their artists – more so than radio and the music press. For their artists, they would have to get their hair done, buy new clothes and learn how to mime and act. And for the rest of us, they cropped up every half hour on TV, on the just-introduced video jukeboxes in the pub, in the newly created video racks of your average High Street record shop and in video rental shops. It wasn't exactly YouTube, but it *was* a new experience.

The promo for Queen's 'Bohemian Rhapsody' (1975) is often considered music video year zero, but there were plenty of pop promos before that, albeit shot on film not video. Alex Wharton's clip for The Moody Blues' 'Go Now' and Peter Goldmann's for The Beatles' 'Strawberry Fields Forever' were high water marks of the 60s[5], but the early 70s didn't see the artform develop much. The arrival of video cameras and video tape was the game changer, and Bruce Gowers' 'Bohemian Rhapsody' promo set the bar high, even if it only cost £4,500. Even if directors didn't always shoot using video – many still preferred the quality of 16mm or 35mm – they ended up on it. It was cheaper, gave a crisp finish and was easier to store and transport. But it still took a while for British record companies to see the attraction of investing in them when there weren't many outlets beyond Top Of The Pops.

Promos for punk, new wave and disco were serviceable, if rarely works of genius. That would have to wait until David Bowie's 'Ashes to Ashes' (co-directed by Bowie and David Mallet) which had it all: extraordinary indoor sets and outdoor locations, even more out-there costumes, juxtapositions of solarised colour with stark black & white, techy tricks like jump- and freeze-frames, a select cast of new romantics walking in front of a bulldozer – all held together by an intelligent story-within-a-story and, lest it not be forgotten, a great song. But that was an expensive exception (at the time, the most expensive pop video ever made). Most promos were cheap, crude and still not considered worth investing serious amounts of thought, time and money given the limited outlets. That all changed with the arrival of MTV in 1981. Although, initially, only watchable in the States, it propelled music videos into the mainstream. Suddenly there was not just a programme, there was a *whole channel*, playing hundreds of them a day, 24/7.

In terms of commissioning videos, the US record industry was actually behind the UK's which was already firmly established, and consequently most of MTV's early content came from Britain. The people behind MTV were also completely inexperienced in television; most came from radio. In many ways, MTV was like visual radio. But it had Warners and American Express money and the kind of devil-may-care start-up mentality that just willed itself to happen. When they launched (famously with The Buggles' 'Video Killed the Radio Star' at midnight on 1 August), they said they were in three million homes, but they weren't; it was more like half a million. They weren't even in New York where MTV was based; the nearest place was across the Hudson in New Jersey or Midwest cities like Tulsa. And at first they had hardly any content. 'When we went on the air', said one executive, 'we had something like 165 videos. And thirty of them were Rod Stewart'[6]. 'To be honest, we'd play pretty much anyone with a video', said another.[7] It helped of course that, initially, the content was free; record companies fell over themselves to get their artists on the new channel, but they wised up later in the decade. But thanks to an innovative 'I Want My MTV' campaign featuring stars like Jagger, Bowie and Idol, more and more cable companies started to offer MTV. By September 1982 it was available in New York, and Los Angeles followed soon after.

MTV was seemingly everywhere, and everyone wanted to be on it, including Bowie, here quizzing VJ Mark Goodman on why they didn't show black artists.

It was perfect timing for the UK music scene having just entered the new pop phase with its heavy focus on image. British labels, bands and their managers were eager for success in the States and here was a platform that was not only a shop window but hungry for content. Another factor in choosing MTV over traditional media was that the latter were either difficult to penetrate or limited in number. US radio, with its spread out, multiple local stations, payola[8] and conservative playlists, was hard to crack; and aside from the fortnightly Rolling Stone and monthly Creem and Trouser Press magazines (the latter underground and about to fold[9]), there was no national music press in America. So in 1982 and 1983, promos by Spandau Ballet, Duran Duran, Human League, ABC et al flew across the Atlantic like flocks of seagulls. It was Britain's new pop that initially gave MTV its cutting-edge kudos. It was win-win: MTV needed the content, British bands needed the exposure. It's hard not to underestimate the effect of MTV on the British invasion, especially in the expanse of land between east and west coasts, as one Anglophile (later a video-maker himself) growing up in the midwest testifies: 'A lot of the bands would simply have never made it if not for their image/video. Slogging the college circuit was the norm but even that typically translated into east/west coast success. The battle was won in the midwest and that's what MTV achieved. MTV was cable, so not everyone had it, but it was so cool you would go to people's houses just to watch it. From the middle of America it was a way to discover new acts'[10]. That's what MTV was: cool. Right down to its seemingly hand-made logo which was all over its programmes, T-shirts, baseball caps, even on the moon – thanks to a genius ident featuring an astronaut planting an MTV flag into the lunar surface. 'Yes, even here' it seemed to boast.

Not everyone was happy. Some felt that videos 'seemed to mean the replacement of rock values (sincerity, musical dexterity, live communion) with old pop conceits (visual style, gimmickry, hype)'[11]. And Joe Jackson spoke for many when he said, 'Things which used to count, such as being a good composer, player or singer, are getting lost in the desperate rush to visualize everything. It's now possible to be all of the above and still get nowhere, simply by not looking good in a video or, worse still, not making one'[12]. If he was speaking about older, balding blokes like himself, he'd forgotten Phil Collins who wasn't complaining. Nevertheless, he had a point, and with record companies' energies focussed on getting their money back for two or three videos per album, it meant cutting back elsewhere, including reducing the number of artists on their labels. The number of acts on CBS, for example, dropped during 1980-85 from 375 to 200[13]. This may not have been solely attributable to the video age, but it was probably a major factor.

They also restricted the meaning of a song. Pre-MTV, songs were entwined with people's memories of when they first heard them or could mean different things at different times. But from the early 80s onwards people tended to think of the video when they heard the song, its image usurping one's own imagination. Nevertheless, it became US and UK industry wisdom that a place on the MTV playlist could substantially increase sales[14] and that exclusion from it meant no sales at all. It was also helped by the fact that, from the very outset, MTV labelled the songs at their beginning and end.

Record labels were very controlling about making records – from the recording process to the marketing – but when it came to video, they didn't have a clue. The job was given to promotions assistants or secretaries, mostly female, together with a budget averaging £18,000 and they'd have to find out what a video director was and how to get one, and let him (and it was usually a him) and the artist get on with it.[15] Julien Temple: 'The record companies had no control over the videos. They were very film ignorant, as long as you could agree on an idea with a band, you were free to do what you wanted. It was very exciting to have an idea as you fell asleep and two weeks later see it all around the world on MTV'.[16] The term 'music video' started to connote a specific set of qualities: aggressive directorship, edgy editing, vivid colours, nonsensical juxtapositions and gratuitous glamour.

MTV was at the centre of it all. '1984 was our tipping point. It was an incredible year for music: Bruce Springsteen, Michael Jackson, Prince, Madonna, Van Halen […] Artists were selling tens of millions of records, in no small part due to video. And finally, *finally*, after three years, people understood what we'd been pitching them'.[17] It was also the year when MTV finally started regularly playing music by black artists. They'd played Michael Jackson's 'Billie Jean' and 'Beat It' the year before on limited rotation, defending their stance by saying they were a rock music channel and there were hardly any African Americans playing that kind of music. Herbie Hancock's hip-hop 'Rockit' *was* a hit, but it featured can-can-ing robot legs in preference to any black people. David Bowie was one of the few white voices in rock brave enough to criticize them directly, saying in an interview with VJ Mark Goodman: "I'm just floored by the fact that there's so few black artists featured on [MTV]. Why is that?"[18]. The floundering Goodman's non-answer prompted the company to re-think; that and the impact of Jackson's 14-minute 'Thriller' featurette released just before Christmas 1983. This wasn't so much a video to promote the single (which in any case came out a month later), it was a declaration of Jackson's superstardom and a television 'moment'; even in Britain it was listed in TV schedules. Thereafter Prince, Lionel Richie, Stevie Wonder, Tina Turner, Chaka Khan, Ray Parker Jr, and countless others swamped MTV in 1984. As for black video directors, as far as the record industry was concerned, there weren't any. Don Letts's experience said it all. 'I'm in New York and I get a call from MTV. They want to interview me about making videos for The Clash. When I get to the studio, everyone looks at me like I've shit myself. After an embarrassing five minutes, a guy sits me down and says, 'I don't know how to tell you this, we can't do the interview. We didn't realise you were black'.[19]

In April, MTV started running London Calling, a monthly hour-long show (hosted by Steve Blacknell and produced by PMI, the audio-visual division of EMI), but tellingly, this was the year when British acts started to relinquish their dominance of MTV programming and the US charts. David Mallet: 'It started with a British sensibility and then the American sensibility took over – ie. money'[20]. In came the heavy metal video with its emphasis on performance and musical authenticity. Or as one academic put it: 'Between the edits of fingers buzzing up and down fretboards, denim-clad musicians getting on and off tour buses, and the fans sweating and swaying in the stadia of North America, anti-narratives and anti-realism quickly faded into MTV history'[21].

Of course, it wasn't all about MTV, even in America. There were other music video programmes, if not channels, springing up all over the place, including Video Jukebox on HBO (1981-86) and Friday Night Videos on NBC (1983-2002) which was regularly watched by 50 million people. Media mogul Ted Turner even tried to take on MTV when he launched Cable Music Channel in October 1984, but it haemorrhaged money and closed after just five weeks. MTV itself started a sister channel Video Hits One (VH1) on 1 January 1985.

Meanwhile, the marketing departments of London-based labels had their own front yard (sorry, garden) to consider, with its boom in music programmes on the four terrestrial channels (see Chapter 13), as well as the European market, Australia and Japan. Nevertheless, it cannot be denied that MTV opened the floodgates and by 1984 the western world was awash with music videos.

The two holy grails for any UK record label were getting a single onto Radio One and Top Of The Pops. But if the former was still tough and involved pluggers, lunches and gimmicks, at least video offered an alternative entry point into the latter, as well as a growing bunch of other television shows. The music press was still important, especially Smash Hits, but video was now king. It was all about combining sound and image. It also offered complete control of an artist's image. You could negotiate a major feature in NME or Sounds, but you couldn't control what they'd write about you.

*****

So the demand was there and now the platforms, but who in 1984 was actually making all these videos? It was still a fledgling industry and the entry points were diverse. Some came from film and television, and some were from advertising (a medium famous for client pontification; with music videos they could do anything they liked). Some were photographers or graphic designers. Some were musicians, and a few were from the record industry's own marketing departments. Still others had no training at all and just blagged and hustled their way in. Some would focus first and foremost on telling a story, while others would approach the brief from a marketing point of view (what's going to sell this single?). Others would be interested in playing with different mediums and techniques (performance, animation, early computer graphics) while others simply wanted to impose their own auteur vision and to hell with the brief, if there was one. It was all utterly up for grabs.

Russell Mulcahy's story goes back to the world's first music video programme, Sounds Unlimited, created by ex-Radio Caroline DJ Graham Webb, and broadcast on Channel 7 in Sydney from 1974. It was a great idea, but there weren't an awful lot of videos around at that time, so Webb asked Mulcahy, who was working in the newsroom at the time, to go out and shoot some generic three-minute films of anything and everything which could then accompany the records. The ploy was so successful that bands started to ask Mulcahy to make videos for them, sometimes with money, and even a brief. He soon left Channel 7 to become a freelance music video director, at first for Australian bands, before moving to London in 1976 and making videos for XTC's 'Making Plans for Nigel', The Vapors' 'Turning Japanese' and, crucially,

Buggles' 'Video Killed the Radio Star'. 'No-one really knew what they were doing, including me'[22]. His big break, however, was Ultravox's 'Vienna', shot in the Austrian capital, pre-gentrified Covent Garden and Kilburn of all places.

From then on Mulcahy became the archetypal 80s music video director working with Duran Duran, Spandau Ballet, Elton John and numerous others. 1984 saw him at his most indulgent and extravagant, helming Duran's 'The Wild Boys' and Culture Club's 'The War Song' for example. The former has gone down in pop culture history as one of *the* videos of the 80s. With a budget of one million pounds (or dollars, depending on who you read), Mulcahy went big – installing a massive dystopian set in Pinewood Studios complete with metallic pyramid, windmill, water tank and a phalanx of dancers choreographed by Arlene Phillips. The inspiration came from William Burroughs' 1971 novel, *The Wild Boys: A Book of the Dead*, which Mulcahy wanted to turn into a feature film, using the promo as a teaser to find a Hollywood backer. The movie came to nothing but if he ever saw the video, Burroughs might have managed one of his poker-faced grins when witnessing the five Duranies being caged, strapped, dunked in water and attacked by giant amphibious maggots. But of course they came out on top (of what was not clear) riding upon a vintage Rolls in a ticker-tape parade. It was bonkers mad but as a spectacle was hard to beat.

If Mulcahy's video for Culture Club's 'The War Song' wasn't *quite* as extravagant, it still boasted a full-on military-chic catwalk show filmed at the half-demolished Beckton Gas Works[23] in east London, hundreds of schoolchildren dressed as skeletons marching down Shad Thames[24] and Boy George in four different wigs. Style-wise, Mulcahy was particularly known for split frames, body paint (both famously, and excessively, in Elton John's 'I'm Still Standing' in 1983), jump-cuts and fake widescreen effects. He would later go on to direct *Highlander*, a promising start to what turned out to be a rather disappointing feature film career.

'Ashes to Ashes' was a difficult act for David Mallet to follow, but Bowie continued to send work his way ('Fashion', 'Let's Dance', 'China Girl') while he also worked with the likes of Peter Gabriel, Def Leppard and Tina Turner. Aside from another Bowie commission (the overdone 'Loving the Alien'), 1984 would see him make three videos for Queen: the anthemic *Metropolis* trailer 'Radio Ga Ga', a straight-forward but genuinely thrilling performance of 'Hammer To Fall' and arguably his *second* most famous video, 'I Want To Break Free'. Many remember the band in drag sending up Coronation Street, but few recall the fantasy sequence in the middle where a de-moustachioed Mercury plays Nijinsky in 'L'Après-midi d'un Faune'. From then on Mallet seemed to limit himself to working with AC/DC or filming entire concerts.

Son of film scriptwriter and director Zelda Barron[25], Steve Barron followed in her footsteps and was very nearly a conventional film maker, working on a number of big 70s features. But when punk came along, he found himself drawn to the music scene, hanging out with The Jam and Siouxsie and the Banshees at the Speakeasy Club, and directing his first video, 'Another Girl Another Planet' for The Only Ones. As the new decade dawned, he shifted gears, forming a production company, Limelight, with his producer sister Siobhan. Barron's early 80s CV is astonishing, managing to juggle alternative UK acts like Human League ('Don't You Want Me'), Heaven 17 ('Let Me Go') and Simple Minds ('Promised You a Miracle') with big US acts like Michael Jackson ('Billie Jean'), Toto ('Africa') and Madonna ('Burnin' Up').

On set: Russell Mulcahy & Duran Duran's John Taylor (*Arena*) and Steve Barron & Michael Jackson ('Billie Jean').

1984 was the beginning of Barron's shift away from music videos, directing his first feature film, *Electric Dreams*, a fluffy love triangle between a guy, a girl and a computer – 30 years ahead of Spike Jonze's *Her*. It was the first production for Virgin Films, and felt like it (although its oft-quoted comparison to a very extended video was strange; there may have been an accompanying soundtrack album featuring music by various Virgin staples, but their music didn't figure in the film).

At the same time Barron was becoming more drawn to animation. 'I was always a big fan of Disney's *Pinocchio* growing up. When I started doing videos, animation became the Holy Grail, being able to control the images and movement frame by frame. It always seemed to fit better on a tempo level with most music, more so than most live-action…'[26]. The following year he would use very different types of animation in two of the best-known videos of all time. A-ha's 'Take On Me' had been released in 1984 but both song and video had failed to make an impression. Cue Barron's inventive remake using a technique called rotoscoping (drawing over filmed frames) to create *that* video: a cute love story literally straight out of a comic book. On the other hand, Dire Straits' 'Money For Nothing', recorded in December 1984, presented a very different challenge. Mark Knopfler hated music videos but his record label was desperate to get the band on to MTV with something other than just their frontman playing guitar. In the end, Barron won the argument and created one of the first computer animated music videos when it was released in 1985 and one of the most played videos on MTV ever. Sting's 'I want my MTV' refrain probably helped.

If Barron was on the edge of the punk scene, Julien Temple was in the thick of it. And in the spirit of the times, untrained but with oodles of self-belief, he skipped promos and went straight to directing *The Great Rock 'n' Roll Swindle*, the infamous mockumentary which presented *one* side of the Sex Pistols story. From then on it was promos for as diverse a bunch of artists as you could imagine, from Gary Numan and his great love, The Kinks, to Neil Young and *seven* promos for Judas Priest.

Temple's thing was telling stories, perfectly illustrated by The Kinks' 'Come Dancing' (Ray Davies as the perfect spiv) and The Rolling Stones' 'Undercover of the Night' (Central American kidnappings, summary executions and church shoot-outs – which may have scared MTV but was enough to give the Stones some much needed street cred). ABC's 55-minute *Mantrap* (1983) should have given Temple plenty of time to spin a yarn but it turned out to be 95% 'The Look of Love' performed in rococo-and-red-velvet European concert halls and 5% silly spy caper. Sade's 'Smooth Operator' in 1984 was possibly even sillier. But he raised his game again with another extended video, *Jazzin' for Blue Jean*, which was designed to promote David Bowie's 'Blue Jean', his first single since *Let's Dance*'s trio of blockbusters a year earlier. *Jazzin'* starred Bowie as both incompetent 'nobody' Vic and drug-addled rock star Screaming Lord Byron, roles he played with some aplomb. What also makes it different from most videos – aside from its 17-minute length (it was screened alongside the feature film *Company of Wolves* in cinemas) – was Bowie poking fun at himself and the fact that it didn't have a cop-out ending. In fact, the ending is wonderfully self-conscious, as the camera pulls out to reveal the film crew and Vic / Bowie arguing with the director: 'Look, it's my song, my concept, my neck! I told you before, Julien, if she gets into the car with the rock star it's far too obvious…', until finally Temple shouts 'Cut!'[27]. Temple of course went on to make *Absolute Beginners* (again featuring Bowie – and Ray Davies and Sade for that matter), but really found his metier in later rockumentaries[28].

Temple didn't have a monopoly on the extended format. To accompany their *Labour of Love* covers album, UB40 commissioned Bernard Rose to make a 30-minute film which not only showcased every song on the album but managed to fuse them into an understated, fairly convincing storyline of Ali Campbell and his mates out and about on the wrong side of the law in their beloved, blighted Birmingham. It worked as a whole, and *kind of* individually ('Red Red Wine', 'Cherry Oh Baby' and 'Please Don't Make Me Cry' all used extracts as separate promo videos). Shot in late 1983 in black & white and released the following year, it made a refreshing change from the glitz and glamour of most other videos.

However, Rose's most important video, which made realism even more real, was for Bronski Beat's 'Smalltown Boy'. If you failed to pick up the gay theme of the song, then the video made it abundantly clear, yet still in a commendably understated and poignant fashion. A young man (Somerville) eyes up another at the swimming pool, the latter returning a smile, but it is a trick as he and his mates later beat Somerville up. The police take him home, bloodied and bruised, and it is there that his shocked and ashamed parents learn of the truth. He leaves home, taking a train to London – as Somerville did in reality in 1979, aged 18, not telling his parents where he was for three months. It ends in hope as the two other guys in the group join him on the platform as the train is about to depart for a new life in a perhaps more forgiving city. It is an astonishing video in many ways, bringing homosexuality and everyday homophobia into the pop mainstream, its images understated, almost mundane, and in complete contrast to most of the glamorous promos of the time[29]. It might have disappointed, even concerned, some record companies, but London Records were extraordinarily supportive; their Managing Director, Colin Bell, who was gay, even appeared in the video as a policeman. Also unusual was the fact that, without the song, it was essentially a silent film, with no lipsynch singing, sound effects or dialogue, despite being highly narrative. 'Smalltown Boy' became a gay anti-anthem and, thanks to the video, probably the most 'political' song in this book[30]. *And* it was great to dance to, *and* it reached #3 in the charts.

Bronski Beat's brave 'Smalltown Boy' directed by Bernard Rose. Tim Pope and Talk Talk dumb down 'Dum Dum Girl'.

Tim Pope was one of the first students to take O-level Film when it was introduced to British schools in the early 1970s. Like Temple, he hustled his way into video-making, debuting with the extraordinary 'Sex Dwarf' by Soft Cell, commissioned by Some Bizzare. The importance of new, free-thinking labels like Some Bizzare, 4AD and Factory to young, wannabe film-makers cannot be overestimated. Mavericks like Stevo, Ivo and Wilson effectively gave people like Pope carte blanche to do what they wanted, and they found willing collaborators in their artists. By 1984 Pope was on a role, knocking out a video a month: China Crisis's 'Wishful Thinking', The Cure's 'The Caterpillar'[31], a couple for Siouxsie and the Banshees, Queen's bonkers 'It's a Hard Life', Strawberry Switchblade's dotty 'Since Yesterday' and three for Talk Talk. The latter were particularly perverse, highlighting the band's increasing disinterest in playing the marketing game, which Pope was happy to encourage. 'Such a Shame' was relatively conventional, with a rooted-to-the-spot Hollis somehow managing to appear both manic and bored; 'It's My Life' was simply some wildlife films occasionally juxtaposed with Hollis looking glum in London Zoo; and 'Dum Dum Girl' was the weirdest of all with the band filmed in a field, no instruments, occasionally breaking out into Cockney banter, probably looking forward to a pint in the village pub. And then of course there was Pope's own attempt at pop stardom: the whimsical 'I Want to be a Tree', written with Robert Smith, the video of which – one long take of Pope wedged into a tree stump – must have cost all of fifty quid.

Kevin Godley and Lol Creme were something else again. Formerly one half of 10cc, the pair re-invented themselves as phenomenally successful video directors for the new decade. Their angle was not so much to tell a story but to make an impression – and in that way were not far removed from advertising men. 'Girls on Film' (kinky sex), 'Every Breath You Take' (candles) and 'Rockit' (robot legs) were all very different but had that big idea. This continued into 1984 with Frankie Goes To Hollywood's 'Two Tribes' (Reagan and Chernenko lookalikes fighting it out in the ring[32]) and 'The Power of Love' (nothing less than the birth of Jesus, done surprisingly straight and reverential – even if the song wasn't about religion). They would arguably hit a creative peak the following year with their own 'Cry', again employing one big idea: a constantly evolving sequence of morphed faces mouthing along to the song's words.

If Godley and Creme were the Saatchi & Saatchi of pop, Anton Corbijn was – at this early stage in his career at least – an auteur with a distinctive style. Born near Rotterdam, Corbijn started out as a music-mad photographer, moving to London in the late 70s when new wave was at its peak. He found work with the NME and quickly became synonymous with Britain's grey landscapes and grim bands: Cabaret Voltaire, Echo & The Bunnymen and most famously, Joy Division. Almost inevitably Corbijn started making videos and 1984 was to be his foundation course starting with The Art Of Noise's 'Beatbox' (a messy assemblage of eccentric London street scenes) and Propaganda's 'Dr Mabuse' (an ill-advised Fritz Lang pastiche). He got it almost right with David Sylvian's 'Red Guitar', a homage to another master photographer, Angus McBean, whose famous 1950 portrait of Audrey Hepburn's head and naked shoulders sticking out of the ground Corbijn copied – with a half-buried Sylvian – to suitably surreal effect.

Next to come calling were U2. Having already commissioned Corbijn to provide the cover photo of 'Pride (In the Name of Love)', they asked him to shoot the video too. The result was a deeply claustrophobic promo filmed in a dark basement which had Bono doing his worst Ian Curtis impression, and the band wisely ditched it. But finally Corbijn just about nailed it with Echo & The Bunnymen's 'Seven Seas', which placed the band on a fin de siècle stage dressed as penguins, a fish and Mac as an utterly convincing blonde beatnikette. Corbijn would juggle photography and video-making for many years to come: continuing to work with the Bunnymen, U2 and Depeche Mode (for the latter alone he has shot over 20 videos) as well as Metallica, Nick Cave and Coldplay, before going on to direct feature films, including, coming full circle, the Joy Division biopic *Control*.

There were of course many others. Andy Morahan managed to combine the arty (The Art Of Noise's 'Close to the Edit'[33]) with pop ('Wake Me Up Before You Go Go') before going on to direct Pet Shop Boys, Guns 'n' Roses and scores of others. Peter Care started making videos with Cabaret Voltaire and Scritti Politti (their 'Sensoria' and 'Hypnotize' singles in 1984 both using an innovative and disorientating 180-degree camera-on-a-boom trick). He would later go on to work with ABC, Depeche Mode, and R.E.M. amongst many others. Nigel Dick started off as press officer at

Stiff Records in the late 70s but moved to Phonogram and in 1984 ended up directing Band Aid and Tears For Fears' videos. The randomness of storylining was perfectly encapsulated by the latter's 'Head Over Heels'. 'Roland Orzabal told me what he envisaged: 'I see myself in a library, there's a beautiful girl, we'll grow old together, and there's all this random stuff like a rabbi and a chimp'. And I'm rapidly scribbling on a piece of paper: 'Chimp, rabbi.''[34] Like many, he then moved to the US and directed Britney Spears ('Baby One More Time'), Cher ('Believe') and around 300 others.

Some got bored of making music promos. Having co-directed, with Thomas Dolby, the MTV favourite 'Hyperactive', and helmed *Madonna Live: The Virgin Tour*, Daniel Kleinman swapped music videos for commercials before designing every James Bond title sequence after *Golden Eye*. Duncan Gibbons had directed promos for Eurythmics' 'Who's That Girl?' and George Michael's 'Careless Whisper' amongst others, the latter's initial cut famously scrapped because Michael had a bad hair day. (At least he could laugh about his bouffant locks: 'Some days I made the covers of the tabloids. Some days Princess Di made the cover of the tabloids. Some days I think they just got us mixed up'[35]). Gibbons then headed off to the States to direct proper films[36]. Brian Grant had made videos for the likes of Queen, Human League and XTC before directing Duran Duran's worst video, 'New Moon on Monday' in January 1984. He was best making videos for female artists – Kim Wilde, Olivia Newton-John, Donna Summer, Tina Turner, Whitney Houston – but by the 90s had moved to a career in US television.

On the other side of the camera, women were a rarity, at least in Britain. One woman who certainly was key to the UK's music video industry, however, was Tessa Watts, who helmed Virgin Records video production division. Alongside Simon Draper, Watts was instrumental in moving Virgin away from prog and krautrock to the hipper end of new wave, commissioning over 1,500 videos[37] in a long and distinguished career. On the directorial side, a key figure, Sophie Muller, was just starting out. After obtaining her Masters at the Royal College of Art, she was the third assistant on 1984's *Company of Wolves* film but would go on to specialise in music videos, initially almost exclusively for Annie Lennox and Eurythmics. Branching out in the 90s, she has directed over a hundred videos for major international artists, including Sade, Björk, PJ Harvey, Sophie-Ellis Bextor, Gwen Stefani and even some men. In the US there were a few directors: Mary Lambert, for example, who directed most of Madonna's early videos, and Tamra Davis (married to Mike D of Beastie Boys) who shot Depeche Mode's 'But Not Tonight'.

There was also Annabel Jankel who, with her partner Rocky Morton (known collectively as Cucumber), had started producing back-projections for punk bands, before directing proper music videos like Tom Tom Club's 'Genius of Love' and the animation tour-de-force, 'Accidents Will Happen' for Elvis Costello. 1984 saw them shoot a video for Miles Davis who wanted 'something glamorous, with dancing girls in a desert... We had to imply that, in our opinion, it wasn't dignified for the world's greatest trumpet player to devalue his iconic status with a bunch of gallumping girls'[38], and he had to make do with moody black & white close-ups instead. But aside from that they spent much of 1984 writing a book about computer graphics and developing (with sci-fi writer George Stone) a faux computer-generated[39] character called Max Headroom. The latter would host a 30-minute music video show on Channel 4 the following April, his gibberish in-between-promo patter mocking DJs and chatshow hosts and prompting various spin-offs in both the UK and US and a video game.

Of course, there was a lot of rubbish too. Behind the Max Headroom concept 'was the realization that video need do no more than exist. MTV has demonstrated that people [...] will sit and watch an unending stream of appalling promo clips in the hope that a good one will come up next'[40]. Most of 1984's top 50 best-selling singles in the UK had at best 'serviceable' promos and in some cases utter abominations.

******

Outside of mainstream video-making was a small but interesting coterie of independent outfits, mostly based in the north of England. Ikon (1980-89) was Factory Records' video offshoot, releasing a couple of dozen titles during its ten-year lifetime, two of its most interesting being 1984's *The Final Academy Documents*, a collection of William Burroughs' short films and spoken word (the latter recorded at Manchester's Hacienda two years earlier) and *Feverhouse*, a Lynchian short film with music by Biting Tongues[41]. Doublevision was both a video and record label set up by Paul Smith in Nottingham and Cabaret Voltaire in Sheffield in the early 80s. 1984 saw it at its peak with a string of releases by Throbbing Gristle, Chris & Cosey, 23 Skidoo, Tuxedomoon and The Residents. Also the excellent *TV Wipeout*, an ahead-of-its-time compilation of leftfield promos, interviews and extracts from arthouse films. Within its 60 minutes running time Bill Nelson and David Bowie rubbed shoulders with Psychic TV and Cabaret Voltaire; excerpts from Andy Warhol's *Heat* and *Plan 9 From Outer Space* vied with Japan and Marc & The Mambas; and there was even an ad for 'competitor' Ikon[42]. (The following year Smith would go on to set up the highly influential Blast First label, introducing US noise bands like Sonic Youth, Big Black and the Butthole Surfers to the UK). Jettisoundz, based in Lancashire, started out in 1983 releasing crude one-camera-only live punk videos, but by the following year were filming and retailing videos by Hawkwind and Black Flag. They're still going.

Having directed the punk film, *Jubilee*, it was almost inevitable that Derek Jarman would shoot promos but not that he would conform. His promos for Orange Juice's last single 'What Presence?' and Marc Almond's 'Tenderness Is A Weakness' were fairly conventional. Reassuringly more perverse was his preference to use low-budget 8mm film, re-editing some home movie footage for a Wang Chung promo and shooting a fearsomely arty (one might say arty-farty) featurette to accompany The Smiths' *The Queen Is Dead* album in 1985. That neither had anything to do with the songs' subject matter was beside the point. Jarman was an artist first, promo maker second (or possibly ninth).

76

Video as art: Anton Corbijn's 'Red Guitar' for David Sylvian, and Eno's *Thursday Afternoon.*

Even further away, to the extent that it wasn't promotional, nor a documentation of a concert, nor trying to tell a story, nor even really a 'music video' (although was comprised of both music and video), but definitely art, was what Brian Eno was up to. On moving to New York in 1980, Eno had started to experiment with 'video paintings', making two short works, *2 Fifth Avenue* and *Fences*, followed by the more developed *Mistaken Memories of Medieval Manhattan*. The latter, a tightly framed view of the Manhattan skyline with slowly shifting clouds above an eerie foreground of rooftops and water-tanks shot from his 13th floor apartment on Broom Street and accompanied by a suitably ambient soundtrack, was in complete contrast to MTV's frenzied programming of bells-and-whistles promos which had debuted around the same time. Eno's videos ended up doing the rounds of art galleries and, unlike his records, you couldn't buy them. That started to change in 1984 when Sony commissioned a new work, for sale on sleek laserdisc in Japan as well as clunky VHS in North America. For this, Eno filmed seven different versions of actress/photographer Christine Alicino sitting naked in the bath on a Thursday afternoon in San Francisco. Like *MMoMM*, it was slowed right down and heavily treated so as to become almost abstract (but crucially not *quite*) and designed to be viewed vertically[43]. The year saw some eight installations in mainland Europe and Canada, but it wasn't until 1986 that his first major UK installation, *Place #11*, took place at Riverside Studios in London. This took the video format to another level. Comprising a large, blacked-out space with translucent perspex frames and three-dimensional structures suffused with slowly-changing coloured light generated by concealed video monitors, it still remains one of his most satisfying 'video works'. 'Video for me is a way of configuring light, just as painting is a way of configuring paint', Eno explained at the time. 'What you see is simply light patterned in various ways. For an artist, video is the best light organ that anyone has ever invented'.[44]

But of course, music videos were not really about art, they were there to sell product. They were different from advertising though. A regular 10-second ad on TV showed the product and straightforwardly urged you to buy it. A music video lasted the length of the song and presented a visual fantasy – artist in glamorous / dramatic / humorous settings – which it was hoped you'd want to buy into. In comparison, purchasing the actual piece of black vinyl could be disappointing. Most were highly standardized due to constraints of time, budget and imagination; and there wasn't much longer-term thinking (odd, given the amounts of money being 'invested') of using video to create and maintain a particular image of the artist.

Although music videos would continue to be hugely important devices in selling artists' records, the late 80s and early 90s saw the novelty factor wear off and boredom set in with MTV diversifying to include programmes like Unplugged, Beavis and Butthead etc. 'In ten years' time', suggested Simon Frith in a 1987 lecture, 'I am sure, straight promo-video channels like MTV and Music Box will have ceased to be.[45] He wasn't far wrong.

Chapter 5: Punk's Not Dead
Punk, anarcho-punk and the angry brigade

This Is What You Want… This Is What You Get
PiL

You're Already Dead
Crass

Eight years after 'Year Zero', where were the punks? By 1984, it all seemed a very long time ago. Of the two leading lights, the Pistols had split up at exactly the right time, but The Clash soldiered on, dogged by internal tension and management problems. At the height of new pop, they released their last decent album, *Combat Rock* (1982), which yielded two hit singles in 'Rock the Casbah' and 'Should I Stay Or Should I Go', but soon afterwards began the slow, painful disintegration. Topper Headon was first to go, incapacitated by a heroin habit, and Mick Jones was fired for unspecific reasons (though non-punctuality and constant feuding with Strummer were at the root of it). Replacements were found and in January 1984 they kicked off a world tour that took in the US (twice), most of mainland Europe and the UK, ending up with a benefit show for the striking miners. But the band was living on borrowed time. When it came to writing new material, they struggled badly. Mick Jones had been the main songwriter, and when manager Bernie Rhodes started taking on some of the songwriting and production duties, you knew the game was up. *Cut the Crap*, released in 1985, was unanimously panned and the band split the following year.

Meanwhile, John Lydon's Public Image Limited were also in a sorry state of affairs. Since 1981's *The Flowers of Romance*, there had been aborted sessions with guitarist Keith Levene, bassist Pete Jones and drummer Martin Atkins, after which Levene was sacked (heroin again) and Jones left soon after. By 1983 one of the tracks, 'This Is Not a Love Song', had been reworked by Lydon and Atkins, becoming a surprise hit (PiL's highest charting single at #5). Things then got really strange with Levene releasing – in limited quantities – a version of the earlier sessions as the album *Commercial Zone* in PiL's name, while Lydon and Atkins re-recorded the same sessions, excising Levene, as *This Is What You Want… This Is What You Get* in July 1984. The album was not well received although there were some good moments, not least the doomy, minimal 'The Order of Death', written for (but not in the end used in) the movie of the same name[1]. The summer saw Lydon move from New York to LA where he started recruiting for a new band, which very nearly included an unknown 21-year-old bassist called Michael Balzary. He passed the audition but decided to stay with his own group who were about to release their debut album but whose future was by no means assured. They were called Red Hot Chilli Peppers[2]. Nevertheless, a band of youngsters had been recruited and PiL were back in business, embarking on a four-month tour which took in the US, Australia and Japan. Lydon even found time to collaborate with Afrika Bambaataa and Bill Laswell as Time Zone, their sole release, 'World Destruction', coming out in December and joining the early examples of the great rap and rock's coming together.

If The Clash and Lydon's output was still punctuated by ire and cynicism, The Stranglers – previously arch exponents of punk's belligerence – had mellowed into an easy-on-the-ear Philly-soul pop group. For some this was the end – and certainly *Aural Sculpture*, released at the end of 1984, was no *Rattus Norvegicus*. In came producer Laurie Latham who had helmed Paul Young's *No Parlez*, softening everything: Burnel's previously Stranglers-defining, snarling bass was dropped low in the mix, Jet Black was largely replaced with a drum machine and lite horns were introduced, all wrapped up in preposterous sleeve notes. That said, 'Skin Deep', the first single, was gorgeous, the album's only saving grace. The Stranglers were if nothing else perverse, their own men, impervious to criticism. Some blame it on Hugh Cornwell coming off heroin; it was enough to make you want him to get back on it.

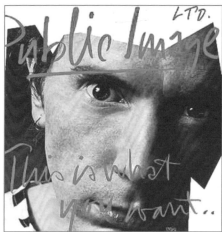

New York residents John Lydon and Billy Idol: moving in different directions.

By 1984, The Damned had become punk caricatures, albeit funny, loveable ones. There was creature-of-the-night Dave Vanian still dressed up as a vampire, mad Rat Scabies on drums, loony Captain Sensible still wearing his red beret and, er, two others. They were perfect for a pantomime or, as turned out to be the case, an episode of *The Young Ones*, the semi-anarchic BBC sitcom which was in its second series that year and which regularly hosted a band midway through each episode[3]. Otherwise it was a quiet year for the group releasing just the one single, 'Thank You for the Night' in June, which scraped the Top 50 – although they'd be back with a vengeance with an album and hit single in 1985. At the same time Captain Sensible was still putting out solo singles: his first, 'Happy Talk', had made #1 in 1982 while the jolly 'Glad It's All Over' (actually a belated anti-Falklands War song) reached an equally respectable #6 in March 1984. It wasn't therefore too much of a surprise when he left the group after their festival appearance at Brixton's Brockwell Park in June to concentrate on Weetabix ads and two more solo singles including, somewhat inevitably, a Christmas song that sank without trace. (Mind you, it was up against formidable festive fodder from Band Aid, Wham! and Queen). Perhaps the strangest change of direction, though, was Vic Godard and Subway Sect's move from punk to (briefly) northern soul and then to the 1940s-style swing-time of *Songs For Sale* (1982), after which Subway Sect became the rockabilly-soul act, JoBoxers. Godard meanwhile recorded a crooner jazz album in 1984 called *T.R.O.U.B.L.E.*, produced by Simon Booth of Working Week. Ironically, the year's jazz revival didn't help and the album remained unreleased until 1986. Nevertheless, a Rough Trade compilation of early Godard material more than compensated.

Central to punk, if only in terms of personnel rather than critical or commercial success, had been Generation X. By 1981 they'd split, with James Stevenson joining Gene Loves Jezebel, Terry Chimes re-joining The Clash and Tony James eventually going on to form Sigue Sigue Sputnik. But it was frontman Billy Idol (originally 'Idle', at school) who went on to have the most success. Moving to New York, he secured the services of a shrewd, go-getting manager (Billy Aucoin, ex-Kiss) and in-vogue producer (Keith Forsey) and set about 'cracking America'. With his good looks, punctuated by pop's best, gravity-defying snarl, Idol's metamorphosis was perfectly timed for the MTV explosion – a safe, stylish punk for the video age. 1984 was his year, at least in the States: 'Rebel Yell' (Meat Loaf with attitude), 'Eyes Without a Face' (soft rock), 'Flesh for Fantasy' (Jim Kerr meets Prince) and 'Catch My Fall' (could have been anyone) all went Top 50 in Billboard; the videos are hilarious. They fared less well in Britain, although reissues of 'White Wedding' and 'Rebel Yell' both hit #6 the following year.

Rare examples of first generation punk bands surviving into the 80s and successfully continuing to play in the original punk style were few and far between, but included: UK Subs, ironic, given frontman Charlie Harper was originally a blues singing Magma fan and already in his thirties first time round and turned forty in 1984; The Vibrators and 999, who'd moved from major to minor labels; The Homosexuals, who changed their name from The Rejects and *finally* released their debut album on, of all labels, Recommended Records, better known for groups like Henry Cow and Faust; Abrasive Wheels, from Leeds, whose more pop-punk *Black Leather Girl* album in 1984 was their last; and Angelic Upstarts, who had got through their strange period of wearing swastika armbands – and perhaps even stranger era of ex-Roxy Music Paul Thompson on drums – and moved into oi! territory, more of which later.

More interesting was the second wave from around 1980 onwards which, depending on your viewpoint, existed in a 'punk's not dead' time-warp complete with zips, safety pins and either spikey hair or mohawks, or was a more genuine take on the genre: harder, faster, angrier. Much denigrated at the time, the second wave ironically had an authenticity that the first lacked. The first generation were influenced by The Stooges and The Faces, mod and pub rock, while the second was influenced by, well, punk – in effect, more punk than punk. Born in an angry age of early Thatcherism and inner-city riots, it was also more politically hardcore, branching off into anarcho-punk. And whereas the first wave had been signed by majors, the second wave was almost totally, defiantly, independent. As John Finch of the band Lunatic Fringe said: 'The first wave was an umbrella which could include bands of vastly differing influences and musical styles, whereas second wave bands were moving towards a much more uniform (some would say entrenched) sound and look'.[4]

There were hundreds of groups, and like the post-punk scene, were scattered all over the country, largely invisible to the majors and media in London. Some of them enjoyed considerable success, if invariably confined to the independent charts and touring Europe in clapped-out vans. A few even made it to America. Bands like GBH, The Exploited and Anti Nowhere League had large, loyal followings. Others like The Accursed and Action Pact (who sounded punk but looked mod) existed only between 1982-84.

Some, like Discharge and English Dogs, were as much influenced by metal (especially Motorhead) as punk. Indeed, although on the one hand diametrically opposed (clothes, haircuts, lyrics and to some extent musical ability), there were similarities with Def Leppard, Samson and other NWOBHM bands, both scenes arising at around the same time and both essentially keeping the focus on fast and furious guitar riffs. There were very few women in the scene, the exception being Beki Bondage of Vice Squad and, on leaving them in 1982, her subsequent underachieving acts, Ligotage and Beki and the Bombshells[5]. Most bands operated in the what-the-hell netherworld of juggling day jobs or dole, playing small local venues and recording on small local labels (or, if they were lucky, a few bigger labels like Riot City, No Future and Clay).

A few, like Toy Dolls, relied on novelty, their 'We're Mad' single of 1984 a sort of manifesto, reinforced by the surprise re-released thrash hit of 'Nellie the Elephant' and providing the theme tune for kids programme Razzmatazz. The Adicts, too, distinguished themselves from the rest of the punks by looking like a cross-between The Doctors Of Madness and the house band of *A Clockwork Orange* complete with droog henchmen. To reinforce the latter connection, their album *Smart Alex* (recorded in 1984, released in 1985) was named after the droog's leader Alex DeLarge. But they weren't averse to compromise, changing their name from Adicts to ADX in order to secure a major label release.

*****

Other bands, attracted by punk's anarchistic tendencies, had become 'anarcho-punks'. Crass were the prime movers, putting politics before music, ethics before age, attitude before class. Co-founders Penny Rimbaud (a then 35-year-old middle class ex-art teacher) and Steve Ignorant (a self-confessed teenage yobbo) couldn't have been more different, and yet 'they meant it maan', living a post-hippy, proto-crusty communal existence in Dial House, on the north-east edge of London. With various other residents, who drifted in and out, Crass espoused gradual, purposeful revolution rather than the shock tactics of punk and encouraged people to think for themselves. Other bands followed their lead, the black clothes, Pay No More Than… ethos, but Crass didn't want to be seen as inventors of anarcho-punk. 'We never separated ourselves; we were a part of it, at one with it. There were those that tried to force that sense of leadership onto us, but I think we were very successful in never, ever accepting that role'[6]. Nor did Rimbaud or Ignorant see themselves as frontmen; indeed Eve Libertine and Joy De Vivre often took on the vocal duties in line with the group's pro-feminist stance. Crass's records, tours, publications and many political activities made them both famous and infamous, and by 1984 they were worn down by the attentions of the police[7] and the stresses and strains of communal living, disbanding after a final single, 'You're Already Dead', that summer.

One of Crass's final concerts in Cumbria, May 1984. Flux of Pink Indians' *The Fucking Cunts Treat Us Like Pricks* (note section of it in the banner behind Crass).

Having initially been 'signed' to Crass Records, Flux of Pink Indians effectively grabbed the baton from Crass, releasing the infamous and almost unlistenable *The Fucking Cunts Treat Us Like Pricks* in the spring of 1984[8]. The double album, and other records (including *Penis Envy* by Crass and *Frankenchrist* by the Dead Kennedys), were seized by Greater Manchester Police from Eastern Bloc, the record shop charged with displaying "Obscene Articles For Publication For Gain", but it never went to court. Flux's bassist Derek Birkett went on to form One Little Indian Records the following year, initially for other leftfield Crass-related acts but soon to be home of The Sugarcubes and Björk. There were scores of other bands, the best known probably being The Mob, Zounds, Subhumans, Rudimentary Peni and Chumbawamba (years before their 'Tubthumping' single went to #2 in 1997); several female singers and bands like Annie Anxiety, Rubella Ballet, Poison Girls and Lost Cherrees (their 1984 single 'A Man's Duty, A Woman's Place' was produced by jazz-rocker Jon Hiseman of all people); and female-*fronted* bands like Antisect, Dirt, and Hagar The Womb.

The key period (or 'glory years' as punk documenter Ian Glasper describes them) for second wave and anarcho-punk was 1980-84, paralleling the first five years of kicking against Thatcherism. Once the miners had been defeated and Thatcher's power consolidated, or possibly because the movement had simply run its course, bands like

Crass and Flux of Pink Indians split up, while others like GBH, Discharge and Exploited had identity crises and went in a more metal direction. 'Across the pond Slayer and Metallica were starting to make waves, and offering a new level of intensity. I think they – and many other UK bands – saw 'crossover' as a way to reinvent themselves and introduce new elements to their sound without losing sight of their punk roots'[9].

One associated movement which didn't stick around for long or develop into something else was oi!. Originating in punk, oi! was named and championed by Garry Bushell of Sounds, but its heyday was the late 70s and early 80s. Mostly London-based, male, white, working class and forever associated (rightly or wrongly) with white nationalist movements and football terrace yobbism, by 1984 it was largely a spent force. Bands like Cock Sparrer, The Business, Cockney Rejects, The 4-Skins and Combat 84 were still releasing albums that year but the latter two split straight afterwards and the scene went even more underground than it was at its 'height'. (Bushell also attempted to champion another male, white, working class genre called casual, somehow managing to get a band called Accent onto the front cover of Sounds in May. Identified more by their anything but casual obsession with neat, neo-mod sportswear than their ordinary pre-indie music, the band in question lasted one single).

*****

Of the more accessible end of the Class of 77's angry brigade – or at least the *top* of the Class, the ones who'd had some chart success, and weren't really punk at all – most were no longer active in 1984. Sham 69, The Adverts, Wire, Buzzcocks, Eddie and the Hot Rods, Stiff Little Fingers, The Jam had all run out of ideas and done the right thing, the Gang of Four as late as midway through the year. There have been reunions – long-lasting in the case of Buzzcocks and astonishingly prolific and creative in Wire's.

Of all the splits, The Jam's, at the end of 1982, was the most shocking, the one that left a gaping hole and the one most perfectly timed. That Paul Weller would go on to interesting things was never in doubt – although you feared for Bruce Foxton[10] and Rick Butler – but it was difficult to imagine something as different as The Style Council. Weller had teamed up with Mick Talbot (ex-Merton Parkas and Dexys Midnight Runners) to create something genuinely new. Not the individual elements perhaps – pop, jazz, soul, funk, rap and definitely no rock – but in terms of their combination and Anglicization. Four singles in 1983 prepared the way, but their peak was in 1984 with their debut album proper, *Café Bleu*, which was so eclectic it seemed like a various artists compilation.

Some found the variety distracting at best, irritating at worse. And it's true, there was a lot of affectation, not least the silly sleeve notes by 'The Cappuccino Kid' (aka NME scribe Paolo Hewitt). But ignore the posing and what you had were 13 thrillingly distinctive tracks. What really stood out was not so much the variety of styles but the variety of *moods*: the exuberant 'Headstart for Happiness' and four (count them) instrumentals, one of which even has a drum solo; the introspection of 'The Whole Point of No Return' (for some reason omitted from the sleeve) and the Tracey Thorn-sung 'The Paris Match'; the forthrightness of 'A Gospel' and 'Strength of Your Nature'; the Dexys-ness of 'Here's One That Got Away'; the Mantovani-ness of 'Blue Café'... And that's not even mentioning the two singles: the achingly beautiful, stripped-down piano-only version of 'My Ever Changing Moods' and the soppy but irresistibly groovy 'You're the Best Thing'. And there was more. 'Shout to the Top' was another singular slice of positivism released in the autumn.

Calling his band The Style Council prompted accusations that Weller was putting style – the sharp clothes, the cycling gear, the slick sleeves – before (socio-political) substance, but as Robert Elms commented: 'I don't see any contradiction between wanting to look good and being left-wing. [...] So I loved it when Weller, while being at his most political, became his most overtly stylish. I also thought that his message was internationalist and that was important; embracing Europe-ness was very anti-Thatcher.'[11] Right at the end of the year Weller brought together musicians including Martyn Ware and Jimmy Ruffin, calling themselves Council Collective. The one-off single, 'Soul Deep', was in aid of the striking miners. Just before that, Weller had contributed to Band Aid, and indeed throughout the year he was seen as pop's social conscience, whether he liked it or not.

Having returned Le Monde to the café table, Mick and Paul check out the chart competition.

Of course it wasn't all roses. Polydor weren't sure of the album at all, the videos were terrible, Weller broke his arm on April Fool's Day, packed in Respond Records[12] and continued to shoot his mouth off in the music press. The latter had great respect for

Weller, but also unreasonable expectations, expecting him to speak for his generation, musically and politically, which led to some strains, like this exchange with X Moore of the NME (aka Chris Moore of The Redskins) on the release of *Café Bleu*:

> *Moore: Presumably this album is what you reckon to be definitive.*
> *Talbot: No, it's just the LP we have made this year.*
> *Weller: There will be no definitive Style Council sound.*
> *Moore: Ever?*
> *Weller: Ever. Why should there be?*[13]

Also not shy of speaking his mind, Elvis Costello had a bad year. He was going through a divorce, there were tensions with The Attractions and he was fed up with the music business. Nevertheless it was a surprise when, entering the studio in February, he announced his next record would be his last. 'I was really down about lots of other things and I really just decided I wanted to do this one record, and I was asking [producers Clive Langer and Alan Winstanley] to make a record they weren't really set up to do, which was essentially a 'live-in-the-studio' record. And then we had a loss of nerve about that and started to edge it back towards the kind of production they did anyway'[14]. The result was the miserable *Goodbye Cruel World*, often regarded as his worst. It did, however yield the rather beautiful if melancholic 'I Wanna Be Loved' complete with backing vocals by Green Gartside and an innovative video by Godley & Creme. Two other singles failed to reach the Top 40. Of course Costello didn't retire. Live Aid coaxed him back and the following year he released not one but two albums. He's still going (relatively) strong.

We've already seen how The Fall fared, but it's worth repeating how Brix Smith had ushered in a more melodic, sartorial, try-for-a-hit approach – despite her husband's singular, critical-of-everything attitude[15] – and many feel this mid-80s period was their peak. The theatrical dalliance with Michael Clark Dance Company made them all the more interesting.

Punk and the theatre made intriguing bedfellows. Joe Strummer starred in a couple of Alex Cox films in the late 80s; Ian Dury trod the boards with the Royal Court; and Adam Ant, Siouxsie Sioux, Gene October, Toyah Wilcox and others had famously 'starred' in Derek Jarman's *Jubilee*. Wilcox would go on to have parallel careers in acting and music. 1984 was a watershed year for her, appearing alongside Laurence Olivier in the television drama, The Ebony Tower, breaking up Toyah, the band (and at the same time releasing *Toyah! Toyah! Toyah!,* a final best of album) and reinventing herself as a solo artist. It was also around this time that she met Robert Fripp, 12 years her senior and so utterly different that their marriage in 1986 seemed perversely logical. Hazel O'Connor was also managing to combine singing and acting, although struggled to match the lead role success of 1980's *Breaking Glass* for which she also wrote the music (not quite a first in movie history, but impressive[16]) Nevertheless, 1984 saw her star in *Nightshoot* at the Hammersmith Lyric Theatre, as well as release two albums (*Smile* and *Greatest Hits*) and four singles.

Punk, Clockwork Orange style: The Adicts and Sigue Sigue Sputnik.

Punk in the next century was apparently going to sound like Sigue Sigue Sputnik, a band formed by former Generation X bassist Tony James. Before signing to a label or releasing a record, the NME interviewed James in 1984, billing the band as 'hi-tech sex, designer violence, and the fifth generation of rock 'n' roll', the bandmates chosen for their looks rather than anything else. And their image was extraordinary, brilliantly described by Tom Bromley in The Guardian as 'Clockwork Orange meets My Little Pony'. PR'd to within an inch of their lives – by James's then girlfriend, Magenta Devine – they signed to EMI ('Would You pay '£4m' for this crap?' screamed the NME's front page) and after one of the longest band gestation periods ever, their debut single 'Love Missile F1-11' was released in 1986. Three years later they split up. Needless to say, it wasn't the future of punk.

Chapter 6: Rock in Opposition
Pop and politics

Pop is a more radical purveyor of political messages than rock.[1]
Bono

Being spokesman for a generation is the worst job I ever had.[2]
Billy Bragg

War is stupid
Culture Club

Arguably, 1984 was British rock and pop's most politicised year, before or (at time of writing) since. Whether it was responding to unemployment, privatisation, the miners' strike, Northern Ireland, gay rights, nuclear brinkmanship, famine and Apartheid in Africa, travellers and free festivals, or basically anything that Margaret Thatcher said or did, it was a heady old year.

Since the 80s, protest songs have declined in quantity, potency and (some may argue) relevance. Nowadays, most discontents prefer to argue the case on Facebook and Twitter with its instant access to millions, rather than releasing a single with a message, much less strapping on a guitar and singing from a street corner like Billy Bragg used to do. Also, in the 90s, the ideological gap between (New) Labour and Conservatives became much narrower. Even rap has become strangely de-politicised, although there have of course been exceptions. But back in the 80s, things were very different.

Following victory in the Falklands and the ensuing General Election, Thatcher had become in her own mind, and near enough in reality, invincible. Nothing and no-one would get in her way. She was a great target: intransigent and hectoring; the Iron Lady who wasn't for turning; or simply 'that bloody woman'. People hated her, but liked having someone to hate, and she had the thickest skin of any politician. Thatcher simply didn't care what people thought of her, barely read the newspapers, and everyone be damned – including members of her own cabinet. And yet if everyone hated her, how did she get voted in? The truth of course was that Britain was divided straight down the middle: those who approved of her free market policies, reduced state intervention and curbing the powers of unions, and those who saw her as the destroyer of Britain's manufacturing industries, unions and even society itself.

Artists generally fell into the latter camp – creators against the destroyer – and musicians were to the fore, despite, on the face of it, conforming to the very values Thatcher espoused: entrepreneurs who got on their bikes to spearhead the great rush from manufacturing to service industries. Many were Labour voters, including, for instance, Everything But The Girl: 'Ben and I were successful young people during the era she was in power: economically we thrived; she lowered our taxes. It's that awkward thing [of] voting against your best interests.'[3] There *were* a few who confessed: Tony Hadley, Jon Moss, Errol Brown, Gary Numan – the latter pilloried for his politics as much as his music and the fact that he flew a plane. Of all types of artists, musicians (especially lyricists and singers) have generally been the most successful at raising awareness of political issues. Actors and writers come close, but in the right hands, a song can speak more immediately and powerfully than a book, play, film or artwork.[4] Three minutes and it's out there: on records, radio and TV.

People think of the 60s as pop and rock's politicized highpoint, and in America that may have been true with musicians' involvement in the Civil Rights Movement, Black Power, the sexual revolution and festivals like Woodstock. But in Britain music and politics hadn't come together in quite the same way. Nor would they in the 70s. The Bay City Rollers never supported the miners' strike in the winter of 1973/4; ELP never played benefits for Northern Ireland; the Sex Pistols never stood shoulder to shoulder for CND; and the only major music festival to support a political cause was George Harrison's Concert for Bangladesh in 1971 – and that was in New York. It's often said that the 80s were the 'me' generation, but it could easily apply to the 70s too (as Tom Wolfe did in his influential essay, *The 'Me' Decade,* which described a shift away from communal, progressive politics to 'atomised individualism'). The 70s were indulgent times, and it seemed the only campaigns were for Real Ale.

By the end of the decade, however, pop and politics were beginning to come back together again. Bob Marley had become a political force to be reckoned with, speaking for the downtrodden of Jamaica and helping to inspire the Rock Against Racism movement in Britain that brought punk and reggae bands and fans together to fight the rise of the far right. (Meanwhile, Eric Clapton had gone the other way with his drunken 'Keep Britain White!' outburst at a concert in Birmingham in 1976). The punk explosion was high on energy and slogans, but aside from the many things it was against, it was unclear what it was *for*. Was wearing a swastika pro-National Front or a Brigade Rosse T-shirt[5] pro-terrorism, or just a silly pretence to shock? The Clash liked to think they were political but it was very unclear what their politics actually were. They didn't walk the talk. At least the Sex Pistols were honest enough to admit that they themselves 'weren't anarchists, just wallies!'[6]

Rock Against Racism, alongside the linked but more overtly political Anti-Nazi League, played a significant part in neutering the ambitions of the National Front. After the latter's poor showing at the 1979 election, bands turned their attention to other causes, mainly fighting against the person who had won the election. One spin-off was the ska revival, based around Coventry's 2-tone label and half-white, half-black bands like The Beat, The Specials and The Selecter. Their songs had rarely dealt explicitly with racism (they hadn't really needed to – it was implicit from their line-ups); they were more mini-critiques of an increasingly divided Britain, with songs like The Beat's 'Stand Down Margaret' and The Specials' 'Ghost Town', the latter a #1 during the riots of the summer of 1981.

Thatcher's 1979 election victory politicised pop, and the DIY ethos of punk had inspired those with something to say, *to say it*: on records released by the many small independent labels that had sprung up, and to a sympathetic music press who were now generally more interested in a band's politics and the books they read rather than the instrumental intricacies of their songs. And if 1980-83 was the training ground, occasionally distracted by the *apparent* style over content of the new romantics, 1984 was the real coming together of pop and politics – not just in a general opposition to the Conservative Government and a loathing of its leader, although both were central, but in all sorts of other areas.

*****

True to script, 1984 was dominated by the threat of global war, principally of a nuclear variety. The year of George Orwell's novel had finally arrived and cultural commentators busied themselves making comparisons between fiction and fact. The novel is set a few decades after an atomic war, with the three super-states of Oceania, Eurasia and Eastasia tacitly agreeing to keep up a Cold War instead of finishing each other off. It was a fiction not *too* far removed from reality, the US and Soviet Union having the means to unleash Armageddon but just about holding off. However, it only needed one loose cannon, or perhaps a stray balloon, to set it all off. Nena's '99 Luftballons', a global hit in February 1984 (and #1 in Britain) was about exactly that. A boy and girl innocently release a clutch of balloons into the air, it's picked up on radar, the military jump to conclusions, international governments panic, and a nuclear holocaust is triggered. However, there was more controversy about Nena's armpit hair than the song's lyrics.

Pop music's response to the Cold War wasn't just a one-off from Nena, however. It was everywhere. Hot on Nena's heels, Ultravox's #3 hit 'Dancing with Tears in My Eyes' was about a nuclear power plant meltdown rather than nuclear war, but by the summer the sirens of Frankie Goes To Hollywood's 'Two Tribes' were the real thing, accompanied by a video of Reagan and the new Soviet leader Konstantin Chernenko slugging it out in the ring. Phil Oakey was seen wandering around a deserted, post-apocalyptic London in the video for the Human League's 'Life on Your Own'. Nik Kershaw's 'I Won't Let the Sun Go Down On Me' talked about a forefinger on the button. Elvis Costello and Ian Dury chipped in with 'Peace in Our Time' and 'Ban the Bomb'. Even Queen were moved to comment, with 'Hammer to Fall' ('You just got time to say your prayers while you're waiting for the hammer to fall'). In July, the Soviet Union boycotted the Los Angeles Olympics while in August, during a microphone check for his weekly radio address, Ronald Reagan made his off-air joke about bombing them. In September, the BBC broadcast *Threads*, a startlingly realistic dramatization of a nuclear attack on Sheffield that did little to lighten the mood. Even Bucks Fizz got in on the act, with the prosaically titled 'Cold War'.

And that was just the *threat* of war. There were plenty of real ones going on in various parts of the world: Afghanistan, Iran-Iraq, Lebanon, Sri Lanka, Sudan, Ethiopia, Angola, Western Sahara and so on. Pop music's response to *these* was almost zero, except the Human League's 'The Lebanon', which surprised just about everyone. But what was pop trying to say other than – courtesy of Frankie Goes To Hollywood and Culture Club – "War, what is it good for?" and "War is stupid"?

Nine years after Hiroshima and Nagasaki, rock & roll's first contribution to the nuclear debate was a naive little tune recorded in 1954 by Bill Haley about the delights of a nuclear explosion that had left one man and – ho ho – 'Thirteen Women' (the song's title) alive. Incredible though it may seem in hindsight, the atomic age, bombs and all, was seen by many as exciting. In Britain, ignorance was also bliss. However, by the end of the decade many were becoming fearful of the increase in the number of countries which 'had the bomb' and the after-effects of nuclear testing, and in 1957 the Campaign for Nuclear Disarmament was formed in London[7]. Its first five years were very active, supported by jazz and skiffle musicians, but its image (lefty, earnest, middle-class radicals in duffle coats), failed to appeal to young people in the 60s and 70s, during which time it ticked along quietly and unspectacularly.

Reagan and Chernenko battle it out in Frankie Goes To Hollywood's 'Two Tribes', while scores of bands performed for the benefit of CND at Glastonbury.

In the early 80s, things changed. With Reagan and Thatcher emboldened by office, and Brezhnev on his last legs (he died in 1982), western governments sensed the upper hand in the Cold War. Plans were put in place to base Cruise missiles in Britain and other European NATO countries. Alarmed, there was a sudden grass-roots 're-interest' in nuclear issues. Michael Eavis, the Somerset farmer (and therefore perhaps the grassiest of them all), had run the relatively minor Glastonbury Festival on and off (mainly off) during the 70s. As Britain and its music scene became more politicised in the early 80s, Eavis teamed up with CND, placed their logo above the pyramid-shaped stage and got in some hipper bands. The 1984 festival featured speakers such as Bruce Kent and local MP Paddy Ashdown, performers like Elvis Costello, The Smiths, Ian Dury, The Waterboys, Billy Bragg and even Howard Jones – alongside the more expected John Martyn, Fairport Convention, Weather Report, Joan Baez and Fela Kuti. Groups on EMI were struck off the list because the label was owned by Thorn which made guidance systems for Trident missiles. Nevertheless, 35,000 tickets were sold[8] raising £60,000 for CND and local charities. After that, Glastonbury went from strength to strength.

In 1983 Paul Weller chose to unveil the Style Council at CND's Festival for Peace in Brockwell Park in south London and the organization also benefited from proceeds from their second single, 'Money Go Round'. Heaven 17 donated royalties from a track off their *How Men Are* album and hung a huge banner outside Air Studios on Oxford Circus saying 'Heaven 17 Say No To Cruise Missiles'. And so on. Of course it couldn't be compared with the Greenham Common women who had camped out on the air base's perimeter from the beginning of 1983, when cruise missiles were announced to be coming (and who stayed for literally years), nor Katherine Hamnett wearing an oversized '58% Don't Want Pershing'[9] T-shirt when she met Margaret Thatcher at Downing Street in February 1984. But it was what musicians did best: raising awareness, especially amongst young people.

There was another war closer to home, in Northern Ireland. It might have been called the 'Conflict' or the 'Troubles', but for nearly 30 years it was, essentially, a war. Folk musicians had sung about the division for decades, but following the introduction of British troops in 1969, internment without trial in 1971 and Bloody Sunday[10] in 1972, there was a small flood of Troubles-related records. One of the first was Paul McCartney & Wings' debut single 'Give Ireland Back to the Irish' (which topped the Irish charts and, despite being banned, went Top 20 in the UK), followed a few months later by a couple of tracks on John Lennon's *Some Time in New York City* album. All three were cack-handed, but at least it showed that Britain's two principal songwriters of the 60s were interested in what was going on across the Irish Sea – or Atlantic Ocean in Lennon's case.

Glossing over Boney M's trite 'Belfast', late 70s punk gave birth to a few bands – notably the Protestant Stiff Little Fingers and the Catholic Undertones – who encouraged both sides to their concerts, while the early 80s saw a few Troubles-related songs turn up in the UK charts – Kate Bush's 'Army Dreamers'[11], The Police's 'Invisible Sun', Fun Boy Three's 'The More I See (The Less I Believe)' – some more specifically related than others. Closer to home, Clannad's 'Theme from Harry's Game' (a 1982 TV mini-drama about the Troubles) took a neutral stance, and at time of writing is still the only UK hit single to be sung entirely in Irish Gaelic. U2 used to play it at the end of every concert in the mid-80s, and their own song, 'Sunday Bloody Sunday', needs no introduction. Other musicians, like Dublin-born folk singer Christy Moore were more one-sided, not least on his 1984 album *Ride On* which featured two songs written by Irish Republican prisoner Bobby Sands[12].

Politically, 1984 was a defining year in the Northern Ireland conflict. In March, Sinn Féin MP Gerry Adams was shot and wounded in Belfast; in May the New Ireland Forum published a report presenting three possible solutions to the conflict, all of which Margaret Thatcher turned down; and in October the IRA bombed the Grand Hotel in Brighton where Thatcher and her cabinet were staying for the Conservative Party Conference, killing five people and injuring 31.

Amidst all this, a single by Bananarama might have seemed puerile, but their 'Rough Justice' was heartfelt. Although not specifically about the Troubles, it was inspired by a friend of theirs, Thomas 'Kidso' Reilly, who was shot dead by a British soldier the summer before. They'd all attended his funeral; Kidso had been Bananarama's road manager and the brother of Jim Reilly from Stiff Little Fingers, who Siobhan Fahey was dating at the time, so it had hit hard. It coincided with the group wanting to be taken more seriously, reflected in some of the lyrics and the slightly lower chart positions, although the effervescent 'Robert De Niro's Waiting' hit #3. Unfortunately, Mark Knopfler's music for *Cal*, a film about the Troubles, *was* a bit bland, even if in the film it manipulated or shadowed the emotions effectively enough. And confusingly, Madness's 'Michael Caine' was not about Michael Caine at all, but about an informer during the Troubles (sung by Chas Smash who, as Cathal Smyth, had Irish family connections). It was a strange song: a contentious subject made less so by linking it to Caine's Harry Palmer spy persona in the *The Ipcress File*.

Both Stiff Little Fingers and The Undertones left Northern Ireland for London where there was already a large Irish population including a number of bands that had come up through punk and were playing pubs and small clubs. The best known of these was Pogue Mahone[13], changing their name to the Pogues in time for debut album *Red Roses for Me* and a support slot on The Clash's 1984 tour. Their music – traditional Irish folk played with ramshackle punk energy – was completely unfashionable and not particularly political at the time, at least not regarding the Northern Ireland issue. That would come later with 'Birmingham Six' (1988), a protest song about the imprisonment of six Irishmen following the bombing of a Birmingham pub in 1974 which killed 21 people. Plenty more songs would follow in the late 80s, including from a band formed in Northern Ireland in 1984, The Adventures, whose 'Broken Land' went Top 20 in 1988.

*****

Sectarianism is not far removed from racism and there was plenty of the latter in Britain in 1984. Of course, pop and rock had their origins in black music, and its various genres have always played an indelible part in the black population's struggle for equality. It gave them a voice and because it was something that was initially sung

93

in the fields (the blues) or in church (gospel) in the American south, it flourished, largely unhindered. Rock & roll did much to bring American whites and blacks together when it started out in the mid-50s. 'Rock & roll does help to combat racial discrimination', said Bill Haley. 'We have performed to mixed groups all over the country, and we have watched the kids sit side by side just enjoying the music while being entertained by white and Negro performers sharing the same stage'.[14] Artists like Chuck Berry, Little Richard, Muddy Waters and Bo Diddley then paved the way for soul, funk and disco.

Black influence on British music was slower to take hold and was heavily influenced by what was coming out of the US, as well as the introduction of ska and rocksteady from Jamaica[15]. In the 70s this led to northern soul, disco, reggae and a ska revival. But if the music was integrated into the British charts (black artists were occupying the #1 singles slot for 11 weeks in 1978, for example), Britain by the end of the 70s was still waylaid by everyday racism and discrimination with words like 'wog' and 'paki' still in common usage. Rock Against Racism and the 2-tone bands helped spread a certain amount of tolerance and were especially effective against the National Front but ultimately there wasn't a great deal that music could do in what was a complex mix of economic, cultural, historical and institutional issues.

If there were few British musicians writing about racism in the early 80s – Peter Gabriel's anthemic 'Biko' and Paul McCartney and Stevie Wonder's saccharine 'Ebony and Ivory' excepted – then 1984 upped the ante a bit. U2's *The Unforgettable Fire* had not one but *two* songs about Martin Luther King. Smiley Culture's Top 20 hit 'Police Officer' managed to be both funny and serious, an autobiographical tale of how Smiley was arrested for the possession of cannabis but then let off in return for an autograph when the policeman recognised him as a famous reggae artist.[16] Another interesting flashpoint was when the young reggae poet Benjamin Zephaniah hit the road in support of the miners' strike. At some gigs he encountered racism from the local communities, but when they discovered he was performing without a fee or expenses and that working-class Caribbeans were collecting money for them, it became an education lesson.

What *did* bring musicians together in the fight against racism was what was going on 9,000 kilometres away in South Africa. Apartheid had been in force since 1948 but a long-delayed UN resolution in 1980 was beginning to have a positive, isolationist effect[17]. In music's case, this meant that bands were 'discouraged' from playing there and those who did went into the UN's little black book. Not everyone agreed with it. Some wanted to visit and find out for themselves (which was fine as long as they didn't perform), while others wanted to make a point and perform with black musicians. By the same token, South African artists, black or white, weren't 'allowed' to perform in the UK, though again some did, including Shikisha (who also recorded an album in Kenya in early 1984 with Robin Scott of M and 'Pop Musik' fame)[18].

The most contentious (or at least publicly known) issue was Sun City, a Las Vegas-style entertainment complex a couple of hours' drive from Johannesburg. In order to attract international talent, generous performance fees were waved around, enticing the likes of Status Quo, Elton John and Rod Stewart in the early 80s. Even black artists like Millie Jackson and The Real Thing flew over. Queen's run of shows in October 1984, therefore, wasn't unprecedented, but it backfired badly on them. Brian May's limp 'We've thought a lot about the morals of it and it is something we've decided to do'[19] hardly endeared them to their fans back home, let alone the media[20], despite being contrite enough to regret it later on for all the right reasons. A little earlier that summer, Paul Simon had been given a cassette by South African group the Boyoyo Boys. Intrigued, he later watched a BBC documentary, *Rhythm of Resistance: the Music of South Africa*, filmed secretly in 1979 by Jeremy Marre, flew out to Johannesburg to find out more and later recorded with black musicians both in Johannesburg and New York, which eventually became his *Graceland* album released in 1986. Simon got his wrists slapped for that but others supported him, including star South African trumpeter Hugh Masekela.

But what of Anti-Apartheid songs themselves? Strangely there had been very few in the early 80s that directly addressed the issue, or at least that the West knew about. There was 'Biko' of course, but otherwise it was a long wait until the Special AKA's 'Free Nelson Mandela' – a joyous, celebratory song, produced by Elvis Costello, that became a rallying cry around the world, reaching #9 in the UK, although was curiously described as 'lightweight' in the NME[21]. Others followed: Artists United Against Apartheid's 'I Ain't Gonna Play Sun City' (which had the added effect of chastising a number of fellow musicians), Youssou N'Dour's 'Mandela', Stevie Wonder's 'It's Wrong' and Microdisney's rather less subtle *We Hate You South African Bastards!* – followed by the Mandela 70th Birthday Tribute at Wembley Stadium in 1988. Music's contribution to his release from prison a year and a half later is difficult to quantify, but suffice to say it was significant.

*****

Political songs were everywhere. Robert Wyatt's EP *Work in Progress*, released in August, featured only politically-orientated songs: aside from a stripped-down, plaintive version of 'Biko', there was a commentary on the US invasion of Grenada, a song by Victor Jara, the revolutionary Chilean composer of 'Venceremos' (itself covered by Working Week that year), and another by the Cuban songwriter Pablo Milanes. It had the galvanising effect of kick-starting work on *Old Rottenhat,* his first solo album since the brace of *Rock Bottom* and *Ruth Is Stranger* ten years earlier.

The debate about whether protest pop could attract the younger post-punk generation was an interesting one. Most post-punks poo-pooed the folky, archaic language, acoustic guitars and tin-whistles, while the folkies argued that their songs were more radical and that rock was basically conservative. But somehow they worked it out, much like the punk and reggae bands did at the Rock Against Racism festivals in the late 70s. One singer-songwriter[22] was particularly passionate about bringing the two styles together. Billy Bragg had a love of both Dylan and The Clash and his debut mini-album *Life's a Riot with Spy vs Spy* was a salvo of short, spikey tracks, some politically-charged ('To Have and Have Not'), some love songs ('The Milkman of Human Kindness'). It reached #30 in January 1984[23]. Bragg played everywhere and anywhere, with electric guitar and microphone plugged into a rucksack ampstack. A one-man band, he was loud, passionate, opinionated and mobile – the troubadour brought right up to date. Released towards the end of the year, a second album, *Brewing Up with Billy Bragg*, continued in the same vein, although this time he was accompanied by three others, including The Smiths' Johnny Marr, but still no drums. 'It Says Here' was a biting attack on the tabloid press while 'Island of No Return' was an anti-war song. It did even better than the debut, reaching #16. And right at the end of the year, Kirsty MacColl had a hit with a cover of 'New England', undoubtedly the best song from his first album. Her folk roots ran deep: her father was folk-singer and activist Ewan MacColl who, aged 74, was still active, supporting the miners' strike and releasing the cassette album *Daddy, What Did You Do In The Strike?* (Having a famous father and a famous husband – producer Steve Lillywhite – made it hard for MacColl to be accepted in her own right, 'The token daughter, the token wife', as she sang on a much later song[24]).

Billy Bragg, late 20th Century troubadour. Nelson Mandela, late 20th Century prisoner.

Bragg's grassroots, leftist politics were forged as a teenager, especially seeing The Clash in 1977, but were sealed by Labour's landslide defeat in the 1983 national election and the miners' strike the following year. The latter was probably the most bitter and divisive strike in British history, with union leader Arthur Scargill and the miners on one side, the champions of market forces, Margaret Thatcher and Ian MacGregor (Head of the National Coal Board) on the other, and a supporting cast of miners' families, the police, flying pickets and the media slugging it out in the middle. The dispute was about the slow death of the mining industry, uneconomic pits facing closure, state intervention versus market forces, preserving communities versus Thatcher's 'no such thing as society', and ultimately it became a show of strength between two hardliners on opposite ends of the political spectrum. There had been miners' strikes in the 70s (which the miners had won without too much trouble), though then there wasn't much of a link with music. But the strike in 1984 had an almost instant effect on musicians, partly, simply, to oppose Thatcher and partly to help support the miners themselves who were in dire financial straits. Benefit concerts and festivals took place up and down the country: Wham!, Big Country, Working Week and The Style Council performed at the Royal Festival Hall in London; and at the tail-end of the year The Clash played two benefit gigs at Brixton Academy. Some artists (appropriately including the Flying Pickets) went even further, joining the miners outside colliery gates. Even Bruce Springsteen, who was on a massive world tour which wouldn't reach Britain until the following year, donated.

The support extended to records too. Paul Weller formed the one-off Council Collective (with Mick Talbot, Dee C Lee, Martyn Ware, Vaughn Toulouse, Junior Giscombe, Dizzy Heights and Jimmy Ruffin - whose father was a miner) to record the benefit single 'Soul Deep'[25]. There were obscure, well-meant compilations[26]. And of course Billy Bragg was not to be left out: his version of 'Which Side Are You On?'[27] encapsulated the general mood of the country.

Not every song was about giving money. Sometimes they were simply inspired by what was going on and ended up informing the lyrics of later songs: The Style Council's 'A Stone's Throw Away' on *Our Favourite Shop*, Sting's 'We Work the Black Seam' on *The Dream of the Blue Turtles* (both released just after the strike had ended) and U2's 'Red Hill Mining Town' on *Joshua Tree* a little later. Even into the 90s and 00s, bands were still penning songs about the strike: Dire Straits' Battle of Orgreave-referencing 'Iron Hand', Manic Street Preachers' '1985', Pulp's 'Last Day of the Miners' Strike' and Funeral For A Friend's 'History' for example.[28]

The miners' strike prompted benefit albums and concerts, the latter sometimes combined with a gay theme.

Experimental bands also got involved. Test Dept recorded with the South Wales Striking Miners Choir, releasing an album, *Shoulder to Shoulder*. Robert Wyatt (again), members of Henry Cow and poet Adrian Mitchell got together for *The Last Nightingale* mini-album with all proceeds going to the Miners' Strike Fund. The Enemy Within[29] (John Dogood, Marek Kohn, Keith LeBlanc and Adrian Sherwood) even sampled bits of Arthur Scargill's speeches on the edgy, vaguely danceable 12-inch, 'Strike'. It was similar to Le Blanc's 'No Sell Out', although Scargill's words and tone were rather less poetic than Malcolm X's. Scargill also cropped up on an album by former Hawkwind singer, Robert Calvert. *Freq* was an unlikely post-punk tour-de-force, interspersing uneasy minimal, electronic songs about machinery and struggle – 'Work Song' is a minor (miner?) classic – with union speeches and field recordings from the picket lines.

Ultimately, it was all to no avail. After 358 days, the strike ran out of steam. Thatcher and MacGregor had won, Scargill and the miners had lost. The other losers were the Labour Party who had been made to look utterly impotent. This after a relatively young new leader, Neil Kinnock (who came from a Welsh coal-mining town), had taken over Labour's leadership after their disastrous defeat in the elections the year before. However, he had learned some lessons and seen pop's galvanising effect, particularly on young people. He actually liked rock music[30]. Over the next three years he would actively seek the help of musicians in campaigns around the Youth Training Scheme and Red Wedge, with bands inviting be-suited, dad-at-the-disco MPs (they were mainly men) to their concerts to engage with audiences. Whether it was successful or not was open to question. They still lost the next general election.

*****

The blame for Britain's declining manufacturing industries, the miners' strike, escalating Cold War tension, the Troubles in Northern Ireland and a host of other issues were all laid at the door of Government and particularly Margaret Thatcher. In September 1984, UB40's 'If It Happens Again' single, referring to her election victory the year before, continued '…I'll pack my things and go'; the Human League's 'Betrayed' from the *Hysteria* album was similarly gloomy; The Duvet Brothers, an early scratch video act, used New Order's 'Blue Monday' as the soundtrack to three and a half minutes of images of toffs in top hats, royalty, riots, police, missiles, graveyards and marching soldiers to make their point. Subtle it was not.

Unemployment in Britain in 1984 was the highest since records began with a peak in June of 3,260,000 or nearly 12% of the workforce (a figure yet to be surpassed). By the end of 1984, nearly 700,000 young people were on special government training and job creation schemes with an average wage of less than £30 per week[31]. From 1981-84 the number of young people (16-24) out of work for more than a year tripled.

The early days of any struggling, aspiring musician were frequently punctuated by impoverished spells on the dole[32]. 'Dole culture' provided both money and time (enough to survive and create respectively), and the music scene would simply have not been the same without it. 'Unemployment brings out the guitar in everyone'[33], was a maxim that literally struck a chord. UB40 even named themselves after the dole claim form. It was better being in a band than sulking at home, walking around town all day or resorting to petty crime. Many of those signing on also felt empathy and a desire to help affect change, or at least continue opposing Conservative Party policy that was seen to be at the root of the problem. Others took advantage of the Enterprise Allowance scheme which aimed to reduce unemployment figures by encouraging entrepreneurial types to start their own businesses, as remembered by film critic Mark Kermode, then a struggling musician in Manchester: 'In return for staying off the dole, the government would give you a moderate financial stipend, along with some amorphous 'business advice' and the promise of expert mentoring'[34]. Alan McGee and Jazzie B were two such beneficiaries.

The need for jobs became the rhétorique du jour at countless free festivals. To some extent, it was preaching to the converted, but they created a sense of purpose and camaraderie. A major free festival, Jobs for a Change, was organized by the Greater London Council – itself under attack from Thatcher – on 10 June featuring The Smiths, Billy Bragg, Mari Wilson, Hank Wangford, Aswad, The Redskins and The Pogues. There was also a jazz concert at the Royal Albert Hall, a large Christmas Party in Finsbury Park featuring Madness, Ian Dury, Marc Almond and Imagination, and other smaller affairs in town halls. And then there were other GLC-organized festivals which didn't fall under the Jobs for a Change banner, but might as well have. If musicians hated Thatcher and weren't sure about Kinnock, they loved Ken Livingstone, GLC's leader. There was even a rap record named after him by Law Lords International (aka Attila the Stockbroker and friends): 'The GLC has got to stay, that's what the Red Ken Fan Club Say, cos he's the coolest guy around, we're rapping to the Red Ken sound.' Singer Sarah Jane Morris, about to join The Happy End and, a bit later, The Communards agreed: 'We were just fascinated by Ken Livingstone. He had such energy and conviction and we liked what he stood for. Nearly every weekend there was some kind of multicultural festival going on. Just generally living in London in the eighties was very exciting when you were an artist'[35]. But it wasn't just about the GLC, nor London. Up and down the country, artists like Billy Bragg, The Three Johns and The Redskins were constantly doing benefits for whatever cause was top of the agenda that week. Some of these were at festivals, but most were in small clubs in mining communities.

Not all free festivals were linked to campaigning for jobs, supporting CND, protesting against Apartheid or trying to bring the two sides of Northern Ireland together. Free festivals like Stonehenge and others that attached themselves to the 'commercial' fests like Glastonbury and Nostell Priory were deeply alternative – not in the musical sense, but as part of a way of life. If anything, they were anti- rather than pro-jobs, and in that sense alone formed a whole other political agenda in mid-80s Britain. The so-called new age travellers could be traced back to the hippies of the counterculture 60s, but by the early 80s had been augmented by anarcho-punks and what would later be termed 'crusties', mini-tribes on the edges of society. Attracted by the idea of communal living, they travelled in convoys of clapped-out buses, lorries and cars, pitching up at music festivals and fairs. Music was an important part of the lifestyle and certain groups sympathetic to the travellers' ideology (Hawkwind, Roy Harper, Here And Now, A Flux of Pink Indians etc) would play for next to nothing.

1984 was a defining year for the freebie fests. Stonehenge Free Festival, for example, had taken place every year since 1974, held around the same time as the Druid Order's Summer Solstice ceremonies, and growing in size year by year. Back then you could camp and play right by the stones and the minimal police presence was tolerant of the (mainly) soft drugs openly on sale. But by 1984 attendance had grown to tens of thousands and took up an area the size of a small town. On the positive side, it was a fascinating example of organization: funded by a 'tax' from traders and contributions from hash dealers and then shared out amongst the rubbish collecting teams, the kids areas, St John's Ambulance and production of the main stage – on which played free festival favourites like Roy Harper, Hawkwind and Here and Now, together with the less obvious Twisted Sister, Brilliant and Thor. But on the negative side, hard-drug dealers were now present and by the end of the four days the site looked like a rubbish tip with a dozen burnt-out or abandoned vehicles (some of them being owned by heroin dealers, rough justice having been dispensed by vigilantes). It was the last time a music festival would take place at Stonehenge, English Heritage having obtained a high court injunction to prevent a similar gathering the following year[36].

Crass were the link between counterculture hippies and punk's angry brigade. Both sets, and others in-between, would meet at free festivals across Britain, including the last Free Festival at Stonehenge in June 1984.

Two months later, a similar occurrence took place on the perimeter of the major Nostell Priory Festival in West Yorkshire, but this time five hundred police swooped on the camp (run, claimed the Daily Mail, by 'an evil drug-pushing cult') and that was the end of that festival too. Interestingly, the police had come from nearby Orgreave, site of a more famous pitched battle with striking miners. Free festivals were basically over by 1984, although they would be revived in a different form – the rave – in the early 90s, most of which were not free, but the Government dealt with them in largely the same heavy-handed way.

Many of those who attended free festivals were the aforesaid hippies and anarcho-punks, on the one hand diametrically opposed to each other but in reality becoming almost indistinguishable. Both were reacting against capitalism generally and the new urban phenomena of yuppies[37], sloanes and gold-collar workers. And for both, music was central to their lives. Crass were typical. Formed in 1977, they were both a band and a collective living together at Dial House, an open community in the north-east suburbs of London. They formed their own label, designed their own sleeves (Gee Vaucher's brilliant graphics and videos, and Dave King's iconic logo, were a major part of their mystique), took part in the Stop the City demonstrations in 1983 and again in 1984[38], a forerunner of the anti-globalisation protests of the 90s. They even tricked a teenage romance magazine into containing a flexi-disc of their song, 'Our Wedding', from the band's third album, *Penis Envy* – and as parodies go, it was so realistic as to have defeated its original anti-marriage purpose.

Crass's *Penis Envy* ended up at the centre of a censorship court case when, in early 1984, copies of the album, along with records by the Dead Kennedys and A Flux of Pink Indians, were seized by the police in Manchester's Eastern Bloc record shop under the Obscene Publications Act. The legal cost of defending themselves and internal friction between those who supported pacifism and those who supported violent action culminated in Crass's breakup in July. A similar incident took place in August when police raided Spectrum Records in Northwich, Cheshire, seizing 19 records. Shop owner Graham Cheadle was found guilty under the above Act but on appeal it was quashed, the judge deciding that the records were indeed "crude, vulgar and they consist to a large extent of abusive rubbish but they don't tend to deprave or corrupt"[39].

*****

Censorship and pop music share a long history, especially in the area of broadcasting, and particularly in the nannying decisions of the BBC. George Formby's 'When I'm Cleaning Windows' (1936) was an early 'oo-er vicar' example of a BBC Radio ban[40], but the arrival of rock & roll in the 50s threw programmers into a panic. When early, smutty rhythm & blues music was directed at blacks no-one minded, but when white youth began to be attracted, the moral majority grew concerned. In Britain, the 50s saw an extraordinary amount of songs banned as BBC Radio struggled to cope with the evil connotations of, for example, 'Walk Hand in Hand' (1956) by Tony Martin. Inconsistency was rife: Serge Gainsbourg's heavybreathing love-in, 'Je T'aime... Moi Non Plus' (1969) with Jane Birkin, was deemed too risqué for broadcast, while Lou Reed's 'Walk On The Wild Side' (1972) was deemed fine, presumably because the powers that be didn't know what 'giving head' meant. Judge Dread was arguably the most censored artist in pop history with 11 songs banned, but his cod-reggae, innuendo-laden 'Up with the Cock' escaped since Dread *of course* meant 'up at dawn'. (Both Gainsbourg and Dread, interestingly, had controversial releases in 1984: the former released a dodgy duet with his 12-year-old daughter Charlotte called 'Lemon Incest', while the latter covered 'Relax' just months after Frankie's original had left the charts).

Censorship wasn't monopolised by sex, however. Songs – or sleeves or music videos – that featured swear words, blasphemy, politics, homosexuality, violence, devil worship, drugs, guns, terrorism, product placement, copyright infringement or simply political incorrectness have all been reason enough to arouse authoritarian umbrage. The Sex Pistols' 'God Save the Queen' (released during the Queen's Jubilee celebrations and therefore in 'gross bad taste'), Heaven 17's 'We Don't Need this Fascist Groove Thing' (potentially libellous), Split Enz's 'Six Months in a Leaky Boat' (released during the Falklands War) and myriad songs by anarchist groups like Crass, A Flux Of Pink Indians and the Anti-Nowhere League have all fallen foul of the censors, denying air time to minority opinions. In some ways 1984 was no different, though it kicked off with one of the most celebrated bans in British pop history. On 11 January Radio One's Mike Read suddenly took exception to the lyrics and sleeve of Frankie Goes To Hollywood's 'Relax' and announced he wouldn't be playing it anymore. A BBC radio and television ban followed and the single immediately went to #1 and by mid-year became a million-seller. That the ban ironically 'made' Frankie was no comfort to others whose careers were stymied by BBC censorship. Needless to say, there was no right of appeal.

It wasn't just the BBC, although in 1984 they were the dominant national broadcaster. Many independent radio stations played 'Relax' but had playlists which were even more limited than Radio One's, thereby practising another type of censorship. Other forms included Woolworth and Boots refusing to stock The Smiths' debut album and the single 'Heaven Knows I'm Miserable Now' because both contained a track, 'Suffer Little Children', about the Moors Murders and followed complaints from one of the victims' family. HMV and Woolworth also refused to stock The Ex Pistols' 'Land Of Hope and Glory' single by Sex Pistols' early producer/soundman Dave Goodman because of obscenities on the back cover.[41] After 13 years of annual events, the 1984 Reading Festival was banned by the local Conservative Council, re-instated only when Labour took control two years later. Even the GLC became would-be censors, declaring at the beginning of 1984 that it would ban from its halls any artist who had broken the anti-Apartheid cultural boycott (although no major event seemed to have been affected).

Mostly, however, censorship *was* about sex. Across the Atlantic, Prince and Madonna's early nooky-obsessed songs courted controversy but mostly escaped censure. In fact, compared with his 1980 *Dirty Mind* album, the former's massively successful *Purple Rain* was reasonably uncontroversial. Except, that is, for the track 'Darling Nikki' ("I knew a girl named Nikki, I guess you could say she was a sex fiend. I met her in a hotel lobby, masturbating with a magazine") which provoked the fabulously named Tipper Gore, wife of presidential hopeful Al Gore, into forming the innocuous sounding but in reality very powerful pressure group Parents Music Resource Center (PMRC) the following year. Citing links between rape, teenage suicide and teen pregnancies with the lyrics of certain rock records, PMRC called for self-restraint from record companies, which in effect was self-censorship, and parental advisory stickers. Several songs from 1984 made it on to the PMRC's Filthy Fifteen list including 'Darling Nikki', Sheena Easton's 'Sugar Walls' (also written by Prince), Twisted Sister's 'We're Not Gonna Take It', Judas Priest's 'Eat Me Alive', Vanity's

'Strap On 'Robbie Baby'', W.A.S.P.'s 'Animal (Fuck Like A Beast)' and Cyndi Lauper's 'She Bop'.

If the portrayal of heterosexual sex (demeaning to women or otherwise) ran the risk of censorship, presenting what went on between gays and lesbians was a complete no-no. Indeed, up until the end of the 70s, simply coming out was considered a bad career move. In the new decade however, gay artists became more public, and pop music found itself playing a prominent role in increasing the understanding of and tolerance towards gays and lesbians. 1984 had its fair share of hit singles either by openly gay pop stars (Boy George, Marc Almond, Pete Burns, half of Frankie) or not yet openly gay ones (Elton John, George Michael, Freddie Mercury, Limahl, Hazel Dean). The gains, though, were countered by (largely) media-driven paranoia about AIDS. With 'only' 108 cases – but a chilling 46 deaths – reported in Britain in 1984, the disease was perhaps still too new and taboo to galvanise a response from musicians[42]. Indeed, none of the above artists chose to include gay and lesbian issues in their songs.

The song that really did that was Bronski Beat's debut single 'Smalltown Boy', released in June. It was an intriguing combination of elements: singer Jimmy Sommerville's plaintive falsetto cutting across a beautifully crafted, toe-tapping electronic beat; lyrics which may have been open to interpretation; and a video which didn't need interpreting at all. The video was extraordinarily ordinary: a powerful yet almost mundane narrative of what it was to be gay, a victim of homophobia, and facing up to shamed parents. It reached #3 in the charts. A second single, 'Why?', continued the theme but was angrier in tone and with a more confrontational video. An album, *The Age of Consent*, referring to the legal age at which gay men could have sex (21 in England and Wales[43], 16 in most other European countries), followed in October. This information was helpfully printed on the inside sleeve together with a telephone number for gay legal advice. Extraordinarily, one of the companies the designers commissioned for typesetting objected to the content, but they found another to do the job.

When journalist Paul Flynn set out to write *Good As You: From Prejudice to Pride, 30 Years of Gay Britain*, the year 1984 was the obvious starting point. 'I was looking at one of the charts for that year and you had Frankie's 'Two Tribes' at Number 1, George Michael's 'Careless Whisper' at Number 2, and 'Smalltown Boy' by Bronski Beat at Number 3', he says. 'Then when I looked down the chart there was Animal Nightlife, The Associates and Blancmange and they all had gay members. Then of course at the time you also had Pet Shop Boys and Culture Club. I was just fascinated by why there was such a glut of gay men making pop music and what was it they were trying to get out of their system by doing it in pop songs'[44]. Things were changing. By the end of the year, Chris Smith became the first gay MP to publicly 'out' himself.

It was indeed a heady old year. Of course there have been politically charged years since then – including, as I write, the awfulness that is Brexit, Trump and the rise of the far right – but where are the protest songs? Certainly not in the charts. Of course there are activists, but aside from stars like Stormzy, they don't seem to be choosing music as a medium for expression. Interestingly, 1984's most powerful example of activism wasn't actually political in that it was largely responding to a natural disaster rather than one brought on by the government. It was of course Band Aid, but we shall return to that later in the book.

Chapter 7: The Politics of Dancing
Dance music and club culture

The politics of dancing
The politics of ooh feeling good
Re-Flex

[Techno] wasn't designed to be dance music, it was designed to be a futurist statement.
Jeff Mills[1]

I think that's what the warehouse party scene did: it allowed people to express themselves; allowed people to dress how they wanted, because there was no one on the door….[2]
Terry Farley, club promoter

In 1984, dance music was a vague description rather than the bona fide genre it became by the end of the decade. Contrary to what one read in the style magazines, the music most people danced to was Top 40 pop music, so at a typical run-of-the-mill disco[3] the majority of the great British public would be dancing around handbags to the mainstream synth-funk of Duran Duran and Shakatak, the black soul of US heavy-hitters Michael Jackson and Prince, and the blue-eyed British soul of Culture Club and Wham!.

But for the hipsters, there were options. Certain clubs would 'keep the faith' –northern soul nights were still extant for instance. Others served the more recent sub-cultures: goths still headed for the Batcave in London, the Phono in Leeds and Berlin in Manchester. Jazz-funk had its hardcore scene (see Chapter 19). Many clubs would cater for all sorts: Steve Strange and Rusty Egan for instance had moved on from the new romanticism of Tuesday nights at Billy's, Blitz, Hell and Club for Heroes and into the 1,400-capacity Camden Palace with a different theme each night. We'll return to clubland later on, but first the actual music.

Looking beyond mainstream pop music, the most exciting dance music in the first half of the 80s was hip-hop, emanating from New York. Hip-hop was actually a wider cultural entity embracing DJing, rap, street art, breakdancing, bodypopping and fashion, originating in the rougher neighbourhoods of the Bronx and Queens. Its musical form went back to the early 70s with DJs like Kool Herc (aka Jamaican-American Clive Campbell) using two turntables to loop and accentuate the instrumental and beat-heavy portions of funk records. When words were needed, Jamaican-style MC-ing became rap – assertive and angry – and before long the music was central to 'block parties' before being embraced by Manhattan's edgier clubs like Paradise Garage. By the early 80s artists like Grandmaster Flash, Afrika Bambaataa and Run DMC were not just messing around with other people's music but, using drum-machines, synthesizers and other effects, making their own.

It has been endlessly described how influential Kraftwerk, Giorgio Moroder and Yellow Magic Orchestra were on the early 80s sound of hip-hop. And certainly the former's 'Trans Europe Express' and 'Numbers' were a double blueprint for the genre, particularly the *sub*-genre of what became known as electro-funk, or – in Britain only – simply electro. Electro was a relatively short-lived (roughly 1982-84) phenomenon which bridged the gap between the hip-hop funk of Afrika Bambaataa's Planet Rock and the hip-hop rock of Run DMC's eponymous debut album. In between there were hits like 'Rockit' by Herbie Hancock (with the stellar scratching of GrandMixer D.ST), 'No Sell Out' by drummer Keith LeBlanc (issued as 'by' Malcolm X, whose political diatribe provided the track's lyrics) and 'Jam On Revenge' by Newcleus.

Many Brits made the pilgrimage. Inspired DJs brought back boxes of 12-inch singles and made mixtapes for broadcasting on pirate radio; New Order and Factory created the Hacienda; Charlie Ahearn's hip-hop film *Wild Style* made it over to selected cinemas; and Martha Cooper and Henry Chalfant's *Subway Art*, the first book to document New York City's graffiti movement, published in 1984, made it into bookshops and galleries on the other side of the Atlantic. Also key was Malcolm McLaren's surprisingly brilliant 'Buffalo Gals' which, with the not inconsiderable production help of Trevor Horn and Anne Dudley who laid the beats and sampled The World's Famous Supreme Team, went Top 10. It also raised questions about authenticity. Could hip-hop be white?[4] Was it cultural theft? Nothing new there, then.

In parallel, a few mainly London-based artists tried to replicate the New York sound in their own recordings. First-wave British 'crews' (as they were often called) included the London-based Family Quest[5], Cookie Crew and Faze One – and, in Manchester, Broken Glass[6] . Their activities were generally limited to live sets rather than recordings, the exceptions being Dizzy Heights' 'Christmas Rapping' (1982), DJ Newtrament's vocoder-heavy 'London Bridge is Falling Down' (1983) and City Limits Crew's 'Keep It On' (1984). These first singles showed artists feeling their way into a 'borrowed culture' and the dilemma of 'keepin' it real'. Should they adopt American accents and the vocabulary of the Bronx or create London and Manchester vernaculars?

For those who wanted the original article, the main problem was getting hold of the records which were on fairly obscure US labels like Tommy Boy, Prism and Sunnyview. In 1983, an entrepreneurial Anglo-Indian, Hong Kong-born hustler called Morgan Khan saw the gap and started licensing key tracks for his Street Sounds compilation albums. Particularly influential was the *Electro* series of ten albums[7] which peaked in 1984 with *Electro 3,4,5* and *6*, featuring Herbie Hancock, Newcleus, Run DMC, Divine Sounds, Imperial Brothers, Fresh 3MCs, Radio-Active, Cybotron (which, if we're splitting hairs, was early techno) and many others. The quick-fire release schedule, modest price, stylish graphics, full-length tracks which segued flawlessly into each other and 'Electro is Aural Sex' strapline were an instant success with London's fashion-conscious style set, including The Face which put them on the cover in May 1984[8]. In essence, they helped electro – and indeed hip hop – cross over from cult status to the mainstream in the UK[9].

Morgan Khan's StreetSounds compilations defined the cool new sound of electro in the UK, quickly picked up (and mimicked) by The Face.

Khan saw StreetSounds as the 'mood of a nation playing catch up to what was going on in the States'[10]. By June 1984, he felt that maybe the UK *had* caught up, so he released *UK Electro*, an album which had an unlikely genesis in ex-Magazine and A Certain Ratio musicians Martin Jackson and Andy Connell, recently retired Manchester DJ Greg Wilson and the dance crew he managed, Broken Glass. 'Morgan told us he wanted to release an album called *UK Electro*, using six of our tracks, plus a further track that Mastermind (who mixed the Electro albums) recorded under the name The Rapologists. To give the illusion of a thriving electro scene developing in Britain, he asked us to think up different artist names [and] Morgan came up with the colourful aliases that appeared as the various production and songwriting credits'[11]. The truth was that the Brits *hadn't* caught up and the *UK Electro* series ended up as a series of one. Jackson and Connell went on to form Swing Out Sister, while Khan would continue licensing US tracks for the main *Electro* series, start up another, *Hi-Energy*, compiled by Ian Levine (paralleling the hi-NRG singles Stock Aitken Waterman were just starting to put out), and release the first Chicago house records in the UK. Somewhere in the midst of this – between electro and hi-NRG – was Paul Hardcastle, whose first four electro singles released in 1984 didn't do much, but the following year hit the jackpot with '19', a UK #1 for five weeks.

Straight-ahead hip-hop by largely anonymous DJ-production crews may not have reached the heights of New York, but – as was so often the case with borrowing Stateside – British artists turned the style into something else. The Wild Bunch was a sound-system and loose collective of DJs and rappers performing in Bristol between 1983 and 1987. Although – like most of the crews in London – they barely recorded anything, their shows at the Dug Out and private parties, mostly in the St Paul's area, were hugely influential in terms of combining hip-hop, rare groove, soul, reggae and rock, opting for a slower (typically 90bpm), laid-back vibe than their other British equivalents. Members included Nellee Hooper (who went on to produce Soul II Soul, Björk and Madonna), Grant Marshall, Robert del Naja and Andrew Vowles (aka Daddy G, 3D and Mushroom, who formed Massive Attack), Tricky (who went solo),

Miles (Milo) Johnson and Claude (Willy Wee) Williams. Combined, and individually, theirs was a very different sound and style to what had gone before.

The Wild Bunch at the Dug Out, Bristol, 1984. From left: Milo, Daddy G, Nellee, Willie Wee and 3D.

Aside from the DJs and crews, electro influenced a number of unconventional white bands. The Art Of Noise, an intentionally faceless London-based 5-piece comprising ZTT's producer, engineer, programmer, arranger and journalist, did as their name suggests. They mixed beats and sophisticated samples with flourishes of musicianship and almost classical arrangements. They were the Yes of hip-hop. Debut EP, *Into Battle With The Art Of Noise*, released in November 1983 was their manifesto (almost literally; Paul Morley's sleevenotes read like one) and its two main tracks, 'Beatbox' and 'Moments in Love', would form the basis of the various singles and, arguably, a whole album which followed in 1984. Top 10 hit 'Close to the Edit' pretty much *was* 'Beatbox'. That said, it was fun, clever and 'Moments in Love' was gorgeous. Also clever was a piss-take or homage, depending on your viewpoint, called *Into Trouble with the Noise of Art* by the similarly faceless Mainframe. Released on Ying Yang Yumm Records and including its own manifesto, as parodies go it was a bull's eye. Less playful, more northern-austere, New Order's 'Thieves Like Us', Section 25's 'Looking from a Hilltop', Cabaret Voltaire's 'Sensoria' and Eric Random & The Bedlamites' 'Mad as Mankind' married electro to post-punk, replacing the funky rap of the Bronx with the less convincing, sung affectations of Manchester and Sheffield.

Closely aligned with hip-hop and its electro offshoot was breakdancing. And in a refreshing twist, it was towns like Nottingham, Manchester and Huddersfield which led the way. In 1983, the New York dance troupe, WFLA crew, performed in

Nottingham's Old Market Square, inspiring tracksuited youngsters to do their own thing, sometimes on lino in public spaces but also once a week in a club called Rock City. Here the Rock City Crew were formed and went on to perform around the world, supporting the likes of hip-hop legends, Afrika Bambaataa, Run DMC and Grandmaster Melle Mel. (Claude Knight, who was the Crew's rapper, later made a film about the scene, *NG83: When We Were B-Boys*).

In 1984, a young Brit by the name of Paul Oakenfold had been hanging out in New York working as a courier and mixing with the hip-hop set. On returning home, he helped set up the London All-Star Breakers who entered the Swatch world breakdancing competition. 'We all flew to New York! We found ourselves at the Roxy, England's entry to the world competition, battling the Rock Steady Crew. We didn't win, but we did well'[12]. At the same time, a teenage Goldie appeared on TV as both graffiti artist and a member of the Wolverhampton B-Boys breakdance crew. In Manchester, Broken Glass and Street Machine led the way, the former also involved in jazz dance, the latter breakdancing upstarts. Street Machine's Evo (aka Stephen Evans), three times British breakdancing champion, pointed out the difference between the American and British styles: 'In New York they would dance to original funk breaks, James Brown, stuff like that. Over here it was electro, and that changed the way we danced.'[13] Another of Street Machine's dancers was Jason Orange who would later join Take That.

But what really took breakdancing into the mainstream were the films: two of which were released almost simultaneously in June 1984: *Beat Street* which featured Africa Bambaataa and Grandmaster Melle Mel and a classic B-Boy battle between the New York City Breakers and Rock Steady Crew; and *Breakin'*, a #1 box office comedy which included Ice-T's first ever appearance on film. The latter was sniffily dismissed in Black Echoes as '…one of those movies […] that buries what it comes to praise'[14]. Astonishingly, a sequel, *Breakin' 2: Electric Boogaloo*, was released before the year was out. In fact, 1983 and 1984 were big years for dance-themed Hollywood movies and their attendant soundtrack albums, *Flashdance* and *Footloose* combining to increase dance class memberships and sales of legwarmers across the UK. And that's leaving aside the dance-peppered soundtracks of *Purple Rain* and *Ghostbusters*.

*****

Electro's younger, longer-lasting brother was techno. Like electro it originated in the US and was heavily influenced by Kraftwerk and Moroder, as well as the early 80s British synthpop of Gary Numan, Yazoo and Human League – but not, it would seem, the parallel genre of electronic body music (EBM) that was coming out of Belgium, Germany and the UK at roughly the same time, of which more later. Techno's origins were not the block parties of the Bronx but the bedrooms of Belleville, a small white-collar town 30 miles west of downtown Detroit where Juan Atkins, Derrick May and Kevin Saunderson hung out together. They were middle-class black kids hooked on the electronic music coming out of Europe rather than the hip-hop of New York, and what is often cited as the first techno record, 1981's 'Alleys of Your Mind', was actually a collaboration between Atkins and a white Vietnam Vet called Rick Davis under the name of Cybotron. But unlike electro's loose crews of producers, DJs, rappers and breakdancers, techno was mostly the domain of individual artists. Atkins, May and Saunderson may have helped each other initially but they never formed a group or crew. The stylistic differences between early electro and techno were blurred (the *Electro 3* compilation featured Cybotron's 'Techno City' for example), but over time techno would dispense with rapping (and vocals generally), focussing on a minimal, trance-like sound with a machine-perfected 4/4 beat. In 1984, however, techno was still in its infancy, didn't even have a name and as far as a UK movement was concerned, wouldn't properly take root until the early 90s.

One of the intriguing things about the development of techno has been the lack of critical reference to EBM. Groups like DAF, Nitzer Ebb and Front 242 were playing an aggressive, dark form of pumping electronic dance music in the early 80s which must have been picked up in Detroit but is rarely mentioned. The genre had its genesis in the so-called industrial music scene but developed into a style which shared much in common with techno: minimal, pure, pulsating electronic rhythms often with a dystopian sci-fi theme. Where it differed was that it was white, group-based, veered towards rock and adopted an aggressive sexual aesthetic. If techno wasn't named in 1984, EBM definitely was, with the sleeve of Front 242's *No Comment* album proudly proclaiming: 'Electronic Body Music Composed And Produced On Eight Tracks By Front 242'. Belgium was full of EBM and it became the dance music of the black-clad, sunglasses-after-dark crowd in the claustrophobic clubs of Brussels and Antwerp. It would eventually mutate into the slower new beat and the electronica of labels like R&S.

EBM, however, never *really* caught on in Britain and was a bit late in trying. Bands like Essex's Nitzer Ebb and south London's Hard Corps released suitably assailing debut singles ('Isn't It Funny How Your Body Works' and 'Dirty' respectively) before 1984 was out. The former were dedicated exponents of the genre, surprisingly uncompromised by recording with Phil Harding of PWL, and are still going; the latter took the genre into a more pop-oriented direction (like Kraftwerk meets Depeche Mode in a seedy Châtelet alley – the singer was French) but split up before achieving a success that seemed to be on the cards.[15] Portion Control's excellent 'Rough Justice' and 'Go-Talk' singles, Data's[16] disco-porn 'Blow' and even Depeche Mode's 'In Your Memory' (B-side to 'People Are People') toyed with EBM, but ultimately the genre was too dark to catch on in British clubs and it was left to Belgium to fly the flag.

If EBM was dark, negative and alternative, hi-NRG was bright, positive and mainstream. It wasn't new – 70s singles by La Belle Epoque, Baccara, Boney M, even Donna Summer – were effectively hi-NRG, but 1984 was a big year for the genre in Britain, dominated by the production trio of Stock Aitken Waterman, then new kids on the block. Typified by uptempo rhythms, a trebly sound (as opposed to bass-heavy techno and EBM), fervent-bordering-on-shrill vocals, and a harking back to disco (as well as a nod to the contemporaneous Italo-disco scene), hi-NRG was white dance music made for the singles charts and adopted by the gay community. Hazell Dean, Divine and Dead Or Alive – all SAW productions – were all Top 10 in 1984 *and* favourites in the clubs. Other singles like Bronski Beat's 'Why?', Kim Wilde's 'Second Time' and Pet Shop Boys' first two singles – the original Bobby Orlando-produced versions of 'West End Girls' and 'One More Chance' – could also be described as hi-NRG. It was also akin to the upbeat sound of Motown and therefore embraced by Northern Soulsters and DJ-producers like Ian Levine. In fact Levine, who ruled the roost at Heaven, was producing hi-NRG records before SAW came along, but it was the latter who turned it into the perfect mainstream package. And mainstream it became: cue double page spread in Smash Hits and BBC Radio One's Peter Powell calling it 'the sound of '84'.

Although Levine was hugely influential, in the early 80s the cult of the DJ was still an underground, not a mainstream phenomenon. But spinners like Chris Sullivan, Jay Strongman and Paul Murphy, London's Soul Mafia, Greg Wilson playing Northern Soul, and of course crews manning (and they *were* all men) the sound-systems were highly respected if not highly remunerated. DJs like Tim Westwood played hip-hop on pirate radio; others like Roger Johnson and Chad Jackson focussed on its technical spin-off, scratching. It was only when Danny Rampling and Paul Oakenfeld came along that DJs began to become superstars.

******

As for the clubs, 1984 was – like the music scene – a mix of everything. London tends to dominate club talk given its position as home of the music industry (the majors and biggest independents), media and fashion, its large black population (at the vanguard of most dance music) and simply the size of the place. And certainly – with obvious exceptions like northern soul – there's a strong case in arguing that most club 'scenes', dance movements, even whole youth cultures (new romantics at Billy's and Blitz[17] and goths at the Batcave, for example), started off in the capital. The new romantic era was effectively over as early as 1982, as Visage lost momentum, Spandau sported suits and Japan ('who weren't new romantics') split up. The scene propagated by Steve Strange and Rusty Egan had of course been tiny, exaggerated a hundred-fold by the style magazines, MTV, coffee-table photo books and retrospectives that continue to this day. Strange and Egan tried replicating the formula with Club for Heroes at 1 Baker Street, Hell in Covent Garden and Slum It In Style at Camden Palace, the latter lasting well into 1984. The last hurrah was surely Leigh Bowery's Taboo which gestated throughout the year until finally opening in January 1985 in Leicester Square. Taboo was all about the look, combining new romanticism with the avant-garde, often to grotesque extremes. Door-minder Mark Vaultier would hold up a mirror to Taboo-wannabes and ask "Would you let yourself in?" But the era of trailblazing synthpop and extreme make-up, hair and clothes was on its way out.

Instead, the dancefloors were full of electro, funk and soul at London clubs like the The Wag, Mud Club, Heaven, The Dirt Box, White Trash and the Hippodrome. Some had a symbiotic relationship with the jazz revival (see Chapter 19), while The Ace in

Brixton even catered for roller-dancing. Most had regular nights in fixed locations, but some flitted between addresses.

Warehouse[18] clubs came into fashion, especially in London, motivated by the desire for bigger, more alternative venues and to get out of the chrome-and-mirrors West End. They democratised the capital's nightlife, taking place in London's hinterlands and attracting a whole new wave of clubbers, their 'here today gone tomorrow' status only adding to the allure. 'Switching location from one week to the next heightens the appeal', cooed The Face. 'If you're not on the right grapevine you simply won't know where to go'[19]. For a while they were known as speakeasys but it didn't stick. It wasn't really new – reggae sound-systems had been peripatetic for years – but it did add a more egalitarian dimension to the club scene: raffle ticket or bring-your-own booze policy, music that catered for all tastes and no dress code. On the downside there was no health and safety, very little security and more than likely no toilets. The Dirt Box was in an old West Indian drinking den in Earls Court, up some stairs above a chemist's shop, before moving around, one step ahead of the police. The Circus and Wharehouse were bigger affairs: the former, involving Jeremy Healy of rastadickensians Haysi Fantayzee, presented their last one, in 1984, at Bagley's Warehouse behind Kings Cross – which would become a mega, legit venue in the 90s. The latter, run by Frank Kelly and Dave Mahoney, ended up with a permanent residency at Camden's Electric Ballroom. Also around this time and in the vicinity, two Irish brothers, Noel and Maurice Watson, started throwing parties in a disused school in Battle Bridge Road behind Kings Cross with the help of Rip, Rig & Panic's Sean and Andrea Oliver and Neneh Cherry. Terry Farley, another promoter, remembers the scene fondly:

> *The parties were in dilapidated, ex-industrial areas like the Docks, Hackney Road, Old Street and Curtain Road (which had a lot of warehouses because of the commercial rag trade), Lots Road in Chelsea and even places out in the suburbs, like Wembley. It was a reaction against the West End and the license laws. People wanted to get away from the restrictions of the West End. It was very hard to get into clubs for the majority of people. [...] I remember going to Billy's [...] and that opened until 4:30, which seemed really late, but if you went to a warehouse party you could go on well after the sun rose. It felt brilliant. It felt lawless. There was a huge buzz going to a party in Lots Road, just as an 18-year-old would have felt going to their first acid house party in Southwark six years later. Being somewhere where you're not constrained gives people a freedom... It was more varied than in a trendy club in Soho. There was a greater social mix. You had a much better fashion mix. London was awash with tribes back then and it was really cool to go to a warehouse party and see some goths and rockabillies and a few casuals in the corner keeping their heads down.[20]*

Other warehouse events were more theatrical affairs. Funkapolitan's Tom Dixon and Nick Jones, for example, joined forces with sculptor/set-designer Mark Brazier-Jones to organize astonishing parties in disused factories featuring junk-sculpture and live welding. There were parallels with the metal-bashing scene of Test Dept and SPK, the theatrical Mutoid Waste Company which was founded that year, and Spain's La Fura Dels Baus, whose debut UK show in a massive East Docklands warehouse in 1985 involved chain-sawing a car and fireworks whizzing inches above people's heads. In any case, it was how Dixon became an internationally renowned furniture designer – self-taught rather than at college. The warehouse scene survived long enough to influence rave but it became harder and harder to find venues as the developers moved in, property prices went up and London gentrified.

Although you wouldn't know it from reading the London-centric style magazines, there were thriving club scenes elsewhere in Britain. Manchester's wasn't just the Hacienda; Liverpool's revolved around The State (formerly a ballroom where tea dances took place in the 1930s), Quadrant Park and 051; Leeds The Warehouse, The Orbit and Tiffany's; Glasgow had Panama Jax and Cinder's[21]; Newcastle had Mr M's at Tiffanys and Rockshots; and so on.

Nightlife: Chris Sullivan and Ollie O'Donnell, founders of London's Wag Club. Madonna at Manchester's Hacienda.

And then of course there was northern soul, the scene within a scene, its collectors, DJs and dancers devoted to obscure American soul acts and labels that had long been forgotten in their homeland. Since the end of the 60s and throughout the 70s, the music was danced to, traded and celebrated in clubs like Manchester's Twisted Wheel, The Torch in Stoke, the Blackpool Mecca and Wigan Casino, intense nights powered by amphetamines and self-righteousness. Towards the end of the 70s the British media became interested, which had the effect of the purists closing ranks and going underground again. The mid-80s saw the scene move around, even to the distrusted south, even to *London* where the 100 Club put on northern soul all-nighters. One of those who frequented was journalist Stuart Cosgrove who was then writing for Black Echoes, NME and The Face. In his book *Young Soul Rebels* he recalls the die-hards from Preston who'd travel down to London for the weekend or the rush to the decks when DJ Ady Croasdell played an impossibly rare record – a scenario that's hard to imagine nowadays.

If amphetamines (aka speed) was the northern soul drug of choice, then a new substance was about to hit UK clubland. Known to chemists as 3,4-Methylenedioxy methamphetamine, and to clubbers as MDMA or ecstasy or simply E, the drug was in use in New York and Boston in the early 80s and still legal in 1984[22]. In the UK, MDMA fell under the 1971 Misuse of Drugs Act, so it was already outlawed as a Class A substance when small quantities started arriving from America. In the early 80s it was still very small-scale in British clubs, brought over by a few party animals, but in the sun-kissed Balearic Islands it was gaining popularity. One of these clubs was Amnesia on Ibiza where Alfredo Fiorito had started DJing in late 1983. The synergy of decent weather, holiday vibes, euphoric music and bliss-inducing ecstasy helped usher in a new kind of club culture, picked up by visiting British DJs and exported back to Blighty.

Chapter 8: In the Studio
From analogue to digital

All music is based one way or the other, or influenced through the ages, on technology.[1]
Hans Zimmer

The great benefit of computer sequencers is that they remove the issue of skill, and replace it with the issue of judgement.[2]
Brian Eno

On January 24th, Apple Computer will introduce Macintosh, and you'll see why 1984 won't be like 1984.
The ad that launched the Mac

Before 1984 the world of music – and life generally – was mostly pre-digital. Musical instruments were almost exclusively analogue (even if they were increasingly electronic), recording equipment was still based on magnetic tape, and the finished product was made available on vinyl and cassette. After 1984 the music world marched inexorably towards ones and zeroes.

On the face of it, the basic instrumental triumvirate of pop and rock – guitar, keyboards, drums – had barely changed in thirty years. What *had* changed were, firstly, the keyboards which had moved on from pianos, organs and the occasional exotic Mellotron or Mini-Moog, to increasingly sophisticated kit which could synthesise completely new sounds or sample existing ones. They weren't there simply for melody either – they filled out a composition adding colour, texture and atmosphere. The second thing that changed was the way rhythms were constructed. In the early 80s, the beat, so essential in pop and rock, began to be created (or augmented) by drum machines and sequencers, much to the chagrin of most drummers but to the delight of producers and engineers who sought perfection. The third was the plethora of effects and recording and mixing techniques, including that most 80s of sounds, 'gated' drums[3]. And the fourth was MIDI (Musical Instrument Digital Interface), which enabled all of the above to 'talk' to each other; by 1983 it was standardized and by 1984 it was increasingly the norm.

But let's start with those keyboards and the way they not only became more sophisticated but also digital. As we have seen, analogue synthesizers were fairly widespread in the early 80s but the introduction of digital equivalents was slow, their performance erratic and the price high. The Synclavier ($13,000 at the time) was the first in 1978, with producer Mike Thorne an early user – you can hear it on Soft Cell's 'Tainted Love' and Michael Jackson's *Thriller* (the 'gong' at the beginning of 'Beat It'). The Fairlight CMI ($25,000) followed in 1979 and was different in that it was as much a sampler as a synthesizer and had a flashy screen on which you could 'draw' the waveform you wanted. Peter Gabriel, Stevie Wonder and Kate Bush were early users and you can hear it all over Yazoo and The Art Of Noise. The Emulator ($10,000) arrived in 1981 and was essentially a sampler with keyboard, used extensively by Depeche Mode, Ultravox and New Order, as seen when the latter played 'Blue Monday' live on Top Of The Pops. But it was the Yamaha DX7, debuting in 1983, which would – because of its simplicity, reliability and $2,000 price tag – become the most widely used digital synthesizer for the rest of the 80s. It didn't sample, but its electric piano, bass and marimba sounds were ubiquitous, particularly in ballads. Older keyboards were analogue – they actually went out of tune – but the DX7 was 100% digital with, for better or worse, no harmonic distortion. It was perfection for a producer.

The first programmable drum machine to sample sounds was the Linn LM-1 ($5,000) debuting in 1980 with early users including Prince, Heaven 17 and Human League (extensively and famously on *Dare*), quickly followed by the LM-2. However, pre-set drum-machines were still popular, like the Roland TR-808 which, used with the 303 Bass Line, would prove hugely influential. In 1984, the LMs were succeeded by the 9000 and the 808 by the 909 (both unsuccessfully as it turned out), while the rare British-made Movement Percussion Computer, so expertly used by Eurythmics, bowed out altogether. And then there was the none-more-80s Simmons electronic drum kit with its hexagonal pads, played by the likes of Roger Taylor of Duran Duran and Rik Allen of Def Leppard, the latter's customized to let him play it one-armed after he lost the other in a car-crash.

It wasn't just synths and drum-machines. Synonymous with the mid-to-late 80s was the Steinberger Bass: a thin, stumpy, minimal-futurist looking guitar that was the first radically different bass design since the inception of the electric bass by Leo Fender in 1951. Following prototypes in the early 80s, by 1984 they were becoming as ubiquitous as the DX7 keyboard. Traditionalists hated the truncated look; there was no machine head at the end of the neck, strings just ended like they'd fallen off a cliff. It looked like a children's guitar, albeit a very techy one, and like everything in the 80s it was in designer black.

And then there were the hybrids. Guitar synthesizers had been around for a while, but they'd looked like regular electric guitars. Making its debut in 1984, however, the Roland G707 looked very different. Alongside the neck it had a 'stabiliser bar' prompting its alternative name, the 'dalek's handbag'. It certainly looked futuristic which is why it was anathema to The Smiths and perfect for Sigue Sigue Sputnik. If the G707 was naff, the SynthAxe was naffer. Developed by a small company in England in a joint venture with Virgin, it was incredibly sophisticated but unfortunately looked like a hi-tech grass strimmer. Only 100 were sold. Naffest of all, though, was the keytar – half keyboard, half guitar, all cringe. Although developed in the late 70s, it became uniquely identified with the 80s, played by the likes of Jan Hammer, Herbie Hancock and Howard Jones, a heroic attempt to make the keyboard as cool and unfettered as the guitar. It is difficult to understand its naffness – I mean, why? – but it just was. And even though it's enjoyed something of a (knowingly ironic?) revival in recent years, it remains the epitomy of uncool.

However, it was the arrival of MIDI and sampling which shifted the balance of artistic power from songwriters and instrumentalists to producers. MIDI allowed control of keyboards and drum machines through a computer, so you could step-sequence a song in perfect timing. Sampling allowed producers to dispense with orthodox instruments and use pre-recorded sounds from their own record collections or sample new, non-musical ones (the metal bashing fad, for example). They could become artists in their own right. The key was not just sampling the sounds but ordering them, slowing them down or speeding them up, reversing them, turning them into rhythms, playing them back in a different key. As already mentioned, early digital synthesizers like the Fairlight and Emulator were essentially samplers. They came with keyboards, but with MIDI you didn't need to have them combined. Before too long, the sampler was basically a box (like the Akai S900) and you could play back the sounds on any digital keyboard you happened to have in the studio. Sampling had the same empowering effect as punk. You didn't have to be much of a musician to play three chords; now you didn't have to be a musician at all. You could use someone else's music and make it your own – the legal issues of which would occupy the music industry for years to come. It required some technical skill, and it was really about recording rather than performing, but it could be quickly learnt.

Kate Bush with Fairlight, Steve Jobs with Apple Macintosh, and the much-mocked keytar.

Meanwhile, on 24 January 1984, Apple launched the first Macintosh computer. Despite the sophisticated ad[4] directed by Ridley Scott and broadcast during the Super Bowl, the computer itself looked and (compared obviously with now) *was* pretty basic, and initial sales were poor. But west coast tech geeks Peter Gotcher and Evan Brooke bought one. The pair had founded DigiDrums to sell drum sound clips for sampling synthesizers and wondered whether the Macintosh could be used to edit the sound files. It was clunky but it worked. It was the beginning of Pro Tools (launched seven years later) and the game-changing world of digital audio workstations where music could be created entirely 'in the box' without the need of expensive studios.

*****

But that was the future. For musicians, engineers and producers in 1984, the recording studio was the be-all and end-all. London alone had around ten major studios at the time. Sarm West (formerly called Basing Street, and before that Island) was the studio of choice for Trevor Horn's ZTT productions, and was where most of the Band Aid single was recorded. It also had a sister studio, Sarm East at the bottom of Brick Lane in the East End. The Virgin-owned Townhouse on Goldhawk Road in Shepherds Bush played host to countless artists including Elton John, Queen, Duran Duran and The Jam, and was where Phil Collins's famous 'In the Air Tonight' drum sound was captured. Others included George Martin's Air Studios on Oxford Street (Heaven 17, Madness), Olympic in Barnes (Elvis Costello, Spandau Ballet), Trident in Soho (Nick Cave), Britannia Row (owned by Pink Floyd) in Islington, Odyssey near Marble Arch (Kate Bush, Alison Moyet), and Wessex in Hampstead (Bronski Beat, Scritti Politti). CTS in Wembley claimed to be the world's first all-digital recording studio[5]. Ironically, the most famous studio of them all – Abbey Road – was somewhat in the doldrums before reinventing itself in the 90s.

There were of course many well-known studios outside of London, including Amazon in Liverpool (OMD, Echo & The Bunnymen); The Manor in Oxfordshire (XTC, PiL – and of course where *Tubular Bells* was created a decade earlier); Rockfield near Monmouth in Wales (Robert Plant, Adam and the Ants), Strawberry in Stockport (New Order, The Smiths), the just-about-to-close Cargo in Rochdale near Manchester (The Fall, The Teardrop Explodes), Castlesound near Edinburgh (The Blue Nile, Simple Minds), and the former Bovril factory and snooker club, Windmill Lane Studio in Dublin (U2, Virgin Prunes). For tax reasons or simply because they liked a change or because the studios had a special atmosphere (or pool), British bands would also record further afield: Hansa in Berlin (Depeche Mode, Killing Joke), Miraval in the south of France (Sade, Wham!), the appropriately named Mountain in Switzerland (Bowie, Queen), Compass in the Bahamas, Air in Montserrat and so on. And of course many artists ended up in often legendary studios of New York and LA.

Once in the studio, the producer was king (rarely queen). The artists maybe had demos but it was the producer's magic that turned the rough cuts into hits – or not as the case may be. By the mid-80s, the blurring of musical instruments, effects and recording equipment produced pop that was 'perfect', not a note out of place. The trick was to somehow retain enough of the song's character and emotion – usually the vocals or perhaps the well-placed inclusion of a conventional instrument – for it not to sound too machine-like. The following studio situation – it happened to be The Go-Betweens but it could have been anyone – was typical:

Then started the dreaded discussion of live versus programmed drums and suddenly we were face to face with eighties recording hell. Little was getting done as [the producer] manoeuvred [the drummer] into accepting the use of drum machines.[...] The era of the obsession with time-keeping was upon us, automated recording and mixing desks and synthesizers forcing the requirement of absolute accuracy in the drums; no 'feel' was allowed. It came down to what kind of music you wanted to make – modern pop or music with an old-time feeling. And that led to what kind of band we were in April 1984. We weren't [...] Einstürzende Neubauten. We had pop songs and one of them [...] sounded to [the producer and record label] like a hit single. [...] But this wasn't a decade when pop hits were recorded live in the studio. Now they were intricate constructions, taking days or weeks to build, and the first thing to go was the drummer. A rhythm machine was programmed and the other members of the band took turns in fitting their part to a giant gyre of sound so complicated that a pair of hands couldn't hope to mix it.[6]

Describing the process of making a record was anathema to the music press. It was just too technical, too muso, too boring. Even the musician pages at the back of Melody Maker were the butt of jokes from NME and Sounds staff. And strangely, the most technically precise producer of the day, Trevor Horn, agreed: 'All of that is just so boring. It's all very well reading about some guy saying he prefers to mic a bass drum this way, but that stuff is irrelevant to making a single – not the day to day reality of it, but to the magic of it'[7]. And yet, was talking about Deleuze and Barthes more interesting? Ultimately though, Horn was right: it was about the people: producers, engineers and artists.

*****

Trevor Horn had been a session musician in the late 70s, then one half of The Buggles, before producing albums for Dollar, ABC, Malcolm McLaren and Yes. If any producer could claim 1984 as his own, then Horn was front of the queue. Frankie Goes To Hollywood would have been a footnote in pop history were it not for his transformation of middling songs into megahits. The 12-inch versions, particularly, allowed Horn to stretch the bare essentials into magnum opuses. 'It was all this technology that was just exploding at that time, and 'Relax' was probably the pinnacle of all that stuff. It was a combination of [the Fairlight's] Page R [...] and locking it to a Linn drum machine'[8]. In this form, 'Relax' was pumping, extended foreplay, while 'Two Tribes' was less a song (it's not until well over half way through the 12-inch that Holly Johnson actually gets to sing) and more a set of instructions – set to an electro beat, sirens and 'Rite-of-Spring' crescendos – for surviving a nuclear attack. 'The sound of the end of the world', as Capital Radio's DJ Roger Scott remarked. 'I had one of the very first 24-track Sonys in 1984', explained Horn. 'And 'Two Tribes' I think was the first number one single on a Sony 24-track digi. 'Two Tribes' was completely digital'[9]. The title track of the ensuing album was pure indulgence, punctuated with bird noises and Steve Howe's acoustic guitar, stretched to over 13 minutes, while the 12-inch single version features a spoken word introduction of Nietzsche's *The Birth of Tragedy*. Of course, much of this tomfoolery – and certainly the wordplay – could be attributed to Paul Morley, but there couldn't have been many

119

producers so open-minded as to actually go along with it. Single-minded perfectionism, however, often results in casualties. Holly Johnson ended up being the only band member to perform on the recording of 'Relax', for example, and the amount of time Horn spent in the studio meant whopping great bills for Frankie.

Horn's dictum that he was only interested in creating hits was tested by Morley's signing of Propaganda, a German band whose first single, 'Dr Mabuse', was about a character from a 1922 Fritz Lang film. Horn responded by throwing everything at it: thick bouncy basslines, heavily processed drums, epic synth lines, reversed vocals. It was almost certainly the only time German Expressionism went Top 30. The Art Of Noise looked even less likely to land ZTT hit singles: a largely instrumental 'band' comprising a producer, engineer, programmer, arranger and journalist whose publicity photos had them hiding behind masks. Their sound was near enough entirely based on sampling and looping, using the Fairlight to create massive breakbeats from recordings of drums (Yes's Alan White's being the most identifiable). The Fairlight may have been high-end but it was still only capable of capturing 1.2 second soundbytes. As arranger Anne Dudley explained, "That's why The Art Of Noise's music is so stabby"[10]. It was ironic, somehow fitting and very post-modern that the group would themselves become one of the most sampled in pop.

Trevor Horn at Sarm West studios, and Anne Dudley, fellow member of The Art Of Noise and arranger extraordinaire.

Anne Dudley's role outside of the group in crafting the perfect single is one of the most overlooked in pop. Debuting with arranging the strings on ABC's *Lexicon of Love* and co-writing 'Buffalo Gals', Dudley went on to sprinkle her magic on Frankie's 'The Power of Love', Lloyd Cole's *Rattlesnakes* and April Showers' sublime-though-ignored 'Abandon Ship'; keyboards on George Michael's 'Careless Whisper', synth for Paul McCartney's 'No More Lonely Nights' and David Gilmour's *About Face*; a co-write for Five Star and on and on. And this was just 1984. The last 30 years have seen her arranging for everyone, from Pulp and Pet Shop Boys to Seal and Boyzone, scoring music for countless TV programmes and films (including an Oscar for *The Full Monty*) and releasing her own albums. Neil Tennant described her style as 'Beauty and harmonic richness from the English pastoral and church tradition with a little flavour of jazz'[11] (which could also apply to the music of Virginia Astley come to think of it). But back to the men – and in the field of production, engineering and mixing, it was always men.

Steve Lillywhite had been on the staff at Island, producing Ultravox, the first three U2 albums and Peter Gabriel's third, and in 1984 helmed Simple Minds *Sparkle in the Rain* and Big Country's *Steeltown* amongst others. These were the 'big sound' bands, the ones whose albums had signature drum and kerrang guitar sounds, and this was largely down to Lillywhite. But he never went beyond 24 tracks. And he would produce 'small-sounding' artists too: Kirsty MacColl's cover of Billy Bragg's 'A New England' in December for example.

Another producer with a signature drum sound was Keith Forsey, who started off as a session drummer in the 1970s, working mostly in Germany with the likes of Boney M and Giorgio Moroder. In the early 80s he moved to New York and – right place at the right time – teamed up with Billy Idol who'd also just moved across the Pond. The result was two hugely successful albums and a fine start to Idol's solo career. Forsey then got into soundtracks, co-writing *Flashdance... What a Feeling* and, in 1984, contributing to *Ghostbusters* and *The Breakfast Club*. One of the songs he wrote for the latter was 'Don't You (Forget About Me)', which, after The Fixx, Bryan Ferry and Billy Idol had all turned it down, ended up being reluctantly recorded by Simple Minds, tossing it off in a three-hour session in a north London studio before promptly forgetting about it. When the film and single were released the following year, it broke the band in America. But one of Forsey's – and 1984's – most overlooked albums was *Mirror Moves* by The Psychedelic Furs who, like Idol, had fancied their chances in New York, moving there in 1982. Drummer Vince Ely had just left the group so Forsey handled both drums and production. And yet he left plenty of room for John Ashton's guitar and the album comes across as both warm and edgy, particularly on the wonderful 'Heaven'.

Some producers who'd worked throughout the 70s, with both prog and new wave groups, successfully adapted to the 80s way of doing things. Both Chris Thomas and John Leckie, for example, had started out as tape ops in Abbey Road Studios, and both worked on *Dark Side of the Moon*. Thomas went on to produce several Roxy Music albums and *Never Mind the Bollocks* while Leckie got his production chops with new wave bands like The Adverts, XTC and Magazine. 1984 saw Thomas working with Elton John, The Pretenders and finishing off Human League's *Hysteria*, while Leckie, returning from a year or so on an ashram, still wearing red and fully beaded, helmed albums by The Fall (three in a row) and Felt. Both would go on to produce late 20th Century milestones: Pulp's *Different Class* (Thomas) and *The Stone Roses* (Leckie). Born in the same year (1947) as Thomas, 1984 was a breakthrough year for Rupert Hine, producing Howard Jones's *Human's Lib*, The Fixx's *Phantoms,* Chris De Burgh's *Bird on the Wire* and contributing to Tina Turner's *Private Dancer*. Hine and Jones hit it off immediately – perhaps because Hine had prog roots and a parallel career as a solo synth artist. He embraced technology, although later on would bemoan some of the interfaces, the sitting in front of screens, the tiny drop-down menus. For

Hine, musicians work in two different modes: creative and editorial. He felt that musicians 'were forced too quickly into editorial mode by many forms of new music technology. [It] is so enticing that it often starts leading the way. It's so easy to get sidetracked.'[12]

Another producer with prog roots, Rhett Davies had moved on from producing Eno, Camel and King Crimson to Dire Straits, OMD and Roxy Music, and in 1984 he was busy helming Bryan Ferry's *Boys and Girls*[13]. Recorded in six different studios and featuring 30 musicians, Ferry's 'solo' album was a hallmark of mid-80s uber-production, all languid vocals over multi-tracked guitars and melancholic ambience, the moodiness just about rescuing it from soporific easy listening. Davies and mix engineer Bob Clearmountain had first worked together on Roxy's *Avalon*, and in truth *Boys and Girls* continued in much the same vein.

Ex-Roxy synthesist, Brian Eno, was back to producing other people's albums for the first time since Talking Heads' *Remain in Light* in 1980. U2 were looking for a new producer and in stepped Eno, but only after a long period of hesitation and only if he could bring in Daniel Lanois as co-producer (and backup if it all went pear-shaped). Work began on *The Unforgettable Fire* in Slane Castle in Country Meath in May 1984 before moving back to their customary Windmill Lane Studios in Dublin the following month, with everything wrapped up in August and the album released in the autumn. (In those days that was leisurely; these days, despite – or because of – the technology, it ends up taking infinitely longer). Eno had encouraged the group to experiment with atmosphere and textures, with The Edge's guitar, often heavily processed, reduced to equal footing with the other instruments – including, for the first time, a Fairlight. It was the start of a highly successful alliance.

Eno was typically receptive to all the new technology around, particularly digital recording and playback. 'I'm interested in digital recording for the most boring technical reason, which is that a lot of my music is very quiet and the lack of background hiss you get in a digital studio set-up really makes quite a big difference'[14]. As for the finished product, the compact disc was perfect for Eno's ambient music. 'I dread getting vinyl test pressings. It's the most depressing thing. When I get this shitty piece of crap back from the factory and put the needle on it and it goes 'krrcccczzzzkkrrrshh' – they've never really reached the standard that I want'[15]. Eno's next release, *Thursday Afternoon*, would be released on CD only.

Of the younger generation, producers like Steve Levine and Mark Ellis quickly progressed from tape ops to running the show. Levine was hugely influential in nailing Culture Club's sound, producing all their records from first single to *Waking Up with The House On Fire* (and quite a few since), but his attempts to be a pop artist in his own right fell at the first hurdle – the tepid synth-reggae of single 'Waiting In Line' failing to impress or chart. Mark Ellis – better known as Flood[16] had no such delusions. Starting out as a runner at London's Morgan Studios at the end of the 70s, he quickly stepped up to producing Some Bizzare artists Cabaret Voltaire, Psychic TV and Marc And The Mambas, and in 1984 came of age with Nick Cave's debut on

Mute. These early albums were on the dark side, and he would continue that way with albums for Depeche Mode, Nine Inch Nails and PJ Harvey, but *alongside* 'lighter' albums with U2 and Erasure. 'I dislike the fact that people know what I do, in the same way you hear a Trevor Horn production and you know it'[17]. Although no luddite, Flood maintains an analogue attitude to recording, or what he calls a 'tactile approach': hardware like modular synthesizers are preferable to software instruments, pedals are preferable to plug-ins, knobs and faders are meant to be twisted and pushed with fingers rather than a mouse, and he believes in committing to sounds before recording, rather than 'fixing them in the mix'.

Brian Eno and Stock Aitken Waterman: opposite ends of the producer spectrum.

On the more pop side, there were scores of producers helping to shape the slick sound of the 80s, not least those who worked as a team. Jolley & Swain had produced a string of hits for Imagination in the early 80s before moving on to Bananarama, Spandau Ballet and Alison Moyet, each of whom had major releases in 1984. The year also saw the start of the UK's ultimate production team, the occasionally (almost grudgingly) respected but mostly reviled Stock Aitken Waterman. Mike Stock and Matt Aitken were good but jobbing musicians who decided they wanted to write and record songs for others, while Pete Waterman had worked as a DJ and in A&R before setting up PWL (Pete Waterman Limited), in effect signing up the other two. Their first efforts as a trio were inauspicious: Cyprus's entry to the Eurovision Song Contest ('Anna-Maria Lena' by Andy Paul if you're interested; it came 15th) and a single in a ripped-off 'Relax' sleeve by the preposterously named Agents Aren't Aeroplanes which disappeared off the radar, both released on the small Proto label. However, in July, all of a sudden, they had two hits on their hands. The music for 'You Think You're a Man' by drag queen Divine was the first of a seemingly endless stream of cowbell-infused hi-NRG backing tracks with interchangeable vocals, but you couldn't take your eyes off the 20-stones of Harris Glenn Milstead (his real name) squeezed into spangly dress, his gravelly voice adding a peculiarly compelling menace to the whole confection. Coming from Chelmsford in Essex, Hazell Dean was less exotic, more the girl next door, and had been active for nearly ten years without a hit[18]. But after a surprise Top 10 with 'Searchin' (I Got to Find a Man)'[19], again on Proto, SAW saw potential and rushed out 'Whatever I Do (Wherever I Go)', which hit #4. At this point, SAW were recording either in the Marquee Studios in Soho or at Mike Stock's suburban home studio. It wasn't until the following year that they would set up their own PWL studios in a particularly unglamorous, semi-industrial cul-de-sac in Borough in south London. By the end of the year, with the release of Dead Or Alive's 'You Spin Me Round (Like A Record)'[20], they were a force to be reckoned with, and in a nod to Motown, they started calling themselves the Hit Factory. And with some justification: the rest of the decade saw them garner a dozen #1s and countless Top 40s. The sound may have been Motownesque, but SAW wasn't a label, preferring to license their product through the likes of Epic, RCA and EMI. SAW's production methods were cool and calculated, with total control over the whole process: write the song, stick to formula, use the latest technology, hire boy-or-girl-next-door singers (Divine and Dead Or Alive excepted), control the publishing and so on. It was uber catchy, quick turnaround, Poundland pop or 'choons for ordinary people with Woolworth's ears'[21], and it sold like hotcakes. When they called it a day in the early 90s, the joke going around was the split was due to musical similarities.

Not all producers had a good a good time in the mid-80s. For Tony Visconti, temporarily shunned by David Bowie, it was 'frustrating, disheartening [and] ultimately downright awful for my career'[22], 'reduced' to producing Elaine Paige and the Moody Blues. The best years were behind Mickie Most and Chinn & Chapman (glam), Roy Thomas Baker (Queen), Glyn Johns (The Who), and even George Martin was largely treading water, forever producing Paul McCartney albums. It was also a year when, despite or because of the new technology, productions started to sound 'samey' as producers and engineers sought perfection in a new digital world, often resorting to pre-set synth sounds, unimaginatively programmed drum machines, limited sampling and ubiquitous effects, none more so than the gated drum. 1984 was the first year when *all* chart-topping singles (at least in the US, with the UK's not far behind) featured synths. However, it wasn't totally synthetic or digital. Saxophones were everywhere, and not just because of the jazz revival; the fretless bass was still in vogue; there was a minor marimba craze (from Thompson Twins to Bowie); and there were still hundreds of bands who remained analogue and idiosyncratic for several years yet. It was also still a long way from compression, autotune and microphones that are so good that you can tell whether the singer just swigged a whisky that was single malt or blended.

Chapter 9: In a Big Country
The second sound of young Scotland

There's something which has been written out of music history [...] and that's that Scotland – from around 1978/9 to 1984 – just ruled the fucking world. Wiped the floor with England, Wales and Ireland. You had, off the top of my head, The Associates, Orange Juice, Josef K, Aztec Camera, The Skids, Simple Minds, Big Country. Need I go on? Scotland, for a seven-year period, dominated the post-punk world. There's never been a book about it; there's never been a Mojo piece about it...[1]
James Dean Bradfield (Manic Street Preachers)

Scotland isn't big. But with its highlands, islands and wild, wide open spaces it seems bigger than it is. Its two principal cities also seem somehow larger than their geographical area and populations; all those sandstone tenements and imposing civic buildings. Bands like Simple Minds, Big Country and The Waterboys (the latter typified by their 1984 single 'The Big Music') seemed to get their widescreen inspiration from their surroundings. And Americana: The Byrds, country, soul and the blues were all much bigger influences in Scotland, particularly in Glasgow, than they were south of the border.

The 80s saw a boom in Scottish bands, way beyond what had been going on in the 60s (Lulu, The Beatstalkers, Donovan) and 70s (Sensational Alex Harvey Band, Nazareth, Bay City Rollers). Granted there were individuals who'd made a mark, but most of them had moved south at a young age, while Rod Stewart, for all his Scottish affectations, was a Londoner. Punk brought forth The Rezillos, The Skids and Johnny and the Self-Abusers, but it was the dawn of the new decade that ushered in a wave of post-punk and new pop bands. Some moved down to London to be closer to the main labels and media, but many stayed or at least retained certain aspects of Scottish identity, culture, accent and attitude. The sheer number and quality of 80s bands was totally disproportionate to Scotland's overall population. And when one considers the vast majority came from just two cities, it's even more impressive.

By 1984, Simple Minds had skilfully navigated their way to the top of the heap, via three edgy, non-hit albums on Arista and two plusher, more European-sounding ones on Virgin. The very title of the last of these, *New Gold Dream 81-82-83-84*, summed up that four-year evolution of new pop: modern, shining, forward-looking. The music too was glorious, ecstatic. It was Simple Minds' finest hour. *Sparkle in the Rain,* the album that followed in early 1984, was transitional. There were still moments of sprightly splendour, but also lumpen lambast – Mel Gaynor's monumentally clattering drums signalling the call of arena-rock. As Kerr himself said, "I think it is a snapshot...not a landmark... I think [it] was en-route to somewhere."[2] Tracks like 'Book of Brilliant Things' and 'Speed Your Love to Me', however, were enough to keep it more than interesting.

In a way, Simple Minds were moving into territory occupied by fellow Scots[3] Big Country. Frontman Stuart Adamson had been in the modestly successful Skids, but from the outset his new group were more Celtic, more rock. With a successful debut album in 1983 under their belt, the band began 1984 with the rousing Top 10 single, 'Wonderland', followed by two more which didn't do as well, but put that to rights with *Steeltown*, produced by Steve Lillywhite (the same man who had helmed Simple Minds' album), which went straight in at #1. Much has been made of their 'bagpipe' guitar sound but mostly they sounded like Thin Lizzy, Celtic roots and all, but with clean melodies and harmonies supplanting hoary old R'n'B. Unloved by the music press, other musicians came to Adamson's defence, including James Dean Bradfield of Manic Street Preachers:

> *I just loved the way he put myths and folklore – Scottish folklore – into music, but he also linked it up with the modern day era. Lots of musicians have done that in different guises, but because Big Country was wrapped up in a certain Scottishness in the music, and what some people have called the Celtic mist in their music, they were utterly pilloried in the press. I love the music press and I love music journalism, but sometimes the music press have to be called to account, and they should give the musical kudos and reparations to Big Country and Stuart Adamson, who's sadly not with us[4].*

As with so many bands (Frankie, Wham!, Duran, Bunnymen etc), Big Country peaked in 1984, thereafter following the traditional path of recording in LA in the hope of breaking America, failing and by the mid-90s were a minor band. The title of their seventh album, *Why The Long Face*, said it all.

Simple Minds and Big Country shared a similar sound in 1984, thanks to Steve Lillywhite's productions.

It wasn't all about big productions though. The early 80s had seen a small independent Glasgow-based label champion the opposite. Postcard Records was very short-lived (barely two years) and released just a dozen records by four groups – Orange Juice, Josef K, Aztec Camera and (from Australia) The Go-Betweens – and only one of these an album[5]. However, its idiosyncratic helmsman, Alan Horne, had good taste and marketing instincts ('The Sound of Young Scotland' was the label's strapline), even if he was hopeless with money and unwisely made an enemy of John Peel. The three Scottish bands found their way onto the NME *C81* cassette and together they unknowingly set the foundations for indie: crisp, sour, arty, retro-sounding songs somewhere in between The Velvet Underground, The Byrds, Television and Talking Heads[6], dominated by clipped, brittle guitars and played by pale, androgynous young men with great haircuts. But it was a small operation and only a matter of time before one of them flew the coup. First to go were Orange Juice, signing to Polydor; Aztec Camera and The Go-Betweens went to Rough Trade; and Josef K split up.

Orange Juice quickly made their mark with two albums in 1982 and the Chic-inspired hit single 'Rip It Up' the following year, but internal differences led to departures and by 1984 frontman Edwyn Collins was struggling to hold the band together. They kicked off the year with the so-so mini-album *Texas Fever* and ended it with an album for which they couldn't even find the inspiration to give a proper title (*The Orange Juice*). It was a fine swansong, though, with producer Dennis Bovell lending it a dry, dubby feel, sounding like a cross-between Talking Heads and The Style Council. It was even advertised on Channel 4. Its three singles all bombed, however, despite an uncharacteristically goofy video by Derek Jarman for one of them. But they did better than Collins' side-project with Paul Quinn: a straightforward cover of the Velvet Underground's 'Pale Blue Eyes' on Alan Hornes' new, short-lived Swamplands label which he'd established under the aegis of London Records that year, on which the remnants of Edinburgh band The Fire Engines – renamed (unwisely) Win – also failed to prosper. Collins announced the end of Orange Juice at a miners' benefit in early 1985; his subsequent solo career would lurch from under- to overachieving (the Iggy Pop-esque 'A Girl Like You' was a 90s hit on both sides of the Atlantic), but the insouciant innocence of Orange Juice was behind him.

Josef K's frontman, Paul Haig, meanwhile, had gone solo[7], signed with Belgium's Les Disques du Crépuscule and embraced synthesizers. Despite early praise from Paul Morley at the NME, Haig struggled to find his niche, seemingly not wanting to be at the centre of things while Crépuscule wanted him to be exactly that. A series of singles made little impact, even when gathered together on the Island-distributed *Rhythm of Life* album. Nevertheless, 1984 saw two more singles, the upbeat 'Big Blue World' (produced with Alan Rankine) and clubby 'The Only Truth' (produced by New Order's Bernard Sumner and A Certain Ratio's Donald Johnson), a collaboration with Cabaret Voltaire and a self-titled mini album. But still no hit. And that's been Haig's lot: fine, accessible, groove-ridden records, great suits and a haircut to die for, but no hits.

Aztec Camera, the third of the Postcard trio, fronted by the young Roddy Frame, succeeded where the other two (largely) failed. Debut album *High Land, Hard Rain* and a top 20 single, 'Oblivious', set the bar high in 1983 before Frame switched from Rough Trade to WEA. Still only 20, he nevertheless had the precocity to hire Mark Knoppfler as producer of a second album, *Knife*, the following year. It was a polished, mainstream affair, including another hit ('All I Need Is Everything'), a B-side cover version of Van Halen's 'Jump' and a 9-minute title track. There was a sense that he was acting older than his years. Four more albums – and one more hit single, 'Somewhere In My Heart' – would follow before he dissolved the band and went solo.

Other remnants of Postcard's extended family included Paul Quinn, who had been to school with Edwyn Collins, sung with The Jazzateers and The French Impressionists, and guested with Orange Juice and Aztec Camera, before finally forming his own group, Bourgie Bourgie. They were less jangly and more akin to the direction Billy Idol was going in. In fact, Quinn and Idol had a lot in common: good looks, impossibly wide mouths, similar voice and a US-friendly sound. But despite a promising start to 1984 (a deal with MCA[8], Peel session, and an appearance on The Tube), the band split up before the year was out. Quinn's two singles with Collins and (in 1985) Vince Clarke also underachieved. The Happy Family, a spin-off group from Josef K, featuring Nick Currie, had also experienced unhappiness with a London label, though the fact that it was 4AD was a surprise. 1984 saw a posthumous cassette album of demos, *This Business of Living*, on Les Temps Modernes, before Currie went on to a solo career as Momus.

Postcard had been a very male affair, if resolutely anti-macho. Occasionally a female in the orbit would join or form a band, one such being April Showers comprising Beatrice Colin and Jonathan Bernstein[9]. Their one and only single, 1984's 'Abandon Ship', backed by members of Orange Juice and produced by The Art Of Noise's Anne Dudley (complete with gorgeous strings), was a minor classic. ''April Showers' came out of the blue. I was 19, at university and all of a sudden we got a record deal, were being flown down to London and going to parties with pop stars like Wham! and Duran Duran. It was very strange and sort of unreal. What I did learn very quickly is that your shelf life in the business is very, very short. We were there and then we were gone'[10]. The same went for Glasgow female-fronted new-pop acts Sunset Gun, Talking Drums, Sugar Sugar and Fruits of Passion, lured south by the majors, but to no avail. Rather longer-lasting, but still only one-hit wonders, were Glaswegians Rose McDowall and Jill Bryson, aka Strawberry Switchblade. Formed in late 1981 as a foursome, they recorded Peel and Jensen sessions that October, were managed by Bill Drummond and David Balfe, released a debut single (featuring Roddy Frame) on indie label 92 Happy Customers, switched to Korova and played support on a Howard Jones tour which was not as surprising as it sounds. Their first major single, 'Since Yesterday', finally came out in November 1984. A jaunty, sprightly tune with downer lyrics ('And as we sit here alone, looking for a reason to go on, it's so clear that all we have now, are our thoughts of yesterday'), it was a #5 hit. Visually they were startling, adopting a Japanese look that spliced Yayoi Kusuma dots and circles with Harajuku-chic lace and ribbons. An album followed in 1985 but it failed to live up to expectations, except in Japan where they couldn't get enough of them. They'd be playing 3,000-seaters and it was almost worth just focussing on Japan. But not quite, and they split in 1986.

Postcard's legacy may have been 'jangly indie', but none of Orange Juice, Paul Haig or Aztec Camera continued in that vein. In fact, it seemed to trigger a reaction across

Scotland against Postcard's 'puritan pop'. Glasgow-born Alan McGee was one of those who railed against both Postcard and synthpop, advocating instead the sound of the two eras he loved most, 1965-67 psychedelia and 1976-77 punk, preferably at the same time. McGee grew up on punk and during that time played rudimentary bass in a couple of make-believe bands, The Drains and Captain Scarlet and the Mysterons ('We never played a gig – we were the audience *and* the band'), before a short stint in a proper group, H2O. In 1979 he left and formed another, Newspeak, the group moving down to London where they quite quickly split up. There would be another few years of operating on the fringes of the capital's post-punk scene before he finally bottled the sound he was looking for and, in 1984, launched (with Joe Foster and Dick Green) a label, Creation, to go with it. That he had to do so in London separates him from Alan Horne whose Glasgow-based Postcard label seemed to consciously *represent* Scotland in a way that Creation never would. It wasn't that McGee himself lost his Scottish identity – his famously thick Glaswegian brogue and the fact his label's early releases were mostly Scottish acts were evidence of that – but somehow Creation was more about a certain sound than a place. And for that reason, the likes of The Jesus and Mary Chain, Primal Scream, The Pastels and The Jasmine Minks are discussed in Chapter 16.

Returning to new pop, Billy Mackenzie and Alan Rankine as The Associates had had their moment of fame in 1982 with *Sulk*, a brilliantly decadent, melodramatic, almost hysterical (in the true sense of the word) take on synthpop. But on the eve of a world tour and possible superstardom, the contrary and complicated Mackenzie preferred to stay at home in Dundee with his whippets. Rankine left to work with Paul Haig and formed the short-lived Pleasure Ground, while Mackenzie kept The Associates name, signed to Warners and racked up a huge studio bill while working – on and off, mostly off – with various musicians and producers for a year or two. Finally, in June 1984, a single was released. Produced by Martyn Ware, 'Those First Impressions' was decent but barely scraped the Top 50. The clubbier 'Waiting for the Loveboat' and the beautiful 'Breakfast' didn't do much better. It seemed that The Associates had had their moment, and when the album, *Perhaps*, finally slipped out in February 1985, it peaked at #23. And yet, for all its long gestation and (it has to be said) overlong tracks, the album wasn't far off the quality of *Sulk*, and Mackenzie's voice was as extraordinary as ever. Sadly, his label, Warners, were less forgiving and he was dropped[11]. Two other synth-based bands with Glasgow-reared singers as distinctive as Mackenzie were The Blue Nile and Bronski Beat, both already described in Chapter 2. In the case of Bronski Beat, it was the escape from Glasgow to London (and London Records) that made them.

The Bluebells were on London Records not Postcard, but they sounded similar to and had toured with Aztec Camera, and 1984 was just as big a year for them with three Top 40 singles and an album, *Sisters*, which peaked at #22. Their biggest hit, 'Young At Heart', was co-written by guitarist Bobby Bluebell with Bananarama (when he was going out with the latter's Siobhan Fahey), first appearing on Bananarama's debut album. The Bluebells' version was the hit[12], however, complete with violin solo that harked back to the Dexys. But relations with London soured and the band's brief career ended in late 1985.

Too young to have hung around the Postcard set, but equally enthralled with the clean sound of guitars, Del Amitri were regulars at the Warzika Club in Glasgow and their first recorded output was a flexi shared with The Bluebells. Their first proper single was 'Sense Sickness' on Glasgow's No Strings Records but by 1984 they'd signed with Chrysalis, then (after a couple of years of hand-to-mouth existence) to A&M, whereupon a reasonably successful career ensued which combined post-punk and the folky vibe of their biggest hit 'Nothing Ever Happens' five years later. Meanwhile, there was instant success for a Derbyshire-born guitarist studying English and Philosophy at Glasgow University. Lloyd Cole, backed by fellow students, The Commotions, was quick to secure a record and publishing deal with Polydor and before anyone knew it, debut single 'Perfect Skin' went top 30, an album *Rattlesnakes* hit #13, and two more singles scraped the charts before the year was out. Cole's name-dropping of cultural icons (Simone de Beauvoir, Eva Marie Saint, Truman Capote, Greta Garbo, Joan Didion etc) grated with some critics, but lines like 'She's got cheekbones like geometry and eyes like sin, and she's sexually enlightened by Cosmopolitan' (the last's fifteen syllables rattled off in a space better suited to eight) were very different from Morrissey's but equally thrilling to experience on Top Of The Pops.

Glasgow's The Wake and Grangemouth's Cocteau Twins are perhaps better known, rightly or wrongly, as 'Factory and 4AD bands' and as such are discussed in Chapter 15. But Grangemouth yielded another group, Dead Neighbours, managed by Robin Guthrie's brother Brian. Their 1984 debut album, *Harmony in Hell* sounded just like that, a cross between The Cramps and (inadvertently) The Jesus And Mary Chain. The Cocteau Twins connection continued too, with original bassist Will Heggie joining them that same year, resulting in a change of direction and name – Lowlife. Similarly obsessed with the Americana of The Stooges and MC5 were The Primevals who, after a self-financed debut single, 'Where Are You?', ended up on the French New Rose label, ironically alongside Johnny Thunders and The Cramps.

Having grasped the opportunity (or survived the ignominy) of being crowned Young Band of the Year on children's TV show Saturday Banana in the late 70s, Edinburgh band The Questions went on to be closely linked to Paul Weller's Respond label, on which they released several of their own soul-infected pop singles – three in 1984 alone – as well as writing for Tracie Young. All looked good with three songs included on Tracie's debut album, but their own debut, *Belief*, bombed and they split by the end of the year. Friends Again had been on the periphery of the Postcard set, playing in pubs, before landing a deal with Phonogram and releasing a couple of polished singles in 1983, and four in 1984, plus an album. If Orange Juice paid lip-service to soul, Friends Again were a little more upfront, a little syrupy, complete with female backing singers and even a flute, but the album, *Trapped and Unwrapped*, struck a good balance between sweet and sour. Unfortunately, tension between co-writers Chris Thompson and James Grant resulted in them splitting by the end of the year with the former forming The Bathers and the latter forming Love and Money who would release four fairly successful AOR albums in the late 80s and early 90s.

When Altered Images split up towards the end of 1983, Clare Grogan resumed her acting career in another Bill Forsyth film *Comfort and Joy* (she had famously starred in his *Gregory's Girl* three years earlier) while guitarist Johnny McElhone formed Hipsway with Harry Travers and Graham Skinner (the latter from The Jazzateers), joined later by Pim Jones. The band would plough the same pseudo soul furrow as Love and Money.

Strawberry Switchblade, Billy Mackenzie and The Bluebells.

Post-1984, blue-eyed soul kicked in big time, with everybody starting to look and sound the same. Endgames had been around since the beginning of the decade and were typical of a group regarded by the industry as 'of high commercial potential', shunted from one major to another (WEA, Mercury, Virgin). By 1983 they'd teamed up with dance pop duo The Quick who produced their debut album, followed by a second in 1985 with fairly predictable hi-fidelity contributions from Julian Mendelsohn, Stewart Levine and Anne Dudley. But neither sold and they split two years later. Early concerts by Vortex Motion (as post-punk a name as you could invent) included songs by The Clash, Squeeze and Magazine. By 1984 they had changed their name to Wet Wet Wet, after a line in a Scritti Politti song, and attracted the attention of Rough Trade's Geoff Travis and Elliot Davis, who helmed Precious, a local indie label with as yet no records. But a post-punk or indie path was not to be. Instead, they became more soulful, attracting the attention of Phonogram, Davis ended up managing them and the band's pop career eventually took off with seven top 20 singles before the decade was out, to say nothing of 1994's worldwide smash 'Love is All Around'. Hue and Cry (formed in 1983) followed a similar trajectory, as did 1984-formed Dundee band Spencer Tracy, changing their name to Danny Wilson on the eve of their 1986 debut album release. Deacon Blue settled for a mid-Atlantic niche with a nod to Springsteen and Prefab Sprout, while The Big Dish, after providing the support slot on Big Country and Lloyd Cole tours, sold their soul to the MOR sound of US FM radio. Along with south of the border groups like Johnny Hates Jazz and Curiosity Killed the Cat, this was to be if not *the,* then certainly *a,* soundtrack to the second half of the 80s.

And then there were scores of well-meaning but largely anonymous new pop bands. Fiction Factory may have been one-hit wonders but the gorgeously melancholic '(Feels Like) Heaven' was a deserved #6 hit at the beginning of 1984. Fellow synthpoppers The Messengers (a duo of Danny Mitchell and Colin King) had evolved from an earlier incarnation, Modern Man, whose one album had been produced by Midge Ure. The Ure connection endured with The Messengers supporting Ultravox on tour and Ure producing their first two singles. But 1984's self-produced 'Frontiers' single was tepid and Chrysalis turned down an album. And that was that – except for Mitchell co-writing Ure's 'If I Was' the following year. Passionate Friends and White China were not dissimilar, the former supporting big acts like The Police, Rod Stewart, Big Country and Nik Kershaw, but they only got to release a couple of singles each before splitting up.

H_2O could point to the faintly embarrassing fact that Alan McGee had briefly ('three weeks, four gigs') played in their original line-up. Then they were post-punk; in 1984 they were full-blown romantics kitted out with synths, vocoders and haircuts. After a couple of dreamy Top 40 hits they released debut album *Faith* but this, and another two singles, flopped and it was all over by the following year[13]. Likewise Positive Noise were once interestingly post-punk, but by 1984 were releasing bland singles like 'A Million Miles Away' (complete with miming-in-the-glens video), and by 1985 no more. Formed in 1984, Sideway Look made a promising start with impressive U2/Big Country-type guitar work all over their second single, 'Knowing You From Today', and a decent eponymous debut album. Virgin brought in Queen's Roger Taylor to produce a follow-up before they were inexplicably dropped and the album shelved. Similarly unsung, east coasters APB released a string of singles throughout the early 80s on Aberdeen's Oily Records, only for their new-wave-funk to end up more recognised on the US east coast than their own. Their 1984 singles, 'Danceability' and 'What Kind of Girl Are You?', were in the same this-side-of-the-pond NY funk league as A Certain Ratio, the latter as radio-friendly and catchy a single as anything in the charts that year. Certainly the above could hold their own with The Armoury Show, Richard Jobson's post-Skids band which, although also boasting John McGeoch and John Doyle of Magazine, struggled to live up to the promise. 1984 singles 'Castles in Spain' and 'We Can Be Brave Again', plus album *Waiting For The Floods*, were all, sadly, bland bombast. As were debut singles 'Trigger Happy' and 'Carry Me', by the One O'Clock Gang, both dominated by the mid-80s creep-in of inflated vocals, portentous lyrics and plodding gated drums.

The post-punk electronic dance of New Order, Cabaret Voltaire and others was much less evident in Scotland. Secession, led by the troubled Peter Thomson, seemed like the band most likely to succeed but after a promising start with the Joy-Div-meets-synthgoth 'Betrayal' single in 1983, the following year saw them pursue a blander, synthpop direction with 'Fire Island' and 'Touch'. A switch from Beggars Banquet to Siren didn't help and after a decent but poorly promoted album In 1987 they split. Thomson took his own life in 2001. It was left to two other bands, both formed in 1984, to take Scottish proto-electronica forward. Alone Again Or, named after a 1968 song by Love, released two cringingly titled singles, 'Drum the Beat (In My Soul)' and 'Dream Come True', which were actually decent electronic dance numbers. They then changed their name to The Shamen, going on to become major participants in early 90s rave. Finitribe's first EP, *Curling and Stretching*, on their own Finiflex label, would do the same, displaying elements of industrial funk and EBM before moving onto bangin' rave.

Meanwhile, in Edinburgh, Bob Last's turn-of-the-70s labels Fast Product and Pop Aural, and the bands that were on them, were already history. Instead, a very different, incestuous cottage industry scene was, if not exactly asserting itself, then occasionally putting its hand up. Rote Kapelle ('Red Orchestra', named after a Second World War anti-Nazi resistance movement) had been a trio plus whoever else was around since the early 80s. They didn't release anything until 1985: the urgent *The Big Smell Dinosaur* EP on their own label – followed by more releases on Marc Riley's In-Tape until splitting in 1990. However, two of those who 'were around' ended up forming The Shop Assistants[14] whose exultant 2-minute debut single 'Something To Do', complete with double handclaps on the chorus, was released on The Pastels' short-lived Villa 21 label in 1984 – along with the latter's own re-release of their first single, 'Songs for Children'. But that was it for Villa 21, although it would be quickly replaced by 53rd & 3rd, a label run by Stephen Pastel, David Keegan (The Shop Assistants) and Sandy McLean (Fast Product). The Pastels continued releasing records on a multitude of independent labels, including Creation. The scene would beget The Soup Dragons, The Vaselines and BMX Bandits and, separately, Goodbye Mr Mackenzie whose first single in 1984, 'Death of a Salesman', had been released as part of the Government's Youth Training Scheme but who would become better known as the group Shirley Manson was in before joining US band Garbage in the early 90s. Glasgow, too, had retained a scene of small, independent bands like Apes in Control, The Suede Crocodiles and The Wee Cherubs releasing what turned out to be one-off singles (the latter's 'Dreaming' was woefully ignored), all on the short-lived Bogaten Records. Mention must also be made of Robert King's Pleasantly Surprised and Cathexis labels, the former hosting a prime series of compilation cassettes, the latter soon to be home to the excellent if obscure Vazz, a kind of Scottish successor to Wales's Young Marble Giants.

*****

So far, so new pop and post-punk-going-on-indie. But there was also an increasing interaction between pop, rock and Scottish folk music in the mid-80s. Formed in 1973, Runrig had been playing the folk-rock circuit but in the new decade gradually switched to rock, still with heavy folk leanings and a mixture of songs in English and Gaelic, but definitely with broader appeal. Robert Bell of The Blue Nile had produced their transitional third album, but by their fourth, *Heartland* (1985), they'd made the transformation. Newer on the scene, Mike Scott formed The Waterboys in 1983, releasing their debut eponymous album that year and a second, *A Pagan Place*, in 1984 together with a single, 'The Big Music', which came to describe their output generally. Sort of acoustic-U2 but with all the passion. Scott even looked like a cross between Bono and Geldof. The Proclaimers were also formed that year, although their twin, thick Leith brogues wouldn't be heard on record until three years later. Originating in Oban in western Scotland in 1984, Capercaillie released their debut album, *Cascade*, in the same year, combining Scottish folk music, electric instruments and haunting vocals to considerable success. It was also the beginning of Fairground Attraction, who were more skiffle than folk, although were based in London not Scotland. Glaswegian Eddi Reader had been a backing singer with The Gang of Four, Eurythmics and Alison Moyet (and made her recording debut with the bizarrely named and utterly obscure Outbar Squeak in 1984) before hooking up with Welsh guitarist Mark Nevin to form Fairground Attraction, achieving brief but massive success four years later with the single 'Perfect' and album *The First Of A Million Kisses*.

The Waterboys and Runrig in suitably glennish surroundings.

But if you wanted a real Scot, a cartoon Scot, wearing kilt and helmet and brandishing a 5lb claymore with a 4ft blade while running through the highlands, then that would have been Jesse Rae. Hailing from the village of St Boswell, uncomfortably near the English border, and well-known for its annual gypsy fair, Rae actually learned his craft whilst drifting around America, working with disco groups like Odyssey[15]. He then hit upon the idea of wearing a kilt and after a couple of false starts (his second single was largely sung in Russian), settled into a puzzling musical style of what could reasonably be described as Scottish Tourist Board funk. His 1984 single, '(It's Just) The Dog in Me' was dire and flopped, although 'Over the Sea' reached #65 a year later. *Much* later he tried his hand at politics, standing for election to the Scottish Parliament, but failing.

What made the Scottish scene so vibrant? Partly it was a sense of cultural confidence, but mixed with sticking two fingers up to London, in much the same way that Tony Wilson did with Factory Records. Many bands didn't feel the need to sing in that kind of mid-Atlantic accent that was accepted in both England and the States. The Proclaimers, when they got going, made a point of retaining and rejoicing in their heavy accents. Songs were lyrically often political, but rarely nationalist or urging independence, and very very few bands sung in Gaelic, which would have been a political as much as a cultural point. (Indeed, possibly the most heard song in Gaelic in 1984 was a track on Ultravox's *Lament*, 'Man of Two Worlds', sung by Mae

134

McKenna). Perhaps it's more about how Scottish rock and pop has always wanted to emotionally connect, influenced by its own folk culture and Americana rather than the somehow more 'removed' popular music south of the border, its tending towards the sincere and the heartfelt, as well as the gruff and the melancholic.

Chapter 10: The Unforgettable Freur
Post-punk in Ireland and Wales

How long must we sing this song?
Bono, U2

I just ran away. But I felt guilty. That's the thing about traitors.[1]
John Cale

If, in the early 80s, popular music in Scotland was thriving, the same could not really be said of the Irish and Welsh scenes. Punk had shaken things up, but what followed – post-punk, 2-tone, synthpop, industrial, new romantics – never really took hold in the same way that it did in England or Scotland. It was difficult to pinpoint why. Perhaps cities like Belfast, Cardiff and Swansea weren't big enough to sustain a scene, resulting in the more ambitious bands moving to London. Dublin was larger, and it also had the advantage of having its own music press[2], national charts and record industry (which, being frivolous for a second, contributed to Ireland winning the Eurovision Song Contest seven times, at time of writing more than any other country), as well as the catalysing force that was U2, which we'll come on to soon.

There were connections – the Celtic influence of course, although this generally manifested itself in the more traditional form of folk or newer form of 'world' rather than post-punk (although there was a semblance of it in the expansive sound of U2 and The Alarm whose 'big music' vied with that of Simple Minds and Big Country) – but essentially the Irish and Welsh scenes could be characterised more by their differences than their similarities.

*****

By 1984, the Northern Irish punk-and-new-wave glory days of Terri Hooley's Good Vibrations shop and label (romanticised in the eponymous hit film of 2013) were over. It was always a small scene, and smaller still when Stiff Little Fingers and The Undertones moved to England, joining the many other artists with Irish heritage, including Costello, Morrissey, Marr, Lydon and Rowland, to name just a few. Good Vibrations went bankrupt in 1983[3] and the two bands in question split up the same year. The Undertones's Feargal Sharkey teamed up first with Vince Clarke and Eric Radcliffe as the short-lived The Assembly (a kind of Yazoo Mk2), and then with members of Madness for his first 'solo' record, 'Listen To Your Father' in 1984; while the O'Neill brothers formed the more-true-to-their-punk-roots That Petrol Emotion who would release their debut single the following year. Other early Good Vibes regulars like Cruella de Ville and Billy Idol lookasoundalikes The Outcasts also closed their vinyl account in 1984, the latter with an EP on the label New Rose from France, a country where they were almost popular. Northern Irish labels like Rip Off, Budj and It Records had ceased functioning – the latter's Portadown office damaged when an IRA car bomb exploded nearby.

Northern Ireland's music scene was not immune from The Troubles, and because of the constant tension many bands chose not to be lyrically explicit, fearing reprisals, though a few did stick their heads above the parapet. The 70s had been grim with music venues struggling to stay open, most English and American bands giving Belfast and Derry a wide berth. Musicians from both sides of the sectarian divide were subject to verbal intimidation, but also occasionally beatings, or worse. (In July 1975, when returning from a concert in County Down, three members of The Miami Showband, a successful south of the border band who'd been around since the 60s, were assassinated on their way home from a concert in Belfast).

Punk, with its air of couldn't-give-a-shit rebellion, emboldened a wave of new bands. Most were not overtly political, but a few were, or at least wrote a few songs that were. In the early 80s, on the Republican side, The Defects tackled the subject of Castlereagh, the British Army's infamous interrogation centre, in their 1982 single, 'Brutality'. On the Loyalist side, Ruefrex's single, 'Wild Colonial Boy', was an attack on NORAID, the IRA's American fund-raisers – though generally their stance was laudably anti-sectarian; they even made the front cover of Melody Maker. Less inclined towards seeing both sides of the argument, the repertoire of oi band Offensive Weapon included unambiguous songs like 'Gestapo RUC' and 'Bulldog'. Their bassist, Johnny Adair, joined the Ulster Defence Association in 1984 and later fronted the paramilitary Ulster Freedom Fighters' Shankill Road 'C' company.

Meanwhile, anarcho-punk groups Stalag 17 and Toxic Waste railed less about the Troubles specifically and more about society generally, though of course it was difficult to separate the two in Northern Ireland. One-man band The Hit Parade (aka Dave Hyndman) recorded two 12-inch singles and an LP with Crass in London. Unusually, he chose synths and drum machines to back his political messages, which included berating the Troubles from both sides of the fence. The first two 12-inchers were a bit crude but the 1984-recorded album, *Nick Knack Paddy Whack*, was extraordinary. The opening track, 'What Friends', sounds like Vangelis on steroids before moving into the kind of post-metal bashing territory SPK had just vacated.

Graduating from Cambridge University in 1984, Belfast-born singer-songwriter Andy White addressed the Troubles head on. Signing to Stiff Records, he released debut EP *Religious Persuasion* the following year and has since gone on to collaborate with Sinead O'Connor and Peter Gabriel amongst many others. Rather more mainstream, The Adventures have the dubious distinction of being one of the first signings by Simon 'Pop Idol' Fuller. Two singles, 'Another Silent Day' and 'Send My Heart', were catchy but neither made it into the Top 40, likewise the debut album which followed in 1985 – although a later single, tellingly titled 'Broken Land', did better. Understanding the Northern Ireland music scene was difficult for those not actually based there: the scene was small, the politics complex. So in the wake of October

1984's Brighton bombing, the NME dispatched one of their own, Andrew Tyler, to Belfast and Derry, with That Petrol Emotion's John O'Neill as his guide. The resulting 6,000-word feature, titled 'Bomb Culture', offered a neutral, well-intentioned lay perspective but it hardly mentioned the two cities' music scenes.

Northern Ireland's Big Self and The Adventures could have made it on either side of the Irish Sea, but didn't.

In mainland Britain there was the occasional song that touched upon the Troubles (as we have seen in Chapter 6) and south of the border, away from the violence, musicians spoke more freely. U2's 'Sunday Bloody Sunday' was angry but neutral[4], while others offered a Republican slant. The most outspoken songwriter in Ireland was Christy Moore, whose 1984 *Ride On* solo album was one of his best – heavily political, with two songs written by IRA prisoner Bobby Sands who had died in the Maze Prison hunger strike three years earlier. Moore's passion and energy, however, was actually more concerned with broader Irish history.

A few bands retained a cool post-punk edge while also embracing new pop. The Bank Robbers were a West Belfast powerpop band with a couple of singles on Good Vibrations under their belt, but in 1983, after appearing on The Tube's Belfast Special, they were picked up by EMI and moved to London. Their first single for the major involved a publicity stunt centred around printing fake £50 notes with the band's logo on it, a prank which saw them fined a real £50 in court. It seemed to work, though, as single 'Jenny' reached #8 in the UK independent charts. But in the long run it wasn't enough and after another single, 'Problem Page' in 1984, they were dropped, returned to Belfast and promptly split up.

Big Self were one of those should-have-made-it bands, beloved by John Peel and the likes of NME and Sounds. Debut and only album *Stateless* was recorded in Dublin's Windmill Lane Studios in early 1984 (although the band was living in London at the time) and a single, the excellent 'Vision', seemed to put them in the same orbit as Talk Talk or Echo & The Bunnymen. But a delayed release meant that they lost impetus and their performance at the Irish concert Self Aid in 1986, where they shared the stage with U2 ,Van Morrison, Elvis Costello, The Pogues and others, turned out to be their last.

Formed in 1984, Colenso Parade were also promising, and their debut single that year, 'Standing Up', was redolent of New Order. But they too split in 1986, guitarist Terry Bickers going on to join House Of Love and singer Oscar declining to replace Ian McCulloch in Echo & The Bunnymen. That honour went to Noel Burke of another Belfast band, St Vitus Dance, but only after they had moved to Liverpool, released a decent debut album and then split. Perfect Crime, led by Gregory Gray were flamboyant, even camp, and made some headway, but their only two singles, 'Brave' (1983) and 'I Feel Like an Eskimo' (1984), both on MCA, flopped and they split soon after.

Rather more successful, Silent Running modelled themselves on Simple Minds. It was shameless: the 'big' sound, the vocal mannerisms, the carbon-copy single 'Young Hearts', they even toured with them. Debut album, 1984's *Shades of Liberty*, received a five star review in Melody Maker, but it failed to chart, they were dropped by EMI, signed to Atlantic and split up after a second album which didn't do any better. Continuing the mass appeal trajectory, mention should be made of Jimmy McShane, a Derry-born dancer-cum-singer who ended up fronting italo-disco act Baltimora, formed in 1984 by Milanese producer Maurizio Bassi. The execrable 'Tarzan Boy' topped the charts in several European countries the following year. However, they turned out to be one-hit wonders and McShane returned to Northern Ireland, where he died of an AIDS-related illness in 1995.

*****

Meanwhile, south of the border, by 1984 U2's Bono Vox (aka Paul Hewson) saw the band at a crossroads. In the seven years since their formation they had released three critically acclaimed albums, made considerable in-roads into America, been expertly steered by manager Paul McGuinness and still were able to base themselves in Dublin. Bono, particularly, had developed into a man on a mission, a spokesperson for his generation, communicating to audiences with a passion bordering on evangelism. But musically they needed a change. All three albums had been produced by Steve Lillywhite and they were in danger of simply regurgitating what they'd done before. To their credit they took a risk, eventually persuading Brian Eno to produce their next album. Eno had spent the previous four years in New York but was returning to Europe. *The Unforgettable Fire,* collaboratively produced by Eno and Daniel Lanois, would give them the sophisticated, yet still edgy, sound they were looking for, especially to 'crack' America where 'Pride' became their first Top 40 single and the album went Top 20. But it wasn't until 1987 with the release of *The Joshua Tree* and appearing on the front of Time that they were catapulted into big league status.

U2 never moved to London, preferring to play a central role in the Dublin scene. However, the temporary (or in some cases permanent) move to the UK capital was no less common than the flow of bands from Northern Ireland, attracted by the much larger music scene and the city's big Irish population which provided a helpful support structure. Thin Lizzy had taken their mix of Dublin folk and Belfast blues to London in the early 70s and The Boomtown Rats had been in London since punk days, and in frontman Bob Geldof's case, earlier. Geldof's relationship with his home country was ambivalent to say the least, having denounced the church and corrupt politicians on Irish television in 1977. Attempts to play in Dublin two years later were thwarted by the authorities and when they finally did, a riot ensued. Geldof responded with the song 'Banana Republic', which suffice to say *wasn't* about a volatile central American state. It was their last Top 20 hit, yet they were still somehow together and in 1984 released *In the Long Grass*, a title that smacked of being kicked out to touch. No less than four singles were inflicted on a disinterested public, none of which made the Top 40. Not even Geldof's huge public profile after Band Aid and Live Aid at Wembley (at which the Rats performed) could avert their demise, which inevitably came in 1986. Indeed, after those two events, no-one really wanted to hear Geldof sing or talk about music. Unwittingly, he had a new role in life.

The UK capital even had its own Irish label, Kabuki Records, which released early singles by London-based Irish bands like Kissed Air, Five Go Down To The Sea and Microdisney, but ran out of steam in 1984. Microdisney stayed, and that year recorded no less than three John Peel Sessions and two albums for Rough Trade (debut *Everybody is Fantastic* followed by a compilation of early singles, titled, somewhat less positively, *We Hate You South African Bastards*). Interestingly, none of the six founding members of that most Irish of bands, The Pogues, were born in Ireland, not even Shane McGowan. A product of post-punk London, in 1984 they released their debut album, *Red Roses for Me,* which most definitely *was* an Irish album, described perfectly by Sounds as 'a satisfyingly impure, purposefully imperfect and totally irresistible collection of lasting resentment, rebellious roars, watery-eyed romance and uproarious jigs'[5]. It was both traditional and modern, boorish but cultured, falling over but full of life, and utterly against the grain. Above all it is heartfelt. The full-throated roar of "What will you have? I'll have a pint. I'll have a pint with you sir!" perfectly captures the bonhomie of drinking culture, and to hell with the hangover, work next day and longer-term health prospects. Perhaps the most restless band, however, were the just-formed My Bloody Valentine. Having recorded their first demo in Dublin in March 1984, they moved to Holland[6], then Berlin where in December they recorded their debut mini album, *This Is Your Bloody Valentine*, then back to Holland and finally to London. Theirs however was a music practically devoid of nationhood, all heavily treated guitars and a vocal delivery redolent of Nick Cave.

The majority of Irish bands, however, stayed put. U2's influence was considerable, particularly in Dublin which was big enough to accommodate scores of bands but small enough for them to all know each other[7]. Keen to support them, Bono and The Edge helped out with occasional demo and production assistance. In 1984 they took the next step and formed a record label, Mother Records. The plan was only to release singles by Irish bands with the intention that, once noticed, they would move on to bigger labels. The first release (on 1 August) was In Tua Nua's 'Coming Thru', a gorgeous slither of lilting Celtic tinged pop. Before long, with Mother Records' job done, they'd signed directly to Island and then Virgin, enjoying both mild fame and frustration, splitting up before the decade was out. Other bands starting out on Mother would include Cactus World News (Bono producing their debut single 'The Bridge' before they moved on to MCA), Tuesday Blue and The Hothouse Flowers. Eventually the label would become independent of U2 and release non-Irish artists as well as albums.

Gavin Friday of The Virgin Prunes, live in Paris; U2's 'Pride'; and Microdisney live in London.

Mother didn't have a monopoly. Elvira Butler's Reekus Records stepped in to release the debut album by The Blades, a cross between late Jam and Squeeze, whose earlier signing to Elektra had ended unhappily. Another label, Hotwire, established by former Horslips drummer Eamon Carr, also provided friendly competition. The label's first album was a 1984 compilation, *Hip City Boogaloo*, though most of the featured artists didn't last beyond the year let alone the decade. John Peel favourites The Stars of Heaven, who were more akin to R.E.M. or Violent Femmes, released their finger-pickin' debut single 'Clothes of Pride' on Hotwire the following year. However, the label was best known for The Golden Horde, a psychedelic punk band whose zany debut single 'Dig That Crazy Grave' in 1984 prefaced an even zanier mini-album, *The Chocolate Biscuit Conspiracy,* with Robert Anton Wilson, the following year.

Also helped on their way by U2 (The Edge produced a demo), 1984 saw Blue in Heaven release a couple of singles (both produced by Hugh Jones) and a debut album (helmed by Martin Hannett) which placed the band in the same orbit as New Order and Echo & The Bunnymen, but they too would split before the end of the decade. Zerra 1 were more influenced by U2 and The Cure, having supported both in 1982. Their debut single 'Let's Go Home' and The Cure's 'Let's Go To Bed' shared more than similar titles. By 1984 they'd signed to Mercury who secured Todd Rundgren to produce their eponymous debut album, spawning three singles, none of which charted. A second album and a tour with Ultravox followed in 1986 but they broke up at the end of the year. The Fountainhead were a duo occupying a fairly interesting space between electro goth and Billy Idol. Their 1984 self-released debut single 'Rhythm Method' attracted China Records' attention and thereafter they slipped into a blander second-half-of-the-80s sound. Auto Da Fa, fronted by Gay Woods (ex Steeleye Span) somehow combined folk with synthpop and after a few early 80s singles produced by Phil Lynott (gathered together on the dreadfully named 1984 compilation *5 Singles & 1 Smoked Cod*) they released their first album proper, *Tatitum*, the following year. Les Enfants, a fairly typical mid-80s mannered synthpop outfit, signed to Chrysalis, releasing a single 'Take the Girl' and album *Touché* before promptly disappearing. Mention must also be made of a young Sinead O'Connor who in her early teens had featured in an embryonic version of In Tua Nua and then, as a 17-year old (in 1984), in an unrecorded band called Ton Ton Macoute. This brought her to the attention of Mother Records' Fachtna O'Ceallaigh and U2's The Edge, guesting on the latter's first solo album, a soundtrack, *Captive*. The rest, as they say, is history.

Of all the U2 connections, the Virgin Prunes were the closest. The bands grew up together in the mid-70s, sharing an in-joke fantasy world which would be mysteriously referred to in early interviews. Their singers assumed the names Bono Vox and Gavin Friday (real name Fionán Martin Hanvey), while the Prunes' Dik Evans was The Edge's brother. However, the Virgin Prunes would take a more experimental path. Interesting on record but utterly compelling and unpredictable live, 1984 saw them in typical contrary form: touring Europe, losing two members and abandoning the recording of an album, *Sons Find Devils*. One member, former child actor Daniel Figgis (known in the band as Haa-Lacka Binttii) had left to form Princess Tinymeat, releasing debut 'Sloblands' on Rough Trade that year. The single was a raucous coming together of the Prunes and Einstürzende Neubauten but was perhaps better known for its sleeve showing Figgis in trash-transvestite full frontal pose. The group split in 1987 but Figgis continued his career as a largely uncategorisable artist with fingers in lots of pies. (There are parallels with Simon Fisher Turner here, also a child actor).

Even more experimental were Operating Theatre, partly a real theatre company and partly a musical outlet for Roger Doyle, director, actor and one-time member of early-70s avant-jazz group Supply Demand And Curve. Works like 'Rapid Eye Movements' and 'Fin-estra' (1978) would be released by Nurse With Wound's United Dairies label in 1981[8], after which Doyle discovered the Fairlight and gave piano lessons to Bono[9]. Perhaps the strangest of all mid-80s Irish artists, though, was Stano (real name John Stanley), a carpenter by trade, but who became drawn to making the kind of leftfield music that the era had a knack of encouraging. His first two albums either side of 1984, the unfeasibly named *Content To Write I Dine In Weathercraft* and *The Protagonist 28 Nein - Seducing Decadence In Morning Treecrash,* sounded like Cabaret Voltaire meets The Residents. All of these artists had, at some stage, been involved in The Project Arts Centre which, after being formed in 1967, had several homes in Dublin. The multi-media performance art of Nigel Rolfe was typical of the experimentation the Centre encouraged, his self-produced electronic opus *Island Stories* project eventually being released by Reekus Records in 1986.

Celtic music had always played a major role in Irish pop and rock (Horslips, Planxty, Moving Hearts), but the mid-80s saw a distinctly new age influence creeping in, less reels and jigs, more mist and mystery. Influenced by what was being released on Californian labels like Windham Hill, the Irish variation focussed on the voice: a sort of late millennium plainsong, sung in Gaelic, English or simply wordless, with a modern instrumental backing that smoothed out all edges. In fact, Van Morrison had hinted at the direction with *Astral Weeks* (1968) and his 80s albums, especially 1983's *Inarticulate Speech of the Heart* with its instrumentals and spiritual themes, dabbled in the area. However, it was Clannad who took it further. After a decade of fairly straightforward Celtic folk, their 1982 'Theme from Harry's Game', featuring heavily multi-tracked voices[10], became an unlikely hit on both sides of the Irish Sea. It was the main piece of music from a Yorkshire Television programme about the Troubles, and a year and a half later they received another commission from English television – this time to score the music for a 26-episode drama, *Robin of Sherwood*, released as an album, *Legend*, in 1984. It won them a BAFTA. Like many Irish folk groups, Clannad were a family affair: three siblings and their twin uncles. A younger sibling, Enya, had joined them in the early 80s but had struck out on her own just before 'Harry's Game'. In 1984 she released her first solo recordings on the little-known *Touch Travel* compilation as well as music for an equally obscure Anglo-French film, *The Frog Prince*. Humble beginnings for what would turn out to be a massively successful solo career of mild and moody 'feather-on-the-breath-of-God' vocal pop.

*****

Of course, Ireland in the mid-80s had more than its fair share of pap pop (émigres, The Nolans), MOR (Chris De Burgh) and once great now struggling 70s stalwarts (Rory Gallagher and Phil Lynott)[11] – exactly the kind of staid musical reputation Wales was suffering from. Ex-milkman Shakin' Stevens (more time in the UK charts in the 80s than any other artist) and Bonnie Tyler (still the only Welsh artist to have a US #1) ruled the airwaves, while Tom Jones had gone country and Shirley Bassey released the perfectly titled album, *I Am What I Am*.

Whither the voice of a leftfield music scene? There was plenty to fight against: a decade of mass redundancies, pit closures, English second homes, the erosion of the Welsh language – all in the context of a prime minister with little personal interest in Wales and a Government which never won a majority there. In the early 80s there were a few residual punk groups[12], but the post-punk scene was small and scattered. Cardiff had Young Marble Giants, the cool but short-lived Z Block Records, and Spillers, the oldest record shop in the world. Cardigan was home to the band Ail Symudiad (Second Movement) and their Fflach label. The small north-west town of Bethesda hosted not only two Peel favourites, Maffia Mr Huws and Anhrefn (the latter also starting a label of the same name), but also the Welsh-language music magazine, Sgrech (Scream)[13]. Bangor was the base for Central Slate Records, formed in 1984. And on a slightly larger scale, the Caernarfon-based label, Sain, had been releasing Welsh-language records since 1969, but were rather more folk and choral than pop or rock, including the first recordings by a 14-year-old, pre-*The Snowman* Aled Jones. Radio and TV helped – especially the creation of BBC Radio Cymru in 1979, with its nightly show, Hwyrach (Later – though not with Jools Holland), and the Welsh equivalent of Channel 4, Sianel Pedwar Cymru (Channel Four Wales), or S4C, in 1982 – but their programming was too conservative for most post-punk's taste. In academic and economic terms, 'Welsh popular music was […] built on an amateur aesthetic for a home audience; the place shaped the business'[14].

Alternatively, you moved to London. Green Gartside moved from Newport, via Leeds, to form Scritti Politti in London. Stephen Harrington left the mining town of

Newbridge to become Steve Strange and form Visage. Gene Loves Jezebel took the yellow brick M4 east to become a moderately successful goth band. The Partisans moved to London in 1983, releasing the album *Time Was Right* the following year but split up immediately afterwards[15]. It had always been thus: back in the 60s, John Cale had studied music in London before moving to New York where he joined the Velvet Underground. Still based in New York, the old Welsh punk released two albums in 1984, their bland titles – *Caribbean Sunset* and *John Cale Comes Alive* – sadly giving a clue to their contents (neither has had a CD release).

Welsh-language post-punkers and Peel favourites, Datblygu and Anhrefn.

Many of the bands that stayed put chose to sing in Welsh. To do so was a political statement. As the academic Sarah Hill pointed out, 'Popular music was a central component in the modernization and survival of the Welsh language… [It] made the Welsh language more relevant to the cultural needs of the younger generation of Welsh speakers'[16]. Dafydd Iwan's 1981 single 'Yma O Hyd' ('Still Here') was a key song, especially its defiant chorus: 'We're still here, we're still here, in spite of everyone and everything'. '[T]he song occupies a position of near-ubiquity in Welsh culture; its lyrics can be found, either wholly or in part, on T-shirts, greeting cards and even tea towels'[17].

The mid-80s saw the real, belated beginnings of a Welsh-language post-punk scene, with three key bands. Datblygu (Developing) were at the time limited to cassette albums and dubbed 'the most influential Welsh band never to succeed'[18]. David Edwards' vocals were visceral approximations of spoken Welsh, totally unlike anything heard in Welsh pop. They would end up recording five Peel Sessions and bridge the gap between sung and rapped post-punk. Y Cyrff (The Bodies) were formed while still at school in 1984, debut single 'Yr Haint' (The Infection) being released the following year; the two central members, Mark Roberts and Paul Jones, went on to form Catatonia in the 90s. Anhrefn (Disorder) recorded three Peel Sessions and ran a label with the same name. Like The Alarm's Mike Peters, Anhrefn's bassist Rhys Mwyn wanted to promote his music outside of Wales. Before releasing anything, he went to London with a demo tape of four bands, personally giving a copy to John Peel, who started playing more and more alternative Welsh music on his show. In 1984, the label put out its first record, a double A-side by Anhrefn, 'Dim Heddwch' / 'Priodas Hapus' (No Peace / A Happy Marriage), followed by a couple of compilation albums, ten singles and finally a vinyl album by Datblygu in 1988, whereupon it went into extended hibernation[19]. But the scene had been set, paving the way for 'Cool Cymru' and the likes of Catatonia, Gorky's Zygotic Mynci, Manic Street Preachers, The Darling Buds, Stereophonics and Super Furry Animals in the 90s.

Of course, you could make political statements without singing in Welsh. The Alarm were probably Wales's most successful post-punk group, stepping into the vacuum The Clash had left, their big sound characterized by playing acoustic guitars with pickups, their English lyrics a bluster of generic protest. On the last point, they had affinities with U2, supporting them in the UK and US. This turned out to be both a help and a hindrance, gaining a sizeable following in America but being accused by the English media of sounding too like their Irish friends. Actually, they sounded more like The Clash and looked like renegade country and westerners. 'The press never liked us and we never worried about it', said frontman Mike Peters. And in truth they attracted a fervent fan base, not just in the States but in their homeland. Debut album *Declaration* made #6 in the UK charts in February 1984. They never bettered it. Later in the decade they would become more interested in language, becoming the first Welsh band to simultaneously release an album in English (*Change*) and Welsh (*Newid*).

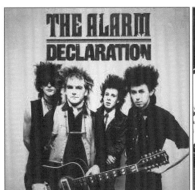 

A study in 80s hairstyles: The Alarm anticipate Chapter 11 while Freur model an extraordinary range of cuts.

Another English-speaking Welsh band who were typical of the legions (from all over the UK) who signed to majors in the hope of hitting the mid-80s big time were Freur[20]. Formed in Cardiff, the group moved to London, were signed by CBS, had a minor hit with 'Doot-Doot' in 1983, were momentarily big in Italy, let the success go to their heads, were a fashion car-crash, decided they were too cool to do press, and when the follow-ups didn't chart, were dropped. Had they been a bit more level-headed, stuck to the original game plan (synth-experimentation), perhaps signed to an independent and not gone chasing fame, who knows what would have happened. In any case, they just about managed to survive the rest of the 80s, changed their name to Underworld, moved to Essex and completely reinvented themselves at the dawn of the new decade, seduced by rave, returning to the game plan and signing with an independent. But they weren't typical of Welsh bands – or perhaps *any* band.

Musically, the mid-80s were not particularly inspiring times for Wales or Ireland (north or south of the border). There were plenty of bands, particularly in Dublin where the success and patronage of U2 helped shape a scene of sorts, but there was nothing to compare in Belfast or Derry, Cardiff or Swansea. Nevertheless, 'Cool Cymru' would put Wales on the map in the 90s and Ireland would continue to punch well above its weight with U2, Sinead O'Connor, Enya, The Cranberries, Boyzone and Westlife.

Chapter 11: First and Last and Always
Post-punk goth-style

*That whole romanticism of death! Anyone who's ever experienced death first hand could tell you
there's nothing romantic about it.*[1]
Robert Smith

It goes against the grain of popular perception, but I remember it being humorous.[2]
David J of Bauhaus, talking about The Batcave

Batley, West Yorkshire 1984. An earnest narrator guides the viewer through the
dilapidated streets of a once-prosperous northern industrial town. To the strings of
what sounds like Mantovani (but turns out to be John Lennon's 'Woman' played by
the James Last Orchestra or similar), the camera alights on a half-decent building the
60s planners spared, prompting the narrator to continue his tour. 'This architectural
masterpiece […] is now a first-class disco. The owner, Mrs Ann Swallow, invites you
to a special disco evening'. Mrs Swallow appears in evening dress by the
underwhelming front door. Is it Michael Palin in drag? Ushered inside, we see a
traditional pub-like bar, velvet stools and a mirror ball. Mr and Mrs Swallow are
interviewed. 'What type of clientele do you get?' 'Erm, mainly futuristic and way-out
young people […] A lot of people don't seem to get on with our customers, but we're
happy with them, they're no trouble at all'.

You'd be forgiven for thinking this excruciating video, which you can find on
YouTube, is a long-lost episode of Ripping Yarns, but it's dead straight (and, at over
two hours, dead long). Entitled, in all seriousness, *The Height of Goth 1984: A Night
at the Xclusiv Nightclub, Batley, West Yorkshire UK*, it was commissioned by the
club's owners and sold for two quid each. A veritable time capsule, it presents the
more mundane side of goth. There's a bit of back-combed hair, ripped fishnets and
interesting makeup but mainly it's just normal looking people dancing to post-punk,
goth and a bit of glam. At one point two goths are asked what their favourite type of
music is. 'I don't know really... Glenn Miller and.... Cabaret Voltaire' says the bloke.

I stumbled upon the video by accident, as you do on YouTube, and only later realised
that it's become a bit of a pop culture document. Mostly it's cringeworthy or boring,
but in its banality it also says something about how music can transcend our often
mundane lives, how a hundred or so locals can momentarily leave the realities of life
in mid-80s West Yorkshire behind. We will return to West Yorkshire later, but first,
what exactly was goth?

Both a sub-genre of post-punk and a sub-culture beyond music, goth was perfect for
the loner-teenager with an attraction to the dark side. The name goes back to the

Goths, an ancient Germanic people who resisted the Roman Empire. But by medieval times it had become the adjective 'gothic', used to describe a type of architecture: the pointed arches, flying buttresses and ribbed vaults of churches, but also palaces (London's Houses of Parliament) and even cities (Gotham). All emphasized verticality, the reaching up to the heavens.

However, gothic was also entwined with our voyeuristic attitude to death and the afterlife, which was more inclined to be hell than heaven. We can see this in art (Rackham, Dore, even the Pre-Raphaelites), literature (Poe, Shelley, Dickens), film (Murnau, Lang, Burton) and television (The Addams Family, The Munsters, Buffy the Vampire Slayer). Film played a particularly important role in cementing the archetypal gothic experience, combining original literary source, gloomy set designs, distorted camera angles, atmospheric lighting, minor chord music and ominous sound effects. In a novel like *Dracula*, one could have sympathy for the Count, but on celluloid he could turn into a heartthrob. Death, or its possibility, became something alluring, even romantic. Most gothic stories have an element of horror, but not necessarily the other way round. A zombie film isn't gothic. Similarly with rock: Bauhaus are gothic, Impaler are schlock horror.

The look of goth was heavily influenced by these films, particularly *Dracula*. The palest of skin, for both men (Count Dracula never got out much) and women (all the better to contrast the red trickle of blood on compliant white neck), was de rigueur. Clothes-wise, because many of the novels and the films they spawned were set in the 19th Century, some latter-day goths went for formal, funereal Victoriana: stiff, buttoned-up suits, satin bodices under long velvet dresses, elbow-length lace gloves, and always, *always* (well, almost always) in black[3]. This would be latched onto, in extremis, by the teenage Takeshita-dori set in Tokyo. But another more practical starting point was punk: torn fishnet tights and tops, and black spikey hair. Hair and make-up were out of control, heavily influenced by Siouxsie (for the girls) and Robert Smith (for the boys). And to complete the picture: sunglasses, swathes of dry ice mimicking foggy 19th Century London streets and the mist that crept around castles, and definitely no smiling.

Musically, the term 'gothic' began to gain currency when describing the late 70s post-punk of Joy Division, Siouxsie and the Banshees, The Cure and The Damned, but actually it goes further back to the Velvet Underground, Leonard Cohen and Nico. Nico, particularly, with her sonorous voice, lugubrious harmonium and don't-talk-to-me aloofness, was seen by those in the know as the high priestess, the real thing (inadvertently helped by the fact that in the 80s she was living in Manchester, its city centre still panoramically Victorian). Bands fixated or playing around with the occult and other psychic forces – Black Sabbath, Psychic TV, Current 93 – weren't goth as such. In any case, the term didn't really catch on until Bauhaus released their debut single, 'Bela Lugosi's Dead', in 1979. The importance of this song in the goth canon cannot be overstated. Even though it was about the *actor* who played Dracula, the rest of their songs had nothing to with ghouls and initially the band wore jeans and T-shirts, Bauhaus would become synonymous with the dark side – and would play up to it. At one point, Peter Murphy's stage persona and the character of the somnambulist (played by Conrad Veidt) in *The Cabinet of Dr Caligari* were virtually inseparable. But there was still no scene as such and 'gothic' had yet to lose its 'ic'. The Birthday Party's 'Release the Bats' single and The Cure's *Faith* album were key musical milestones while the new romantic movement influenced its look, albeit in a manner that was more dandy than dark. The final nail in the coffin (so to speak) was probably Ian Astbury of Southern Death Cult in 1983 using the term 'goths' to describe Sex Gang Children's fans, which was then picked up by NME writer David Dorrell.

Another defining moment, both musically and visually (the latter crucial), was the opening on Wednesday[4] 21 July 1982 of the Batcave at the appropriately named Gargoyle Club, 69 Dean Street, in London's Soho. The brainchild of Olli Wisdom and his band Specimen, it quickly became the meeting point for pale, thin misfits dressed in Victoriana or fetish-wear, with heavy black makeup and hair big and back-combed[5]. Here they could listen to resident DJ Hamish McDonald playing a continuous soundtrack of Bauhaus, Siouxsie, The Cure and Killing Joke sprinkled with T.Rex, Iggy Pop and The Cramps. It was a live venue too, so you could also see lesser-known bands in the flesh, safe in the knowledge that there were many others who looked and felt like you, before running the gauntlet of the night bus home. And yet it wasn't just a goth hangout: Test Department played their first concert there soon after it opened, even Whitehouse played there. But it will forever be associated with its two effective housebands: Specimen, who were fronted by Wisdom, formerly of Bristol punk rockers The Unwanted[6], and Alien Sex Fiend, formed by another Batcave employee, Nik Wade, and his wife, Christine. Specimen were pervy fishnet glam who released a few records either side of 1984, while Mr & Mrs Fiend were max-factored zombie electronic, releasing three singles and two albums in 1984 alone. *Both* were camp and kitsch rather than doom and gloom. Musically the Batcave was Division Two: the main bands didn't mind propping up the bar but they wouldn't be seen dead playing there. Visually, it was influential, but as with Billy's and Blitz, the media exaggerated the scene. By 1983, the club had outgrown its Dean Street venue and moved to the top floor of the Subway Club, 28 Leicester Square, then Fouberts off Carnaby Street, and then the Cellar Bar underneath Charing Cross Station. It also went on tour. There were Batcave nights at Planets in Liverpool, the Hacienda in Manchester and (appropriately) the Belfry in Leicester.

*****

London's Batcave may have been the one in the media but the goth strongholds – bands and fans – were actually in northern England, and specifically, for reasons unknown, in the West Yorkshire towns of Leeds (The Sisters Of Mercy, The March Violets), Bradford (Southern Death Cult who became Death Cult who became The Cult), Keighley (Skeletal Family) and Barnsley (The Danse Society). The dark satanic mills and desolate, windswept moors[7] may have had something to do with it, although for some reason there was no equivalent scene across the border in equally industrial, windswept Lancashire.

Although the bands were almost exclusively male[8], the genre gained a large female following, attracted by its fashion but also its gender egalitarianism. As with the new romantic movement, both sexes liked to dress up. At the extreme end, it is easy to scoff at the looks of Specimen (which, transformed from black to blazing colour, would influence Sigue Sigue Sputnik, also just beginning to stir in 1984) and the kinky looks *and* names of Alien Sex Fiend, Sex Gang Children and Rudimentary Peni (the last more anarcho-punk than goth) but in reality most goth bands were curiously asexual.

After Bauhaus split in the summer of 1983, Peter Murphy paired up with Mick Karn to form the intriguing but flawed Dalis Car project, their 'career' of one album and a single (see Chapter 23) competing with the Sid Presley Experience as this book's shortest. The rest of the 80s saw Murphy release three solo albums but struggle to find his niche. Meanwhile Daniel Ash and Kevin Haskins continued with side project Tones On Tail releasing four singles and their only album – the ironically titled *Pop* – in 1984 before forming (with fellow Bauhaus member David J) the more conventional rockers Love and Rockets – who would go onto major success in their States, eclipsing Murphy, at least commercially.

The Damned, The Cure and Siouxsie and the Banshees became the mainstream goth trinity, certainly in terms of looks, although musically they were dallying with pop and psychedelia, even breaching the Top 10. The Damned had the perfect goth credentials in ex-gravedigger, horror-movie-loving, Dracula-attired[9] Dave Vanian, even if the rest of the band were still pantomime punk. Goths simply couldn't wear red berets or fluorescent jumpers. 1984 was a quiet year for them, with just the one single, 'Thanks For The Night', and Captain Sensible leaving midway through to concentrate on his solo career.

The year saw The Cure in a period of transition. After the top-yourself bleakness of *Faith* (1981) and *Pornography* (1982), the group had slimmed down to Smith and Laurence Tolhurst, who'd moved from drums to keyboards, and had embarked on a whimsical trio of singles: the poppy 'Let's Go to Bed', the New Order-ish 'The Walk' and the jazzy 'The Love Cats'. Collected, with B-sides, on *Japanese Whispers* at the tail end of 1983, they had lightened up a bit. Would Smith cross the line and deliver a full pop album? As it turned out, *The Top*, released in April 1984, hedged its bets, combining a bit more whimsy ('The Caterpillar', the album's sole single), a return to doom and gloom – slow ('Shake Dog Shake') and fast ('Give Me It') – together with some trippy psychedelia and even a spot of fife-and-drum marching music. It divided the critics and perhaps as a response, the live album that followed, *Concert*, recorded in London and Oxford in May, featured only two tracks from *The Top*, the rest staple favourites from earlier. Augmented by Andy Anderson on drums, Phil Thornalley on bass and Porl Thompson on guitar, the album rips through their back catalogue in imperious fashion. It was as if Smith suddenly realised he could do pessimism *and* pop – a combination perfected on their next album, 1985's *The Head on the Door*, which also broke them in America.

Who said goths were too serious? Odd couples: Nick Cave and Nic Fiend, Robert Smith and Siouxsie.

For the first half of 1984, Smith was also still a member of Siouxsie and the Banshees, having joined them in late 1982, post-*Pornography*, and also formed the short-lived The Glove project with Steve Severin the following year (while Sioux and Budgie had their own offshoot, The Creatures). In effect, he was working on both *The Top* and the new Banshees album, *Hyaena*, at the same time. The latter took the psychedelia of The Glove and 'Dear Prudence' single and created an intriguing, experimental if slightly complacent album with 'Swimming Horses' and 'Dazzle' being standouts – duly released as singles. It wasn't every day that Top Of The Pops audiences heard lyrics like 'He gives birth to swimming horses' as they did on 29 March, or watched its video in which the four of them forsook their customary black and dressed entirely in white, the men masked and looking like inmates from a lunatic asylum while Siouxsie writhed in front of them.

Smith's tenure in the band couldn't last though. By May he was suffering from exhaustion and his doctor's note doubled as a resignation letter to Sioux and co enabling him to focus on The Cure alone. Siouxsie and the Banshees were therefore back to their favourite occupation, looking for a guitarist, and found one in John Carruthers, ex-Clock DVA. The omens were good. *The Thorn* EP, released in the autumn, featured four older tracks reworked with strings. It suited them perfectly, giving them a rich, expansive, even filmic sound while doubling up as a curtain closer to their first seven years.

Although The Birthday Party played an influential role in early goth, on splitting in 1983 it was obvious Nick Cave was leaving the fold, even if he'd ever been part of it. True, his dalliance with the ghoulish, New York-based Immaculate Consumptives – alongside Marc Almond, Jim 'Foetus' Thirlwell and Lydia Lunch – *looked* goth, but it was a short-lived, live-only distraction and by mid-1984 his new band, the Bad Seeds, with Mick Harvey (ex-The Birthday Party), Blixa Bargeld (on loan from Einstürzende Neubauten), Barry Adamson (ex-Magazine), Hugo Race (ex-Plays With Marionettes) and Anita Lane, had released debut album *From Her To Eternity*. Musically the album was far from goth, more garage blues than anything else, and on stage they were still wild and shambolic, rather than the studied, mysterious cool of goth. Lyrically it was highly literary, referencing a confused space that existed between Americana and the Old Testament. There was also a single, 'In The Ghetto', a cover of Elvis Presley's 1969 comeback hit (as grim a US Top 10 as ever there was).

As a statement of intent, the album and single couldn't be bettered, and The Bad Seeds would serve Cave well for the rest of his idiosyncratic career.

The Birthday Party had started out on 4AD which had strong gothic associations even though it wasn't a goth label. Rather it embraced the melancholy and mystery of the genre. Despite their name, Dead Can Dance weren't goth (though co-vocalist Brendan Perry had a gothic voice to die for) and neither were Cocteau Twins (largely because you couldn't understand what Liz Fraser was singing about), but Xmal Deutschland were. If you weren't a German-speaker, you couldn't understand what Anja Huwe, their striking peroxide version of Siouxsie, was singing about either, but a quick translation of one song turns out to be a veritable goth template:

> *You are alone, you are alone*
> *Just as the night is dark*
> *No star in the heavens*
> *Your white skin shines like porcelain*
> *You are darkened like the night alone*
> *You find no light, there is no sun*
> etc[10]

The band released two albums on 4AD, 1983's *Fetisch* and 1984's *Tocsin*, the latter seeing them at their peak before petering out by the end of the decade. Having supported Dead Can Dance on tour in 1984, Dutch band Clan Of Xymox signed to 4AD that year and released their first full self-titled album the following year. Gloomy vocals, portentous washes of synths, New Order-esque beats and a gauzy, haunting sleeve saw them tagged goth too. 4AD's 'supergroup' This Mortal Coil, meanwhile, were graceful goth, combining the wistful compositions of its own stable of writers with intelligent covers of delicate songs by Tim Buckley, Alex Chilton and Roy Harper. Likewise, the sleeve for debut album's *It'll End In Tears* was mystery incarnate.

Borderline goths, Killing Joke had one foot in post-punk, the other in metal, and started 1984 like they meant business. Released in April, 'Eighties' was a huge, vaguely Nietzschean-sounding single with a slick production which paradoxically pointed to a more accessible, if not chart-friendly sound (though it peaked prematurely at #60). The song's killer riff was famously plagiarised by Nirvana on 'Come As You Are'. A follow-up single, 'A New Day', was not quite in that class, but the *Night Time* album, recorded in Berlin in the autumn (although not released until early 1985) was their biggest selling album, going silver. They never bettered it.

In reality goth was niche, but there were still other bands who flirted with its look and sound. Formed in Bradford in 1981 and over time truncating their name from Southern Death Cult to Death Cult to simply (in January 1984) The Cult, the group were a curious mixture of post-punk, heavy rock, the macho posturing of Jim Morrison and a touch of goth, the last element rooted not in 19th Century Victorian romanticism but 19th Century native American shamanism. Singles 'Spiritwalker', 'Go West' and

152

'Resurrection Joe' seemed to reinforce this, as did 'Horse Nation', the opening track of their debut album, *Dreamtime* (the lyrics of which were lifted almost verbatim from Dee Brown's seminal book, *Bury My Heart at Wounded Knee*). But coming from Bradford, people still thought they were goth, probably not helped by goth-friendly Zigzag magazine voting them Best Group and Best Live Act of the year, though by 1985 they were more like Led Zeppelin. If The Cult were the Indians then Fields of the Nephilim were the cowboys, complete with 'dust'-covered hats and weather-beaten coats. Formed in 1984, they combined the Spaghetti Western look with Crowley- and Lovecraft-inspired lyrics, a sound that was classic goth noir and a name that came from the Hebrew Bible. The fact that they didn't look black as much as brown (on account of all the dust – actually it was flour) and came from the small town of Stevenage didn't seem to hold them back.

Another Bradford band operating on the (long, unconditioned) fringes of goth, were New Model Army. They too romanticised the past, but NMA were rooted in England, naming themselves after the English 17th Century Parliamentarian militia. Their music was as mixed up as The Cult's but with an added 'crusty punk' element, evident in their look and leftist lyrics. Debut album *Vengeance* was released in April 1984 and made the top of the Indie Chart – this when their first two singles hadn't made the charts at all. (They would inspire another English Civil War-inspired band, The Levellers, who formed in 1988).

Thorns, stars, runes: Goth bands always had the best logos.

At the forefront of nouveau-goth were Leeds' The Sisters Of Mercy. Formed in 1980, it took three years for them to release their first couple of singles – including another goth milestone, 'Alice' – and establish a reasonably stable line-up of Andrew Eldritch, Wayne Hussey (previously in an early version of Dead or Alive), Gary Marx and Craig Adams. In Eldritch they had the voice of goth and with Hussey, who wrote most of the music, they reflected a world of Cold War paranoia and acid rain, and the promo for their June 1984 single 'Body and Soul' – black clothes and shades amongst toppled pillars and dry ice under a darkened sky – became a benchmark for all goth videos. Recording of their debut album, *First and Last and Always*, rife with drug intake and tension, dragged on through the summer, missed its scheduled October release and ended up coming out in early 1985 whereupon the band predictably disintegrated. But like similarly post-apocalyptic Arnold Schwarzenegger[11], they (or rather Eldritch) would be back.

Fellow Leeds band The March Violets' first singles were on Eldritch's Merciful Release label but later they formed their own, Rebirth. They'd started with the rather unusual line-up of two lead singers, the huge, bearded Simon Denbigh and the rather more compact Rosie Garland, guitars and drum-machine. 1984 saw the appearance of two singles and a debut album, *Natural History*, together with the disappearance of both singers, replaced by one: the more upbeat, conventionally glamorous Cleo Murray. Many goth bands at this time tried to lose the goth tag, as Siouxsie and The Cure successfully did, and for the next two years the Violets followed the rather predictable route of moving to London, signing with a major, making videos which focussed on Murray (who looked a bit like Kim Wilde), and watering down their sound. They fizzled out in 1987.

The same happened to The Danse Society, who scraped the charts in early 1984 with an album *Heaven is Waiting* and a cover of the Stones' '2,000 Light Years From Home' (as opposed to 20 miles from Barnsley). Like The Sisters, they were heavy on drum-machine-and-sequencer riffs which secured them floor-play in clubs. They were miserable as hell. Formed at the beginning of the decade by identical Welsh twins Michael and Jay Aston, Gene Loves Jezebel went through several line-up changes[12] before reaching some sort of stability in 1984. That year saw them release two singles, the prosaic 'Shame' and the broody 'Influenza' (which sounds like T.Rex on valium with a beautiful marimba back-rhythm, 1984's exotic instrument of choice), a tour with fellow Welshman John Cale, the inevitable Peel session and the commencement of work on their second album, *Immigrant*. They would become big(ish) in America but much of recent history has seen *two* Gene Loves Jezebels, fronted by each of the twins, one in the UK, one in the US. Armed with the perfect goth name, The Lords of the New Church were formed in 1982 with ex-members of The Damned, Sham 69, The Barracudas and The Dead Boys, as a kind of belated punk 'supergroup'. By 1984 they were onto their third album, *The Method to Our Madness*, but in reality they were more metal than goth and more American than Brit, and were massive underachievers in the UK, splitting up in acrimony at London's Astoria in 1989. They never got a hit – not even when covering Madonna's 'Like A Virgin' – but inevitably they'd reform in the new millennium.

Other notable goth releases in 1984 included Flesh For Lulu's eponymous debut album and a couple of singles, 'Subterraneans' being the better of the two; Bone Orchard's *Jack* which seemed to be a meeting point between The Birthday Party and Lemon Kittens; Skeletal Family's debut album, *Burning Oil*, which turned out to be their peak; Play Dead's *From the Promised Land* (their next would be produced by Conny Plank); Party Day's 'The Spider' single (prefacing two fine albums before they split in 1986); the eponymous debut album by The Cure acolytes And Also The Trees (and incidentally one of the few early-80s-formed bands to make it through the ensuing decades without splitting up); debut single 'The World of Light' by Balaam and The Angel who comprised three Scottish brothers relocated to Staffordshire; two singles by Brum goths Ausgang before they split up in 1987; an eponymous mini-album by Furyo, formed from the ashes of punk band UK Decay; and the very gothically named Sunglasses After Dark's debut single 'Morbid Silence', the sleeve of which featured the vaulted arches of an unnamed church. Perfect.

After 1984, many goth bands switched their attention from Britain and the rest of Europe and focussed on 'cracking' the US. In so doing they became less overtly goth and more like American hair metal[13] or even soft rock, signing to majors, spending fortunes on videos, playing indoor sports arenas and the occasional trashing of hotel rooms. The Mission, The Cult, Gene Loves Jezebel, Flesh For Lulu all followed this route. As did Love and Rockets who were more pop and The Cure who swung between pop and goth. In fact the 'gothiest' of British bands active Stateside may well have been Depeche Mode who had been attracting the black hordes since 1984's *Some Great Reward*. The one act who resisted was The Sisters Of Mercy, Eldritch apparently preferring to 'watch suspect Japanese films and listen to cricket all day'[14]. By the 90s the US would lead the way with Trent Reznor and Marilyn Manson's combining of goth with industrial, electronic and metal.

But Yorkshire is still a safe haven for goths. As the crow – or bat – flies, it's 80 miles from Batley to the North Yorkshire port of Whitby, where Count Dracula arrived with his 50 boxes of Transylvanian earth. Bram Stoker would never have believed that 100 years later there would be a Whitby Goth Weekend. But there is and it endures, presenting many of the class of 1984 alongside the next generation. Truly goth is the undead.

Chapter 12: Better by Design
The rule of the 12-inch sleeve

I never had to answer to anyone.[1]
Peter Saville

It is getting a bit silly when the sleeve is more important than the record.[2]
Jon Savage

No one minds when Jack Kerouac's On the Road *gets a new cover design. [But] woe betide the marketing genius who one day decides that* Sergeant Pepper *needs a graphic makeover.*[3]
Rick Poynor

In the last four decades of the 20th Century, the best record sleeves were more than just graphic design, protecting the vinyl inside, or communicating information to the consumer. They formed a symbiotic relationship with the music, the sleeve being inextricably linked to the experience of identifying, enjoying, interpreting and remembering the music within. Many have since become key signifiers in the development of popular culture. Some, like *Sergeant Peppers* and *Dark Side of the Moon*, have become art.

Today, music has become largely de-objectified. It exists in the ether, as MP3s, FLAC or on Spotify. You can still buy it on a CD, just, or even, making an extended comeback, on vinyl, but it is the exception. Most people stream or download music, and the in-between stage has largely gone. Back in 1984, a single or an album was still an object. You went into a shop, fingered through the racks and possibly bought something on impulse because of an interesting cover. You'd get it home, slip the vinyl from its sleeve, pop it onto the record player, drop the needle and then, while your speakers did their stuff, settle down to study the sleeve: the track titles, the lyrics, who played on it, where it was recorded. The format of 12 inches square (actually 12 and three-eighths) would make it easy to read and over the years became a kind of perfect size for a designer, an artist or a photographer to play with. Perhaps if the first records were five inches square then we might be saying that that was the perfect size, but I doubt it and they weren't[4].

The album might be a gatefold (almost certainly if it was a double), but by the 80s that was considered a bit passé, a bit prog – although many a designer yearned for the opportunity. It might have cut-outs, fold-outs and embossing. Or it might be a DIY effort, with a photo or illustration stuck onto a plain sleeve, either because the label and band couldn't afford anything more or because the designer thought it somehow captured the band's (or the music's) essence. It might also have some extra bits: an inner sleeve with lyrics, a folded poster, a postcard, a mail order flyer advertising a must-have T-shirt, or, if the band was feeling pretentious, a 'limited edition art print'. It might even smell. My copy of Madonna's *Like A Prayer* still whiffs of patchouli. When we talk about great sleeves, we mostly mean album covers: the grand, roughly annual statement. Singles were still usually seen as a bit throwaway, although sometimes you'd get a decent sleeve for the 12-inch format, and occasionally there would be a successful reduction to the 7-inch version. Rarely would a cassette cover be judged in the same light: the canvas of 4 x 2½ inches hidden behind plastic casing was just too limiting and record companies were mostly unwilling to lavish the same attention and money on something which seemed somehow temporary, even if cassettes sold more than records. By 1984 the compact disc was coming in but few designers (and commissioning record companies) made a real effort to produce something specifically for the new five-inch square format. Almost all of the early examples of CD sleeves were hidden, like cassettes, behind plastic jewel cases with illegible 6pt text and a dry, dull page devoted to the disc's technical specifications.

So the 12-inch canvas ruled. Moreover, graphic designers were being recognised as never before. Up until the mid-60s, they didn't exist. They were called commercial artists, 'little men with Brylcreemed hair, toothbrushed moustaches and sleeve garters... [so that's where Ron Mael got his look!]. After years of being commercial artists they all woke up one morning and announced they were graphic designers'[5]. In the late 60s and early 70s, however, it was still quite rare to see design credits on record sleeves – with major exceptions like Hipgnosis, Roger Dean and Barney Bubbles[6] – but with punk and the early 80s advent of style magazines, graphic designers became an important part of youth culture's visual language. There was illustration and photography of course, and these were used (and abused) as never before. Labels like Stiff and Chiswick were the first to re-introduce picture sleeves and customized labels. But what really changed in the post-punk years was the use of type. Ever since Jamie Reid appropriated ransom note letters and stuck them on Sex Pistols sleeves, type was up for grabs. Words and individual letters became illustrative, serifs were combined with san-serifs, lower case randomly juxtaposed with upper case. Extraordinary new typefaces were created. It also helped that most graphic designers were music lovers. Faced with a choice of annual reports and food packaging or the wide-open brief of a record sleeve, many young graphic designers opted for a career in the latter.

1984 was arguably a watershed year for graphic designers working in the music industry. The year before had seen the death and dissolution of, respectively, Barney Bubbles and Hipgnosis. Of the new generation, set free and energised by punk, many had adopted a more refined style, plundering neoclassicism and Russian constructivism, in response to new pop's sophistication and briefs that required the artist to look more worldly-wise, less a band and more a brand. Of course, there was a lot of bad or lazy design around in the 80s. The best-selling album in the UK in 1984 was Lionel Richie's dully dressed *Can't Slow Down*, while the cover of Roger Waters' *The Pros and Cons of Hitch Hiking* continued the tradition of sexist artwork that had been so common in the 70s[7].

Some bands or labels, or even the designers themselves, had, if not a house style, then at least an aesthetic consistency. New Order records rarely featured their name or title on the front cover; Cocteau Twins sleeves were delicate and mysterious. The key designers were Peter Saville, Neville Brody and, in the guise of agencies, Malcolm Garrett of Assorted iMaGes and Vaughan Oliver and Nigel Grierson of 23 Envelope (though the names sounded more like bands – Altered Images or 23 Skidoo – than companies). Between them they went a long way to help visually shape the era.

*****

Peter Saville's obsessively clean, ordered, minimal, *auteur* designs were the anti-thesis of punk's wild abandon. Enrolled in Manchester Polytechnic's graphic design course with Malcolm Garrett (though he would later state that 'Roxy was my BA [and] my MA started the day I picked up *Pioneers* [*of Modern Typography*] from Malcolm's desk'[8]), Saville met Tony Wilson at a Patti Smith concert in January 1978 who asked him to design a poster for a series of four concerts he was organizing[9]. Soon after, he joined Wilson and Alan Erasmus as partners in Factory Records, and designed the sleeve of their first release, the EP compilation, *A Factory Sample*[10], and a year later the label's first album, Joy Division's *Unknown Pleasures*. Whilst continuing to design Factory sleeves, Saville moved to London, designing the first few releases on Virgin offshoot DinDisc, including OMD's beautifully conceived debut album, in collaboration with architect Ben Kelly. He then branched out, creating a body of work which captured the essence of the era: Joy Division's *Closer*, Roxy Music's *Flesh + Blood*, Eno & Byrne's *My Life in the Bush of Ghosts*, a lot of Ultravox and every release by New Order, including of course the iconically-sleeved 'Blue Monday' and *Power Corruption and Lies*.

By 1984, Saville was operating as Peter Saville Associates with Brett Wickens (who had been in Canadian synthpop band Spoons), photographer Trevor Key and others. His intriguing sleeve for Section 25's *From the Hip* album consisted of 20 colour-coded metal poles shot on location in Snowdonia, while two New Order singles, 'Thieves Like Us' and 'Murder', continued the fine art appropriation – this time Giorgio De Chirico. But Saville was moving on. The front cover of OMD's *Junk Culture* album set blurred but vibrantly coloured flowers in a background of fathomless black, the sleeve for Ultravox's *Lament* was simply gloss black typography on matte-black card and, lest it be forgotten, he also designed Wham! sleeves in 1984. Saville would go on to work in fashion, join Pentagram and even become Creative Director of the City of Manchester but his legacy will always be wrapped up in record sleeves.

Malcolm Garrett had designed his first record cover, Buzzcocks' debut single, 'Orgasm Addict', a year before Saville. It looked punk – an appropriation (in the style of Dadaist Hannah Höch by illustrator friend Linder Sterling) of a female torso with an iron for a head set against day-glo yellow – but the type was placed 'just so' and he'd even, at his first attempt, created a logo of the group name which is still being used today. Around about the same time he set up his own company, Assorted iMaGes, the name of which would grace an extraordinary array of sleeves in the late 70s and early 80s, including Magazine, 999, The Pop Group, John Foxx, Simple Minds and Duran Duran's first four albums. If Saville would be forever associated with Joy Division and New Order, then Garrett and Assorted iMaGes would be strongly linked to Simple Minds and Duran Duran. The early 1984 sleeve for the former's *Sparkle in the Rain* album was classic Garrett. Simple Minds were moving from alternative new wave synth group to a bigger 'arena-rock' sound. The album cover, with its bold, modern coat of arms in gold, orange and blue set against clean white, seemed to announce their new, royal, A-list standing.

Duran Duran were already pop royalty, helped as much by their good looks, and the fact they were Princess Diana's favourite group, as their music. But they didn't always put their mugs on the covers nor ape Roxy Music with photographs of glamorous models (the *Rio* girl, remember, was a decidedly unraunchy illustration). 1984's 'New Moon on Monday' and 'The Reflex' singles were pure graphics, but another single, 'The Wild Boys', and a live album *Arena*, acquiesced to a group photo amidst all the squares, circles and viewfinder frames that Garrett and others were fond of at the time. His sleeve for Thomas Dolby's *The Flat Earth* looked positively Hipgnosis-like in its conception. Garrett would continue to lead Assorted iMaGes into the next decade, and they would be one of the first graphic design studios to go completely digital in 1990, but would leave to set up the interactive media production company AMX in 1994.

Peter Saville, Malcolm Garrett and Neville Brody sleeve designs for New Order, Simple Minds and Cabaret Voltaire.

Although Saville and Garrett wrestled with the intricacies, placement and aesthetics of type (Saville to the point of preferring to leave it out whenever he could), it was Neville Brody who became most associated with the visual concerns of type and typefaces. Brody had studied at the London College of Printing and started designing sleeves for new wave and alternative acts like Cabaret Voltaire, Clock DVA, 23 Skidoo, even Depeche Mode's early single, 'I Just Can't Get Enough'. But actually, Brody was better known as a magazine designer. In 1980, at the same time as he was designing fairly obscure record sleeves, former NME editor Nick Logan had invited Brody to become designer and art director of his new venture, The Face. Within a few years, his page layouts had become extraordinarily inventive; sometimes with just the first word (or even its first letter) taking up a whole page, serif & san serif typefaces

159

(often including his own) might be mixed in one word, some might be upside-down; while a photo would be cropped to within an inch of its life. The look then transferred to the High Street. As design curator Catherine McDermott noted: 'The impact became particularly noticeable in 1984-5 when the banks and building societies produced a series of free magazines in the style of i-D and The Face. […] Barclays Supersavers [leaflets] were sent out to 3,000,000 teenagers.' Others included Go! Magazine for Midland Bank and TSBeat for the Trustees Savings Bank. [11]

Brody still found time to do the odd sleeve and in 1984, having been responsible for the majority of Cabaret Voltaire's record covers, he designed their album *Microphonies.* A figure, face heavily-bandaged, the whole tinted a grainy blue and with a view-finder grid of red crosses, suggests something sinister, but what? The sightline of a hi-tech rifle? The Cabaret Voltaire logo Brody created for this sleeve, an angular combination of upper and lower case in what looks like a font of his own, is perfectly positioned on the right. So satisfying is it that it takes up the whole of the cover of their subsequent single, 'James Brown'.

Brody would continue to combine his design work for magazines and record sleeves together with work for other non-music clients and creating new fonts, and by 1988 he was the subject of a Thames and Hudson monograph edited by Jon Wozencroft and an exhibition at the Victoria and Albert Museum. There were some who felt he'd 'got above his station' and that some of his typefaces were illegible[12], but his influence was undeniable and he still produces startling work as Brody Associates whilst also teaching the next generation of graphic designers at the Royal College of Art's School of Communication.

However, it was Vaughan Oliver and Nigel Grierson, collectively known as 23 Envelope, who were the most obvious aspirants of 'design as art'. Both had studied graphic design at Newcastle Polytechnic then moved to London – Oliver to work freelance (for all sorts of products, including early 4AD sleeves), while Grierson secured a work placement at Hipgnosis before deciding to take an MA in photography and then in film. In 1981 they formed 23 Envelope, and on a freelance basis started contributing sleeves for 4AD bands, starting off with Modern English's *Mesh & Lace* before graduating to Cocteau Twins and Colourbox (and occasionally for other non-4AD bands like Yazoo's *You and Me Both*). In 1983 Oliver became 4AD's in-house designer, still working with Grierson as 23 Envelope but one of them was now full time, the other still freelance (a curious arrangement which contributed to later complications). The next year saw them produce some of their most renowned and recognised work, including Cocteau Twins' *Treasure* and This Mortal Coil's *It'll End in Tears.* The former was a gorgeous chiaroscuro concoction of filigree, light, shadow and meticulously crafted typography on the outside with the attention to detail carried over onto the inner sleeve and labels within – or, as Oliver modestly said, '…boiled down, it's a bloody mannequin with a few bits of lace around it!'[13] For *It'll End in Tears,* Grierson's soft focus, black & white, then tinted, photograph of a friend-of-a-friend[14] (originally shot for a Modern English sleeve, but not used) is perhaps the ultimate 4AD sleeve: beautiful, utterly mysterious, melancholic, and seemingly from another age and place. In truth, 23 Envelope's work was actually extremely varied – Colourbox and Wolfgang Press sleeves, for example, were ultra-colourful and modern – and would get even more varied as the decade progressed. But tension over credits would see Grierson leave, with Oliver reducing the name to v23 thereafter.

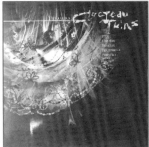

23 Envelope's sleeves for Cocteau Twins and This Mortal Coil; 8vo's for The Durutti Column.

Another graphic design company who'd juxtaposed the letter V with a number was 8vo, founded in London in 1984 by Simon Johnstone, Mark Holt and Hamish Muir. The three of them were obsessed with Swiss and Modernist typography. Both Muir and Johnstone had studied in Basel while Holt had picked up the basics of Modernist typographers Piet Zwart and Jan Tschichold in San Francisco. Their first sleeve was for Factory, The Durutti Column's *Without Mercy* (coincidentally FAC84), an elegant combination of pulp card onto which was glued a postcard-like image by Matisse and some exquisite letter-pressed typography. On the reverse, the refined, swirling track titles were similarly stuck onto postcard-sized paper, in effect the back of the postcard. Given the apparent luxury of complete creative freedom, 8vo's response was to set themselves a very tight brief of their own making. 'It's quite difficult to find a starting point when you could start anywhere', said Muir. 'So actually using the production process, and trying to deconstruct it, saying, 'We've never done this, so why don't we do it and see how it shapes the project', can narrow the brief and make it easier'[15]. 8vo had made an impressive debut and would go on to design pretty much every release by The Durutti Column as well as publish the influential, if short-lived, typographic magazine, Octavo.

*****

All these designers had recognizable styles and their sleeves were seen as creative calling cards. However, it wasn't all Swiss typography and Modernism. Many designers simply responded to briefs and turned out decent work, often centred around a photograph of the artist because that's what the label wanted. Founded by Rob O'Connor in 1981, Stylorouge struck lucky with very early commissions, Siouxsie and the Banshees' *Juju* followed by their compilation, *Once Upon a Time - The Singles* – as fine a pair of covers as any that year. But thereafter they struggled a bit and had to accept some less than inspiring commissions including, in 1984, Chris Rea, Clannad and Gary Glitter – though their cover for Alison Moyet's *Alf* was at least highly visible. They are still going, still churning out hundreds of sleeves, including George Michael's *Faith*, Blur's *Parklife* and Pink Floyd's possibly final studio album *The Endless River*.

Aside from Saville, Garrett and 8vo, another important designer in Factory's formative years was Martyn Atkins. Having designed sleeves for A Certain Ratio, Section 25 and, lest we forget, *co*-designed (with Peter Saville) Joy Division's *Closer*, as well as non-Factory acts like Teardrop Explodes and Echo & The Bunnymen, Atkins set up Town & Country Planning Design, which would work extensively with Depeche Mode, often with photographer Brian Griffin. Their 1984 singles 'People Are People', 'Master and Servant' and 'Blasphemous Rumours', and album *Some Great Reward* were all designed by T&CP (as it came to be called). But that same year they also provided the intriguing *Mange Tout* cover for Blancmange (whose in-joke hieroglyphic 'code' set fans off in a vain deciphering quest) as well as sleeves for artists as wide-ranging as Penguin Café Orchestra and Severed Heads, with Echo & The Bunnymen (still) and The Pale Fountains in-between. When Atkins moved to the US in 1989, he sold the company to Stylorouge where it still resides as a sister company.

Yet another Saville and Garrett associate, Keith Breeden spent the early 80s designing sleeves, both freelance and as part of Assorted iMaGes, for the likes of The Gang of Four, Spear of Destiny and Blancmange, but it was his work for ABC that got him noticed, particularly his bold, brash, cartoon-like graphics for 'How To Be A Millionaire' in 1984 – a reaction to the rather austere sleeve for *Beauty Stab* the year before. The year also saw him set up his own agency, Design Keith Breeden, and during the second half of the decade his studio was responsible for the sleeves of more ABC, Scritti Politti's *Cupid & Psyche '85* (almost certainly the best sleeve of that year), Fine Young Cannibals, The Communards and others. Then, in 1992, he closed down DKB, moved to a cottage in north Wales and became a portrait artist.

Possibly the only graphic designer to have his mugshot on a sleeve (League Unlimited Orchestra's *Love and Dancing*, 1982), Ken Ansell designed many covers for John Foxx, DAF, Japan, XTC and Human League, before setting up The Design Clinic with Dave Dragon. As Ansell remembers: 'Sleeves in the 80s were all about style, creating a look to accompany the sound. Dave and I never had a 'house style' and consequently we were commissioned by Virgin to work on a number of sleeves where the bands wanted to have creative input. All of the Human League sleeves were designed in close collaboration with Phil Oakey and the band, and similarly XTC's with Andy Partridge. We enjoyed solving problems and collaborating. It helped at Clinic where we ended up solving problems for clients beyond the record industry'[16].

XL Design was started by two designers: Royston Edwards, who'd worked in illustration and magazines, and Tom Watkins, who was actually a furniture designer and had worked for Terence Conran, and even designed the interior of Sarm Studios. Which was how he met Trevor Horn, Jill Sinclair and Paul Morley, just as they were about to start ZTT. A commission to design the label's first release, 1983's *Into Battle*

With The Art Of Noise EP, led them to effectively become ZTT's in-house design team. In terms of record sales and public profile, 1984 was as much XL Design's year as any of those just discussed. David Smart, who'd joined them early on, described the adventure: 'I loved the bonkersness of it all (if that's a word) and I loved that anything seemed possible. I have always held on to that notion when designing. Frankie represented for me a subversive way of being and designing. The Art Of Noise had a mysterious madness and a charming playfulness. But actually I loved all of ZTT's acts as they all had a character and spirit that seems missing in much of contemporary music'[17]. Certainly, working with Paul Morley must have been a whole different ball game to working with the A&R departments of, say, EMI or CBS. 1984 saw a continuous stream of playful, irreverent and experimental product issued from their Poland Street office. Aside from having to keep up with the umpteen variations of sleeves for all the 12-inch remixes, there were posters, ads masquerading as manifestos and (famously) 'Jean Genet' boxer shorts, 'Virginia Woolf' vests and 'Andre Gide' socks. And then there were the Frankie Say T-shirts, which were not so much designed as screamed. That summer they were everywhere.

Somehow that year the company managed to design for artists on other labels too: Nik Kershaw, Nick Heyward, Kim Wilde. As Watkins confessed: 'Sometimes it worked, sometimes it didn't'. The sexing up of Kim Wilde didn't. 'The leather dress looked like a bin liner, with a belt wrapped around the middle'[18]. They played safe with another artist, though, providing the sleeve for Pet Shop Boys' debut, 'West End Girls'. The link would be enduring as by that time Mark Farrow[19] had joined the XL team and would go on to become almost synonymous with the long-term visual identity of Pet Shop Boys. Equally importantly, towards the end of 1984, Tom Watkins became the group's manager and would steer them to success through to the end of the decade.[20] Financial problems and Watkins' non-design preoccupations saw XL Design fold in 1986 with Edwards and Smart forming Accident Design, which provided them with the opportunity to credit their work as 'Designed by Accident'.

While Tom Watkins had gone from designing bands' sleeves to directly managing a group, graphic designer John Warwicker would join the actual ranks of a band – Freur (or 'squiggle') – as keyboard player, just in time for their one and only minor hit single, 'Doot-Doot' (1983). At the same time he joined another designer, Al McDowell, in setting up the Da Gama agency who would provide not only all the artwork for Freur, but also for Siouxsie and the Banshees and, in 1984, sleeves for Bananarama, Lloyd Cole, Psychedelic Furs, Thomas Leer, Savage Progress and Shriekback (the latter's *Jam Science* being one of the best sleeves of the year). Warwicker would leave Freur in 1986 to re-focus on design, and five years later left Da Gama, to co-found the creative collective Tomato[21].

Another designer-musician (or the other way round) was The Cure's Porl Thompson who, along with photographer Andy Vella, formed Parched Art. Together they would provide the majority of The Cure's artwork including, in 1984, 'The Caterpillar' and *The Top*. Vella was also made Art Director of The Cure's label, Fiction Records. Artist Russell Mills, known at first for his Royal College of Art thesis which exhaustively illustrated all of Brian Eno's 70s lyrics, and then for his association with Wire members Bruce Gilbert and Graham Lewis (he performed with them on their 1982 album, *MZUI*), became better known for his exquisite album covers – of which 1984's *The Pearl* by Harold Budd and Brian Eno and *Exorcising Ghosts*, a posthumous Japan compilation, were an aesthetic watershed. He would later return to music in the 90s with his Undark project (involving many of the musicians he'd designed for)[22]. Another artist and fellow Kurt Schwitters fan, Chris Morton, had been design director during Stiff Records' heyday before going freelance in 1982. Amongst the many relatively straightforward design commissions, he loved to contribute something painted, Working Week's 'Venceremos' being a great example. Going further away from the mainstream was Steve Stapleton, whose music (as Nurse With Wound) and record covers (as Babs Santini) would stretch the boundaries of both. In the late 70s and early 80s, Stapleton worked as a sign-writer in a small graphics agency in London's Soho, although his sleeves (mainly black and white and all the more powerful for it) were more surreal than typographic. 1984 saw him design for other groups too, notably his new friend David Tibet's Current 93, but it's the sleeves for NWW that really stand out.

Da Gama's *Jam Science* for Shriekback, DKB's 'Wood Beez' single for Scritti Politti and Brian Griffin's photograph for Echo & The Bunnymen's *Ocean Rain*.

There were many others of course. Sheffield University philosophy student, Ian Anderson, designed his first proper sleeve in 1984 for Missing Persons, the band he was then managing. It was nothing special, but he would soon set up The Designers Republic with fellow student Nick Phillips. The fact that neither had studied design didn't seem to bother them or their clients. The Designers Republic would go on to become hugely influential in the 90s and 00s. A final mention (almost a felony in its cursoriness) should be given to Benoît Hennebert, Les Disques du Crépuscule's in-house designer, whose beautiful sleeves were an inspiration to many young British creatives and label owners.

*****

Photography, of course, was an essential part of the process of marketing a band. Not every sleeve featured a photo of the artist, or even photography (in the early 80s much was purely graphic). Nevertheless, a photo of a band on the front or back cover or

164

inside sleeve was the preferred choice of many artists, managers and labels – and designers.

Like the graphic designers mentioned, many photographers did other work but music was a powerful magnet for most. Basically, they took four types of photograph: for record sleeves, promotional portrait shots for labels, live shots for the serious music papers and feature shots for the style magazines. Some, like Gered Mankowitz had been working with bands since the 60s, others like Pennie Smith, Jill Furmanovsky and Sheila Rock[23] (the latter's photos featuring on some 25 sleeves in 1984 alone) since the early 70s. But as with the impact of punk on graphic design so too did it create a new wave of photographers in the second half of the 70s.

It was an exciting time to be a photographer. There were so many groups, most of whom were approachable and happy to be directed by someone with a few creative ideas. Initially the money may have not been great, but it was relatively easy to build up a portfolio and establish a style. Stylist par excellence was Dutchman Anton Corbijn who moved to Britain in 1979 and started taking photographs for the NME. His grainy, monochrome shots of Joy Division, for example, perfectly captured the zeitgeist: that of the symbiotic relationship of earnest, black and white weekly music press covering earnest, monochrome post-punk. By 1984, Corbijn was one of Britain's most in-demand rock photographers. He seemed to be able to transform a humdrum musician or band in a mundane setting into thoughtful heroes placed in an elegiac landscape or intense interior. That year, his work featured on some 20 record sleeves, including iconic shots of Echo & The Bunnymen, Frankie Goes To Hollywood, Fad Gadget, David Sylvian, Propaganda, Siouxsie And The Banshees – and of course U2, whose impassioned, grandiose soundscapes wedded to Corbijn's coarse, heroic portraiture would create the perfect mythology (even, later, in colour).

Working in a different style altogether, but equally stylish, Brian Griffin created highly refined, staged, mostly colour shots, often outdoors and with a surreal twist. His classic photographs of a blue-washed Echo & The Bunnymen standing in a rowing boat in Cornwall's Carnglaze Caverns for *Ocean Rain* and the juxtaposition of bride and groom against Round Oak Steelworks near Birmingham on the cover of Depeche Mode's *Some Great Reward* were both from 1984. Peter Ashworth took the iconic *Touch* shot of Annie Lennox as well as Tina Turner's *Private Dancer*, Frankie Goes To Hollywood, Bananarama and lots of Soft Cell and Marc Almond (he even played drums with The The and Marc and the Mambas). Trevor Key was the photographer of choice for many designers, especially Peter Saville. His forte was stills rather than band photography, and as such his input was often overlooked, for example in the case of New Order sleeves. One of his first covers was *Tubular Bells*, and it's a little-known fact that he turned designer himself after scrawling the Virgin logo on a paper napkin. 'That'll do', said Richard Branson. Brian Aris started as a news photographer working in Northern Ireland, the Middle East and Vietnam before moving into celebrity portraiture, including taking the Band Aid official photograph. Terry O'Neill worked extensively with David Bowie and Elton John and Hollywood actors (he was married to Faye Dunaway in the mid-80s). Just starting out, Nick Knight would move into fashion photography and set up SHOWstudio.

There were plenty more, including two photographers best known for their reportage of London's youth culture. Graham Smith, not content with designing Sade's *Diamond Life* and early Spandau Ballet sleeves, photo-documented London's club scene, later collected in *We Can Be Heroes: London Clubland 1976-1984*. Derek Ridgers, too, was a key chronicler, his work constantly in the style magazines, collected in *When We Were Young: Club and Street Portraits 1978-1987*. Kevin Cummins was strongly associated with the Manchester scene and was for many years chief photographer at NME. Bleddyn Butcher, raised in Australia, followed The Birthday Party over to London, and became synonymous for his portraits of Nick Cave alongside other work for the NME. Simon Fowler was principal photographer for Smash Hits, while also shooting around 30 sleeves in 1984 alone and having one of pop's largest portfolios thereafter. Eric Watson succeeded Fowler at Smash Hits and then became strongly identified with Pet Shop Boys, including shooting several of their videos. AJ Barratt was closely associated with ZTT. Ross Halfin shot 70s rock and punk for Sounds, then helped set up Kerrang!, thereafter making a name for himself as metal photographer of choice. There were so many others: Andy Catlin, Steve Pyke, Steve Rapport, Alan Ballard, Bay Hippisley to name just a few more.

But as the 80s morphed into the 90s, things started to change. The canvases shrunk from 12 to 5 inches square; a number of record companies went bust; others merged and became more hard-nosed about promotion with some preferring to spend more on videos than a static cover; and it became harder and harder for a graphic designer to rely solely on music industry commissions. Of course, there was still highly creative work being produced in the 90s: Mark Farrow for Pet Shop Boys, Me Company for Björk, Designers Republic for Warp and others. But come the new millennium, the album as an object was under threat, the artist's image effectively reduced to a tiny square jpg on iTunes or Spotify. That's perhaps an exaggeration, but not far off.

Chapter 13: Sound and Vision
Radio and television

[1984] was the year of the super-pirates – the big new operations that broadcast 24 hours a day on high power across London that for the first time were influencing music in the capital, not just reacting to what was being played.[1]
Stephen Hebditch

Hello, and welcome to another Top of the Pops – another half hour in the company of attractive young people wearing extraordinary trousers.[2]
John Peel

Make it live and give it balls.[3]
Jeremy Isaacs, commissioner of The Tube

In 1984, radio was the medium through which most people listened to music – pop, rock, classical, everything – in the kitchen, at work, in the car. It still is. In this age of on-demand music streaming services, most people *still* listen to radio (terrestrial or internet)[4]. Why? Partly it's because many like the patter, whether about the music, weather or a traffic report. And partly it's the tyranny of choice: Spotify has so much music available that it's hard to know where to start. You want somebody else – a DJ, a chart, any trustworthy authority – to choose. In the mid-80s, you couldn't get more trustworthy, or authoritarian, than BBC Radio One. There *was* independent radio but, incredibly, it was still in its infancy.

Unlike in the States where commercial radio had been in existence since the First World War, and by 1922 had more than 550 commercial stations, Britain opted for a 'public service'. Created, at arm's length from the Government, the British Broadcasting Corporation held a monopoly on radio for some 45 years. Moreover, when rock and teenagers appeared in the 50s, the BBC's response was largely to ignore both. In the 60s, it may have launched Top Of The Pops[5], but radio-wise it was still in the dark ages, relying on the Light Programme[6] which since 1945 had been wowing the great British public with Mantovani and Bing Crosby.

If you wanted to hear decent pop music, you had to tune into Radio Luxembourg or, from 1964, the new pirate radio stations anchored in the murky waters, geographically and legally, off Britain's coastline. The government responded by introducing the Marine Etc Broadcasting Offences Act of 1967, effectively sinking the pirates (although they didn't totally go away) and at the same time handing the pop portfolio to the BBC. At least it now had to 'get with it'. And so in September of that year Radio One was launched, with most of the DJs having been recruited from the pirates, including John Peel, Tony Blackburn, Ed Stewart, Kenny Everett, Pete Murray and Tommy Vance.

Within a few years, Radio One was attracting huge audiences, but it was a monopoly until Independent Local Radio (ILR) finally arrived in the autumn of 1973 – initially with two independent London stations, Capital and LBC, followed a few years later by 17 more scattered around the country. They were local, not national, founded during a time of great economic upheaval and highly regulated by government, but by the early 80s were giving the BBC a run for its money. Kenny Everett left Radio One to join Capital, while David 'Kid' Jensen went the other way, from Radio Trent to the Beeb. By 1984 there were another 34 ILR stations but still no national one. That would have to wait until the early 90s with commercial stations like Kiss FM (who'd been transmitting illegally from 1985), Classic FM and Heart.

Two key things happened to radio in 1984. Firstly, 20 years after the launch of Radio Caroline in 1964, there was a resurgence in illegal *land-based* stations, especially in London, mostly focussing on black or dance music; and secondly the legitimate ILR stations, held a conference to respond to the above while at the same time seeking a loosening of restrictions on their own operations (of which more in due course).

*****

'It was the year of the super-pirates', wrote Stephen Hebditch, Editor of TX / Radio Today, the most popular pirate radio magazine in 80s London. 'Big new operations that broadcast 24 hours a day on high power across London that for the first time were influencing music in the capital'[7] rather than the other way around. In effect it was when they stopped being a hobby and became a business. Whereas previously illegal land-based stations had typically broadcast for just a few hours on a Sunday, rigging up flimsy aerials in trees as much as on tops of tower blocks, many stations became more brazen, aided by advances in simple, cheap but powerful transmitter equipment, which could be set up and taken down quickly, just about staying one step ahead of the police[8].

There were many stations: Radio Invicta ('Soul Over London') and Radio Jackie had been operating since the 70s, while Alice's Restaurant and Dread Broadcasting Corporation had been transmitting since the early 80s; Neneh Cherry was a DJ on the latter. New stations like JFM and Horizon both went 24/7 in February 1984 and hosted a strong roster of DJs, including a very young Gilles Peterson who worked for both[9]. The music covered all sorts, including much that you would never hear on Radio One (John Peel excepted), Capital or most of the other ILR stations. In many ways, pirate radio was far more representative of 1984's wider music scene than the official stations. Dread, for example, run by Leroy Anderson – whose half-sister, Rita, was married to Bob Marley – filled the reggae void. Alice's Restaurant meanwhile played rock which, oddly, had become somewhat marginalised on radio following the rise of new pop. London Weekend Radio was launched by DJ Tim Westwood who focussed on hip-hop, a still-new genre which rarely got aired on the 'majors', In effect, the pirates were providing the same kind of service as indie labels and fanzines, and like them they were all over the country, from Carousel Radio in Wilmslow to Radio Freedom International in Fife. Ethnic minority radio was also on the rise, particularly

Indian and Greek, providing a genuine public service whilst also doing very nicely from local advertising. A few sea-based stations also continued transmitting. The now American-backed Caroline and Laser 558, for example, were still bobbing about on the North Sea relaying hits to south-east England, Holland and Belgium, though their playlists were rigidly commercial.

Typical pirate studio and transmitter/aerial set-up.

In June, meanwhile, the ILR stations convened the so-called Heathrow Conference at which they complained about the pirates, demanded fewer restrictions from the Independent Broadcasting Association (IBA) and talked directly to the Home Office's Leon Brittan. Five years into Thatcher's free market crusade, they found a sympathetic ear, and from this date on there was less control of playlists, more advertising, more competition. In effect, independent radio started to become *commercial* radio. In addition, the following month the Government introduced the 1984 Telecommunications Act, privatizing British Telecom, while at the same time taking the opportunity to amend the 1949 Wireless Telegraphy Act, which finally, legally, allowed them to seize pirate station equipment. The raids increased in the autumn and by the end of the year many stations were forced to close, including Dread. In the following years, some of them would submit bids for licenses, there would be mergers and takeovers (just like in the City), but many preferred to stay underground and continue to play cat-and-mouse with the authorities.

Meanwhile, Capital and most of the other legit independent stations were going from strength to strength. When Chris Tarrant joined Capital in 1984, ratings soared. Tarrant, formerly a presenter on the mildly anarchic children's television programme, Tiswas, was the forerunner of celebrities like Chris Evans and Jonathan Ross. But no-one tuned in for the music he played. For that, people turned to young, music-obsessed DJs like Gary Crowley, who'd already been at the station for four years but was still only 23.

*****

However, it was BBC Radio One that dominated the pop airwaves, reaching 44% of all adults compared with 42% for the *entire* ILR network of stations[10]. DJs like Mike

169

Read, Gary Davies, Janice Long, Dave Lee Travis, Steve Wright, Peter Powell and Annie Nightingale were either household names or were at least famous enough to open a supermarket or switch on the Christmas lights in Yeovil. Mike Read of course was famous for having 'banned' Frankie's 'Relax' on Radio One's prime time Breakfast Show. Except he didn't – he just took exception to the lyrics and decided he wouldn't play it any more. It took ⌐ ⌐meone a lot more senior to actually ban it (Derek Chinnery, Controller of Radio One). Read was ubiquitous, including on TV, presenting Top of the Pops, Saturday Superstore and Pop Quiz. Gary Davies was Radio One's eligible bachelor, a medallion-wearing lothario who took over the lunchtime show in 1984. The buzzword in Radio One(der)land was 'fun'. Producers were instructed to incorporate phone-ins from made-up characters, competitions and comic sketches. And then there were the Radio One Roadshows, enforcing the fun on seaside towns every summer, broadcasting live from an articulated truck to astonishingly large audiences (30,000 was typical). The format was basically the same as the radio shows, except they also had 'live' bands and the pranks were visible. There was even a confined-to-1984 TV spin-off, 1 On the Road.

On the more alternative front, David 'Kid' Jensen presented the early evening show just before Peel, with whom he had formed an unlikely TV double act (of which more later) until leaving in the summer for Capital. His slot was taken by relative newcomer Janice Long[11] – only the second female DJ to be employed by Radio One, after Annie Nightingale, who'd been appointed over a decade earlier. Local BBC Radio stations also played their part. Steve Barker's On the Wire for BBC Radio Lancashire, for example, was first broadcast on 16th September 1984, with Adrian Sherwood and Keith Leblanc in the studio. At time of writing, it's still going: the longest-running alternative music show on UK radio[12].

And then there was John Peel. So much has been written about Peel and his place in championing alternative popular music (he was almost a genre in his own right, yet paradoxically impossible to pin down), that it's easy to forget that in 1984 he was fighting to stay on the air. In truth, this was nothing new: he'd always been treated with a fair degree of suspicion by both BBC senior management and much of Radio One's young audience who viewed him as an old hippy or, conversely, didn't 'get' the new stuff he played either. After the heyday of punk when he was broadcasting five nights a week, by the end of 1978 he'd lost one night to Tommy Vance's Friday Night Rock Show and in October 1984 lost another to the terribly named Into the Music on Thursdays (again hosted by Vance). This was the kind of music Radio Two played, easy-on-the-ear, Adult Oriented Rock, and as such barely lasted a year, replaced in 1985 by a perkier rock show fronted by a young Andy Kershaw[13].

It seemed unthinkable that, by the end of the year, Peel was only on Monday to Wednesdays. And yet, he remained hugely influential, not least to students, NME-readers and those old enough to have been bored teenagers in 1977. He would play a bewildering variety of genres. His first show of the year (2 January 1984) included Frankie Goes To Hollywood (pre-ban, though he continued to play them anyway), Hagar the Womb (punk), The Leather Nun (Swedish industrial goth), Toxic Reasons

(US hardcore) and Zoviet France (ambient avant-garde) amongst many others.

The Peel Sessions were another attraction – to both listeners and bands alike. They had originated in 1967 as a way around an archaic Musicians Union-related rule called Needle Time which meant that the BBC could only play a certain number of hours' worth of records. Specially recorded sessions were the answer. Other programmes had them too – Kid Jensen and Janice Long for instance – but it was Peel's that went down in history.[14] If you were a new band, to have a Peel Session under your belt was reason enough to say you'd made it and you could gracefully disappear without ever releasing a further note (where are you now Autumn 1904, Shoot! Dispute and Chinese Gangster Element, all whom recorded sessions in 1984). But for most it was the perfect stepping stone, and for established bands it was almost unheard of to decline an invitation. Some bands recorded several sessions over a number of years; The Fall hold the record with 24 between 1978-2004. In 1984, some 122 bands made the trip to the BBC's Maida Vale studios where engineers would attempt to capture 15 minutes' worth of songs. A band would normally turn up at noon, set up their equipment, record from 2:30pm until 6:00pm, after which they'd have until midnight to mix the results. For years you could only hear these on the radio, usually two sessions per show (but often repeated). Some of course made it onto bootlegs. It wasn't until 1987 that a label, Strange Fruit, started releasing them officially.

BBC opposites: John Peel and Mike Read, the latter hosting a Radio One Roadshow in sunny Cleethorpes.

Peel was everywhere. Aside from his regular Radio One audience, he reached a much wider one through his half-hour shows on the BBC World Service which he hosted for over 25 years.[15] He could be found playing roadshows all over the country, comfortably presiding over the ICA Rock Week in October and uncomfortably co-presenting Top of the Pops. Towards the end of his life, new technology enabled him to record some of his shows from home; at first it went out live but later some were pre-recorded. It wasn't the same, but it suited his lifestyle. And as the new millennium progressed, radio production changed at a rate of knots. Radio One was overtaken by Radio Two as the Beeb's most listened to station; digital broadcasting ushered in yet more programming, including podcasts, both on BBC and commercial radio; and internet radio and streaming services like Spotify have opened things up even more.

*****

Similar changes have swept through the broadcasting and consumption of music on television. In 1984, watching TV was something you did from an armchair in the front room on a relatively small screen from a choice of four terrestrial channels and in real time. Nowadays you could be watching on a large flat screen in the sitting room, or on a tablet or phone on the train, from a choice of terrestrial, satellite, cable or internet, and whenever you like. Indeed, you can now re-watch multiple episodes of Top Of The Pops on any number of platforms. Back in the 80s, unless you remembered to set the timer on your clunky VCR, you had one shot at it.

Top Of The Pops had debuted in 1964 and twenty years later was still going strong. Like its audio sister Radio One, it was *the* show to be on. In the 70s it was regularly attracting audiences of 17 million every Thursday evening, largely because it had no competition. So important was an invitation to appear that often a band would interrupt a tour in Europe or America and fly back just for that three-minute slot. The rules for inclusion were very simple. It was a chart show: only acts whose records were going up the charts were allowed on; no act was permitted to appear on consecutive weeks (except for the top spot); and every show ended with the #1. But that still gave scope for the pluggers to infiltrate the BBC bar and schmooze with the producers, cameramen and floor managers. Before he became a football agent in the late 80s, Eric Hall was a plugger for EMI, one of the best. 'I used to get champagne for everybody... One time Cliff Richard stood up in the bar, and announced, "Eric Hall's expenses have just gone platinum"... I do miss [it]'[16].

Top Of The Pops opened 1984 with a 20th anniversary special on 5 January, featuring blasts from the past alongside new acts, including Frankie Goes To Hollywood performing 'Relax', six days before the ban. And before the month was out, Madonna made her debut performance with 'Holiday'. As with Radio One, 'fun' was pre-requisite. The 70s era of choreographed dance troupes – Pan's People, Legs & Co, Ruby Flipper, Zoo – were replaced by a non-stop party atmosphere, with streamers, balloons and lots of cheering. At times it looked like an American political party convention. But it certainly wasn't political, as Billy Bragg remembered. 'Steve Wright was hosting the show, and he came over at rehearsal, and asked me to explain the politics of the song to help him with the intro... I talked him through it and he listened thoughtfully and nodded a lot. Then, when he came to it, he just said, "Ladies and gentlemen, it's Billy Bragg!"'[17]

The shows were presented by Radio One DJs, and by 1984 it was always a pair of them. By far the most interesting double act was John Peel and David Jensen. Aside from a cameo appearance 'playing' mandolin with The Faces in 1971, Peel had managed to avoid television for the rest of that decade but was coerced into appearing on a 1981 Christmas special and thereafter was a semi-reluctant regular[18]. Calling themselves the Rhythm Pals, they would send the whole thing up, occasionally wearing fancy dress (the Roman centurion outfits were particularly memorable). Although the more outgoing of the two, Jensen played the straight man to Peel's laconic quips. In 1984 he was on a roll, introducing Duran Duran as 'White boys on port and lemon, lots of ice', and 'At number 12, 'Master and Servant', both by Depeche Mode'. After Jensen left for Capital, he teamed up with Janice Long and the quips got even weirder[19]. If not specifically a high point in Top of the Pops history, 1984 certainly saw it in rude health and it was still a thrill to see your favourite band mime their way through their latest hit. But from the second half of the 80s, it was a slow slide into old age and was rationalized out of existence in 2006.

Odd couple comperes Kid Jensen and John Peel (as the Rhythm Pals) on Top Of The Pops, and Jools Holland and Paula Yates on The Tube. It was hard to tell which duo took more of the piss.

For years, Top Of The Pops had no competition at all, but in the early 80s a new kid was on the block. The Tube was a cooler, edgier, non-chart show broadcast live on Friday evenings from a studio in Newcastle. It had launched in the first week of Channel 4's existence in November 1982, the brainchild of the Channel's founding Chief Executive Jeremy Isaacs and producer Malcolm Gerrie. Isaacs was particularly keen to have edgy content from outside of London and Gerrie delivered it (tweaking the format of an earlier music show, the short-lived *Alright Now* for Tyne Tees Television). By 1984 The Tube had settled into a format of performances from three or four bands, interviews and 'magazine' sections. If Top Of The Pops was production-line slick, The Tube was gloriously ramshackle. Co-presenters Jools Holland and Paula Yates made a strange but watchable couple[20], the former charmingly flippant, the latter fake-ditsy and flirtatious – with a supporting cast of cool, sharp interviewers like Muriel Gray and Leslie Ash[21]. Being live, things invariably went wrong and the bands often sounded terrible, and yet it was thrilling TV – somehow more honest than Top Of The Pops and definitely more hip. Its specials on Belfast, Berlin and (of all places) Hull were excellent.

The Tube couldn't keep going 52 weeks of the year so during its intermittent breaks, other music programmes made brief appearances. Switch had been the first 'gap filler'

173

in 1983, presenting three live acts each week plus magazine features from around the country, hosted by the unfeasibly young Graham-Fletcher Cook (19) and Yvonne French (21). It failed to get a second chance the following year though, and the rather more basic High Band simply broadcast recorded concerts by the likes of Thomas Dolby, Siouxsie and the Banshees and Ultravox. In 1985 it was the turn of something called ECT (Extra Celestial Transmission), dedicated to heavy rock.

This was just the tip of the iceberg. Channel 4 was essentially a commissioning body and around this time launched a mini-torrent of music programmes, all of which were short-lived. The indulgent Play At Home series gave several groups free rein to make a film about themselves, the most interesting being New Order's tongue-in-cheek documentary on Factory Records (which included Gillian Gilbert interviewing a naked Tony Wilson in the bath) and Siouxsie and the Banshee's unsuccessfully surreal take on Alice in Wonderland[22]. Debuting in the spring, Earsay, presented by Gary Cowley, Nicky Horne (both from Capital Radio) and Lesley-Anne Jones, was infamous for the occasion when Horne asked Phil Oakey how much money he had in his bank account. Rebellious Jukebox, produced by Miles Copeland and directed by Godley and Creme, meanwhile, was an attempt to combine music and comedy. Shooting started in the summer in London Dockland's Limehouse Studios, but it didn't work and only two episodes were ever broadcast. The Other Side of the Tracks took the rather safer option of Paul Gambaccini earnestly interviewing a range of artists.

There was plenty happening on the Beeb too. Seventies stalwart The Old Grey Whistle Test had begun life as a kind of televisual version of the NME or Melody Maker, featuring 'album artists' and presented by studious, authentic-rock gatekeepers, the most famous of which was 'Whispering' Bob Harris. As 1984 dawned, a new series ditched the 'Old' and 'Grey', substituted the old title music with something electronic and moved from dependable late night to slightly uncomfortable mid-evening. Bob Harris had long gone, succeeded by a string of sanguine, authoritative presenters such as Annie Nightingale from Radio One and the double act of Mark Ellen and David Hepworth from Smash Hits, which spoke volumes about the direction BBC producers felt they needed to go. It was a very different double act to The Tube's, but Whistle Test was a different type of programme, driven more by journalism than yoof culture. 'It worked well with me and Dave', remarked Ellen, 'but neither of us was a 'huge' personality which TV tends to favour. Things fell into place when the charismatic Andy Kershaw arrived and Dave and I could settle into being the wiser, quieter ones'[23]. Kershaw was a force of nature, a telly natural, even though he'd never done any. During the early 80s he'd booked bands at Leeds University, briefly worked in local radio and for the first half of 1984 acted as Billy Bragg's driver and tour manager. He got the job simply by being with Bragg in the Whistle Test studio one day and obviously made an impression. 'We needed an *enfant terrible*' explained producer Trevor Dann[24].

Like The Tube, Whistle Test mixed performance with interviews and covered a wide variety of genres. In one show you might get The Chevalier Brothers, Blancmange and a special on 20 Years of Pirate Radio, while at the end of the year Lou Reed and Penguin Café Orchestra were rubbing shoulders, together with reports on Peel Sessions and Thompson Twins in Paris. And yet it was the antithesis of both The Tube and Top Of The Pops: it wasn't a chart show, the studio looked like a rehearsal space, in which there was just about room for the band, certainly no audience. At the end of a song, no-one cheered. It just ended. And so too did Whistle Test, victim of Janet Street Porter's appointment in 1987 as BBC Head of Youth Programmes. Presumably, Whistle Test simply wasn't youthful enough[25].

Another hangover from the 70s was Sight and Sound in Concert, broadcast simultaneously on BBC2 and Radio One, usually from a venue called the Golddiggers in Chippenham for some reason. By 1984, it still walked a tightrope between old- (Gary Moore, Curtis Mayfield) and new-school (Blancmange, Wang Chung) but in its favour the concerts were live and not off-the-shelf. Two programmes that were more akin to – and in fact had pre-empted –The Tube were Riverside, broadcast from a Thameside studio near London's Hammersmith Odeon, and Oxford Road Show, from the BBC studios in Oxford Road in Manchester. The former was produced by the Whistle Test team and included elements of broader pop culture. The limited run from 1982-83 was hard to fathom. Its Manchester-based sibling lasted a little longer, trendily truncating itself to ORS84 with bands like The Cure, Simple Minds and The Alarm playing live (this time with crowd), but after ORS85 the plug was pulled on this too. Perhaps it was simply that they weren't different enough from everything else.

It wasn't all concerts and videos. There were also 'panel' shows. At one end of the spectrum, there was the banal but mildly entertaining Pop Quiz, made up of two teams of musicians, with Mike Read acting as question master. Its most famous episode was its last (28 December 1984) when Duran Duran were pitted against Spandau Ballet[26]. At the other end of the spectrum was Eight Days a Week, a music discussion show compered by proper journalist Robin Denselow, his guests ranging from the mildly intellectual or opinionated (Gartside, Bragg, Morrissey) offset by more down to earth characters (Noddy Holder, Holly Johnson, Tracie Young). It was a talking shop but it filled a gap. As its name suggests, Rockschool offered practical tips on music-making, a rare thing on British television. It was limited to two short series in 1983/4 and 1987, and only confirmed that pop music and education make uneasy bedfellows.

And still pop groups were everywhere: on BBC1's Late Night in Concert series (introduced by Annie Nightingale) in the autumn; BBC2's Rock Around the Clock 15-hour special in August; and Jonathan King's Entertainment USA which focussed heavily on music. There would be forced appearances on children's programmes, like Saturday Superstore (although its phone-ins were sometimes risky affairs: Matt Bianco were called a 'bunch of wankers' by one caller), Razzamatazz (presented by a 16-year old Lisa Stansfield, amongst others) and Wide Awake Club (which launched the career of Mike Myers). In addition, appearances on prime-time chat shows like Harty and Wogan could significantly affect the chart trajectory of an artist's latest single, especially if you physically attacked the presenter, as Grace Jones famously did on Harty in 1982. And of course, there was always The Eurovision Song Contest, with playfully acerbic commentary from Wogan. The 1984 contest was won by clean-cut Swedish brothers The Herreys – 'the dancing deodorants', as they were called in their home county – with the nonsensical 'Diggi-Loo Diggi-Ley'; Britain's entry, Belle & The Devotions' 'Love Games' came seventh, booed at the end by a contingent of the Luxembourg audience, still angry about England football fans running riot in the city six months earlier. (Previous UK Eurovision winners Sandie Shaw and Bucks Fizz had eventful years. Seventeen years after 'Puppet on a String', Shaw had a minor hit covering The Smiths' 'Hand in Glove', while Bucks Fizz enjoyed a brief renaissance with 'Talking in Your Sleep' – though the year would end badly for them. Following a tour bus crash, band and crew ended up in hospital, and Mike Nolan only just made it out of a three-day coma).

It wouldn't last. Sight and Sound, Eight Days a Week, Rockschool and Pop Quiz all had their plugs pulled by the end of 1984[27], ORS ended in 1985, Whistle Test and The Tube in 1987, the latter hastened by Jools Holland's infamous and injudicious use of the phrase 'ungroovy fuckers' in a live trailer. The mini-torrent of Channel 4 programmes gave way to yoof shows which were broader in scope but equally short-lived. Even Top Of The Pops started showing its age in the late 80s with various new producers brought in to try to keep it going. For Malcolm Gerrie, who had moved to independent television production, the music scene had lost something and it had affected what he and others were trying to put on the box: 'It was a funny time, actually, the end of the eighties, beginning of the nineties, pre-Brit pop, the fag-end of post-punk…'[28]

Two important comedy series, which also happened to feature a lot of music, were The Young Ones and Spitting Image. The former, an anarchic sitcom in its second series, was set in a squalid house occupied by four undergraduates. Aside from its theme song, a raucous version of Cliff Richard's titular hit, each episode featured a band playing in the house or occasionally on the street outside; in the 1984 series these included Motorhead, Madness and The Damned amongst others. The series also saw two of its stars have hits themselves: hippy Neil (played by Nigel Planer) had an in-character #2 hit with a cover of Traffic's 'Hole in My Shoe', while Alexei Sayle, who played the landlord, had an out-of-character rap hit earlier in the year with 'Ullo John! Gotta New Motor?'.

If The Young Ones played with politics, Spitting Image went for the jugular. Launched in February 1984, the show consisted of grotesque latex puppets which mercilessly parodied Britain's politicians, royal family and pop stars. Mick Jagger always seemed to be high, Ringo Starr always drunk, Phil Collins always self-pitying, and Michael Jackson's skin got lighter with each episode. And as with The Young Ones, there were spin-off singles, kicking off in 1984 with 'Nancy Regan' screeching 'Da Do Run Run', and Sting singing a re-worded version of 'Every Breath You Take', set to a video portraying how terrible world leaders were. The lyrics didn't beat about the bush:

Every bomb you make. Every job you take. Every heart you break, every Irish wake. I'll be watching you.
Every wall you build, Every one you've killed, Every grave you've filled, all the blood you've spilled, I'll be watching you.

Needless to say, it was never released.

If BBC1, BBC2 and Channel 4 were tripping over themselves to cover rock and pop, ITV's contribution was poor. Profiles in Rock (Toto!), The Best of Saturday Night Live (Carly Simon!), and the unthrillingly titled Rock Concert (Sad Café!) – although they redeemed themselves with the South Bank Show's high culture specials on Malcolm McLaren, Weather Report and Paul McCartney's *Give My Regards to Broad Street* (about which it tried to be kind). But it did have ads, and from 1984, both current and heritage pop would play an increasingly important part in the selling of product. At the beginning of the year Michael Jackson could be seen promoting Pepsi (even if he never drank the stuff), and the following year Marvin Gaye's 'I Heard It Thru the Grapevine' was appropriated for Levi's Jeans 'Laundrette' ad.

Spitting Image, The Young Ones and Miami Vice: required viewing for mid-80s hipsters.

Satellite and cable TV were slow to start on this side of the Atlantic – the main reason why MTV didn't launch a UK version until 1997. A fledgling Sky started business transmitting to 10,000 homes in Swindon in January 1984 (with Kate Bush, of all people, cutting the ribbon), followed a couple of months later by Music Box which ran a pan-European 24-hour cable and satellite channel from offices in London. But it took a number of years for the infrastructure to arrive and audiences to sign up. In the meantime, the nearest equivalent to wall-to-wall videos, The Chart Show (1986), wasn't on cable or satellite, but terrestrial (Channel 4). Another reason why the UK was slow to ape MTV was down to an existing culture of music programmes like Top Of The Pops and Whistle Test which focussed on bands performing and being interviewed in the studio, *supplemented* with videos.

*****

If music programmes reached a high point in 1984, in terms of quantity if not quality, then the same year saw a big increase in the way television series and films –

177

particularly in the US – used pop music as an integral part of the production. Traditionally most producers commissioned new or library music, but the American crime drama Miami Vice broke the mould. From its first episode in September 1984, music director Jan Hammer peppered each episode not just with his own incidental music but dozens of recent hits, spending thousands of dollars in the process[29]. People would watch it as much to check out that week's music selection as the story. In fact, in terms of promotional influence, having a song included on Miami Vice was even better than MTV. The soundtrack album, for instance, stayed on top of the US album chart for 11 weeks. And Phil Collins in particular was strongly linked to the series. American audiences visually associate his 'In the Air Tonight' much more with Crockett and Tubbs driving through Miami at night than the song's rather dull promo video of three years earlier. Collins even acted in a later episode.

In feature films, and again especially in Hollywood where the budgets were bigger, things really took off. 1984 was the year when pop and films got it together big time. *Against All Odds, Beverley Hills Cop, Ghostbusters, Romancing the Stone, The Woman in Red* and *Sixteen Candles* were indiscriminately filled with pop songs, designed to attract ever younger audiences and to sell the accompanying soundtrack album, which in turn re-sold the film. In the case of *Purple Rain, Footloose* and *Breakin'*, the film and soundtrack were almost inseparable. Giorgio Moroder turned Fritz Lang's 1927 *Metropolis* into what was effectively a heavily extended remix on coloured vinyl, having added synth rock and colourised the film's original monochrome print. Even that year's *Repo Man* (second division punk), *Dune* (Eno, Toto, Sting in a codpiece), *Paris, Texas* (Ry Cooder's spaghetti western guitar twangs) – films which weren't cashing in on mainstream pop – were discussed very much in terms of their soundtracks; and when they weren't, as in the case of Brad Fiedel's underrated score for *Terminator*, they should have been. As, obviously, was Talking Heads' *Stop Making Sense*, possibly the best concert film of all time.

Often the soundtrack album was more successful than the film: *Eddie and the Cruisers* was a critical and commercial flop but the album went quadruple platinum. It could work in reverse too, as in the curious case of *This is Spinal Tap*. If the film seemed real, the album sounded even realer. So perfect was the parody that on first impressions it seemed indistinguishable from any other competent heavy metal album, thus rendering it (the joke) nigh-on pointless. For British bands trying to break America, having a song in the right movie could make or cement a reputation. Simple Minds' 'Don't You Forget About Me', Psychedelic Furs' 'Pretty in Pink' and OMD's 'If You Leave' were mid-80s, middle-of-the-road tipping points for all three bands – having featured in anglophile director John Hughes's early teen films, *The Breakfast Club* and *Pretty in Pink*.

Britain was much slower to pick up on the trend. True, 'pop' musicians were being commissioned to score films   Peter Gabriel (*Birdy*), Mike Oldfield (*The Killing Fields*), Mark Knopfler (*Cal, Comfort and Joy*) and even Eurythmics (*1984*) all made their debut soundtracks in 1984 – but they were predominantly 'traditional' instrumental affairs. To pepper a film with recent hits just wasn't done this side of the

Atlantic, though Julien Temple would try with *Absolute Beginners*. As for television, there was no mid-80s equivalent of Miami Vice in the UK, although Echo & The Bunnymen might have sounded good accompanying a car chase in, say, Morecambe Vice[30]. The Young Ones was probably the only case of including pop music as a core element of the production.

Of course the 90s saw its fair share of decent music programmes – The Word, The White Room and Later – and the internet has utterly changed the way we experience music on screen. But it was hard to beat the early 80s central triumvirate of Top Of The Pops, The Tube and Whistle Test, plus supporting cast, partly because of the way we watched TV then – the ritualistic anticipation of a once-a-week viewing and the less-is-more factor of only having four channels to choose from – and partly simply because of the music going on at the time.

Chapter 14: Generals and Majors
Multinational record labels

In 1984 people were just crazy for records. [1]
David Hepworth

The music industry is a strange combination of having real and intangible assets: pop bands are brand names in themselves, and at a given stage in their careers their name alone can practically guarantee hit records.[2]
Richard Branson

It is somewhat unfashionable to write about the role major record companies have played in shaping the British music scene. It's far more interesting, especially in the 80s, to document the role of the maverick independents, the labels who were closer to the bands and were in it for the love of music rather than as a business. And it's true, the story of Rough Trade, Mute, Factory, 4AD and a host of others *is* more interesting, and is discussed at length in the next chapter. But the majors were once independent, or near enough, made it up as they went along and signed most of the artists who have made popular music what it is now. Anyone who signed The Beatles, Pink Floyd, Kate Bush and Radiohead can't be all bad.

It also gives us the opportunity to look at the economic context of the wider music industry, the introduction of the compact disc (a godsend to the majors), the importance of the charts, and the place (literally) of record shops in a pre-download and streaming age. It also needs to be pointed out that the division between majors and independents was often blurred, with myriad deals and agreements existing between the two, especially in the areas of marketing and distribution. It's true that the majors played at higher stakes, foisted terrible contracts on naive young bands who just wanted to get a record out and then dumped them as soon as the first single didn't sell or held them to ransom if it did, but independents didn't always hold the moral high ground. As John Peel said, 'There's an awful lot of crap gets issued by indie labels and a lot of the stories I hear from the bands who've got involved with some of the bigger, allegedly indie labels, are as horrifying as those from bands involved with established major record companies'[3].

In the late 70s and early 80s, the UK music industry had been in the doldrums. Set against a struggling economy and high inflation, record companies had spent recklessly, often from lavish expense accounts, and punk had eroded the support for the established acts but not sold enough of their edgier product to compensate. Revered companies like Decca and Pye drifted into acquisition by Polygram, pressing plants closed. But in 1984, it had something to smile about. In the context of a slightly improving economy[4], expense accounts being reined in and the ever-increasing marketing power of music videos, sales were up 14% on the previous year[5].

On the 'export' front, British bands were still enjoying the fruits of the so-called Second British Invasion of the US (the first being the Beat groups in the mid-60s) aided by the advent of MTV which needed content for their round-the-clock programmes which the visually strong British artists were perfectly placed to provide. In March 1984, 24 of the US Top 50 singles were by British artists. It wasn't just about videos, however. The new pop of ABC, Human League, Eurythmics and Culture Club[6] sounded sophisticated but also cool and edgy, appealing particularly to audiences in New York and Los Angeles who were more accepting of many of the groups' fey or gender-bending personas. At the same time, the more commercial end of post-punk (Billy Idol, The Cure, Psychedelic Furs) were embraced by the college set, and old-wavers Yes, Genesis and Phil Collins went pop and started appealing to middle America.

It was a boom year for singles. Six of them – Band Aid's 'Do They Know It's Christmas', Frankie Goes To Hollywood's 'Relax' and 'Two Tribes', George Michael's 'Careless Whisper', Wham!'s 'Last Christmas', and Steve Wonder's ' I Just Called To Say I Love You' – sold over a million copies each, something that had never previously happened, and that was just in Britain. They were aggressively marketed by videos and also increasingly being bought in the more expensive 12-inch format with their bigger sleeves, extended versions, extra tracks and better sound quality (and that year accounted for nearly 30% of UK singles sales)[7]. Exploiting the song beyond one release became commonplace: 'Two Tribes' came out in at least five different mixes. It mainly suited artists whose songs were aimed at, or at least stood a chance on, the dancefloor, prompting a never-ending variety of club, dub, hi-NRG, extended or, most boring of all, instrumental versions of songs. To be fair, others used the opportunity for a different kind of instrumental: the arty ambient track which cropped up on scores of synthpop B-sides. China Crisis were particularly proficient at these, but also OMD, Depeche Mode, Howard Jones, Ultravox and Japan. But not everyone saw the point of a 12-inch. The Smiths and Lloyd Cole, for example, hated them. Album sales, on vinyl and cassette, also increased (up 6.6% from the previous year) even if only a small amount of the nearly 6,000 new releases were hits.

The record industry was also taking note of the new compact disc (CD) format, developed by Philips in the Netherlands and Sony in Japan. Like vinyl, the CD was a disc but the audio was converted into binary digits, played with a laser, started in the middle, ended at the outer edge, and varied its speed from 500 to 200 rpm (as opposed to a consistent 33 or 45rpm).

Nimbus, the bespoke south Wales-based record plant, famous for its hi-fi recordings and pressings of classical music on vinyl, had been an early advocate of the CD. Instead of buying a mastering lathe from Philips at £1.5 million it decided to make its own for a tenth of the price. It took nearly a year, but in May 1984 the Nimbus plant, only the second in Europe[8], produced its first test disc. Three months later, on 22 August, the first mass-produced CDs in Britain came off the production line, just ahead of America's first run, Bruce Springsteen's *Born in the USA*, manufactured at the CBS plant in Terre Haute, Indiana in September. For Nimbus, it was only modest

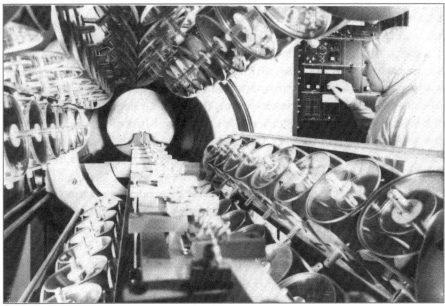

Located near Monmouth, Nimbus was the UK's first CD-pressing plant.

quantities at first: 200 a day, then 20,000 a month, then 20,000 a day and by 1987, when they opened a plant in the US, they were hitting 400,000 discs a day.

This was all very well, but the industry had to convince consumers to buy the hardware. Sales of CD players in Britain amounted to just 19,000 in 1983, rising to 33,000 in 1984. Using similar technology, RCA's 12-inch videodisc hadn't caught on and the player was discontinued in April 1984. But after Philips and Polygram launched a joint marketing campaign in October (promoting, respectively, the hardware and software), and a month later Sony introduced the world's first portable CD player, the Discman, the only way was up. By 1986 there were over half a million players in Britain, and Ford had started to put them in cars.

Some industry figures fretted about the implications of an indestructible disc, like the union leaders and bosses in the Ealing comedy, *The Man in the White Suit*. If they were so perfect, wouldn't shops or libraries simply rent them out, confident in the knowledge that the sound quality of the 100th loan would be the same as the first? As it turned out, no. The public bought into them and indeed started buying CD versions of LPs they already had. As one executive said, 'To sell a recording to a customer once is good business; to sell it to him twice is sheer heaven'[9]. Especially when the recording costs were already covered and, in the early days, the effort put into printing the new-format sleeves cheapskate.

Still, there *were* things to worry about, like the cost of producing video promos[10] (even if the industry was beginning to get its act together in retailing compilations of them), cheap imports undercutting UK-manufactured records, and the big unknown that was home computers. By the end of 1984, it was estimated that there were 2.5 million home computers in the UK, a penetration rate of nearly 20% of households – the highest in the world[11]. Would computer games compete with album sales? No-one knew.

There were the occasional lawsuits around plagiarism, mostly in America[12], but at least they didn't have to worry about the legalities of sampling which was a few years off. And there was a spate of legal cases brought by artists, mostly regarding 'unfair' contracts 'forced' onto artists without offering proper legal advice – the better-known ones being Wham! v Innervision, Elton John v Dick James Music and The Beatles v EMI. This would continue to be a major industry issue, made even more public in the 90s when George Michael sued Epic and Prince sued WEA. One artist – Robert Fripp – who managed to extricate himself from particularly complex management and publishing contracts and form his own company took to including the following erudite statement on all his subsequent releases:

> *The phonographic copyright in these performances is operated by Discipline GM on behalf of the artist, with whom it resides. Discipline accepts no reason for artists to give away such copyright interests in their work by virtue of a "common practice" which is out of tune with the times, was always questionable and is now indefensible.*

Basically, artists started to get smarter. They hired lawyers, challenged contracts, got serious about publishing and called the tune as much as their managers. By the end of the decade they were finally figuring out that they could license their recordings to a record label rather than simply hand them over and lose ownership of them. Pet Shop Boys were good examples of a new breed of business-savvy musician: by *Behaviour,* the blurb on the back sleeve read: 'The copyright in this sound recording is owned by Pet Shop Boys Partnership under exclusive licence to EMI Record Ltd'. But that was in 1990; in the mid-80s there was still some way to go.

The other major issue which continually vexed the record industry was home-taping. By the early 80s, cassettes were hugely popular, easily playable on the move, both in car and pocket – the latter thanks to the introduction of the Sony Walkman in 1979. In fact, pre-recorded cassette sales were as high as those of LPs. It was the blank tapes that were the 'problem'. For several years the record industry complained to anyone who would listen (which wasn't many) about lost sales. In 1982 they launched a campaign, "Home-taping Is Killing Music – And It's Illegal", claiming that it was losing them as much as £300m a year in lost revenue. However, there was no evidence to back up its theory that people taped records instead of buying them. On the contrary, there was every reason that people bought records they particularly wanted and taped the ones they were undecided about. The Government was lobbied, a 10p levy on blank cassettes was proposed, and eventually a Green Paper was published in 1988, with various recommendations, but none of it came into practice[13].

Other industry figures complained about bootlegging (unofficial releases, often secretly recorded at concerts), but this was incredibly niche. The record company lost no sales because the record was never in their catalogue, and never would have been. Interestingly, the early Virgin Records shops openly sold vinyl bootlegs and Richard Branson himself was fined £1,045 for doing so way back in 1973[14]. Vinyl bootlegs, however, were rare and in the 80s were overtaken by the easier-to-duplicate cassettes, sold in markets and outside concerts, and in the 90s by CDRs. Now, of course, official live recordings (many available immediately after the concert ends), demos and outtakes are part and parcel of a markedly different industry.

*****

By 1984, the major record companies operating in Britain comprised EMI, CBS, WEA, RCA, MCA and Polygram, collectively known as the 'Big Six', as well as Island, Virgin and Chrysalis. The difference between them was size, history (some of which was pre-World War Two) and the Big Six's bewildering structures which were often further complicated by geography, mergers and buy-outs. They all had multiple labels, most had their own distribution and some had their own pressing plants. They were perceived as 'The Man': acronymed multinationals, business first music second, executives in suits, and women confined to the typing pool, reception or PR[15]. This wasn't strictly true but not far off. Only one was British, four were American and one Dutch-German, although this would change within the year.

EMI (Electric & Musical Industries) had been founded in 1931, at first making recording and broadcasting equipment (the artist Richard Hamilton was an employee during the war) before diversifying into all sorts of manufacturing, and then the music business. By the beginning of the 60s EMI dominated the British music industry courtesy of The Beatles, Abbey Road Studios, its own HMV record shops and celebrated labels like Parlophone, His Masters Voice and (from the turn of the decade) Harvest[16]. It wasn't until 1972 that they actually had a label called EMI. Alongside Pink Floyd's *Dark Side of the Moon*, the 70s brought them Queen and Kate Bush, but by the end of *that* decade they were struggling and were forced to merge with the electronics firm, Thorn, resuscitating them in time for early 80s new pop, signing Duran Duran and re-launching the careers of David Bowie and Tina Turner. By 1984 they were selling off peripheral activities and the following year signed the Pet Shop Boys.

Of the American companies, CBS (Columbia Broadcasting System) were the biggest. It had been founded in New York in 1962 to promote the much older Columbia Records label outside of the US, including artists like Bob Dylan, Simon & Garfunkel, and later Bruce Springsteen and Michael Jackson. In the UK, 1984 was its annus mirabilis having just added Paul Young, Wham!, Alison Moyet and Sade to its Epic roster, and overtaken EMI in terms of market share[17]. But if you weren't one of the above, then it was likely you struggled. Typical, perhaps, were Sunset Gun, a trio of sisters Deidre and Louise Rutkowski and multi-instrumentalist Ross Campbell whose beguiling Alan Rankine-produced debut single 'Be Thankful' was somewhere in between Carmel and Sade. When Deidre married CBS's A&R man Gordon Charlton, the label presented them with a plaque which advised 'Hits Before Kids'. They lasted a few singles and one album.

WEA was made up of Warners, Elektra and Atlantic and after a long period of resting on their laurels (70s behemoths Led Zeppelin, The Eagles, Fleetwood Mac) were catching up fast, thanks largely to their energetic young Managing Director, Rob Dickins, who signed artists like Howard Jones and Aztec Camera, as well as setting up cool, semi-independent sub-labels like Korova (Echo & The Bunnymen, Strawberry Switchblade) and Blanco Y Negro (Everything But The Girl, Jesus and Mary Chain). Having Madonna and Prince on the mother label didn't do them any harm either. RCA (Radio Corporation of America) could trace their origins back to 1901 and were of course famous for signing Elvis Presley in 1955 (and keeping him) and as the home of David Bowie throughout the 70s. However, the former's death and the latter's switch to EMI America contributed to a downturn in their fortunes and in 1986 they were subsumed into the Germany-based Bertelsmann Music Group. Bertelsmann were better known for publishing but were about to become serious players – as BMG – in music, also acquiring Arista and Ariola. MCA (Music Corporation of America) were the smallest of the Six and had the most convoluted history of them all, but suffice it to say, they were on their uppers by the mid-80s – new signings included (somewhat desperately) The Damned and (bravely) Chakk – and in the 90s were absorbed into Universal.

Jointly owned by the Dutch and German tech giants Philips and Siemens, Polygram was a merger of two of their music companies, Polydor (Roxy Music, The Jam) and Phonogram (ABC, Soft Cell). Also brought into the fold were Mercury and Fontana (acquired in the 60s and 70s) and Decca and A&M (bought at either end of the 80s). Polygram's strength lay in its owners' development of the CD, both the disc and the player, and they were central to getting it introduced to Britain. Sticking his neck out, Managing Director Jan Timmer proclaimed that 'The black disc will be dead by 1989'. Put yourself in the 90s and that didn't seem wildly exaggerated.

*****

Of course the majors weren't just the Big Six. In fact, Virgin and Island (and to a lesser extent Chrysalis) were probably more influential and certainly better known than most of the aforementioned multinationals, thanks to their enigmatic founders, impressive rosters and – crucially – semi-independent cache[18]. No-one outside of the industry knew who steered the Big Six, but most people knew of Richard Branson and many Chris Blackwell.

By 1984, Virgin Records had been in existence for a little over ten years. Branson had started a mail order outlet, then a small record shop, and then a label, much the same way Geoff Travis would start Rough Trade. Despite hitting the jackpot with its very first release, Mike Oldfield's *Tubular Bells,* it shouldn't be forgotten that Virgin's first few years were dominated by comparatively less lucrative, leftfield, post-hippy

185

albums by the likes of Tangerine Dream, Gong and Henry Cow. Singles were an afterthought. But they were quick to react to punk and new wave (signing Sex Pistols and XTC), new pop (Human League, Japan, Culture Club) and new old pop (Phil Collins). Sub-labels were added: Front Line for reggae (Branson even took John Lydon to Jamaica to advise on who to sign[19]), 10 Records, and he even bought Charisma, on which sat incongruous bedfellows Julian Lennon and Malcolm McLaren. By 1984 they were on a role with a roster that also included OMD, Heaven 17, Scritti Politti, PiL, Simple Minds, China Crisis and David Sylvian, as well as others through smart licensing deals: UB40 (via DEP), The Blue Nile (via Linn), Madness (via Zarjazz), Cabaret Voltaire (via Some Bizzare) and Eurythmics' soundtrack to *1984* (Virgin Films).

The first of the *Now That's What I Call Music* album was released in December 1983, starting the most successful compilation series of all time, here with the poster which gave it its name. By June 1984, Richard Branson was starting another successful Virgin initiative.

It was also the start[20] of the phenomenally successful *Now That's What I Call Music* compilations which Branson – or rather Simon Draper, who *really* ran the music side – jointly conceived with EMI. The title came from a poster in Draper's office, bought in Portobello Market just across the road. It showed a pig listening to a chicken with said words across the top. In marketing terms, 'Now' was a wonderfully strong word. Who needed an advertising agency? Of course there had been compilations aplenty before, including the *Top of the Pops*[21] ones with their dolly-bird sleeves and featuring cover versions played by session musicians, as well as the 'original artists' ones released by K-Tel, Ronco, Arcade and others. With their 20+ tracks crammed onto two sides of vinyl, these were the Spotify of the 70s. *Now That's What I Call Music* was different in that they featured half as many tracks again but spread over a double album, which gave better audio quality and a gatefold sleeve for more pictures and text. They were compiled by Ashley Abram who had been working for Ronco but joined the *Now* team in 1984. 'The first *Now* album had the whole year to choose from but there was only a limited period of time to compile *Now 2* and a more limited pool of tracks'[22]. Securing them was not easy. David Bowie and Eurythmics declined to be on the first one, but by the summer's *Now 3*[23] the series was on a roll and everyone wanted to be on it. Except for WEA and CBS who started to refuse tracks by their

186

artists while they activated their own series in November, the rather more prosaically titled *Hits*. Others jumped on the bandwagon: Chrysalis, MCA and Polygram pooled their acts on the equally perfunctorily named *Out Now!*, while K-Tel re-entered the market with *Hungry For Hits,* which ended up being a series of two and one respectively. For a while, *Now* and *Hits* were neck and neck, with two-to-three releases a year. However, by the end of the decade, the *Now* brand surged ahead and it's now the world's most successful compilation series ever, having just passed number 100 in the series.

1984 was a defining year for Virgin. Having been on the brink three years ago, money was now rolling in, and Branson was itching to invest and diversify. He'd already tentatively moved into books but brought in a couple of professionals from Macmillan to start Virgin Publishing, ditching the novels and focusing on non-fiction, including, obviously enough, books about music. He was also beginning to take an interest in films. *Electric Dreams*, *1984* and *Secret Places* were all released in 1984, the first two with strong tie-in soundtrack albums. Their success inspired Branson to invest heavily in *Absolute Beginners* but its flop in 1986 curtailed further film production forays, although a video distribution arm proved very successful. However, the real game-changer was that year's launch of Virgin Atlantic and its flights between London and New York. The airline's success established Virgin as a brand that could be applied to almost anything. Consequently, the record company began to take a bit of a back seat (not least because Branson and Draper had fallen out over the airline) and in 1992 Branson sold it to Thorn EMI for £560m.

*****

Island Records' first release was nothing like *Tubular Bells*. It was an LP of jazz standards by a Jamaican pianist, Lance Hayward, recorded in 1959 by a 22-year-old ex-pat Englishman, Chris Blackwell. Blackwell established a small office in Kingston and a few more releases followed before he shifted the operation to London, acquiring the rights to the recordings of Jamaican sound-systems and selling them to Jamaican immigrants in Britain. Millie Small's six-million-selling 'My Boy Lollipop' (licensed to Fontana) followed, before Blackwell switched to late 60s album-oriented, underground rock (Traffic, Free), folk-rock (Fairport Convention, Richard Thompson), glam (Roxy Music, Sparks) and, in the mid-70s, reggae (Bob Marley, Burning Spear). As the 70s turned into the 80s, Island had branched out into post-punk (U2), post-disco (Grace Jones) and post-western world (King Sunny Ade).

1984 was an exceptional year for Island, but it could have turned out very differently. Blackwell, like Branson, was becoming interested in films but needed cash. He was financing a new label, ZTT, which by the end of 1983 had delivered an instrumental EP by faceless, studio boffins and an expensively produced single by an unknown Liverpool band which was hovering just outside the charts (more of which later). So he did a perverse thing: he bought 50% of Stiff Records. Stiff had been the archetypal late-70s independent label, nurturing The Damned, Elvis Costello and Ian Dury and, with the Stiff Tours, introducing – to the UK at least –the idea of 'label as family' and promoting it aggressively via campaigns like 'If It Ain't Stiff, It Ain't Worth A ****'. But in 1983, Stiff was in the doldrums, so it's Director, Dave Robinson, was open to Blackwell's offer. Only it came with a big catch. Because of Island's cashflow problems, Robinson ended up lending Blackwell a million pounds in order to buy his own label. In the process he also lost Madness who set up their own label, Zarjazz, through Virgin. On the plus side he signed The Pogues and was boss of both labels for the whole of 1984. Whether it was Robinson's stewardship or simply good timing, Island raked in the cash thanks to the double whammy of Bob Marley's *Legend* and (via ZTT) Frankie Goes to Hollywood's three #1 singles and #1 album. On the downside, Robinson lost his grip on (or interest in) Stiff, and it went bust fairly soon afterwards. 'To cut a long story short, 1984 was great, 1985 was shit because all the money had gone'[24].

In 1984 Chris Blackwell was juggling Island, film (here on the set of *Countryman*), Stiff and ZTT – the latter, run by Jill Sinclair, Trevor Horn and Paul Morley, enjoying its annus mirabilis.

ZTT[25] was one of the year's great stories. Dreamt up by Trevor Horn, Jill Sinclair and Paul Morley in 1983, it was a very different kind of label, acting like a cross between an independent and a major. They were cool and fleet of foot but also brash and confident, knowing that they had serious distribution and Island's money behind them. They wanted to shake things up *and* be commercially successful. Horn had been a session musician before forming The Buggles, joining Yes and producing groups like ABC; Sinclair was Horn's manager, wife and sharp-as-nails businesswoman whose interest in pop music was, by her own admission, 'very little' ('I'd never bought an album before I joined the music business'[26]); and Morley was the NME's star scribe, though by that time he'd resigned his staff position and was more interested in signing and marketing bands rather than just writing about them.

Of the five first signings – Frankie Goes To Hollywood, The Art Of Noise, Propaganda, Anne Pigalle and Andrew Poppy – only the first seemed to have any chart potential, the others being more easily and damagingly described as (respectively) instrumental, German, French and (despite his name) the antithesis of pop. It was a bold, some might say, foolhardy (ad)venture, but that's what it became: a mad-as-a-hatter rollercoaster ride, dominated by Frankie in 1984, but peppered with obtuse, always-interesting releases by a strong, if occasionally neglected supporting cast. And all wrapped up in marketing-speak which was in turn amusing, irritating and bewildering. It was one of the things that made the year so much fun: a pop label that was passionate, intelligent and sophisticated, yet flippant, pretentious and patronising. There hasn't been anything like it since.

Mention must also be made of Chrysalis, founded in 1968 by Chris Wright and Terry Ellis (Chris Ellis, geddit?), first as a booking agency, then management company, then label. They reacted quickly to new wave (Blondie, Generation X), struck a smart deal with 2 Tone Records and hit their stride with new pop, signing Spandau Ballet and Ultravox who in 1984 had eight Top 30 hits between them and in the latter's *The Collection*, a triple-platinum compilation. That year they also bought Ensign Records, home of the Boomtown Rats, The Waterboys and a plethora of black artists ranging from Phil Fearon to Light of the World, A&Rd by DJ Chris Hill. After investing in television (the quirky Max Headroom), Ellis disappeared to pursue film projects, leaving the label in the hands of Chris Wright who eventually sold the label in 1990 to EMI.

*****

These then were the majors, the establishment so-to-speak, linked for the most part by complex multinational identities, distribution and pressing plants and, on occasion, more money than sense. They were also members of the British Phonographic Industry (BPI) which provided a discussion forum, lobbied government, liaised with the Musicians Union and certified platinum, gold and silver discs. Aside from the Big Six and the likes of Virgin, Island and Chrysalis, its 125 members[27] included independents like Rough Trade, Cherry Red and Beggars Banquet (though not Mute and Factory), as well as dozens of lesser-knowns. And once a year it held an awards ceremony. The 1985 Awards (covering 1984) were held at London's Grosvenor Hotel, and for the first time were televised live to an audience of 11 million. Winners aside – there were no surprises[28] – the event was probably best remembered for Prince's monosyllabic acceptance speech for Best International Artist, accompanied by his shock-haired, vest-wearing, 6ft 8ins bodyguard 'Big Chick' Huntsberry, and Neil Tennant filing one of his last reports for Smash Hits. Next year he'd be up on the stage receiving Best Single of the Year for 'West End Girls'.

Central to the music industry – especially for singles – were the charts. In Britain, these had existed since 1952 and in the years that followed they grew in number (Top 20, 40, 75), genre (pop, dance, country, indie etc) and format (singles, albums and now include downloads and streaming). They also grew in sophistication. The first chart had involved Percy Dickins, Editor of the NME, ringing up 20 shops for a list of their ten best-selling songs. For the rest of the 50s and most of the 60s numerous periodicals published their own charts and it wasn't until 1969 that *one* official singles chart was established, compiled from postal returns of sales logs from 250 shops[29]. In 1983, a company called Gallup took on the coordination and computerized the whole process. For a record label, especially a major (given the amount of money involved), getting an artist's single into the charts was the be-all and end-all. It was a vicious circle: to get into the charts you had to be on Top of the Pops and mainstream radio, and to be eligible for both, especially BBC Radio One, you had to be in the charts. If it was a great song and you employed skilled pluggers and had the marketing budget for a half-decent video and Smash Hits put you on the cover and there wasn't much competition that week, and a dozen other variables, then you might be lucky.

Hyping singles up the charts was commonplace. Sometimes this was at the shop end (exaggerating figures of records that *weren't* selling with the hope that it looked like they were and would sell 'even more' next week), but mostly it was at the record company end. Typical were the singles which came with cut-priced or free gifts. In 1984 there was even a board game, Hype, subtitled 'The only board game with all the slime and grime of the music business', marketed by Virgin Games[30]. Gallup's new computerized reporting helped, replacing the manual sales diary, but there were a few high-profile cases which caught out the do-badders, one of which resulted in WEA's Chairman resigning his post. 1984 was no better and no worse than other years, and it still happens today.

One single which didn't need any hype was Band Aid's 'Do They Know It's Christmas?' Apart from the speed with which it went from idea to recording, it was an unprecedented example of how well the record industry worked together, even if it took Bob Geldof's hectoring to act as the fast-forward button. Never mind the overdressed pop stars, to get the record in the shops a week after its recording was a phenomenal logistical achievement, especially given the quantities involved and that it was during the run-up to Christmas. Phonogram had all five of its European factories pressing vinyl round the clock; the printers, Robert Stace in Tunbridge Wells, did the same; and the distributors worked overtime to get them to the shops. If some of the retailers moaned about foregoing their mark-up, it was probably because they were worried about it creating a precedent, which of course it did. Seven charity singles followed in 1985 alone, compared to almost none before.

In mid-80s Britain there were around 6,000 shops that sold records, split between High Street chains like HMV, Virgin and Our Price; multipurpose stores like Woolworth, Boots, WHSmith and Menzies; and around 2,200 independents. Of the chains, HMV had been in existence since 1921 and by 1984 had 37 outlets, the same number as Virgin[31]. HMV would reach its zenith in 1986 with the opening of arguably the biggest record shop in the world (all 60,000 square feet of it) at 150 Oxford Street in London, while Virgin had already rebranded itself as Megastores earlier in the decade, although in most cases they were far from it. Our Price had started in London in the early 70s, although initially was called The Tape Revolution, before changing its name in 1976 and selling vinyl. By 1984 it had become the second largest retailer of records and tapes (after Woolies), floated on the London Stock Exchange and was acquired by WH Smith two years later. American chain Tower Records' first appearance in the UK was in Kensington High Street in 1984, followed the next year by a 25,000-square-foot flagship outlet at 1 Piccadilly Circus. And it wasn't just the big boys. Andy's Records started out as a stall on Felixstowe pier in 1969, before moving into bricks & mortar shops all over East Anglia, and thereafter the midlands and the north.

By the early 90s it had become the UK's largest independent music retailer. Music Zone, founded in 1984, had a chain of shops in and around Manchester.

So the mid-80s saw both national chains and regional independents in fairly rude health, not just because people were buying more records but, in the years to follow, buying CD versions of records they already had. But in truth the former were becoming more alike, bulk-buying and focusing on the Top 40, resulting in the latter struggling to compete. Come the new millennium, and the onset of music without product, it would all come crashing down. Tower Records and Andy's both went bust in 2003, Our Price a year later, Virgin's 130 shops in the UK and Ireland became something called Zavvi (which lasted just 15 months before going bust) and only HMV limped on. Independent shops fared even worse' as consumers switched to downloading MP3s or simply not consuming. From 948 stores in 2003 to 408 in 2007[32], it looked like they were heading for extinction – until the vinyl revival from around 2010, but that's another story.

1984 was, in that classic phrase, a transitional time for the record industry. On the one hand it had bucked the economic downturn of the early 80s, with new pop still selling well, especially in America, aided and abetted by promo videos. The compact disc looked like it was going to be a success. And pop was getting bigger and bigger: production-wise, media-wise (now very much in the tabloids) and budget-wise. However, some of the majors were spreading themselves too thinly, distracted by film and airlines, so that by the turn of the decade, Island was sold to Polygram and Chrysalis and Virgin were taken over by EMI. But majors weren't the only model.

At the beginning of the year, Music Week published its 100 UK Acts Tipped For '84, the result of a survey polling radio DJs and producers, critics from the music press and journalists from national and provincial newspapers – acts they had picked up on in 1983 and felt deserved success in the new year. The list (see Timeline and Charts at end of book) was interesting for a number of reasons. Firstly, Music Week couldn't count: there were 86 acts, not 100, and two weren't from the UK at all. Secondly, the predictions were very wide of the mark – a good half of the artists disappearing within a year or two. But perhaps most interesting of all was the fact that over 60% of the acts were on independent labels. For every Sade and Kershaw on a major, there was a Billy Bragg, Cocteau Twins, Cabaret Voltaire, Pulp and of course The Smiths on a minor. True only the last-named would regularly dent the charts, but it said something about where the arbiters-of-taste's allegiances lay. And it is to the independent labels that we now turn to.

191

Chapter 15: Cowboys and Indies
The independent labels

Nobody had a clue about running a record company and that was the best thing about it… and I try to know as little about running a record company today.[1]
Daniel Miller, Mute Records

Factory wasn't a record company, it was just a group of people with some mad ideas, the imagination to have the mad ideas, and the balls to commit themselves to the things they'd dreamt up.[2]
Vini Reilly, The Durutti Column

We just wanted to have a place to go where we could hear the music we loved. […] The whole idea was for people to hang around, there was no pressure to buy anything.[3]
Geoff Travis, Rough Trade

For a while, we participated in something pure and unique. Those records will vibrate long after I've ceased to do so.[4]
Ivo Watt-Russell, 4AD

The 80s were the heyday of independent labels, giving the majors a run for their money and encompassing a wide variety of genres: from post-punk to proto-electronica, pop to rock, reggae to soul. In January 1984, it was estimated that there were between 5,000 and 7,000 indie labels in existence in Britain[5] – a staggering number. Most (but not all) starting in the late-70s' crucible of punk and new wave, the independents grew in size and importance, sniffing out the best new leftfield bands, often working together and figuring out how to turn hobbies into 'businesses'. Unlike the majors, who were all based in London, the independents were all over the country, presenting local bands to local audiences. Several of them joined an informal network jokingly called The Cartel, which helped mesh labels, shops and distribution. Some labels died, others remained tiny, but a surprising number became serious concerns.

'Independent'[6] meant independent of the multinational 'Big Six', with separate distribution channels like The Cartel, Spartan, Pinnacle and IDS. However, the delineations were always blurred and as the 80s progressed became ever more so. Some independents had 'M&D' agreements whereby a major might manufacture and distribute the record.[7] In turn, very small labels might have similar deals with some of the bigger independents, particularly Rough Trade. Some major labels had so-called 'independent' subsidiaries, boutique labels as we might call them now, which they either created themselves or bought up existing ones. These were seen as 'cooler' to artists and fans alike, but also often acted as a testing ground for a band who might 'graduate' to major label status once they'd 'proved themselves'. It is often forgotten that labels like Island, Chrysalis and Virgin were the epitomes of independence in the previous decade but fairly early on they secured distribution from the majors and by the next decade were wholly owned by them[8].

Key to the 'independence' question was distribution. In 1984, the Big Six had 80% of the distribution of that year's new releases, but it still left about £146m worth of business for the independents[9]. Rough Trade was initially a shop and then a label and then got into distribution, which became as important, if not more so, than the label. But they couldn't cover the whole of the UK, so came to arrangements with other independent, regional set-ups like Red Rhino in York, Revolver in Bristol, Fast Forward in Edinburgh, Probe in Liverpool and Backs in Norwich (the 'Small Six'?), collectively known as The Cartel. As Sean Mayo of Revolver remembered: 'It was friendly. We were all into it for the same reasons. It was about the music. But not just the music – it was independent, and all that represented. It was doing it for all the right reasons'[10]. As another Revolver employer, Jeff Barrett (now the boss of Heavenly Records) reminisced, 'Things were so exciting musically – the first Smiths album came out, the Cocteau Twins, Aztec Camera'[11]. Most local independent distributors had started as shops, then set up labels, then became regional distributors, often juggling all three. As Derek Chapman of Backs recalls, 'Distribution was the main business, that's where all the efforts went. The label was how we *lost* the money we made'[12]. However, distributors could lose money too, and 1984 saw one of the key independent players, Pinnacle, go bust.

However, this was all behind the scenes. Most consumers didn't really care how records got from A to B. But they did care about the label. The ones described in this chapter were usually created by one person, inspired by punk and the DIY ethos it espoused. They 'understood' their artists and were music fans first, business people second. That said, they had learned quickly and several had grown in terms of staff, catalogue and turnover. By 1984, there was a handful that seemed to be leading the pack. What differentiated 4AD, Factory, Rough Trade, Mute, Beggars Banquet, Cherry Red and their contemporaries from other indies that came before and after was 'their ability to sustain a position in the mainstream'[13].

*****

For better or worse, some artists are so identified with their record labels that they end up getting grouped that way. When a label is known to foster a particular genre then this is perhaps understandable (you know roughly what you're going to get with Motown, ECM or Fax) but it happens to labels with diverse musical styles too. 4AD, an offshoot of another independent label, Beggars Banquet (see, ironically, later), is – or perhaps *was* – the label par excellence of a certain sound, a family of artists. 1984 was the early apotheosis of this[14], even if the groups were in reality very different from each other. 4AD's roster included Cocteau Twins, Dead Can Dance, Modern English, Dif Juz, Colourbox, The Wolfgang Press, Xmal Deutschland and This Mortal Coil, none of whom on the face of it sounded similar. What held them together was the guiding influence of the label's quietly spoken supremo, Ivo Watts-Russell, who created a kind of extended family united by a common aesthetic – or 'brand' as one would call it now.

The year before, Ivo[15] and designer Vaughan Oliver (it says something about the former's aesthetic vision that the first full-time employee he took on was a graphic designer) moved from Hogarth Road in Earls Court where they'd been since their inception in 1980, to Alma Road in Wandsworth – actually only three miles due south, but positively suburban in comparison. (Mute, Rough Trade and Cherry Red remained in the more urban west of London). The basement was converted into a rehearsal space where different bands hung out; and before the year was out there'd be a shared album, but more of that later.

An early signing, Cocteau Twins had moved from the Scottish refinery town of Grangemouth to London, shed their bassist, and then released the well-received *Head Over Heels* album and *Sunburst and Snowblind* EP, both drenched in Guthrie's beloved reverb. In 1984 Simon Raymonde[16], who'd worked at the Beggars Banquet shop, joined on bass. A single, 'Pearly-Dewdrops' Drops', came out in April and was their first to make the Top 30, prompting an invitation to Top Of The Pops which they snootily declined, although acquiesced to a video. For their third album the idea of bringing in producer Brian Eno and his new sidekick Daniel Lanois as engineer was discussed but both sides agreed it was better Guthrie do the honours again. Recorded in the summer, *Treasure* was a landmark album, at least in the view of their fans (one of whom was Robert Smith, who was obsessed by it and played it while getting dressed on his wedding day), although the group claim it was rushed and sounds of its time. Both may be true, but what a rush and what a time. 'Persephone' was a restless quick-step, 'Pandora' a waltz, while 'Donimo', the album's closer, is the perfect marriage of light and dark, calm and intensity. The moment when the heavily multi-tracked, chiming guitars come in at 2:22 still gives me goose-pimples[17]. Such was the closeness of the 4AD family that the album's opening track would be titled 'Ivo'. It's almost impossible to imagine the head of any other label receiving the same homage. Culture Club's 'Richard' anyone?

Another early 4AD signing, Dif Juz didn't actually release anything in 1984 but nevertheless seemed to be everywhere, contributing to This Mortal Coil and playing live with Cocteau Twins and Dead Can Dance. Despite not having a focal point – they were a guitar-and-drums instrumental outfit only – their live shows were nonetheless thrilling ('The best live band I'd ever seen', claimed Simon Raymonde; and I saw them three times that year) in a strange, ambient-dub kind of way, and in Richie Thomas they had one of the finest drummers around. Their two early 80s 12-inch EPs were fantastic, rough-and-ready, guitar-driven affairs but their first full 4AD album, *Extractions*, released in 1985, was sadly flawed, muddied by Robin Guthrie's saturated production which didn't suit Dif Juz's dry live sound.

The exact opposite was true of Colourbox who existed (and sounded fabulous) in the studio and never played live. Comprising brothers Martyn and Steve Young, plus singer Debbie Curran (later replaced by Lorita Grahame), they really ought to have been bigger but suffered from studio perfectionism. Still, their two singles in 1984, 'Say You' and 'Punch', were quality dance music, veering from reggae to funk and heavily influenced by New York electro – a 4AD anomaly. A decent, if slightly over-produced album followed a year later, and they would have their 15 minutes of fame in 1987 as one half of MARRS which produced the solitary though highly influential 'Pump Up the Volume', after which they promptly split. One can't help thinking they had more to offer.

The unfortunately named Dead Can Dance – fuel for those who thought 4AD was the home for goths – were a half-Australian, half-British/New Zealand duo. On stage Lisa Gerrard was ghostly, in flowing white dress, playing a Chinese dulcimer and from out of her mouth came the most devastating wordless vocals, a sort of classical version of Liz Fraser. Brendan Perry meanwhile was a fine guitarist with a rich baritone voice. They were an odd couple, but together created a music that seemed to have more in common with ancient Greece or Wagner than mid-80s British pop. Eventually, after an almost hand-to-mouth existence, they signed to 4AD, supported Xmal Deutschland and in January 1984 released an eponymous album. It was a fine debut, if a little under-produced. An EP, the warmer, more accomplished, and earnestly titled *The Garden of the Arcane Delights*[18], followed, and Dead Can Dance were on their way. By the end of the decade their albums would be 4AD's biggest sellers, a majestic bridge between Joy Division and world music.

4AD's Ivo, Cocteau Twins and Dead Can Dance.

Bands didn't always stay. Modern English had been one of 4AD's first signings and had had major US success with a single 'I Melt With You' in early 1983 on the back of its inclusion in the film *Valley Girl* and its accompanying soundtrack. 1984 saw them release their third album, *Ricochet Days*, and they were involved in This Mortal Coil, but the temptation of making it big in America led them to leave 4AD for Sire, move to New York and, unfortunately for them, disappear into obscurity. Ivo had signed Xmal Deutschland in 1983, a band in thrall to Joy Division and Bauhaus, fronted by Anja Huwe, Germany's peroxide answer to Siouxsie Sioux. They sang in German, released a debut album, *Fetisch*, and opened for Cocteau Twins. 1984 saw them release *Tocsin* which was more of the same. They tried remixes and singing in English, like Nena had done with '99 Red Balloons', but still the records sold poorly and Ivo let them go the following year.

The 'group' and album to truly cement the 4AD aesthetic, however, was This Mortal Coil. Conceived as a kind of house band to play Ivo's favourite songs, it had achieved instant success at the end of 1983 with a cover of Tim Buckley's 'Song to the Siren'[19]. Liz Fraser and Robin Guthrie's version was exquisite: Fraser's passionate but languid voice (and discernible lyrics for once) over understated guitar ambience. It went on to sell half a million copies. In 1984 Ivo went a stage further and gathered together a dozen or so 4AD stalwarts plus a few outsiders (Howard Devoto, Gini Ball and Martin McGarrick) to record a full album of 70s covers (the aforementioned Tim Buckley plus Big Star and Roy Harper[20]) and self-penned tracks by the 4AD artists themselves. Despite the variety, *It'll End in Tears* came across as a single, homogenous whole, heavy on melancholy – a quality that would be applied to much of 4AD's output – but mysterious, sensuous and lush. Troubled aesthetes, romantics and loners bought it by the bucket-load, helping it reach #1 in the UK Indie Charts and #38 in the UK main album chart. There were two more albums, until Ivo called it a day in 1991[21], but *It'll End in Tears* was the one.

And then there were the sleeves. Perhaps more than anything, more than the so-called similarity of the bands or production, it was the ethereal graphic design of 23 Envelope[22], the name Vaughan Oliver and photographer Nigel Grierson used for their collaborative work, that unified 4AD and set them apart from any other label. The sleeve of Cocteau Twins' 'Pearly Dewdrops' Drops' was marbled Victoriana, while *Treasure* was all lace, darkness and light with a fine attention to typography. *It'll End in Tears* was similarly spectral. But others were utterly different. The sleeves for Colourbox's 'Say You' and 'Punch' singles were starker, more typographic, more 'now', while The Wolfgang Press's *Scarecrow* EP looked like Hockney on acid. Dead Can Dance refused to use 23 Envelope and consequently their two very monochrome 1984 sleeves look different still. And yet somehow Oliver and Grierson created a house style and people would often buy 4AD records simply because of the sleeves.

For Ivo, and most of the 4AD stable, 1984 was a highpoint. Everybody and everything was seemingly in harmony. Musicians guested on each other's albums, went on holiday together, and in the case of Modern English and Colourbox, even shared a house. Of course it couldn't last. There were complaints about royalties, especially concerning This Mortal Coil. Robin Guthrie's relationship with Ivo began to sour over money and control issues. But in a very British way, none of it was brought out into the open and it festered quietly into the second half of the decade. 4AD carried on releasing some superb albums – three more from Cocteau Twins, six more from Dead Can Dance, and would diversify by the late 80s with American signings Throwing Muses and Pixies, but for sheer creativity 1984 was their watermark.

*****

Back in 1983, Channel 4 asked New Order to make a documentary about themselves and their home town – part of a series called Play At Home. They chose instead to make one about Factory Records, possibly because the label was more interesting than the band. Broadcast on 19 August 1984, it opened with the titles 'Factory Records, a partnership, a business, a joke', followed by a clothed Gillian Gilbert interviewing a naked Tony Wilson in the bath.

Like 4AD, Factory was, by 1984, fast becoming a legend within its own lifetime, courtesy of its larger-than-life partners (Tony Wilson, Rob Gretton, Martin Hannett, Peter Saville and Alan Erasmus, "five extremely heterosexual men, all in one way or another in love with each other"[23]), the rise of New Order from the ashes of Joy Division, the opening of the Hacienda, and the simple but hugely important fact that it was all happening in Manchester not London. No disrespect to the other associated bands, designers and staff (including Mike Pickering who from that year would become increasingly influential in terms of A&R and as Hacienda in-house DJ), but these five people, the band and the building went a long way to defining Factory. 4AD had its head honcho, defining band and designer[24], but they went about things in a more restrained, rarefied way. Factory was more in your face. Certainly Tony Wilson was a spokesman and provocateur par excellence, in complete contrast to Ivo's quietly cultivated culthood, deliberate or otherwise.

Founded in January 1978 (at the height of industrial decline, in mid-winter – perfect), Factory was actually modelled on another Manchester label, Rabid Records, but quickly usurped its mentor, establishing itself as an exemplar of northern cool. Its first four releases, the *Factory Sampler* EP, A Certain Ratio's 'All Night Party', OMD's 'Electricity' and Joy Division's *Unknown Pleasures* set the tone both aurally (Hannett) and visually (Saville). Factory celebrated Manchester's post-industrial bleakness, wearing it as a monochrome badge of honour. But it was bleakness as romanticism rather than any kind of political statement, except as a kind of two fingers up to London. Its romanticism extended to the way it was run – naively ('we had a heroic attitude to artistic freedom', reflected Tony Wilson[25]) – and of course to Ian Curtis's suicide in 1980, the ultimate in poetic statements. Wilson's enthusiasm and provocations meant that the label was becoming more interesting than the groups, a situation which Wilson was content to perpetuate. Faced with the prospect of uninteresting interviews with dour bands, Wilson was a godsend, even if you sometimes wanted to wring his neck.

As the early 80s progressed, Joy Division became New Order, and with the change of name and a trip to New York, hanging out at Danceteria and Funhouse, came a more hi-tech, hip-hop-influenced, electronic dance-oriented sound, a style also taken on by new signings Section 25 and Quando Quango. Although Martin Hannett had produced New Order's glum *Movement*, he'd had no hand in 'Blue Monday' (produced by the band themselves), an irony not lost on Hannett as he railed against Wilson's decision to build the Hacienda instead of a state-of-the-art studio. Hannett left under a cloud in 1982, sued for unpaid royalties (settled out of court in 1984), became increasingly bitter, but returned in 1988 to produce The Happy Mondays' *Bummed*. He died in 1991, officially of heart failure but it was the drink and drugs that did it.

1984 was in many ways a stop-gap year for New Order, with just one single, 'Thieves Like Us' (two, if you count the pointless instrumental, 'Murder', only available on import). The previous summer had seen them in New York working with Arthur Baker, resulting in the beat-heavy, slightly unsatisfactory 'Confusion'. That collaboration had also yielded a very rough 'Thieves Like Us', though properly recorded without Baker back in London in the new year, and released in April 1984 in a plush, if po-faced, De Chirico-influenced[26] Saville sleeve. If the cover continued to present the group's efforts as art, the band would do its best to bring things down a peg with lyrics like 'Oh, love is found in the east and west, but when love is at home it's the best'. There were no words on the single that followed a month later on the Factory Benelux subsidiary. Dressed in another De Chirico-influenced sleeve, 'Murder' was a strange, inconsequential affair, and that it wasn't released on Factory proper was perhaps just as well. But the year was important in the development of the group's sound. Ensconced in the studio from October to December, they threw off the New York homeboy beats and set about defining their rock guitars and synth sound, resulting in *Low Life*, released in May the following year. And in response to pleas from their new American label to, for the first time, 'put their fucking faces on the cover', Peter Saville did just that – albeit stretched and distorted on wraparound tracing paper.

Tony Wilson and New Order: Factory's mouthpiece and most successful band.

If 1984 was a quiet year for the group, its individual members were busy producing other (mostly) Factory bands under the name Be Music. Between 1983-84 Bernard Sumner helmed releases by Section 25, Quando Quango, Shark Vegas, Marcel King, Surprize and Foreign Press; Hooky oversaw Stockholm Monsters, The Royal Family and the Poor, Lavolta Lakota, Nyam Nyam and Some Now Are; while Stephen and Gillian (the Other Two) produced 52nd Street, Thick Pigeon, Life and Red Turns[27].

With New Order temporarily out of the limelight (and for that matter A Certain Ratio too, who were in flux, with members leaving to join Kalima or Quando Quango, yet still somehow releasing a couple of classy funk-latino singles, 'Life's A Scream' and 'Brazilia'), it provided the opportunity for other Factory groups who were ploughing a similar furrow to come to the fore. Shark Vegas were an Anglo-German group who had supported New Order on a European tour in the Spring of 1984. The group featured Alister Grey and Mark Reeder who had both moved to Berlin. Reeder had played a bit part in Mick Hucknall's The Frantic Elevators and was now Factory's 'official representative' in Germany, sending electronic mix-tapes to Bernard Sumner. Sumner returned the favour by producing Shark Vegas's single, 'You Hurt Me', later that year, a decent slab of New Order-style electro-angst which nonetheless flopped. Reeder also acted as guide to Muriel Gray's Berlin special on The Tube in March, introducing viewers to Die Tödliche Doris and a reassuringly unhinged Blixa Bargeld amongst others[28]. Section 25 had been with Factory since 1980, but it wasn't until 1984 that they really found their sound and an audience. Their third album, *From the Hip*, and particularly the remixed single, 'Looking from a Hilltop', both produced by Bernard Sumner (the latter also with Donald Johnson of A Certain Ratio), were state of the art electronic dance, let down by weak vocals. 'Looking from a Hilltop' was big in the clubs but the band couldn't follow it up and split the following year. Quando Quango were formed by Mike Pickering with Dutch siblings Reinier & Gonnie Rietveld while the former was on a sojourn in Rotterdam. Two early singles had shown they had a groove, and by 1984 the line-up had changed considerably with Simon Topping of A Certain Ration, amongst others, joining. Single 'Atom Rock' certainly had the right ingredients, including Johnny Marr on guitar, and went down well in the clubs, but it was essentially a rhythm looking for a tune. Work started on their debut album, *Pigs + Battleships* (featuring second guitarist Vini Reilly), released the following year, but like Section 25 they fizzled out. Mike Pickering, however, went on to become increasingly influential as Factory's A&R man, Hacienda's in-house DJ and co-founder of Deconstruction Records and the band M People.

New Order soundalikes Stockholm Monsters released their only album, the Peter Hook-produced *Alma Mater*, and a couple of singles ('All at Once' and the archly titled 'How Corrupt is Rough Trade?[29]), but like Section 25 and Quando, they didn't have staying power and had split by 1987. The Wake were probably the pick of the bunch. Beyond the mildly interesting fact that frontman Gerard McInulty used to be in Altered Images and Bobby Gillespie played drums before being asked to leave in 1983, The Wake are a good example of a good band that could have been great. Their overlooked March 1984 single 'Talk About the Past' was catchy and the album that followed, *Here Comes Everybody*, released the following year, perfectly mixed funky post-punk and melancholic synthpop. The track 'O Pamela' has since been covered by Nouvelle Vague which is as fine an example of belated recognition as any.

Factory's first release of the year was a 12-inch single by Manchester band Kalima. Formerly known as Swamp Children, the band changed their name in 1983, drafted in most of A Certain Ratio and released the latin-jazz influenced 'The Smiling Hour'. A monochrome video of fruit & veg shopping did its best to undermine the warm, lilting song. Another incongruity was soul singer Marcel King's 'Reach For Love' – a heinously overlooked, hugely accessible dance number, produced by Bernard Sumner and Donald Johnson (see also Chapter 20). Meanwhile, away from post-punk, The Durutti Column continued to work outside the parameters of fashionable pop or rock. Their 1984 album, *Without Mercy*, was a meandering jazz affair inspired by a Keats poem, though words were conspicuously absent. Aside from the ever-present Reilly and percussionist Bruce Mitchell, they were augmented by strings (Blaine

199

Reninger of Tuxedomoon and Caroline Lavelle) and a 4-piece brass section. The album itself was a bit of a yawn. Even Reilly disowned it. '*Without Mercy* is a joke. That album's terrible. It was all Tony Wilson's idea to make it more classical'[30]. As was his idea to place an ad in the music press saying 'The Durutti Column piss on The Art Of Noise'.

It is often forgotten that James began life with Factory, with their 3-track single 'Jimone' (geddit?) in 1983. The following year they toured with The Smiths and a second single, the prosaically titled 'James II' was recorded in October (released at the beginning of 1985). The A-side, 'Hymn from a Village', already showed the band had a great future ahead, including some wonderfully perverse lyrics:

> *This song's made up, made second rate*
> *Cosmetic music, powderpuff*
> *Pop tunes, false rhymes, all lightweight bluffs*
> *Second-hand ideas, no soul no hate*
> *Wasn't meant to be, built on complacency.*

Wilson pressed for an album, but they were a bit sniffy about Factory and passed.

Also-rans that year included a swathe of incestuous, mostly short-lived projects: The Royal Family and the Poor's patchily gorgeous, preposterously titled *The Project Phase 1 (The Temple of the 13th Tribe)*; a single, 'Too Crazy Cowboys', in possibly the worst Factory sleeve ever, by Thick Pigeon (aka New Yorkers Miranda Stanton and Carter Burwell[31] who also recorded for Crépuscule); the still-born Life (their one single, 'Tell Me' featured Andy Robinson who became New Order's co-manager after the death of Rob Gretton); a Minny Pops dance offshoot, Streetlife's sub-Cabaret Voltaire *Act of Instinct*; and to cap it all, a 'novelty' cover of 'Telstar' by a group calling themselves Ad Infinitum which turned out to be Peter Hook, two members of A Certain Ratio, Eric Random and Lindsay Reade (Tony Wilson's ex-wife). Perhaps the most interesting of all Factory's releases in 1984 was Biting Tongues' *Feverhouse* album, which, despite Wilson's arty rhetoric, was Factory's only nod to outright experimentalism. The soundtrack to their own film of the same name, shot in monochrome and released as a video by Factory offshoot, Ikon, the music sounded like a cross between 23 Skidoo and (seriously) Magma. The group's Graham Massey went on to form 808 State.

So was there a Factory sound? Certainly in 1984 the influence of Joy Division was still there, and several groups were following New Order into clubland. But on the other hand, The Durutti Column and Kalima were nothing like them, and Martin Hannett was no longer in-house producer. As with 4AD, it was more an attitude and a strong design aesthetic. But, less like 4AD, there was a certain prankster humour involved, including the infamous catalogue numbers which extended beyond the records, with some attributed to events, concepts or, in the case of Fac 99, a visit by Rob Gretton to the dentist[32]. Mostly, however, it was the fact that most of the bands came from Greater Manchester.

As for Fac 51, The Hacienda club had been set up in May 1982 in response to New Order's (and particularly their manager Rob Gretton's) love affair with Manhattan clubs. They wanted to create a similar experience in Manchester, found a large space in the centre of the city, brought in Ben Kelly to apply Factory's cool industrial aesthetic to its interior design, hired Mike Pickering to book the acts and waited for punters to flood in. They didn't. Partly because it wasn't sure if it wanted to be a club, a live venue or an arts centre, partly because the initial sound system was terrible, and partly because it was run by amateurs. But slowly people began to accept the ambiguity and on 27 January 1984 it became the setting for Madonna's first televised performance in the UK[33], dancing and miming to 'Burning Up' and 'Holiday', and broadcast live by The Tube that evening. Of course no-one had the slightest idea who Madonna was: most people were there for the TV cameras and the Factory All Stars (a kind of Factory supergroup with members from Quando Quango, The Durutti Column and, inevitably, A Certain Ratio). In the crowd was a 21-year-old Norman Cook (pre-Housemartins and Fat Boy Slim): 'She mesmerised the audience. She won a huge number of friends that day'[34]. Later that year, Mike Pickering created the Nude Night and would help usher in the era of house, raves and an early incarnation of the Happy Mondays who lacked Factory's trademark angst and who Pickering convinced Wilson to sign, ultimately giving Factory a new lease of life. Wilson marketed them as the people's band. In came acid house, ecstasy and suddenly the Hacienda was having it large in one non-stop party. For a label that *didn't* sign Buzzcocks, The Fall, The Smiths and Stone Roses, it was somehow ironic that they *still* represented Manchester, but they did – no other label got even close – even after going bust in 1992.

*****

Unlike Factory, Rough Trade was a shop first, then mail order and distribution, before becoming a label in 1978. It was founded by Geoff Travis (a Cambridge graduate like Tony Wilson, but more influenced by Marxism than the Situationists) and operated as a kind of collective[35] which would have been considered hippy if they hadn't been the first to stock punk, industrial and reggae records. Travis was a champion of punk's DIY ethos and the need to revolt against the majors. There was no master plan, profits were shared 50/50, they didn't insist on copyright, didn't even think about publishing and paid all the staff the same salary. And yet, for all their naivety, Rough Trade did well from the off. Their first album, Stiff Little Fingers' *Inflammable Material*, was the first indie label album in Britain to sell over 100,000 copies.

However, in the early 80s as Rough Trade became more successful, questions like 'What kind of music should we be releasing?' and 'How do we hold onto bands?' became ever more pressing. The bands were changing too. Scritti Politti decided they wanted to make intelligent pop music for as many people as possible rather than the small lefty audience they'd so far been catering to; likewise Aztec Camera. Both stayed with Rough Trade long enough to release debut albums but in the end were tempted away in 1983 by Virgin and WEA respectively. There were cashflow problems, they brought in an accountant and had to sell the shop (thankfully to their own staff). The collegiate atmosphere had gone, records had become 'units', and there was a growing schism between the label and distribution.

Their saviours were The Smiths. In April 1983 Johnny Marr had travelled down from Manchester to force a demo tape on Travis with the words: 'You won't have heard anything like this before'. It was a perfectly timed marriage. It was also the first time the label proposed a long-term contract (four albums) and a serious marketing plan. 'Hand in Glove' and 'This Charming Man' set the scene and, as 1984 dawned[36], the love affair with Morrissey, Marr and the other two went into overdrive. Three crisp Top 20 singles – 'What Difference Does It Make' (January), 'Heaven Knows I'm Miserable Now' (June) and 'William It Was Really Nothing' (September) – together with an eponymous debut album and a collection of singles and sessions, *Hatful of Hollow*, made sure they were never out of the news.

Rough Trade's Geoff Travis and The Smiths.

The Smiths seemed to oppose new pop: pitting back-to-basics guitars-bass-drums against synthesizers and drum-machines, utilitarian clothes against designer suits, a proud miserablism against dumb optimism, looking back instead of forward. And yet they were definitely pop stars, or at least Morrissey and Marr were. Morrissey's NHS specs, hearing aid and gladioli sticking out of his back pocket may have looked nonchalant and the antithesis of Boy George's clothes-horse look, but they were equally considered[37]. Morrissey stood for the glamour of the ordinary, of Jimmy Porter in John Osbourne's *Look Back in Anger* (1956) and the succession of British kitchen sink dramas which followed in the 60s. And yet he also obsessed over James Dean and Jean Marais, who clearly weren't ordinary or British. Always good for a quote, whatever Morrissey said ended up in Sounds, NME and Melody Maker the following week. Marr, with his shades and studied cool may have made him look like a Velvet Underground extra, but he wore more jewellery. Of course without Marr's exquisite guitar work, The Smiths wouldn't have been The Smiths, but without Morrissey they wouldn't have been given the time of day. Morrissey's lyrics *were* anti-pop. Lines like 'I was looking for a job, and then I found a job, and heaven knows I'm miserable now' and 'What she asked of me at the end of the day, Caligula would have blushed', showed humour, intelligence and a language that spoke to quiet sixth-formers and university students throughout the land, all sung with a world-weariness just the right side of pathos. 'Hand in Glove' was a great song, but sung by anyone else – even swinging sixties queen Sandie Shaw – it just didn't cut it. Even Shaw was nonplussed about it. 'Has the single influenced your daily life?' asked a journalist. 'Not a lot', she replied[38].

The speed in which Morrissey, Marr, Joyce and Rourke took The Smiths from nothing into both public conscience and music press approval took Rough Trade by surprise. In one sense they were the perfect label – very indie and right on – but in others they just weren't equipped to keep up with the demand for orders, let alone exploit the band to the full. The other problem was that the band, for all their self-confidence, had effectively no management and had internal problems of their own: Morrissey & Marr being the creative force, Joyce & Rourke effectively hired hands. Also, the debut album was a disappointment, particularly when compared with their live delivery. The choice of producers was strange to say the least. The first attempt was by Troy Tate who'd played keyboards in Teardrop Explodes and Fashion but who had very little experience of producing[39]. The sessions were scrapped and John Punter was brought in. Punter had more experience but a CV that included Japan, Judie Tzuke and Re-Flex didn't make much sense either. However, it was too late to try someone else and out it came: muddy and compromised. The tightly cropped, blue-tinted photo of American actor Joe Dallesandro from Andy Warhol's *Flesh* seemed an odd choice too[40]. Much better and much more representative of the band's crisp, urgent sound was *Hatful of Hollow*, a collection of singles, B-sides, and sessions, released at the tail end of the year.

One Manchester band Rough Trade reunited with, and then lost again within months, was The Fall. *Perverted by Language*, their sixth album, was released at the very end of 1983, but they fell out and moved to Beggars Banquet. Whether it was over a full-length video the band wanted to make, or Smith's irritation of Rough Trade's political correctness, or Geoff Travis's fixation with The Smiths is open to question. But, as we saw in Chapter 3, they would go on to even greater things later in the year.

Another band that left and came back again were The Raincoats. Their wonderfully shambolic post-punk had graced a couple of Rough Trade albums at the turn of the decade, but it wasn't until the beginning of 1984 that a third, *Moving*, appeared. An easy-on-the-ear, vaguely funky/world music workout, it would be their last album for a dozen years, in-between which founding members Gina Birch and Vicky Aspinall formed a pop group called Dorothy, ostensibly the antithesis of The Raincoats, though with tongue firmly in cheek. Their split went largely unreported but fan Kurt Cobain's 'famous' visit to the Rough Trade shop in 1992 in search of a new copy of the debut album resulted in a reunion for Rough Trade a few years later[41].

Rough Trade were still open to M&D deals with smaller, start-up labels, and towards the end of the year Paul Smith from Nottingham (not *the* Paul Smith from Nottingham) approached them about releasing a hardcore band called Sonic Youth from New York. Smith was already running the Rough Trade-distributed Doublevision[42] label, which wasn't right for hardcore, so he proposed a new label called Blast First. A deal was done over a pint, and out came the *Bad Moon Rising* album in the New Year. However, following their topless model-sleeved single, 'Flower', Rough Trade passed and the deal transferred to Mute. For all Rough Trade's expansion since the Marxist years of Notting Hill, they were consistent in their anti-sexist principles. Political correctness, we'd call it now.

If The Smiths saved Rough Trade, it came at a price. The label became formally known as Rough Trade International (thankfully, the RTI acronym never stuck) and in March 1984 moved out of its spiritual home in Notting Hill to new offices in Kings Cross. Qualified professionals were brought in, the staff count hit 100, a new business language started to be talked… and yet everyone was *still* being paid the same salary. It couldn't last. Rough Trade went bust in 1991, a year before Factory. But unlike Factory, there was a happy ending when Geoff Travis bought back the name and, with Jeanette Lee, ex-PiL, resurrected it in 2000. A combination of astute signings (The Strokes, Libertines, Arcade Fire), management deals (Jarvis Cocker), a slimmed-down staff reminiscent of the early days and, later, a partnership with Beggars Banquet has put Rough Trade back where it was.

*****

Mute Records was another label with an identifiable sound, if not image. Founded by Daniel Miller in 1978 – the year, or thereabouts, of a plethora of debut leftfield electronic singles by the likes of Human League, Cabaret Voltaire, Throbbing Gristle, Robert Rental, Thomas Leer, OMD, File Under Pop and Non – Mute's first release was his own 'band' The Normal's Kraftwerk-meets-Ballard 'TVOD / Warm Leatherette'. As a signifier of the label's intentions, it couldn't have been bettered. Austerely electronic yet danceable, the next couple of years' releases walked a tightrope between outright experimentalism and synthpop, the latter coming to the fore in the shape of Depeche Mode and Yazoo. However, 1984, saw a diversification in direction as Mute started to embrace non-electronic artists like Nick Cave and the Bad Seeds and German metal bashers Einstürzende Neubauten (the latter discussed in Chapter 26).

Of those earlier class-of-78 acts, Miller remained an enthusiastic fan, putting out records by Robert Rental[43], signing File Under Pop's Simon Leonard's new project I Start Counting (whose debut single, 'Letters To a Friend', came out in 1984) and, much later, becoming the back catalogue custodian of Cabaret Voltaire and Throbbing Gristle – and Can for that matter. Mute's second release had been a single, 'Back to Nature', by Fad Gadget who continued to issue a steady stream of alternative synthpop records combined with concerts that were more performance art than pop. 1984 saw an album *Gag*, a single 'Collapsing New People' (featuring Einstürzende Neubauten), and – after abandoning the Fad Gadget moniker and reverting to his real name Frank Tovey – a collaboration with Non (aka Boyd Rice), *Easy Listening for the Hard of Hearing*[44], which is conveniently self-descriptive. From this time onwards Tovey would largely abandon electronics and in doing so lost half his audience, but Miller remained intensely loyal.

Mute Records' Daniel Miller, Depeche Mode and Fad Gadget.

Miller was a big fan of and friends with Wire and when, post-EMI, the band was looking around for someone to release the 'difficult' *Document and Eyewitness* album, it was surprising in a way that it ended up on Rough Trade rather than Mute, or 4AD for that matter. During the group's hiatus between 1980-84, however, two of its members, Bruce Gilbert and Graham Lewis, had started to record much more experimental semi-electronic music under various names (Dome, Duet Emmo, P'o, Cupol, their own) for various labels. Halfway through this period, they teamed up with Miller for the patchily brilliant, though sadly one-off, project Duet Emmo (an anagram of Dome Mute); and in 1984 Gilbert released his first solo album on Mute, *This Way*, mostly taken up with an austere electronic work commissioned by the dancer Michael Clark, in the same year that he was working with The Fall. The following year when Wire reconvened as a group it was no surprise that they signed with Mute, releasing several albums through the late 80s and early 90s with them.

Of course, all this was in the background to a year dominated by the continued success of Depeche Mode which (as previously described) saw the group maintaining its purposeful transformation from light synthpop to heavy synthgoth. Mute would go on to carve an enviable and highly successful niche for itself, balancing the experimental with the accessible, the latter in effect funding the former. Thanks largely to Depeche Mode and Erasure they managed to keep going through the collapse of Rough Trade Distribution in the early 90s (which saw Factory and Rough Trade Records go bust), temporarily selling out to EMI, and are still going strong.

*****

Beggars Banquet never quite had the cache of its offspring 4AD, nor Factory or Rough Trade, which does the label a disservice and certainly its owner Martin Mills, as astute and successful an indie label boss as any in Britain. Founded in 1977, there were comparisons with Rough Trade in that it had initially been a shop (actually several, all in west London). Gary Numan's arrival in 1979, firstly with Tubeway Army and then solo, benefitted the label financially but made it difficult for them to emerge from his shadow. The press had never been kind to Numan, and to some extent Beggars got tarred with the same brush. The early 80s saw them try to address the problem by setting up sub-labels, 4AD and Situation Two, the latter releasing the early Associates singles before becoming the home of goth. The mother label, however, remained compromised by, on the one hand, bands like The Fall and The Mighty Wah! while, on the other, less credible groups like Freeez and a slew of proto new age artists (the latter moving to another subsidiary, Coda, the following year). It was all good business though and Beggars would outlast labels like Factory and Rough Trade – indeed in the new millennium, would bring the latter, resurrected, under its wing.

Cherry Red Records had been founded in 1978, by Iain McNay and Richard Jones, and had its first success with the Dead Kennedys' debut album in 1979. But it wasn't until Mike Alway joined as A&R in 1980 that the label forged a strong identity for itself with alternative acts like Eyeless In Gaza and Thomas Leer alongside the very English clean, melodic guitar sound of The Monochrome Set, Felt and Everything But The Girl, all of which ended up on the 99p epoch-defining *Pillows and Prayers* compilation[45]. Cherry Red was poised for great things, but 1984 was the year they temporarily blew it. The label lost its auteur sheen when Alway got itchy feet and set up Blanco Y Negro with Geoff Travis of Rough Trade and Michel Duval of Les Disques du Crépuscule, taking Everything But the Girl and The Monochrome Set with him. It would be 'the first quality indie-major of the 80s: art and commerce working together, with art – naturally – having the upper hand'[46]. At roughly the same time McNay took some time off to join the Rajneeshpuram community in Oregon. Consequently, Cherry Red temporarily lost direction and apart from albums by Felt and Holger Hiller, the year's releases[47] were disappointing.

The Blanco y Negro adventure turned out to be a disappointment too, at least for Alway, and the following year he returned to Cherry Red with his tail between his legs, setting up the sub-label él. This initially became a home for alternative bands like Shock Headed Peters, Momus and The King of Luxembourg (see Chapter 17) but soon turned into an excuse for indulging in his passion for hazy corners of Englishness[48], football fanzine culture and (much later) an obsession with 60s European esoterica released in Crépusculish sleeves set in a non-existent London café society. The Japanese loved it. Cherry Red *and* él would of course reinvent themselves as excellent reissue labels as well as canny curators of alternative pop history.

As would Les Temps Modernes (better known now as LTM), whose first vinyl releases came out in 1984. At the time, founder James Nice was in between school in Edinburgh and university in Glasgow, but it wasn't and never would be a Scottish label. Its first two singles originated from Essex ('Gunpoint'/'Perversion' by A Primary Industry, who would later become Ultramarine and prove adaptable to the dance-oriented 90s[49]) and the Netherlands (Minny Pops). However, it was Belgium's Les Disques du Crépuscule that Nice drew inspiration from, and as soon as he graduated he moved to Brussels to work directly with them. (For more on Crépuscule and its associated labels, see Chapter 26).

Back in Blighty, and continuing with the leftfield, labels like Fetish, Illuminated and Some Bizzare had taken inspiration from Mute, and in the case of Some Bizzare it too had its big-selling synthpop group which helped keep the label going. Fetish, had started by licensing Throbbing Gristle records and then gone on to establish their own small roster of acts like 23 Skidoo, Clock DVA and Stephen Mallinder, but by 1984 they had run out of steam and their last release was a compilation fittingly entitled *The Last Testament* (complete with inserted goodbye letters written by journalists Jon Savage and Sandy Robertson). Fetish had always paid careful attention to their artwork, much of which was designed by a young Neville Brody before he went on to art-direct The Face. The same could not be said of the strangely faceless Illuminated Records whose sleeves were mostly 'serviceable'. This was a shame, as by 1984, the label had an enviable roster of artists including 400 Blows, Portion Control and Fetish emigrés 23 Skidoo (all of whom are discussed in Chapter 18), unsung Euro-synthpoppers Data, goth bands Sex Gang Children and Dormannu, and several others, between them releasing around ten albums and 20 singles that year. It wasn't to last. In 1986 Illuminated disappeared as mysteriously as it had arrived.

If Keith Bagley, Illuminated's supremo, was in the background, Stephen Pearce (aka Stevo) of Some Bizzare, was in your face. Leaving school at 16, unable to read or write, Stevo's music career started with an internship at Phonogram, followed by DJ residencies at Chelsea Drugstore and the Clarendon where he cleared the floors with early Human League, Throbbing Gristle and Cabaret Voltaire (which nevertheless resulted in two electronic music charts for Record Mirror and Sounds) and then decided to put together a compilation album of new, undiscovered electronic acts. His first signing was Soft Cell who he somehow convinced to let him manage them. He was 17. Aside from Soft Cell, *The Some Bizzare Album* (1981) included The The, Blancmange and the first ever recording by Depeche Mode. In the end, Stevo thought Depeche Mode too poppy and they were signed by Mute, and Blancmange went to London Records, but he stuck with The The and over the next three years signed up an enviable roster of leftfield artists.

Some Bizzare was different from most of the labels so far described in that, generally speaking, it didn't manufacture or distribute the records itself[50]. That was left to the majors (Phonogram, WEA, Virgin and CBS) to whom Stevo licensed the product and played them off against each other to secure the biggest advance possible. It says a lot about his persuasive qualities and their – and the early 80s' – appetite for risk, that a major like CBS would sign a band like Psychic TV. But given the success of a group as contrary as Soft Cell who knew what might chart?[51] 1984 was a pivotal year for Some Bizzare: the end of Soft Cell, the make or break of Cabaret Voltaire and the ushering in of Test Dept, Coil and Foetus (the last three dealt with in Chapter 18).

To no great surprise, Soft Cell began the year by announcing that they were splitting up. Both Marc Almond and David Ball had already dabbled outside of the group (Almond's side-project, Marc and the Mambas; Ball's *In Strict Tempo* solo album). A farewell concert at the Hammersmith Palais (January), a single, 'Down in the Subway' (February), and an album, *This Last Night in Sodom* (March), made sure they went out with a bang, but it was painful stuff. The album, recorded in mono, was a dirge of death, dirt and despair, sung with wicked glee by Almond over a cranked up sleazy electro backdrop. An Almond solo deal was struck through Phonogram and in true Stevo fashion, instead of attending the meeting, he sent a teddy bear with a tape recorder attached to it. The demands included a year's supply of sweets. Still stuck in the gutter, but a lot more palatable and less electronic, a succession of solo[52] singles swiftly followed: the excellent 'Tenderness Is A Weakness', the escalating 'You Have' (addressed to a friend who had committed suicide) and the average, cowboyish 'The Boy Who Came Back'; also an album from which they all came, *Vermin in Ermine*. 'People talk about this interest in sleeze', he said, 'but what interests me is the loner, the loser, the misfit, the survivor and the underdog of society'[53].

One of Almond's more unusual tracks was the 17-minute long B-side, 'Split Lip', propelled by incessant drumming similar to labelmate The The's nearly 10-minute long 'Giant' from *Soul Mining*. Released in November 1983, *Soul Mining* was an astounding album: skittish but accessible, marvellously melodic, confidently produced, post-punk at its most assured and sophisticated. Although The The was essentially just one person, 22-year-old Londoner Matt Johnson, he was joined by an esoteric choice of musicians whose inspired contributions – Jools Holland's stunning piano solo on 'Uncertain Smile', Thomas Leer's synth, Jim Foetus's epic percussion, Paul Wickens's accordion, Anne Stephenson's violin, etc – gave the album drive, variety and soul. It also managed to balance grim ('I've Been Waitin' For Tomorrow (All Of My Life)') with upbeat ('This Is The Day'). The bar was set so high that Johnson seemed flummoxed by how exactly to follow it. Eventually, the trenchant, heavily political *Infected* arrived in 1986 but it lacked the variety of its predecessor – although bizarrely it sold a lot more.

Some Bizzare, Cherry Red (Iain McNay and Mike Alway) and Go Discs.

Another of Stevo's great hopes were Cabaret Voltaire whom he'd lured from Rough Trade towards the end of 1982. Stevo encouraged them to move away from abrasive guitars and into the New York club sound that New Order had adopted. On *The Crackdown*, with help from David Ball, production from Flood, a big studio to play in and Virgin's backing, they did just that. But if they were to really trouble the charts, they needed songs rather than (excellent) rhythms with menacing vocals over the top. Early 1984 saw them produce a single by Six Sed Red, a duo featuring Soft Cell backing singer Cindy Ecstasy and B-Movie instrumentalist Rick Holliday. 'Shake It Right', their only recording[54], was a sexy slab of electro, and deserved to do better than its instant disappearance. Expectations were that 1984's *Microphonies*, again licensed to Virgin, would do the trick. Certainly its lead single 'Sensoria' boded well with its incessant, sophisticated beat, backing vocals by Shikisha and inventive promo video, but the album was a bit disappointing. Another album and a double EP followed but, after moving to EMI and flirting with house, they split in the early 90s. And that was Some Bizzare's fate. Whereas Mute had been able to rely on the chart success of Depeche Mode and Yazoo to keep it afloat and help develop the roster, Stevo struggled without Soft Cell, even if he did still have Marc Almond. Cabaret Voltaire and The The had the potential but perhaps not the intention to make it much beyond the indie charts, and the rest of the roster were just too leftfield.

*****

There were hundreds of other labels contributing to a healthy independent scene. Alan McGee's Creation Records kicked off properly at the beginning of 1984 (see Chapter 16), while the year before, Andy MacDonald and Lesley Symons's Go! Discs kick-started Billy Bragg's career, before going on to sign The Housemartins (whose first gig was in 1984), The Beautiful South and The La's. The label felt working class and slightly irreverent, on the one hand urging people to Pay No More Than £2.99 (for Bragg's debut) while on the other sponsoring a football team (Viz comic's Fulchester United, in which star striker Billy The Fish would plug Go! Discs releases). Tot Taylor's Compact Organization was also playful in its marketing, but adopted a make-believe Anglo-European 50s/60s aesthetic which sat perfectly between the equally retro worlds of él and Crépuscule. Its tiny roster was led by two female singers. Neasden's Mari Wilson alternated between upbeat Motown and torch standards but always from underneath a vertiginous beehive, a look which pigeonholed her. 1983 was her year. Sweden's Virna Lindt fashioned a more monochrome Vogue-meets-*Ipcress-File* look, but a proto Saint Etienne sound couldn't disguise a weak voice and her early 1984 *Shiver* album would be consigned to cultdom.

Chris Parry's Fiction Records was marketed and distributed by Polydor and in the 80s focussed almost exclusively on The Cure, but diversified later. Dave Kitson's Red Flame and Ink Records had deals with Virgin's 10 Records and were home to the likes of Carmel, The Moodists and Anne Clark. Founded by Clive Solomon and Sounds journalist Johnny Waller, Fire Records' first release was 1000 Mexicans' excellent 'Diving for Pearls' in 1984, followed by Pulp, Blue Aeroplanes and others. Nick Ralph's Midnight Music was occasional home to Robyn Hitchcock and Cindytalk. Abstract Records and Glass Records may have been based in north London but gave the impression they were from, respectively, the north of England and the midlands. Abstract seemed to focus on the crusty-goth of New Model Army, Three Johns, 1919 (all with 1984 releases) while Glass concentrated on The Jazz Butcher, In Embrace and Bauhaus emigré David J. Food Records was set up in 1984 by ex-Teardrop Explodes' David Balfe, who later took on Sounds journalist Andy Ross as his partner, their first releases including Brilliant and The Woodentops. Originally wholly independent, the late 80s saw Food become more closely linked with the majors, which probably helped them sign a band called Seymour, who changed their name to Blur, and in the mid-90s EMI bought them out completely. Formed in the early 80s and part of the bigger Zomba Group so barely indie, Jive Records put out singles by A Flock Of Seagulls and Q Feel before switching to hip-hop.

Of course there were hundreds of labels operating outside of London, often originating in record shops and some of them achieving success beyond their immediate locale. It's impossible to do them all justice here, but it's worth mentioning a dozen. Kitchenware and Volume were both founded in Newcastle in 1982, but with very different agendas. The former linked with majors and had success with Prefab Sprout and The Kane Gang amongst others; the latter were almost entirely about one group, The Toy Dolls, whose astonishingly successful re-release of 'Nellie the Elephant' in 1984 kept the label in business for many a year. Another quirky band similarly paid the bills for Geoff Davies's Probe Plus label in Liverpool. 'The period from '84 onwards is the period I'm happiest about. Most of them were flops, but what made all the money was Half Man Half Biscuit'[55]. Red Rhino in York was perhaps best known as a distributor, but it had a flourishing label too, its mid-80s releases including The Mekons, Red Lorry Yellow Lorry, Hula, Pulp's debut album and some goth. But the real home of goth was Leeds-based Merciful Release, created by Andrew Eldritch for Sisters Of Mercy albums and singles, but also putting out product by the March Violets. Nottinghamshire-based Ron Johnson Records put out vinyl by edgy post-punk bands like Big Flame, A Witness and Stump. Ex-Fall Marc Riley's In-Tape label was evidence that Manchester wasn't just about Factory, its eclectic roster of bands best summed up by the title of its compilation, *Just A Mish-Mash*. West Midland's Graduate Records were famous for signing UB40, but were on the slide by 1984. As was Bristol's Y Records, best known for The Pop Group, The Slits, Pigbag and Shriekback. Its founder Dick O'Dell carried on with band management as well as humouring himself (though very few others) with a group called Disconnection whose two cover singles – 'Bali Hai' (1982) and 'We Love You' (1984) – should perhaps have remained on the ideas shelf.

Despite the legion of successful Scottish bands plying their trade in the mid-80s, there were very few Scottish independent labels of note. Even Fast Product and Postcard in their turn-of-the-decade heyday had been tiny, and the few that followed in their footsteps (Oil City, Statik, Linn) struggled to live up to their legacy, most bands choosing English labels. It was the same in Northern Ireland with Good Vibrations ceasing business in 1982, though south of the border was healthier with Reekus and U2's Mother Records. Wales was a similar story. Independent labels are usually associated with post-punk, but there were plenty catering for other genres: Greensleeves (reggae), Hi-Lo (mod), Neat Records (heavy metal) and Street Sounds (electro) were just a few. And lest it not be forgotten, Stock Aitken Waterman's hits were released on the independent PWL which licensed them to majors.

The second half of the 80s saw the birth of indie, the genre. It was linked to independent labels in that, at the beginning it would be found on them, but in time became a meaningless catch-all. The general consensus is that it started with the NME's C86 cassette, but you could just as easily say it started with The Smiths. As Richard King, author of *How Soon Is Now?* said: 'A sympathetic understanding of indie music is to see it as a morass of signifiers: guitars, fringes, young or youngish groups of mainly white people connecting the highlights of their music collection in an ever-shifting reconfiguration of the past. A more critical assessment would be that indie is the pinnacle of disengaged, querulous solipsism'[56]. Ouch.

Indie was accessible, and therefore attracted the major labels. But they relied on the independents to discover the bands, later waving their chequebooks at either the band or the label. Buying into independents became common practise, EMI's relationship with Food Records being a good example. EMI could be indie without being independent; Food could focus on A&R without worrying about the money. This made it difficult for the 'real' independents to compete, and in their efforts to do so they spent too much money trying to expand. It took a few years, but in the early 90s, the Cartel had collapsed, Rough Trade and Factory went bust and Alan McGee and Ivo Watt-Russell went AWOL. The fact that indie went mainstream in the form of Britpop didn't really benefit the independents as most of the bands were being bankrolled by majors. 4AD struggled on (without Ivo who sold up and moved permanently to the States), Creation sold out to Sony and ceased trading by the end of the decade, and Mute sold out to EMI at the beginning of the new millennium[57]. Interestingly, it was Beggars Banquet and Cherry Red, run by businessmen rather than the guys with the A&R vision, who best negotiated the choppy waters. Beggars became Beggars Group, ironically bringing a new-look Rough Trade into the fold, and Cherry Red[58] transformed itself into a successful custodian of popular music's past.

Indie ushered in a wave of guitar bands who felt comfortable – now – in this in-between time that 1984 seemed to represent, to reference the 60s. Not the beat groups or blues, but mod and psychedelia. It is to those bands and one particular new label we turn to now.

Chapter 16: Swingeing London
From psychedelia to psychobilly

When I tell you about psychedelia, you can forget all the Peace-Love-Dove shit.[1]
Julian Cope

Creation Records seeks pop groups with fantastic songs and a hatred for the current pop scene.
Ad in Melody Maker

In December 1983, having emerged from what was effectively a year-long acid trip after the split of The Teardrop Explodes, Julian Cope submitted an article to the NME called *Tales from the Drug Attic*. It introduced its youngish readership to American mid-60s psychedelic bands, using the infamous *Nuggets* compilation (1972) as a starting point: The Seeds, Thirteenth Floor Elevators, Chocolate Watch Band, Electric Prunes as well as, from Britain, the first Pink Floyd album, *Revolver, Sergeant Pepper*, The Creation, The Misunderstood and others, all in Cope's (then little-known) ecstatic-mind-dump style. The purpose of the article was celebratory, educational and a rallying call. What had prompted this? Certainly, Cope was reacting against the new pop that he had been a part of, but basically he was on a crusade to unearth a music that he felt was being ignored and that the time was ripe for reappraisal.

There had been a revival of sorts two years earlier, but it was short-lived, limited to central London and focussed more on the look rather than the music. Its real reference points were Swinging London, The Prisoner TV series and films like The Monkees' *Head*, rather than the studious appreciation of the original music which Cope was calling for. This first look back was itself modelled on the mod revival of 1979, the two genres coming together in a mix-up of stripey trousers and floral shirts, fish-tail parkas and hussar jackets. Its beating heart was the Groovy Cellar club in Soho, aided and abetted by two others, The Clinic and Le Kilt. Escapist, like the parallel, peaking new romantic scene, but less cliquey, it was like 1967 frozen in time with a lot of waving around of arms and fingers to the likes of Syd-Barrett-singles-era Pink Floyd and current bands like Mood Six. A 30-minute film, *The Groovy Movie* (1981), captures the idiosyncratic scene perfectly, including a boat trip 'happening' down the Thames. In short it was very Austin Powers. Things looked like they were coming together when WEA put the likes of Mood Six, High Tide, The Marble Staircase, The Barracudas and The Times onto a neo-mod/psych compilation called *A Splash Of Colour*[2] at the start of 1982. But by spring the scene was already over, too idiosyncratic and niche to cross over into the mainstream.

It never totally went away, however, and in 1983 the mainstream success of Siouxsie and the Banshees's 'Dear Prudence'[3], as well as Robert Smith and Steve Severin's side project, The Glove (named after the giant flying gloves in the *Yellow Submarine* film), helped rekindle interest in psychedelia. In the autumn a new club called Alice In Wonderland opened in Soho and by the end of the year Cope had written his NME essay. But this time it wasn't about the look. This time it was about the music, its part in the rise of indie and its commentary on the tensions and divides of mid-80s Britain. Less swinging and more swingeing. *Swingeing London* was the title of one of artist Richard Hamilton's best-known works, its subject Mick Jagger handcuffed to art dealer Robert Fraser, shielding their faces from the cameras as they arrived by car at Chichester Crown Court following the Redlands drug bust in 1967. It was a study of fame, the media and the establishment, and captured the country at the moment when one version of the 60s (peace, love, optimism and a buoyant economy) was about to end, and a version of the 70s (strikes, pessimism and economic crises) was about to begin. Like Warhol, Hamilton had produced numerous variations of the same image from 1968, around the time of the Stones' strained, psychedelic *Their Satanic Majesties Request* and The Beatles' 'difficult' *'White Album'* (the cover of which Hamilton also designed). If the first psyche revival had been about the cool, hedonistic Swinging London, the second reflected the tension of 1968.

Punk had adopted a scorched-earth, kill-your-heroes, never-trust-a-hippy approach to rock and pop heritage. But as post-punk began to fade, it had started to become permissible to look back. In truth, punk was itself retro, modelled on a mixture of mod and The Stooges. But now it became increasingly acceptable, even fashionable amongst the new underground scene that was taking shape, to reference *Nuggets* et al. The same was happening in the US with hardcore's acknowledgement of pre-punk heritage and the beginnings of the so-called Paisley Underground scene. In April 1984 Sounds ran a special on Paisley – bands like The Long Ryders, Rain Parade and so on – as well as the nascent British scene, including an enthusiastic one-pager on the Alice In Wonderland club by David Tibet.

The Alice club had been gaining in popularity, with bands like Naz Nomad (aka The Damned), Scarlet Party (featuring Mark Gilmour, brother of the Pink Floyd guitarist) and Jeremy's Secret (Simon Fisher Turner and Colin Lloyd – see also next chapter) playing live. The Groovy Cellar's DJ and compere, The Doctor (aka Clive Jackson), had been retained, and his group, Doctor and the Medics, became the new club's house band. The club started putting on specials: film festivals at the Scala in Kings Cross and 'mystery trips', the latter involving being bussed to Chislehurst Caves in Kent (where Doctor and the Medics played a suitably claustrophobic set) and the so-called Alice in Wonderland Trip to Fairyland, which turned out to be the old Decca Records factory in Battersea.

A couple of other movers and shakers from the first revival were school-friends Dan Treacy and Ed Ball and their two groups, Television Personalities (mainly Treacy) and The Times (mainly Ball). Television Personalities had debuted with the EP 'Where's Bill Grundy Now', which also included the semi-classic 'Part Time Punks', in 1978, but by the early 80s were resolutely (if ramshackle) psyche, epitomised by albums *And Don't The Kids Just Love It* and *They Could Have Been Bigger Than The Beatles*. But 1984 saw them at a low point. *The Painted Word*, was a strange, droney, even dreary record which even the tongue-in cheek arty video for the title track couldn't lighten; and it was followed by a lacklustre live album, *Chocolate Art*, recorded on tour in Germany, and snidely subtitled 'A Tribute to James Last'. They also ran into trouble with Pink Floyd's David Gilmour who asked them to support him on tour having heard their single 'I Know Where Syd Barrett Lives'. Unfortunately, Treacy really did know where Barrett lived and chose to read out the address to a bemused audience, after which they were promptly dropped. However, they bounced back, and are one of those rare bands of the post-punk era that made it into the 90s and, after several dark years out of the public eye, into the new millennium.

Although Ed Ball had played with Television Personalities in the early years, he left in 1982 to concentrate on The Times[4]. If the former were psyche, the latter were mod. Titles of records alone were indicative – 'I Helped Patrick McGoohan Escape', *Pop Goes Art!* and *This is London* – but the music too placed them in a Swinging London timewarp. The title of 1984 album *Hello Europe* may have bucked the titular trend, but it was still steadfastly mod in sound. Ball continued to record as The Times, changing his style a bit by the 90s, forming other groups, working for Creation Records, and even briefly re-joined Television Personalities in the new millennium. Mod had already enjoyed a revival in the late 70s, spearheaded by The Jam and the release of the *Quadrophenia* film. When Paul Weller called time, the scene went underground, but reappeared around 1984. Some of the bands who'd aped The Jam's split reformed again (eg. The Purple Hearts), some had never gone away (The Times, The Prisoners, The Reaction) while others were new (The Truth, Makin' Time, The Jetset); even Steve Diggles's post-Buzzcocks band Flag of Convenience were effectively mod. Like the earlier psychedelia revival, the look was hugely important, as DJ and publisher Paul Hallam remembers: 'When the whole mid-80s mod revival started to happen, it became all about getting your shoes and shirts handmade. We were looking back at the '62 mod, studying Richard Barnes's book, we weren't listening to The Who, we were sitting in bars in Shoreditch, reading French newspapers'[5]. When he wasn't hanging around in Soho cafes or DJ-ing at Sneakers in Shepherds Bush, Hallam documented the scene with his Olympus Trip camera, collected much later in in a book, *Odds and Sods*. Sounds also ran a big mod revival feature in July, but like the 1979 media-induced attempt, the scene never went mainstream. Which kept it fresh: '…it was a rejection of 80s pessimism and an attempt to adopt the forward-looking, optimistic state of mind so obviously present in the 60s'.[6]

Aside from the on-off playing in each other's bands, Dan Treacy and Ed Ball had also formed Whaam! Records (referencing Lichtenstein rather than Michael and Ridgeley). Ironically, it was less a conduit for their own music and more a home for others', releasing around ten albums and a dozen singles by bands like The Direct Hits (named after The Who's early compilation of B-sides and sounding like it; their 1984 debut album *Blow Up* was another steal from the era), and debut singles by The Pastels and Doctor and the Medics. These and more were collected on that year's compilation *All For Art… And Art For All,* which turned out to be the label's final release. The 'more' included The Laughing Apple and Revolving Paint Dream, two groups who were central to another leading force in the scene.

*****

On moving to London in 1979, Alan McGee and fellow Glaswegian guitarist Andrew Innes had dissolved one band, Newspeak, and formed another, The Laughing Apple, surviving long enough, with different line-ups, to release three singles, all of which sounded typically post-punk rather than psychedelic. They split up in early 1982 and McGee went back to his British Rail day job. Not to be put off, he turned his hand at promoting concerts, putting on a series of Sunday shows at the London Musicians Collective in Camden in the autumn of 1982 featuring, amongst others, Television Personalities, The Go-Betweens and Eyeless In Gaza, compered by The Legend! (aka NME scribe, Jerry Thackray). It didn't make any money, but it proved he had the organizational talent. He called it The Communication Club.

McGee now went into overdrive, forming yet another band, Biff Bang Pow!, named after a song by The Creation, starting a fanzine called Communication Blur (in which he laid out his stall: 'Only two periods have meant anything to me in recent years: 1965-67 and 1977-78') and in the summer of 1983, re-locating The Communication Club to a tiny room above the Adams Arms pub on Conway Street in central London, two months later changing the name to The Living Room. It quickly became the centre of a nascent 'scene', although it was never cut-and-dry psyche, as appearances by the likes of Death In June, 1000 Mexicans and Three Johns testify. Thackeray continued to act as host, while also performing a kind of acapella post-punk as The Legend and his Swinging Soul Sisters. Next on the cards that summer was the almost inevitable setting up of a record label, Creation Records[7], formed with Biff Bang Pow! bandmates Dick Green and Joe Foster. Its first release, however, was a false start – The Legend!'s '73 in 83' single – an amateur-hour white rap which even McGee panned (albeit much later).

As 1983 drew to a close, with Cope's essay appearing in NME, McGee sensed that the following year everything would come together and in a press statement declared that Creation would be 'The Next Projected Sound of 1984'. Thanks to an ad in Melody Maker ('Creation Records seeks pop groups with fantastic songs and a hatred for the current pop scene'), the *real* launch of Creation arrived in January 1984 with the near-simultaneous release of four singles[8]: '50 Years of Fun' by Biff Bang Pow!, 'Flowers are in the Sky' by The Revolving Paint Dream (helmed by Andrew Innes, with occasional input from McGee), 'Something's Going On' by The Pastels, and 'Think!' by Aberdeeners-in-London, The Jasmine Minks. Whereas The Living Room's signature sound was quite wide ranging – the new year kicked off with The June Brides (post-punk), The X Men (garage/psychobilly) and Surfadelic (surf) – Creation Records honed in on psychedelia. Stephen Pastel had told the NME that he wanted his group to 'sound like a 60s group with an element of bubblegum in it'[9] and Edwin Pouncey made 'Something's Going On' Single of the Week in Sounds, comparing it and them to the Velvet Underground and Love.

Straight after the release of this first batch of singles, The Living Room's Adam's Arms residency fell foul of fire regulations and had to switch to sporadic outings at, for instance, the Union Tavern in Kings Cross and Oxford Arms in Camden, before settling into the Roebuck Pub on Tottenham Court Road[10]. Meanwhile, in early summer, the next batch of Creation releases included Biff Bang Pow!'s second single, another by The Jasmine Minks and a garage rock-out called 'Do the Ghost' by The X-Men which turned out to be Creation's best-selling single that year.

Whaam!'s Dan Treacy and Creation's Alan McGee; The Jesus and Mary Chain live.

However, the band that put Creation on the map were coming up in the fast lane. Wild, truculent and permanently in shades, The Jesus and Mary Chain – aka East Kilbride brothers Jim and William Reid and residual others – were perfect for McGee and Creation. After spending the early 80s on the dole dreaming of being in a band, they eventually formed one, The Daisy Chains, and in late spring 1984 sent a demo to McGee. He wasn't that impressed but invited them down to London anyway, the brothers changing their name before they arrived. On 8 June they played their first ever gig, a short, shambolic, feedback-drenched set at The Living Room supporting Microdisney. 'After one song I knew they were genius', McGee proclaimed[11], and signed them on the spot. There followed a Peel Session in October, debut single 'Upside Down' in November and a 'riot' at the ICA Rock Week in December. They may have shared Postcard's love of The Velvet Underground, but their other influences were more The Ramones and the Shangri-Las – the wall-of-sound composite drenched in feedback. There were melodies in there – some curiously reminiscent of the Beach Boys – but they were buried under half a ton of attitude. Unlike the Postcard bands' disdain for drink and drugs, the Reid brothers were demons for both. McGee, who was also acting as their manager, encouraged their antics, and the press, looking for the next big thing, jumped on them. With manager's hat on, he saw that Creation was too small for them, so let them go to Blanco y Negro – until the next two truculent brothers came along.

The Jesus and Mary Chain's 'residual others' included, for a while, Bobby Gillespie on drums. Or possibly drum. As a teenager he'd been in The Drains with McGee, then roadied for Altered Images and played bass with The Wake before joining the Reid brothers – all this while trying to get his own band, Primal Scream, off the ground. Primal Scream at this stage were essentially a live band, but 1984 saw them record an obscure would-be debut single ('The Orchard', with vocals by Judith Boyle because

Gillespie had a cold), shelve it, sign to Creation and release the more considered 'All Fall Down' in early 1985. In line with the rest of the Creation roster, their music was heavily 60s influenced but wasn't quite ready for chartdom. That would come much later with *Screamadelica* in 1991. Not so lucky were The Loft who despite releasing 1984 debut single 'Why Does the Rain?', almost a template for what many considered to be the 'Creation sound', split up spectacularly onstage the following year.

So, by the end of 1984, Creation had established itself and yet it was still small fry compared with the likes of Go! Discs and Red Flame, let alone Rough Trade and Mute. Through hard work, a maverick PR style and sheer force of will, McGee would steer the label through the ups and downs of the second half of the decade trying to break bands like Felt and The House Of Love, before striking gold with the indie/dance crossover *Screamadelica*, My Bloody Valentine's *Loveless* and, of course, Oasis in the mid-90s.

Of course there was more to the British psyche scene than Creation and Whaam!. The Pink label, for instance, released The June Brides' first two singles, 'In The Rain' and 'Every Conversation'. They had played in The Living Room and seemed destined for Creation, but McGee reputedly decided not to sign them as it would have been 'too obvious'[12]. XTC jumped on the bandwagon with side-project The Dukes of Stratosphear (see next chapter). The Playn Jane finally released debut album *Friday The 13th (Live At The Marquee)* followed the year after by their one and only studio album *Five Good Evils*. Mood Six, who'd been at the centre of the earlier revival, had signed with EMI but it didn't work out and were soon back to indie-label status, releasing debut album *The Difference Is...* in 1985 on Psycho Records. Ace Records' Big Beat imprint put out the more garage end of psyche, bands like The Sting-Rays and The (sometimes Thee) Milkshakes.

Medway stars: The Milkshakes, The Delmonas, Billy Childish and Tracey Emin.

The Milkshakes were at the centre of a vibrant, self-contained and purposefully amateur scene-within-a-scene in the cluster of Medway towns in North Kent. The band's driving force was musician, painter, poet and all-round renaissance man Billy Childish who steered them through nine albums between 1981-84 (five in 1984 alone). In truth, their sound was as much 50s rock'n'roll as 60s psyche. During this time,

Childish's lover was fellow Medway artist Tracey Emin, the two influencing each other's activities. Also around at the time was all-girl group The Delmonas who originally sang backing vocals with The Milkshakes. When the latter split, they switched roles, with The Milkshakes becoming the backing band for The Delmonas. Debut single 'I'm Comin Home' could have been straight out of *Pulp Fiction*.

The importance of 1972's *Nuggets* has already been noted, but there were other US psyche revival compilations that followed in its wake, most notably the *Pebbles* (1978-88) and *Mindrocker* (1981-86) series. These mined obscure tracks from the second half of the 60s, often copied straight from the vinyl, and inspired a whole new American scene dubbed Paisley Underground – bands like Rain Parade, The Dream Syndicate, The Long Ryders, Thin White Rope and Opal. Many of these were licensed to Peter Flanagan's Clapham-based Zippo Records and in turn greatly influenced the UK's psyche scene. In truth, they were tighter and more professional than most of British bands who still adopted punk's ramshackle DIY ideology.

*****

Moving further away from psychedelia and mod, but still in thrall to punked-up Americana, psychobilly was the early 80s lovechild of rockabilly and punk by way of Bill Haley and the Comets, The Cramps and Stray Cats. The Cramps had the smut but not the crucial upright bass, and the Stray Cats[13] had the upright bass but not the smut. Psychobilly, a largely British phenomenon, had both. And the band with the mostest were south Londoners The Meteors whose image of horror schtick and B-movie sleaze made for intense live performances. Of the countless albums they've put out – at time of writing they're still going – 1984's *Stampede* is as representative as any. Hot on their heels were other bands like Guana Bats (just starting), King Kurt (whose cover of 'Mack The Knife' graced the charts in 1984), and The Polecats (whose third album, *Cult Heroes,* was released by Nervous Records that year). Nervous were also responsible for a key compilation, *Hell's Bent On Rockin!,* also released that year, and featuring Demented Are Go, Frenzy and The Sharks amongst other fly-by-nights. In truth, some of these were more rocka- than psychobilly.

The real heart of psychobilly was at the Klub Foot Nightclub in the art-deco ballroom of the Clarendon Hotel in Hammersmith, running from 1982 until the building was demolished in 1988. A live compilation album entitled *Stomping at the Klub Foot –* four bands with four tracks each – was released in 1984, semi-documented the scene[14]. As with psyche and mod, the clothes were crucial: for the guys sleeveless leather jackets, checked shirts, heavily faded jeans, brothel creepers and flat tops or quiffs; for the girls tight, hot-rod outfits and either Bettie Page hair or (in the case of the Shillelagh Sisters' Jacquie Sullivan) 'the biggest fuck-off quiff you could manage, preferably bleached'[15]. Both sported vintage-themed tattoos.

From psychobilly to cowpunk was either a leap or a hop depending on how you defined the latter. Essentially it was a cross between country, bluegrass, skiffle, folk and punk, and occasionally known as roots music. Again, the principal antecedents were American – Hank Williams and Patsy Cline for instance, and newer bands like X and Lone Justice – but also British skiffle artists like Lonnie Donegan and Mungo Jerry and other folk/roots music of the 60s and 70s. In any case, 1984 saw a short-lived but intense 'revival' (actually, it had probably never come together in such a way before) very much centred in London. Arguably its prime movers, The Pogues had formed in 1982 but didn't get into their stride until two years later when they found themselves supporting The Clash, signed to Stiff and released debut single 'Dark Streets of London' and album *Red Roses for Me*. The B-side of the former was a punked-up version of 'And The Band Played Waltzing Matilda', a paean to the 1915 Gallipoli tragedy by Scottish-born Aussie Eric Bogle which used elements of the 19th Century song. Another of Bogle's First World War homages, 'The Green Fields of France', was covered by The Men They Couldn't Hang, a band who had recently moved to London from Southampton, signing to Elvis Costello's Imp label. Surprisingly for a debut single and with a subject matter that was at odds with Top Of The Pops, it was an instant success, topping the indie charts and voted #3 in John Peel's Festive 50 that year. The band would go on to release an album a year for the remainder of the decade, become live favourites, including supporting David Bowie in 1990, before splitting up a year later.[16]

Psychobilly at the Klub Foot Nightclub in Hammersmith, London; cowpunkers The Shillelagh Sisters.

By day, gynaecologist Dr Samuel Hutt, by night Hank Wangford, the latter has probably done more to promote country & western (if not cowpunk) than any other person in Britain. Although he and his band only released two albums in the 80s, 1984 saw them constantly touring: supporting the miners' strike as Hank, Frank and Billy (with Frank Chickens and Billy Bragg); performing at a benefit concert for the GLC (where they were attacked on stage by a group of right-wing skinheads); and being nominated for a Perrier Award for their Edinburgh Fringe Festival show. After a long absence, even classic post-punkers The Mekons returned with an alt-country sound, incorporated fiddle, steel guitar and harmonica. Based in Leeds, one of the heartlands of coal mining, the band had been re-ignited by the miners' strike and felt that 'rootsy' instruments were somehow more appropriate for the times – though to say it was cowpunk would be stretching it a bit. The same could be said of Martin Stephenson & The Daintees or even Billy Bragg, though that would be stretching it even more.

However, for a while, there was a genuine scene, mostly in London, centering on half-a-dozen short-lived groups who in 1984 *all* released debuts and *all* recorded Peel Sessions, and yet *all* split up the following year. As their name-suggests, the Boothill Foot Tappers were a lively act whose debut single 'Get Your Feet Out of My Shoes' was a minor hit. The Shillelagh Sisters were an all-girl[17] group with links to the Polecats, who managed to secure a deal with CBS, but their two singles, 'Give Me My Freedom' and 'Passion Fruit' flopped. Singer Jacquie O'Sullivan later joined Bananarama. Cowboy/girl-fixated Yip Yip Coyote (formed by Carl Evans, previously of Brighton band The Chefs) also managed to release a couple of singles, *and* an album, the rather good *Fifi*, some of which was produced by Tony Mansfield and Anne Dudley (though not together), but they didn't last the course either. Bucking the London trend, Terry and Gerry came from Birmingham, played in black suits and ribbon ties, and managed to record *three* John Peel Sessions, five singles and an album before splitting at the end of 1985. Also ex-The Chefs, Helen and the Horns started off as cowpunk but their two 1984 singles, 'Footsteps at my Door' and cover of Rodgers & Hammerstein's 'The Surrey with the Fringe on Top', were more like old-time jazz. An eponymous album the following year somehow managed to combine both. Tub-thumpers Skiff Skats were a 7-piece with links to Madness who put out one fine album and performed in the loos at the Alternative Country Music Festival in the Electric Ballroom in the spring of 1984. Around the same time London Weekend Television broadcast a 'cowpunk' special called South of Watford, presented by a young Ben Elton and featuring most of the above. Both had the effect of making the scene slightly more than coincidence, but only in London. Appearances on The Tube followed, but there was no cowpunk compilation and the 'scene', if not necessarily the music, started to fizzle out by the end of the year.

We have come a long way from psychedelia to psychobilly to cowpunk – let alone the minor diversion of mod. But what they all had in common was a British punk revision of Americana, be it based on (the original) garage, rockabilly or country. And for some reason it all hit a peak in 1984. Quite why this happened virtually simultaneously is hard to say, but a very significant factor was the reaction against new pop and synthpop, and the welcoming back of guitars and 'authenticity'. Of course, it wasn't totally authentic but it was perhaps the beginning of British popular music's 'retromania' (to use Simon Reynolds' term). The late 70s and early 80s had seen a wave of genres – not just post-punk, new pop and synthpop, but also industrial, EBM, hip-hop and early techno – which were all clearly forward-looking. Of course, most popular music looks back to some extent, but 1984 seemed to represent a tipping point.

Chapter 17: English Eccentrics
Pranksters and poets, misfits and mavericks

Eccentric (adj): *deviating from the recognized or customary character, practice, etc.; irregular; erratic; peculiar; odd.* (noun) *a person who has an unusual, peculiar, or odd personality, set of beliefs, or behaviour pattern.*

My mission was always intended to be slightly outside the public eye, because that makes me appear more interesting than I really am. A lot of people don't realise that merely by staying away, you can create a myth.[1]
Julian Cope

Using the word weird implies that there is a norm.[2]
Robyn Hitchcock

For one reason or another, the British – and especially the English – are famous for being eccentric. Certainly history has a long list of moneyed men (rarely women; too busy) of leisure with time on their hands, intrepid explorers, double-barrelled squires and cracked actors, to say nothing of Quentin Crisp and Monty Python. If one thinks of eccentricity in British popular music, the names most often thrown up are those with origins in the 60s. The surrealist Bonzo Dog Doo Dah Band and its core members Vivian Stanshall and Neil Innes[3]; the lugubrious harmonium-accompanied songs and poems of London-based Scot, Ivor Cutler[4]; obsessive, manic-depressive oddballs like Joe Meek and Screaming Lord Sutch; self-destructive characters like Keith Moon. They are often assumed to be funny, though the last three were more tragic than comic. Most creatives are eccentric to some degree: they have wacky ideas. Some become so thanks to the absurdity of the rock & roll lifestyle, whether through taking vast quantities of drugs or people saying you're fantastic all the time; others play up to it as a career choice.

Sometimes eccentricity is manifested in appearance. In the early 70s David Bowie fitted the picture when he donned a dress and a flash, but in the mid-80s when he wore suits and looked like an advertising executive it was less apparent. Glam rockers and new romantics didn't really qualify since this was largely an example of career choice and at their height 'everybody' looked like them. Apparel had to be unique and, better still, unfashionable: Ivor Cutler in his plus fours and badge-covered beret, or Jarvis Cocker in his brown corduroys are better examples. Sometimes, though very rarely, a whole group could be labeled eccentric – The Bonzos being a case in point – but mostly it's an individual whose strong personality dominates the others. Even then, were Boy George or Morrissey eccentric, eccentrics, or simply mavericks?

By the mid-80s, the English eccentric was under threat. The free-spiritedness of the 60s had long gone, replaced by conformity and the beginnings of political correctness.

The dwindling number of aristocrats were forced to spend time maintaining their crumbling stately homes; even train spotters seemed to be a disappearing breed.

Malcolm McLaren was more a provocateur than an eccentric, but many of his actions could be seen as pranks even if they were at the same time serious and culturally significant. With Vivienne Westwood and the Sex Pistols he introduced, respectively, outré street fashion and punk to the mainstream; when the Pistols imploded he took on Bow Wow Wow and then immersed himself in New York's hip-hop scene, releasing the highly influential single 'Buffalo Girls' and album *Duck Rock*. But where to next?

The surprising answer came in 1984 when the 'inventor' of low-art punk sought to introduce high-art opera to the masses. McLaren took the romance and tragedy of Puccini (and it was mostly Puccini), replaced strings with Fairlight, kept the sopranos and tenors but also added hip-hop vocals, and hired producer Stephen Hague to make sense of it all. A sumptuously produced single, 'Madame Butterfly', arrived in the summer, with soprano chorus by Betty Ann White, hip versing by Debbie Cole and the strange half-Cockney-half-country narration by McLaren as the caddish Pinkerton. It had the scale and grandeur of romantic-era opera but at the same time was utterly contemporary, and hit #13 in the charts[5]. The following album, *Fans*, didn't live up to the single, but it was a brave experiment. 'Not the revolutionary blend of cultures Malcolm would have us believe it is', wrote Melody Maker, 'But you *can* dance to it and it *is* hugely entertaining'. The US release was accompanied by a provocative (or defeatist?) ad: 'We don't care if you hate this record. We love it'. McLaren would continue to dabble in music projects (*Waltz Darling* in 1989 and a homage to Paris in 1994, for example) but the dalliance with opera – and particularly 'Madam Butterfly' – was his last great musical achievement.

From early-80s reluctant teen-idol to crouching naked under a turtle shell while peering at a vintage toy truck – now that was eccentric. After the disintegration of the Teardrop Explodes, Julian Cope spent most of 1983 in the small village of Drayton Bassett amassing a large collection of vintage toys before releasing not one but two solo albums the following year. *World Shut Your Mouth* was not wildly different from the sound of his former group (and a single, 'The Greatness and Perfection of Love', should have done better than its #52 position), but *Fried* was less sure of itself. The turtle and toy sleeve[6] fronted a mostly sparsely instrumented, vaguely psychedelic collection of non-hit songs. Whatever the intentions behind it, he was promptly dropped by Phonogram and went on to become a paradigm of non-conformity. He would continue to have the odd hit, but 1984 saw Cope become something of a shaman. 'Frank Zappa could be the most talented musician – I didn't like his music, but I can see he was very talented – but he did not declare himself as a shaman. Jim Morrison could be one of the most inept people in the world, but he declared himself a shaman. You've got to declare it'[7]. Cope practised what he preached, combining continued drug experimentation, occasional self-harm[8] and, later, the penning of two learned tomes on British archaeology, to say nothing of two autobiographies and two books about experimental music from Germany and Japan.

222

Malcolm McLaren and Julian Cope.

Eccentrics can come from anywhere[9], but many of the examples in this chapter came from – and chose to remain in – smallish provincial cities and towns, away from the trendiness and distractions of London or Manchester. Bill Bryson's first book, *Lost Continent*, opens with the line 'I come from Des Moines. Someone had to'. In a Channel 4 documentary in 1984, XTC's Andy Partridge said much the same thing about Swindon, an unremarkable town somewhere between the West Country and the Midlands: 'You've got to come from somewhere'. XTC had been a spikey new wave band but by the early 80s had stopped touring[10] and had moved towards a more 'pastoral' direction, exemplified by 1982's *English Settlement*'s sleeve of Uffington Horse (a 3,000 year-old chalk figure carved into a hill near Swindon, which Cope would have identified with) and 1983's charming 'Love on a Farm Boys Wages' single. Instead of touring Partridge now rejoiced in painting toy soldiers and designing board games, while writing-deputy Colin Moulding turned to fishing. In early 1984 they negotiated a cheap studio and set about crafting their seventh album, *The Big Express*, which would hopefully pay back the huge debt they found themselves in with Virgin. The first single, 'All You Pretty Girls', turned out to be a fabulous sea shanty but despite its irresistible hooks and an expensive, if preposterous, video, it failed to make the Top 50. Neither did the wonderful 'This World Over' (which was practically prog); nor third single 'Wake Up'. Partridge loved the album, the others hated it. Perhaps its most unlikely success was inspiring a Japanese band to name itself after one of the tracks, 'Seagulls Screaming Kiss Her, Kiss Her'.

The end of the year took a strange double twist, however. In desperation, Virgin recommended that Partridge work with John Leckie to produce young Canadian singer Mary Margaret O'Hara at Rockfield Studios in Monmouth. But a combination of musical and religious differences (O'Hara was a devout Catholic, Partridge an atheist, and Leckie a follower of the Bhagwan Shree Rajneesh) resulted in their services being terminated at the end of the first day[11]. At a loose end, they booked themselves into a nearby cheap studio, ironically owned by a Christian organization, with a budget of £5,000 to record a piss-take, psychedelic project with Moulding and Gregory (and Gregory's drummer brother), but it wouldn't be an XTC record. Calling themselves the Dukes of Stratosphear, they knocked out an album in a fortnight and somewhat to their surprise, Virgin loved it. *25 O'Clock* was released on April Fool's Day in 1985 and to their relief, as well as embarrassment, it easily outsold *The Big Express*.

Early XTC keyboard player Barry Andrews had left the band at the end of the 70s, initially to play in Robert Fripp's League of Gentlemen before forming Shriekback in 1981 with ex-Gang of Four bassist Dave Allen and Carl Marsh (guitars, vocals). Their first two releases, *Tench* and *Care*, were scrappy, brilliant affairs on a small label, but it was 1984's *Jam Science* on Arista that took them into the potential main league, 'shifting clinical ass' (as NME deftly put it[12]). The album had a relentless, insistent synthpopsoulfunkdub groove which worked a treat when occasionally played on the dancefloor. Two singles, 'Hand on My Heart' and 'Mercy Dash', go from A to A without the need for middle-eights or anything. Andrews sings on just one track, the closing 'Hubris', although he would take on all the vocal duties when Marsh left during the recording of 1985's *Oil and Gold* (which was even better, certainly one of the year's best albums).

Were Shriekback too clever for their own good? Anyone who can rhyme nemesis with parthenogenesis is worthy of attention, but frustratingly – for both band and fans – they never made the Top 50. Andrews: 'It's really that what I've always tried to do with music – specifically *songs,* which are a brilliant art-form and still nowhere near exhausted – is create new places, funny little aquariums where the rules of the outside world no longer apply. Bear in mind that this is not sheet music, it's recorded music, so all sorts of subtleties and inflections are possible […]. What I mean is that songs are perceived sonically, primarily – then we add the strata of meaning. But, as with all good art-forms the most fun is in the grey areas'[13]. Shriekback would become essentially an Andrews solo vehicle from the 90s onwards (occasionally reuniting with former members), along with his solo work, sculpting, furniture-making and blogging.

Like Partridge, Martin Newell decided long ago to stay in the provinces (in his case Colchester, which is where John Cooper Clark ended up – need I say more?) and started in a band before punk came along. The unfortunately named Mighty Plod didn't go anywhere, and neither did his second band Gypp, so the new decade saw Newell narrow his horizons and hook up with drumming neighbour Lawrence Elliot to form The Cleaners from Venus. Fed up with the record industry they joined the throng of early 80s bedroom bands in releasing cassette albums while building up a minor fanbase in West Germany. 1984 saw them release *Under Wartime Conditions*, subtitled *A Collection of Pop Songs*. And they were, however lo-fi. Great songs that could have flowed from the pen of Partridge, Ray Davies or Robyn Hitchcock – very 'English' affairs accompanied by clear, incisive guitar over basic drum machine. One of the tracks, 'Johnny the Moondog is Dead,' would become their first single released on a proper record label, albeit a small German one called Modell Records. Newell was a 'one-man music-biz resistance unit', as Giles Smith (soon to join the Cleaners on keyboards) wrote in his fabulous book, *Lost in Music*: 'This was Newell's way of 'subverting the corrupt, inept and lazy music-industry system'. One day, he thought, all music would be made this way'[14]. And so it would turn out. Smith didn't stay around for long, but Newell has continued to plough his own furrow, occasionally writing with Captain Sensible, recording with Andy Partridge, publishing poetry (he is said to be the most published living English poet), and making a reasonable living from a manager-less cottage industry music career which is now the norm rather than the exception. 'Because I never got mega-successful, I never got too polluted by the industry, I never got jaded by fame or corrupted by money, and so the boyish enthusiasm with which I first went into doing something creative, like music or writing, is essentially still there'[15].

XTC's Andy Partridge, The Cleaners From Venus's Martin Newell and Robyn Hitchcock

One day older than Newell, Robyn Hitchcock is often associated with Cambridge, just up the road from Newell, where he'd formed the Soft Boys in the late 70s, although he's lived all over the place, including the States where he became a lot more popular than in Britain. 'Captain Sensible said it best, that we were doing the right thing at absolutely the worst time. While the rest of England shaved their heads and pummeled out punk progressions, we were playing long guitar solos and harmonizing under our very long hair. We didn't appeal to the British press, and it killed us, leaving us with only spats of vague trendiness'[16]. In 1984 he was pulling himself out of a two-year stupor brought on by the failure of his second solo album, *Groovy Decay*. Keeping himself afloat by working with Captain Sensible, Hitchcock eventually found his muse again and decided to record an all-acoustic album in as quick a time as possible. *I Often Dream of Trains* was full of short, quirky psychedelic folk songs ranging from the cautionary-absurdist 'Uncorrected Personality Traits' to the just plain surreal 'Furry Green Atom Bowl', recorded almost entirely by himself on piano and guitar. Packaged in a rather dull sleeve, the album nevertheless succeeded in re-invigorating his career and soon after he formed a band, The Egyptians (including two former Soft Boys). Ironically, the year also saw the belated release of the Soft Boys' first ever recordings, made in 1977, as an EP, *Wading Through a Ventilator*. Needless to say, neither made it into Smash Hits, although the magazine's traditional end-of-year quotes included one from Hitchcock: 'It's such a weird coincidence to wake up every morning as the same person... I'd quite like to wake up as the Isle of White ferry'.

If band and song names were yardsticks of eccentricity, then Prefab Sprout and their first single, 'Lions in My Own Garden: Exit Someone'[17] are quite hard to beat. So for that matter was frontman Paddy McAloon's pre-band career choice, that of training for the Roman Catholic priesthood. The Church's loss was music's gain and so started a yo-yoing pursuit of peerless pop. In keeping with the chapter's provincial sub-theme, the band came from the rural backwater villages of Consett and Witton Gilbert in County Durham and have been based in the area ever since. 1984 saw the release of their first album, the mature-before-its-time *Swoon*, pitched somewhere between Steely Dan and Aztec Camera, as well as three singles. The first two, 'Couldn't Bear to be Special' and 'Don't Sing', were, respectively, ploddingly odd and more conventionally upbeat, but the jewel in the crown was 'When Love Breaks Down', as perfect a piece of pop that ever was. And yet it took four separate releases before it became a hit a year later. In the autumn the band teamed up with Thomas Dolby to start work on a second album, *Steve McQueen*, and thereafter the Prefabs seemed destined for stardom. There were hits, yes, but their third album was shelved, becoming their fourth, and after writing their fifth – a double album of songs about ABBA, Elvis and death – McAloon disappeared for seven years, during which time he wrote a then-unreleased album about God. He would later take on a Godlike appearance himself, complete with all white suit, shirt, flowing hair and beard, and staff. His studious search for 'otherness' may have been pop's loss, but you have to admire his determination. 'I'm prepared to be bloody-minded about it, even to do without an audience to make the music I want'[18].

Time to move south to Birmingham and the indie-before-indie Felt or, more specifically, main man Lawrence (like Madonna or Prince, never to knowingly use his surname)[19]. Felt were the classic early 80s Cherry Red band, switching to Creation halfway through the decade, and issuing a total of ten singles and ten albums[20]. Full of jangly guitars and instrumentals, 1984 saw them at possibly their peak, certainly their most prolific, with two mini-albums, The *Splendour of Fear* and *The Strange Idols Pattern and Other Short Stories* and two singles. The idiosyncratic Lawrence gave great copy in interviews ('CDs are rectangles, you see, and that's why I hate them, because I hate rectangles'[21]) but ironically Felt's music never seemed to say much. It was always more about mood and meandering Johnny-Marr-and-Vini-Reilly-ish guitarscapes. Even John Leckie, who produced *The Strange Idols Pattern*, passed on doing a second album; 'They're all the same, they just seem to start and then stop'[22].

And yet, there was something thrilling, possibly important, about Felt. 'We used to say in the 80s, all these bands are clogging up the airwaves, and none of us can get on there. And then in the 90s we all got on there! Yeah, what we'd all worked so hard for, it had become this thing called Indie, and it became a brand. Really, what we'd all worked for, all of the early Creation bands too, we'd fought them wars, you know, for the Oasis generation... [But] The poet in the garret was made for me. I was quite happy to be on my own composing and writing the words and writing the music, just waiting for fame'[23]. At the end of the 80s, Lawrence dissolved Felt and started Denim and at the end of the 90s he dissolved Denim and started Go Kart Mozart. He's still in the garret, awaiting fame.

'Englishness' was a theme that ran through many bands, but perhaps none more so than three north London acts who came to represent three consecutive decades. Lawrence again: 'I'm in that Ray Davies camp. You know, I love the England of, what's it called, *The Village Green Preservation Society*. I'm that kind of songwriter. I long for that kind of past, that time when you were a child. And you cling onto that really, but you try to live in a modern world as well'[24]. Ray Davies's fixation with – and songs about – English history, culture and class continued to show itself as The Kinks approached the 20th anniversary of their first single. In the early 80s they had experienced a renewed sense of purpose, and with 1982's 'Come Dancing', their biggest hit for years, Davies played the spiv, bringing back the 50s. But it wasn't to last and 1984 saw only a so-so album, *Word of Mouth*, released towards the end of the year, together with two singles, 'Good Day' and 'Do It Again'. Solo-wise, however, Davies was more enterprising, directing his first film for which he also provided the music and even made a cameo appearance (along with a young Tim Roth). Titled *Return to Waterloo*, the made-for-TV film was not so much a sequel to their 1967 hit as a slightly creepy take on commuter culture – in this case suggesting that the dull looking suburbanite played by Kenneth Colley might not be quite what he seemed. But in those days of one-time screenings it passed by largely unnoticed.

Ian Dury's glory years were also behind him though he too managed an album and a film. The former was the weak, long-delayed *40,000 Weeks' Holiday*, backed by The Music Students who had replaced the disbanded Blockheads[25]. The latter was his first screen acting role in *Number One,* a film about snooker starring Bob Geldof. It flopped, but it would set him on the path for more substantial roles in the second half of the 80s, particularly in Jim Cartwright's play, *The Road*, and Greenaway's film, *The Cook, The Thief, His Wife and Her Lover*.

Both Davies and Dury were major influences on Madness[26] whose very English brand of modern-day music hall was approaching the end of Act I. None-more-English than Michael Caine turned out to be the title, if not the subject, of their first single of 1984, a song about an informer during the troubles in Northern Ireland with its accompanying video referencing Caine's role in the 60s spy thriller *The Ipcress File*. Madness had always had a melancholic thread running through their on-the-face-of-it jolly oeuvre, whether it was the nostalgia of 'Our House' or the genuinely depressing 'Grey Day', but by the mid-80s they had brought it to the fore. Their next single, the innocent-sounding 'One Better Day', was a song about homelessness:

> *Arlington house, address: no fixed abode*
> *An old man in a three-piece suit sits in the road*
> *He stares across the water, he sees right through the lock*

But on and up like outstretched hands
His mumbled words, his fumbled words, mock

And yet the group had a clever knack of combining earnest lyrics with witty, entertaining arrangements and the song still made the Top 20. The album, tellingly titled *Keep Moving*, as if they were aware of imminent stagnation, peaked at #6. It was their last for Stiff Records, the band forming their own label Zarjazz (through Virgin). Keyboardist Mike Barson also left, and the end credits were beginning to roll. One more album, 1985's *Mad Not Mad*, closed things for a while, but there would be more acts and intervals to follow.

Certainly eccentric (but more Celtic than English), Kevin Rowland had wanted Dexys Midnight Runners[27] to be different from anything else in the early 80s. And that they were, characterised by a retro, soulful, free spiritedness but also by continuous band in-fighting, putting statements out as adverts instead of doing interviews, and Rowland's obsession with the band's 'look' – from *Mean Streets* donkey jackets & woolly hats to gypsy dungarees & leather waistcoats (never mind 1999's infamous album cover of Rowland in lingerie), donned and discarded according to Rowland's shifting strategizing. By 1984 they were stuck in the studio trying to follow up *Too-Rye-Ay*, a painfully long, slow process with too big a budget. *Don't Stand Me Down* would eventually be released the following year complete with yet another new look – Ivy League suits and frat haircuts – to a generally bad reception, its spoken word parts too weird for 1985, yet now enjoying something of a reappraisal. "I live for my music. It's the main thing in my life. It comes before relationships and all that sort of stuff, for better or worse. Sometimes for worse"[28].

Felt's Lawrence, Dexys Midnight Runners and The Monochrome Set's Bid

'English alternatives', rather than eccentrics, would perhaps be a better description of exact centre-of-England, Nuneaton-based duo Martyn Bates and Peter Becker. Named after a novel by Aldous Huxley (who certainly was an eccentric), Eyeless In Gaza had come through experimental post-punk but an English folk aesthetic coupled with a deep sense of nostalgia and minimalism ran through albums like *Photographs As Memories*, *Pale Hands I Loved So Well* and *Drumming the Beating Heart*. They were often photographed in fields or country churches. Caught at a T-junction – turn left for more of the same or right for commercial success – they decided to try out the latter. The early 1984 single, 'Sun Bursts In', was an uplifting piece of pop ("Perfect!" said Joe Leeway of the Thompson Twins in Smash Hits, "It's got that barefoot feel to it… More chart oriented than previous offerings") but it didn't chart, and it was the three short melancholic songs on the B-side that many people still turned to. Live, they got into MIDI interfacing and running stuff from floppy discs, but still seemed fetchingly human and ramshackle. Another wonderfully uplifting single, 'Welcome Now', followed the year after and the recording of an album, *Back from the Rains*, but Eyeless In Gaza and pop didn't work out and in 1987 they took a break from each other, reforming six years later. They're still going, stronger, wiser, and not terribly interested in fame.

Cherry Red label-mates in the 80s, The Monochrome Set were the great could-have-beens and, like Eyeless, they saw 1984 as their chance at cracking the charts. When Mike Alway left his A&R job at Cherry Red to set up – with Geoff Travis and Michel Duval – Blanco y Negro, with the enticing financial backing of Warners, he took The Monochrome Set with him. "The Monochrome Set were going to be enormous. I thought Bid (their India-born frontman) was in a different class completely. He had absolutely everything – the intelligence, the looks, the attitude, the humour, […] and he produced these absolutely astonishing records"[29]. 'Jacob's Ladder', was a 'sure-fire' hit. Like Bid, it had everything: a twangy Shadows middle section, a bit of Gospel and yet English to the core (including the church bells opening), but Warners messed up the release and against all the odds it flopped. An album followed in 1985 but that didn't sell either and the band retreated to the shadows.

Another artist, also orbiting planet Cherry Red (in fact he was a press officer there for a while), was Simon Fisher Turner, a true English original. Turner had been a child actor, then would-be pop star, groomed by Jonathan King. But by the end of the 70s he found himself becoming increasingly drawn to alternative music and its synergies with film. In the early 80s, as Jeremy's Secret and fictitious 'French' duo Deux Filles (both with Colin Lloyd Tucker[30]), he dabbled in psychedelia and ambient respectively, while slowly and fortuitously being pulled into Derek Jarman's orbit, first as a driver and then, as could only happen on a Jarman project, scoring his films. "Derek was very good to me. I never expected to do the music for the films and it was always peculiar and strange. But he was generous with his trust"[31]. Turner's career as alt-soundtrack provider would go from strength to strength while at the same time experimenting with other forms – his skewed 70s songs as the King of Luxembourg being a tongue-in-cheek return to his 'pop star' roots.

Born in Paisley, near Glasgow, and peripherally involved with the Postcard scene, Nick Currie is obviously not an English eccentric – any more than Billy Mackenzie was. Indeed, although he moved to London in 1984 and hung out with Cherry Red and él's rank of misfits, he has since seemed more at home in Osaka, Paris and Berlin. The move south followed the demise of The Happy Family, an Edinburgh-based band comprising himself and ex-members of Josef K, whose one album and single on 4AD failed to stir much interest. A posthumous cassette album of demos, *The Business of Living*, was an early release by LTM the year of his move, at which point he became Momus (after the Greek god of satire and mockery). On the 159 bus into central London, he mused on Kierkegaard and started devising an album about bread and circuses, "the way popular entertainment is used to pacify and placate the masses", which eventually appeared on él. It was the first of countless albums, the lyrical content of which made Morrissey's seem like a Loaded editorial. Critically appreciated rather than commercially rewarded has been Momus's lot. The Moshe Dayan eyepatch only added to the mystique.

If wearing horse brass and appearing naked and lupine in Neil Jordan's *The Company of Wolves* could be considered eccentric, then Karl Blake and Danielle Dax should be considered here. After the 'aggressively absurdist'[32] records of their early 80s group, The Lemon Kittens, the two split but continued to live up to the description: Blake to form Shock Headed Peters and Dax to go solo as well as continue a parallel painting career. 1984 promised much for both. Shock Headed Peters' first release was the single 'I, Bloodbrother Be' – a thrillingly tense piece of alternative pop, NME 'Single of the Century' and a very early production by Stephen Street – followed by the equally out-there album *Not Born Beautiful* the following year. Needless to say, neither charted but Blake would heroically persevere with SHP, other projects and wearing horse brass. Dax had beaten him to it with her *Pop Eyes* album (with eye-popping cover), followed in 1984 by the wonderfully titled *Jesus Egg That Wept* (a surreal but real newspaper headline). Dax didn't play to the rules. Her startling looks contrasted with a voice that was half scary half siren, her image veering between goth (when she hung out at the Batcave) and a sort of skewed hippy-raj chic. In 1984 she almost made it, appearing on The Tube and in the aforementioned *The Company of Wolves*, but ultimately she didn't fit into a particular box and the record-buying public turned the other way. The title of a later compilation said it all: *Comatose-Non-Reaction*.

Karl Blake's Shock Headed Peters debut single, Danielle Dax and The Cardiacs.

Formed in 1977, The Cardiacs were that rare thing: a group who were genuinely uncategorizable. One could say that they operated in a parallel world where a mixture of the post-punk energy of XTC, the dada of The Residents, the time signatures of Henry Cow, the riffs of Def Leppard and the cabaret of the Tiger Lillies made sense, but in mid-80s Britain it didn't. As with Martin Newell, early releases were cassette only, on their own Alphabet label, including the extraordinarily odd early 1984 album, *The Seaside* (and accompanying video *Seaside Treats*). The media either didn't know what to make of it or ignored it completely. Marillion, however, were brave enough to invite them as support act on their extensive end-of-year tour although their fans hated them. The same year saw founder and frontman Tim Smith, wife Sarah and William Drake embark on a largely acoustic side project called Sea Nymphs, their first album prosaically called *Mr and Mrs Smith and Mr Drake*. The Cardiacs were out of time with their times, an acquired taste, a red rag to a critic who liked things compartmentalized, but they had their loyal fans – Damon Albarn of Blur being one of them.

Eccentricity is usually associated with humour, so if you wanted 'funny' – but not Black Lace (whose 'Agadoo', incidentally, was the eighth best-selling single of 1984) – then we could start with two post-punk bands fixated with football, drinking and British popular culture, one just about to split, the other just beginning. Serious Drinking had formed in Norwich[33] in 1981 and three years later were on to their sophomore album, *They Might Be Drinkers Robin, But They're Still Human Beings*, together with a single, 'Country Girl Became Drugs and Sex Punk' a cautionary tale of a local lass who falls for the temptations of the big bad city, which was actually both funny and very real. They split the following year but not before passing the baton to the wonderfully named Half Man Half Biscuit who formed in Tranmere in 1984[34]. A debut album, *Back in the DHSS*, arrived twelve months later and thereafter the band have issued albums every other year or so. The wit of Nigel Blackwell's lyrics lies in the closely observed loser-culture of life on the dole, picking up on B-list TV 'stars', the half-surreal, half-toilet humour of Viz, and championing the underdog. Early song titles like 'Fuckin' 'Ell, It's Fred Titmus' and 'I Hate Nerys Hughes – From the Heart' struck a chord with lovers of cricket and bad 70s sitcoms, but would have met with incomprehension from anyone else. And yet they aren't 'zany'. On stage, for example, they are deadpan and unsmiling, which has made their comical songs come across as all the more bizarre. They are also fiercely protective of their anonymity. Needless to say, they were great favourites of John Peel.

Joining Norwich and Tranmere on rock's cultural (if not geographical) perimeter was Leicester, a town best known, musically at least, for Showaddywaddy and Engelbert Humperdink. It was also the birthplace of Monty Python's Graham Chapman and hosts the Leicester Comedy Festival, the largest in the UK. Sometimes a whole city can be considered eccentric and certainly a surreal sense of humour has permeated a number of Leicester bands. Showaddywaddy may have been conservative, but they were surely the only group to have two singers, two drummers, two guitarists and two bassists; and Engelbert Humperdink's appearance at the Eurovision Song Contest in 2012 at the age of 76, finishing second to last, is the stuff of legend.

At the centre of Leicester's post-punk scene was *Printhead*, a fanzine dedicated to the best the city and environs had to offer, which in 1984 was surprisingly considerable. That year the zine released *Let's Cut A Rug*, a compilation featuring 13 local bands. Most sank without trace, but a couple stuck around to make their presence felt both within Leicester and beyond. Yeah Yeah Noh were formed around a nucleus of Derek Hammond and Printhead co-editor John Grayland, debuting in early 1984 with the appropriately titled *Cottage Industry* EP, whose short-but-sweet 'Bias Binding' track would make #32 in Peel's Festive 50 that year. Hammond loved weird track titles, 'Startling Pillowcase, And Why' being a contender for this book's strangest. Meanwhile Deep Freeze Mice were resolutely post-punk in a lo-fi psychedelic, almost Dadaist kind of way, as well as being fiercely independent, releasing records on their own label, Mole Embalming Records. So independent that they didn't even have a telephone number. They existed as long as the decade and made an album a year. "I can't think of a band, before or since, that sounded as anywhere near original as we did. We were quite amateur, but very committed, and we were enthusiastic."[35] Bassist Mick Bunnage went on to work for *Loaded* magazine and co-created (with Jon Link) the *Modern Toss* comedy series on Channel 4. Another formed-in-84 band who were nevertheless too late to be included on the compilation were Gaye Bikers On Acid whose first album *Drill Your Own Hole* was pressed without a hole in the centre. You could say it was a clever marketing ploy but given the numbers pressed it was more likely a 'What the hell, why not?' kind of decision.

The links between indie and football were very close, centred on a love of the amateur-in-spirit, self-deprecating underachiever – something that British culture in general holds dear, from the Ealing Comedies to Eddie the Eagle. Indie felt closer to lower division football rather than the big guns, and editors of football fanzines (the best ones often being for lowly teams) were often music fans, and vice versa, the two existing in a kind of symbiotic harmony. Liverpool-based fanzine The End, edited by Peter Hooten of The Farm, covered both music and football in a style that became known as terrace culture. One of Half Man Half Biscuit's great acts was to decline an invitation to perform on The Tube because Tranmere Rovers were playing that evening, while Go! Discs 'sponsored' the Billy the Fish strip in Viz. Later, Mike Alway would co-compile[36] a double album of lower league club songs, *Flair 1989: The Other World of British Football*; and much later, Yeah Yeah Noh's Derek Hammond would write a book, *Got Not Got: The A-Z of Lost Football Culture*. An alternative title for either might have been 'Now That's What I Call Quite Good'.

But back to 'odd'. David Cunningham's Flying Lizards[37], were a pop group which existed in a kind of parallel universe where yesterday's hits were minimised into automated, deadpan 'actions' that were either Dadaist or postmodern depending on your viewpoint. They'd had a surprise hit with a cover of Barrett Strong's 'Money' in 1979, followed by an equally skewed version of Eddie Cochrane's 'Summertime Blues' and a couple of albums, but the joke had a limited shelf-life and in 1981 Cunningham put the project on hold – only to revive it again three years later with reassuringly bizarre covers of 'Sex Machine' and 'Dizzy Miss Lizzy' and an album, *Top Ten*. Had the group not done 'Money' then either would have been extraordinary, and certainly the videos are worth viewing on YouTube, but they had and the joke was finally put to bed. Cut from the same cloth, it's also worth mentioning oddball 4AD band The Wolfgang Press's cover of Otis Redding's 'Respect' on their 1984 *Scarecrow* EP, though respectful it wasn't.

Half Man Half Biscuit and Shelleyan Orphan, just starting out.

If The Flying Lizards poked fun at history, Shelleyan Orphan were deadly serious about it – which, as their name suggests, went back a lot further to the early 19th Century and a minor fixation with Shelley, Byron and their circle of poets. Formed by Caroline Crawley and Jemaur Tayle in Bournemouth at the beginning of the decade, their very English inspirations were more literary than musical, their songs set to string ensemble and oboe. The only vaguely similar act at the time was Virginia Astley whose records would successfully bridge the gap between chamber classical and pastoral pop (see Chapter 23), while Shelleyan Orphan got a rough ride for being 'pretentious'. That said, 1984 saw them get their first break with a Richard Skinner session on Radio One and, right at the end of the year, the most unlikely double-billing, possibly in the history of pop, supporting The Jesus and Mary Chain at an ICA rock week. The Orphans got an encore, the Reid brothers flying beer bottles. In the audience was Geoff Travis who signed them to Rough Trade (which was the same time Virginia Astley recorded a beautifully whimsical one-off EP for them), but it took another year and a half before their debut release, 'Cavalry of Cloud'[38]. By then, the first half of the 80s' freespiritedness had given way to less adventurous times and the music press could only describe them as Pre-Raphaelite. They would release three albums, perform on The Tube with a painter and support The Cure on their 1989 *Disintegration* tour until petering out in the early 90s when Rough Trade went bust. But like so many bands in this book, they reformed in the new millennium, older and wiser, and really not caring about those accusations of affectation[39].

If Shelleyan Orphan were dabbling on the edge of poetry, there were others who were doing the real thing, if sometimes combining spoken word and singing. Of the older generation, Ivor Cutler, as mentioned earlier, was doing nicely (including his 13th Peel Session in February 1984), but 'punk poets' John Cooper Clarke and Patrik Fitzgerald, who'd shone either side of the old/new decade, were now sadly on their uppers. Clarke had a serious heroin habit (not helped by living with Nico at the time) and hadn't released any records for two years, though he did perform at New Order's miners' benefit concert at the Royal Festival Hall in May. Fitzgerald meanwhile had shifted more towards songs à la Billy Bragg but sadly for him very much under the radar; his *Drifting Towards Violence* album that year was released unnoticed on a tiny Belgian label and towards the end of the decade he worked as a waiter in the House of Commons.

A new generation fared better. If Attila the Stockbroker (an album and two EPs in 1984) and Steven Wells (aka Seething Wells, Swells and Susan Williams, an NME journalist who made his performing debut that year) carried the punk poetry torch, others diversified. Joolz Denby set her words to music written with Jah Wobble & Ollie Marland (she also helped form New Model Army). Anne Clark somehow set hers to synthpop, working with David Harrow (she was particularly popular in Germany). And then there were the Medway Poets who included Billy Childish, whose poetry jostled for pole position with his painting and music (his band The Milkshakes released *five* albums in 1984). Mention must also be made of Edward Barton, a genuine eccentric, whose gem-like *Jane and Barton* on Cherry Red was one of the most original albums of 1983. On it, Barton's minimalist poetry was sung by Jane Lancaster with occasional flute and piano accompaniment. One of the songs, the acappella 'It's A Fine Day', was later a hit for house act Opus III. An obscure single, 'Mulch', as Barton and Harry (Stafford, of the Inca Babies), appeared in 1984, followed by very occasional releases through to the end of the decade, at which point he found himself directing a suitably surreal video for James's 'Sit Down'.

Additionally, dub poetry – with its focus on Jamaican patois – was doing well through Linton Kwesi Johnson (*Making History* album on Island) and Benjamin Zephaniah ('Big Boys Don't Make Girls Cry' single, mixed by Mad Professor). None of this was necessarily eccentric but, with the possible exception of Anne Clark[40], was a particular take on, if not Englishness (Cutler was Scottish, Johnson and Zephaniah Jamaican[41]), then Britishness – from all sorts of angles. Much of their writing was political which struck a chord (or a panchromatic meter?) with the times. Certainly it is hard to imagine a scene as rich as this now.

Finally, a mention of Richard Strange who, with John Otway, had actually toured as The English Eccentrics, to America, earlier in the 80s. Strange had fronted The Doctors of Madness in the mid-to-late 70s who fell foul of never fitting into one particular genre, one day supporting Be Bop Deluxe, the next being supported by the Sex Pistols. But in the early 80s, Strange found his true calling: organizer and compere of the wonderfully eclectic Cabaret Futura nights in Soho and Mayfair[42] which featured quirky cabaret (Frank Chickens and Hermine Demoriane[43]), avant-garde post-punk (Lemon Kittens), performance art (Bow Gamelan, The Event Group), comedy (a young, naked Keith Allen) and very early, fresh-faced synthpop (Soft Cell, Blancmange and Depeche Mode). By 1984, Strange was recording his own skewed brand of synthpop, as The Engine Room, while commencing an acting career. Cabaret, or multi-genre shows, were briefly the rage. Bill Nelson's autumn 1983 UK tour was called The Invisibility Exhibition and featured himself with Frank Chickens, Richard Jobson reciting poetry and the Yorkshire Actors Company performing *The Cabinet of Dr Caligari*. Vivian Stanshall went even further, he and his wife Pamela 'Ki' Longfellow converting a ship in Sunderland and sailed it to Bristol Docks where it became a floating theatre, The Old Profanity Showboat. They even staged their own comic opera, *Stinkfoot*, there the following year.

One set of performers at Richard Strange's Club Futura were the Neo Naturists, a group of three women – sisters Christine and Jennifer Binnie and Wilma Johnson – which grew out of the new romantic, Fitzrovia squat scene, although celebrating their rounded, ruddy 'Earth-mother' painted bodies they were actually the complete opposite of the thin, pale, dandy Blitz Kids. Their semi-improvised performances were more like 60s counter-culture happenings than part of some contrived, careerist contemporary art plan, and, as critic Louisa Buck remarked, 'cocked a good-humoured snook at both the earnestly exquisite dandyism of Steve Strange et al, and the streamlined pneumatic amazons of Helmut Newton' [44]. In the Thatcherite 80s, the Neo Naturists, all in their 20s, were an incongruous presence but could be seen to be part of a wider group of on the one hand older (mostly male) artists who had been part of late 60s and 70s counter culture (Derek Jarman, Andrew Logan, Bruce Lacey, Genesis P-Orridge etc) and a younger feminist crowd (The Slits, The Raincoats).

Between 1983-86 Christine and Jennifer lived in a squat in Crowndale Road in Camden, along with Jennifer's boyfriend Grayson Perry and a host of other contributing, leftfield creatives including Marilyn, artist Cerith Wyn Evans, film-makers Sophie Muller and Angus Cook, as well as others like David Holah and Stevie Stewart of BodyMap, the artist Firewolf, DJ Princess Julia, and film-maker John Maybury who would float in and out. Some of their most infamous performances took place in 1984, including Valentine Sexist Crabs at the Fridge club, Neo Naturist Mermaids with Marilyn at the Henley Regatta, and Swimming and Walking Experiment in the Centre Point fountains on Tottenham Court Road.

Of course, eccentricity – or at least strangeness – was at the core of the experimental music scene, and we shall turn to that next.

Chapter 18: How to Destroy Angels
Experimental music and cassette culture

I'll lead depressionist youth mass to mock rebellion for a fee
Choose choose choose choose your weapons, we're in a calamity crush
Foetus-Art-Terrorism 'Calamity Crush'

The local rag and bone men [...] used to come past our squatted house in Nettleton Road and
drop off old water tanks, car springs, sheet metal, gas cylinders anything that had a sonic
resonance and could be hit with force with metal drumsticks or sledge hammers.[1]
Test Dept

Wildness, you know, let's have a bit of wildness again.[2]
Genesis P-Orridge

One of the most important and interesting outcomes of punk was not punk rock but a wave of alternative, experimental, electronic music, mostly on small independent labels or self-released. Throbbing Gristle led the way with a series of uncompromising albums in the late 70s and early 80s which simultaneously questioned the very nature of music while single-handedly establishing a new genre which became known as 'industrial', partly named after the group's own label and partly because much of the music sounded like the grinding of machines in a factory.

Actually, TG's formation in 1976 was coincidental to punk, having pre-existed as performance art collective COUM Transmission for several years beforehand. But their reinvention as a 4-piece *band* and change of name was well-timed. It was a complete break with the past, instrumentally, sonically, lyrically and visually, while at the same time soundtracking the end of Britain's industrial era. Instrumentation comprised of basic synthesizers, tapes, rhythm generators, processed cornet and heavily modified guitar, overlaid with lyrics and imagery that were fully intended to shock. Punk's confrontation was kindergarten stuff compared with TG's cocktail of sonic terror, recordings of death threats, pornography, sado-masochism and the occult. And yet it attracted countless kindred souls who formed their own groups and labels and would outlast TG who had the good sense to split in 1981 having 'accomplished their mission'.

As Simon Reynolds wrote, 'Being a Throbbing Gristle fan was like enrolling in a university course of cultural extremism'[3] with De Sade, Lautreamont, Crowley, Bataille and Burroughs as set books. Their importance was such that their influence was felt well beyond their immediate disciples and reached out into the pop, rock and even the dance world. Soft Cell, the Sheffield electronic acts, most of the groups on Mute, the Electronic Body Music movement and post-industrial artists like Nine Inch Nails, were just a few beneficiaries. Another aspect was the thrill of seeing them and,

236

after they split, bands associated with them, live, in suitably unusual settings. Responsible for many of these events which were mostly in London was the promoter, Final Solution, which grew out of the Small Wonder record shop and label in the late 70s. Using weird and wonderful flyer graphics, they put on memorable events like Throbbing Gristle at Butler's Wharf near Tower Bridge and all-nighters at the old Scala Cinema, underneath the Post Office Tower, before it moved to Kings Cross. Their last event was Psychic TV, Monte Cazazza and films by Derek Jarman and Cerith Wyn Evans on 23 December 1984 at Heaven on Villiers Street, a relatively conventional venue for them. Nevertheless, it seemed like the end of an era.

Post-TG, the four members essentially split into two: Genesis P-Orridge and Peter Christopherson formed Psychic TV with Alex Ferguson, releasing two albums on major labels, via Some Bizzare, in 1982 and 1983. Christopherson then left to form Coil with Geoff Rushton (aka John Balance), opening their account with an EP, *How To Destroy Angels*. The A-side was a 17-minute piece of dark, rhythmless ambience performed live in the studio on 19 February 1984 which continued the themes of ritual and magick (always spelled with a K) started by Psychic TV. "[W]e have tried to produce sound which has a real, practical and beneficial power in this modern Era" they explained. "Specifically, it is intended as an accumulator of male sexual energy". The B-side had no groove at all. Literally, it was unplayable. An album, *Scatology*, followed before the year was out. Co-produced with Jim Thirlwell, musically it struck a balance between continued low-key ambience and rhythmic, jolting forays on a Fairlight. Lyrically it was subversive, if not overtly sexually, then psychologically. 'A vast proportion of what we do and the way that we live our lives would probably freak out the majority of civilised people, simply because it's out of the norm of their experience […] I think it must be that we have a different threshold'[4]. Coil would continue their explorations of ritualised sound for another 20 years until Balance's death in 2004.

Post-TG projects: Psychic TV, Chris & Cosey, and Coil.

Psychic TV meanwhile had reverted to independent releases – eight in 1984 alone – and would plough their own particular counter-cultural furrow, filming their own sex-cult rituals while also veering towards acid house in the late 80s. The other half of TG, Chris Carter and Cosey Fanni Tutti, formed two groups: the prosaically named Chris & Cosey whose more accessible, proto-techno *Songs Of Love And Lust* in 1984 was their third for Rough Trade; and Creative Technology Institute (CTI) which combined music and video and brought in outside contributors – their first two, *Elemental 7* and *European Rendezvous*, released as both VHS and LPs on the fledgling Doublevision at the tail end of 1983 and mid-1984 respectively. They were still edgy, but away from the stress of TG and particularly the demands of Genesis, they had moved from London to Norfolk, found domestic contentment and it was reflected in their output. By the end of the year Cosey also decided to stop doing her striptease action projects.

There were some unlikely meetings of minds. Chris & Cosey collaborated with Eurythmics on the little-known single 'Sweet Surprise'; Rose McDowell of Strawberry Switchblade started hanging out with Psychic TV and Coil; Jim Thirlwell and Derek Jarman worked with Orange Juice. Sometimes the radical instrumentation of the alternatives got taken on by more mainstream artists. 1983 had seen the birth of 'metal bashing' with bands like Test Dept and Australasian exiles SPK as well as (from Germany) Einstürzende Neubauten and Die Krupps, using scrapyard objects and live welding to create a rhythmic cacophony. The creative effect of which was not lost on Depeche Mode. Their *Construction Time Again* album was full of the sound of pipes being hit and extended to 1984's 'People Are People' single, the video of which showed the Basildon boys bashing bits of HMS Belfast, as well as a corrugated sheet of iron being rattled on stage as part of the *Some Great Reward* tour. Sometimes it was the other way round. In the early 80s SPK were a highly experimental outfit, but used metal bashing as a mainstream reinvention. Live, they were still edgy, as evidenced by their chaotic appearance on The Tube in February 1984 and a health-and-safety-curtailed show at the ICA in October. But on record they, like Depeche Mode, used samplers to tidy it up and the resulting album, *Machine Age Voodoo*, was a vapid affair. Main man, Graeme Revell, was at least honest about it, describing the album's tracks as "commercial aberrations"[5], but the major label advance enabled him to buy a Fairlight, fund much more experimental side projects and then head to Hollywood where he began a hugely successful career in composing film soundtracks. A calculated move if ever there was one.

Test Dept[6], however, were the real thing. Unlike SPK, the only hits they were interested in were physical, requiring a fitness regime that rivaled that of Japan's Kodo Drummers. The group was formed in Deptford, London in 1981, an area full of derelict factories and scrap metal merchants. Their music echoed the environment, but instead of dealing with death and decay it took a positive stance, looking back to 1920s Soviet Collectivism and Modernism for inspiration, exalting the worker as part of a mass movement. There were just a few of them, but it seemed like an army, bashing the hell out of whatever they could find in the scrapyards. And yet the music was well-crafted and their concerts amazing spectacles[7], often staged in unusual venues like rail and bus stations (in effect carrying on from where Final Solution left off). Test Dept were at their best live, but Some Bizzare's Stevo saw potential in putting their sound onto vinyl and it worked surprisingly well. There had been two cassettes, before signing to his label and releasing the 12-inch single, 'Compulsion' in 1983, but it was *Beating the Retreat*, a boxed 2EP set with lots of inserts and capital letters, which acted as their manifesto for a much wider audience. There was a video too, *Program*

238

for Progress 82-84, released on Doublevision. In the year of the miners' strike, Test Dept felt like kindred spirits and both toured throughout the country with the South Wales Striking Miners Choir, all profits of which went to support the strike, and released the album *Shoulder to Shoulder* before the year was out.

Even more creative onstage were Bow Gamelan Ensemble, the often overlooked (partly because they didn't record much) east London collective which included the twice Turner Prize nominee Richard Wilson. Although best known for their fantastic mainly outdoor performances on barges and the like, their debut recording was an eponymous cassette recorded in April 1984 featuring track titles like 'Tumble Drier With Mixed Contents', which kind of says it all. As does Tools You Can Trust, the name of another metal-bashing band, this time from Manchester, based around the core duo of Ben Stedman and Rob Ward. Theirs was a fairly obscure mid-80s existence, confined to a few singles and a couple of albums on their own label, although they also recorded no fewer than three Peel Sessions. Salvaging junkyard debris crossed over into design too, with Ron Arad and bass player and DJ turned designer Tom Dixon creating hybrid furniture like the former's Rover Chair and record player set in concrete which both became design classics.

Test Dept, Bow Gamelan and 23 Skidoo.

North Londoners 23 Skidoo's interests in the sound of scrap metal was matched by their enthusiasm for world music, martial arts and funk – which all came together in 1984 when, drafting in bassist Peter 'Sketch' Martin from soul-funk band Linx and switching from Fetish Records to Illuminated, they released three career-defining records. 'Coup' was Cabaret Voltaire meets James Brown, adroitly described by Sounds as "hopping through the city ruins, ghetto-blaster in one hand, shrapnel grenade in the other"[8], while a second single, 'Language', continued their bass-driven explorations of dubby leftfield dance. Meanwhile, an album, *Urban Gamelan*, was split between following the above direction (including a peculiar reworking of 'Coup') and a second side of ambient industrial gamelan music. Confounding fans and critics alike, it was reflecting a year that saw them at their peak.

The idea of ambient industrial – the buzz of pylons, the reverb of an emptied factory, the opposite of metal bashing – was taken up by a number of other groups who'd formed in the early 80s, a trio of which emanated from the north of England. Newcastle-based Zoviet France released esoteric, exquisitely packaged albums of atmospheric, restless soundscapes – their 1984 album, *Eostre*, cradled in a silk and latex sleeve, being typical. In the same year, fellow Tynesiders The Hafler Trio released their debut album, *BANG - An Open Letter*, comprising fifteen tracks of what were essentially field recordings. Titles like 'Echoes in the Body' and 'Owl Ionisation Recording' gave clues but the group have always been hard to pin down, like their line-up, initially listed as 'Dr Edward Molenbeek' and 'Robert Spridgeon' who turned out to be Andrew McKenzie and ex-Cabaret Voltaire Chris Watson, the latter leaving after this album. And from Leeds, the inexplicably named O Yuki Conjugate also released their debut album, *Scene in Mirage*, in 1984, going on to issue numerous instrumental albums which could be described as ethno-minimalist. And as the 80s turned into the 90s, other names like illbient or dark wave came into fashion.

Combining the crushing beats of metal bashing with the shock-tactic themes of industrial music, Jim Thirlwell, aka Foetus, also came to the fore in 1984. Like SPK's Graeme Revell, Thirlwell had moved from Australia to London a few years earlier, recording under numerous variations of the Foetus moniker[9] before teaming up in New York with Marc Almond, Lydia Lunch and fellow Melbourne émigré Nick Cave at the end of 1983 in a kind of alt-cabaret act named The Immaculate Consumptives. Whilst the project was ultimately a failure, and certainly short-lived, Thirlwell's stock was high enough to get him on the cover of the NME in February 1984 and sign with Some Bizzare. There followed a breakthrough single, the rockabilly-Stravinsky of 'Calamity Crush' (as Foetus-Art-Terrorism), and an equally abrasive industrial-country album, *Hole* (as Scraping Foetus Off The Wheel). Both benefitted from Some Bizzare's marketing although he was too leftfield, still, to be licensed to a major, and the artist name put paid to significant radio play. As, perhaps, did the title of Coil's debut album, *Scatology*, if radio programmers knew what it meant; some thought it referred to vocal jazz. Thirlwell would soon move to New York and at time of writing has released around 15 one-word / four-letter albums – but 1984 was the year that put him on the map.

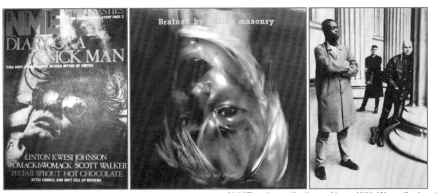

Foetus was everywhere in 1984, including on the cover of NME and contributing to Nurse With Wound's deeply strange *Brained by Falling Masonry*. 400 Blows meanwhile went from experimental to electro-funk.

Equally propulsive and shouty were south Londoners Portion Control who had several home-released cassettes to their name before signing with Illuminated in 1984 and releasing the excellent 'Rough Justice' and 'Go-Talk' singles as well as a slightly disappointing debut album proper, *Step Forward*. Depeche Mode and Blancmange picked them as support acts for their 1984 tours, but despite the year's reasonably high profile somehow it all fizzled out by the following year. The same happened to labelmates 400 Blows whose string of 12-inchers, 'Declaration of Intent', 'Groove Jumping' and 'Pressure' were fine examples of alternative 1984 electrofunk, though their debut album couldn't quite decide whether to be experimental or commercial. By the following year they'd decided on the latter, issuing a trio of ferociously funky, slickly produced 12-inchers, including a cover of Brass Construction's 'Movin'', but still success eluded them and they split by the end of the decade.

Mention must be made of Sudden Sway, a deeply strange music-cum-performance art group from Peterborough who contributed what may be two of the most esoteric Peel Sessions ever: the first in November 1983 was a kind of 15-minute exercise tape which traced evolution from amoeba to lizard; the second the following September sounded like a cross between The Hitch-Hikers Guide to the Galaxy and a spoof Open University lecture, until the last 3 minutes when it sounds like Talking Heads. They would go on to release *Sing Song V1-V8*, eight different versions of the same song on Blanco y Negro, and perform three one-minute songs on the Whistle Test in a kind of prefab jukebox. Put it this way, they weren't Madonna.

*****

A lot of the bands, labels and fanzines operating in this area were promoted by Dave Henderson's regular Wild Planet! column in Sounds and two era-and-genre-defining 'difficult music' compilations, *The Elephant Table Album* and *Three Minute Symphony* (1983 and 1984 respectively). These were both double albums on a decent label (Illuminated), but what Wild Planet! really helped unearth was something called cassette culture: a sprawling, alternative scene of bedroom artists and bands whose sonic experiments were issued only on tapes[10].

The cassette wasn't of course the exclusive domain of experimental music makers – it was a highly popular medium, outselling vinyl[11]. In 1980 Bow Wow Wow had released their first single as the appropriately titled 'C30, C60, C90, Go', while the NME's cassette compilations *C81* and *C86* were markers for post-punk and indie respectively (although it's often forgotten that there were many others in between – six in 1984 alone). However, the format *was* particularly attractive to purveyors of the weird as it was often the only medium by which it could realistically get released, distributed almost exclusively by mail or sold at performances. A few independent shops like Rough Trade stocked them but it was easier to sell direct to the customer – small and lightweight, a jiffy bag was all you needed. It was a logical step and much cheaper than getting a record pressed. You could record straight onto a C45 or C60, and then copy it to order. Sometimes the music (a few tracks or maybe an album's worth) could be acquired simply by sending a blank tape and a stamped addressed envelope. But there were also small autonomous labels which slowly accrued a modest catalogue, professionally duplicated with properly printed covers and inlay labels. A major inspiration had been (again) Throbbing Gristle, with their methodically released cassettes of live performances, reaching a pinnacle when collected together as the *TG24* box set in 1980. But there were others: in terms of surveying the scene, Third Mind's *Rising from the Red Sands* compilation pipped *The Elephant Table Album* to the post. And a few cassette labels became as important as record labels. Touch, founded in 1982 by designer Jon Wozencroft and Mike Harding, released well-curated, classily presented cassette-only compilations before eventually switching to vinyl and CDs. But by the mid-80s cassette culture was tailing off, with successful artists graduating to vinyl and the unsuccessful ones for the most part calling it a day.

Experimental music wasn't all bedroom doodling. Some were willing and obsessive enough to invest in decent studios to create meticulously produced recordings which would stand out from the herd. The doyen of them all was arguably Nurse With Wound whose music was genuinely unlike anyone else and whose high aural and visual standards led the way. Although originally a 3-piece, NWW had quickly settled into a vehicle for the surreal imagination of Steven Stapleton, who drafted in other artists as and when needed. 1984 saw the first releases – mini-album *Gyllensköld, Geijerstam And I at Rydberg's*[12] and 12-inch EP *Brained by Falling Masonry*[13] – to feature Diana Rogerson and Current 93's David Tibet as regular collaborators. Aside from the A-side of 'Brained', which also featured a histrionic Jim Thirlwell and was the closest NWW ever got to 'rock', both were typical of NWW's early style: carefully constructed collages of music, voices, found sounds and other sonic bric-a-brac, heavily influenced by dada and surrealism.

If Nurse With Wound were on another planet, most – or at least *many* – other experimental groups formed in the aftermath of punk tended, still, to be lumped in with 'industrial' even if they were far from it. It is beyond the parameters of this book to describe even a fraction of them. Certainly groups like Whitehouse, Nocturnal Emissions, Bourbonese Qualk, Organum, New Blockaders, Unkommuniti (Tim Gane's early noise group which begat McCarthy, which begat Stereolab), Muslimgauze and Konstruktivits were a million miles from rock and pop – and perhaps they would argue a million miles from each other. And yet they shared an austere, challenging, cheerless sound and monochrome look[14] which was attractive to many (myself included). Others like Death In June and Current 93 would, later in the 80s, veer towards folk.

Dozens of labels operated in this field. Some, like Mute, Some Bizzare and Illuminated (discussed in Chapter 15) released experimental stuff because they had other artists who would in effect act as subsidisers. Others like Gary Levermore's Third Mind Records, founded in 1983, led a precarious existence but would have enough of a mainland European and alt-American fanbase to get by and occasionally thrive. There was also an older, parallel scene based around Chris Cutler's Recommended Records which brought together the remnants of leftfield prog and post-punk artists (eg. Henry Cow and This Heat, respectively). Its 1984 release schedule included albums as varied as South Africa's renegade Kalahari Surfers, south London punks The Homosexuals, Henry Cow spin-off group News From Babel and a miners' benefit EP *The Last Nightingale* featuring Robert Wyatt and others.

Other musicians associated with Recommended came from the hermetic world of improv. Artists like guitarist Derek Bailey, saxophonist Lol Coxhill, the group AMM, and all those who dipped in and out of the London Musicians Collective operated in a timeless parallel world to most of the names discussed in this chapter. It would be stretching the brief of this book to start exploring the esoteric nature of this sub-genre, but it's certainly time now to look at what it sprang from, and how, for a while at least, it came to be embraced by pop. And that's jazz.

Chapter 19: Smooth Operators
The jazz revival

Sade doesn't want to be an overnight sensation. She wants to be around for a long time.[1]
The Guardian

At the moment this music is fashionable but there will never be a big revival.[2]
Maurice Chevalier of the Chevalier Brothers

Jazz was almost the big thing in 1984. Hyped to within an inch of its life, it became – after many years in the doldrums – cool again, smoothing the sounds of Sade and Matt Bianco, rasping the grooves of Working Week and The Special AKA, and getting everyone dancing at select, hipster clubs across the land. It wasn't just the bands with brass sections or men in zoot suits, which you'd see on Top Of The Pops or in The Face, it was the real deal in certain clubs. There was certainly something going on.

Jazz in Britain was never as big as in the US or continental Europe. It had been hip for a while in the 50s, centred around the Flamingo Club and Ronnie Scott's in London's Soho, but was largely ignored by pop and rock fans in the 60s. It developed into fusion and jazz-rock in the 70s, while its difficult sister, improv, more or less abandoned the audience altogether.

But by the early 80s, things started looking up and jazz began to make its influence felt in pop and youth culture generally. This was partly in reaction to synthpop, partly about style (cool suits in Soho photo-shoots peppered the new style magazines), and partly about a serious form of clubbing and dancing which rivalled the intensity of the Northern Soul phenomenon. Films like *The Jazz Singer* (1980) and *The Cotton Club* (1984) had made a mark too, while Capitol Records started re-releasing Frank Sinatra's mid-50s jazz-influenced albums like *Songs for Young Lovers* and *In the Wee Small Hours*. The summer of 1984 saw a three-day international jazz festival at Brixton Academy; a package of Ella Fitzgerald, Oscar Peterson, Joe Pass and the Count Basie Orchestra (Basie himself had died in April) played the Royal Festival Hall; as did Miles Davis a few weeks later as part of the JVC/Capital Jazz Parade; Herbie Hancock, Weather Report and Chick Corea visited, showcasing new, jazz-fusion albums. And by the end of the year talks took place about reviving the Blue Note label (which duly happened the following year).

It wasn't all about major US stars though. A few UK post-punk groups that were jazz-influenced, exhibited elements of sultry cool *and* frenetic free-jazz. And they weren't just from Soho – they were from all over Britain. The Pop Group, from Bristol, had combined punk-funk, dub-reggae and free-jazz in the late 70s and the band that came out of their split in 1981, Rip Rig & Panic (named after a jazz album by Roland Kirk), took those jazz elements much further. Soon joined by singer, Neneh Cherry, step-daughter of trumpeter Don Cherry, they released three 'out-there' albums before they in turn split up in 1983. Cherry went on to form the disappointing and bewilderingly named Float Up CP, releasing a single, 'Joy's Address', in 1984 and an album the following year, before *they* split and she embarked on a much more successful solo career. The same year saw Rip Rig's pianist, Mark Springer, release a debut album, prosaically titled *Piano*. Occupying an area somewhere in between free-jazz and classical, Springer's post-punk credentials were seemingly absent, but on closer listens you can hear him break up Chopin-esque melodies with wild abandon. Bassist Sean Oliver, meanwhile, went on to co-write 'Wishing Well' with Terence Trent D'Arby.

Operating in the same orbit and timespan as Rip Rig, Pigbag were formed in Cheltenham, 40 miles up the road from Bristol, and had an instrumental hit with 'Papa's Got a Brand New Pigbag' in 1981 (which made an even bigger impact when re-released the following year), but like Rip Rig they split up in 1983. Three of them went on to form Instinct, signing to ZTT where they played fourth fiddle to Frankie, The Art Of Noise and Propaganda, confined to releasing just one track, and that was on a compilation.

The Scottish early 80s post-punk dalliance with jazz was linked to Postcard. Pianist Malcolm Fisher had formed the French Impressionists (aka Frimps) in 1981 and its initial incarnation saw musicians like Paul Quinn, Edwyn Collins, Roddy Frame and Campbell Owens help out. They may not have released anything on Postcard but a single and EP the following year fitted perfectly on Belgium's Crépuscule. Alas, they couldn't keep it together and split up in 1983. Short-lived member Beatrice Colin joined April Showers, their one great string-drenched 1984 single 'Abandon Ship' sounding like a groovier Everything But The Girl; and Malcolm Fisher would resurrect the Frimps in name only in the new millennium as a vehicle for his own piano instrumentals, similar in style and tone to fellow early 80s classical impressionists Virginia Astley and Robert Haigh. Confusingly, another Glasgow band, the Jazzateers, weren't jazz at all, and in 1984 morphed into Bourgie Bourgie who sounded like they might be jazz but weren't either.

When Cardiff-based Young Marble Giants split in 1981, no-one imagined that singer Alison Stratton would form the jazz-pop Weekend with Simon Booth and others, but she did and for a while they were almost as revered (and short-lived) as YMG. When Stratton left to become a teacher, Booth (who'd originally worked at Jazz Mole record shop in King's Cross in London) turned Weekend into Working Week, and in 1984 released the singles 'Venceremos - We Will Win' and 'Storm of Light'. The former, a bossa nova tribute to Chilean protest singer Víctor Jara, featured guest vocals from jazz sympaticos Robert Wyatt and Tracey Thorn; the latter free-jazz singer Julie Tippetts. Both were self-penned and released on Paul Murphy's newly set up Paladin label, but sounded mature and chartworthy, even if confined to the lower reaches.

Also briefly part of Working Week was Corinne Drewery who would go on to form another jazz-pop group, Swing Out Sister, in late 1984. Indeed, it was a more slick, commercial take on jazz that took root. Zoot-suited Blue Rondo à la Turk were an early 80s latin jazz group with a strong live reputation, but an album and a couple of singles didn't set the world on fire and in 1983 the band split into two: a slimmed-down Blue Rondo (they lost the Turk), releasing another couple of singles and an album which did no better; and Matt Bianco who did rather well, having enlisted Polish singer Basia Trzetrzelewska. The band name was a fictional character conjuring up a world of 60s secret agents and martini cocktails. In 1984 their first three singles – 'Get Out of Your Lazy Bed', 'Sneaking Out the Back Door' and 'Half a Minute' – all went top 50, and they're still going, hugely popular in Japan. Chris Sullivan of Blue Rondo, meanwhile, started a jazz night on Mondays at the newly opened Wag Club in Soho, more of which later. Occupying roughly the same area, Animal Nightlife were a loose collection of East Enders and habitués of The Face and London's club scene, fronted by Andy Polaris, who had shared the same squat as Boy George and co. By 1984 they'd slimmed down from a 9- to a 5-piece, switched from Innervision to Island and in the summer the polished but cheesy 'Mr Solitaire' became their first hit. A couple of albums followed but they weren't able to maintain the momentum and split in 1988.

Working Week, Matt Bianco and Carmel.

Meanwhile in Birmingham, Swans Way (named after the first volume of Proust's *Remembrance of Things Past*, which made a change from, say, Mud) had formed in 1982 but had their brief moment in the sun in early 1984 with the curious 'Soul Train'. After ten seconds of aggressive double bass scrapings, it bursts into life, exuding a raw desperation. The suits and dresses softened the edges a bit, but still, it was a surprising Top 20 hit. Sadly, the next two singles didn't do as well and by the time their debut album, *The Fugitive Kind*, came along, the impetus had been lost and they split up the following year. Not far on in style, and just up the M6 in Manchester, Swamp Rats were another early 80s jazz-influenced band who included members of A Certain Ratio and had by 1984 changed their name to Kalima. In January they released the excellent 'The Smiling Hour' single in January, based on a Sarah Vaughn standard, with the Jazz Defektors on backing vocals. Its black and white video of peroxide singer Ann Quigley gazing across a grim, grey Manchester skyline conformed to one set of stereotypes, but its fruit'n'veg shopping, mixed race supporting cast and latino-jazzy groove signposted something new. They didn't quite cash in first time round but made a slightly better fist of it when moving to London in time for the later acid jazz scene.

Staying in Manchester, Carmel were formed in 1981 by art student singer Carmel McCourt, bassist Jim Parris and drummer Gerry Darby. Less latin than Kalima, let alone Blue Rondo or Matt Bianco, they combined jazz, blues and gospel and had reasonable success in 1984 with the single 'More More More' and brave, blustering debut album *The Drum is Everything*. McCourt dressed down, looking like she'd stepped out of a late-50s social-realist film (they even hired John Schlesinger to direct the video for 'More More More', all monochrome northern streets, culminating in a working men's club). But the British media never totally warmed to them, so they spent more more more time in France where they achieved considerable fame.

Conversely, a couple of French singers tried their luck in Britain, and although they weren't *strictly* jazz, it was certainly an influence. Isabelle Antena combined latin with jazz but her stay was short (see Chapter 26). Anne Pigalle's sojourn was longer, having moved to London in the early 80s, recorded an EP with jazz pianist Nick Plytas, sang on a short Channel 4-commissioned 'operavideo' by Michael Nyman and Paul Richards, and in 1984 signed to ZTT. Great things were expected: she certainly looked the part – straight out of Vogue, the darling of i-D, a fashion iconette – but, as with ZTT's other artists waiting in Frankie's shadow, it took an age to release her debut album, *It Doesn't Have to be This Way*, and her pop moment passed[3], though she took on an interesting, if less-known role as a leftfield multimedia performance artist.

But it was Sade who would be seen as central to the jazz revival. Born to mixed Nigerian-English parentage, Sade Adu shimmied into 1984, somehow fully-formed yet seemingly from nowhere. The truth is she'd studied fashion at Saint Martin's School of Art and then sang backing vocals with a group called Pride, until she and three of them split to form Sade, playing their first concert at Ronnie Scott's in December 1982 and signing with Epic ten months later. Rightly or wrongly, Sade came to typify the London jazz 'boom': 'unthreatening lounge-jazz made by an exotic, sexy chanteuse and her white male sidekicks for the consumption of yuppies and urban sophisticates', as The Quietus ironically put it[4]. However, they were no flash in the pan. Where Matt Bianco were fluffy and Carmel rough around the edges, Sade were cool and understated. It helped having the 'face of the 80s', a producer (Robin Millar) who absolutely nailed the perfect sound for them, and the timing was perfect, but ultimately they had some very good songs and the band's longevity speaks for itself. Debut single 'Your Love is King' hit #6 in February 1984, 'When Am I Going to Make a Living' managed #36 in May, and 'Smooth Operator' (originally the B-side to 'Your Love is King') made #19 in September. But it was the album, *Diamond Life*, which everyone bought. Six million of them. Adu's aloof singing style and image was formed by her character: she wasn't interested in the trappings of pop stardom and hated doing interviews, and this would serve her well for the rest of her career: sophisticated and alluring but haughty and untouchable. "We are a band – Sade is a band not an individual – we write our own material, have played countless gigs before the [first] single was released, we've worked hard […] We didn't just emerge out of the marketing department at Epic"[5]. And the music, eschewing the vogue for synthesizers and drum machines, harked back to the era of Billie Holiday, but with a modern production that smoothed out the edges.

Sade Adu and Everything But The Girl.

Coincidentally, Robin Millar produced Everything But The Girl's debut album, *Eden*, in the same studios at roughly the same time. EBTG's first single, in 1982, had been a cover of Cole Porter's 'Night and Day' which felt almost subversive. "It was part of that whole thing that came along in the wake of punk when people were discovering all sorts of other forms of music, and jazz was one of them. We felt there was something equivalently radical about doing a jazz standard"[6]. *Eden* was a female-voiced, jazz-influenced affair, particularly the first single 'Each and Every One', but the comparisons with Sade ended there. Ben Watt and Tracey Thorn's sound was rougher, dryer and augmented by an unusual array of guest musicians, from Simon Booth (Working Week) to Charles Hayward (This Heat). Watt and Thorn set some rules: no snare drum (too rock), no electric bass (only double bass), no acoustic guitars (too folk), no piano (too 70s rock ballad), and no backing vocals (too glossy). Production-wise, Millar described *Eden* as a bizarre hybrid of jazz, and at the same time still influenced by the Buzzcocks. *Diamond Life*, on the other hand, was purebred. "Which is why it won the Best Brit Album Award that year, while we sat at home in a rented flat, watching the whole ceremony on a rented telly"[7]. In any case, Everything But The Girl were already moving away from the influence of jazz and instead seeing kindred spirits in The Smiths.

Of the slightly older generation, Joe Jackson had infused spikey jazz elements into his late 70s new wave albums, and carried on doing so in the 80s, gradually shifting to a smoother latino style with 1982's *Night and Day* – still his best-selling album – and 1984's *Body and Soul*. The latter's cover (if not the music) aped the sleeve of *Sonny Rollins Vol.2* and included one great, mouthful of a single, 'You Can't Get What You Want (Until You Know What You Want)', but in truth Jackson was heading off into AOR and, ultimately, classical territory.

Sting of course had impeccable pre-Police jazz credentials and on splitting up with Summers and Copeland, was able to show them off on his debut solo album which he started writing in the second half of 1984 and recording in the new year. Sting went the whole hog, drafting in America's finest young session musicians: Omar Hakim (drums, Weather Report), Darryl Jones (bass, Miles Davis group), Kenny Kirkland (keyboards) and Branford Marsalis (saxophones, brother of high-flying Wynton). Joni Mitchell had gone down this route in the mid-70s with self-consciously earnest results, but Sting's pop pedigree meant that he wanted to appeal to everybody while at the same time be taken seriously. The jazz vibe was prevalent throughout but there were many other elements too: rock, calypso, reggae, gospel, even a bit of vaudeville and Prokofiev. It worked, though he found it hard thereafter to shrug off accusations of pretentiousness – never mind the tantric sex and saving Amazon tribes.

Others flirted with jazz. The Style Council's *Café Bleu* was peppered with it. David Sylvian's *Brilliant Trees* featured top British jazz sessioners Kenny Wheeler, Danny Thompson and Phil Palmer, as well as American trumpeters Mark Isham and Jon Hassell. Mari Wilson had had chart success with her highly stylized jazz-tinged torch songs but her two 1984 singles flopped (like her beehive), although she hit exactly the right austere tone for the title song for the 50s-set film *Would You Dance with a Stranger* the following year. More funk than jazz, Level 42 would have Top 20 hits with the single 'Hot Water' and album *True Colours* (and for frontman and bass slapper Mark King a debut solo album, *Influences*), while Shakatak went Top 10 in July with 'Down on the Street', prompting Smash Hits to run a feature titled, 'This group have sold 1.25m records in the UK. Bet you don't know who they are.'

Deviations aside, for many the real jazz scene – in London at least – was to be found in clubs, pubs and bars. Formed in 1982, bands like The Chevalier Brothers played jumpin' jive jazz in places like the Dublin Castle in Camden[8]. They didn't take themselves too seriously (with stage names like Maurice Chevalier, Ray Gelato, Roger Beaujolais and Clark Kent, how could they?), and it wasn't until 1984 that they got around to recording a couple of singles: 'I Like 'Em Fat Like That' and 'Bar Tender'. The Big Town Playboys, formed in 1984, were a similar act, although they were more boogie-woogie than anything else. Both bands' debut albums were recorded live at the Dublin Castle within three months of each other in early 1985. Other artists played at Ronnie Scotts (celebrating its 25th anniversary in 1984) and the surprisingly influential and long-running Pizza Express Jazz Club[9]. In the same year, an early version of the Jazz Café opened up in Stoke Newington before moving to Camden in 1990.

Away from pop, British jazz was driven by a new generation of musicians like Django Bates, Steve Berry and Chris Batchelor, who were at the core of 1984-formed Loose Tubes, an extraordinary, leaderless (white) ensemble of anything up to 20 players. Their concerts would cover the whole gamut of jazz, introduced by an irreverent compere, and they did much to win jazz a new audience. They also released four albums, but the sheer numbers of musicians involved was just too much to manage and they split by the end of the decade[10]. There continued to be jazz festivals like Jazz

Parade at the Royal Festival Hall, the Bracknell International Festival, Now's The Time in Brixton, Midsummer Jazz at Ronnie's and the excellent Actual at London's Bloomsbury Theatre, as well as four great jazz shops in Covent Garden[11] which, with neighbouring Soho, became the epicentre of the revival. Some emigrant jazzers, like Andy Sheppard, returned to Britain, but many of the older generation – Stan Tracey, Evan Parker, John Stevens, AMM and so on – struggled as much as they had always done, playing free or (contradictory sounding) classical modern jazz. Mike Westbrook even turned to a curious kind of jazz cabaret.

At these concerts, it was all about watching and listening, but there was a whole other scene which was about dancing. Centred around a posse of DJs, clubs and dancers, not just in London but all over the country, jazz dance became an important, serious, almost religious sub-culture to some, and simply fashionable to others, building up like new wave and post-punk through the late 70s and early 80s and peaking around 1984. Jazz Dance came out of jazz, funk and latin fusions of the 1970s, played in clubs like The Goldmine on Canvey Island and The Lacy Lady in Ilford where, in the late 70s, coachloads of people from as far away as Glasgow would come to experience DJ Chris Hill spinning soul, funk and jazz. At the same time, George Power held his Friday lunchtime jazz residency at Crackers in Soho[12] and Colin Curtis held court at the Highland Room in the Blackpool Mecca as well as Rafters, Berlin and Cassinellis in Manchester. They were playing everything from Astrud Gilberto and Art Blakey to Miles Davis and Chick Corea, and inspiring a new generation of DJs like Paul Murphy (from Essex) and Winston Tong (Kent).

Paul Murphy had started at the Kingswood Club in Ilford, organized buses to all-nighters or -dayers like at Alexander Palace or Knebworth, before securing a residency at The Horseshoe on Tottenham Court Road in the early 80s. Working at Our Price in Leicester Square was never going to satisfy his quest for crucial jazz so he'd shop at places like Contempo on Hanway Street, before becoming a dealer in his own right and then opening his own tiny shop, Fusion, at Exmouth Market in Clerkenwell (20 years before the area became trendy & gentrified). But his big break came when George Power offered him a residency at the Jazz Room at Camden's Electric Ballroom in August 1982 where he played hard, no-compromise, contemporary jazz to a mostly black crowd. The nights became legendary: dark and intimidating, with ultra-serious dancers battling against each other, often ending in violence. Even good dancers would stand against the wall for weeks before they could pluck up the courage to do their stuff. "It was a very dark room with a very black crowd but it was so intimidating in there because of the music. It was intense, the atmosphere was intense. There'd be black guys that were too scared to go in there"[13].

In January 1984 Murphy also took on Monday nights at The Wag in Soho, Tuesdays at the Sol y Sombra, Thursdays at Legends, Saturdays at Brighton's Jazz Room, finally handing over the Electric Ballroom gig to a young Gilles Peterson in April. That summer he closed Fusion only to open another shop (with Den Hulme) in Soho, which also doubled up as a label, both called Paladin. The latter saw their release of Working Week's 'Venceremos' and 'Storm of Light' singles and an EP by Onward

International. Murphy left The Wag the following year to start at the Comedy Store and Blue Note, but ended up returning to Electric Ballroom in 1986. His influence on the scene was seismic.

Jazz DJs Paul Murphy and Gilles Peterson (with Chris Bangs behind).

Gilles Peterson was born Gilles Jerome Moehrle to a French mother and a Swiss father whose work took the family to south London when he was very young. Like Murphy, he started DJ-ing at a young age, but differed in that he got into radio very young too. With a neighbour, he set up a small pirate show called Civic Radio with an aerial rigged up on Epsom Downs, before moving on to Radio Invicta, KJAZZ, Solar Radio and Horizon. At the same time he was DJ-ing at a few clubs including The Jazz Junction on Oxford Street before taking over from Paul Murphy at the Electric Ballroom, aged 19. Murphy was a tough act to follow. "When I first started there I was terrible. It was the most daunting and disillusioning DJ night I'd ever had. I was scared shitless."[14] He quickly got his act together though, and from there, he went on to DJ at Special Branch and Dingwalls' jazz nights before getting into serious radio (Mad on Jazz show on BBC London, and Kiss FM), record labels, mixing, production and the rest is history.

There were plenty of other players in the jazz dance scene in 1984. A2 Connection outfit organized all-dayers at the Maze Club above Ronnie Scott's (including spots for Murphy, Peterson, Ed Stokes and IDJ), and Nicky Holloway started Special Branch in the second half of the year at the Royal Oak on Tooley Street for instance. But it wasn't just about London. In Manchester, Colin Curtis ruled the roost (in clubs like Rafters, Legend, Smartys and Berlin), along with Hewan Clarke who became the first DJ at the Hacienda. The Factory connection was peripheral but important, with A Certain Ratio and Kalima part of a strong jazz scene which also included the Jazz Defektors (more of whom soon), Carmel and occasionally Mick Hucknall.

Birmingham was also important, not least because it had the earliest and best jazz dancers and clubs like the Locarno and The Rum Runner club. Leeds had the Coconut Grove and Bradford The Checkpoint; Nottingham had Rock City and Sheffield had Jive Turkey nights at the Mona Lisa; Bristol had Reeves, and Kent had Pete Tong who, like Peterson, would become a successful BBC radio presenter. The Scottish scene was centred around Glasgow with DJs like Kerrso playing at Chippendales. There'd be wild jazz nights in the most unlikely places, like The County Inn in Canbuslang, south east of the city, which ran every Sunday night from 1978-84 and its sister pub, The Glen Ruth ("People would come from all over the west of Scotland... It was rammed; a lock-out. We all went there, all of us"[15]).

Jazz, be-bop and that latin beat: The Jazz Defektors and IDJ.

For many people, however, it wasn't about the DJs, it was the dancers who made the jazz scene. Influenced by the choreography of West Side Story and Bob Fosse, northern soul, disco, martial arts films and the Jackson Five's moves, 80s jazz dancing came to be known as fusion or simply jazz dance. The moves were acrobatic, balletic and often bewildering, involving shuffling, pirouetting, knee spins, cutting, foot-tapping, splits, something called 'the cockroach crush', even kicking. It was serious business with 'challenges' or 'battles' between very young dancers, who were initially white but then mainly black (once racist door policies were finally consigned to history). Some dancers became well known: Trevor Shakes, Paul Anderson, Milton McAlpine (who was just 15), Blue Rondo's Chris Sullivan and scores of collectives. For many of them, it was their whole life, forever practicing, buying the right clothes, sometimes the records, sizing up the opposition – and it could often get violent, with personal or 'area' pride at stake. At times it would resemble tag wrestling.

The Jazz Defektors were formed in Manchester in 1982 and hung around with Factory bands A Certain Ratio and Kalima, and actually started singing backing vocals before dancing. But by 1984 they were supporting Sade at The Ritz in Manchester, performed on The Tube, became favourites at The Wag, and would later appear in *Absolute Beginners* and Falco's 'Rock Me Amadeus' video – as well as tour Japan, before splitting up around 1988. I Dance Jazz (usually abbreviated to IDJ) were arguably the most successful dance crew of the genre, coming out of the Electric Ballroom. Their first show as a team was at the invitation of Simon Booth, performing with Working Week at Camden Jazz Festival in 1984, then appearing in their 'Venceremos' video (directed by Julien Temple). Later in the year they featured in the Special AKA's 'Free Nelson Mandela', and were due to appear in *Absolute Beginners*, but ended up on the cutting room floor. There were plenty of other crews: The Untouchable Force (TUF) were early on the scene in 1981; Birmingham seemed to specialize in brothers: Carl & Lance Lowe, The Twins (Rick and Ty Hassell), the Baptist Brothers and Brothers in Jazz; and there were others which didn't even have names. This may be stretching a point, but the jazz dance moves of the film and musical *Billy Elliot*, set during the miners' strike, must have come from somewhere – and it probably wasn't the brass bands of the collieries.

The 1984 jazz scene was such that it became an integral part of Julien Temple's vision for a musical based on Colin MacInnes' book *Absolute Beginners*. Talks took place with financial backers; Sade, Bowie and Ray Davies were cast, along with oddballs like Alan Freeman, Tenpole Tudor and Lionel Blair; an unknown 16-year-old Patsy Kensit[16] was spotted at an early Eighth Wonder gig by Temple and producer Bruce Wooley and offered the role of Crepe Suzette; extras were eyed up at The Wag; The Face hyped it up… but when production started in 1985 it was already a million pounds over budget, Temple lost control and it couldn't live up to the hype. The film was finally released to unanimously bad reviews in April the following year.[17]

The media's role in promoting and reporting the jazz revival was crucial, but it was often divided. The Wire was at that time only a few issues old and was more interested in old school than new, but was gracious enough to give some column inches to Paul Murphy's residency at The Wag. '"You don't have to be a buff" said Murphy, as the opening strains of Duke Pearson's 'Jeannine' inspired the mixed throng in attendance to dispose of their beverages and take to the floor'. In a review for The Wire, Mark Webster couldn't help but agree: 'Let us not forget the fundamental thing here: the music is getting played - it's getting played a lot and a lot of people are getting, well, well into it'[18]. Webster also wrote the jazz dance pages for Blues and Soul and Black Echoes magazines, but for these he used a pseudonym so his provocative opinions didn't rebound on him. Robert Elms, writing for The Face and going out with Sade Adu at the time, 'got a lot of grief from it. On the one hand you had the serious jazz buffs complaining that we're riding the band wagon and also getting grief from the club kids who just thought it was the latest trend'[19]. It was a very contrasting scene with hard-core on the one side and placid jazz on the other, and Elms in the middle. 'We all hung around together […] and although Sade was never going to go in that [extreme] direction, it would've reinforced what she was into. Remember also you had bands like Working Week and even Style Council, so it was penetrating the mainstream…'[20]

The Jazz Dance scene wound down around 1986 for all sorts of reasons: Murphy and Peterson leaving the Electric Ballroom, violence in Birmingham clubs (linked to football hooliganism which was at its peak in the mid-80s), *Absolute Beginners* flopping, Colin Curtis retiring thru ill health, house music coming in, and so on. The jazz revival didn't end abruptly, rather it mutated into something called acid jazz: another scene, a label, a perfume even, leading to 90s acts like Stereo MCs, Galliano and Jamiroquai. At its height in 1984, guitarist Maurice Chevalier warned: "At the moment this music is fashionable but there will never be a big revival. A few bands will do it for a few months but they'll get bored of it afterwards". And so it was.

Chapter 20: Chasing the Breeze
UK soul and reggae

One say: *"Shall we put him in the van or in the back of the Rover?"*
Me say: *You can't do that, ca' me name Smiley Culture.*
Smiley Culture 'Police Officer'

We were the second generation of black people over here and did what came naturally to us. Whatever had been thrown into our pot went into making lovers rock.[1]
Janet Kay

When the computers came in, that's when the amateurs took over.[2]
Dennis Bovell

In the early 80s British soul turned white. Whether it was Phil Collins covering 'You Can't Hurry Love' or duetting with Philip Bailey, or the Motown pastiche of Wham! or the bluesy torch songs of Alison Moyet, or the faux-gospel vocal acrobatics of Annie Lennox, to say nothing of Culture Club, Spandau Ballet, ABC, Style Council and slightly later acts like Simply Red and Lisa Stansfield, soul seemed to pass from black to white artists, at least as far as the charts were concerned. Of course, this was nothing new: most white rock and pop is derived from black rhythm & blues, but even so, it was galling for British black musicians. Why couldn't they get the deals, the media, the hits? Some of it was about talent, or not diversifying enough, or because American black artists were better, or bad management, or whatever reasons most acts fail to make it, but a lot of it was about racism, institutional or otherwise.

It was also because 'black music' – whatever that meant – was going through a stylistically messy time. Soul, funk, disco, blues and reggae were mixing with lovers rock, hip-hop, rap, electro and (soon) house. By the end of the decade much would simply be called dance. So, the mid-80s were uncertain times with no one style dominating. On the one hand that made things interesting, but also confusing as artists, producers and record labels hedged their bets and waited for the next big thing.

Black music in Britain had always played second fiddle to black music's standing in America. Rod Temperton, ex-Heatwave and scribe of three tracks for Michael Jackson's *Thriller*, described American soul music as having "a direct link to its African roots, whereas British soul, in its original form, came with a heavy dose of Caribbean influence"[3]. In the 60s and 70s, the UK looked to the sounds of Stax, Motown and Philly, but as the 70s progressed, British home-grown funk bands like The Equals, Osibisa, Cymande, Kokomo, FBI and others[4] vied with Jamaican reggae to become something unique to Britain. In the late 70s, disco – although not specifically a black phenomenon – proved a colourful distraction, though on a smaller scale than across the Atlantic. But when disco tailed off at the turn of the decade, the artists reverted to funk or soul again[5].

In parallel with the demise of disco was the turn-of-the-decade revival of ska, also known as 2-tone thanks to the bands' mixed-race line-ups[6] and the name of the record label some of them signed to. Ska also doffed its pork pie hat to punk – punk and reggae having forged a kind of mutual respect and rebellion society. Centred in Coventry and Birmingham, ska burned brightly but briefly, with key bands The Specials, The Beat and The Selecter having split by 1983. The Specials briefly became The Special AKA and had a top 10 hit with 'Free Nelson Mandela' in March 1984, while The Beat split into two bands, General Public and Fine Young Cannibals at about the same time. More durable was the reggae-based music of Birmingham-based UB40, who were also mixed race. After three successful early 80s albums showcasing their own songs, they released *Labour of Love* in 1983, featuring covers of songs that had inspired them to form the band in the first place. It went to #1 and yielded four Top 20 singles. But 1984's *Geffery Morgan*[7] saw a return to self-penned songs in a style that was more mainstream than roots. Still, they helped popularize reggae and took control of their own affairs with their own label (DEP International), studio and film subsidiary, all housed in an ex-meat factory.

Ninety-nine per cent of reggae, however, was black. And for many, the only authentic reggae was Jamaican, not British. But in the early 80s, following the death of Bob Marley, politicised 'roots' reggae was on the wane, up against a UK (and US) record industry that wanted to reach wider audiences. One reaction to roots reggae machismo had been lovers rock - a more inclusive, accessible style of reggae, not 'feminised' exactly, but with male *and* female singers. It was essentially a UK-only genre, initially an informal underground phenomenon on small labels, played at sound system events. Its influence also crept into the music of established British reggae bands. Most of the singers had day jobs and stayed in them, but a few went on to achieve mainstream success. One was Janet Kay who had an early lovers rock hit with 'Silly Games' in 1979 and, in 1984, the equally infectious (though non-charting) 'Eternally Grateful'. Between 1983-85 Kay had a parallel acting career, starring in No Problem!, Channel 4's first sitcom and the first comedy series specifically to address the lifestyle of Britain's black community.

But back to reggae. So, while there were no successors to Bob Marley's crown (Peter Tosh, the man-most-likely-to, failed to step up to the plate), the early 80s saw British reggae diversify. It was different from what was going on in Jamaica, having developed in another culture and taken some of that culture on board. The ska revival was one thing but aside from ska, three #1 hits towards the end of 1982 sealed reggae's continuing popularity and influence. Eddy Grant was an established figure in British reggae[8], although ironically he'd just moved *back* to the Caribbean when 'I Don't Wanna Dance' became his first #1, followed quickly by a #2 with 'Electric Avenue'. Hollywood came calling and his theme song for *Romancing the Stone* in 1984 did well in the US charts but, unexpectedly removed from the actual film, it peaked at only #52 in UK. Thereafter he became more of a producer. At the opposite end of the spectrum, Birmingham youngsters Musical Youth were novices, but their sophomore single 'Pass the Duchie' was massive. The intensity of the fame thrust on so young a band (their average age was 13 at the time) meant that they struggled to maintain the momentum. Three singles in 1984 barely charted and they split acrimoniously the following year. The way had been paved, however, for a group which could combine the sleekness of Grant and charm of Musical Youth whilst adding a talking-point frontman, all wrapped up in a fashionable new pop image. It duly arrived in the form of Culture Club's reggae-lilting 'Do You Really Want to Hurt Me' and the wholesale appropriation of black music by white boys, which we will return to later.

Of course, Bob Marley's absence was still keenly felt, not least by Island Records. So in May 1984, the three-year-dead legend was metaphorically exhumed and repackaged. *Legend*, the compilation, was a phenomenon: the third biggest selling album in the UK that year, and by far the best-selling reggae album ever. It took reggae into the mainstream, bought more by white people than black. 'One Love' became a #5 single, its Kings Road-set video featuring cameos from Paul McCartney, Bananarama, Aswad, Musical Youth and Madness. If ever there was a moment when Marley really crossed the colour border, this was surely it. To make sure it worked in the US, five of the album's tracks were remixed. Other Jamaican acts sharpened up their sound too, with increasing use of synthesizer and electronic rhythms. Black Uhuru's 1983 *Anthem*, for example, was remixed for an international audience the following year, winning a Grammy for Best Reggae Recording. But overall, reggae productions actually got *weaker*, thanks to the lazy use of digital technology including the introduction of the Casio whose preset rhythm dominated Wayne Smith's 1985 hit 'Under Mi Shengnan Ten', the first reggae record not to have a bass-line. Sly and Robbie, Jamaica's foremost rhythm section and production duo, were critical of the new direction: "As the eighties went on, the music took a dip, took a nosedive [...] When the computers came in they think you don't even have to try, like the computer will do it all for you."[9]

The legend of Bob Marley was both an inspiration and a tough act to follow for British reggae bands like Aswad and Steel Pulse.

Meanwhile, British reggae bands were also refining their sound even if they retained their political toughness. A month into 1984, the release of Steel Pulse's fifth studio album *Earth Crisis* lived up to its title, which for good measure depicted Reagan,

Andropov, the pope and the Klu Klux Klan on the sleeve. For all the proselytizing, however, it was upbeat. Aswad's 1984 *Rebel Souls* album may have shared the requisite disaffected title, but singles like 'Chasing for the Breeze' (with its Neville Brody sleeve) and ska standard '54-46 Was My Number' – their first to chart, albeit in the lower reaches – showed a more mainstream approach even if it was through a ganja mist of languorous bass and brass. They even appeared on Pop Quiz and Eight Days A Week. Meanwhile, Southall-based Misty In Roots' mellow, radio-and-white-friendly sound was countered by a fierce independence, never signing to a major; they even disappeared to Africa for a while which in turn influenced mid-80s albums *Earth* and *Musi-O-Tunya*. From Bristol, Black Roots' *The Front Line* was also a key album that year, which they promoted on a European Tour supporting UB40. Of the younger generation, Maxi Priest was different again, combining reggae with feelgood lovers rock and rhythm & blues on his 1984 debut singles 'Sensi' and 'Throw My Corn'.

1984, then, saw reggae diversify, at least in the UK, echoed by Ini Kamoze, who was being trumpeted as the next big thing from Jamaica: "With our heads so deeply buried in the roots [of reggae], we don't seem to notice how far and wide the branches are spreading"[10]. It also saw the first staging of Reggae Sunsplash in London. The festival was in its seventh year in Jamaica but it was new ground for London, presented in Crystal Palace, sponsored by Capital Radio and featuring a mix of Jamaican and British talent. The long hot summer was perfect for reggae, at its best booming from street sound systems and festivals, with a strong, upbeat Notting Hill Carnival, as well as those in Leeds and St Paul's in Bristol, concluding things at the end of August.

Capital Radio's support of reggae was the exception rather than the norm. Most stations weren't interested, although John Peel and Kid Jensen continued to champion reggae on Radio One[11]. The big change was pirate radio, especially in London. Some of these illegal stations had been transmitting for years, but often only for a couple of hours at a time, using weak transmitters and continually being forced off air by the authorities. Also, those that played black music (Invicta, JFM, Horizon, LWR and others) were mostly white-owned, aligned to the Soul Mafia DJs and weekender crowd. The exception was Dread Broadcasting Corporation, Britain's first black-owned radio station, broadcasting from a Notting Hill eyrie, 22 floors up. As one DJ explained, "At the time there was a big gap between the black community and the guys who were doing pirate radio. It was a 'them and us' situation […] they were all good presenters and good friends y'know, but there was just this gap – there were no black presenters as such"[12]. There was a similar situation in the music papers: most of the writers at Black Echoes and Blues & Soul were white.

This started to change. In his book, London's Pirate Pioneers, Stephen Hebditch, described 1984 as the year stations smartened up their acts and brought in more DJs, including more black ones, and also started paying them. LWR for example brought in future rap stars Derek Boland, Joe Douglas, Daddy Ernie and Barry Bee. Towards the end of the year Dread Broadcasting Corporation went out of action, but it was less for being busted and more because their Ranking Miss P was offered a weekly reggae show on BBC called Culture Rock. Soon stations started bidding for bona fide licenses, but the flipside was that the legit stations became less edgy, more mainstream.

Not so the sound systems which dated back to the yard and street parties of Jamaica, and became popular in Britain – mainly London, but also cities like Bristol and Manchester and (bizarrely) Huddersfield[13] – in the 70s. By the early 80s there were scores of sound systems operating, usually set up in community centres or empty houses often depending on whether they could get the massive speakers through the doors. They would play important roles in breaking a record and testing the metal of up-and-coming singers and DJs in front of no-nonsense, unforgiving audiences.

Sir Coxsone Outernational was probably the most established and was largely responsible for introducing lovers rock to sound system culture; it also had a short-lived label, S.C.O.M., releasing a dozen singles confined to 1984/85. But there were others like Trouble Funk, Madhatters, Fatman, Jah Shaka, Funkadelic and Saxon Studio International. The last-named was where toasters like Tippa Irie, Papa Levi and musicians like Maxi Priest honed their art, some of which can be heard on *Saxon Studio International: Coughing Up Fire!!!*, released in November 1984, the only official recording of Saxon[14]. In a fit of exuberance, reggae documenter John Masouri saw the sound system as key:

> *"The 1980s were the best decade ever for reggae in this country; it was this huge explosion of talent, not just in London but all over the country. [...] You had real storytellers emerge. [...] That was such a talented generation with the MCs and the singers on systems like Saxon. In 1984 Papa Levi had a number one hit in Jamaica with 'Me God Me King'. That had never been done before – in fact, it has never been done since – but it was just amazing. A young guy from South London, from Lewisham, who learnt his craft in local youth clubs, and suddenly he's got a number one hit in Jamaica – the home of reggae sound systems, the home of reggae culture"*[15].

Another artist honing his talents as part of the Saxon posse was David Emmanuel, aka Smiley Culture, a young toaster from south London, his first two 45s becoming key reggae releases of 1984. Debut single 'Cockney Translation' was an extraordinary single, mixing the Cockney dialect from east London with Jamaican patois in a fast-flowing 'chat' style that had originated in Jamaica. And yet it was absolutely about what it was to be black *in London*.

> *The translation of cockney to understand is easy*
> *So long as you don't deaf and you listen me keenly*
> *You should pick it up like a youth who find some money*
> *Go tell it to your friends also your family*

And they did. In fact it was later used in schools as an example of how immigration has affected the English language. The follow-up single 'Police Officer' was equally impressive, managing to be both politically adroit *and* funny. Supposedly based on a real-life incident, Smiley re-enacts a conversation with the police who are preparing to arrest him for possession of cannabis:

One say: "Shall we put him in the van or in the back of the Rover?"
Me say: You can't do that ca' me name Smiley Culture
"You what? Did you do that record Cockney Translator?"
In the reggae charts number one was it's number
"My kids love it and so does my mother!
Tell you what I'll do. A favour for a favour
Just sign your autograph on this piece of paper"

Sadly, Smiley couldn't keep up the momentum and ironically, tragically, he died of a self-inflicted stab wound in 2011 while the police were searching his house in connection with a drug offence.

Jah Shaka, Dennis Bovell and Smiley Culture.

Racism was a fact of life for most black musicians, British, Jamaican or otherwise. It hindered record deals, media exposure and simply going out, which was one of the reasons sound systems were so important – most black youths couldn't get into the clubs, especially in London's west end. However, rather than retreat into the ghetto, some young entrepreneurial operators got hip to doing things differently. Strangely, amidst the gloom of Thatcherism, unemployment and the miners' strike, a new sense of individual and small-collective positivity emerged. One of these can-do youngsters was Trevor Romeo, aka Jazzie B, who in his teens worked with friends on the Jah Rico sound system before re-naming it Soul II Soul in 1982. "It wasn't all about sufferation or being dowdy or downtrodden. It was about being optimistic, doing quite well for yourself and having a bit of swagger".[16] It was also about appealing to a white audience, but run by black people, unlike the big out-of-town soul all-dayers and weekenders run by white DJs like Chris Hill and the rest of the Soul Mafia. In essence, Jazzie B and company were doing what Thatcher was espousing: getting out there and doing it for themselves[17]. Firstly the sound system, then the clothing line and (but not until the end of the decade) their own recorded music, all with a cool sheen of optimism: "A happy face, a thumping bass for a lovin' race" as their motto proclaimed. Paradoxically or not, punk too was an influence: "One of the reasons we're all here today is because of punk", Jazzie B admitted. "None of us would be accepted unless punk came along, because punk helped black music penetrate the media"[18]. In Bristol, The Wild Bunch were doing something similar, later becoming Massive Attack, although theirs was a less optimistic vibe.

On the dub side – the subtraction of tracks, including vocals, and the addition of echo and other effects – Jamaican pioneers like King Tubby and Lee Scratch Perry were being superseded in the early 80s by UK-based producers like The Mad Professor and Jah Shaka (indeed they released a joint album *At Ariwa Sounds* in 1984). There was also increasing interchange between black and white producers and remixers. 'White dub' pioneer Adrian Sherwood, who used to drive a van delivering reggae acetates to shops like Rounder in Bristol, produced Akabu's 'Watch Yourself', the first British release on New York's Tommy Boy label. And dub versions of white pop (eg. Groucho Smyckle's remixes of Shriekback's 'Hand On My Heart' and Blancmange's 'Murder') could be found on the B-sides of mainstream 12-inchers, although in truth, most of the latter were simply remixes rather than dub.

Dennis Bovell was perhaps the best example of (literally) mixing it. Having produced both black and white artists in the early 80s (including, famously, The Slits), he continued in 1984 with Linton Kwesi Johnson on the one hand and Orange Juice on the other. Another example was Adrian Sherwood's dub productions of loosely concocted, interconnected groups from the OnU Sound stable. The year was a busy one: Singers and Players' *Leaps and Bounds* featured over a dozen musicians including Bim Sherman amongst its four singers, while two Dub Syndicate albums, *North of the River Thames* and *Tunes from the Missing Channel*, shared some of the musicians, the latter also including two post-punkers in Jah Wobble and Keith Levene, in-demand session keyboard player Nick Plytas and even improv musician Steve Beresford.

*****

If reggae was in rude health, British soul artists were still very much in the shadow of their US counterparts. There were no equivalents of the legion of American stars. The closest was Billy Ocean. Born in Trinidad but raised in Essex, he'd started his career in the mid-70s and had an early hit with 'Love Really Hurts Without You' in 1976. But it was 1984 that really saw him achieve transatlantic success with 'Caribbean Queen', complete with its borrowed 'Billie Jean' rhythm. In an interesting marketing ploy, the title was changed to 'European Queen' in European territories and 'African Queen' for South Africa. In any case, it won him a Grammy, and the album, *Suddenly*, went gold in the UK and double-platinum in the States.

The rest was a mixed bag. As disco-soul-funk music by bands like Heatwave, Hot Chocolate, Hi-Tension, Central Line and Light Of The World was coming to an end, the mid-80s was a time when black British soul seemed to lose itself. After Linx's split in 1983, for example, David Grant tried desperately hard to model himself on Michael Jackson, and failed; backing singer Junior Giscomb also went solo, as well as, in 1984, working with the Council Collective and Phil Lynott; and bassist Peter Martin joined avant-funksters 23 Skidoo. Phil Fearon & Galaxy were having hits with what was essentially still disco. Loose Ends represented Virgin Records' first serious investment in a British black music act, but their debut 1984 album heralded a run of barely-charting, average records. And then there was Five Star – three girls, two guys, one family – slavishly modelled on the Jacksons, who had a kind of parallel sound to Stock Aitken Waterman. The only promising British female soul singer seemed to be Jaki Graham whose uplifting 'Heaven Knows' went completely unnoticed in 1984 and almost as unnoticed when it was re-released a year later, although by then she was ironically enjoying a string of lesser quality hits. The parlous state of affairs was reflected in Blues & Soul magazine's choice of 1984 cover stars, *all* of which were American – an extraordinary editorial decision despite the situation[19].

Billy Ocean, Jaki Graham and Loose Ends.

Contender for best soul song that never made it, indeed possibly the best British soul single of 1984, was Marcel King's 'Reach for Love'. King had had some success in the mid-70s with Manchester group Sweet Sensation, but nothing was happening for him in the early 80s. Attempting to revive his career on Factory Records was an odd move, but New Order's Bernard Sumner – still heavily in thrall to New York's club music – provided blissful production. It should have been a hit, but Factory didn't put their weight behind it, which didn't stop Tony Wilson declaring it "one of the best records on Factory – one of the high spots of the entire collection"[20]. Nearly as good was fellow Manchester band 52nd Street's 'Can't Afford', also on Factory but this time produced by New Order's Stephen Morris. Again, Factory couldn't quite get behind it and they moved to 10 Records and had some success in the States. Colourbox were another example, also on a trendy, 'white' label (in their case 4AD), Lorita Grahame providing the gutsy vocals on 1984's 'Punch' and 'Say You' singles. Signed to Virgin and with a Don Was-produced 1984 debut album in the bag, the more mainstream, Floy Joy were tipped to go far, but the two Sheffield white boys behind the music couldn't seem to get the right black, female singer (they went through three in three years[21]) and split after a second album.

Somewhere between funk and hip-hop, Black Britain were another mixed-race group formed in 1984, playing in clubs like the Wag before signing with 10 Records. Their songs were a slightly confusing mix of smooth ('Real Life') and political ('Ain't No Rockin' in a Police State'), the latter becoming their first single two years later. Perhaps the strangest twist was new band View From The Hill, formed by Patrick Patterson of 70s Brit-funksters Cymande. Their 1984 debut single 'I'm No Rebel' sounded like Van Morrison.

White jazz-funk-soul musicians had always worked with black musicians: Rod Temperton in Heatwave, Harvey Hinsley in Hot Chocolate, for example. In the case of Shakatak (their biggest hit, 'Down On The Street', in 1984) and Level 42 (whose 1984 album, tellingly called *True Colours*, yielded the Top 20 hit 'Hot Water') they were *all* white. As we have seen, white men playing black music is an oft-made criticism of early-to-mid 80s new pop. But it was nothing new: so were The Beatles and the Stones. It also applied to white DJs who specialized in black music, particularly the aforementioned Soul Mafia in the south of England and Stuart Curtis, Mike Shaft and others in the north. Even the perennially old northern soul scene started to change a bit, particularly though DJ Ian Levine who tried to introduce new sounds, including hi-NRG (northern soul with a thumping disco beat). His move into writing and production resulted in the several million-selling, genre-defining 'High Energy' sung by Evelyn Thomas which would in turn provide Stock Aitken Waterman with their trademark sound for the next year or so.

When black Chicago-based musicians and DJs started playing house in 1984, it took some time to catch on in Britain but by 1987 it had established itself in both clubs and charts, before transforming itself into the ecstasy-influenced Acid House. By which time it had been commandeered by a largely white rave culture. Plus ça change.

Chapter 21: It Says Here
From NME to Smash Hits

A stylish, thoughtful, hedonistic pop era flourished, and Smash Hits was its house magazine.[1]
Neil Tennant

Part of the pleasure of popular culture is talking about it.[2]
Simon Frith

It's a beautiful thing, the destruction of words.
Syme, in George Orwell's *Nineteen Eighty-Four*

When you wake up to the fact that your paper is Tory
Just remember: there are two sides to every story
Billy Bragg, 'It Says Here', 1984

In this age of Facebook, Twitter, Wikipedia, Discogs and thousands of music blogs, it is hard to imagine a world, not really that long ago, when information about rock and pop was mostly printed and available once a week at best. A decade away from the internet and two from social media, those wanting to keep in touch with the music scene could nevertheless choose from a healthy array of publications. In 1984 there were *seven* UK weekly music papers: Melody Maker, New Musical Express (NME) and Sounds were all 'serious' broadsheets; Record Mirror had in 1982 downsized from semi-serious broadsheet to a more pop-focussed colour magazine, joined by the similar Number One a year later[3]; Echoes was a soul and reggae weekly; and Music Week was a not-without-interest industry publication. There was also the fortnightly Smash Hits, Blues & Soul (which in 1984 subsumed its former rival Black Music and Jazz Review), and the 180,000-print-run Soundcheck (delivered free to live venues), scores of specialised monthlies and hundreds of fanzines. And that's aside from the extensive music content of the nascent style monthlies, teen zines and the increasing pop gossip of the tabloid dailies.

The three weekly broadsheets – Melody Maker, NME and Sounds – had been in existence since 1926, 1952 and 1970 respectively, and although they differed somewhat in the extent and intensity of their coverage of popular music, their appearance hadn't. Aside from their names in red, all three were basically printed in black & white on rough 13-inch x 17-inch newspaper stock. They would acquire more colour as the 80s progressed, much like Britain's daily newspapers, but it has to be said that most front covers looked way cooler in moody monochrome. If the 60s was largely about conveying information about pop, often in a groovy, hyperbolic style, more akin to press releases than criticism, then the 70s was the era of more serious rock journalism. In America, the counter-culture had sired three new music magazines – Crawdaddy (founded 1966), Rolling Stone (1967) and Creem (1969) – introducing a whole new style of hip writing ('gonzo journalism' as Hunter S Thompson called it) which accentuated the first person singular, took a relaxed approach to objectivity and frequently went off at tangents bringing in wider cultural references[4]. Writers included Richard Meltzer, Lester Bangs, Paul Williams, Tom Wolfe, Greil Marcus and Nik Cohn. "This was a time when the vocation of a music journalist could be an elevated pursuit"[5], wrote Patti Smith, herself a contributor to those magazines.

British writers like Richard Williams, Caroline Coon, Ian MacDonald, Nick Kent and Charles Shaar Murray also started to elevate popular music to a lofty cultural platform, interwoven with politics, literature and cod-philosophy. For some it went to their heads – and over others'. Lest we forget, these writers, together with John Peel, were the absolute arbiters of taste; in 1973 the NME, for example, had a circulation of 300,000 and Peel was listened to by millions. If you add the privileges of hobnobbing with rock stars, label-funded jaunts to album launches in LA (this was the era of record company largesse) and the imbibing of substances backstage after gigs, then it was perhaps little wonder the prose turned purple.

But for many that was rock's appeal. Bands like Led Zeppelin and Pink Floyd weren't like normal people. They were up there with the gods, chimerical and untouchable, a position contrived and perpetuated by journalists, labels, managers, the bands themselves (though some would deny it) and the record-buying public. But Icarus-like, it all came crashing down when punk arrived in 1976. The record-buying public realised that rock didn't have to be that way: anyone could form a band. And so they did, in their hundreds.

Sounds was the first of the weeklies to embrace punk, followed quickly by NME and, grudgingly, Melody Maker. Some journalists got rid of their flares and cut their hair short. NME's editor Nick Logan brought in hip, young things like Tony Parsons and Julie Burchill. As Parsons himself remarked: 'They were picking people who looked the part more than anything. It was about the image, about the NME as a brand, about it being cutting edge and dangerous'[6]. But he also confessed that the period before he joined [roughly 1972-75] was when the paper was creatively at its strongest. 'I don't think the writers who came after – including me – were anywhere near as good as Nick Kent, Charles Shaar Murray or Ian MacDonald'.[7] Between punk and the end of the decade a whole wave of savvy writers arrived: at NME Danny Baker (initially as receptionist), Paul Morley and Ian Penman; Sounds brought in Jon Savage, Vivien Goldman, Garry Bushell and Dave McCullough; Melody Maker had Ian Birch, James Truman and Mary Harron[8].

Despite the influx of a new scene, new bands and new writers, the circulations of all three papers in the late 70s were actually declining. In 1979, the NME was down to about 200,000 per issue, Melody Maker 150,000 and Sounds 120,000, and the trend continued into the new decade so that by 1984 those figures were nearly halved[9]. There were two main reasons for this: firstly competition from the new, 'lighter', full-colour magazines like Smash Hits and Number One (which we'll come on to later); and secondly the increasingly impenetrable, theory-driven text of some of the monochrome weeklies' 'serious' critics. If people thought punk's stripped-back ethos would be reflected in the prose that was written about it, they were wrong. If anything, punk upped the word count and semiotics. Reviews became less about the artists' new record or concert and more about what the journalist was reading at the time (Barthes, Foucault, Situationism). It could be interesting and entertaining, but it could also be cruel or utterly incomprehensible. Ian Penman's review of Blondie's 'Rapture' single, for instance, included the line: 'Is it at all possible – the reciprocity of sensations between mythical Debbie Harry and your solitary wallpaper self?'[10]; while the first half of Paul Morley's 9,000-word feature on Devo is him in a taxi on the way to the interview worrying about his sexuality and the state of the world[11].

The early 80s saw many of these writers switch papers or go freelance. Jon Savage went from Sounds to Melody Maker to The Face, Chris Bohn and Paolo Hewitt from Melody Maker to NME; Parsons and Burchill wrote columns for the national press before becoming successful novelists; Bushell went to The Sun, Baker to television and Paul Morley, having championed new pop, switched from full-time journalism to maverick A&R at ZTT. Rather than writing about pop, he would unearth and manufacture it.

New pop had re-introduced colour and ambition after monochrome new wave, but the broadsheets were still largely printed in grubby black and white and were fickle about which groups to support. ABC were OK because they were arch and ironic, but Spandau Ballet were not because they were clothes horses. NME writer Paolo Hewitt summed up the dilemma: 'You had Smash Hits taking off and we didn't know what to do with people like Boy George and Simon Le Bon and Duran Duran. There were no rock acts and the NME was just flummoxed'[12].

*****

Smash Hits, however, knew exactly what it was doing. It had launched in 1978, cashing in on the lively new wave scene and putting Blondie on its first front cover. Its founder, Nick Logan, had been the editor who had recruited the hip young punk writers to the NME, but he had seen the future and the future was pop. The new, fortnightly A4-sized magazine was full-colour, fun and unashamedly frivolous – but not so anodyne as to be bland, Logan instilling in it a light-hearted irreverence. Not for Smash Hits the cynical death-by-a-thousand-words: a flippant ten-word put-down would do the trick, and even then it wasn't meant earnestly. It was full of glossy photos and lyrics; single reviews were 50 words, albums the same; the pen-pal section had real addresses; the letters page probably wasn't made up. The relationships Smash Hits conducted with the bands through the press departments of the big labels (and it was mostly the majors) were win-win for both. Logan left after only two years to set up another ground-breaking magazine – The Face in 1980 – but, regardless, its circulation steadily soared, from 166,000 in 1979 to over half a million in 1984. Clearly a list of Andrew Ridgley's Top 5 Favourite Cars and a news item announcing that Susanne Sulley had passed her driving test were what people wanted to read. And the frivolity wasn't just limited to 'lightweights'. In the regular Personal File we learned that Morrissey bought his shirts in a ladies outsize shop in Kensington High

Street and in a later issue he astonishingly (ironically?) made Duran Duran's 'The Wild Boys' Single of the Fortnight. We also learned that Siouxsie would like to meet JG Ballard. 'I must say', she said, 'I do like this idle chit-chat. It's much better than a real interview...'[13].

Smash Hits, Record Mirror and Number One – the toppermost of the poppermost.

By 1984 Smash Hits was being helmed by Mark Ellen, while also presenting BBC's revamped Whistle Test, and there were two Assistant Editors, Melody Maker émigré Ian Birch (Features) and Neil Tennant (News). Tennant, soon to leave to try his hand at being a pop star himself, has always looked back fondly at his time at the magazine:

I was lucky enough to work for Smash Hits in a golden age for British pop, between the end of punk and Live Aid. This was the period when young, intelligent pop stars had learned the lessons and ideas of punk and decided to link them to the glamour of pop, stardom and nightlife. A stylish, thoughtful, hedonistic pop era flourished, and Smash Hits was its house magazine.[14]

Tennant's arch style was a combination of Jackie and Noel Coward. Artists doing well were 'on the giddy carousel of pop'; struggling bands were 'down the dumper'. When Tennant left Smash Hits he was presented with a mock issue with the headline: 'How I Left Britain's Brightest Magazine To Form My Tragic Pop Group, Went Down the Dumper and Asked For My Job Back'. Nine months later he was on the cover for real.

Smash Hits didn't have it all to themselves though. Record Mirror went way back to 1954 and had been the first music paper to have a full colour front cover (The Beatles, inevitably). By the mid-70s it had expanded to a broadsheet and had swallowed up another title, Disc, but by 1982, with circulation declining, it reduced its size and went glossy and pop. Its best-known writers were probably Dylan Jones, Betty Page and Nancy Culp[15]; the latter two used to dress up in rubber and were active in the Skin Two scene, the club in Soho which had started in 1983 (by David Claridge, who would shortly be the hand inside Roland Rat) and the magazine which was launched a year later. Midway through 1984 Record Mirror introduced a free monthly supplement

267

called VID covering music video, computer games and television. It must have seemed a good idea at the time, its first editorial presciently announcing that 'Just like pop music, audio visual entertainment is here to stay'. But its editorial and design were a bit dull and VID lasted just three issues. Number One had no pedigree at all, brazenly launched in 1983 as direct competition to Smash Hits. By the end of the decade its circulation was more than any of the serious music papers, but by 1991 and 1992 respectively, both Record Mirror and Number One had folded.

The self-importance and real importance of Britain's music press was unique. No other country could boast so many. There certainly were good, unpretentious writers still plying their trade. The problem was what to cover? Smash Hits had nailed its pop colours to its mast; the NME now looked to The Face for inspiration. A quick check of the former's front covers in 1984 reflects an increasing eclecticism, or some would say confusion. Take this run of five consecutive front covers in the spring of that year: a heavy metal special, The Style Council, Foetus, Culture Club and Hugh Masekela. Sprinkled throughout the year, there were non-musical cover stars too: Rik Mayall of The Young Ones, Robert De Niro and Charlie Nicholas of Arsenal. The paper was also becoming not just politicised (in terms of where its writers' sympathies lay) but editorially *political* – a 'viable way of communicating left-wing politics to the mainstream', as Billy Bragg commented[16].

But music remained at the core, and there were good, solid writers in Chris Bohn (as Biba Kopf), Steven Wells (as Seething Wells, Swells or Susan Williams), Danny Kelly (who would later become Editor), Mat Snow, Don Watson[17], Stuart Cosgrove as Media Editor (who would later spend 20 years at Channel 4), David Quantick and Barney Hoskyns, to name a few. There was still room for polemical diatribes, including the constant obsessing about the 'faceless folk of pop'. In September, Ian Penman wrote a suitably dense piece called The War on Pop while earlier Richard Cook had written a centrespread feature called Identikit Pop.[18] In it he interviewed usual suspects Nik Kershaw and Howard Jones, who came across as patient, positive, intelligent people compared with Cook's cynical stance.

In 1984 Melody Maker was similarly unsure of which way to go. Some weeks it would look like a broadsheet version of Smash Hits, with Wham!, Sade and Human League on the cover, the next week it would return to the more earnest Paul Weller and Lloyd Cole. Earlier in the 80s it had changed its masthead from Melody Maker to MM but in 1984 reverted again to the name in full, albeit in reassuringly modern block letters. At the back it still had its muso section ("Hi-tech Guitars: 8-page Special") and famous small ads (through which, as 1984 gave way to 1985, Vince Clarke secured the singing services of Andy Bell for example), but it would drift somewhat until Chris Roberts arrived from Sounds and Simon Reynolds and David Stubbs joined from university via the dole office.

Both NME and Melody Maker were published by IPC Magazines, but that didn't make them allies. In fact, they were often at each other's throats, not helped by the fact that Melody Maker staff were paid more, simply and inexplicably by being in a different division of the company (they were in 'Hobbies', NME was in 'Youth Titles'). Halfway through the year, a problem of a different kind arose. Partly to seek better pay and conditions and partly out of sympathy with the miners, writers from both papers went on strike for much of June and July. Even this didn't bring them together. Melody Maker staff returned to work a good two weeks earlier than NME's, earning scorn from the latter.

The 'inkies' – NME, Melody Maker and Sounds.

It was a frustrating time for NME editor Neil Spencer: 'It's very hard to make a paper good and very easy to lose readers. It really damaged us and I don't think NME ever really recovered [...] My beef with IPC was always financial. They wouldn't give us more pages – Sounds had more pages of editorial, which is one of the reasons why they gave NME a good run for a while'.[19] Spencer left in the New Year and started writing about stars from an entirely different angle. Astrology.

At Sounds, there was less agonizing and both staff and freelancers got on with the business of interviewing musicians, reviewing albums and reporting on gigs. There was perhaps less debate and naval-gazing, and as a result its editorial direction was a bit of a mystery, but at least everyone more or less got on. Chris Roberts joined at around this time and would quickly become one of its star writers before moving on to Melody Maker. Old hand Sandy Robertson was still writing about Aleister Crowley, and Edwin Pouncey was contributing his faintly grotesque but popular cartoons as Savage Pencil. Johnny Waller had helmed Fife's first music fanzine, Kingdom Come, before joining the paper while also setting up Fire Records in 1985. Andy Hurt (real name Ross) was filling in time before being recruited by David Balfe for his new label Food Records which he'd set up in 1984 and which would soon be the home of Blur. David Tibet and this author covered the alternative end as freelancers, which was an odd affair given that they already had staffer Dave Henderson championing the weird and experimental through his influential Wild Planet column. If ever there was a strange album or gig that needed reviewing, the cry was usually 'Give it to one of the three Daves'. (I have to confess that I was in awe of many of the writers and was occasionally guilty of slipping into an affected style which was trying too hard to be cool. So if there are any bands out there who didn't understand the piece I wrote about them, sorry!) It also had rather more female writers: Carole Linfield, Robbi Millar, Jane Simon and Mary Anne Hobbs amongst others. Sounds front covers were often stupendously unfashionable: while the other three took it in turns to put The Smiths, Echo & The Bunnymen and Depeche Mode on the cover, Sounds put Rubber Rodeo, Swamp Things and Marillion on theirs, although to be fair their going-out-on-a-limb approach also included 'hipper' artists like 23 Skidoo, Cabaret Voltaire and Test Dept.

The music that many people associated with Sounds, however, was Heavy Metal or, to give it its Sounds moniker, New Wave of British Heavy Metal, unhelpfully abbreviated to NWOBHM. The term had been coined by Alan Lewis, editor at the end of the 70s, and then championed by his successor Geoff Barton both within Sounds and in subsidiary magazine, Kerrang!, which launched in 1981. Many of Sounds' journalists would snigger as they passed the Kerrang! desks on their way to file copy, but Barton and his small team would have the last laugh. Sounds would fold in 1991 and Kerrang! is *still* going strong.

Interestingly, none of the main music papers discussed how music was made: the recording process, producers and studios, the new phenomenon of sampling. It was somehow boring, even irrelevant, best left to the specialist muso monthlies. Nor was it particularly interested in investigative journalism. There were stories crying out to be written about pop and censorship (following the banning of 'Relax'), 'Smalltown Boy' and LGBT, even the Island-Stiff merger. As Simon Frith said: "They're quick to voice opinions – on home taping, say – slow to gather fresh information to support such opinions"[20].

*****

Monthlies-wise, there was nothing really equivalent of today's Mojo or Uncut (or the recently deceased Q) which effectively cover what the 80s weeklies used to. However, there were a couple of exceptions. Zigzag was founded in 1969 by Pete Frame, famous for his Rock Family Trees. Initially it covered the underground scene, had a brief mid-70s pub-rock phase, then, under Kris Needs' editorship, devoted itself to punk, but by 1982 it had closed down. Just two years later, with Mick Mercer as editor, it was re-launched, with a vaguely alternative post-punk and goth focus. But with its lack of major backing and glossy fanzine feel it wasn't too much of a surprise when it folded again in 1986.

One of the more unusual magazines of the time was Debut, almost exclusively confined to 1984. Promoting itself as an 'LP Magazine', it was exactly that: a 12-inch square magazine covering a broad array of new pop, together with an LP featuring many of the songs that it wrote about. It had originally been conceived just for the German market, with the first issue published there in November 1983, but a UK version quickly followed from April the next year. The name Debut was supposed to reflect the space given to new bands: in the first UK issue, for example, there were tracks/articles on unknowns Kudos and Niagara Calls, both of whom promptly and unhelpfully disappeared, as well as a section in the magazine called Demos featuring yet more no-hopers[21]. Otherwise it was a not uninteresting mix of chart-friendly fayre, alongside an article on, say, the Video Recording Bill and, bizarrely, a travel feature on Egypt, plus ads for, amongst others, Gitanes and Greenpeace. Subsequent issues continued in this vein, but production and distribution costs were always going to be a challenge and by the end of the year the German edition had shut down. The UK version tried reducing its format to a 10-inch square but it too ceased publication in February 1985. Production costs were only half the story though; bluntly speaking, it was poorly written. A successful successor to Debut would not come until the beginning of the 90s with the excellent Volume and Trance Europe Express series, although the obvious advantages of the CD format were perhaps offset by the tiny type of their accompanying booklets[22].

Meanwhile, there were plenty more specialist magazines and fanzines to choose from. In 1984, Mixmag was into its second year as the first British monthly magazine aimed at DJs. The Wire, then covering pretty much jazz only, was into its third year but it was only in the autumn that it went monthly. Record Collector was at this time a rather dull-looking five-year-old resource for the serious vinyl collector, before its broader appeal rejuvenation in the new millennium. There was HMV's free magazine The Beat, along the lines of Smash Hits, and of course scores of magazines like Guitarist and One Two Testing aimed at musicians and techies.

And then there were the fanzines: mouthpieces of the fan, bulletins from the frontline, precursors to today's blog. It's often said that 1977 was their heyday, and it's true, there were a great many that started thanks to punk's DIY manifesto. But hardly any of the original zines lasted into the 80s. It was more a case of constant replenishment, *and* some. For every one that died, two would spring up in its place, so that by 1984 there were hundreds of them, selling for 50p or so. The tatty, influential Manchester-based City Fun and Newcastle's Eccentric Sleeve Notes, for example, were just finishing, but just starting up were scores of others, and mostly from 'the regions'. From Leeds, Attack On Bzag! was edited by James Brown who went on to create Loaded; from Manchester there was Dave Haslam's Debris, as well as the longer-lasting (1984-94) Ablaze!, the title of which became the commandeered surname of its editor Karren.[23] These were the relatively well-known ones, but often just as interesting were the ones from small towns across the land, edited by 'the only punk in town' and often covering not just music but the local subculture (such as it was): Blaze from Peterborough, Mucilage from St Albans and A Trip into Realism from Whitby – the latter's looking-back editorial including the immortal and doubtless accurate 'Not a lot has happened in Whitby since'.

Of those that *had* started in punk's heyday, John Robb of The Membranes was still putting out the rough-and-ready Rox, while Tony Stewart's Jamming had become (in autumn 1983) a swish bi-monthly magazine and then, a year later, monthly. But it was too fast too soon and went bust by the end of the year, although carried on for another twelve months under different ownership.[24] Stewart moved to the US and began

271

writing biographies of bands like Echo & The Bunnymen, R.E.M., The Clash and The Smiths. Vague, conceived in the closing months of 1979, continued to combine music and psychogeography, mining the pop-and-rock history of west London. Just as didactic, was Monitor, edited by then students Simon Reynolds, Paul Oldfield, David Stubbs and Hilary Little. Suitably verbose, it was a portent of great things to come from all three writers. Like Stewart, Reynolds moved to the US and commenced a career penning brilliant, intelligent music books; Stubbs too, from London.

There were scores of others: The Legend!, cobbled together by Creation Records associate and future NME scribe Everett True; the debut issue of Alphabet Soup, co-edited by Miki Berenyi and Emma Anderson who at the end of the decade would form shoegaze band Lush; the enigmatically named Trout Fishing in Leytonstone (a nod to the first novel by Richard Brautigan, who committed suicide in 1984); as well as the likes of Hungry Beat, Slow Dazzle, Noise Annoys, The Underground, Adventure in Bereznik, To Hell With Poverty, Bombs Away Batman and so on. Humour was an important part of fanzine culture – the underdog-championing ethos to be found in the parallel world of footie fanzines, or the more scatological wit of Viz. It was the end of an era for the Tyneside comic. 1984 was its last year as a home-produced fanzine, sold in Newcastle pubs and clubs; the following year it 'sold out' to a major, Virgin.

*****

At the opposite end of the spectrum, yet still a key source of music information, was the so-called style magazine. Back in 1980, three were launched almost simultaneously – The Face (May), i-D and BLITZ (both September)[25] – and they would go on to dominate the genre for the rest of the decade. Style was something that mods understood, but for most young men (and it was aimed at men as much as women), glossy magazines were either What Car? or on the top shelf. As we have seen, Nick Logan had started The Face after successful stints helming NME and Smash Hits, so when he announced a 'new-wave Life magazine for 16-to-25-year olds', the publishing industry sat up and took note. From the off it was full colour and monthly, with (the following year) crisp art direction, design and typography by Neville Brody and all the best writers like Savage, Parsons, Burchill and Elms. If at first it focussed mainly on music, by 1984 its front covers were alternating with fashion. These were styled by Ray Petri and the Buffalo collective, a loose team of mostly mixed-race photographers, hair and make-up artists, musicians and models, the latter taken from the street rather than agencies (including a 14-year-old Naomi Campbell). Midway through the year, Brody started customising typefaces, in effect using type as an alternative to photography and/or illustration. Advertising revenue grew, and yet they occasionally turned down ads that looked boring. In short, The Face was doing very well.

Founded by Terry Jones, i-D magazine took some time to shed its punky, hand-stapled, landscape-formatted fanzine appearance (a surprisingly casual look given Jones's previous job as art director of Vogue), and for the first four years it was published irregularly. By early 1984 it was beginning to look like The Face, went bi-monthly in April, monthly in September and Time Out's Tony Elliott became a publishing partner before the end of the year. The difference was that i-D was more hip street style while The Face was classier, especially in its art direction.

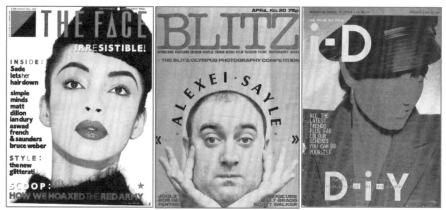

The style trio: The Face, BLITZ and i-D.

In a way, BLITZ was a forerunner of Monitor fanzine, founded by students Carey Labovitch and Simon Tesler at Oxford University in 1980. Its first three issues were limited to a print-run of 2,000 each and sold from market stalls in Covent Garden, Portobello Road and Brick Lane. But it had an ambitious, quirky editorial featuring interviews with, for example, David Puttnam, Barry Norman and Barbara Cartland, and guest writers Sheridan Morley and Alexander Walker. In the autumn of 1981 it secured distribution from WHSmith, went quarterly and by 1984 it was a monthly. Its front covers that year ranged from obvious pop (Frankie and Boy George), to the slightly more alternative (David Sylvian and Peter Murphy) and the distinctly non-musical (Rupert Everett and Alexei Sayle – excepting the latter's single, 'Ullo John, Gotta New Motor?' which hit #15 in March). Its writers included Fiona Russell Powell (who in the February issue asked Simon Lebon: 'How does it feel to know that you are the masturbation fixation of thousands and thousands of pubescent girls all around the world?') and Paul Morley (who before the year was out started a regular column – 'So I stopped interviewing other people and I let them interview me' – opposite a piss-take of a fashion spread with girlfriend Claudia Brücken).

The influence of this holy trinity cannot be overestimated. Their wider take on youth culture, pronouncements on what was in and what was out, the championing of design and the promulgation of something called *style* (different from fashion) set the scene for the rest of the decade, and transferred readily to the High Street. Whether there was room for three style magazines, however, was answered as the next decade dawned and BLITZ folded in 1991.

The casual music fan, however, probably got most of its information from teen magazines (My Guy, Look In and the just-launched Just Seventeen), weekly city listings (Time Out, City Limits) and the increasingly pop-fixated tabloids. In the latter's case, a pop star like Boy George was a godsend: articulate, visually arresting and great for a quote, he was rarely out of the papers in 1984, although his world would begin to go pear-shaped by the end of the year courtesy of overexposure and a lame album. Most of the 'news' was simply gossip, and much of that simply untrue[26]. The go-to page for such titbits was The Sun's Bizarre column, edited by John Blake from 1982, and succeeded in early 1985 by former Sounds writer Garry Bushell, who had made his name championing NWOBHM and oi! bands. Blake meanwhile had set up a pop column, White Hot Club, at the Daily Mirror. Even the broadsheets were increasing their coverage of popular music. At the Sunday Times, Simon Frith was appointed rock critic to complement Derek Jewell's position as pop critic – although one had to wonder why it wasn't the other way around.

1984 was in many ways a watershed year for Britain's music papers. It effectively signalled the end of the cult of music writer as personality, to be replaced by efficient, fairly faceless journalists who weren't espousing manifestoes or blowing trumpets. It also saw diversification. Britain's 15-25 year olds were becoming more discerning, more wide-ranging in their tastes. There was music, yes, but there was also fashion, films, video, computer games, even politics. Most of these 'distractions' weren't new of course, but the 80s were bringing them to the attention of ever younger consumers, and style magazines like The Face, BLITZ and i-D had risen to the challenge of covering them. The weekly music papers would face a real struggle to keep up and stay relevant as the decade passed the halfway mark.

Chapter 22: Monsters Of Rock
From NWOBHM to Spinal Tap

Metal is the feeling of being an outsider, but still being part of something huge.[1]
Brian Posehn, actor and comedian

Heavy metal is a universal energy, it's the sound of a volcano. It's rock, it's earth shattering. Somewhere in our primal being we understand.[2]
Billy Corgan, The Smashing Pumpkins

These go to eleven.
Nigel Tufnel, Spinal Tap

There is very little middle ground with heavy metal. It's either love or hate. In 1984, aside from Sounds and Kerrang!, the music papers hated it but heavy metal nevertheless attracted hordes of followers, an older generation weaned on its Black Sabbath, Led Zeppelin, Deep Purple and Judas Priest roots in the late 60s, and a younger generation inspired by the New Wave of British Heavy Metal (NWOBHM) resurgence in the late 70s. It's often forgotten that the latter was inspired by punk. Iron Maiden, Def Leppard, Saxon and others were all formed around 1977. Indeed there was sometimes little difference, musically, between the two. Both were fast and furious, guitar-driven and 'from the street'. For a while they shared a penchant for leather and studs, both tended to sing about rebellion and alienation, and pressed their own records. The Pistols' Steve Jones was the greatest riffer heavy metal never had.

And yet there was also a world of difference. Heavy metal musicians liked to show they could play while punks hated the idea of showing off their chops (if they had any). Metal heads liked Flying V-guitars, enormous drum kits and massed banks of Marshall amps; punks generally liked everything as basic and as unostentatious as possible. When not singing about rebellion and alienation, heavy metal frontmen avoided politics and screamed about the devil and death, while punks avoided fantasy and screeched about society. Heavy metal acts were often misogynistic or at least sexist[3], punk and new wave bands less so. Heavy metal fans retained the long hair of the anti-establishment hippy era, while punks went short and mod – unless parading for the tourists on Kings Road, in which case it was Mohican or dayglo spiky. Heavy metal clothes would soon veer away from leather to spandex and denim while punks experimented with ripped T-shirts, bin-liners and tartan trousers tied together at the knees. All the above veers towards stereotype but there's truth in every cliché.

The new version of heavy metal grew rapidly and widely and by the end of 1978 John Peel, at the height of his championing of new wave, had forfeited one of his five weekday slots to Tommy Vance's metal (or at least hard rock) promulgating *Friday*

Rock Show. NWOBHM wasn't actually named as such until May 1979 when Sounds' Geoff Barton penned a review of Iron Maiden, Samson and Angel Witch at the Music Machine in London, although the spiritual early home of NWOBHM was Neal Kay's Heavy Metal Soundhouse at the Bandwagon pub in north west London – about as blandly suburban as you could get (and coincidentally a stone's throw from where Wham! were about to hatch their plan for world domination). By 1980 Iron Maiden had signed to EMI and Def Leppard to Phonogram, with both going on to conquer America with, respectively, *The Number of the Beast* (1982) and *Pyromania* (1983). None of the other NWOBHM bands made it to this level.

An interesting by-product of the NWOBHM boom was its galvanising effect on older bands: not Led Zeppelin, Black Sabbath or Deep Purple, who either limped into the 80s or split up, but rather the likes of Judas Priest, Motorhead and AC/DC who all had their origins in the first half of the 70s. Judas Priest had formed in 1970 but really only made it big when they adopted a kinky black leather-and-studs look (courtesy of Rob Halford, who was not only gay, but had short hair – both distinctly un-metal), went for a more commercial sound and cashed in on the NWOBHM boom by naming their 1980 breakthrough album *British Steel*. Motorhead's 1980 album and single, *The Ace of Spades*, would also be regarded by many as their best. AC/DC had similarly ridden the late 70s metal resurgence and not even the death of singer Bon Scott could stop their ascendancy. The first album with Geordie frontman Brian Johnson, 1980's *Back in Black*, would remain their biggest seller, helped along by producer Mutt Lange, who would nail the mainstream metal sound with Def Leppard, Foreigner and Bryan Adams.

Iron Maiden's *Powerslave*; Def Leppard.

However, by 1984 most of the above groups, first *and* second wave, had hit a creative impasse. Judas Priest released the middling *Defenders of The Faith*, AC/DC were in between the so-so *Flick Of The Switch* and *Fly On The Wall*, Motorhead could only manage a compilation, and Def Leppard were still touring with 1983's *Pyromania*. True, Iron Maiden released the platinum-selling *Powerslave* which put a metal spin on Egyptology and a 13-minute interpretation of *The Rime of the Ancient Mariner*, followed by a gruelling 11 month world tour. But with the disintegration of Rainbow, Bad Company, Thin Lizzy, Status Quo and The Who, and the retreat from the limelight of others like Uriah Heap, Wishbone Ash and Nazareth, it was clear that 1984 was not a good year for British hard rock, and that NWOBHM had run its course.

If Britain's metal scene was in the doldrums, the US scene was on the rise, heavily influenced by NWOBHM. Such was the devotion of one fan that, aged just 17, he flew to London on his own to see his favourite band Diamond Head play in the Woolwich Odeon in the summer of 1981, and ended up sleeping on their floor having made no other accommodation plans. The boy's name was Lars Ulrich. Two years later he formed Metallica and in 1984 they played their first concerts in Britain, secured some serious management and signed to Elektra. Other bands like Anthrax, Slayer and Megadeath were also on the up. This was basically thrash metal, the ascendancy of which was paradoxically slow and methodical.

Rather quicker, and more opportunistic, was the parallel scene of glam metal, which became as big as the hair and platform boots of its main exponents. The genre had its origins in Alice Cooper, New York Dolls and Kiss. Indeed, bands like Van Halen had started to glamorize their music at the turn of the decade, but 1984 was the moment it became cartoonised, monetised and everywhere. Top of them all – at least in terms of heel height, depth of make-up and drink'n'drug intake[4] – were Mötley Crüe who enjoyed their first Top 20 single ('Looks That Kill') that year; W.A.S.P. and Ratt released their eponymous debut albums; and Quiet Riot were still riding high on Slade covers. Even Kiss were back in the frame with their *Animalize* album.

Attracted like moths to a flame, bands from the East Coast (Twisted Sister, Poison) cashed in and even overseas bands like Hanoi Rocks (Finland) and Krokus (Switzerland) moved to LA or at least secured US labels and management. Influenced by the glam of a decade earlier and the effeminacy of the in-vogue new pop, bands dressed up as chicks, with make-up and hair that was out of control. LA Strip's Rainbow, Troubadour, The Whisky and Roxy clubs were full of them. It was kind of pop. It was certainly in the charts. Before this particular scene, heavy metal had been pretty much for boys only, but now it attracted the girls, even if they were largely objectified. MTV played its part: Mötley Crüe's 'Looks That Kill' video featured caged girls while Van Halen's 'I'll Wait' was basically a video version of FHM.

Van Halen were the smartest. Not only did they have the best guitarist in Eddie Van Halen and most narcissistic frontman man in David Lee Roth, but at the beginning of the year they released 'Jump', which had an uber radio-friendly riff, and it was played on a *synthesizer*. The single, and the *1984* album it came from, were huge hits. They didn't go in for Satan, spurned black and actually smiled. Their songs had strong melodies, harmonies and glossy keyboards. In short, they mainstreamed or 'Americanised' heavy metal. A close second were ZZ Top whose 'Legs' single from the previous year's massive-selling *Eliminator* album, went Top 10 in the US and Top 20 in the UK. This was hard(-ish) rock, again with synthesizers, but most of all humour. Sure the 'Legs' video featured sexy pegs, but it was the identikit beards and spinning, furry guitars that won it an MTV award.

Van Halen's soft metal wasn't a million miles from bands like Bon Jovi who released their debut album in January, Bryan Adam's 'Run To You' in April, or even MOR acts like REO Speedwagon whose *Wheels Are Turnin'* album went Top 10 at the end of the year. It was the dawn of the soft metal power ballad, templated by Jennifer Rush's 'The Power of Love' which closed her debut album that year[5]. But it wasn't just female artists. Foreigner's plaintive, massive-selling 'I Want to Know What Love Is' was a classic example. Bon Jovi, too, would soon ditch the fantasy and macho aggression, replaced with rugged romantic vulnerability, a more positive outlook, jeans instead of spandex, and conditioner. This was more attractive to female fans and propelled the band into the Top 40 singles charts. It was still metal, still had the power chords and postures, but reached out to a wider audience – a deliberate move perfected with 'Living on a Prayer' in 1986.

Foreigner were half British while Whitesnake were wholly from the UK but, like Def Leppard, had modelled their sound on America. Their 1984 *Slide It In* would be their biggest selling album to date. Frontman David Coverdale had been in Deep Purple who (without him) reformed in 1984 after an eight-year hiatus, resulting in a highly lucrative album and tour. Meanwhile Black Sabbath were touring their *Born Again* album complete with preposterously oversized Stonehenge props (the measurements having been written down in metres instead of feet[6], a scarcely believable reversal of the undersized version which appears in *This Is Spinal Tap*), and ex-Sabbath frontman Ozzie Osbourne was touring with Mötley Crüe in one of the 'craziest drug and alcohol-fueled tours in the history of rock & roll.'[7]

Many of these bands came together for the annual Monsters of Rock festival-in-a-field in England. By 1984 it was in its fifth year and had become a well-oiled machine hosting 60,000 denim-clad head-bangers. The enormous PA was deafening but in the days before large video screens all you could see was the aura of Lee Roth's ego. It was also the first to be designed as a touring package: so, after AC/DC, Van Halen, Gary Moore, Ozzy Osbourne, Mötley Crüe and Accept had done their stuff in Britain's metal heartland, it toured Europe (a model adopted by, amongst others, Amnesty International's Conspiracy of Hope tour). One of the curious things about Monsters of Rock, apart from its custom of hurling plastic bottles of warm piss, was the lack of NWOBHM bands: none in 1984 and desultory showings in the previous four line-ups[8]. It was either OWOBHM or 80s west coast.

AC/DC's use of mock canons on stage was of course very Spinal Tap, the phrase possibly already an adjective by the summer. Released in March 1984, *This Is Spinal Tap* was the mockumentary film par excellence. Although the work of a US director, Rob Reiner[9], and starring American actors, Michael McKean, Harry Shearer and Christopher Guest, it told the story of a British heavy metal band, Spinal Tap (who might as well have been a down-on-their-luck Sabbath) on tour in the States. As a piece of satire it was uncannily perfect, complete with intra-band musical differences, hapless manager, interfering girlfriends, the aforementioned Stonehenge prop and – perhaps the scene most bands identified with – getting lost between the dressing room and stage. It was so close to home that many people thought the group really existed

– and in fact it did. Actors McKean, Shearer and Guest[10], played all the music on the accompanying album and, alongside their continued thespian careers, would go on to perform as Spinal Tap for many years. On an Everything But The Girl tour across the States, Tracey Thorn spotted its genius, the fundamental truth that 'beneath the pomposity and delusion and ludicrous self-aggrandisement, it is eventually a levelling experience. Whether you were a successful headline band or the measliest support act, you'd still have to experience many of the same discomforts and indignities'[11].

Spinal Tap: the poster, the actors, the stars.

As 'Tap' as any band, Led Zeppelin had been dormant for four years. Robert Plant had formed The Honeydrippers but it took until 1984 to release anything, the dully titled, ironically one-off *The Honeydrippers, Volume One* EP. The same year saw Jimmy Page form The Firm with former Free and Bad Company singer Paul Rodgers, but the two albums they mustered are best forgotten. John Paul Jones, meanwhile, contributed to Paul McCartney's *Give My Regards to Broad Street* fiasco, although to be fair, he would distinguish himself with a post-Zep career of intriguing collaborations and productions with everyone from Brian Eno and the Butthole Surfers to La Fura Dels Baus and Diamanda Galas.

Of all the British hard rock bands around this time, The Rolling Stones were the most adrift. *Undercover* had been released at the end of 1983 and although its first single 'Undercover of The Night' had been a hit, the album divided critics and was the first studio album not to top the US charts since 1969's *Let It Bleed*. There was no tour to support it, the Jagger-Richards fissure was growing, and the former spent much of 1984 writing songs for his first solo album and even found himself singing with The

Jacksons. Towards the end of the year Charlie Watts socked him in the jaw in an Amsterdam hotel after Jagger had referred to him as 'my drummer'. It would be another five years before they jelled again, with *Steel Wheels*.

If Van Halen were the smartest of the US heavies, then Queen were the smartest in Britain. In their formative years they were essentially a heavy rock band, but as the 70s progressed they became much more diverse incorporating pop, funk, even disco into ever more sophisticated productions, although had lost their way by the early 80s. 1984, however, saw them rejuvenated and selling by the million again, at least in the UK. *The Works* album went triple platinum, spawning four hit singles. Together they seemed to represent all of Queen's musical styles: 'Hammer To Fall' (hard rock), 'It's A Hard Life' (power ballad), 'Radio Ga Ga' (synth anthem) and 'I Want To Break Free' (pure pop). And as early masters of the promo video, they made sure the visual aspect was as professional as the musical production. 'Hammer To Fall' presented them in a thrilling, no-nonsense live setting; Tim Pope's 'It's A Hard Life' was completely bonkers with a set and extras straight out of Versailles and Mercury looking like a giant prawn; David Mallet's 'Radio Ga Ga' was set in Fritz Lang's Metropolis[12]; 'I Want To Break Free' (Mallet again) saw the band in drag parodying Coronation Street. The last was all too much (or possibly just too British) for MTV, who banned it, but otherwise they were never off the screens.

But it wasn't all roses. They were castigated for playing at Sun City in South Africa during the height of Apartheid, Roger Taylor somehow found time to release a dull solo album, and they divided critics. BBC DJ Stuart Maconie described them as "horrible boot-clicking music for torchlit rallies"[13] while Sounds' David Tibet (of all people) thought they were hilarious. In any case, 1984 was as much their year as anyone's. They ended it with 'Thank God It's Christmas' and famously trumped everyone else at Live Aid the following summer, by which time they were more pop than rock and certainly not metal.

But let us leave the gladiators battling it out in a fantasy, male-centred world which had suddenly gone mainstream, and move on to the mixed-up world of the mid-80s auteur.

Chapter 23: Art for Art's Sake
Art rock, new age and neo-prog

It's not important to me that people understand me.[1]
Kate Bush

The public so often want to freeze the artist at a moment in time when they were at the peak of their commercial success. They want the artist to revisit that period repeatedly as if it was something of greater authenticity than anything subsequently produced.[2]
David Sylvian

Not everything in 1984's popular music scene stemmed from late 70s punk, new wave, soul or dance. Nor was it strictly 'popular'. But there were hundreds of uncategorizable artists who operated on the periphery. Sometimes, inadvertently, they'd make fleeting appearances in the lower reaches of the charts, but mostly they were happy to follow their muse, creating music principally for themselves and a small but loyal audience. It wasn't the extreme music of Chapter 18 which had largely come out of DIY punk culture. It was more muso, more auteur, often by artists who'd been around in the 70s and were constantly reinventing themselves, or by those who had experienced pop stardom and turned their back on it. Some were from the classical world but embraced new technology, liked the immediacy of pop and preferred small ensembles (their own) rather than large, unwieldy orchestras. Others had been part of, or were inspired by, the progressive rock era and were still drawn to its creative options yet somehow making it work in the less forgiving 80s. Still others were from jazz or folk backgrounds who became, often unwittingly, disciples of mood music.

One of the most interesting cases of reinvention was that of former Be Bop Deluxe frontman and axe-hero Bill Nelson. After the band split in 1978, Nelson embraced the new wave scene, got a haircut and formed a post-punk band (so far, so Robert Fripp): the short-lived Red Noise who released one album, the abrasive *Sound On Sound*. By the 80s, however, he'd ditched the band and became a fully-fledged renaissance man, handling everything – guitar, vocals, bass, drums and keyboards - as well as dabbling in painting, photography, video and Rosicrucianism. Coinciding with the new romantic movement, he suddenly found himself operating in the same orbit as Japan, A Flock Of Seagulls and Yellow Magic Orchestra, even though he was a little older than them. His early 80s albums, *Quit Dreaming and Get on the Beam*, *The Love That Whirls (Diary of a Thinking Heart)*[3] and *Chimera* were progressively lush affairs featuring heavy use of synthesizers. But despite sounding contemporary and being critically well received, they were just not quite mainstream enough.

By early 1984, Nelson had been dropped by Mercury in the UK but decided to have one more crack at the US, promoting the CBS compilation, *Vistamix,* with a band that included his brother Ian (sax), Preston Hayman (drums), Ian Denby (bass) and

William Gregory (keyboards)[4]. While in New York, Nelson asked disco producer John Luongo to remix 'Acceleration', a catchy, standout from 1983's *Chimera*. Given he was now a free agent, it came out on Cocteau Records, the label he'd set up in 1980 for occasional instrumental albums and singles by himself and others (including A Flock Of Seagulls' debut). In a parallel world, 'Acceleration' might have gone Top 10, but Cocteau lacked the marketing power and it slipped by unnoticed.

Far from disheartened, Nelson went into independent overdrive releasing a 4LP instrumental box set, *Trial by Intimacy*, also on Cocteau. Packaged with a glossy 54-page book of Nelson's poetic, vaguely erotic photography and paintings on postcards, the album containing 83 tracks ranging from delicate ambient vignettes to aggressive electronica. It was a very impressive work, perfect for television documentaries, ads or plays[5] and should have kept him in PRS royalties for life. Not content with that, Nelson released a double compilation of remixes, B-sides and demos called *The Two-Fold Aspect of Everything*, again on Cocteau; started a side project, Orchestra Arcana, which would release a couple of sample-heavy albums during the second half of the 80s; and began recording what would turn out to be his last attempted mainstream major-label album, *Getting the Holy Ghost Across*, a torturous process (it wasn't released until 1986).

One of the most interesting associations Nelson fostered in 1984 was with Man Jumping whose debut album, *Jump Cut*, he released on Cocteau at the end of the year. The 7-piece band, formed out of the wilfully obscure but brilliant 26-piece The Lost Jockey, sounded like a cross between Steve Reich and Herbie Hancock – 'systems funk' as someone labelled them. Someone else described them as the "most important band in the world"[6]. Be that as it may, *Jumpcut* is a wonderful album, as foot-tapping and utterly accessible as it is complex and intelligent. The group would only last about four years but most of them would go on to interesting things in theatre, dance and television[7].

Bill Nelson kept very good company around this time, particularly with Japan, both the country and ex-members of the band, although it wasn't until 1984 that he first met David Sylvian, going on to contribute to the latter's *Gone To Earth* album in 1986. For Sylvian, 1984 was the start of his solo career and the release of the brilliant *Brilliant Trees*, a year and a half after splitting up Japan. With their first two albums being called *Adolescent Sex* and *Obscure Alternatives* (both 1978), Japan could have qualified as new wave, but actually they'd formed a few years earlier and with their long hair and rockist pose, they looked and sounded much more like the New York Dolls than your average post-punk band. That they then switched, seemingly overnight, to a sophisticated image and sound that was at first decadent Euro-disco and then quasi-East Asian, culminating in the fabulous *Tin Drum*, was one of those wonderful anomalies that just seemed to happen in those days.

Sylvian, however, wasn't enjoying being a pop star and split the group at the peak of their powers at the end of 1982, much as Paul Weller had done with The Jam at exactly the same time. He spent a year getting his head together, travelling, taking polaroids, listening to jazz[8]. He knew he didn't want to form a band but he also knew he didn't want to record alone. The musicians he ended up calling were highly indicative of the direction his career would take: Ryuichi Sakamoto, Steve Jansen and Richard Barbieri were perhaps obvious[9], but Holger Czukay, Jon Hassell, Mark Isham, Kenny Wheeler and Danny Thompson were not. The last four were essentially from the jazz world, but although *Brilliant Trees* was influenced by jazz, it doesn't sound like jazz. It was perfect for the summer: a warm, hazy, languid album. The first side featured relatively straight-forward songs, three of which Virgin chose as singles. 'Red Guitar', which had preceded the album, made #17, but 'Ink in the Well' and 'Pulling Punches' barely charted. In between was 'Nostalgia' which sounded, well, nostalgic, but overall the first half of *Brilliant Trees* was uplifting. Side two was more experimental and meandering, largely improvised with Hassell's processed trumpet seemingly the dominant instrument and no bass at all. By the last song, the title track, any semblance of rhythm has gone, at least for the first half of its eight-and-a-half minutes, and Sylvian is at his most existential: 'My whole life stretches out in front of me, reaching up like a flower, leading my life back to the soil.' It ends with Hassell's breathy trumpet colourings over an extensive, muted Fourth World workout.

David Sylvian, Simon Jeffes (of Penguin Café Orchestra) and Bill Nelson.

Brilliant Trees was a brave, challenging and deeply personal record and no-one could have been more surprised than Sylvian himself when it entered the album charts at #4, one place higher than Japan had ever reached. Of course Virgin took advantage of the 26-year-old's good looks despite his wish to hide. The sleeves for the singles outlined the dilemma: should he play the game and put his mug on the sleeves or just put some art on them instead? In the end he did both. On 'Red Guitar' he is in moody shadow, cigarette in hand; on 'Ink in the Well' he is captured, seemingly without knowing, underneath a poster for a Picasso exhibition (a *French* poster); while on 'Pulling Punches' he stares direct at the camera on the front cover while hiding behind a Jean Cocteau ceramic on the back. The accompanying videos for 'Red Guitar' and 'The Ink in the Well' were shot by Anton Corbijn, photographer of choice for those wanting arty black and white stills, but fairly new to directing videos. 'Red Guitar' was the better of the two, complete with cameo by Angus McBean whose classic photograph of Audrey Hepburn seemingly growing out of the ground, was a major inspiration for the promo. Quite what Top of the Pops audiences thought of it has never been recorded. A third video, for 'Pulling Punches', was just dull.

Coinciding with the album's July release, Sylvian presented an exhibition of his polaroid collages at the Hamilton Gallery in London's Mayfair. There was also a plush catalogue. Unfortunately, they were uncannily similar to David Hockney's polaroid work of a year or two earlier. The fans loved it, the critics cried copycat or, worse, dilettante. But it didn't spoil the party. David Sylvian had proved he could cut it as a solo artist. In November he was in Japan recording music for two short films: the first a philosophical affair called *Preparations for a Journey* with Seigen Ono; the second an abstract take on the city of Tokyo called *Steel Cathedrals* with Ryuichi Sakamoto[10]. One final event of what must have been a deeply satisfying year for Sylvian was Virgin's decision to release a double compilation of Japan tracks, intelligently selected, packaged in a beautiful Russell Mills sleeve and tellingly titled *Exorcising Ghosts*.

Not to be outdone, Japan colleague Mick Karn had also been busy in 1984. Karn had actually beaten Sylvian to recording a solo album by two years with the halfway decent, politely received *Titles*. Since then he'd recorded with Gary Numan, Bill Nelson and Midge Ure amongst others, but for 1984 he chose to form a group with Peter Murphy who'd just dissolved Bauhaus. It was a curious pairing which never quite worked. First off, they decided to call themselves Dalis Car; one could forgive the pretentiousness and denial that it had anything to do with the Captain Beefheart track, but not the missing apostrophe. A single, 'The Judgement is the Mirror', appeared in October. It was intriguing without being captivating, a rather plodding, vaguely Eastern tune dominated by Murphy's obscure lyrics, Karn's liquid, fretless bass and a suitably baffling video. It reached #66. But nothing could have prepared Japan fans for the album to follow. Titled *The Waking Hour*, it was completely out of time with the zeitgeist, from its gatefold cover reproducing Maxfield Parrish's painting *Daybreak* on one side (which The Moody Blues, for godsake, had used just the year before) and nasty blue centre spread with Roger Dean-like typography, to the lugubrious music within. It was almost prog. To be fair, it *was* interesting, not least the rhythms, and it had its moments, but it died a death. Check out their performance of 'His Box' on Whistle Test on YouTube and they look bored as opposed to coolly nonchalant. Murphy himself described the collaboration as 'a very introverted project in every respect... Obscure but listenable'.[11]

The same description could be applied to the Penguin Café Orchestra: obscure, in that they were essentially a chamber ensemble whose first album had been released on Eno's Obscure label, but much to everyone's surprise (including the group's) they turned out to be very accessible.[12] Helmed by multi-instrumentalist Simon Jeffes, PCO's music was instrumental, acoustic, charming (without being whimsical), warm, quirky and very English. A kind of folk meets minimal music although it was essentially unclassifiable. Diverse musicians drifted in and out of its ranks: Steve Nye (producer of *Brilliant Trees*, and Roxy Music and Japan before that), Geoffrey Richardson (Caravan), Ryuichi Sakamoto, Nigel Kennedy and many others. They'd even supported Kraftwerk at the Roundhouse in 1976, and Jeffes had worked as an arranger with Sid Vicious, Adam Ant and Bow Wow Wow. In short, for a chamber ensemble, they were mighty cool.

But they still weren't that known. *Broadcasting from Home*, released midway through 1984, changed that, particularly the opening track, 'Music for a Found Harmonium', which ended up being used in numerous films and documentaries. The album introduced many pop and rock fans to music that was outside their immediate sphere. Jeffes died of a brain tumour in 1997, but his son, Arthur, still carries the torch as the Penguin Café (having dropped the Orchestra).

One of several interesting records Bill Nelson contributed to in 1983 was Monsoon's third single, a cover of The Beatles' 'Tomorrow Never Knows'. An indipop (as opposed to indie pop) trio based around teenage actress-turned-singer Sheila Chandra, producer Steve Coe and guitarist Martin Smith, they'd had a surprise dancefloor hit with 'Ever So Lonely' in 1982, followed by three more singles and an album. But disagreements with Phonogram over artistic control split the group up. Chandra decided pop music wasn't for her, and who can blame her? Check out the videos of them performing on German and Dutch TV complete with sand dunes, camels and Egyptian sphinxes[13]. (As an aside, there were plenty of other indipop groups, mostly based in the Midlands, and although their releases were usually on cassette only, this still amounted to very considerable sales given Britain's large South Asian population and its already well-established cassette culture. A particular genre, Bhangra, started to make its mark in 1984 with debut albums by two of its soon-to-be stars: Punjab-born Maltit Singh's *Nach Gidhe Wich* and Neera's *Jagh Wala Mela*. Bhangra would come of age in the late 80s and early 90s, thanks in part to the parallel dance wave).

Meanwhile, 1984 saw Chandra embarking on a solo career, supported by a devoted Steve Coe (who also ended up her husband), releasing records on their own Indipop label. The first, *Out on My Own*, issued at the beginning of the year, was a half-step on from Monsoon mixing uptempo mostly English language songs with more introspective Indian music. On the cover, 19-year-old Chandra is pictured wearing her sari, standing barefoot and stock-still, hand on hip, defiant amidst the rush of London commuters. "I am Indian and proud of my culture" she seemed to be saying. But it wasn't until her second album, which followed just a few months later, that she really found her own voice. *Quiet!* was a revelation. Gone were the beats and lyrics; instead the focus was on Chandra's wordless vocals, some it in spoken 'bols' style, others more hymn-like, and backed by a beautifully recorded and symbiotic mix of Indian and western instrumentation. This was new territory and anticipated her later work on the Real World label. You could also make a case that she influenced Enya. If there was one problem with *Quiet!* it was the lurid lime green and pink cover – a contender for 1984's worst sleeve.

From one strong, young woman to another. Kate Bush, had spent the late 70s and early 80s as pop's equivalent of Emily Brontë or Angela Carter – bewitching pre-Raphaelitism meets magic surrealism. Still only 25, she shut herself away for the whole of 1984 recording what many people believe to be her career high, *Hounds of Love*. After the relatively poor sales of *The Dreaming*, Bush had taken a break before deciding to build her own 48-track studio in an old Kentish barn, next to the 350-year-old house in which she was born and brought up. Working with engineer and bassist

Del Palmer (they were then also an item), and a host of other musicians largely from outside pop's sphere of influence, she took her time. Recording sessions were, though, largely idyllic. Away from London's cramped, smoky studios with takeaways and the clock ticking away the pounds, Bush was able to craft, layer and experiment, with her mum, dad and brothers constantly popping in with ideas, tea and cakes. There was a trip to Windmill Studios in Dublin for some additional recording. By June the recording was over, but many months of overdubbing and mixing followed.

Sheila Chandra and Kate Bush.

It was divided into two suites: *Hounds of Love*, comprising five chart-friendly songs, four of which were released as singles; and *The Ninth Wave*, consisting of seven more experimental songs which essentially hung together as one long track. Finally released in 1985, it had EMI breathing a sigh of relief, especially regarding side one, even if the lyrics were as impenetrable as ever. There was a song about swapping genders through a 'deal with God'; another about a rainmaking machine, inspired by the real-life experiments of Wilhelm Reich; another about medieval witch trials. *Hounds of Love* couldn't have been made by anyone else. It spoke of the past and yet was thoroughly modern, it was outside of pop and yet accessible, it was very English and yet went to #1, #2 and #3 in Holland, Germany and Switzerland respectively. In the UK it went straight into the top spot, replacing Madonna's *Like A Virgin*. 'I know there's this big theory that goes around that you must suffer for your art [but] I don't believe this, because I think in some ways this is the most complete work that I've done [...] and I was the happiest that I've been compared to making other albums'[14].

The nearest male equivalent to Bush, in terms of creativity and stature (if not style or age), is often thought to be Peter Gabriel. They had worked together – Bush provided backing vocals on his third album – and would do so again, famously, on 'Don't Give Up' in 1986. But that was all ahead of him. 1984 was a quiet year for Gabriel with one dull single, 'Walk Through the Fire' (written for the equally dull film, *Against All Odds*, which also featured contributions from Gabriel's old Genesis muckers Phil

Collins and Mike Rutherford) and his first full soundtrack, *Birdy*. The latter marked Gabriel's first work with producer Daniel Lanois, fresh from co-helming, with Eno, U2's *The Unforgettable Fire*. Totally instrumental and combining reworkings of old tracks together with new material, *Birdy* was a strange, claustrophobic album serving a strange, claustrophobic film, and is often passed over by fans and critics alike, certainly in comparison with his next soundtrack, the more mature *The Passion* (1989). In truth, Gabriel was in transition between four decent, somewhat experimental studio albums plus a live double that could be seen as a conclusion to what went before, and the quest for something more accessible, which he would achieve in no uncertain terms with his next album, *So*.

Just around the corner from Gabriel's base in Bath[15] and somewhere in between his rhythmic instrumentals and the funky systems music of the aforementioned Man Jumping, were Bristolians, Startled Insects. Comprising Bob Locke, Tim Norfolk and Richard Grassby-Lewis, their first release was a self-titled 12-inch EP in 1984 on the local Antenna Records. It was miles from the mainstream but it did influence a number of artists, not least those in Bristol and indeed there would be connections with Massive Attack[16], Portishead, Goldfrapp and even Madonna a decade or so later. But for now, Startled Insects' records (they would sign to Island's New Antilles label in 1987) and concerts were cherished by the few. Fellow Bristolian and ex-Rip Rig & Panic member, Mark Springer, was also on the outside.

In March 1984, Scott Walker released his first solo album in ten years, *Climate of Hunter*. As one-third of the US-born Walker Brothers, he'd had considerable success in the UK in the 60s and 70s, but by the mid-80s was almost forgotten. 'I don't write songs for pleasure. I can only write when I have to – like I'm under contract, or to finish an album'[17]. The album was unlike anything else at the time. Half of its eight songs lacked either titles or easily identifiable melody, and when there *was* a melody it was kept a closely guarded secret from most of the musicians involved. An unusual choice of musicians – from Evan Parker to Billy Ocean was a wide spectrum to put it mildly – contributed sparingly and seemingly at odds with Brian Gascoigne's orchestral arrangements and Walker's operatic voice, and yet it was an incredibly intriguing album, sealing his cult status. Intriguingly, Brian Eno was lined up to work on Walker's next album but it was abandoned after several sessions. Patient fans had to wait 11 years for *Tilt* which was even more removed from pop.

Since 1980, Eno had been living in New York City, infiltrating the No Wave scene, recording with David Byrne and Talking Heads, while at the same time ploughing his ambient furrow and becoming increasingly immersed in video. A key collaborator in this period was Daniel Lanois, who would spend much of 1984 at Eno's side. March saw the release of *The Pearl*, an ambient collaboration with pianist Harold Budd (co-produced with Lanois). Eno and Budd had worked together off and on for six years and in truth the new offering didn't break new ground, but – as was so often the case with Eno – would be a catalyst for other Budd collaborations, notably with Cocteau Twins and Bill Nelson. It was also, simply, gorgeous. 'I would set up a sound', said

Eno, 'he would improvise to it, and occasionally I would add something to it: but it was mainly him performing in a sound world I had created.'[18]

In April, Eno flew to San Francisco to film a friend sitting naked in a bath, as you do. It was the fourth in a series of video paintings and the first to be commissioned (by Sony TV in Japan). For the music he headed off to Lanois's studio in Ontario. The soundtrack, named *Thursday Afternoon,* was one very long (61 minutes) track of semi-random clusters of sounds subdued to the level of a murmur. Combined – video and music – it was designed to be as ignorable as it was interesting, like a painting on the wall, only this one changed, audio-visually, ever so slightly each time you passed by. Eno also embraced the opportunity to release an audio-only version on CD, his first release on the medium, the following year. American critic Dave Segal has written about the therapeutic effect it has had on him personally, as a regular migraine sufferer:

> *Listening to it has become a ritual over the past 20 years. In that enfeebled condition, I require something more salubrious than silence, but nothing too disruptive sonically. [...] Why this Eno album instead of others? [...] It's down to the cleansing sparseness of the piano motifs, the calming feng shui of the notes, the benevolent drone of the foundational drone, the Zen patience with which Eno [...] deploys each palliative unit of tones.*[19]

A month later Eno and Lanois were in Ireland co-producing U2's *The Unforgettable Fire*, working through the summer. They even found time to contribute a track to David Lynch's *Dune* film. And after that, Eno was back in London for good.

*****

Many of the above artists forwent vocals and focussed on instrumentals that were sufficiently rhythmic, complex, dynamic and interesting enough to avoid being called new age, although not many people were aware of that term in 1984. The idea, if not the name, goes back to the hippy 60s and the Western take-up of Eastern philosophies, yoga, meditation, natural healing, spiritual enlightenment and generally opting out of the rat race. It quickly became reflected in the music, literature and to some (bad) extent the visual arts, and by the 70s was influencing progressive rock and jazz, if not pop.

But new age as a genre in its own right was harder to pin down. Mike Oldfield's *Tubular Bells* (1973) was seen by some as an example, but if new age was supposed to be calming and Zen-like, then the caveman grunts and 'two slightly distorted guitars' didn't fit the bill[20]. Tangerine Dream's *Phaedra* (1974) was certainly minimal, glacial and spacey, but it was also dark and tense – two adjectives at odds with new age's credo of positivism. Brian Eno's *Discreet Music* (1975) was serene and relaxing, but so ignorable-as-it-was-interesting that the listener was barely aware that it was on – a type of 'barely music' (though, paradoxically, still with an edge) that Eno would explore and make his own for the next four decades. No, the generally agreed starting point for new age was the hippy birth-state of California and Steven Halpern's *Spectrum Suite* in 1975, an album of understated free-form melodies played on a Fender Rhodes that were designed to relieve stress while at the same time energize the body's chakras. It's very easy to be cynical and – like much new age – it *is* insipid on many levels, including the sleeves and titles, but in a hospital or at the end of a hard day or as background music, it served a purpose for many.

New age's next milestone was the creation of Windham Hill Records in 1976 by former builder and carpenter William Ackerman, and Anne Robinson, initially simply to release the former's delicate acoustic guitar music, but would later provide a home for musicians of various styles, although still homogenously soporific. Another key moment was Kitaro (whose first album appeared in 1977) and the role synthesizers would play in the development of new age. There were other synth players who'd been at it earlier, particularly Deuter, but Kitaro was a million-seller.

It's not known when the term 'new age music' came into common currency, but it was probably around the beginning of the 80s, and certainly in 1981 Tower Records started labelling a small section of racks New Age Music. Some radio stations ditched AOR for NAM, rebranding themselves as a 'mood service' and by 1984 new age had 'commandeered', at least in marketing terms, elements of jazz (eg. Keith Jarrett), folk (Claire Hammill), world music (Incantation), classical (George Winston) and something called contemporary adult instrumental (Vangelis, Yanni, Jean Michel Jarre). Needless to say, new age and compact discs were perfect bedfellows.

1984 was a defining year for new age, in both America where it was commercially more advanced, and the UK where it was just being introduced. On the US west coast it saw the founding of Hearts of Space Records – a natural next step on from Stephen Hill's successful radio show of the same name, created a decade earlier. HoS would release largely electronic or 'space' music by the likes of Michael Stearns, Steve Roach, Robert Rich, Kevin Braheny and Constance Denby – barely new age at all (these artists created music with real tension) but it got marketed as such. Also founded that year, Narada Records focussed on instrumental piano music and smooth jazz. On the east coast, former Tangerine Dream member Peter Baumann launched Private Music, a 'home for instrumental music', initially signing artists like Patrick O'Hearn, Yanni and (ironically) Tangerine Dream, but soon widened its musical base as long as it was by older, established artists. Windham Hill on the other hand was a label more in keeping with new age's tranquilising traits ("An Antidote to Urban Madness") and remained the market leader.

In the UK, new age was just beginning to be recognised as a genre. In 1984, Nick Austin of Beggars Banquet and sub-label Coda Records had set up the latter's Landscape Series: its first clutch of albums by largely anonymous session musicians and engineers[21] was sedentary at best. The following year, Windham Hill started to be distributed in the UK through a deal with A&M. And the London-based label, Pan East, specialising in instrumental music from Japan (both the country and two former members of the group) would start in 1986.

Meanwhile, over in Ireland, Eithne Padraigin Ni Bhraonain was morphing into someone called Enya. Originally part of Clannad (see Chapter 10) with some of her brothers & sisters, she recorded two solo instrumental pieces for the 1984 compilation album *Touch Travel* – the only released music under her real name – before switching to Enya when writing some of the music for the Anglo-French film, *The Frog Prince*, also released that year. Enya's multi-tracking of vocals and keyboards in a style that was both Celtic and calming would become a winning combination three years later with the single 'Orinoco Flow' and album *Watermark* and launch a thousand 'mood music' compilations. New age lent itself well to notions of travel, becoming a kind of affiliate of world music. As with Enya or Red Box's 1984 single 'Saskatchewan', it could be the combination of voice and synth that did the trick. Or the addition of an exotic instrument: the panpipe group Incantation instantly transported listeners and – when used in television documentaries (which was often) – viewers to the Andes.

As an aside, the mid-80s saw the term 'world music' start to gain currency in the UK record industry, become a genre if you like. The name had existed since the 60s but rather more for ethnomusicologists than the record-buying public. A controversial term, it was essentially indigenous music, sometimes influenced by western pop, rock and jazz but not necessarily. Crucial to its development in Britain was the World Of Music And Dance (WOMAD), founded by Peter Gabriel and others in 1980, with its first festival held in Shepton Mallet in 1982. Albums by artists like King Sunny Ade were available on license, but the mid-80s saw the establishment of several new UK labels, including Triple Earth Records (Khaled), DiscAfrique (Bhundu Boys), GlobeStyle (Ofra Haza), Earthworks (Youssou N'Dour) and World Circuit (Ali Farka Touré). Paul Simon's *Graceland*, recorded with South African musicians, helped things along, as did the introduction of world music sections in record shops, charts in the music papers, industry awards, Gabriel's Real World label, and the phenomenal rise of Lonely Planet and Rough Guide books. In the 90s World Circuit's Buena Vista Social Club would do the rest.

But back to new age. Miraculously, in the 90s, the genre rescued itself from critical oblivion by being partially associated with 90s ambient house (including the pseudo-mystical prog of The Orb and the KLF's *Chill Out*), the 'world dance' pop of Enigma and Deep Forest, even trip hop.

*****

Virginia Astley's music wasn't a million miles from *some* of new age's characteristics (quiet, calming, vaguely minimalist), but luckily wasn't marketed as such and was in any case punctuated by fragile vocals and experimentation. 'Chamber neo-classical' might be a more apt description. She came from a musical family[22] and studied at London's Guildhall College of Music before briefly joining south London band Victims of Pleasure in 1980 and then forming The Ravishing Beauties with Kate St John and Nicky Holland. The latter never released a record but seemed to be everywhere, supporting Teardrop Explodes and OMD, recording a Peel Session, and contributing to NME's Mighty Reel cassette compilation. Meanwhile Astley had worked on a number of other projects before releasing her solo debut, the sublime, all-instrumental *From Gardens Where We Feel Secure*. With its sounds of summer (birdsong, peeling bells, a creaky swing, bleating sheep), it set Astley's delicate piano and flute amidst a languid English pastoral scene. On the one hand it was deeply conservative & traditional, on the other playfully experimental and as far removed from pop or rock as you could imagine.

In 1984, Astley continued to contribute to other projects (keyboards on tour with Prefab Sprout and session work for half a dozen other artists) and was also invited to perform at the Everyman Cinema as part of an intriguing series where a musician played live followed by the screening of a film of his/her choice (Astley selected *Elvira Madigan*). It wasn't until the end of the year when she finally managed to get some studio time for herself to record a follow-up to *From Gardens...*, the equally, achingly beautiful *Melt the Snow* EP which sounds like it was recorded in either a Victorian parlour or a Viennese ballroom. She would go on to sign with WEA, working with sympaticos Ryuichi Sakamoto and David Sylvian and focussing more on *songs*, but in truth she never bettered these two.

Virginia Astley and Robert Haigh.

Astley's erstwhile bandmates, Kate St John and Nicky Holland, had gone on to other things, the former joining the Dream Academy (whose debut album was recorded in 1984 which included the hit single 'Life In A Northern Town', the chorus of which must surely have influenced Enya), the latter working with Fun Boy Three, Strawberry Switchblade and Tears For Fears before releasing a couple of solo albums in the 90s.

Astley's piano approach was 'minimal classical', as was that of another pianist, Robert Haigh, who modelled his style on Satie and Chopin. Formerly in obscure, short-lived early 80s groups Truth Club and Fote, Haigh then created a solo project called Sema[23] which after four albums culminated in 1984's *Three Seasons Only*, followed by three more similar albums under his own name. Bizarrely, the 90s saw him reinvent himself as a drum'n'bass supremo under the name Omni Trio before reverting again to minimal piano vignettes. It was one of popular music's more unusual career paths. But not as unusual as that of another pianist, Morgan Fisher. Fisher had been in glamrockers Mott The Hoople, took an experimental left turn and, inspired by punk and The Residents, created the fictitious Hybrid Kids, formed his own label, masterminded the legendary *Miniatures* compilation in 1980 and released an ambient album with Lol Coxhill. Fisher then found inspiration in transcendental meditation and the Bhagwan Shree Rajneesh before moving to Japan in 1984. His first album as Veetdharm, *Look At Life*, that year was full of the joys of spring and the single it spawned, 'Happy Again' / 'Lord Of The Full Moon', was genuinely uplifting, but too busy to be called new age.

Approaching the piano from yet another angle, Michael Nyman had been on Fisher's *Miniatures* and released a debut album, *Decay Music*, on Eno's Obscure series in the mid-70s. That had been slow and minimal. What Nyman was now considering was *fast* and minimal, something akin to the repetitive pulsating music of Steve Reich and Philip Glass[24]. It wasn't until 1982 that, almost by accident, he hit upon the 'Nyman style' when, forced to come up with some music for a looming concert performance, he rearranged 16 bars of Mozart's *Don Giovanni* and hammered them out Jerry Lee Lewis style. 'One minute it didn't exist and the next minute it did.'[25] The piece of music was 'In Re Don Giovanni', released as a single and included on a self-titled album, swiftly followed up by a score for Peter Greenaway's *The Draughtsman's Contract* – a kind of hi-NRG interpretation of Purcell. By 1984 he was on a role, scoring another film for Greenaway (*Making A Splash*), a video opera for Channel 4 (*The Kiss*), a US made-for-TV film (*The Cold Room*), an ad to promote new town Milton Keynes, and performing regularly with his Michael Nyman Band. His reputation growing, the soundtrack for *The Piano* (1993) would cement it.

Michael Nyman, Man Jumping and Andrew Poppy

The American minimalist composers had influenced many other young British composers and performers. Groups like Regular Music and The Lost Jockey had formed at the turn of the decade, performing regularly but recording sporadically[26]. Most of their members had parallel work in the theatre or in television or occasionally as arrangers in the pop world. One such, indeed a co-founder of both groups, was Andrew Poppy, who had worked with Psychic TV and Strawberry Switchblade. Leaving a demo of his own music at ZTT's Sarm West reception desk in early 1984, Poppy found himself, a 'serious composer', signed to a five-year, five-album deal on the same label as Frankie Goes To Hollywood. 'I put dots on paper and traditionally trained musicians play them, but on the other hand I work with tape and computers in a studio and I like multi-tracking the sound. Because of that, I didn't take my scores to publishers, I took my recordings to record companies, and Trevor Horn and Paul Morley at ZTT liked what they heard.'[27] Poppy's *The Beating of Wings* – a rapturous mix of orchestral excursions, minimal piano, beats and electronics – came out the following year, and he was part of ZTT's wacky The Value of Entertainment show at the Ambassadors Theatre in May. A second album followed in 1987 but by then ZTT was a different beast and soon after they went their separate ways. It had been an interesting, unusual liaison, taking contemporary classical music (for want of a better term) to a mass audience.

*****

Whither progressive rock? Prog had famously been 'swept away' by punk, but had it? ZTT's Trevor Horn was not only involved in the prog-dance of The Art Of Noise and the vorsprung durch technik of Propaganda, but also revitalised the career of Yes. The group had undergone various line-up changes, with Horn on bass and vocals for a while before switching to producer, and it was in the latter role that he steered them to a massively successful comeback with the album *90125* in late 1983 followed by a new year US #1 single, 'Owner of a Lonely Heart'. Jon Anderson had been tempted back but Rick Wakeman remained absent, so it sort of sounded like the old Yes, but without the flamboyant keyboards. They were there, but buried under several feet of Trevor Horn mix with guitars instead to the fore. The timing and production were perfect for the new American blend of radio-friendly, over-produced, middle-of-the-road adult-oriented pop. Never mind *Close to The Edge* and *Tales from Topographic Oceans*, *90125* was (and remains) their biggest-selling album[28]. Genesis too had continued their transition from prog-rock to pop, by the mid-80s better known for their singles than albums (but then it was hard to embrace a mid-career album simply called *Genesis*) and that Phil Collins was effectively moonlighting from his solo career.

However, most of the old wave were on their way out. In 1984 King Crimson Mk2 released the final album of an early 80s trilogy. Gone was the occasional emotive quality that punctuated the best of Mk1 to be replaced by a technical, soulless brilliance that was influenced by post-punk and informed a new generation of math- and post-rock. It would be ten years before Crimson were resurrected again. Pink Floyd were also disintegrating. Effectively a Roger Waters solo album with a bit of Gilmour, hardly any Mason and no Wright, 1983's *The Final Cut* was the final album from the four-piece line-up that had dominated prog in the 70s. Waters' miserablism plunged new depths and it must have been a relief, even for Waters, that the game was up. In 1984 he released his first proper solo album, the dreary *The Pros and Cons of Hitch-Hiking*; Gilmour released his second, *About Face*; Richard Wright formed the mercifully short-lived Zee with Dave Harris of new romantic outfit Fashion, releasing the one-off album *Identity* – an 'experimental mistake' Wright later confessed[29]; and Nick Mason started recording with 10cc guitarist Rick Fenn, resulting in the passable *Profiles* the following year – although he spent much of 1984 racing his classic car collection[30]. ELP, meanwhile, were attempting to get back together again having spent the first half of the 80s dormant, but there was a problem. Carl Palmer was off playing with Asia so they were forced, in theory if not in practise, to place an ad asking for 'heavy drummer, surname must begin with P'. Fortune shone in that Cozy Powell was available, but the formation only lasted one album.

Neo-prog, meanwhile, was just getting under way. A bit like NWOBHM, with which it had quite a lot in common, and existing in an unfashionable bubble, second generation prog groups like Pallas, Pendragon, and Solstice (great prog names one and all) released debut albums that year. The former's *The Sentinel* was surely the most suitably prog-titled and sleeved[31], but also the most compromised, their epic live track 'Atlantis Suite' being reduced to a 'mere' eight minutes by EMI. None of them produced singles and none made the top 40 albums either. In short they were niche, and not terribly different from the prog that had gone before. Which was fine for their fans. The last thing they wanted progressive rock bands to do was progress.

The only neo-prog band to impact on the charts were Marillion who in 1984 released two top 10 albums, *Fugazi* and the live *Real to Reel,* and would go mainstream the following year with a #2 single, 'Kayleigh', and #1 album, *Misplaced Childhood*. Marillion almost single-handedly resurrected prog as a going concern. From their Tolkien-derived name, concept lyrics, time-warped sleeve designs and Genesis-homaged music, they were impervious to critical hostility from the press, snide mockery from pop and indifference from most others – and yet enjoyed a parallel world of success regardless. Which just went to show that you could make it without the fashion police's stamp of approval. And yet Marillion's plagiarism was so obvious – 'like a quiz night at a Genesis fan's convention'[32] – that you felt for other neo-prog groups who were trying to do something new-ish. (Two such under-the-radar, cassette-only outfits were Karma and Altamont, unremarkable except for the fact that both featured a 16-year-old Steven Wilson, who of course would go on to form No-Man, Porcupine Tree and be the doyen of prog for decades).

Conversely, some initially straightforward pop or rock artists went slightly prog. Sting, who'd played in the short-lived prog band Strontium-90 just before joining The Police, started writing his first solo album *The Dream of the Blue Turtles* in late 1984, and although it would be rightly known for its jazz influences, there is a whiff of prog about it too (his cribbing of Prokofiev for 'The Russians' had echoes of ELP borrowing from Mussorgsky for example). Likewise Kate Bush's *The Hounds Of Love*, was half a concept album. And then there was Dalis Car, Modern English,

Heaven 17, Thomas Dolby and even Frankie Goes To Hollywood, who all toyed with prog. The latter's *Welcome To The Pleasuredome* was heavily influenced by the sound of Yes's *90125* thanks to Trevor Horn's make-it-big production and guest appearances from Yes axemen Steve Howe and Trevor Rabin.

This plushly-produced, soft rock end of prog went down well in the States. And it is to America we turn to now – although way beyond the confines of prog.

Chapter 24: Born in the USA
American mainstream

From Prince to Madonna to Michael Jackson to Bruce Springsteen to Cyndi Lauper, 1984 was the year that pop stood tallest.
Rolling Stone magazine

Black stations, white stations
Break down the doors
Stand up and face the music
This is Nineteen Eighty-Four
M+M 'Black Stations, White Stations'

Although this book is about rock and pop in Britain in 1984, given the symbiotic nature of the Anglo-American music scenes, especially at that time – Second British Invasion going one way, dance culture the other – it's necessary to at least take a peak across the Atlantic. In fact, it was just as eventful a year in the US as it was in the UK. Thirty years on, Rolling Stone magazine declared 1984 as American Pop's Greatest Year[1]: 'From Prince to Madonna to Michael Jackson to Bruce Springsteen to Cyndi Lauper, 1984 was the year that pop stood tallest. New wave, R&B, hip-hop, mascara'd hard rock and 'Weird Al' Yankovic all crossed paths on the charts while a post-'Billie Jean' MTV brought them into your living room'[2]. Certainly it was a year of massive-selling albums[3], each yielding multiple singles, the dawn of huge, sponsored, never-ending tours, films becoming like extended videos and the first break-even year of MTV as well as the debut MTV Awards.

It was also the year when black dance and white rock music came together. Michael Jackson had effectively started it with *Thriller* – cameo appearances by Paul McCartney, Eddie Van Halen and even Vincent Price, attracting crossover appeal which in turn eventually led to 'heavy rotation' on MTV, after the channel originally all but censored videos by black artists. By early February 1984 *Thriller* had sold 25 million copies making it the world's best-selling album, and later that month it won seven Grammys and remained at the top spot in the album charts until mid-April, a year and a half after it was originally released. The black-white mix was beginning to show in his appearance too. By April he was on his third nose job even if his skin was still black and hair still curly – even more so after it caught fire during the filming of a Pepsi ad in January. He was also beginning to wear strange outfits (the electric blue jacket with epaulets and sash he wore to the White House in May made him look like one of Reagan's military attachés), and of course there was the adoption of Bubbles the monkey. But for all the boy/man, man/woman, black/white indeterminacy, Jackson was now a resolutely mainstream artist rather than a soul one, even if 1984 turned out to be a stop gap year. Aside from some ten-year old archived recordings Motown had unearthed and his contribution to the very ordinary *Victory* album by the

Jacksons, he released nothing new in 1984. Almost the entire second half of the year was spent on the road with his brothers on the cash-cow Victory Tour, an unhappy experience which turned out to be the last time they performed together. From here on, it was all about the one Jackson (although Janet gave him a run for his money). And yet, at the age of 25 he'd already hit his peak. From the mid-80s onwards this incredibly talented performer became increasingly estranged from reality even as he continued to sell records by the million.

If 1984 saw Jackson on the slide, it was the year that made Prince. True, his first five albums released in consecutive years from 1978-82 were successful to a point, but it was *Purple Rain* – album, single, film – that truly made him a global star. It was hard to tell whether the album was the soundtrack to the film or the film the extended music video of the album. Either way, both dominated the charts. In fact the album was #1 in the US charts from the beginning of August right through to the end of the year. And then there were the singles – 'When Doves Cry', 'Let's Go Crazy', 'I Would Die 4 You', 'Take Me With U' and of course the anthemic all-rock-zero-funk title track – all becoming global hits. He even found time to write hits for others: 'I Feel For You' for Chaka Khan, 'Sugar Walls' for Sheena Easton, 'Manic Monday' for The Bangles (a #2 hit two years later) and 'Nothing Compares 2 U' for The Family (also a #1 for Sinead O'Connor six years later). Like Jackson, Prince was attracting a crossover audience, but instead of drafting in Caucasian cameos and the plush production skills of Quincy Jones, he was essentially a one-man operation: writing, playing, singing and producing. Even the musicians he surrounded himself with looked more like sexy marketing, although in fact they could definitely play.

Jackson may have attempted to loosen up with the 'Thriller' video, pretending to be a werewolf, but nobody believed for a second that he was 'bad' or 'dangerous', which turned out to be the very titles of his next two albums in a vain attempt to reinvent himself. Prince, however, was the real thing: edgy, unpredictable, sexy. The film, audaciously conceived and directed by first-timer Albert Magnoli, was a stranger affair. In it Prince was everywhere and yet nowhere, hogging the action but wavering, sullen, almost ghost-like. Of course, this was the character (The Kid) he was playing but he was also playing himself. Like Jackson, he would become increasingly estranged from reality, surrounding himself with a large, fawning retinue and later changing his name to symbol or The Artist Formally Known As Prince. There would be more hits and brilliance but never another year to compete with 1984.

A whole host of black artists were also making the crossover. Ray Parker Jr went synthpop with 'Ghostbusters'; Lionel Richie combined latino pop ('All Night Long (All Night))' with smooth soul ballads (the maudlin 'Hello'), its parent album occupying the US Top 10 for the entire year; and The Pointer Sisters had four Top 10 pop-crossover hits, their last to reach those heights. The extent and nature of the shift varied. Some, like Philip Bailey, Jody Watley and Tina Turner chose to work with white British producers in London studios: Bailey's 'Easy Lover' hit single with Phil Collins, Watley with Bruce Woolley on her debut single 'Where the Boys Are' (which inadvertently got her drafted into Band Aid) and Turner's *Private Dancer* album with a range of producers. Turner's reinvention was wholesale, transforming herself from a fading R&B singer seemingly in the twilight of her career (she was in her mid-40s) into an A-league star pumping out plushly produced, cross-genre songs that were hits all over the world. It was odd that chief amongst the British producers responsible for the makeover were alternative synthpoppers Martin Ware and Ian Craig Marsh, yet also somehow unsurprising that another was Mark Knopfler. (As an aside, it was David Bowie who helped get her contract with EMI renewed the year before; Turner returned the favour by covering '1984' from *Diamond Dogs*).

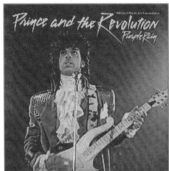

Prince's all-conquering *Purple Rain*, the Jacksons Victory Tour in name only, and the Boss.

Other artists like Womack & Womack ('Love Wars'), Ashford & Simpson ('Solid as a Rock'), as well as Luther Vandross, Teddy Pendergrass, Alexander O'Neal and Glenn Jones stuck closer to the soul genres. As did female singers like Phyllis Nelson ('Move Closer', originally released in 1984, but not a hit until the following year), Thelma Houston and Jenny Burton. Jimmy Jam and Terry Lewis, meanwhile were beginning to form a formidable songwriting and production partnership, embracing white as well as black artists[4]. But it was also a year marked by Marvin Gaye's tragic death in April and Stevie Wonder's 'I Just Called to Say I Love You', easily the most banal of his career.

If 1984 was the year Prince effectively relaunched himself after several years of grind and paying his dues, Madonna's ascent to stardom was relatively quick and certainly canny. Early singles 'Holiday', 'Lucky Star' and 'Borderline' had been aimed squarely at the dancefloor but it was 'Like a Virgin' (US #1) and 'Material Girl' (#2) that propelled her into a broader popular conscience. Nile Rodgers had been brought in to ensure a more sophisticated, cross-genre, radio-friendly sound. And crucially she was *video*-friendly, like Prince using her sexuality to blatant, successful effect. The 'Like a Virgin' promo was a tease, frolicking around in Venetian gondolas, while in 'Material Girl' she mimicked Marilyn Monroe in *Gentlemen Prefer Blondes*. Her performance on the first MTV Music Video Awards in September was calculatedly controversial, writhing around on the floor in a wedding dress, white stockings and boy toy belt. In truth it was embarrassing and there were plenty in the industry who didn't take her seriously, but she got away with it. Even her comparatively weak voice was treated as a minor detail. There was nobody more ambitious than Madonna. "I want to conquer the world" she said in an MTV interview in the same month. It didn't take her long. At the end of the year the *Like a Virgin* album went straight to #1 in the US, UK and most of Europe. The autumn also saw her working on her first major[5] film, *Desperately Seeking Susan,* released the following year. It was perfect for her. Like Prince in *Purple Rain*, she basically played a version of herself – a trampy, listless New York punk – but unlike Prince it seemed like she could really act. Unfortunately for Madonna, from then on it turned out she couldn't, at least outside the comfort zones of her own videos. But acting was but a minor distraction compared with her incredible, all-consuming ambition to be the biggest music star on the planet. Within a year or two, she probably was.

The other great white female hope that year was Cyndi Lauper. She seemed to arrive from nowhere, with mix-and-match clothes, off-centre attitude and a puzzling but powerful voice. Most people had no idea she'd been in a failed late 70s / early 80s band called Blue Angel. Cue solo career and a new image which emphasized a combination of fun and feminism. *She's So Unusual* was the knowing title of her debut album, spawning five singles including the monster hits 'Girls Just Want to Have Fun' and 'Time After Time'. Despite the kookiness, Lauper seemed more real than Madonna. She was pretty but didn't flounce her sexuality, speaking to teenage and twentysomething women in a direct, natural way – even if she'd turned 30 herself.

The astonishing invention of Madonna, reinvention of Cyndi Lauper and re-reinvention of Tina Turner.

On the blue-eyed soul front, Daryl Hall and John Oates were coming to the end of their phenomenally successful early-80s period with a #1 single, 'Out of Touch' and #5 album, *Big Bam Boom,* punctuated by a techy production, including a cameo from Arthur Baker. It would be the last time they'd reach such heights. Billy Joel was also coming to the end of a purple patch. Album *An Innocent Man* and singles 'Tell Her About It' and 'Uptown Girl' were huge hits on both sides of the Atlantic in 1983 but it wasn't until the end of the decade that he matched that chart success.

The same age as Joel, Bruce Springsteen's blue-collar rock dominated 1984. And in the same way that Prince had been 'relaunched', so too had Springsteen. *Born to Run* was the album that had made his name in 1975, but *Born in the USA* turned him into a superstar. It was all about scale. Big topic, big production, seven top ten singles (although most of them sounded like album tracks), and a seemingly endless tour (61 cities in 11 countries seen by 4.7 million fans). Ironically, the title track 'Born in the USA' was a critique of the US government's indifference to its Vietnam vets, but was commandeered by Reagan and the Republicans as a patriotic rallying call in the run-up to the Presidential elections, and also interpreted as such by the majority of the great American public. Originally it had been acoustic but such was the bluster of the song's new production and the stars and stripes that dominated its sleeve, you could understand why Reagan's team went for it. In any case, it didn't do Springsteen any harm. And as politics requisitioned the Boss, so too did the nostalgia industry, his songs requisites for classic jeans and classic beer ads, and featuring heavily on the lite and gold radio stations which yearned for the 'certainties' of mid-20th Century America.

The return of rock was responsible for numerous comebacks: Foreigner ('I Want to Know What Love Is' #1), ex-Eagles' Glenn Frey ('The Heat Is On' #2), ZZ Top ('Legs' #8), a Huey Lewis album that yielded four top ten singles, and so on. Rock was becoming more like pop. Or soft rock. It was perfect for undercover cop TV series Miami Vice which premiered in September, peppering its Jan Hammer soundtrack with soft rock hits by all the above and a whole lot more. Such was the importance of the soundtrack, the visuals were cut to fit to the music rather than the other way round. Even heavy metal went mainstream, with Van Halen's 'Jump' ushering in synth riffs.

While punk in Britain had kick-started a series of overlapping, radio-friendly genres termed new wave, ska, synthpop, new romanticism and new pop, as well as the more 'artsy' post-punk, punk's succession in the US was simply called new wave or new music and would remain known as such through to the mid-80s. Most of the Second British Invasion was termed new wave, and included a few artists who were more successful in the States than at home. Modern English and The Fixx, for instance, had had early success across the Atlantic while struggling for recognition at home (the latter's 1984 *Phantoms* album failed to chart in the UK but went Top 20 in the US). Mentioned elsewhere, Billy Idol and The Psychedelic Furs were also more popular with American audiences at this time. John Waite, ex-singer of non-entities The Babys, had a huge 1984 solo hit in 'Missing You'. Wang Chung had success with a re-recording of a previous flop, 'Dance Hall Days', and album *Points on the Curve*. Their accessible sound appealed to US FM radio and, like the Furs, Simple Minds and OMD, they benefitted from inclusion in mid-80s mainstream film soundtracks. Actually, they went one better, when William Friedkin commissioned them to write the whole soundtrack for *To Live and Die in L.A.* in 1985, which became their third album.

Of the original US class of '77, Talking Heads continued to attract a broader and broader audience with the excellent *Stop Making Sense,* which was both a film and live album; The Cars' *Heartbeat City*, recorded in London, sired their biggest ever single 'Drive', remembered more for its use at Live Aid a year later; and after a mildly interesting early 80s period of sounding like a slightly speeded up Ultravox, Berlin finessed their 'Europeanness' with their March 1984 album, *Love Life*, and would go on to greater success with the Giorgio Moroder-penned 'Take My Breath Away' two years later. Ministry went the other way, transitioning between Anglophile synthpop and Euro EBM and would go on to influence Nine Inch Nails and their ilk.

Others threw in the towel. Blondie had split up just over a year earlier, but 1984 saw several once-happening bands follow suit, including The Go-Go's who'd gone from surf punk to watered down new pop, and Romeo Void whose album *Instincts* and 'Girl in Trouble' single were ironically their biggest hits. Like in Britain, synthpop bands were the biggest casualties: Devo released the poor *Shout* album after which they were dropped by Warner Bros; San Francisco band Units split after their second (mini) album *New Way To Move*, part-produced by Bill Nelson; The Comateens bowed out with their third and final album *Deal With It*, despite featuring the irresistible single 'Don't Come Back'); Our Daughter's Wedding split up after a final single, 'Take Me'; and Iam Siam somehow managed to form *and* split within the year leaving just one great single, 'I Can Hear You Now', for posterity.

It was also the end of ZE Records which had been set up by <u>Michael Zilkha</u>, British-born son of Selim Zilkha, founder of Mothercare, and Frenchman Michel Esteban to record the new, knowing fusion of punk, disco and new wave that was coming out of (mainly) New York. Licensed in Britain by Island (Chris Blackwell was a friend of Esteban's then-girlfriend, Anna Wintour), at its peak around 1981/82, it was releasing the coolest, cleverest records in town – Kid Creole and the Coconuts, Was (Not Was), The Waitresses, the compilation, *Mutant Disco* – although they were generally more successful chartwise in the UK than US. One of their last releases was by Cristina (full name Cristina Monet-Pilaci). Harvard drop-out, wife of Michael Zilkha, she'd flirted with trashy disco at the beginning of the decade, disappeared and then resurfaced with the deeply strange *Sleep It Off*, produced by Don Was and sounding alternately like the Sex Pistols, Nina Hagen and the Flying Lizards. Jean-Paul Goude's sleeve design, stretching Cristina's neckline to giraffe-like proportions, was so good he repeated it for Grace Jones's *Slave to the Rhythm* a year later, while Madonna copied the back cover virtually wholesale for the front of 'Material Girl'. The two had much in common, although Madonna's lyrics were never so controversial as 'My life is in a turmoil / My thighs are black and blue / My sheets are stained, so is my brain / What's a girl to do?'. She would never better it. In fact she would never record again.

*****

If the US had largely abandoned new wave, then Canada was still holding out. Martha & the Muffins' had slimmed down to Martha Johnson and Mark Gane, in the process truncating their name to M+M, and released the excellent 'Black Stations White Stations'. Aside from its irresistible groove, its lyrics – "Black stations, white stations break down the doors, Stand up and face the music, this is 1984" – were a comment on radio stations' racist playlists, echoing what was happening on MTV. Synthpop bands like Men Without Hats, Platinum Blonde and Spoons were still enjoying chart success while others like Rational Youth, Psyche and Nash The Slash[6] were taking a leaf from Depeche Mode and going dark and contrary.

But the real innovation was coming from three female artists Jane Siberry, Mary Margaret O'Hara and k d lang. Siberry and O'Hara had been in bands in the late 70s but had gone solo in the new decade. Siberry's eponymous 1981 debut album was well received but it was her art-pop second, *No Borders Here*, which broke her in 1984, attracting comparisons with Kate Bush. O'Hara, meanwhile, had been picked up by Virgin Records and in 1984 work began on a debut album with Jon Leckie and XTC's Andy Partridge co-producing. After an inordinately long gestation (Leckie and Partridge only lasted a few days and replacement Joe Boyd just a little longer), it eventually saw the light of day four years later, produced by fellow Canadian Michael Brooke, and has rightly been considered a classic. Less innovatory but in the end far more consistent was k d lang, who after forming a short-lived Patsy Cline tribute band released her debut album, *A Truly Western Experience* – attributed to k d lang and the reclines (all in lower case, even then) – in 1984.

Three Canadian singer-songwriters just starting out: Jane Siberry, Mary Margaret O'Hara and k d lang.

Country music was the one genre which wasn't expected to change, and it didn't disappoint. Willie Nelson, Kenny Rogers, Dolly Parton, Crystal Gayle and a host of others continued to do what they did best: simple storytelling full of traditional values, an overlying reference to its past, and music a distant second. It was, of course, a mirror of the conservative times. Nowhere was country's uneasy relationship with other music genres more pronounced than the video of Ricky Skaggs' 'Country Boy' single, shot in New York where country boy Skaggs makes fun of the city. Coincidentally, Neil Young was also stuck in a country rut having completely changed direction after the experimental, electronic *Trans*. But the countryfied *Old Ways* was even more of a commercial flop. It even required two attempts to release it, Geffen (his new label) having vetoed the first. Another quasi-country artist ill-at-ease in the 80s, Bob Dylan was in-between the so-so *Infidels* and distinctly underwhelming *Empire Burlesque*, in part attributed to its soulless digital production which Dylan hated.

*****

If new wave was over and country stagnant, hip-hop was in an unstoppable ascent and about to enter a new phase. In the early 80s it had embraced rapping and scratching

302

as well as the wider cultural expressions of graffiti art and breakdancing. But the really big scene-shifter was its embrace of rock.

The Beastie Boys had been a hardcore punk band before messing around with rap. In early 1984 they made a total switch with a by now steady line-up of Michael Diamond, Adam Yauch and Adam Horovitz, adopting hip-hop monikers Mike D, MCA and Ad-Rock respectively. The other piece of the jigsaw was meeting Rick Rubin, who co-produced their break-through single 'Rock Hard' which pitched hard-edged white-boy rap over sampled AC/DC riffs. Rubin was a student at NYU but had started releasing unlabelled records in his spare time. In early 1984 he was joined by promoter-producer Russell Simmons and they gave the label a name: Def Jam (New York slang for 'the definitive sound'). 'Rock Hard' was the first to feature the distinctive and still-used Def Jam Records logo[7].

Simmons meanwhile was producing another up-and-coming crossover act, Run DMC, which featured his brother, Joseph. Only this time the crossover was the other way round. Run DMC were black hip-hop artists but Simmons convinced them to integrate heavy metal riffs. Not only did it work, their eponymous debut was the first hip-hop album to go gold. Both groups were also largely responsible for a change in the look of hip-hop too. Whereas old school artists like Afrika Bambaataa or Grandmaster Flash tended to look sci-fi or fetish flashy, the Beastie Boys and Run DMC were much more street: the former adopting a downtown delinquent 'aesthetic' (baseball cap, T-shirt, loose trousers), the latter donning black hats, gold chains on top of Adidaswear. By the end of the year, Def Jam had distribution through Columbia Records and the label was on its way to becoming the most influential purveyor of hip-hop in the US.

Beastie Boys, Run-DMC and Roxanne Shante.

Old school hip-hop producers were also appropriating rock, Africa Bambaataa teaming up with John Lydon and Bill Laswell (as Timezone) to release 'World Destruction' at the end of 1984. Even Bruce Springsteen, steering the good ship authenticity, called in Arthur Baker to mix the 12-inch of 'Dancing in the Dark'. The year also saw hip-hop become increasingly politicised. Keith LeBlanc's 'No Sell Out'[8] combined sections of a speech by black activist Malcolm X with a heavy drum-machine beat. It was nothing if not confrontational and was reissued in the UK in support of the miners' strike. LeBlanc was white, but there were plenty of black artists who followed suit, the most political of them all, Public Enemy, forming around this time, although it would be three more years before they garnered significant public attention with their debut album and supporting the by then extremely successful Beastie Boys.

One of the most extraordinary crossover acts was ESG, four young mulatto sisters from the Bronx (plus an extra percussionist) who played infectious stripped-down post-funk, yet were also post-punk without knowing it, opening for UK bands like Gang Of Four, PiL, even Young Marble Giants. Inevitably, Tony Wilson made the connection and before long had them recording a self-titled EP, jointly released by 99 Records and Factory. In late 1983 they released their debut album, *Come Away with ESG*, as cool and danceable as any hip-hop release, yet made entirely without drum-machines and synthesizers. Regrettably, they split the following year – though they remain one of the most sampled bands in hip-hop (and have occasionally reformed).

However, it wasn't all crossover. 'White Lines (Don't Do It)' was a fairly straight-forward, wonderfully melodic hit for Grandmaster Flash and Melle Mel, although originally it naughtily didn't have the bracketed suffix, was a bigger hit in the UK, confusingly didn't feature Grandmaster Flash at all and in any case was a pretty much direct rip-off of Liquid Liquid's 'Cavern' the year before. Africa Bambaataa handed over the mensch-machine baton to Newcleus whose 1984 'Jam on Revenge' and 'Jam On It' singles were brilliant examples of incessant Roland TR808 rhythm programming, better known as electro. The year also marked the debut single, 'Roxanne's Revenge', by 14-year-old rapper Roxanne Shante and the battle between Queens and Bronx crews each claiming that their neighbourhood was the business. And there was still space for older funk bands like Cameo and the Dazz Band to have hits ('She's Strange' and 'Let It All Blow' respectively). However, if there was one hip-hop sub-genre that truly marked the year, at least in the popular imagination and especially on film, then it was break beat, or, to be more precise, its dance manifestation, breakdancing. 1984 saw the craze move out of the bloc parties and onto the streets and screens. There were three breakdancing films in 1984 alone.

Clearly, this has been a whistle-stop tour and does not do the mainstream US scene justice. But the themes were clear: the end of the British Invasion and new wave, the return of rock, the rise of the solo superstar artist who morphed pop and rock, the ascent of hip-hop which, though not mainstream at the time, would be within a few years, and the increasing infiltration of latin pop into the US charts[9]. The next chapter looks briefly at the flipside: America's version of post-punk and its connections with both indie and art-house experimentation, particularly in New York.

Chapter 25: Big Black Flag
American underground

Our band could be your life.[1]
Minutemen

Give them what they need not what they want.[2]
Greg Ginn, Black Flag

After London had wrestled the title of 'punk capital' away from New York in 1977, America's idea of post-punk was half-hearted. Bands like Blondie, The Cars and The Knack were maybe punk in attitude, but musically fairly mainstream. The small minority that stayed close to the punk spirit, in both music *and* attitude, became hardcore (which we'll come onto shortly). The area in between, underground but accessible, the area which had been so successfully colonised by British bands in the late 70s and early 80s, was almost non-existent in the States. New England art-housers Talking Heads headed up the small contingent which bucked the trend (like Wire, they had been post-punk *during* punk), but as they became accepted by Joe Public and grew in stature, they would hand the baton over to, on the face of it, a band without the obvious credentials.

R.E.M. were not from one of the big urban centres but revelled in their provincialism, away from the record industry hipness of New York or Los Angeles. Formed in Athens, Georgia in 1980, it took three years for their debut album, *Murmur*, to appear but their intention was clear: to achieve success on their own terms, stay with an independent label for as long as possible and champion alternative, 'midwest' Americana[3]. As Tony Fletcher wrote in his biography of the band: "…if they were going to climb that ladder, they wanted to bring the new underground up with them"[4], inviting bands like The Dream Syndicate and the dB's on tour with them and including other bands' songs in their setlists. Second album *Reckoning*, recorded in 12 days and released in April 1984, was the perfect combination of studied alternative cool. Its singles, the countryfied '(Don't Go Back To) Rockville' and 'So. Central Rain', gained plenty of college radio play while an arty 6-track video *Left of Reckoning,* shot around folk artist RA Miller's farm home, kept them at arm's length from the mainstream. The massive success of *Out of Time* and *Automatic for the People* was still several years off but they had made their mark. In short, 1984 was the year that R.E.M. became the "superstars of their own cult."[5]

In their jangly wake were debut albums from the likes of Let's Active (led by Mitch Easter who'd co-produced the first two R.E.M. albums), The Bangles, The Long Ryders, Guadalcanal Diary, The Del Fuegos and a debut EP by Throwing Muses, but – like R.E.M. – their peak, at least in terms of commercial success, would come later.

The post-punk scene that *really* defined 1984, if only for a limited audience, was the blooming of hardcore.

Born in the early 80s hardcore was the new punk – aggressive, nihilistic and raucous. If the Ramones played songs that were fast, short and loud, then hardcore played them faster, shorter and louder. And whereas punk attracted the media, hardcore was utterly underground, kept alive by a coterie of labels like SST and Homestead, fanzines like Forced Exposure and Conflict, and relentless gigging in small clubs up and down the country. There would be just enough money for drink and drugs, gas to get the beaten-up van to the next concert which might be 400 miles away, but rarely enough for food and hotels. It was very male and white. For many, the work ethic was the driving force, like a manifesto, and a few groups even went so far as adopting a puritan "Don't smoke, don't drink, don't fuck" ethos.

1984 was both a peak for hardcore, with several career-defining albums released, and at the same time a change in direction. The early bands, those formed in the late 70s or early 80s had, in the spirit of punk, been anti-heritage. But the newer ones started to look back and were comfortable in referencing Neil Young or the Stones. Pure hardcore, based on speed, lost its intensity. Some bands signed to majors, mostly unhappily, and others split up. This was not to say that hardcore joined the MTV age – it was still resolutely underground.

R.E.M. and Black Flag.

At hardcore's hard core were Californian bands Dead Kennedys and Black Flag, both formed in the late 70s, alongside the independent labels, Alternative Tentacles and SST, they set up. Dead Kennedys were the archetypal provocateurs, satirizing the political establishment, but by 1984 were focussing more on touring and releasing other bands' music. They returned with *Frankenchrist* in 1985 with its infamous Shriners parade cover (which resulted in a lawsuit) and inserted poster of HR Giger's *Penis Landscape* (which resulted in an obscenity trial). Financially and emotionally exhausted, they split in 1986. The less political, more existential Black Flag revolved around guitarist, founder and SST helmsman Greg Ginn and frontman Henry Rollins, who joined in 1981. Their early albums were fast and furious, but by 1984 they'd got slower, more like contorted 16rpm heavy metal, with Rollins's stage presence becoming extremely intimidating, his pumped-up physique and nihilist outpourings usually provoking violence of some kind, either between him and the audience or self-administered. 'Give them what they need not what they want' was the stark message. The year saw them release *three* albums: *Family Man, Slip It In* and *My War* – and a *Live 84* cassette released the following year. However, the constant grind of life on the road, sleeping on floors and Rollins's increasing estrangement wore them down and two years later they split.

From Black Flag to Chicago's Big Black was but a tormented step away. Blatant bigot or cruel satirist (it was hard to tell which), frontman Steve Albini also liked to bait the white liberal crowd that made up his audience. The fact that, unlike all the other hardcore bands, they used a drum machine instead of a drummer, made them all the more inhuman. The year saw the release of their third EP, *Racer X*. They would keep going for another three years, peaking with *Songs About Fucking* before inevitably imploding.

Meanwhile in Minnesota's twin cities, two 1979-formed bands were about to release their masterpieces. The Replacements were a ramshackle bunch from Minneapolis whose power-trash songs perfectly encapsulated what it was like to be immature, couldn't-give-a-toss teenagers, yet were delivered with a strangely innocent empathy that drew you in. Calling their 1984-released third album *Let It Be* was both a piss-take and homage. Nothing was sacred. From St Paul, the three-piece Hüsker Dü were also breaking out of the local scene and before too long had signed to SST. By 1984 they were at their peak, releasing a cover of The Byrds 'Eight Miles High' in May and in July their coloured-in-xerox masterwork *Zen Arcade*. It was recorded in a remarkable 45 hours, mixed in 40 and all for $3,200. Rapturously received, Hüsker Dü were, if not catapulted then, nudged into the alternative national consciousness, extending to the college crowd and not just the limited hardcore fanbase. *Zen Arcade* was that most un-punk of artefacts, a concept double album, about a young guy running away from home on a voyage of self-discovery, or as David Fricke in Rolling Stone described it, "a kind of thrash *Quadrophenia*". Not resting on their laurels, they followed it up with another album, *New Day Rising*, barely six months later. The following year, both bands signed to majors. Somewhat inevitably, the moves didn't work out – big label pressures, internal bickering, drugs – and both bands split before the decade was out. Hüsker Dü's Bob Mould himself blamed it on *Zen Arcade*: "It was the best record we ever made, but it was the one that we emulated."[6]

Another three-piece, Minutemen were formed in 1980 (their first gig opening for Black Flag) in San Pedro south of LA. They were regular working-class guys who played fast & furious skewed punk influenced by Wire, The Pop Group, Pere Ubu and Captain Beefheart. They weren't so much hardcore as multi-directional, juxtaposing abrasive mini political paeans with Blue Öyster Cult covers. They didn't look like punks either: plaid and jeans, grunge before grunge. 1984 was the year they came of age with third album *Double Nickels on the Dime*, released on SST. Like Hüsker Dü's *Zen Arcade*, it was a double (in fact, both were released on the same day) and cost even less to record. The sequencing of the 45 tracks was in (ironic or sincere, you never could tell which) homage to Pink Floyd's *Ummagumma* or ELP's *Works Volume One*, each member compiling a side with the fourth simply labelled 'chaff'. Most of the songs were under two minutes, but it somehow encompassed spikey but tuneful punk, abrasive funk, alt-country and even jazz, while lyrically spanning everything from left wing politics and the Vietnam War to racism and linguistics. One track, 'History Lesson Part II' contained the line, "Our band could be your life" which would become a rallying cry for the whole scene. They would never better it. The following year saw the release of the disappointing *3-Way Tie (For Last)* and then, just before Christmas, tragedy struck when singer and guitarist D Boon was killed in a car-crash. There was no question of the band continuing; they burned brightly but shortly.

 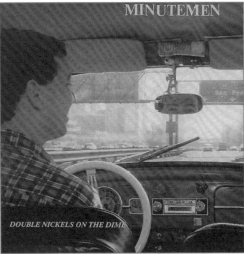

Hüsker Dü *Zen Arcade* and Minutemen's *Double Nickels on the Dime*, simultaneously released by SST on 1 July 1984, were arguably hardcore's zenith.

Across the border in Arizona, Meat Puppets, based around brothers Curt and Cris Kirkwood, took their warped punk into a swamp-rock-bordering-on-country direction on their second album, 1984's *Meat Puppets II* (three tracks of which were eulogised by Kurt Cobain on Nirvana's *Unplugged*, with the brothers helping out on stage). Unlike most hardcore bands, Meat Puppets lasted the course, give or take a couple of temporary splits. A couple of states further east, Texan band Butthole Surfers had been in some sort of existence since the turn of the decade, but it wasn't until 1984 that they debuted with the delinquent mayhem of *Psychic... Powerless... Another Man's Sac*, plus the EP *Live PCPPEP*. That year, Dinosaur Jr represented hardcore's next generation. Too young to have grown up with punk, they didn't harbour the year zero distrust of earlier rock heritage. They were at ease with the 60s and early 70s – frontman J Mascis even used a wah-wah pedal – and their dressed-down stoner, slacker, nonchalant demeanour influenced the UK's Madchester and shoegazer scenes.

*****

Inspired by the early 80s 'no-wave' and the hi-brow dirge of Glenn Branca, New York's hardcore scene was always more arty. And slower – to the point of crawling in the case of Swans. Led by Michael Gira, Swans played heavy, aggressive, torturously slow laments. 1984 saw the release of two, early seminal records, the album *Cop* and the *Young God* EP which took some of the themes that Henry Rollins and others were proselytising – punishment, humiliation, revenge – but played them out at 16 rpm. Sonic Youth operated in the same orbit (they even toured together) but by 1984 were becoming interested in, if not melody then, a more defined structure. In September they went into the studio to record the album that effectively kicked off their 'career': *Bad Moon Rising*. Like a number of hardcore bands, this was the beginning of references to an earlier era in rock music – the album was named after a 1969 single by Creedence Clearwater Revival, and its first single, 'Death Valley 69' referenced the Charles Manson killings of the same year – helping to create a revived interest in the dark underbelly of Americana. The album was released the following year simultaneously in the US and UK.

Swans, and Sonic Youth's Kim Gordon and Thurston Moore.

Sonic Youth's Kim Gordon was one of the very few women in hardcore. Others included the all-girl band Ut who'd temporarily based themselves in England, and Diamanda Galas who wailed like a banshee but was more artcore than hardcore, her eponymous sophomore 1984 album not for the feint-hearted. Ex-Teenage Jesus and the Jerks' Lydia Lunch, was another, although like Galas she moved in wider circles. In late 1983, she'd joined Nick Cave, Jim Thirlwell and Marc Almond in the short-lived Immaculate Consumptives, and her links with Swans and Sonic Youth were close: she'd collaborated with Michael Gira on a spoken-word cassette, *Hard Rock*, in February 1984 and sung on Sonic Youth's 'Death Valley 69'. She also collaborated with Thurston Moore on an album, *In Limbo,* which featured music by Moore, with Lunch adding the vocals at Cabaret Voltaire's Sheffield studio and released on their and Paul Smith's Doublevision label. While in England, Lunch gave Smith a cassette of Sonic Youth's then unfinished. *Bad Moon Rising*. It became the first release on his new label, Blast First, thus kick-starting the wholesale release of US hardcore albums in the UK. Meanwhile, at the less rocky end of hardcore, some bands added elements of free jazz or even contemporary classical. Glenn Branca's dirgy, cacophonic guitar 'symphonies', played by (amongst others) members of Sonic Youth and Swans, or Jeffrey Lohn's perfectly titled 'Dirge', from his one album, 1984's *Music from Paradise*, were typical. 'Avant-garde music you could shake your fist to'.

It was more likely you'd shake your head to the music of John Cage who, at 72 and zen to the core, was still writing prolifically and with the rule book thrown out long ago. Check out *Music for* _____, seventeen parts with no score. The next generation, led by Steve Reich and Philip Glass, on the other hand, were becoming less confrontational, more mature, grander. Glass was everywhere, having succeeded – especially with his *Koyanisqaatsi* soundtrack the year before – in reaching out to both classical and pop audiences. 1984 saw premieres of a full opera (*Akhnaten*) and part of another one (*the CIVIL warS*); music for the opening ceremony of the Olympic Games in Los Angeles[7]; and some song settings for poems by Leonard Cohen, Octavio Paz and Raymond Levesque (*Three Songs for Chorus*). The last work inspired Glass to collaborate with more pop musicians, the following year seeing the release of *Songs from Liquid Days* featuring Suzanne Vega, Paul Simon, Laurie Anderson, David Byrne, Linda Ronstadt and others.

Steve Reich, Philip Glass and Laurie Anderson.

Nowhere was this cross pollination of hi- and lo-brow more evident than on the strange one-hour television special, *Good Morning Mr Orwell,* which brought in the new year. Conceived by artist Nam June Paik, it was a kind of South Bank Show on acid presented live by satellite from New York and (for some reason) Paris. The combination of Glass, Cage, Anderson, Merce Cunningham and Allen Ginsberg with Yves Montand, Oingo Boingo, Thompson Twins and breakdancing was well-intended, even if it didn't work. On that show, Laurie Anderson and Peter Gabriel premiered a new song 'Excellent Birds', a working relationship that would see co-written tracks on both Anderson's *Hunting Mister Heartbreak* that year and Gabriel's *So* a couple of years later. But the biggest arthouse release in 1984 was undoubtedly Anderson's monumental 5-LP box set *United States Live*, a culmination of nearly a decade of her one-woman shows recorded in a two-night performance.

The record labels at the centre of all this were a mixture of major and independent, but there was a whole level below that. Like in Britain, one of the fascinating characteristics of the American early-to-mid 80s alternative scene was its cassette culture. Reach Out International Records (ROIR), run by Neil Cooper, specialised in live recordings, demos and sessions, 'in-between album stuff' as he put it, usually for existing bands but sometimes for new artists as a 'calling card'. Production costs were low so although the label was niche, as a business model it worked well, eventually 'going CD' at the end of the decade. 1984 releases included cassettes as disparate as Richard Hell, Prince Far I and Einstürzende Neubauten. Another label was Tellus (1983-93), which was actually a cassette-zine covering not only the Manhattan noise scene but also audio art and even drama. Debuting in 1983, it ran for ten years and was not so much a business as a public service, supported by New York State Council of the Arts among other funders. It was even available in public libraries. ROIR and Tellus were at the more professional end of American cassette culture, but there were legions of small, amateur labels operating out of apartments and garages across the land – Al Margolis's pre-eminent Sound Of Pig which started in 1984 and went on to release hundreds of titles, and the rather more prosaically named Ladd-Frith to pick two.

Another of the great things about New York's early 80s music scene was its eclecticism. Musicians seemed to be open to everything and anything, and none more so than Bill Laswell. Aside from helming his own group, Material, Laswell played on albums as diverse as Eno & Byrne's alt-funk, proto-world music *My Life in the Bush of Ghosts* and Eno's own ambient *On Land,* and by 1984 was flitting between releasing his debut solo album, another one as Praxis and a hip-hop 12-inch as Timezone with John Lydon and Afrika Bambaataa, as well as producing a second album for Herbie Hancock (on the back of 1983's *Future Shock*), and on his days off he played bass on numerous other artists' albums. Which included John Zorn, whose own career was equally difficult to pin down. His radical 1984/85 re-workings of Ennio Morricone film compositions, *The Big Gundown*, was the one that made his name. Meanwhile, ex-no waver Arto Lindsay had dallied with the jazz-infused The Lounge Lizards before forming the latin-flavoured Ambitious Lovers, in 1984 releasing their debut album, *Envy*, planned to be the first of seven albums inspired by the deadly sins, but they disbanded after *Greed* and *Lust* a few years later.

This was all very well if you lived in New York and had your ear to the ground or were dedicated enough to follow the hardcore bands' cross-country, hand-to-mouth adventures. But for most curious Americans, finding out about the bands was no easy matter. There was no equivalent of NME, Sounds or Melody Maker. As Chuck Warner of Hyped2Death said, "The main culprits in America's 'indie failure', if you're looking for them, were the lack of a monolithic national press, and the geographical isolation of its musical scenes. Rolling Stone was useless, Creem couldn't fix on a coherent identity, and the rest were just fanzines"[8]. To be fair, there was Trouser Press on the east coast and Op Magazine on the west, but both folded in 1984, the former due to editorial disenchantment as new wave withered, the latter completing its 26-issues, having from the outset opted for an A-Z sequence rather than numbers! (It did however spawn two new zines: Option and Sound Choice). There was college radio of course, but nothing national like John Peel, let alone a television programme like Whistle Test or The Tube.

But somehow, the disparate nodes of alternative music-making functioned. Away from New York, The Residents, for example, were by now 15 years into their wilfully mysterious career, and chose the year to put hi- and lo-art under the microscope. *George and James (American Composer Series – Volume 1)* – George being Gershwin and James being Brown – was supposed to be the first in a long series, but it didn't quite work and never made it beyond Volume 2 a couple of years later. Much better was their second album of the year, *Whatever Happened to Vileness Fats?,* both a 30-minute video and album originally conceived 12 years earlier. The former is possibly the strangest film ever made, the latter inevitably similarly off the wall.

It is of course impossible to do justice to the US mid-80s underground scene (any more than the mainstream one) in eight pages. A whole chapter could be reserved for Tom Waits who was in the middle of his *Swordfishtrombones / Rain Dogs / Frank's Wild Years* pots-and-pans triumvirate, the middle album written in a seedy basement on the Lower West Side in autumn 1984. But that's another book.

Chapter 26: Foreign Affairs
Links with Australia, Europe and Japan

I come from a land down under.[1]
Men at Work

European pop sounds like Eurovision pop even when it's not from the Eurovision Song Contest.[2]
The New Yorker

Steppin' into Asia, don't be afraid.[3]
Ryuichi Sakamoto

Rock and pop in Britain in 1984 was not just about Anglo-American artists. There may not have been many foreign chart hits, and even those had to be sung in English[4], but the to-ing and fro-ing of artists from Australia, a good chunk of mainland Europe and even Japan made the scene all the more interesting and healthy. London, particularly, was a magnet and some foreign post-punk bands moved there, crashing on floors, living in garrets, maybe finding the support of a music writer, playing the small club circuit and signing to London-based, mainly independent labels. Many found the capital harsh and unwelcoming, the climate and food off-putting, and the whole experience a bit like trying to make it in Hollywood. German bands DAF and Propaganda had a hard time of it, for example. At least for Aussies and Kiwis there was some sort of shared culture, language and support structure in enclaves like Earls Court.

*****

Until the 80s, very few Australian artists made it big in Britain, apart from The Seekers in the late 60s and AC/DC in the late 70s (not counting semi-émigrés like the Bee Gees or Olivia Newton John). Punk changed the mindset, prompting a trickle of post-punk bands to try their luck in London. 1984 was a turning point for many. As already mentioned, The Birthday Party had moved from Melbourne to London in 1980, then to Berlin, before splitting up in 1983, after which Nick Cave formed The Bad Seeds[5] and relocated back to the UK. Also from Melbourne, The Moodists had moved to London in 1983, signing to Red Flame. The label was particularly enamoured of Australian bands, in 1984 releasing *Beyond the Southern Cross*, a double compilation showcasing Aussie post-punk[6]. The Moodists' own, sole album, *Thirsty's Calling,* followed later in the year, but their stylistic proximity to The Birthday Party (perhaps not helped by supporting Nick Cave on tour that year) made it hard for them to create their own identity. Personnel changes saw former Orange Juice members David McClymont and Malcolm Ross join briefly, but it didn't stop them splitting in 1987. Also on Red Flame's compilation were Perth-band The Triffids, who made the move in the autumn of 1984, giving themselves until Christmas to make an impression. Which they did: wowing audiences live, signing a deal with Rough Trade to distribute their two Australia-recorded albums, and gracing the first NME cover of 1985 which it predicted would be 'The Year of the Triffids'. It wasn't, due mostly to record company machinations, but when their London-recorded album *Born Sandy Devotional* finally came out in 1986, they'd delivered on the promise.

Aussies in London: The Moodists and The Go-Betweens.

The Scottish connection had also applied to Brisbane band The Go-Betweens' at the beginning of the decade. Their debut single was released on Postcard in 1980, before switching to Rough Trade in London – where they eventually 'settled'. But by mid-1983 the label's energies were focussed on The Smiths so the band hawked their third album, *Spring Hill Fair*, to Sire, released in September 1984. It looked like their shift from post-punk to a more refined pop sound would bear fruit – 'Bachelor's Kisses' was a gorgeous single – but the album underperformed. They kept at it, with three more fine albums on Beggars Banquet, but failed to find mainstream success, so returned to Australia, a happier band all round. 'We'd spent five years in London – blackness, darkness, greyness and poverty – and suddenly for some reason we seemed to have more money in Sydney, and we all had places to live and being in a city where after five years we can go to the beach in ten minutes'[7]. The logic behind the return was irrefutable.

Another band who initially struggled to make their way in London were Dead Can Dance who arrived in 1982. I remember braving a pre-gentrified Isle of Dogs to interview Brendan Perry and Lisa Gerrard near the top of a pretty rough Council high-rise which nonetheless afforded an amazing view across London. 1984 saw the release of debut album and follow-up EP which set them on the road to inventing a music inspired by a blend of mythology, classicism and pre-world music that was wholly their own. That it became 4AD's biggest seller was both surprising and gratifying.

In the case of two more leftfield artists, London was a stepping stone to two wildly different careers in New York and Los Angeles. Jim Thirlwell was an early emigrant, moving to London in 1978, working at Virgin Records on Oxford Street and releasing a number of shouty leftfield albums and singles using the multi-varied Foetus moniker

314

on his own Self Immolation label. By the beginning of 1984 he'd been namechecked as a member of the short-lived Immaculate Consumptives, made the front cover of NME in February and signed to Some Bizzare before upping sticks and moving to New York. Working roughly in the same field, New Zealander Graeme Revell had moved to Sydney in the 70s before relocating to London in 1980 where he released a series of 'industrial' records by the first incarnation of his SPK group on his own Side Effects label. By 1983 he attempted to 'go commercial', signing to WEA, buying a Fairlight with the advance, and releasing the fairly thrilling 'Metal Dance' followed by the perfunctory *Machine Age Voodoo* in 1984. With wife and baby in tow, he echoed The Go-Betweens' move, exchanging his Vauxhall squat for the sun and the sea – in his case a highly successful career composing Hollywood soundtracks in LA. Another electronic outfit, Severed Heads, who'd signed with Red Flame's sub-label Ink Records, releasing the excellent *Since the Accident* and alternative dance hit 'Dead Eyes Opened' at the beginning of 1984, never felt the urge to move to the UK. There were promotional visits and live appearances but that seemed to suffice.

Of course there were many groups who eschewed basing themselves in Britain, but nevertheless recorded, toured or had chart success there: Joe Dolce's 'Shaddap You Face' and Men At Work's 'Down Under' had topped the charts in 1981 and 1983 respectively, the latter becoming an unofficial anthem for Australia in the process; INXS recorded their fourth album *The Swing* at the Manor in Oxfordshire in 1984. Others tried studios a little further afield: Hunters and Collectors followed the likes of Ultravox, Eurythmics and Killing Joke by recording their 1983 and 1984 albums at Conny Plank's studio in Germany, while Midnight Oil, having recorded their third and fourth albums in London, switched to Tokyo for *Red Sails in the Sunset*, although again produced by Nick Launay[8]. They, along with INXS, Crowded House, Pseudo Echo, Mental As Anything and others, would have more UK chart success in the late 80s as the Aussie scene moved from a raw pub rock sound (which in Australia had much more positive connotations than in Britain) to a slicker, sharper feel. It was like the old guard being 'lined up like miscreant school kids in front of a higher authority', wrote the critic David Nichols, 'being told in no uncertain terms to Get Modern'[9]. Although this didn't apply to AC/DC who carried on in the same vein regardless. The wave of late 80s success would of course include Kylie Minogue, another London habitué.

*****

By the 1980s, the international dominance of Anglo-American[10], English-language rock and pop had been a fact of life for the previous quarter century. For a band to achieve international success, the song almost certainly had to be in English[11]. This was fine for Scandinavian and Dutch artists who often spoke better English than the British and who also often (*mostly*, in the Swedish case) recorded in English even for their own charts. But it was a challenge for some German and most French, Spanish and Italian groups, even if they *wanted* to break into the UK or US charts. Spanish acts actually had no real need as they had a huge additional Hispanic market in Latin America. In terms of Euro new wave or new pop, the British public was more or less ignorant, labels weren't that interested and the music papers barely covered it. And yet there was of course much that was of interest.

Such was the domination of ABBA in Swedish – and European – pop music from the mid-70s until their split in 1982, it was difficult to see who would fill their international shoes. And for a few years no-one did. In 1984, the 'boys' went off with Tim Rice to record the concept album *Chess*, yielding a Top 20 single 'One Night in Bangkok' (sung by Murray Head), a concert version which toured Europe and then, a year or so later, the celebrated West End musical. The 'girls' meanwhile released solo albums, neither of which set the world alight.

Neither did the enigmatic Virna Lindt, whose 1984 debut album *Shiver* affected a chic 50s/60s Eurovision sound for the even more enigmatic British label, Compact Organization, a decade before lounge, Saint Etienne and Stereolab. It was always difficult to tell fact from fiction with Compact's ZTT-like press releases, but Lindt was apparently an ex-model, actress, designer, journalist and interpreter – everything you'd expect of a coolly beautiful Swede. Sadly she couldn't sing, but it didn't matter, it was a playful, capricious conceit. If irony was a new pop concept, it didn't apply to hard-rockers Europe and soft-rockers Roxette whose international hits, 'The Final Countdown' and 'The Look' came later in the decade. Perhaps the most underrated group at the time was synth duo, Twice A Man. Dan Söderqvist and Karl Gasleben had been proggers in the 70s, formed Twice A Man in 1981 and in 1984 released the fine album, *From a Northern Shore,* and single, 'Across the Ocean', both of which could happily have been on 4AD. They are still going, still good, still largely ignored in Britain.

Up until 1984, Norway's pop credentials were largely confined to their terrible performances at Eurovision Song Contests. 'Norway – nul points' became a running joke, and even now they hold the distinction of finishing last more than any other country. But then along came A-ha. 'Discovered' by British producer Tony Mansfield, they moved to London in 1982. Originally, they hadn't used synths, but England was full of electronic groups so their sound changed accordingly. Debut single 'Take On Me' was released in October 1984 and was a hit in Norway – but nowhere else. "It didn't sound like the hit we thought it should sound like. The chorus didn't sound soaring. There was very little emotion."[12] A new producer (Alan Tarney) and, crucially, *that* video turned things around and the following year it became a global smash. They are still, by a long way, the biggest selling band from Norway and at time of writing the only non-Anglo-American artists to record a James Bond theme song[13].

However, there was more to Norway than A-ha. The small Uniton Records label, for instance, nurtured Fra Lippo Lippi, releasing two early 80s albums and three singles, the last of which, 'Say Something' (1984), attracted the attention of Virgin who ended up releasing an album, *Songs*, early the following year. FLL had started out as very Joy Division but over time became more redolent of China Crisis or Black – mellow, slightly MOR but classy with it. In any case, they made it big, not in Britain, but in the Philippines. The year also marked the debut release by Geir Jenssen, later to be better known as Norway's number one electronic act, Biosphere, but then going by the alias E-man (the name of the Depeche Modey album too).[14]

Sweden's Twice A Man, Norway's A-ha and Iceland's Kukl, featuring a young Björk.

In Denmark the choice was fairly limited. Duo Laid Back were perhaps the best known 'new wave' band of the time and their minimal-funk, drug-referenced[15] 'White Horse' single was a surprise US hit in early 1984. The country did, however, host one of Europe's best-known rock jamborees, Roskilde Festival. Even by 1984 it was well established, with that year's headliners including Lou Reed and Paul Young. (The Smiths had cancelled). The days of Björk, Sigur Ros and countless other ethereal bands who seemed to constitute half the Icelandic population were some way off, but there's a case for 1984 having sowed the seeds of Iceland's remarkable standing as one of the key centres for alternative music. Anarcho-punk group Kukl, featuring Einar Ørn and a 19-year old Björk Guðmundsdóttir, released its debut album *The Eye* on Crass Records that year[16]. It was an extraordinary affair: sounding like a cross between Siouxsie & the Banshees (especially the John McGeogh-style screeching guitar) and Henry Cow, and with a bonkers video for one of the tracks ('Anna'). Björk and Einar would go on to form The Sugarcubes in 1986, after which Björk went solo and the rest is more than Icelandic sagas.

Holland's flirtation with the UK charts – Shocking Blue, Golden Earring, Focus, Pussycat, Father Abraham and the Smurfs, all of whom sung in English, except Focus who yodelled – was largely confined to the 1970s. Late-70s-and-into-the-80s acts like rocker Herman Brood and pop group Gruppo Sportivo who didn't impact on UK or US charts were nonetheless huge at home. As were the naffly-named The Nits[17]. Featuring star keyboardist & producer Robert Jan Stips, their style at this time ranged from new wave ('A Touch of Henry Moore' is Squeeze meets Joe Jackson) to the more Parisian-balladic sound of 'Adieu Sweet Bahnhof', their big hit of 1984. Despite singing in English and achieving considerable success in mainland Europe, they barely registered in the UK or US. The Art Company's cod-reggae 'Susanna' was somehow a UK #12 in 1983 but the album which followed a year later... wasn't.

*****

In West Germany (as it was then), two groups made an impact on the UK charts, and neither of them was Kraftwerk. Following Nena's '99 Luftballons' hit at home in 1983, an English version was recorded with slightly different lyrics (including 'Red' substituted for 'Luft') and to everyone's surprise, not least the band's, it was a UK #1 in February 1984[18]. Alphaville's debut single 'Big in Japan' also went Top 10 in August, named after Holly Johnson's pre-Frankie group and with a video directed by Yello's Dieter Meier. Another 1984 English-singing debutante was the big-haired Modern Talking whose first single 'You're My Heart, You're My Soul' occupied Top 10 positions all over mainland Europe but failed to make an impression in Britain[19]. The same applied to Moti Special (named after a meal in an Indian restaurant the group had in London) whose sophomore single 'Cold Days, Hot Nights' was a hit in Germany. Michael Cretu, their keyboard player, would go on to greater things by producing – and marrying – late 80s German mega-popstar Sandra and then forming 90s chillout sensation Enigma, with Sandra providing the breathy French vocals. Breathy German vocals were the preserve of Gina X, whose deviant debut album, *Yinglish,* came out on the UK's Statik Records, with electronic backing by Zeus B Held (producer of John Foxx and Dead Or Alive) and The Art Of Noise's JJ Jeczalik.

Nena and Madonna, Herbert Grönemeyer and Propaganda.

But West Germany's biggest selling album in 1984 (bigger than *Thriller*) was actor-rockstar Herbert Grönemeyer's *4360 Bochum*, named after his hometown. His first four albums had done nothing, but after starring in Wolfgang Peterson's *Das Boot* in 1982, his fifth went stellar and he concentrated on his music career, which, although hugely successful, was confined largely to German-speaking countries. Grönemeyer didn't provide the excellent music for the U-Boat movie – that was Klaus Doldinger, who was also busy in 1984, working again with Wolfgang Peterson on *The Neverending Story*, the album soundtrack of which included input from Giorgio Moroder and Limahl. Grönemeyer's non-celebrity status in Britain resulted in the shameful occasion when Joe Cocker invited him onstage at a festival in 1985. 'I was flattered, he was always my hero. I got up to sing blues with him and the roadies came and pulled me off. They thought I was a drunk fan, a stage invader'[20]. Nevertheless, Grönemeyer moved to London in the late 90s and set up his own label, Grönland, releasing not just his own music but reissues of Neu!, Harmonia and Holger Czukay amongst others, and he continues to flit between music (duetting with Bono) and acting (a cameo in Anton Corbijn's *Control* for example, which he also part-funded).

The early 80s' Neue Deutsche Welle scene – mostly centred around Düsseldorf but with 'scenettes' in Berlin and Hamburg – saw bands like Trio, Ideal, Rheingold, Palais Schaumburg, Der Plan, S.Y.P.H., Belfegore and Die Toten Hosen achieve a degree of success in their home country. A few more tried their luck by moving to London. DAF had been championed by Zigzag writer Bob Giddens and Mute's Daniel Miller, sleeping on their parents' floors and recording their debut album at Rochdale's Cargo Studios while their second became the first album to be released by Mute. They then released their classic proto-EBM trio of albums for Virgin, before splitting in 1983.

The call of the UK music scene was strong and mostly beneficial, but it also resulted in several bands switching from singing in German (part of what made them different) to English. For example, post-DAF, Robert Görl released a somewhat underwhelming English-language solo album in 1984, featuring Annie Lennox on a couple of tracks. Metal-bashers Die Krupps had downed tools and recorded third album *Entering the Arena* in London. The title said it all really. Belfegore also switched to English, releasing their Conny Plank-produced second, self-titled album on Elektra. Even Propaganda, who despite moving to London, being on the right label in ZTT and putting out the excellent 'Dr Mabuse', had a frustrating time of it playing third fiddle to Frankie and The Art Of Noise. But none of these – not even Propaganda – breached the Top 20.

Some groups decided to stick with German. Holger Hiller licensed his *Ein Bündel Fäulnis in der Grube* (helpfully translated as *A Bunch of Foulness in the Pit*) to Cherry Red in 1984 before beginning a long association with Mute, while Xmal Deutschland released two albums, *Fetisch* (1983) and *Tocsin* (1984), on 4AD and were popular on the UK touring circuit – although were dropped the following year. Einstürzende Neubauten didn't move to London, although they might as well have such was their profile there. By late 1983 they had released *Drawings of Patient O.T.* (on Some Bizzare), swiftly followed by the excellent compilation *Strategies Against Architecture* (on Mute). Guitarist/vocalist Blixa Bargeld had also teamed up with Nick Cave, first in The Birthday Party and, when that dissolved, The Bad Seeds. But the event that probably marked Neubauten's real arrival was their infamous performance at the ICA on 31 January 1984 during which they attempted to drill through the stage and into a supposed tunnel system below which was said to lead to Buckingham Palace. The mayhem – described in the NME as "possibly the best gig since the crucifixion"[21] and which also involved Genesis P-Orridge, Frank Tovey and Some Bizzare's Stevo – lasted 25 minutes before the ICA pulled the plug[22].

Kraftwerk, the German group most Brits might have been able to name (had they not known the true nationality of Boney M), had released the sprightly 'Tour de France' single in 1983, a reflection of their new-found obsession with cycling, and it got a reissue the following year thanks to its inclusion in the film *Breakdance*[23], a continuation of their influence on the new dance genres coming out of Chicago, Detroit and New York. A new album, *Technopop*, was on the verge of being released. According to Karl Bartos, it had been mixed in New York, had a catalogue number and was good to go – but then Hütter and Schneider changed their minds. Was it a loss of confidence, a realisation that they were no longer leading the way? Who can tell, but the fact that it took another two years to see the light of day, in presumably altered form, and was dully retitled *Electric Café* didn't help[24].

Einstürzende Neubauten, and Manuel Göttsching's seminal *E2-E4*.

Other former 'krautrock' artists faced similarly uncertainty and quietude. Neu! and La Düsseldorf had long split up, with Michael Rother (sadly) releasing progressively bland albums of Fairlight faffing and the erratic Klaus Dinger becoming ever more so.[25] Although Cluster had gone into hibernation, 1984 saw its more melodic half, Hans-Joachim Roedelius, release the well-received, piano-dominated *Gift of the Moment* on EG records, his first for a British label. Tangerine Dream had just signed to the London-based Jive Electro, the first album of which – a live double, *Poland* – perfectly captured the end of their Virgin era, before ushering in the beginning of a long, slow slide into new-agey semi-irrelevance, although a deluge of soundtracks – three in 1984 alone – weren't bad. Ashra were similarly going nowhere, although a one-hour track, *E2-E4*, recorded at the end of 1981 by its mainstay, Manuel Göttsching, would eventually be released in 1984. Pretty much ignored at the time[26], it would go on to become a celebrated piece of proto-electronica, bridging the gap between minimalist instrumental prog and minimalist instrumental dance.

Formed in 1979 by Carlos Peron and Boris Blank, then bringing in dilettante Dieter Meier on vocals and lyrics, Swiss group Yello steadily developed over three alternative electronic albums, until Peron left to go solo in 1983. It was a watershed year, as Blank and Meier effectively turned Yello into a polished pop group – albeit an idiosyncratic one. An EP, *Live at the Roxy*, recorded in New York in December, was released in 1984 while the duo worked on their fourth album, *Stella*, through to the summer. Set for release in October (though inexplicably put back to January 1985), it was packed with irresistible, dance-friendly songs: 'Desire', 'Vicious Games' and 'Oh Yeah' would all do well in the club charts. Given Meier's pin-stripe suits, banker's moustache and bizarre background (performance artist, poker player, industrialist), and Blank's uncanny resemblance to Mexican comic, Catinflas, you could never be sure how serious they were being. Well actually you could: they

320

weren't. Somehow it all worked and they continued with the formula for many years, often working with guest vocalists like Shirley Bassey and Billy Mackenzie.

If the Swiss music scene was small, the Austrian one was tiny, seemingly forever mothballed by the country's classical music heritage – until Johann Hölzel, aka Falco, whose first record, the German-language 'Der Kommissar', was a huge 1982 hit across Europe, except of course in the UK, followed by a successful album. He got it wrong with single and album *Junger Römer* in 1984, but 'Rock Me Amadeus' put it right again two years later (#1 virtually everywhere, including UK and US). The Mozart reference seemed compulsory.

Yello's stellar Stella, Lizzy Mercier Descloux and Etienne Daho.

French pop was a puzzle to the British record buying public. There was Serge Gainsbourg of course and those 70s synth hits by Jean Michel Jarre, Space and Cerrone, but they were either in English or instrumental, and nobody realised the last two were French anyway. This was all a shame as there was much that was great in French nouvelle vague in 1984. Etienne Daho's 'Weekend à Rome' hit was sultry pop, and was later turned into 'She's On the Phone' by Saint Etienne. Vienna's 'Say You Love Me (Tu as Juré)' was a kind of French Depeche Mode, which made some sort of sense as singer Odile Aeias was dating Martin Gore at the time. KaS Product had just released the thrillingly tense *By Pass*, a sort of Soft Cell-meets-Suicide, recorded in New York, and it helped that he looked like Phil Oakey and she sang in English.

Taxi Girl's 'Dites-le Fort' was leftfield and featured Mirwais Ahmadazai, who would be 'rediscovered' by Madonna in the late 90s. Lizzy Mercier Descloux released the infectiously vivacious South African- and Bow Wow Wow-influenced *Zulu Rock*, recorded in Johannesburg and London, one of the last records to appear on the New York-based ZE Records which had been set up by Frenchman Michel Esteban and Brit Michael Zilkha. As for Gainsbourg, we could expect nothing less than a single called 'Lemon Incest', sung with his then 12-year-old daughter Charlotte (which hit #2 in the French charts). But ultimately, many young French teens and vingtquelquechoses looking for existentialist pop turned to British bands like Depeche Mode, The Cure and Siouxsie & the Banshees. Come the new millennium, French group Nouvelle Vague would start a whole career based on bossanova covers of mainly British post-punk.

321

However, the closest post-punk pop connection between mainland Europe and Britain was Belgium. The pogo-ing Plastic Bertrand had a UK Top 10 with 'Ça Plane Pour Moi' in 1978[27], and the equally amusing Telex had had some minor UK success with their stripped-down YMO-meets-Sparks synthpop soon after (although by 1984's *Toujours l'Amour* they were past their best[28]). But, aside from geographical proximity, the most decisive link was created by two young anglophiles, Michel Duval and Annik Honoré. In 1979 Honoré moved briefly to London, got a secretarial job at the Belgian Embassy by day and saw bands by night, including Joy Division. On returning to Belgium, her long-distance relationship with Ian Curtis, arranging concerts at Plan K (a former refinery next to a canal on – wait for it – Rue de Manchester in Brussels) and the setting up, with Duval, of Factory Benelux and Les Disques du Crépuscule in the summer of 1980 was the real starting point of a mutual love affair between British and Belgian post-punk scenes, as strong as French band Nouvelle Vague's two decades on.

Factory Benelux started off by releasing a mixture of exclusive or cast-off singles and albums by Factory artists but later simply licensed existing Factory releases. In 1984, a dozen records would include the usual suspects: New Order, A Certain Ratio, Durutti Column etc. Crépuscule, however, was something else: a fantastic, wholly individual label. It looked great, courtesy of designer Benoît Hennebert who established a graphic house style as impressive as Peter Saville's for Factory or 23 Envelope's for 4AD. But it was the eclectic approach to A&R that made them so unique, signalled from the off with their first release, the beautifully packaged cassette compilation, *From Brussels With Love*. Focussing heavily on music from across the channel, it featured not only Factory favourites and other new wavers like John Foxx, Thomas Dolby and Richard Jobson, but also the then virtually unknown minimalist composers Harold Budd, Gavin Bryars and Michael Nyman. There were even interviews with Brian Eno and actress Jeanne Moreau. Perhaps only Cherry Red in the UK was casting its net as wide. Subsequent releases would include Cabaret Voltaire, Bill Nelson, Paul Haig and Josef K, plus an increasing number of Belgian groups like Marine (who would become Allez Allez), Soft Verdict and The Names, as well as Antena from France and Tuxedomoon and Anna Domino from the States.

In 1984, Crépuscule released a dozen or so singles and albums and by this time, aside from the British contingent – Paul Haig, James Cuts, Pleasure Ground (an Alan Rankine side-project) and a spoken-word album by Richard Jobson – there was a strong showing from further afield. Soft Verdict was an ensemble created by Belgian composer Wim Mertens. They operated in roughly the same musical field as Michael Nyman: short, accessible tracks of repetitive, minimal music using both chamber instruments and electronic keyboards. 1984 was the year Mertens established himself thanks to his score for Jan Fabre's marathon alt-opera, *The Power of Theatrical Madness*[29]. From the four hours of music, Crépuscule managed to contrive a 12-inch single for sale at the shows and Mertens then went on to record the excellent *Maximising the Audience*. It would be his last with Soft Verdict; from then on it would be his name only.

Arguably, Crépuscule's most successful artist was Parisian, Isabelle Powaga. Initially she was part of the short-lived, electro-bossanova trio, Antena, their first single being a coolly dry, minimal version of 'The Boy from Ipanema' recorded at John Foxx's studio in London in 1982. Live appearances with the likes of Cabaret Voltaire, and a charmingly quirky mini-album of skewed latinesque home-penned songs followed, but they were perhaps too niche. Reducing to a duo and switching to a more Chic style, 'Be-Pop' and 'Life is Too Short' were produced by Martin Hayles, the first potentially benefitting from a licensing deal with Island in late 1983, the second released on Phonogram's Mercury imprint in early 1984. The group moved to London, hoping to ride the current latin-jazz wave, and it also helped that Isabelle sang in English.[30] An album was recorded, but Mercury cooled and the album was shelved. Dispirited, they returned to Crépuscule in Brussels, the group became a solo project and the excellent rejected album was eventually released as *En Cavale* by *Isabelle* Antena – the name she would use from now on. It was a tough year or so, and a lesson learned: the UK music industry can be fickle. She's since gone on to achieve success in France and Japan (in the latter's case initially through Crépuscule's Tokyo-based sister-label).

Belgium's excellent Les Disques du Crépuscule, home to Isabelle Antena and Anna Domino.

Crépuscule had another female artist with a Japanese connection, and she wasn't Belgian either. Anna Domino (real name Anna Taylor) was born in Tokyo where her father was serving in the US army, but was on the move again soon afterwards, arriving in New York in the late 70s where she started making music. A demo tape ended up at Crépuscule and following an NME single of the week, 'Trust in Love', she released the mini-album *East & West* in February 1984 followed by the obsoletely spelled *Rythm* EP in May, backed by Virginia Astley, Tuxedomoon's Blaine L Reininger and Luc Van Acker[31] amongst others. Both records showcased a singer who was half New Yorker with attitude, half Euro chanteuse suffering from ennui. It was an alluring combination and the four albums that followed between 1986 and 1990 were of a similar high standard[32]. Sadly, her career thereafter would be patchy (quantity- rather than quality-wise).

Fellow Americans Tuxedomoon had relocated to Brussels in the early 80s, releasing their third album, *Divine*, on Crépuscule's Operation Twilight offshoot in 1982. Two years later, there were solo records by Blaine L Reininger (the new-wavey *Night Air*) and Winston Tong (*Theoretically Chinese*). The latter was lush and accessible, produced by Alan Rankine and with contributions from New Order's Steven Morris, Jah Wobble and Dave Formula (ex-Magazine) – a far cry from Tuxedomoon's more experimental oeuvre. There were other sub-labels. L.A.Y.L.A.H. put out records by British experimental artists Current 93, Nurse With Wound, Coil, Robert Haigh and The Hafler Trio amongst others, 1984 being its first full year of operation. And then there was él Benelux and the short-lived UK-based Operation Afterglow run by Philip Hoare, before he became a successful writer and academic.

One could be forgiven for thinking that the Belgian music scene revolved around Crépuscule and its myriad subsidiaries, but there was much much more. We've already (in Chapter 7) seen how EBM (Electronic Body Music) took route in the clubs of Brussels and Antwerp, but 1984 also saw the formation of Belgium's R&S label which would specialize in new beat and electronica. But not yet. Its first release was the embarrassingly bad Big Tony performing a cover of 'Can't Get Enough of Your Love, Babe'. The second half of the 80s, however, would see a series of largely underground 12-inchers released by CJ Bolland, David Morley and others; and in the 90s Aphex Twin, Biosphere, System 7, together with its main sub-label Apollo Records. These were much less EBM and much more IDM, the post-rave Intelligent Dance Music sub-genre which Britain's Warp label was also nurturing.

Finally, and possibly even more important than Crépuscule, certainly in terms of its promotion of music from 'non-rock' countries, Crammed Discs were founded in 1980 by Belgian musician Marc Hollander. Early releases included his own avant-garde group Aksak Maboul and the spikily comic The Honeymoon Killers. By 1984, Israeli-Belgians Minimal Compact were one of their most active artists, releasing *Deadly Weapons* that year and *Raging Souls* the next (the latter produced by Wire's Colin Newman, who moved to Brussels and would later work with and marry their bass player Malka Spiegel). A pivotal year for Crammed, 1984 saw the creation of their Made To Measure 'composer' series. As the label explained: 'The rationale behind the MTM series was to release music which had been or could have been written as illustration for films, theatre plays, choreographies etc'. Volume 1 featured Aksak Maboul, Minimal Compact and Tuxedomoon, and further albums would host Hector Zazou, Benjamin Lew, Sussan Deyhim & Richard Horowitz, David Cunningham and many others[33]. Crammed would go onto embrace dozens of musical genres. At time of writing they have released 325 albums by artists from all over the world.

*****

Thanks to the omnipresent US military bases, Japan had been a huge market for western style pop and rock ever since the dawn of rock 'n' roll. Young Japanese either bought them on import or as exquisitely re-packaged domestic releases. Japanese music fans have a well-earned reputation for being obsessive and ultra-curious, creating cliques around obscure genres, tracking down everything. Concert tours, even by little-known western artists, would be sold out. If your career was on the wane back home or if you were in need of a cash injection or ego massage, then Japan was the place. Its homegrown artists, whether western sounding or the more manufactured J-pop, were equally popular, but almost entirely confined to the domestic market. Very very few crossed over internationally. The Sadistic Mika Band had a modicum of success in the UK in the 70s, their albums produced by Chris Thomas, released on Harvest and were the first Japanese band ever to tour Britain, supporting Roxy Music. However, it was the all-electronic Yellow Magic Orchestra in the early 80s who made more of an impression. That said, their only UK hit was 'Computer Game' which peaked at #17 in 1980 and as a group they were always somehow less than the sum of their very creative parts. But their influence on artists like Japan, Bill Nelson and Simon Jeffes was considerable.[34] The Japan-Japan link would remain long after the British band split up at the end of 1982, and after YMO took an extended breather at the end of the following year, which was marked by a double live album, *After Service,* released in 1984 and featuring ABC's David Palmer on drums.

YMO go solo: Sakamoto's *Ongaku Zukan*, Takahashi's *Wild and Moody*, and Hosono's *S-F-X*.

YMO's three individual members had always juggled group and solo projects but now they were able to indulge themselves. Ryuichi Sakamoto had scored the music for *Merry Christmas, Mr Lawrence* (the title theme of which became the exquisite single 'Forbidden Colours' with lyrics and vocals by David Sylvian), as well as acting in it alongside David Bowie. In 1984 he released *Ongaku Zukan*, initially only available in Japan, though it would resurface on Virgin in a slightly different (tighter, better) version two years later as *Illustrated Musical Encyclopedia*, also featuring Thomas Dolby[35]. A drummer himself, Yukihiro Takahashi had a penchant for working with English percussionists: with David Palmer, again, on the live *Time and Place* and with Steve Jansen, out of a job with Japan, on the patchily brilliant *Wild and Moody.* Also playing on both was Bill Nelson who would license the latter album for his Cocteau label (and, while we're about it, marry Takahashi's former wife, Emiko). Haruomi Hosono mixed less with the Brits and more with the French, co-producing Parisian duo Mikado's only (eponymous) album[36] while finding time to release two solo albums, the conventionally toe-tapping *S-F-X*, and the supremely quirky and almost unlistenable *Video Game Music*, which did what it said on the tin. Other groups like Sandii and the Sunsetz and Ippu-Do also appeared briefly on Britain's pop radar[37].

It is often said that humour doesn't travel well, but nobody told Kazuko Hohki when she moved from Tokyo to London in the late 70s. With Kazumi Taguchi, the pair eventually formed Frank Chickens and became regulars at Edinburgh's Fringe Festival. But 1984 was the year that defined them, turning what was essentially a cabaret act into a pop group and releasing an album and two singles. Backed by improv musicians Steve Beresford, David Toop and Dave Hunt amongst others, the result was surprisingly catchy pop with lyrics that played on western perceptions of Japanese popular culture (ninjas, enka and a giant moth called Mothra for example). They even made it into John Peel's Festive 50) and *Smash Hits*, whose conclusion 'Hard to tell if they're making fun of themselves or of us' was spot on.

Chapter 27: Band Aid
1984's denouement

I'm sure it's impossible to write flippantly about something as fundamentally dreadful as the Ethiopia famine.[1]
Melody Maker

One can have great concern for the people of Ethiopia, but it's another thing to inflict daily torture on the people of Great Britain.[2]
Morrissey

The greatest example of the coming together of pop and 'politics' was at the tail end of 1984: Band Aid. Except that it *wasn't* political in as much that it wasn't against something that the Government was directly accountable for. It was, as its central protagonist Bob Geldof frequently pointed out, above politics and more about being pro than contra. It could so easily have turned into a finger-pointing exercise, presenting petitions to No.10 and demanding an increase in aid to Ethiopia and other famine-stricken countries. The fact that it didn't, along of course with the millions of pounds raised and lives saved, was one of its great achievements – that direct action worked.

Most people of a certain age know the story of how Bob Geldof was sitting at home on Tuesday 23 October, watching a BBC news report by Michael Buerck about the famine in Ethiopia. Like everyone, Geldof was appalled. It put his own situation as a declining pop star into some perspective. He brooded and resolved to do *something*. The following morning Paula Yates flew off to Newcastle to film that week's The Tube, but not before leaving a note on the fridge that said "Ethiopia. Everyone who visits this house from today onwards will be asked to give £5 until we have raised £200 for famine relief". Geldof rang her in Newcastle and Midge Ure happened to be there. They got talking and arranged to have lunch the following Monday where the idea of making a charity record came together, but it had to be in time for Christmas. The idea of covering something well-known wouldn't work as they'd have to pay royalties. So together they wrote a song and then Geldof started phoning around for people more famous than he was to join in, both knowing that not many people would have bought a charity record by either of them. It had to have stars. Known for his big mouth, Geldof proceeded to use it to great effect: asking, begging and bullying stars to join. He then asked, begged and bullied a studio (Sarm West), label (Phonogram), cover artist (Peter Blake, who'd co-created probably the most famous album cover of all time), a record pressing factory and printer, all to provide their services for free, or as near as. He even got the Government to 'waive' VAT (strictly speaking, it wasn't waived, but the Government made an equivalent donation), although only after much cajoling.

The basic backing tracks had been recorded at Midge Ure's home-studio before he, Geldof and a phalanx of pop stars descended on Sarm West in Notting Hill on Sunday 25 November, less than three weeks after Geldof and Ure's lunch. Some arrived in limos, Sting walked in clutching the Sunday papers, Bananarama turned up in an old VW Golf, most had been up late the night before, and a flame-haired Boy George turned up in the evening having been woken up in New York by Geldof on the phone and told in no uncertain terms to 'get his arse to London'. Egos were checked in at the cloakroom, but drugs, booze and, above all, hairspray were on hand for those in need. In the room was the cream of British pop – Duran Duran, Spandau Ballet, George Michael, Sting, Bono, Paul Weller, Phil Collins, Paul Young, Bananarama, Heaven 17… and some oddities like the American acts Kool and the Gang (who happened to be in Phonogram's office when Geldof was phoning people up) and singer Jody Watley who'd just moved to England; the fading Marilyn, who wasn't invited but turned up anyway, possibly hoping it would miraculously bring him back into the limelight (it didn't); and Status Quo (who'd actually split up). Others who couldn't make it recorded messages for the B-side.

The Band Aid line-up, photographed during the song's recording on 25 November 1984

The song itself was actually half-decent. It was modern (the looped beat lifted from Tears For Fears' 'The Hurting'), uplifting, a bit like a cool carol. Being a carol, albeit a late 20th Century one, it was a mass sing-in. Some got a line each – Bono's, Boy George's and Paul Young's are the ones most people remember – while others were happy to muck in with the chorus. Phil Collins gave a masterclass in drumming, but most of the rest of it was by Midge Ure, who also stayed up all night mixing it. It was quite deliberately a Christmas single, a cash-in on the tradition of the Christmas #1 which was steeped in British pop history and always sold well. They called the group Band Aid. It was almost called Food For Thought.

Although responding to the Ethiopian famine, the scope of the lyrics was continental ('And there won't be snow in Africa this Christmastime'), even global ('Feed the

328

world'). It was a strange mix of saccharine and serious, sometimes in the same line ('And the Christmas bells that ring there are the clanging chimes of doom'), with Bono assigned a particularly unfortunate line ('Well, tonight thank God it's them instead of you') which he had to be twice persuaded to sing. Yes, you could criticize the words, even the title – around 380 million African Christians (nearly half of the continent's population) certainly *did* know it was Christmas time – but it made an arresting change from mistletoe and wine. And of course it wasn't written with Ivor Novello awards in mind. Its sole purpose was to raise cash. As much cash as possible.

'Do They Know It's Christmas?' was released on Monday 3 December, less than six weeks after Geldof had watched Michael Buerck's report and just a week after the recording session. It was an astonishingly quick turnaround. It was also an astonishingly quick seller: the fastest-selling single of all time. It had longevity too. The following Christmas it was re-released; then there was a Band Aid II featuring a different line-up in 1989, Band Aid 20 in 2004 and Band Aid 30 in 2014. The original record sold four million copies in the UK and a further eight million around the world. Everyone bought the record, even if they didn't like it.

Bob Geldof and Midge Ure's mad idea becomes reality.

Then there was the question of how to collect the money and what to spend it on. Geldof and Ure had to go on a crash course in running a charity and working with other NGOs, and Geldof's meetings with politicians would more often than not end in exasperation, if not castigation. There were question marks about the lack of black artists on the record (just the Americans Kool and the Gang and Jo Watley), prompting the formation of a kind of Anglo-French supergroup featuring members of The Specials, Madness, UB40, General Public and Afrodiziak from one side of the Channel, and an all-star cast of mainly West African musicians on the other.[3] Their single, 'Starvation / Tam Tam Pour l'Ethiopie', was recorded in December while 'Do They Know It's Christmas?' was top of the charts, but for some reason wasn't released until March the following year. On the whole, however, most people naturally sympathised with Geldof's situation. USA for Africa's 'We Are the World', recorded in January 1985, addressed the issue head on with a line-up that was basically half white, half black. Where things got rather more heated was with Live Aid, particularly the Wembley show. One can sympathise with Geldof again, going for famous stars and the fact that there weren't that many mega-selling British black acts at the time[4] and that some were approached but declined, perhaps because they didn't want to be the token black act. It was kind of balanced up by the Philadelphia show, but still, it seemed a missed opportunity.

Band Aid was a turning point for 80s pop. It was the first big pop charity single, after which a flood of others followed: USA for Africa's 'We Are the World'; Canadian supergroup Northern Lights' Tears Are Not Enough' (including the inevitable verse in French); the painfully named Hear'n Aid's 'Stars' (cruelly but amusingly described as "a stage-long knee-slide straight into the waiting arms of self-parody"[5]); Tears For Fear's 'Everybody Wants to Run the World' (Sport Aid); Cliff Richard and The Young Ones' 'Living Doll' (Comic Relief) – and these were just for Ethiopia. There were also singles responding to other disasters, particularly in Britain: The Crowd's 'You'll Never Walk Alone' (Bradford City FC fire), Ferry Aid's 'Let It Be' (Zeebrugge ferry disaster), a group of Liverpool artists' 'Ferry 'Cross the Mersey' (Hillsborough disaster). Of course there were benefit records in other countries too, but Britain did seem to rather corner the market. The biggest-selling charity single of all time was Elton John's 'Candle in the Wind 1997', selling a staggering 33 million copies and raising copious amounts for the Diana Princess of Wales Memorial Fund.

There were concerts too. Most people forget that there was a major Benefit for Ethiopia at the Royal Albert Hall the day before the Band Aid single came out (and way before Live Aid), featuring a motley line-up of Julian Lennon, Nick Heyward, Feargal Sharkey, Mike Rutherford and Alvin Stardust. Perhaps even less known was a benefit in Sheffield the same month including the Human League's first concert in two years, complete with live drums and rock guitars. But like the records, they soon went beyond famine to include Farm Aid, The Prince's Trust, Self Aid, NetAid, ChildLine, Tsunami Aid and so on. Some were more 'political' than others. The Conspiracy of Hope Tour in June 1986, for example (involving U2, Sting, Bryan Adams, Peter Gabriel, Lou Reed and many others), was not about raising funds but simply to increase awareness of human rights and the work of Amnesty International[6]. And there were yet more initiatives that didn't involve records or concerts, like Pete Townsend's anti-heroin campaign.

Of course, being included in something that was not just worthy but all over the media was a useful career move, but most of the musicians seemed to get involved in Band Aid for genuinely altruistic reasons. Most had been called directly by Geldof, not through the filter of management, and at the time there was no real precedent. Later, when charity fatigue set in, musicians had to think carefully about which cause they should support. But in 1984, it wasn't in the handbook.

Early in the new millennium, following a solo concert, Midge Ure received a card backstage. 'On the front was a picture of a 19-year-old black girl. The message was simple: 'You don't know me but this is a girl who received an education via Band Aid. She has just passed her degree, and I thought you might want to see what she looks like…'. I'm often asked, 'Did Band Aid make a difference?' and there was the answer. That girl is the difference. She is alive'.[7]

Chapter 28: Epilogue
1985 and all that

After Live Aid, no record company wanted another Nik Kershaw, or another Yazoo. They wanted another U2, another Sting.[1]
Dylan Jones

Pop culture used to be like LSD – different, eye-opening and reasonably dangerous. It's now like crack – isolating, wasteful and with no redeeming qualities whatsoever.[2]
Peter Saville

'One thing', said Tod. 'How did we get into this mess?'
Anthony Burgess *1985*

As 1985 dawned, new pop and post-punk faded, rock returned, and hip-hop became the dominant force in dance music even if it wasn't yet mainstream. The novelty of synthpop was over. Pale, androgynous men standing statically behind a synth were out; mobile guitar-wielding frontmen were back in, or in a ghastly hybrid variation, strutted the stage playing keytars. Eurythmics got it straight away, shifting from the quirky synthpop of *Sweet Dreams* and *Touch* to the gospel rock of *Be Yourself Tonight* complete with guest appearances by soul legends Stevie Wonder and Aretha Franklin. Annie Lennox may still have been androgynous, but it was the 'right' way round: guys being girls was becoming a bit passé, girls being guys was still somehow novel – Annie as Elvis at the Grammys being a case in point.

Tears For Fears were now heavy on the guitars and their expansive, anthemic songs became perfectly suited to American FM radio, even if (in their video for the huge-selling 'Everybody Wants To Rule The World') their open-top convertible driven under big American skies and parked outside a diner was a quaint Austin-Healey 3000. Depeche Mode adopted a different tact, beefing up their synths and samplers to sound like a rock band, inevitably bringing in guitars a bit later on. The biggest surprise was how frontman Dave Gahan transformed himself from wimpy boy next door into universal rock god. Others also diversified, less successfully, or split up.

New pop's artifice fell out of favour. Duran Duran split into factions; Spandau Ballet moved from Chrysalis to CBS and from soulboy to rock with unimpressive results; Thompson Twins' Tom Bailey had a nervous breakdown and the group drifted into irrelevance; Wham! split up in 1986, delayed for long enough to ensure Andrew Ridgely would never have to work again. Although hardly new pop, XTC's Andy Partridge spoke for many towards the end of 1984: 'Punk was necessary and another big bang is necessary now. To clear away the likes of, well, us I suppose...'[3]

It was arguable whether new pop had simply run its course or whether the return of rock was the nail in the coffin. A bit of both probably. In any case, in the US the authenticity-versus-artifice debate was in many ways a reaction to the Second British Invasion and its emphasis on style and escapism. Ronald Reagan's landslide second presidential victory brought with it a conservative, patriotic entrenchment with country music and a backward-looking rock reasserting itself. Artists were real men making real music. REO Speedwagon, Foreigner, ZZ Top, Bryan Adams, John Mellencamp all enjoyed revivals, none more so than Bruce Springsteen. Alternative acts like Violent Femmes and some of the hardcore bands also started looking back to America's rock heritage. Outside the main cities patriotism and homophobia became bedfellows: 'Flag wavers vs fag wavers', as Joe Carducci of the SST label said, clearly a dig at the British 'haircut bands'.[4] Even R.E.M. weighed in, Peter Buck penning an article entitled 'The True Spirit of American Rock' for US magazine Record and later telling British fanzine Jamming: 'Suddenly an audience has sprung up who don't listen to the British invasion bullshit and are slowly returning to American groups.'[5] Inside the main cities, it was different with Madonna, Prince and hip-hop taking pop and dance's reins.

In Britain the term 'rockist' had been used in a pejorative way by the media, from NME to Smash Hits, but bands like U2 and Simple Minds were now moving into exactly that are(n)a. Where new pop embraced androgyny, rockism accentuated gender difference. As Simon Frith wrote, 'Part of the appeal of the new generation of guitar/pub/roots bands [was] their restatement of old rock & roll truths of sex and gender – rutting, romantic men, mysterious, deceptive women'.[6] A slightly different take on authenticity came from The Smiths. They weren't rockist, but they were against new pop and its attendant synths and videos, and instead plunged themselves into a reverie of late 50s and 60s kitchen sink drama.

One of the exciting things about post-punk, and particularly synthpop with its startlingly radical instrumentation and sound, was its newness, its ability to mix things up, its urge to look forwards. There had literally been nothing like The Human League, The Pop Group or Throbbing Gristle before. Even a mainstream band like Frankie Goes To Hollywood, thanks largely to their gargantuan hi-tech sound, was unprecedented. But when post-punk gave way to indie, the new generation of bands went for a thinner sound and looked backwards, specifically to the 60s. The Jesus and Mary Chain may have reacted against synthpop, and their use of feedback was initially quite shocking, but underneath was a Ronettes and Beach Boys foundation.

The Creation roster dispensed with the feedback and went straight for the 12-string psychedelia of The Byrds, but in truth, bands like The Jasmine Minks, The Pastels and The Loft were resolutely underground for the rest of the 80s. There was a certain amount of 'emperor's new clothes' about this scene. Bill Drummond, working for Warner Brothers at the time, didn't get it, despite Alan McGee's constant evangelising: 'I thought, this is rubbish […], what are you talking about, 'This is the greatest this that and the other'. I can't hear it, these are badly made records, cheaply made records.'[7] It wasn't until the early 90s that Primal Scream, My Bloody Valentine and Oasis became successful. Other indie bands were collected and pigeonholed on the NME's well-intentioned C86. As a successor to post-punk, it seemed fey and wimpy – the very charges being levelled against the synthpop groups.

Indie did, however, appeal to a generation who were too young for punk or post-punk, but still saw it as a genuine alternative to the mainstream. As youth culture documenter Sam Knee wrote, 'It was the last wave of the new wave before the whole E thing came barging in, lobotomizing the youth into a sterile conformity'[8], 'giving way to American imports (such as riot grrrl and grunge) or a diluted state of insipid regurgitation (britpop)'[9]. And it was more interesting than the creeping in of polite, watered-down white soul by groups like Curiosity Killed the Cat, Wet Wet Wet, Simply Red, Hue and Cry, Johnny Hates Jazz and Deacon Blue, who were typical of the second half of the 80s.

*****

The event which truly reflected the zeitgeist and reinforced the divide was of course Live Aid. 'It certainly encouraged the music industry to look away from frail-looking synth duos and concentrate on the kind of rock acts who could carve themselves a proper stadium career'[10]. Nick Heyward – no synthpop artist but at the heart of new pop – was scathing: 'It created an aristocracy, attended by Princess Di. Clapton, Phil Collins, and all hanging out with the Royal Family. Sick making.'[11] Adam Ant, who, unlike Heyward, was invited, though only got to perform one song, went even further: 'Doing that show was the biggest f**king mistake in the world. Knighthoods were made, Bono got it made, and it was a waste of f**king time. It was the end of rock 'n' roll.'[12] There was an element of sour grapes – Adam Ant should really have performed a crowd-pleaser rather than the untested 'Vive Le Rock' – but they had a point.

Of course, the humanitarian sentiment behind it all was unarguable, but it signified another trend. Music was beginning to turn away from the political engagement that had so characterized 1984 and the half-dozen years before that, 'but Live Aid hastened that process, replacing politics with charity, abandoning commitment for the more nebulous concept of caring'[13]. Singles-wise, 1985 was dominated by charity records: USA For Africa's 'We Are the World', Bowie and Jagger's 'Dancing in the Street', Hear 'n Aid's 'Stars', The Crowd's 'You'll Never Walk Alone', Dionne Warwick, Stevie Wonder, Gladys Knight & Elton John's 'That's What Friends Are For' and so on. It also had an effect on the political establishment. Happy to be by-passed by charitable actions, in line with the Thatcherite devolvement of state responsibilities to individuals or the private sector, it became increasingly aware of the power of rock and pop in contributing to the economy and Britain's soft power (Norman Tebbit gave a special BPI award to Elton John and Wham! in January 1986 for playing in Russia and China) and attracting the youth vote (Labour's Red Wedge tour featuring Weller, Bragg and others).

Live Aid also made rock musicianship and middle age fashionable again. The performances of Status Quo, Queen, David Bowie and The Who (and that was just at Wembley, never mind the dinosaurs in Philadelphia) shattered the notion that rock music, like a shark, had to continually move forward to survive. The age of the back catalogue, conveniently re-released on CD, and the long-serving artist as *brand* had arrived. The record industry didn't have to put all their time, money and energy into new stuff; they could simply exploit and re-package the old. And scale it up. As David Hepworth wrote, '1985 was the year the scale of rock changed the nature of rock. The bigger the show is, the more it's about ritual than content'[14].

By March 1985, Thatcher had beaten the miners and, for those on the left, including most artists and musicians, a certain defeatism set in, accentuated by the apparent ineffectuality of the Red Wedge tour and the Conservative party's third election victory in 1987. The vibrant counter-culture which had made the early 80s so interesting effectively disappeared. Not all musicians were dispirited; some were excited by the spirit of entrepreneurism which seemed to be in the air. Stock Aitken Waterman's production line pop became firmly established; their slogan, The Sound of a Bright Young Britain, even sounded like the Young Tories. They boasted it took 40 minutes to write and record Kylie Minogue's 'I Should be so Lucky', and it sounded like it.

The first two months of 1985's UK singles charts were dominated by Foreigner's 'I Want To Know What Love Is' and Elaine Paige & Barbara Dickson's 'I Know Him So Well'. Of course, every year has more than its fair share of top ten tosh. 1984 had 'Agadoo', 'That's Livin' Alright' and 'We All Stand Together' to name but a few, and many would add million-sellers 'Hello' and 'I Just Called to Say I Love You'. And there were also, of course, some gems in 1985 – Kate Bush's *The Hounds of Love,* Pet Shop Boys' superior, re-released 'West End Girls', New Order's *Low-Life,* The Cure's *The Head on the Door,* Propaganda's much-delayed debut album to name a few – as well as moments of innovation in the rest of the decade, especially in dance music. However, it is undeniable that popular music, as a genre embracing a number of distinct strands, lost its way, not least in the *alternative* scene. John Peel spoke for many when he drolly admitted, 'I don't even like the records I like'. Angry, urgent post-punk was making way for languid, largely apolitical indie, and the once thriving independent labels were struggling to compete, losing their artists to, or forced to make deals with, the majors while at the same time trying to expand and diversify.

Even the label that seemed to have the perfect combination of prankster aesthetics and enviable sales turned sour. 'For me', admitted Paul Morley, 'the disappointment with ZTT and Frankie is that I'd got a plan that I wanted to develop over ten, fifteen years. I planned for a quiet period after Frankie's preposterous and absurd beginning. I signed a 'systems music', minimalist composer, Andrew Poppy, and a French torch singer, Anne Pigalle. But because it got so successful so early it became a business thing very quickly […] I had all these ideas and plans, and then The Art Of Noise left ZTT and became a normal group, a novelty group, everything I hated'.[15]

Street culture also underwent significant change. Fashion became more about expensive labels rather than the creative homespun clothes of punk and the second-hand dandyism of the new romantics. Indie wore casual, hip-hop sported sportswear, and, later on, acid house adopted baggy. There were no new pantomimed Adam Ants, kimonoed Boy Georges, ragamuffin Haysi Fantayzees or gypsied Kevin Rowlands. Chains and brands were in. So too shoulder pads and Armani suits, big hair and mullets. Beards were still a fashion no-no, but stubble became almost de-rigueur. Part of the problem was that the style media, which hadn't existed five years earlier, was now a crowded market and they were all saying much the same thing, and to a unisex readership – men became consumers like women. Britain changed from a nation of shopkeepers to a nation of shoppers. Supermarkets became superstores, models became supermodels, cinemas became multiplexes, cereals became healthfoods, and people started drinking bottled water and cappuccinos. 'Britain is now more like everywhere else', wrote 80s style guru Robert Elms, 'more affluent and easy-going, more sophisticated and sensible, more materialistic and meritocratic, […] Less creative, less well-dressed'[16]. He was actually writing in 2005 about the Britain of that time but it could just have easily applied to 1985.

Clubs became less exclusive, clubbers dressed down and everyone was welcome. In a way, Live Aid and warehouse parties ushered in that communal, egalitarian spirit. People had been given permission to be mainstream and this would reach a peak with rave culture as the 80s turned into the 90s. However, there was also plenty to keep you at home. By the end of 1984, the UK had more personal computers per household than anywhere in the world. A lot of young people who bought records also bought computer games, which became ever more sophisticated as the years passed. For many, the imagined worlds conjured up by the music and lyrics of pop and rock became superseded by the technofantasy worlds of Tomb Raider and Super Mario. Football culture went mainstream. In the 80s it had lurched from one disaster after another, but come the 90s with the advent of the Premier League, blanket coverage on Sky TV, communal viewing in chain pubs, and of course big, big money, it seemed everywhere, paralleling the lad culture of sportswear, britpop and magazines like Loaded, FHM and Maxim. These monthlies swallowed up some of the readers who had previously bought the weekly music papers and fanzines which had disappeared in the early part of the decade. True, dance culture has gone from strength to strength, there was jungle, trip-hop, even a renewed interest in folk. But by the end of the century, celebrity culture, reality TV and Pop Idol had taken over, experienced through the prism of the internet, multi-channel flatscreens and eventually smartphones. Everything is now available, but little holds our attention.

*****

What no-one could have predicted was the 80s revival, the tenacity and longevity of which has been extraordinary. As mentioned earlier, many if not most of the bands who'd had their heyday in the first half of the 80s went into extended hibernation in the 90s, only to re-appear, bleary eyed in the 00s. It seemed to coincide with musicians of a certain age finding that they could actually make a decent living out of playing live again, when previously touring had been a loss-leader for selling records. There appeared to be an audience, both patient fiftysomethings with disposable income, and a younger public who were hip to analogue synths and 'got' vinyl. And there were new and practical outlets (own labels, crowdfunding, bandcamp etc) for releasing new stuff outside the largely discredited traditional music industry. True, there had been a proliferation of tribute bands in the 90s interim, but from around 2010 the real McCoy was back and the 80s revival kicked off in earnest.

ABC, Human League, Heaven 17, OMD, Culture Club, Howard Jones, Bananarama, Alison Moyet, Midge Ure, A Flock Of Seagulls and scores of others play the 80s revival tours, often several on the same bill, most also releasing new albums. Others like Duran Duran, The Cure and Depeche Mode have distanced themselves from the retromania, arguing, truthfully, that they'd never been away. Certainly, U2 cleverly managed to stay relevant throughout the 90s. Still others – The Smiths, Frankie Goes To Hollywood, The Style Council, all of whom had split in the late 80s – resisted the reunion urge.

*****

However, all this was some was off. I remember sitting in the Sounds weekly meeting in 1985 with new Editor, Tony Stewart. In a commendable attempt to rally the troops, he tried to convince a frankly sceptical posse of hacks that this was the most exciting time in music. So, if post-punk, synthpop and new pop were dead, and the jazz, psychobilly and cowpunk revivals passing fads, what was the future? For about two seconds it was tempting to say Sigue Sigue Sputnik's 'fifth generation rock & roll' – the post-modern marriage of punk, technology and style over content. Someone probably said indie, another goth – but were they the *future*? I don't think anyone offered arena rock, a term which hadn't yet gained currency. A couple of brave souls said dance, which would have been about right. But hip-hop was still largely underground, and Stock Aitken Waterman would dominate dance, at least on the airwaves if not necessarily in the clubs, for the next few years, until house and acid house arrived. No. What seemed more likely was a kind of smooth corporate pop incorporating a soupçon of blue-eyed soul, a dash of faux-funk, a bedrock of gated drums, lots of DX7, the return of the guitar (even solos), designer clothes, big hair and model-infested videos. Some would call it sophistipop. Think – deep breath – Go West, Curiosity Killed the Cat, Hue and Cry, Johnny Hates Jazz, Brother Beyond, Living In A Box, Belouis Some, Love and Money, Swing Out Sister, Texas, T'Pau, The Christians, Climie Fisher, Wet Wet Wet and a host of others.

Of course, it wasn't *that* bad. Chartwise, there were refreshing anomalies like the brief reign of The Smiths and the meteoric rise of Pet Shop Boys, and one can always find decent alternative music in any era. But at the time, in the charts, after the excitement, innovation and downright contrariness of post-punk, it felt like it.

Notes and Sources

Frontispiece
⑤ Photo of Paul Weller by Eric Watson, courtesy National Portrait Gallery.

Introduction
[1] You can, inevitably, hear it on YouTube.
[2] It would become very young again, mostly involving solo artists featuring other solo artists in the new millennium. The band, particularly the *rock* band, has mostly disappeared from the singles charts).
[3] New Musical Express, Sounds, Melody Maker, Record Mirror, Number One, Echoes, and the industry rag Music Week.
[4] After a brief but spectacular crash, due to over-saturation, in 1983/84.
[5] Mark Ellen in an email to the author.
[6] Short for 'young urban professional' or 'young, upwardly-mobile professional'.
[7] Robert Elms *The Way We Wore* p.238.
[8] Nearly 30% of all singles sold in in the UK in 1984 were 12-inch. And only four of Music Week's Top 100 were released only in the 7-inch format.
[9] By the end of the 80s the record industry downgraded the certified sales levels: platinum from 1m to 600,000, gold from 500,000 to 400,000, and silver from 250,000 to 200,000.
[10] There were a few duos: Strawberry Switchblade, Toto Coelo, Cookie Crew etc.
[11] www.bananarama.co.uk/biography/
[12] Depeche Mode, Siouxsie and the Banshees, The Cure and Propaganda.
[13] Working Week's 'Venceremos (We Will Win)'.
[14] Thomas Leer's 'International' and 'Chasing the Dragon' – the latter an exquisite B-side.
[15] In 1984, its most famous exponent, Mark Fisher, set up the Fisher Park Partnership, later becoming Stufish. U2 would become a major client.
[16] Giles Smith *Lost in Music* p.96.
[17] Paul Morley sleevenotes for Siouxsie and the Banshees' reissued *Hyaena*, 2008.

Chapter 1: Make It Big
[1] Bono interviewed in Trouser Press in 1983.
[2] Band Aid documentary.
[3] Steve Malins *Duran Duran: Wild Boys* p.146.
[4] A term coined by NME journalist Paul Morley.
[5] Holly Johnson, talking to Chris Heath in *Jamming*, April 1985, p.24.
[6] Simon Garfield *Expensive Habits* p.164.
[7] Saxophones were very much part of the 80s sound (Spandau Ballet, Madness, Sade, Matt Bianco, Bruce Springsteen, Men At Work etc). It seemed like every other song on the radio back then featured a sax. And then, come the 90s, inexplicably, they disappeared.
[8] For the full story, read Napier-Bell's *I'm Coming to Take You to Lunch*. The (17) lunches in question were always at the Sheraton Great Wall in north-east Beijing. Thirty years later this author would spend four years in an office literally next door, and would lend minor assistance to Napier-Bell on another Beijing caper.
[9] John Taylor *In the Pleasure Groove: Love, Death & Duran Duran* p.265.
[10] The central character, Sherman McCoy, was originally a writer not a broker.
[11] Boy George shared a house in Carburton Street with Marilyn, music-hall double act Robert Durrant and Robert Laws and their friend 'Loud Mouth Tracy', and Jennifer Binnie who had founded the Neo Naturists, along with Wilma Johnson, Christine Binnie and Grayson Perry.
[12] Released as *The Making of The Unforgettable Fire Documentary* later that year.
[13] Bono interviewed in Trouser Press in 1983, requoted by Simon Reynolds in *Rip It Up*, p.451.
⑤ Photo of U2 and Eno by, and courtesy of, Colm Henry.
[14] Interview with Paul Du Noyer, NME, 10 November 1984.

[15] Roland Orzabal in the sleevenotes for the reissued album, 1999.

[16] The B-side of which was a cover of Robert Wyatt's 'Sea Song' from a decade earlier.

[17] Hugh Padgham quoted in David Buckley *Strange Fascination* p.420.

[18] Nicholas Pegg *The Complete David Bowie* p.370.

[19] He took these duties very seriously and was rewarded when Watford reached the final of the FA Cup in May that year (though they lost 2:0 to Everton).

[20] http://www.rogerebert.com/reviews/give-my-regards-to-broad-street-1984

Chapter 2: Absolute

[1] *I Want My MTV* p.114.

[2] From BBC's *Synth Britannia*, broadcast on 16 October 2009.

[3] It would later be extended to over 15 minutes by producer Patrick Cowley.

[4] Sleevenotes from Bowie's *Sound and Vision* compilation 1989.

[5] OMD and China Crisis B-sides were littered with them.

[6] Stuart Moxham, Young Marble Giants, quoted in AlexOgg *Independence Days* p.373.

[7] In December 1984, they performed a one-off 4-song benefit gig for Ethiopia, at Sheffield City Hall, their first live appearance for two years, featuring a drum kit and second on the bill to Alvin Stardust.

[8] Colin Irwin, Melody Maker, May 1984.

[9] Along with Rupert Hine, Terry Britten and John Carter.

[10] Although Howard Jones didn't fit the Stiff mould, General Manager Paul Conroy saw potential and took the artist with him when he left Stiff for WEA.

[11] Initially, translated by his Japanese record label as 'I'd Like to Force Myself Upon You'.

[12] Smash Hits, 1 March and 22 November 1984.

[13] Adele Bertei had been part of the New York no wave scene and was Brian Eno's assistant there before contributing backing vocals to numerous groups throughout the 80s and 90s.

[14] Email to the author, 6 June 2018.

[15] No relation to the very-popular-at-the-time Linn drum machine. Today Linn Records is an audiophile label, specializing in classical, jazz and celtic music.

[16] Eleven years later Lennox included a song by The Blue Nile on her covers album, *Medusa*. Probably fearing that she couldn't better 'Tinseltown', she chose 'Downtown Lights' from *Hats*. She couldn't better that either.

[17] For trivia fans, it was the last song ABBA recorded together, until they briefly reunited in 2018.

[18] They released one single, 'Never Never', with Feargal Sharkey providing the vocals.

[19] It got an eventual release 15 years later in 1999.

Ⓢ Photo of Scritti Politti by, and courtesy of, Andy Earl.

[20] Nothing to do with the track of the same name which appeared as B-side to 'Private Plane'.

[21] William Shaw, BLITZ, early 1985.

[22] Let's hear it for 50 random synthpoppers who in 1984 were just about still around, releasing records on majors or minors, before unplugging within a year or two: Baby Go Boom, Basking Sharks, Blue Zoo, The Bodhi-Beat Poets, Box Of Toys, Boys Don't Cry, Jacqui Brookes, The Builders, Camera Obscura, The Catch, Charlie's Brother, Classix Nouveaux, Drum Kcor, East Of Java, Eternal Triangle, Fashion, Feelabeelia, Karel Fialka, Final Program, Force Majeure, Freeze Frame, Glass Museum, Ice The Falling Rain, Hambi and the Dance, Illustrated Man, Language, Laugh Clown Laugh, The Mood, Music For Pleasure, Naked Eyes, National Pastime, Native Europe, Pleasure & The Beast, Shadow Talk, Sense, Red Turns To, Person To Person, A Popular History of Signs, Psycon, Q-Feel, Quadrascope, Scary Thieves, Shiny Two Shiny, Sudeten Creche, Testcard F, Those Attractive Magnets, Two, Two Minds Crack, Vicious Pink, Zoo Boutique and Zoom Lens.

Chapter 3: Restless Albion

[1] Tracey Thorn *Bedsit Disco Queen* p.134.

[2] Julian Cope *Repossessed* p.17/18.

[3] Although carried on in the States right through to mid-decade.

[4] Some say 'indie' began with NME's *C86* cassette of likeminded bands, but they were around

before that.

[5] John Robb *Death to Trad Rock* p.8/9.

[6] Paul Trynka, www.nyamnyamhopeofheaven.wordpress.com 17 Nov 2012.

[7] Colin Irwin, Melody Maker, March 1985.

[8] Geoff Taylor, Age Of Chance, *Death to Trad Rock* p.43.

🌀 Photo of Cabaret Voltaire by, and courtesy of, Peter Care.

[9] FON stood for Fuck Off Nazis.

[10] Martin Lilleker *Beats Working for a Living: Sheffield Popular Music 1973-1984* p.237.

[11] Their gig at Sheffield's B-Hive on 18 December, for example, is listed on Pulp's website as 'probably the most shambolic of the 80s Pulp gigs [...] false starts, abandoned songs, a hostile and drunken crowd and an increasingly tetchy Jarvis'.

[12] Russell Senior *Freak Out the Squares: Life in a Band Called Pulp* p.35.

[13] A 3-issue fanzine co-edited by pre-ABC Martin Fry and pre-Quando Quango / M People Mike Pickering.

[14] Peter Hook and local studio manager Chris Hewitt bought Cargo for £1,300 in 1985, and renamed it Suite 16, but it never turned a profit. In recognition of its heyday, a blue plaque was placed on the building in 2009.

[15] They would later collaborate on a much bigger project, *I Am Curious Oranj*.

[16] Clark also featured in Scritti Politti's 'Wood Beez' video, which also manages to squeeze in fencers, a beekeeper, climbing a mountain, black power salutes and the band sitting on a giant bed in their pyjamas.

[17] In addition, Zigzag magazine included the immortal description: 'Not only have The Membranes wiped the floor with the opposition, they redesigned the tiles'.

🌀 Photo of Mark E and Brix Smith by, and courtesy of, Michael Pollard.

[18] Alan Brown of Big Flame, quoted in John Robb *Death to Trad Rock* p.62.

[19] At which Townsend tried to commandeer Reni's services, who was not only a brilliant drummer but also guitarist, bassist and keyboard player.

[20] In 1984, before joining the Carpets, Clint Boon and had been in a group called The Mill with Mani before he joined the Roses.

[21] Liam: 'The first time music ever did anything for me was when I heard The Smiths'; and Noel was still four years away from becoming Inspiral Carpets' roadie (*The North Will Rise Again* p.360).

[22] Except perhaps Bill Drummond.

[23] Ronnie Hughes quoted in Paul Du Noyer *Wondrous Place* p.4.

[24] From 1976-80. Incidentally, Yazoo's *Upstairs at Eric's* album was completely unrelated, not least because Eric's was in the basement.

[25] Though, like Postcard, it only released around a dozen records, almost all of them singles.

[26] M. Parkinson *Liverpool on the Brink*, Hermitage, Berks, Policy Journals 1985.

[27] It was actually Bill Drummond, who came up with the advertising strapline, 'The greatest record ever made'. His reasoning: 'I mean, why fuck around?' (quoted in Richard King's *How Soon Is Now?* p.51).

🌀 Photo of Probe Records courtesy of Geoff Smith.

[28] The soundtrack was written by Alan Gill of The Teardrop Explodes and Dalek I Love You.

[29] Sara Cohen *Rock Culture in Liverpool*.

[30] Exactly 20 years later, however, it somehow ended up in Jonathan Demme's 2004 remake of *The Manchurian Candidate*.

[31] 'Tragedy' may perhaps be too strong a word to describe Trotskyist Derek Hatton's meddling in Liverpool City Council, but the word certainly applied to the Liverpool FC-related calamities which took place in Heysel and Hillsborough stadiums in 1985 and 1989 respectively.

[32] Simon McKay, editor Eccentric Sleeve Notes fanzine.

[33] As told to David Stubbs in The Quietus, 12 June 2012.

[34] www.blabbermouth.net. 17 November 2003.

[35] 100 copies were sold in a local record shop before getting a proper release 11 years later.

[36] In truth, the origins of shoegaze could be traced to Cocteau Twins and Robin Guthrie's row of wall-of-noise-and-reverb foot pedals.

[37] The Wild Bunch and Massive Attack's Robert Del Naja (aka 3D) was a graffiti artist first, musician second, and was a big influence on Banksy.
[38] The backing musicians for the latter album were actually US band Tackhead.
[39] Check out the promo video, which incidentally features the same Hellenic pillars and fires as The Sisters Of Mercy's later 'Body and Soul'. Waste not want not.
[40] Garry Johnson, Sounds, 29 December 1984.
[41] Tracey Thorn Bedsit Disco Queen p.134.

Chapter 4: Close to the Edit
[1] Craig Marks and Rob Tannenbaum I Want My MTV p.566.
[2] As above p.65.
[3] As above p.118.
[4] As above p.149.
[5] You could even go back to Walt Disney's Fantasia in 1940.
[6] Rick Krim, MTV executive.
[7] Gale Sparrow, MTV Director of Talent and Artist Relations.
[8] Payola is the illegal practice of payment by record companies for the broadcast of recordings on commercial radio.
[9] Trouser Press folded in April 1984, which said something about the parlous state of US new wave that year. Creem ceased publication in 1989.
[10] Brett Sullivan, email to author.
[11] Simon Frith 'Making Sense of Video' in Music For Pleasure p.210.
[12] Joe Jackson, Billboard, 22 December 1984.
[13] Simon Frith 'Making Sense of Video' in Music For Pleasure p.210.
[14] A 1983 survey commissioned by MTV owners, Warner-Amex, showed that for every nine albums bought by MTV viewers, four purchases could be directly attributed to watching the video of the artist (Rolling Stone, 8 December 1983).
[15] When Steve Barron had to turn down directing Thomas Dolby's 'She Blinded Me With Science' video (he was busy directing Michael Jackson's 'Billie Jean', so fair enough), his producer sister Siobhan Barron encouraged Dolby to do it himself.
[16] Julien Temple in I Want My MTV p.88.
[17] John Sykes, MTV executive.
[18] Rolling Stone, 13 January 2016.
[19] I Want My MTV p.170.
[20] David Mallet in I Want My TV p.149.
[21] Andrew Goodwin in Fatal Distractions: MTV Meets Postmodern Theory p.52.
[22] I Want My MTV p.65.
[23] A favoured location not only for videos, but also for feature films (For Your Eyes Only, The Last of England, Nineteen Eighty-Four, Full Metal Jacket), as well as the pilot episode of Max Headroom.
[24] Another favoured industrial-cool location, its former warehouses having been occupied by artists like Derek Jarman and Malcolm Poynter in the 70s, as well as hosting a performance by Throbbing Gristle in 1979. By the mid-80s, however, it was beginning to be gentrified and not even Doctor Who's daleks (filmed there in 1984) could save it from that fate.
[25] Mother, son and daughter worked together on Culture Club videos 'It's a Miracle' and 'The Medal Song'.
[26] http://www.efilmcritic.com/feature.php?feature=2536. Barron later got to direct a feature film, The Adventures of Pinocchio in 1996.
[27] Other mildly interesting titbits are the identities of two of the musicians hired to mime as Screaming Lord Byron's backing band: the bassist was Richard Fairbrass (later to find fame as singer in Right Said Fred) and the drummer was Paul Ridgeley (brother of Wham!'s Andrew).
[28] Including The Filth and the Fury which told the other side of the Sex Pistols story.
[29] Including Rose's own video for Frankie's 'Relax' which was more Sodom & Gomorrah than the Brookside narrative and tone of 'Smalltown Boy'.
[30] The digital magazine Queerty called it "arguably the most enduring LGBT anthem ever

released" (28 October 2014).
[31] Pope's relationship with The Cure was almost a monopoly. At time of writing, Pope has directed around 40 of their videos.
[32] Two early ideas had been skinheads smashing up a Rolls Royce and something based on the film *Death Race 2000*.
[33] This was the second promo for the single. An earlier version, directed by Zbigniew Rybczyński featured a heavily made-up pre-pubescent punkette leading three middle-aged men in suits in the destruction of traditional musical instruments – its message: 'Out with the old, in with the new'. It won two MTV Video Music Awards - Most Experimental Video and Best Editing — the following year. However, its somewhat disturbing effect (it was banned in New Zealand), prompted Morahan's largely animated version.
[34] *I Want My MTV* p.231.
[35] George Michael in his autobiography, *Bare*.
[36] The titles of his late 80s debut feature *Fire with Fire* and scripted *Third Degree Burns* turned out to be weirdly prophetic: Gibbons died in a wildfire which engulfed his Californian home in 1993.
[37] Probably her most famous commission was Peter Gabriel's 'Sledgehammer'.
[38] George Cole *The Last Miles: The Music of Miles Davis 1980-1991* p.148.
[39] Actually, Max was largely created using prosthetics and a plastic jacket.
[40] Adam Sweeting *Rock Yearbook Vol VI* p.139/49.
[41] Biting Tongues' Graham Massey also 'starred' in it. Four years later he would hook up with Martin Price and Gerald Simpson to form 808 State.
[42] Needless to say, it's all on YouTube.
🅢 Still from 'Red Guitar' from www.davidsylvian.net
🅢 Still from *Thursday Afternoon* from www.openculture.com
[43] When *MMoMM* and *Thursday Afternoon* were made available on VHS in Britain in the late 80s, I duly heaved my cathode ray tube television onto its side and the colour promptly drained from one end to the other.
[44] Interview with Peter Naysmyth, The Observer colour supplement, 1984.
[45] Simon Frith 'Making Sense of Video' in *Music For Pleasure* p.220.

Chapter 5: Punk's Not Dead

[1] Also known in the US as *Corrupt* and in Europe as *Cop Killer*, in which Lydon also made his acting debut. He made a decent fist of it too, starring alongside Harvey Keitel.
[2] PiL manager Larry White apparently spent a week trying to persuade him to change his mind: *'Listen, this Chili Peppers thing is going nowhere. The best thing you can do is come out with PiL!'* The band's eponymous debut album, produced by the Gang of Four's Andy Gill, was released in August.
[3] The Damned featured in the 29 May 1984 episode Nasty, performing the song of the same name. See also Chapter 13.
[4] Ian Glaser *Burning Britain* p.10.
[5] She reformed Vice Squad in the late 90s.
[6] Penny Rimbaud, talking to Ian Glasper in *The Day the Country Died: A History of Anarcho Punk 1980-1984*.
[7] This was thanks not only to the 1984 seizure by Manchester police of copies of their album *Penis Envy*, but also an earlier hoax telephone conversation purporting to be between Ronald Reagan and Margaret Thatcher about the sinking of the Belgrano, and involvement in the first Stop The City actions of 1983 and 1984.
[8] The album was actually released on their own Spiderleg label, not Crass Records.
[9] Ian Glasper email to author, 21 October 2017.
[10] Foxton released a solo album, *Touch Sensitive*, in 1984 which peaked at #68.
[11] Daniel Rachel *Walls Come Tumbling Down* p.352.
🅢 Photo of Mick Talbot and Paul Weller by Brian Rasic / Getty Images.
[12] The joke du jour was "What's the difference between Respond and The Titanic? The Titanic had a good band on it".

[13] NME, 10 March 1984.

[14] http://www.elviscostello.info/disc/official/gcw/gcw.htm

[15] To date, The Fall's only Top 10 album has been *The Infotainment Scan*, #9 in 1993.

[16] The accolade of first person to play a film's lead role *and* provide the music goes to Charlie Chaplin for all his features after 1918. On top of that, he also wrote and directed them.

Chapter 6: Rock in Opposition

[1] Stuart Bailie *Trouble Songs* p.245.

[2] From https://blogs.loc.gov/folklife/2017/07/billy-bragg-skiffle-historian-and-singer-visits-the-library-july-21/. Bragg confirms the quotation, but says he was just being flippant about the impossibility of being such a spokesman.

[3] Tracey Thorn in Daniel Rachel *Walls Come Tumbling Down* p.344.

[4] Although conceptual artist Jeremy Deller's Battle of Orgreave, a 2001 re-enactment of 1984's actual Battle of Orgreave, turns that argument on its head.

[5] Italian Red Brigade, who had murdered former Italian Prime Minister Aldo Moro in '78. Photo of Billy Bragg courtesy of Billy Bragg Central Office.

[6] Simon Napier-Bell's *Black Vinyl White Powder* p.291.

[7] Britain has a history of founding pressure groups and charities, including CND, Amnesty International, Save the Children, Oxfam, Christian Aid, Free Tibet, War Child and scores of others.

[8] Many more got in free.

[9] Pershing was a type of missile, although not the type that were brought into Greenham Common.

[10] In which 14 unarmed civilians were shot dead by the British armed forces after a march protesting against internment.

[11] Although not specifically about the Troubles, Bush sang the song with an Irish accent.

[12] Maze Prison's hunger strikes were also the inspiration for Police's 'Invisible Sun'.

[13] Kiss My Arse in Gaelic.

[14] William D Romanowski *Pop Culture Wars*, 1996.

[15] With obvious exceptions (from George Harrison to Malcolm McLaren), music from former colonies in the Indian sub-continent and Africa was rather less influential on British pop and rock.

[16] Dick Hebdige *Cut 'n' Mix: Culture, Identity and Caribbean Music*, 1987.

[17] Resolution 35/206: 'The United Nations General Assembly request all states to prevent all cultural, academic, sporting and other exchanges with South Africa. Appeals to writers, artists, musicians and other personalities to boycott South Africa. Urges all academic and cultural institutions to terminate all links with South Africa.'

[18] The album, *Jive Shikisha!*, wasn't released until 1998.

[19] Mark Blake *Is This The Real Life? The Untold Story of Queen*, 2011.

[20] A full year and a half later on Top Of The Pops, John Peel hadn't forgotten. His introduction, 'At 7, the Sun City boys, Queen and 'A Kind of Magic'' was succinct and pointed.

[21] Danny Baker, Singles, 10 March 1984, NME, p.19.

[22] A term strongly associated with a folk and hippy past and rarely used in 80s Britain.

[23] In its re-released form on Go! Discs; it had originally been released on Charisma in May 1983.

[24] 'Bad' from *Titanic Days* (1993).

[25] Which also raised money for the family of David Wilkie, a taxi driver who had been killed while taking a strike-breaking miner to the pit.

[26] Including *Dig This: a Tribute to the Great Strike* and *Which Side Are You On: Music For The Miners, From the North East*, the former featuring The Men They Couldn't Hang, Poison Girls and an early incarnation of Chumbawamba amongst others.

[27] Ken Loach made a film of the same name about the music and poetry of the strike.

[28] And there were several films too: *Billy Elliot, Brassed Off, The Big Man, Pride* etc.

[29] 'The Enemy Within' was named after Thatcher's reference (not publicly aired at the time) to the striking miners. Le Blanc's involvement was initially just inspirational. Dogood and Kohn

344

modelled their cut-ups on his 'No Sell Out' single on Island earlier in the year, then took the basics to Island who turned it down, then to Rough Trade's Geoff Travis who recommended Adrian Sherwood as producer, who in turn asked Le Blanc to contribute the electrofunk rhythm and edits. Full circle.

[30] In fact, before the miners' strike had even started, he'd made a cameo appearance in Tracey Ullman's 'My Guy' promo.

[31] BPI Yearbook 1985.

[32] Frankie Goes To Hollywood, for instance, were still signing on when 'Relax' went stellar. Worried about being spotted on Top Of The Pops by the DHSS, Johnson asked ZTT to put them on £40 a week each. Ironically, at least one of them (guitarist Nasher) was signing on again after it was all over.

[33] *Europe A Go Go* music special, Channel 4, 5 January 1985.

[34] Mark Kermode *How Does It Feel? A Life of Musical Misadventures* p.88. Kermode was in three little-known Manchester bands around that time (Border Incident, Russians Eat Bambi and Fatspeak) but he didn't sign up to the scheme himself, he was describing fellow band members who did. Kermode was a student at the time, so ineligible.

[35] Sarah Jane Morris quoted in Daniel Rachel's *Walls Come Tumbling Down* p.373.

[36] An attempt was made to stage it anyway, resulting in the so-called Battle of the Beanfield at which over 500 people were arrested.

🎵 Photo of Crass flag by, and courtesy of, Gee Vaucher.

🎵 Photo of Stonehenge by Alan Lodge.

[37] Newsweek magazine declared 1984 as 'The Year of the Yuppie'.

[38] The organization Class War were also involved and had links with a number of bands, namely Bourbonese Qualk who early in 1984 occupied a former Ambulance Station on the Old Kent Road in south east London, turning it into a thriving meeting place for anarchists, an office for the local squatters organization and a recording studio and performance space for themselves. I reviewed one of their gigs in December.

[39] Sounds 19 Jan 1985.

[40] It was a favourite of Queen Mary, however, and Formby sang it before the King and Queen at the Royal Variety performance in 1941.

[41] Goodman was also successfully sued by John Lydon.

[42] Many would die from the disease, including Freddie Mercury, Sylvester and Level 42 guitarist Alan Murphy.

[43] The age was lowered from 21 to 17 in 1994.

[44] The Quietus, 24 July 2017.

Chapter 7: The Politics of Dancing

[1] Interview with Bram E Gieben in www.theskinny.co.uk, 1 Feb 2013.

[2] Red Bull Music Academy lecture 'London Warehouse Parties Pre-Acid House: an Oral History', 13 June 2017

[3] The term 'disco' was still in regular usage.

[4] Or, in the case of Roland Rat, a rodent?

[5] Family Quest would eventually release just the one single, 'Sleepwalking' in 1986, produced by the very improv trio of David Toop, Steve Beresford and Paul Philips. Toop's connection with rap, however, ran deep, penning one of the first books on hip-hop, *Rap Attack*, published in 1984.

[6] Broken Glass was actually a dance crew. Their MC was Kermit (real name Paul Leveridge) who would later form the Ruthless Rap Assassins, the Rapologists and (with Shaun Ryder) Black Grape.

[7] The Electro series morphed into the Crucial Hip Hop series, totalling some 22 albums by 1988.

[8] Possibly the only front cover of The Face which was purely typographic, designed, appropriately, by Neville Brody.

[9] Island Records got in on the act too, with the *Crew Cuts* mini-LP featuring Malcolm X, GrandMixer D.ST, The Art Of Noise and others.

[10] Red Bull Music Academy interview, as above.

[11] Greg Wilson, The UK Electro Story, www.electrofunkroots.co.uk
ⓖ Photo of The Wild Bunch by Beezer, and courtesy of Beezer Photos.
[12] Richard Norris *Paul Oakenfold* p.40.
[13] John Robb in The Guardian, 6 October 2006.
[14] Pete Johnson, Echoes 2 June 1984.
[15] Hard Corps were classic should-have-beens with sublime singles 'Je Suis Passée' and 'To Breathe' (both 1985) and tour support slots with The Cure and Depeche Mode.
[16] Data were led by the itinerant Georg Kajanus whose previous project was the naff 70s group Sailor.
[17] Although Birmingham's Barbarella's and Romulus also have a case.
[18] In truth, they were just as likely to be railway arches, factories and vacant offices than warehouses.
[19] Jay Strongman in The Face, January 1984, p.39.
[20] https://www.skiddle.com/news/all/London-Warehouse-Parties-Pre-Acid-House-An-Oral-History/31743/
[21] Which would later become Volcano and feature in the film Trainspotting.
ⓖ Photo of The Wag Club by, and courtesy of, David Johnson, shapersofthe80s.com
[22] It became illegal the following year.

Chapter 8: In the Studio
[1] Quotefancy.com
[2] Musicthoughts.com
[3] The most famous example of gated reverb on drums was Phil Collins' 'In the Air Tonight', credited to Steve Lillywhite and engineer Hugh Padgham.
[4] Ridley Scott filmed it in England using a cast of 'brainwashed' skinheads (the workers) and a young, non-subservient athlete (representing Apple), the latter running through a grey Orwellian set to throw a hammer at a huge screen where Big Brother was espousing a lumpen, corporate vision of IT. The narrator's last words are 'On January 24th, Apple Computer will introduce Macintosh, and you'll see why 1984 won't be like 1984'.
[5] Music Week, 31 March 1984, p.32.
[6] The Go-Betweens recording *Spring Hill Fair* with producer John Brand in April 1984. This extract is from Robert Forster's *Grant & I: Inside and Outside the Go-Betweens*, 2018
[7] Trevor Horn talking to Paul Morley NME, 3 July 1982, p.15.
[8] Trevor Horn interview in Sound on Sound, March 2005.
[9] As above.
[10] Anne Dudley quoted in Simon Reynolds's *Rip It Up and Start Again* p.496.
[11] Anne Dudley website.
[12] Interview with Paul Tingen in Sound On Sound magazine, Feb 1995.
[13] Released in 1985.
[14] Interview with Chris Everard, Electronic Soundmaker & Computer Music magazine (1984) month unknown.
[15] Interview with this author, September 1985.
[16] So-called when he was constantly going out to get tea and sandwiches for the studio's staff and clients. Another, not-so diligent runner was nicknamed Drought.
[17] http://www.trustmeimascientist.com/2012/03/03/producer-profiles-flood/
[18] She'd had two attempts at representing Britain in the Eurovision Song Contest, in 1976 and 1984, but had finished 8th and 7th respectively.
[19] The original single was produced by Ian Anthony Stephens in 1983. It flopped but Ian Levine's early 1984 remix breathed new life into it.
[20] It was a slow burner, however, taking four months for it to reach #1 in March 1985.
[21] Tom Watkins *Let's Make Lots of Money* p.182.
[22] Tony Visconti *Bowie, Bolan and the Brooklyn Boy* p.274.

Chapter 9: In A Big Country
[1] The Quietus, 23 September 2014.

[2] Kieron Tyler, 15 March 2015: www.theartsdesk.com/new-music/reissue-cds-weekly-simple-minds

[3] Although, interestingly, none of the classic line-up was born in Scotland.

[4] The Quietus, 23 September 2014.

[5] The label would be briefly revived in the 90s, expanding its catalogue somewhat.

[6] Talking Heads' David Byrne was, of course, 'Scottish' – born in Dumbarton.

[7] Also working under the moniker, Rhythm Of Life.

[8] Glasgow-based Passionate Friends were also signed and quickly dropped by MCA, splitting up in 1984.

[9] After April Showers, Bernstein formed the even shorter-lived Me And Mrs Jones before moving to the US and would co-write a glossy book, *Mad World*, about 80s new wave pop.

[10] www.cloudberryrecords.com/blog/?p=1383

[11] Receiving the 'We're letting you go' news over a lunch in London he asked for a taxi home. Warners duly phoned up a cab on account, leaving McKenzie with the last laugh. Home in this case meant Dundee.

[12] A re-release would hit #1 nine years later when it was used for a VW Golf ad.

[13] Although, they reformed several times.

[14] Initially Buba and The Shop Assistants.

[15] He wrote their 1982 UK #3 hit 'Inside Out'.

Chapter 10: The Unforgettable Freur

[1] Interviewed by Simon Price in The Independent, 28 February 2010.

[2] Founded in 1977, Hot Press was, and still is, Ireland's key music paper. Its editorial was greatly influenced by what was going on across the Irish Sea as, indirectly, Nick Kelly of the Irish Independent remembered in September 2011: *There was no such thing as the Mercury Prize back in 1984 but if there had been, the jury would have had one hell of a headache choosing between the Bunnymen's pièce de résistance; The Smiths' epochal debut; Cocteau Twins' magical third album* Treasure; *This Mortal Coil's magnificently multi-pronged* It'll End In Tears *(featuring 'Song To The Siren' and some spine-chilling Big Star covers to boot); Lloyd Cole & The Commotions' timeless debut* Rattlesnakes; *Dead Can Dance's ethereal, stately self-titled first album; Madness's fifth LP* Keep Moving, *which spawned singles like 'One Better Day' and 'Michael Caine'; The Fall's* Wonderful And Frightening World Of The Fall; *Billy Bragg's masterful* Brewing Up With...; *U2's* The Unforgettable Fire ... *you can probably come up with half a dozen more of your own.*

[3] The record shop itself closed and reopened a number of times until finally calling it a day in 2015.

Ⓢ Photo of Big Self courtesy of Elvera Butler, Reekus Records.

[4] Weirdly, the A&R man who originally signed U2 to Island had been a British ex-soldier, Nick Stewart, who had served in Northern Ireland before moving into the music business.

[5] Rose Rouse, Sounds, 6 October 1984.

[6] Opening for R.E.M. on one occasion in April 1984.

[7] Neil McCormick, one of the scores of musicians who'd grown up with U2, indeed went to school with them, turned his failed big-time aspirations into a book *I was Bono's Doppelganger* (2004) which was then turned into a film, *Killing Bono* (2011). In 1984 he was in-between two failed groups Yeah! Yeah! and Shook Up! The exclamations didn't help.

[8] Steve Stapleton, mainstay of Nurse With Wound and United Dairies, would up sticks and move to west Ireland at the end of the 80s.

[9] Bono oversaw two Operating Theatre singles in 1986: 'Spring Is Coming with a Strawberry in its Mouth' and 'Queen of No Heart', both more synth-rock than avant-garde.

[10] Engineered by Richard Dodd, who had engineered 10cc's multiple-vocal-tape-loop-masterpiece, 'I'm Not In Love'.

[11] In 1984, The Nolans were in decline, although still big in Japan; Chris De Burgh's *Man On The Line* went platinum in the UK; Rory Gallagher was playing with Box Of Frogs, an 80s version of The Yardbirds, and Phil Lynott had formed the underwhelming Grand Slam after the demise of Thin Lizzy the year before. He died in January 1986.

[12] Mostly of the anarcho variety, collected on *Bullsheep Detector: Welsh Punk 1980-1984*.

[13] Another magazine, Sothach, also started up in Bethesda in 1988.

[14] Sarah Hill *Blerwytirhwng? The Place of Welsh Pop Music* p.32.

[15] Bassist Dave Parsons later found chart success with Transvision Vamp and Bush.

[16] Sarah Hill *Blerwytirhwng? The Place of Welsh Pop Music*, p.42/43.

[17] Craig Owen-Jones *Still Here? A Geospatial Survey of Welsh-Language Popular Music*, p.62.

[18] Sarah Hill *Blerwytirhwng? The Place of Welsh Pop Music*.

[19] It was resurrected in the 00s.

[20] The name actually came from a guttural sound uttered by keyboard player Rick Smith, which was somehow spelled as Freur and for a while was also represented by a squiggle.

Chapter 11: First and Last and Always

[1] *History of the Batcave* (GothCast) mini-documentary on YouTube, published 21 January 2017.

[2] Valerie Siebert, The Quietus, 10 August 2012.

[3] The colour of choice in Victorian England: it didn't show the dirt and after Prince Albert died in 1861, Queen Victoria wore black for the last 40 years of her life.

[4] Midweek, as the scene was hardly mainstream.

[5] At least that's what the media portrayed it as; in truth there were also mortals in jeans with boring haircuts.

[6] The Unwanted's only claim to fame was appearing on 1977's *Live at The Roxy* compilation before imploding a year later.

[7] The setting for Skeletal Family's *Promised Land* video. And while we're about it, there's a case for including Kate Bush's 'Wuthering Heights' in the goth canon.

[8] Exceptions included Xmal Deutschland who in their earliest incarnation were all-female; Skeletal Family (fronted by Anne-Marie Hurst); Bone Orchard (by Chrissie McGee); All About Eve (by Julianne Regan), who formed in 1984 and at least initially could reasonably be described as goth; and, at a pinch, Danielle Dax.

[9] This wasn't just a stage conceit – Vanian had always dressed that way.

Ⓢ Photo of Nick Cave and Nic Fiend by, and courtesy of, Mick Mercer.

[10] An early song, 'Allein'.

[11] The first of the *Terminator* films came out in 1984.

[12] Including Julianne Regan who would go on to form All About Eve in late 1984.

[13] Indeed, goth and metal had (and still have) a lot in common: strict dresscode, loyal fanbase and will last eternal.

[14] Interviewed by Paul Elliott in Classic Rock, November 2016.

Chapter 12: Better by Design

[1] Raf Simon & Peter Saville: A Meeting of the Minds, The Fashion Law website, 5 January 2017.

[2] The Age of Plunder, *The Face*, January 1983.

[3] In a review of *Sampler: Contemporary Music Graphics*, original source unknown but requoted in the second volume of the book, *Sampler 2*, p.6.

[4] Actually, the first records (78s) were 10 inches square, which is also a pretty good size.

[5] The Guardian, 4 January 1985.

[6] Even that most iconic sleeve, *Sergeant Peppers,* was credited to 'MC Productions and The Apple' before adding that it was 'staged by Peter Blake and Jann Haworth [and] photographed by Michael Cooper'.

[7] 1984 saw the last-but-one of the dollybird-fronted Top Of The Pops compilations, replaced by the equally naff designs of the NOW and Hits compilations.

[8] In an interview with Christopher Wilson, *Designed by Peter Saville*, p.27.

[9] The Durutti Column, Jilted John, Big In Japan, Manicured Noise, Cabaret Voltaire, The Tiller Boys and Joy Division - catalogued as FAC 1 in Factory's famous list of record releases and ephemera.

[10] Featuring Joy Division, The Durutti Column, John Dowie and Cabaret Voltaire.

[11] Catherine McDermott *Street Style* p.84.

[12] Sue Shaw, founder and Director of the little-known Type Museum based in south London, once said to me that she believed Brody's contribution to typography had been a disservice.

[13] Vaughan Oliver, *Facing the Other Way* p.162.

[14] Then a model who shared a house with Modern English, now an artist going by the name of Pallas Citroen.

[15] www.eyemagazine.com/feature/article/8vo-type-and-structure

[16] Email to the author.

[17] From an interview, 26 March 2011, posted on www.orbellcomms.wordpress.com

[18] Tom Watkins *Let's Make Lots of Money* p.176.

[19] Farrow had already designed several Factory sleeves.

[20] He would also manage Bros from 1987-91, and East 17 from 1992-97.

[21] With his ex-Freur mates Karl Hyde and Rick Smith, amongst others.

[22] Brian and Roger Eno, David Sylvian, Robin Guthrie, The Edge, Michael Brook, Kevin Shields, to name just a few.

[23] Women photographers were quite rare. As were, somewhat surprisingly, female graphic designers.

Chapter 13: Sound and Vision

[1] Stephen Hebditch, *London's Pirate Pioneers* p.158.

[2] Top Of The Pops, 7 June 1984.

[3] How We Made The Tube, The Guardian, 15 March 2016.

[4] In 2017, live radio accounted for 76% of all listening, compared with music streaming at 7%.

[5] A reactive rather than a proactive decision, responding to ITV's Ready Steady Go. Ironically, independent television in Britain had started in 1955, well before independent radio.

[6] Amazingly, one of its programmes, Music While You Work, was resurrected in 1984-85 under the title Music All The Way on weekday afternoons, while Family Favourites ran interrupted from 1945 to 1984.

[7] Stephen Hebditch *London's Pirate Pioneers*, p.158.

[8] Strictly speaking, the 'policing' was the responsibility of the Home Office, not the police.

[9] In fact, Peterson had set up his own pirate station, Civic Radio the year before, aged 18.

🐝 Photo of pirate radio studio courtesy of www.thepiratearchive.net

[10] JICRAR survey. Reach meaning total number of people who tuned in at any time within the past week.

[11] Bubbly sister of equally bubbly TV presenter Keith Chegwin.

[12] For a while Steve Barker kept the show going from Beijing where his and my jobs at the British Council overlapped.

[13] By the new millennium, Radio Two's audience numbers would surpass Radio One's becoming the UK's most listened-to station.

[14] For the first few years, Peel didn't have his 'own show': he shared the likes of Top Gear, Nightride, Sunday Show and Sounds of the Seventies with others. So although these shows had sessions, they weren't at that stage Peel Sessions. The show called John Peel wasn't named as such until 1975.

[15] I accompanied Peel, his wife Sheila and World Service producer Dave Tate to Sierra Leone in 1989, in connection with a British Council touring exhibition, *Pop! British Music in the 80s*.

[16] Jeff Simpson, *Top Of The Pops 1964-2002*, p.49.

[17] Ian Gittins, *Top Of The Pops: Mishaps, Miming and Music* p.93.

[18] John Peel's compering debut on Top pf the Pops began with: 'In case you're wondering who this funny old bloke is, I'm the one who comes on Radio One late at night and plays records made by sulky Belgian art students in basements dying of TB'.

[19] Referring to Pete Wylie's 'Sinful' in 1986, Peel caused a minor furor by announcing: 'If that doesn't make Number 1, I'm going to come round and break wind in your kitchen'.

[20] Boy George auditioned, in a wedding dress. But it was at the same time that Culture Club had just signed with Virgin; had that not happened, he would have got the job.

[21] Jarvis Cocker was also interviewed for the job.

[22] The series – also featuring Big Country, Level 42, The Angelic Upstarts, The Special AKA, Echo & The Bunnymen, Girlschool and XTC – was broadcast on Channel 4 between 14 August and 16 October 1984.
[23] Email to author.
[24] Andy Kershaw *No Off Switch* p.164.
[25] In an interview with Andrew Smith of Melody Maker, Janet Street Porter confessed: 'I don't really think I make youth programmes […] the programmes we make are for people who don't have a lot of responsibilities'. Melody Maker, 17 June 1989.
[26] Duran won.
[27] There were occasional short-lived revivals for Rockschool and Pop Quiz.
[28] Jeff Evans *Rock & Pop on British TV* p.222.
[29] 328 different songs were used in the five series, costing around $10,000 per episode in rights.
[30] The BBC police procedural series Life On Mars (2006/7) featured extensive use of early 70s pop music.

Chapter 14: Generals and Majors

[1] David Hepworth *Uncommon People: The Rise and Fall of the Rock Stars* p.241.
[2] www.brainyquote.com/quotes/richard_branson_173427?src=t_music_industry
[3] John Peel in an interview with Martin Aston requoted Philip Ogg *Independence Days* p.iii.
[4] Inflation was down to 4.3% (from 16.4% in 1980).
[5] Total sales were £329m comprising £78.8m singles, £141.2m vinyl albums, £104m cassette albums and £5m CDs.
[6] Frank Di Leo, VP of Promotion for Epic, who released Culture Club in the US had a different tactic: 'We didn't release a picture of Boy George until three weeks after the record was released. We sent the record out in a plain white sleeve to the radio stations. Once we got them into the music we let them see him. Like "Oh by the way, this is what he looks like" ' (The Face, January 1984).
[7] In 1984, 12-inch singles accounted for 29% of UK singles sales, the largest ever share before or since. In July it was 36% thanks to Frankie Goes To Hollywood. Of all the records in the Music Week Top 100 for 1984, only four were released in 7-inch format alone (compared with ten in 1983 and 21 in 1982). Source: BPI Yearbooks.
[8] The other one was Polygram in Germany.
[9] Source unknown.
Photo of Nimbus CD-pressing plant courtesy of Nimbus Records.
[10] In 1984, around 500 videos were commissioned in the UK costing, on average, £15-£18,000 each.
[11] BPI Year Book 1985, p.38.
[12] Ray Parker Junior settled out of court with Huey Lewis when the latter deemed 'Ghostbusters' to be a copy of one of his own songs, 'I Want a New Drug'. And in a bizarre twist, Jon Fogerty was taken to court for copying one of his own songs. His 1984 US Top 10 hit, 'The Old Man Down the Road', was judged by his old record company to be too similar to his 1970 song 'Run Through the Jungle' written when he was in Creedence Clearwater Revival. However, the judge ruled that an artist cannot plagiarise himself.
[13] German royalty collection agency GEMA managed to initiate a scheme in 1985 whereby 19 pfennigs was levied on every C60 sold, which was then shared amongst its members.
[14] Clinton Heylin *Bootleg! The Rise & Fall of the Secret Recording Industry* p.9.
[15] Between 1980 and 2000, no more than five women were appointed heads of any UK-based record companies, major or otherwise. Sheila Whitely *Women and Popular Music: Sexuality, Identity and Subjectivity.*
[16] In the 60s, aside from its music-related business, EMI also made domestic electrical appliances, defence equipment, computers, and had interests in film, hotels and pubs. It even owned Blackpool Tower.
[17] Roughly 16% of both UK albums and singles sales.
[18] In his autobiography, Branson described the Virgin of the early 80s as 'the undisputed leading independent record label'.

[19] Front Line was short-lived, but many of the artists remained on Virgin.

[20] Actually, the first *Now!* compilation was released just before Christmas 1983.

[21] Unconnected with the then untrademarked Top Of The Pops TV programme, the series ran from 1968, ending with *Volume 92* and *The Best of Top of the Pops 1984*. Both sported Page Three girls on the cover: Linda Lusardi on the former and an 18-year-old Sam Fox on the latter.

[22] Classic Pop, Issue 35, December 2017, p.60.

[23] *Now 3* sold over a million copies, making it one of the biggest-selling UK albums of the year, and yet almost impossible to review. This author's review in Sounds simply said 'It's out'.

[24] Dave Robinson in Gareth Murphy *Cowboys & Indies* p.309.

[25] ZTT stood for Zang Tumb Tumb, a phrase from a sound poem by Italian Filippo Tommaso Marinetti, founder of the Italian Futurist movement. There were variations on the spelling of the last two words, even by the label itself.

[26] Interview with Barney Hoskins, NME, 13 October 1984, p.26.

[27] Only 25 of the 125 were based outside of London.

[28] Paul Young (Best British Male Artist), Alison Moyet (Best British Female Artist), Wham! (Best British Group), *Diamond Life* (Best British Album), 'Relax' (Best British Single), Trevor Horn (Best British Producer), 'Wild Boys' (Best British Video) etc.

[29] Selected randomly from a much wider pool of 6,000 shops.

[30] The game was conceived by a band called The Technos whose two 1984 singles failed to benefit from any insider knowledge.

[31] That also counted its games stores.

[32] Garth Cartwright *Going for a Song* p.260.

Chapter 15: Cowboys and Indies

[1] As told to Richard King in his *How Soon Is Now?* p.xxiii.

[2] Alex Ogg *Independence Days* p.321/322.

[3] Interviewed in The Guardian, 22 January 2016.

[4] The Guardian, 10 October 2013.

[5] By the Independent Labels Association, founded in 1982.

[6] The shortened 'indie' generally referred to a genre of music which developed from post-punk from 1985.

[7] For example, Beggars Banquet and Blanco Y Negro with WEA, and in the case of Kitchenware, Some Bizzare and PWL, *several* different majors.

[8] Island was sold to Polygram in 1989, Chrysalis to Thorn EMI in 1991 and Virgin to Thorn EMI in 1992.

[9] BPI Yearbook 1985.

[10] Philip Ogg *Independence Days* p.500.

[11] Garth Cartwright *Going for a Song* p.219.

[12] Philip Ogg *Independence Days* p.498.

[13] Richard King in The Guardian, 22 March 2012.

[14] Even the label's name strangely referenced 1984; a kind of word-game, starting from 1980 FORWARD, truncated to 1980 FWD, then 1984 AD, and ending with the final, crisp 4AD.

[15] He was always known by his forename only.

[16] Son of 60s pop arranger Ivor Raymonde.

[17] I remember watching ITV's On The Ball in the autumn of 1984. Greavsie was interviewing Chelsea's Pat Nevin who was frequently held up as an example of an intelligent footballer, and his love of leftfield music led him to be fêted by NME. On the programme he played a bit of *Treasure* as an example of the kind music he was interested in. 'Good player, that Nevin', said Greavsie afterwards, 'but I'm not sure about the music. Was he playing it backwards?'

[18] After a Hieronymous Bosch painting.

[19] It actually started out as the B-side to a couple of Modern English-penned tracks.

[20] It should be noted that these artists were deeply unfashionable at the time; Ivo was partly responsible for their, and others', reappraisal, at least in the UK.

[21] The idea was resurrected in 1998 with The Hope Blister featuring a new generation of 4AD artists.

[22] Named after a packet of envelopes they had on their drawing board. There were 23 left. Oliver took out some Letraset, crafted a logo but there were no more Ss. And that was it.

[23] Tony Wilson, interviewed by James Nice in 2005 for the latter's *Shadowplayers* documentary.

[24] They didn't have a club, although you could absolutely picture it.

[25] In an interview with Sean O'Hagan in 2002, requoted in Alex Ogg *Independence Days* p.321.

[26] Based on (not a reproduction of) *The Evil Genius of a King* (1914/15). The title 'Thieves Like Us' was also from a 'painting', though in this case some New York street graffiti.

[27] All re-released in 2016 on LTM's compilation *Cool As Ice*.

[28] In the 90s Reeder set up the MFS label and 'discovered' Paul van Dyk.

[29] The latter released on Factory Benelux.

[30] As interviewed by Ryan Gilbey in The Guardian, 21 March 2002.

[31] Carter Burwell would become a highly successful film composer, scoring most of the Coen Brothers' movies.

[32] Fac 99, *Molar Reconstruction, Rob Leo Gretton's Mouth*, 1984.

[33] Madonna's first *un*televised UK performance was a PA at Camden Palace on 15 Oct 1983.

[34] The Guardian, 23 November 2005.

[35] Travis had spent time in a kibbutz after leaving university.

[36] New Year's Eve had seen The Smiths play their US debut at New York's Danceteria. On the same bill was Madonna of all people, four weeks before she performed at The Hacienda.

[37] Sam Knee, author of *A Scene in Between* tells a wonderful story about how he deliberately failed an eye test to secure the same NHS specs Morrissey was wearing. 'The look I had been hankering for was finally complete as I triumphantly promenaded down the high street. The migraine that followed was of little significance […] How I looked and the music I listened to was the only thing of importance'.

[38] Debut magazine, issue 2, p.44.

[39] The hiring of Tate seemed to be based simply on the fact that he's produced 'Jeane', the B-side to 'This Charming Man'.

[40] Most people associate The Smiths' sleeves with British icons from the 60s, and indeed Terence Stamp and Viv Nicholson feature on two 1984 singles, but Morrissey had also chosen two Americans (George O'Mara and Joe Dallesandro) and two Frenchmen (Jean Marais and Gilles Decroix) before the year was out. The cover star for 'William It Was Really Nothing' was initially of an unknown model promoting hi-fi speakers but was reassuringly replaced with a 1967 still of Billie Whitelaw.

[41] *Looking in the Shadows* (1996); they have gone on to play festivals and 'one-offs' ever since.

[42] Itself an important label, 1984 saw the short-lived Doublevision peak with vinyl and video releases by CTI, Chakk, Lydia Lunch, The Residents, Tuxedomoon, Eric Random & The Bedlamites, The Hafler Trio, Annie Hogan, The Box and Throbbing Gristle.

[43] Until he withdrew from music altogether in the early 80s.

[44] It was recorded in 1981.

[45] An often overlooked but similarly excellent compilation, *Perspectives and Distortion* (1981), had showcased a more experimental roster of acts, as had the Morgan Fisher-compiled *Miniatures* (1980) which Cherry Red marketed and distributed.

[46] David Cavanagh *The Creation Records Story: My Magpie Eyes are Hungry for the Prize* p.97.

[47] They included the only album by Grab Grab The Haddock featuring ex-Marine Girl Jane Fox, a noodly solo album by Felt guitarist Maurice Deebank, and a couple of Adrian Sherwood projects.

[48] A theme he'd started as early as 1982 with a reissue of Patrick MacNee and Honor Blackman's 1964 camp classic 'Kinky Boots' on Cherry Red.

[49] The sleeve featured a very early example of Nick Knight photography.

[50] EG Records, formed by David Enthoven and John Gaydon, had a similar arrangement. Like Some Bizzare it was both a management agency and record label, but over the years licensed its releases (by the likes of Roxy Music / Bryan Ferry, King Crimson / Robert Fripp, Brian Eno and Killing Joke) to Island, then Polydor and finally Virgin.

[51] Actually, Stevo set up a sub-label for his more esoteric artists: Coil, Swans and Carlos Peron records appearing on the enigmatically named Kelvin 422.

[52] Credited to Marc Almond and The Willing Sinners
[53] Marc Almond in *Tape Delay*, edited by Charles Neal, p.80.
[54] Although their song 'Dream Baby' appeared on Bananarama's second album (the only track not written by them).
[55] Geoff Davies quoted in Alex Ogg *Independence Days* p.495.
[56] Richard King, The Guardian, 22 March 2012.
[57] In a complicated arrangement, Mute became independent again in 2010.
[58] Cherry Red were also clever about owning the publishing. Most independents didn't really bother with that side of the business; it wasn't sexy. But Cherry Red were quick to see the benefits, even if the bands they signed to this side of the business didn't record with them. They did well out of Blancmange and The The for example.

Chapter 16: Swingeing London
[1] NME, 3 December 1983.
[2] Reissued as a triple CD by Cherry Red as *Another Splash of Colour.*
[3] Following 'Helter Skelter', 'Dear Prudence' was the Banshees' second cover of a Beatles song from the *'White Album',* and reached #3, the biggest-selling single of their career.
[4] Before they became The Times, they were briefly known as the Teenage Filmstars.
[5] https://londonist.com/2016/02/suits-scooters-and-punch-ups-with-skinheads-mod-life-in-80s-london
[6] Chris Hunt, editor Shadows & Reflections fanzine, quoted in Sounds, 28 July 1984.
[7] Creation was named in honour of a British 60s band, The Creation; McGee's band Biff Bang Pow! was named after one of their songs; and Creation Records would inevitably release an album by The Creation's original line-up in the 90s.
[8] Five were planned, but Primal Scream's failed to materialise.
[9] NME August 1982, reprinted in *C86 & All That* p.148.
[10] Creation's first album release was an underwhelming compilation, *Alive in the Living Room*, of which the kindest thing you could say about it was that it documented an era.
🏵 Photo of The Jesus And Mary Chain by, and courtesy of, Laurence Verfaillie.
[11] Brian Hogg *The History of Scottish Rock and Pop* p.275.
[12] Neil Spencer, NME, 2 February 1985.
🏵 Photo of Childish and Emin by, and courtesy of, Eugene Doyen.
[13] Interestingly, The Stray Cats chose to base themselves in London until they split up in 1984.
[14] Several more volumes followed.
[15] Giles Smith's *We Can Be Heroes* p.195.
[16] They would reform in 1996 and are still going.
[17] Actually, they had a male fifth member, guitarist Boz Boorer.

Chapter 17: English Eccentrics
[1] From an article by Mayer Nissim: www.digitalspy.com/music/a236462/cope-i-created-myth-by-staying-away/ 1 July 2010.
[2] Numerous quote banks, original source untraceable.
[3] Innes worked closely with Monty Python and fronted Beatles spoof band The Rutles; Stanshall was master of ceremonies on Oldfield's *Tubular Bells* and recorded a series of bizarre, mainly spoken-word solo albums. Both were active in 1984: Innes with a single 'Humanoid Boogie', Stanshall with his last solo album, *Sir Henry at N'didi's Kraal*; and even the Bonzos had a compilation out that year.
[4] Ivor Cutler enjoyed a productive mid-80s revival thanks to Rough Trade. Two wonderful books, the surreal, semi-autobiographical *Life in a Scotch Sitting Room Vol 2*, brilliantly illustrated by Martin Honeysett, and a collection of poems, *LARGE et Puffy*, were both published in 1984.
[5] The 'Madame Butterfly' video could have been amazing but ended up a missed opportunity. Hiring swinging sixties fashion photographer Terence Donovan was an interesting choice but the result was a – literally – steamy scene of languid models in a Turkish bath, to all intents and purpose, a slowed-down version of Duran Duran's 'Girls on Film'. Donovan obviously liked the look of bored, expressionless models as he then went on to create a band of them to back

Robert Palmer in his infamous 'Addicted to Love' video.

[6] Check out the 8mm film for 'Laughing Boy' on YouTube to see the semi-ritualistic background to the turtle shell caper.

[7] From an interview with Jon Savage in the Observer Monthly Magazine, 10 August 2008.

[8] A concert at the Hammersmith Palais in 1984 saw him cut his torso with the twisted remains of the microphone stand he'd just broken.

[9] Including, of course, the US. Frank Zappa, Brian Wilson, Prince and Michael Jackson, and more recently Marilyn Manson and Lady Gaga, the list is endless. But that's another, rather different story.

[10] Partridge's nervous breakdown on stage in the spring of 1982 had transformed them into a studio-only band with time on their hands.

[11] The album eventually got made with Michael Brook as producer and turned out to be one of the best albums of the decade.

[12] Mat Snow, NME, 11 August 1984.

[13] Interview 7 February 2001, Shriekback website.

[14] Giles Smith Lost in Music p.168.

[15] Interview with Rockerzine, 18 April 2012.

Ⓢ Photo of Martin Newell, courtesy of the artist.

[16] Interview with Andy Carvin, 1993.

[17] McAloon wanted a song title where the first letters spelled out Limoges, the French town where his former girlfriend was staying at the time. And why not?

[18] www.johncodyonline.com

[19] It's Hayward by the way.

[20] Lawrence liked symmetry. When a later album inadvertently had 11 tracks on it, he couldn't get his head around it. 'That hurt me a bit, straight away, before I'd even listened to it'. From an interview with Michael Bonner, Uncut, 24 July 2015.

[21] The Quietus, interviewed by Jude Rogers, 6 September 2012.

[22] Uncut, as above.

[23] The Quietus, as above.

[24] The Quietus, as above.

[25] The Blockheads were inadvertently involved in the biggest hit of 1984, as session musicians on Frankie Goes To Hollywood's 'Relax', although only the bass guitar made it into the final mix.

[26] Ray Davies included Madness in his curation of Meltdown in 2011, and Dury's last ever vocal performance was on Madness's 'Dip Fed Fred' from their 1999 reunion album, Wonderful.

[27] Named after dextoamphetamine, the drug of choice for Northern Soul dancers.

[28] Interview with Philip Mason, 3 Dec 2013, www.popmatters.com

[29] Alex Ogg Independence Days p.414.

[30] Colin Lloyd Tucker's 1984-released debut solo album, Toybox, is also an interesting period piece: a meeting point between early, folky Bowie, Alternative TV and Current 93.

[31] SFT website.

[32] Simon Reynolds Rip It Up and Start Again p.209.

[33] Two other quirky Norwich bands, The Farmer's Boys and The Higsons, also released fine records in 1984. The former's very 60s sounding 'In the Country' extolled the virtues of good clean rustic living, hitting #44 in the summer, while the latter released their debut album The Curse of The Higsons which included an irreverent uptempo version of Andy Williams's 'Music to Watch Girls By'. Frontman Charlie Higson would go on to star in the mid-90s comedy sketch show, The Fast Show.

[34] Two members had been in the equally wonderfully named Attempted Moustache.

[35] LeicestershireLaLaLa.com

[36] With Andy Lyons of the football fanzine When Saturday Comes.

[37] The earlier, more successful version of Flying Lizards had included David Toop and Steve Beresford. The three were also in a group called General Strike, releasing their only album (and originally only on cassette), Danger in Paradise, in 1984 on the nascent Touch label.

[38] A more appropriate label might have been Crépuscule or 4AD, and Crawley did end up playing on the latter's This Mortal Coil album, Blood, in 1991.

[39] Caroline Crawley died in 2016.
[40] Clark could best be described as 'European'.
[41] Zephaniah was actually born in Birmingham.
[42] To be accurate, the Mayfair nights were called The Slammer – an Artotheque. He would re-boot Cabaret Futura in 2010 at The Paradise in Kensal Rise.
[43] Hermine Demoriane was French but had been a London-based bohemian since the mid-60s, including writing for International Times, a tightrope walker, performance artist with pre-Throbbing Gristle COUM, actor (as Chaos) in Derek Jarman's *Jubilee*, playwright, even supported Einstürzende Neubaten, and that's only the half of it. After a few singles and EPs, she finally released a full solo album of skewed torch songs, *Lonely at the Top* in 1984.
[44] Louisa Buck, *The Neo Naturists: A Continuing Story*, catalogue essay for the exhibition The Neo Naturists, 8 July – 28 August 2016, at Studio Voltaire, London.

Chapter 18: How to Destroy Angels
[1] Alexei Monroe, The Quietus, 3 October 2017.
[2] Charles Neal *Tape Delay* p.35.
[3] The Guardian, 7 April 2009.
[4] Peter Christopherson in *Tape Delay* p.125.
[5] Graeme Revell talking to David Tibet, Sounds, 17 March 1984.
[6] The second word was usually truncated.
[7] Comedian Vic Reeves was an early member, playing in their debut concert. Co-founder Angus Farquhar went onto form the arts organization NVA at the end of the 90s who have gone on to produce astonishing, large-scale, site-specific arts events.
[8] David Tibet, Sounds, 18 February 1984.
[9] Up to 1984 this included Foetus Under Glass, You've Got Foetus On Your Breath, Foetus Over Frisco, and Philip And His Foetus Vibrations.
[10] Thirty odd years later Dave Henderson revisited the scene with the 4CD box set, *Close to the Noise Floor: Formative UK Electronica 1975-1984* (which also included this author's group, MFH – the only mention permitted in this book, safe in the knowledge that very few people read the endnotes). The most comprehensive curator of the cassette scene, however, has been Vinyl In Demand (VOD), run by Frank Meier in Germany.
[11] It's worth noting that in most of the developing world was the sole means of listening to music.
[12] The winner of the most obscure album title to feature in these pages is a reference to Swedish authors Vilhelm Carlhiem-Gyllensköld, Gustaf Af Geijerstam and Viktor Rydberg, all contemporaries of August Strindberg, and is taken from Strindberg's book *From an Occult Diary*.
[13] There were also two split releases with Current 93: a compilation cassette, *Nylon Coverin' Body Smotherin'* and a 7-inch single 'No Hiding From The Blackbird' / 'The Burial Of The Sardine'.
[14] Sleeves by all these groups, and most others falling under the industrial tag, were printed in black and white out of financial necessity.

Chapter 19: Smooth Operators
[1] The Guardian, 25 February 1984.
[2] Source lost in the mists of time.
[3] Much later Pigalle released a very interesting 10-minute, biographical video of this period – existential and laden with ennui: https://www.youtube.com/watch?v=hifsoLUDN-o
[4] The Quietus, 22 May 2013 – and they *were* being ironic.
[5] Sade Adu, Black Echoes, date unknown p.6.
[6] Tracey Thorn on Desert Island Discs, BBC Radio Four, 18 Nov 2018.
[7] Tracey Thorn *Bedsit Disco Queen* p.125.
[8] The pub was well known for early gigs by Madness, Blur and Amy Winehouse.
[9] Opening in 1969, the basement venue on Dean Street in Soho has played host to countless artists ranging from Buddy Tate and Benny Carter to Jamie Cullum and Amy Winehouse.
[10] They did, however, inspire another large ensemble, Jazz Warriors, formed in 1986 by

Courtney Pine, Gary Crosby and others.

[11] Mole Jazz, Ray's Jazz, and Dobell's and a jazz-only branch of Honest John's. Mole Jazz also had a slightly bigger shop in King's Cross.

[12] An extraordinary hour of the day to run a club. Some dancers apparently lost their jobs bunking off work to attend.

[13] Seymour Nurse, IDJ dancer, from an interview with Mark 'Snowboy' Cotgrove, in *From Jazz Funk & Fusion to Acid Jazz*, p.260.

Ⓢ Photo of Gilles Peterson by, and courtesy of, David Corio.

[14] *From Jazz Funk & Fusion to Acid Jazz*, p.231.

[15] Kerrso, in *From Jazz Funk & Fusion to Acid Jazz*, p.79.

[16] She played her first gig as Eighth Wonder in November 1984.

[17] The parallels with Francis Ford Coppola's similarly stylized & financially disastrous musical, *One From the Heart*, a few years earlier, did not pass unnoticed.

[18] Mark Webster in The Wire, November 1984, p.22.

[19] *From Jazz Funk & Fusion to Acid Jazz*, p.202.

[20] *From Jazz Funk & Fusion to Acid Jazz*, p.202.

Chapter 20: Chasing the Breeze

[1] Lloyd Bradley *Sounds Like London,* p.207.

[2] Lloyd Bradley *Bass Culture*, p.501.

[3] Rod Temperton, The Guardian, 7 July 2011. Temperton was of course white.

[4] Who in turn were influenced by the West African scene, particularly Sierra Leonian producer Akie Deen, his London Years from 1977-82 spurning various disco calypso hits like Bunny Mack's 'Let Me Love You' (Record of the Year in several African countries).

[5] The word 'disco' was still in regular use in Britain in the early 80s, both as a venue (before reverting to 'nightclub') and as a genre (Black Echoes music paper's Soul/Disco chart continued as late as January 1984).

[6] Not all ska revival bands were mixed race: London-bands Madness and Bad Manners, for example, were all white.

[7] The title came from some local graffiti: "Geffery Morgan...loves white girls".

[8] Grant was born in Guyana but moved to London in 1960, aged 12.

[9] Sly Dunbar, in Lloyd Bradley *Bass Culture*, p.513.

[10] Music Week, 28 July 1984, p.37.

[11] Misty In Roots, Papa Levi, Eek-A Mouse and Wailing Souls all did Peel Sessions in 1984.

[12] DJ Smokey Joe, JFM, quoted in Stephen Hebditch *London's Pirate Pioneers* p.185/6.

[13] There was a major sound system scene in Huddersfield, documented in Paul Huxtable and Al Fingers' *Sound System Culture: Celebrating Huddersfield's Sound Systems*.

[14] Recordings of sound systems usually ended up on cassette, if released at all.

[15] John Masouri: https://www.vice.com/en_uk/article/zng9y8/british-sound-system-culture-092

[16] Jazzie B in conversation with Lloyd Bradley in the latter's Sounds Like London p.303.

[17] Famously, Thatcher never believed in the concept of society, but she probably bought the capitalist benefits of the equally nebulous 'lifestyle'.

[18] The Guardian, 7 July 2011.

[19] The UK's weekly reggae music paper, Black Echoes, were rather more accommodating.

[20] Tony Wilson, in John Robb *The North Will Rose Again*, p.123. Sadly King's career revival stalled and he died of a brain haemorrhage in the mid-90s, aged 56.

[21] Elana Harris, Carrol Thompson and Desi Campbell.

Chapter 21: It Says Here

[1] Foreword to *The Best of Smash Hits*.

[2] *Performing Rites: On the Value of Popular Music* p.4.

[3] Another, The Hit, launched in 1985, lasted just nine weeks.

[4] Eric Clapton, for one, noticed the difference. "All during Cream, I was riding high on the 'Clapton is God' myth. [Rolling Stone] ran an interview with us in which we were really praising ourselves, and it was followed by a review that said how boring and repetitious our performance

had been. And it was true! I immediately decided that that was the end of the band." (Paul Gorman *In Their Own Write* p.52).

[5] Patti Smith *Just Kids*, p.178.

[6] Tony Parsons, quoted in Pat Long *The History of the NME* p.104.

[7] As told to Paul Gorman *In Their Own Write* p.190.

[8] For gossip fans, Harron had dated Tony Blair at Oxford, possibly during the time when he was in Ugly Rumours; another music journalist, Mark Ellen, was also in the band.

[9] They were read by a lot more though. A 1984 TGI Readership Survey found that for 15-24 year-old males, Sounds was read by 437,000, NME 397,000 and Melody Maker 302,000 . Source: Music Week.

[10] Ian Penman, NME, 17 Jan 1981.

[11] Also quoted in Pat Long *The History of the NME*, p.170.

[12] As above p.149.

[13] Smash Hits feature, 22 Nov – 5 Dec 1984, p.4.

[14] Foreword to Smash Hits Yearbook.

[15] The last two's real names being Beverly Glick and Gill Smith.

[16] Pat Long *The History of the NME* p.153.

[17] Both would later work for the British Council (albeit briefly in the case of Snow), alongside this author.

[18] NME, 7 April 1984.

[19] Pat Long *The History of the NME* p.153-154.

[20] *The Rock Yearbook Volume VI* p.127.

[21] Wherefore art thou Colourtime, Cocktail Party, Keytones, Dance On Dance and Curious Dream?

[22] Both were helmed by Rob Deacon who, in 1984, was editing a fanzine called Abstract. Its fourth issue would be combined with Third Mind Records' *Life At The Top* compilation, after which Deacon set up his own record label, Sweatbox. For two final issues, Abstract fanzine was accompanied by Sweatbox compilations before Deacon decided to concentrate on the label alone, releasing albums by Meat Beat Manifesto, In The Nursery and The Anti Group amongst others.

[23] A weighty compendium, *The City is Ablaze! 1984-94,* was published in 2012.

[24] Fletcher was also founding member of Apocalypse whose first single, incongruously called 'Teddy', was produced by Paul Weller. They split up in 1984.

[25] Another, New Sounds New Styles, was launched by Emap in July 1981 but it only lasted a year.

[26] A good example being the 1984 story of Andrew Ridgeley's heavily bandaged nose being the result of an ice-bucket fracas with his mate David Austin at Stringfellow's, rather than the nose job he'd been planning for some time.

Chapter 22: Monsters of Rock

[1] www.azquotes.com/quote/1441094

[2] www.quotefancy.com/quote/1146604/

[3] Teenage boys doing their growing up in all-male bands were prone to a particular outlook, as the feminist activist Barbara Ehrenreich wrote: "For young men maturing in a patriarchal world where men dominate the 'real' world while women raise kids, growing up means growing away from women'. (*The Worst Years of Our Lives* 1990). That said, sexism wasn't just confined to metal. There's a lot in rap of course, country music, take your pick.

[4] There were casualties. Towards the end of 1984, Hanoi Rocks' drummer Nicholas Dingley (aka Razzle) was killed in a drink-fuelled car crash, driven by Vince Neil of Mötley Crüe.

[5] It was released as a huge-selling single in 1985.

[6] Geezer Butler interview in www.classicrockrevisited.com, 29 August 2006.

[7] Numerous sources.

[8] Saxon (1980), More (1981), Saxon again (1982), Diamond Head (1983). Even Def Leppard and Iron Maiden didn't play there until 1986 and1988 respectively.

[9] He would go on to direct *When Harry Met Sally* and *A Few Good Men.*

[10] Guest married actress Jamie Lee Curtis that year.
[11] Tracey Thorn *Bedsit Disco Queen* p.198.
🌀 Photos of Spinal Tap by, and courtesy of, David Corio.
[12] Giorgio Moroder would release a restored version of the film that same year.
[13] Stuart Maconie *Cider with Roadies* p.174.

Chapter 23: Art for Art's Sake
[1] www.flavorwire.com/608756/kate-bush-on-creativity-the-role-of-the-artist-quotes
[2] Originally from an interview, Do Gentlemen Still Take Polaroids?, The Guardian, March 2012, but tweaked by Sylvian, and sent to me via Yuka Fujii.
[3] This author's favourite album of 1982.
[4] William Gregory was also working with Tears For Fears, but in another 15 years' time would go on to form Goldfrapp.
[5] He had already released music for *Das Kabinet* and *La Belle et la Bête* for The Yorkshire Actors Company. In fact, the YAC joined him on two British tours in 1981 and 1983 called The Invisibility Exhibition, combining theatre, Jean Cocteau films, Richard Jobson's spoken poetry, the cabaret of Frank Chickens and an instrumental set from Bill Nelson himself, the backing tracks and incidental music of which comprised one of the records in the box set.
[6] 'There's one group I was quoted as saying is the best in the world, which is a bit premature because I've never heard them. Somebody described to me what they do, and it sounds really interesting, so I *think* I'm going to like them. The group's called Man Jumping'. Brian Eno in Spin magazine, September 1985.
[7] Twenty-five years later, one of them, John Lunn, would be responsible for the earworm music of Downton Abbey.
[8] Courtesy of Yuka Fujii, his girlfriend at the time, who had a huge collection.
[9] 1984 also saw Jansen and Barbieri record their first album, *Worlds in a Small Room,* in Tokyo in November, released in Japan the following year, although not in the UK until 1986.
🌀 Photo of David Sylvian by, and courtesy of, Yuka Fujii.
[10] For completists: the two films were for the Japanese market, although *Steel Cathedrals* got a limited release in the UK at the end of 1985. Sylvian worked on the score with other musicians back in London, and over the course of 1985 some of it resurfaced on the limited-edition cassette *An Index of Possibilities* followed by the more readily available EP *Words with the Shaman,* both on Virgin.
[11] Source lost.
[12] Interestingly, back in 1981 Mick Karn and then-girlfriend Yuka Fujii ran a short-lived eaterie within Bloomsbury's October Gallery called Penguin Café.
[13] The German music show was called (fittingly) Bananas, the Dutch show Top Pop.
[14] Rob Jovanovic *Kate Bush: The Biography* p.161.
[15] In 1984 Gabriel was still living and recording at his Ashcombe House home in Bath, but the following year he bought Box Mill which would become his long-term home and sprawling Real World studio complex.
[16] Startled Insects co-wrote two tracks on Massive Attack's second album, *Protection*, and much of the album was recorded at their studio in Redland, Bristol.
[17] Debut magazine, issue 2, p.18.
[18] Mojo 55, June 1998.
[19] Dave Segal, The Wire. I am also a regular listener, especially when writing, although it's more *absorbed* than listened to. It's one-hour duration feels more like five minutes. I've probably played it some 500 times.
[20] Oldfield had a busy 1984, releasing two albums: *Discovery* and the soundtrack to *The Killing Fields,* surprisingly his only full film score.
[21] John Themis, Tim Cross and Tom Newman – the last two Mike Oldfield cohorts.
[22] Her father Edwin Astley composed music for film and TV (including 60s cult series like Dangerman, The Saint and Department S), her older sister Karen married Pete Townsend, and her brother Jon is a record producer.
[23] Sema was an association of artists in the early 20th Century including Paul Klee, Egon Schiele

and others.

[24] Nyman had written about the American minimalists in his influential book *Experimental Music: Cage and Beyond* (1974).

[25] As told to John Gill in One Two Testing, October 1984, p.69.

[26] Regular Music waited six years to release their eponymous debut on Rough Trade in early 1985, while The Lost Jockey issued an LP, EP and cassette between 1982-83, difficult to find then, near enough impossible now. Shockingly, at time of writing, none of their early 80s music has been reissued on CD.

[27] From sleeve notes to *Andrew Poppy on Zang Tuum Tumb*, 2005.

[28] An interesting aspect of post-punk's antipathy towards prog, and Yes in particular, was the fact that The Slits' Ari Up's godfather was Jon Anderson, PiL's Keith Levene roadied for Steve Howe, and John Lydon's hero was Peter Hammill of Van Der Graff Generator.

[29] Broken China interview by M. Blake, August 1996.

[30] Mason finished 36th at that year's Le Mans.

[31] By Patrick Woodruffe, second only to Roger Dean in creating prog fantasy landscapes.

[32] Paul Stump *The Music's All That Matters: A History of Progressive Rock* p.277.

Chapter 24: Born in the USA

[1] http://www.rollingstone.com/music/lists/100-best-singles-of-1984-pops-greatest-year-20140917

[2] As above.

[3] So massive, that the year saw only five albums occupy the Billboard #1 spot: *Thriller* for 15 weeks, *Footloose* for ten, Huey Lewis and the News's *Sports* for one, *Born in the USA* for four and *Purple Rain* for a staggering 22.

[4] Even, famously, Human League in 1986.

[5] The low-budget *A Certain Sacrifice* was filmed in 1980, released in 1985.

[6] Actually, Nash The Slash, whose stage act had him cocooned in bandages, had been weird for a few years.

[7] 'I Need a Beat' by the 16-year-old LL Cool J (Ladies Love Cool James) was the label's first official release in early 1984.

[8] The single was actually attributed to Malcolm X himself.

[9] Spearheaded by Gloria Estefan and Miami Sound Machine's first English-language album, *Eyes of Innocence* and global hit 'Dr Beat' (both 1984). The same year, Sheena Easton went the other way with her album, *Todo Me Recuerda a Ti*, sung totally in Spanish and geared for the Latin market.

Chapter 25: Big Black Flag

[1] A line from their song, 'History Lesson Part II'.

[2] Michael Azarrad *Our Band Could Be Your Life* p.45.

[3] Guitarist Peter Buck was particularly dismissive of the Second British Invasion and irritated by the British media comparing R.E.M. with The Smiths.

[4] Tony Fletcher *Remarks Remade: The Story of R.E.M.* p.113.

[5] As above, p.116.

[6] Bob Mould quoted in *Our Band Could Be Your Life* p.195.

[7] 'Lighting of the Torch' and 'Closing'.

[8] Chuck Warner ran alternative mail-order and reissue label Hyped2Death. The quote is from Alex Ogg *Independence Days* p.488.

Chapter 26: Foreign Affairs

[1] From their single, 'Down Under'.

[2] Anthony Lane, The New Yorker, 28 June 2010.

[3] First line of Ryuichi Sakamoto's 'Steppin' Into Asia', written with Akiko Yano, from *Illustrated Musical Encyclopedia*, 1986.

[4] Nena's 99 'Red Balloons' and Alphaville's 'Big in Japan' were the only artists, both German, to break into the Top 10.

[5] Initially, for six months, called Nick Cave and the Cavemen

[6] Including The Moodists, The Triffids, Tactics, Severed Heads, Whirlywirld, Great White Noise, Upside Down House, Other Voices, Samurai Trash, The Clean, No Sweat Nights, Bring Philip, Sunday Painters and I'm Spartacus.

[7] Gavin Sawford, Rave Magazine, 12 April 1996, p.7–8.

[8] Midnight Oil frontman Peter Garrett also made his first, unsuccessful attempt to enter politics in December 1984, succeeding 20 years later when he was elected as an Australian Labor Party candidate to the House of Representatives.

[9] David Nichols *Dig: Australian Rock and Pop Music 1960-85* p.416.

[10] And Canadian, Australian and New Zealand.

[11] Prior to the 80s there had been a few exceptions: Jane Birkin & Serge Gainsbourg's 'Je t'Aime (Moi Non Plus)' (1969), Plastic Bertrand's 'Ça Plane Pour Moi' (1978) and a few others.

[12] Magne Furuholmen, interviewed in *Mad World* p.222.

[13] *The Living Daylights* in 1987.

[14] One of the more obscure recommendations arising from this book is *Maskindans: Norsk Synth 1980-1988* - a lovingly compiled 41-track, double CD of Norwegian synth esoterica.

[15] "Perhaps the most unconvincing anti-drug song of all time" (Rolling Stone, 100 Best Singles of 1984).

[16] Björk, Einar and others had already released records in previous bands (in fact Björk had recorded her first album aged 11) but they were only available in Iceland.

[17] There was a slight change of name from 1992: they got rid of the definite article.

[18] It also hit #2 in the US Billboard charts, interestingly in its original German-language version.

[19] Their sole UK success was the dire 'Brother Louis' which peaked at #4 in 1986.

[20] Interview with Neil McCormick, Daily Telegraph, 15 October 2012.

[21] Mick Sinclair, NME.

[22] To be strictly accurate, the event was billed as Concerto for Voice and Machinery, and not a concert by Einstürzende Neubauten.

[23] It wasn't included on the soundtrack album, however.

[24] It has since been re-released under its original name.

[25] Dinger's attempt to release a fourth La Düsseldorf album in the mid-80s without his brother and Hans Lampe was one of many arguments that kept Düsseldorf's lawyers busy. In the end the album, *Néondian,* came out under the name Klaus Dinger + Rhenita Bella Düsseldorf", but it sank without trace.

[26] Although not by all; for what it's worth, this author gave it 5 stars in Sounds at the time.

[27] And, at time of writing, was the last French-language song to chart in the UK.

[28] Telex's Dan Lacksman would go on to produce Deep Forest's hugely successful debut album in 1992.

[29] Possibly the most brilliant / excruciating piece of theatre I have ever seen, at the Royal Albert Hall in early 1986.

[30] This was her second stint in London; as a 19-year-old she had been an au-pair for Rick Wakeman's family.

[31] Anna Domino returned the compliment by singing on Luc Van Acker's sophomore album, *The Ship* (1984).

[32] Thereafter her releases were intermittent and none were as Anna Domino.

[33] It would release 35 volumes by 1995 at which stage it took a rest, but has recently been reactivated.

[34] Two Brits, Peter Barakan and Chris Mosdell, who'd moved to Tokyo in the mid-70s ended up (separately) writing English lyrics for a number of YMO releases, while Robin Scott of M and David Sylvian of Japan both released co-written singles with Ryuichi Sakamoto in the early 80s.

[35] Dolby not only co-wrote their joint single, 'Field Work', but also directed the video.

[36] Paris was as big a draw as London to Japanese musicians, especially another Hosono-produced band, Pizzicato Five who were the nearest thing to Mikado in Japan.

[37] Both Sandii and the Sunsetz and Ippu-Do played a part in Japan's final tour, the former as support band, the latter's frontman, Masami Tsuchiya, temporarily joining the ranks of the main act. Like YMO, Ippu-Do, bowed out with a live album: 1984's *Live and Zen*, featuring Steve

Jansen, Richard Barbieri and Percy Jones.

Chapter 27: Band Aid
[1] Allan Jones, Melody Maker, 8 December 1984.
[2] Interview with Simon Garfield in Time Out, 13 March 1985.
꧁ Photo of Band Aid lineup from www.shapersofthe80s.com
꧁ Photo of Bob Geldof and Midge Ure from The Quietus, A World Of Dreaded Fear: Revisiting Band Aid's Lyrical Crime Scene, 10 Dec 2013
[3] Including King Sunny Ade, Hugh Masekela, Salif Keita, Manu Dibango, Youssou N'Dour, Mory Kante and many others.
[4] Sade was there of course, and Billy Ocean played in Philadelphia.
[5] A.V.Club http://www.avclub.com/article/we-care-a-lot-14-overblown-charityadvocacy-songs-b-2217
[6] Amnesty International London office had worked with musicians as far back as the late 70s, as part of the Secret Policeman's Ball comedy events. It was at The Secret Policeman's Other Ball in 1981 that Bob Geldof and Midge Ure first appeared on stage together, along with Sting, Phil Collins, Eric Clapton and others. Although not directly linked, Working Week's debut single in June 1984, 'Venceremos – We Will Win', about the 'missing' people of Chile, was very much in keeping with the aims of Amnesty.
[7] Midge Ure If I Was p.1.

Chapter 28: Epilogue
[1] Dylan Jones The Eighties: One Day, One Decade p.187.
[2] ICON, issue 404, 2007.
[3] Talking to Mick Sinclair, Zigzag autumn 1984.
[4] Joe Carducci Rock and the Pop Narcotic 1991.
[5] Tony Fletcher Remarks Remade – The Story of R.E.M. p.114.
[6] Simon Frith Music for Pleasure p.166
[7] Bill Drummond quoted in Richard King How Soon Is Now p.229/230.
[8] Sam Knee www.blastedjournal.co.uk 30 September 2013.
[9] Sam Knee The Bag I'm In p.9.
[10] Dylan Jones as above p.187.
[11] Nick Heyward, Melody Maker, 27 April 1996.
[12] Adam Ant, Louder Than War 26 August 2011. Retrieved 18 March 2013.
[13] AW Turner Rejoice! Rejoice! Britain in the 1980s p.249/250.
[14] David Hepworth Uncommon People p.248.
[15] Paul Morley talking to Simon Reynolds in the latter's Totally Wired p.335.
[16] Robert Elms The Way We Wore p.265.

Timeline and Charts

Timeline

January
5 – Top Of The Pops 20th anniversary show compered by John Peel and David Jensen.
10 – Soft Cell play the Hammersmith Palais, their final concert before splitting in March.
11 – Mike Read decides he won't be playing Frankie Goes to Hollywood's 'Relax' any more. Two days later the BBC bans it from being played on radio or television.
13 – New series of Whistle Test begins, featuring It's Immaterial, The Truth, Ian Gillan and Julien Temple. And the same evening you can watch The Tube (with Marc and the Mambas, Cocteau Twins) and ORS 84 (Simple Minds, Michael Clark).
16 – The UK's first cable TV station, Sky Channel, begins operation in Swindon.
21 – Jackie Wilson passes away after lengthy coma, aged 49.
24 – Apple Computer launches the Macintosh personal computer in the US.
25 – The Government announces that all personnel employed at GCHQ in Cheltenham renounce Trade Union membership. Under duress, most agree.
27 – While Madonna makes her UK televised debut at the Hacienda in Manchester, Michael Jackson's hair catches fire during the filming of a Pepsi commercial in LA.
28 – *Now That's What I Call Music 1* is replaced at #1 by Michael Jackson's yo-yoing *Thriller*.
+ Island Records and Stiff Records merge; Altered Images split up; Terry Hall unveils his new group, The Colour Field.

February
4 – Nena's '99 Red Balloons' tops the UK charts (the fourth German act ever to do so) while Culture Club's 'Karma Chameleon' tops the US charts.
10 – The Clash begin first British tour in two years.
14 – Elton John marries German sound engineer Renate Blauel, and Torvill & Dean win Winter Olympic gold skate-dancing to five minutes of *Bolero.*
20 – The Smiths' debut album released on Rough Trade.
21 – BRIT Awards held in London. Amongst other categories, Best British Group was won by Culture Club, British Male Solo Artist by David Bowie, British Female Solo Artist by Annie Lennox.
24 – The new-look/new-sound Scritti Politti release 'Wood Beez' single.
26 – The satirical puppet show, Spitting Image, makes its debut on ITV.
28 – Michael Jackson and *Thriller* scoop most of the awards at the Grammys. The Police win Best Song ('Every Breath You Take'), Culture Club are voted Best New Artist, and Duran Duran win Best Video ('Girls On Film' / 'Hungry Like the Wolf').

March
2 – *This is Spinal Tap* film released.
4 – The Police play their last concert (in Melbourne, Australia) before splitting up.
6 – The year-long miners' strike action begins.
12 – Release of *Swoon,* debut album by Prefab Sprout.
16 – Style Council's *Café Bleu* is released.
17 – Half of the US Top 50 singles are by British acts
22 – Andrew Lloyd Webber marries Sarah Brightman
29 – Music Box starts pan-European 24-hour cable and satellite channel from offices in London.
31 – Last ever broadcast of BBC2's Sight and Sound in Concert (Blancmange).
+ Rough Trade moves from its spiritual home in Notting Hill to new offices in Kings Cross.

April

1 – Marvin Gaye is shot dead by his father after a bitter argument, while US music magazine Trouser Press publishes its 96th and final issue.

4 – Bailiffs, backed by police, clear the main women's peace camp at Greenham Common; Government announce plans to reduce the number of job centres from 1,000 to 350.

9 – Pet Shop Boys' original version of 'West End Girls' is released.

15 – Comedian Tommy Cooper dies from a heart attack during a televised performance.

17 – Duran Duran's 5-month *Sing Blue Silver* world tour ends in San Diego; Police Officer Yvonne Fletcher is shot dead outside Libyan Embassy.

23 – US researchers announce their discovery of the AIDS virus.

24 – Talking Heads' *Stop Making Sense* film released.

26 – Count Basie dies.

30 – The Cure's *The Top* released.

+ Roger Waters starts solo career and Mick Jagger starts work on solo album.

May

4 – Echo & The Bunnymen's *Ocean Rain* released; Diana Dors dies of cancer, aged 52.

5 – Jim Kerr and Chrissie Hynde tie the knot, while The Herreys win the 1984 Eurovision Song Contest for Sweden with the song 'Diggi-Loo, Diggi-Ley'.

12 – Billy Graham starts six-week stadium tour of Britain, preaching to over one million people.

14 – Wham! release 'Wake me Up Before You Go-Go', their first UK #1; Mark Zuckerberg is born in White Plains, New York.

19 – Sir John Betjeman, the poet laureate, dies in Cornwall aged 78.

28 – Eric Morecambe dies of a heart attack after a charity show in Tewkesbury.

30 – The Prince of Wales denounces a proposed modernist extension to the National Gallery, London as 'a hideous carbuncle on the face of an elegant and much-loved friend'.

+ Madness leave Stiff Records and set up their own label Zarjazz; David Sylvian launches solo career with 'Red Guitar' single; Robert Smith leaves Siouxsie and the Banshees to concentrate on The Cure.

June

2 – NME journalists begin nine-week strike; a fortnight later Melody Maker writers also down pens.

3 – Ronald Reagan visits his ancestral home in Ballyporeen, Ireland.

4 – Bruce Springsteen's *Born in the USA* album released.

8 – Siouxsie and the Banshees' *Hyaena* released.

10 – 'Two Tribes' by Frankie Goes To Hollywood enters the charts at #1, where it would stay for the next nine weeks.

18 – The Battle of Orgreave is fought between police and pickets during the miners' strike.

22 – Maiden Virgin Atlantic flight from Gatwick to Newark, £99 one way.

23 – Duran Duran's 'The Reflex' is top of the US singles charts.

25 – Release of Prince's album, *Purple Rain* and David Sylvian's *Brilliant Trees*.

30 – Elton John plays the Night and Day Concert at Wembley Stadium while Status Quo play Milton Keynes Bowl, their 'last ever concert'.

July

5-8 – Bob Dylan tours UK and Ireland.

7 – Prince's 'When Doves Cry' begins a 5-week stay at the top of the US singles charts; Crass play their last ever concert in Aberdare, Wales.

9 – York Minster set ablaze by lightning strike.

11 – The pound sinks to low of $1.32.

12 – Robert Maxwell buys The Mirror newspaper for £113.4 million.

16 – Sade's debut album *Diamond Life* released.

25 – Pixar releases its first film, the 2-minute animation, *The Adventures of André & Wally B.*

27 – The film *Purple Rain* premieres in the US.

28 – The 1984 Summer Olympics begin in Los Angeles.

+ Frankie's 'Relax', just behind 'Two Tribes' at #2, becomes Britain's then biggest-selling single of the 80s.

August
5 – Actor Richard Burton dies, aged 58.
11 – During a microphone test, President Reagan jokes that he 'will begin bombing Russia in five minutes'.
18 – George Michael's 'Careless Whisper' knocks 'Two Tribes' off the #1 spot.
20 – The Blue Nile release 'Tinseltown in the Rain'.
22 – First mass-produced CDs pressed by Nimbus.
25 – BBC2's Rock Around the Clock 15-hour special.
30 – Space Shuttle *Discovery* takes off on its maiden voyage.
+ Giorgio Moroder releases a newly restored version of Fritz Lang's 1927 film *Metropolis* complete with synth rock soundtrack and colourised palette.

September
4 – Fela Kuti is arrested at Lagos airport for 'illegally attempting to take out £1,600 in foreign currency' and sentenced to five years in jail.
14 – First annual MTV Awards held in New York.
18 – Dizzee Rascal born.
20 – More than 20 people are killed when an Islamic militant suicide driver rams a car with explosives into the US Embassy in Beirut.
21 – North America's first compact disc manufacturing plant opens in Indiana with Bruce Springsteen's *Born in the USA* first off the production line.
22 – John Waite's 'Missing You' tops the US charts.
23 – Post-nuclear TV drama, Threads, screened.
26 – UK & China sign treaty to return Hong Kong to mainland China.
30 – EMI reports a world-wide loss of $5 million during the last six months.

October
1 – The releases of Big Country's *Steeltown* (straight in at #1), U2's *The Unforgettable Fire* and This Mortal Coil's *It'll End in Tears*.
4 – Into the Music replaces John Peel on Thursdays reducing him to three nights a week; unemployment figures reach record 3.28m (13.6% of workforce).
9 – Thomas the Tank Engine and Friends makes its debut on ITV, narrated by Ringo Starr.
12 – The IRA attempts to assassinate Margaret Thatcher and her Cabinet in the Brighton Grand Hotel bombing.
14 – The film *Nineteen Eighty-Four* premieres in London.
15 – Release of debut albums by The Pogues and Bronski Beat.
23 – Andy Kershaw debuts as a presenter on Whistle Test, reporting from Monsters of Rock Festival, Castle Donnington, while on BBC News Michael Buerck presents a shocking report of the famine in Ethiopia.
25 – Katy Perry born.
29 – Frankie Goes To Hollywood's *Welcome To The Pleasuredome* album released.
31 – Indira Gandhi assassinated by her own bodyguards.
+ Major series of raids on London's pirate radio stations.

November
1 – Cocteau Twins' *Treasure* released.
3 – Billy Ocean's 'Caribbean Queen' top the US singles charts.
6 – Ronald Reagan wins a second term in office as US President, while Malcolm Morley wins the first Turner Prize.
8 – Two separate car crashes kill American musicians Nicholas 'Razzle' Dingley of Hanoi Rocks (in Los Angeles) and Colin Walcott (in East Germany).
12 – Madonna's *Like A Virgin* album released.
17 – Wham!'s 'Wake Me Up Before You Go-Go' hits #1 in the US and will stay there for three weeks.

20 – British Telecom shares go on sale, in an instant doubling the total number of share owners in UK.
25 – Band Aid's 'Do They Know It's Christmas?' is recorded at Sarm West Studios in west London.
28 – UK premiere at Liverpool's Odeon Cinema of Paul McCartney's *Give My Regards to Broad Street* flops. It flops critically and commercially.
+ Pinnacle, one of Britain's leading independent distributors, goes bust.

December
2 – One of London's longest-running pub venues, The Hope and Anchor, closes.
3 – Gas leak from American Union Carbide factory in Bhopal, India kills over 2,000.
8 – Frankie Goes To Hollywood top the UK chats with 'The Power Of Love'. They are the first group since Gerry and the Pacemakers (in 1963) to hit #1 with their first three singles.
11 – Bucks Fizz's tour bus crashes in Newcastle resulting in all four members sustaining injuries, Mike Nolan seriously.
16 – Margaret Thatcher meets rising Politburo star Mikhail Gorbachev at Chequers: 'I like Mr Gorbachev. We can do business together'.
22 – 'Like a Virgin' is Madonna's first US #1. TV's The Young Ones' Neil plays a one-off show at Hammersmith Odeon.
28 – Duran Duran and Spandau Ballet compete in the last episode of BBC1's Pop Quiz. Duran Duran won.
31 – Def Leppard's Rick Allen loses his arm in a car crash near Sheffield.

1984's best-selling British albums

1. Wham! *Make It Big*
2. Sade *Diamond Life*
3. FGTH *Welcome to the Pleasuredome*
4. Thompson Twins *Into the Gap*
5. Queen *The Works*
6. Alison Moyet *Alf*
7. Howard Jones *Human's Lib*
8. Spandau Ballet *Parade*
9. U2 *The Unforgettable Fire*
10. Duran Duran *Arena*
11. Elton John *Breaking Hearts*
12. Culture Club *Colour by Numbers*
13. The Style Council *Café Bleu*
14. The Smiths *The Smiths*
15. Big Country *The Crossing*
16. Nik Kershaw *The Riddle*
17. David Bowie *Tonight*
18. UB40 *Labour of Love*
19. Simple Minds *Sparkle in the Rain*
20. Bronski Beat *The Age of Consent*

NB: excluding compilations
Source: Music Week, 26 January 1985

Author's counter-list

1. David Sylvian *Brilliant Trees*
2. Cocteau Twins *Treasure*
3. Depeche Mode *Some Great Reward*
4. This Mortal Coil *It'll End in Tears*
5. The Blue Nile *A Walk Across the Rooftops*
6. Bill Nelson *Trial by Intimacy*
7. Man Jumping *Jumpcut*
8. Sheila Chandra *Quiet!*
9. Thomas Dolby *The Flat Earth*
10. Shriekback *Jam Science*
11. Talk Talk *It's My Life*
12. Blancmange *Mange Tout*
13. The Smiths *Hatful of Hollow*
14. Echo & The Bunnymen *Ocean Rain*
15. Penguin Café Orchestra *Broadcasting From Home*
16. Coil *Scatology*
17. Brian Eno & Harold Budd *The Pearl*
18. Nick Cave *From Her to Eternity*
19. Siouxsie & the Banshees *Hyaena*
20. Dead Can Dance *Dead Can Dance*

Music Week's 100 UK acts tipped for 1984

At the beginning of the year, Music Week published a list of '100' (actually there were only 86) would-be achievers, the result of a survey polling radio DJs and producers, critics from the music press and journalists from national and provincial newspapers – acts they had picked up on in 1983 and felt deserved success in the new year.

The Alarm	Ian Elliott	David Knopfler	Winston Reedy
APB	End Games	Annabel Lamb	R.E.M.
The Blood	English Evening	Laughter In The	Yip Yip Coyote
Billy Bragg	Eric Goes Fishing	Garden	Sade
Bourgie Bourgie	Faith Global	Lloyd Cole & The	Second Thoughts
Margaux	Fay Ray	Commotions	Seradine
Buchanan	The Fixx	Lords Of The New	Skafish
Cabaret Voltaire	The Go-Betweens	Church	The Smiths
Care	The Gymslips	Mahon	Spice
Paul Carrack	Paul Haig	Mister Savage	Terraplane
Case	Hanoi Rocks	Modern English	They Must Be
CaVa CaVa	The Higsons	Orange Juice	Russians
Cenet Rox	The Icicle Works	Orchestre Jazira	The Three Johns
Sheila Chandra	Impulse	Pallas	The Touch
The Cheaters	Indians In Moscow	Laura Pallas	Toy Dolls
Chevalier	International	Passion Puppets	Ruby Turner
Brothers	Rescue	Passionate Friends	23 Skidoo
China Crisis	It's Immaterial	Payolas	Unity
Cocteau Twins	Keith James	Jonathan Perkins	John Watts
Jess Cox	Kane Gang	Perfect Crime	Wipe Out
Cruella De Ville	Nik Kershaw	Pogue Mahone	
The Decorators	King	Prefab Sprout	
Thomas Dolby	James King & the	Pulp	
Eddie & Sunshine	Lone Wolves	Chris Rea	
Ellery Bop		Red Guitars	

John Peel's Festive 50

1. The Smiths 'How Soon Is Now'
2. Cocteau Twins 'Pearly Dewdrops Drop'
3. The Men They Couldn't Hang 'Green Fields of France'
4. Cocteau Twins 'Spangle Maker'
5. Mighty Wah! 'Come Back'
6. The Membranes 'Spike Milligan's Tape Recorder'
7. New Order 'Thieves Like Us'
8. The Sisters Of Mercy 'Walk Away'
9. The Fall 'Lay of the Land'
10. The Redskins 'Keep On Keepin' On'
11. Nick Cave & The Bad Seeds 'Saint Huck'
12. New Order 'Lonesome Tonight'
13. Billy Bragg 'Between the Wars'
14. The Smiths 'Nowhere Fast'
15. The Sisters Of Mercy 'Emma'
16. Cocteau Twins 'Ivo'
17. The Smiths 'What Difference Does It Make?'
18. The Fall 'C.R.E.E.P.'
19. Echo & The Bunnymen 'The Killing Moon'
20. New Order 'Murder'
21. This Mortal Coil 'Kangaroo'
22. Cocteau Twins 'Donimo'
23. The Smiths 'William It Was Really Nothing'
24. The Smiths 'Heaven Knows I'm Miserable Now'
25. Frankie Goes To Hollywood 'Two Tribes'
26. Unknown Cases 'Masimbabele'
27. The Very Things 'The Bushes Scream While My Daddy Prunes'

28. The Smiths 'Please Please Please Let Me Get What I Want'
29. Billy Bragg 'The Saturday Boy'
30. The Cult 'Spiritwalker'
31. Propaganda 'Dr Mabuse'
32. Yeah Yeah Noh 'Bias Binding'
33. This Mortal Coil 'Another Day'
34. Berntholer 'My Suitor'
35. Robert Wyatt 'Biko'
36. The Smiths 'Reel Around the Fountain'
37. The Jesus & Mary Chain 'Upside Down'
38. Cocteau Twins 'Pandora'
39. Cocteau Twins 'Beatrix'
40. Flesh For Lulu 'Subterraneans'
41. Special AKA 'Free Nelson Mandela'
42. Frank Chickens 'Blue Canary'
43. New Model Army 'Vengeance'
44. The Fall 'No Bulbs'
45. The Pogues 'Dark Streets of London'
46. Hard Corps 'Dirty'
47. Echo & The Bunnymen 'Thorn of Crowns'
48. Bronski Beat 'Smalltown Boy'
49. Cocteau Twins 'Pepper Tree'
50. Working Week 'Venceremos'

Peel Sessions

John Peel's championing of obscure new bands wasn't just about playing their records – he also invited them to record Peel Sessions at the BBC's Maida Vale studios. There were 122 of them in 1984, ranging from the reasonably well-known to those who vanished without trace. The list below is typical of the range of genres covered: from post-punk to dub, cow-punk to industrial dance. The dates indicate when the sessions were recorded rather than broadcast.

4 Jan	Portion Control	5 June	Eleven
10 Jan	Yip Yip Coyote	6 June	Shoot! Dispute
11 Jan	Play Dead	9 June	Papa Levi
14 Jan	Microdisney	12 June	March Violets
17 Jan	The Pastels	13 June	The Higsons
18 Jan	Bourgie Bourgie	16 June	Eek-A Mouse
21 Jan	3 Mustaphas 3	19 June	The Sisters Of Mercy
24 Jan	Guana Batz	23 June	Pink Peg Slax
25 Jan	In Excelsis	26 June	Marc Riley And The Creepers
28 Jan	Inca Babies	27 June	The Meteors
1 Feb	Onward International	30 June	Die Toten Hosen
2 Feb	Jonathan Perkins	4 July	Men They Couldn't Hang
4 Feb	Shoot! Dispute	7 July	The Damned
7 Feb	Craig Charles	10 July	Big Flame
8 Feb	400 Blows	12 July	Yip Yip Coyote
11 Feb	Hagar The Womb	14 July	The Red Guitars
14 Feb	Papa Face	18 July	Savage Progress
15 Feb	Ivor Cutler	21 July	Joolz
18 Feb	Cook Da Books	24 July	The Screaming Blue Messiahs
21 Feb	Billy Bragg	25 July	Helen And The Horns
22 Feb	Misty In Roots	28 July	Yeah Yeah Noh
25 Feb	Autumn 1904	1 Aug	The Smiths
28 Feb	The Farm	4 Aug	The Sid Presley Experience
29 Feb	The Fire	7 Aug	Champion Doug Veitch
3 March	The High Five	8 Aug	The Icicle Works
6 March	The Shillelagh Sisters	11 Aug	Brilliant Corners
7 March	Shriekback	14 Aug	The Farmer's Boys
10 March	White And Torch	15 Aug	Perfect Vision
14 March	The Frank Chickens	18 Aug	Everything But The Girl
17 March	Ex-Post Facto	21 Aug	Inca Babies

20 March	The Folk Devils	22 Aug	Wah!
21 March	Tools You Can Trust	23 Aug	Floy Joy
22 March	Freeze Frame	25 Aug	Alien Sex Fiend
24 March	Boothill Foot Tappers	29 Aug	Cocteau Twins
27 March	Sebastian's Men	1 Sept	Chinese Gangster Element
28 March	Nick Cave	4 Sept	X Men
31 March	Del Amitri	5 Sept	The Folk Devils
3 April	D.O.A.	8 Sept	Woodentops
4 April	Personal Column	11 Sept	Sudden Sway
7 April	And Also The Trees	15 Sept	Syncbeat
10 April	The Pogues	18 Sept	Billy Bragg
11 April	X-Mal Deutschland	19 Sept	Float Up CP
14 April	Microdisney	22 Sept	Skeletal Family
17 April	Three Johns	25 Sept	Bronski Beat
24 April	Guana Batz	26 Sept	Junior Gee & The Capital Boys
25 April	Pink Industry	30 Sept	Guana Batz
28 April	Come In Tokio	2 Oct	Microdisney
1 May	Working Week	7 Oct	Chakk
2 May	Alien Sex Fiend	14 Oct	Cabaret Voltaire
5 May	Chameleons	21 Oct	The Go-Betweens
9 May	Moodists	23 Oct	The Jesus And Mary Chain
12 May	Gene Loves Jezebel	30 Oct	Wailing Souls
15 May	UT	4 Nov	The Popticians
16 May	Skiff Skats	6 Nov	Triffids
19 May	The Membranes	13 Nov	Eton Crop
22 May	The Gymslips	17 Nov	Partners In Crime
23 May	Die Zwei At The Rodeo	20 Nov	Onward International
26 May	Hard Corps	27 Nov	Tools You Can Trust
29 May	Julian Cope	4 Dec	The Pogues
30 May	Dormannu	11 Dec	The Juggernaughts
2 June	Dead Can Dance	16 Dec	The Persuaders

Bibliography

I am an avid reader of books about music and read widely for the writing of this one. I have compiled this bibliography to give due credit to the authors and publishers, and to encourage the reader to explore further. With this in mind, I've tried to make it more navigable by breaking it up into a baker's dozen sections. Happy reading.

Artist biographies
Brown, Allan. *Nileism: The Strange Course of The Blue Nile* (Polygon) 2010
Buckley, David. *Strange Fascination. David Bowie: the Definitive Story* (Virgin Books) 1999
Easlea, Daryl. *Without Frontiers: The Life and Music of Peter Gabriel* (Omnibus Press) 2013
Fish, M and D Hallbery. *Cabaret Voltaire: the Art of the Sixth Sense* (SAF) 1985
Fish, Mick. *Industrial Evolution: Through the Eighties with Cabaret Voltaire* (SAF) 2002
Neil Fraser. *Long Shadows, High Hopes: The Life and Times of Matt Johnson & The The* (Omnibus 2018)
Richard Houghton. *OMD: Pretending to See the Future* (This Day in Music Books) 2019
Jovanovic, Rob. *Kate Bush: The Biography* (Portrait) 2005
Malins, Steve. *Duran Duran: Wild Boys* (André Deutsch) 2005
Miller, Jonathan. *Stripped: Depeche Mode* (Omnibus Press) 2004
O'Dair, Marcus. *Different Every Time: The Authorised Biography of Robert Wyatt* (Serpents Tail) 2014
Paytress, Mark. *Siouxsie & the Banshees: the Authorised Biography* (Sanctuary) 2003
Power, Martin. *David Sylvian: The Last Romantic* (Omnibus Press) 1998
Reynolds, Anthony. *Japan: A Foreign Place* (Burning Shed) 2015
Reynolds, Anthony. *Cries and Whispers 1983-1991* (Burning Shed) 2018
Rogan, Johnny. *Ray Davies: A Complicated Life* (Bodley Head) 2015
Scoates, Christopher. *Brian Eno: Visual Music* (Chronicle Books) 2013
Sheppard, David. *On Some Faraway Beach: the Life and Times of Brian Eno* (Orion) 2008
Twomey, Chris. *XTC: Chalkhills and Children* (Omnibus Press) 1992

Autobiographies and memoires
Clayton, Ian. *Bringing It All Back Home* (Route) 2007
Cope, Julian. *Repossessed: Shamanic Depressions in Tamworth and London 1983-89* (Thorsons) 1999
Dolby, Thomas. *The Speed of Sound* (Icon) 2017
Drummond, Bill. *45* (Abacus) 2001
Forster, Robert. *Grant & I: Inside and Outside the Go-Betweens* (Omnibus) 2018
Maconie, Stuart. *Cider with Roadies* (Ebury Press) 2004
McGee, Alan. *Creation Stories* (Pan) 2014
Ellen, Mark. *Rock Stars Stole My Life!* (Hodder & Stoughton) 2015
Hyde, Karl. *I Am Dogboy* (Faber and Faber) 2016
Kermode, Mark. *How Does It Feel? A Life of Musical Misadventures* (Weidenfeld & Nicolson) 2018
Radcliffe, Mark. *Thank You for the Days* (Simon & Schuster) 2009
Smith Start, Brix. *The Rise, The Fall and The Rise* (Faber and Faber) 2016
Smith, Giles. *Lost in Music* (Picador) 1995
Smith, Patti. *Just Kids* (Bloomsbury) 2010
Thorn, Tracey. *Bedsit Disco Queen* (Virago) 2013
Midge Ure. *If I Was* (Virgin Books) 2004
Tom Watkins. *Let's Make Lots of Money; My Life as the Biggest Man in Pop* (Virgin) 2017
Wobble, Jah. *Memoirs of a Geezer* (Serpent's Tail) 2009

Genres and pop culture
Azerrad, Michael. *Our Band Could Be Your Life: Scenes from the American Indie Underground 1981-1991* (Back Bay Books) 2001
Beadle, Jeremy J. *Will Pop Eat Itself? Pop Music in the Soundbite Era* (Faber and Faber) 1992
Bracewell, Michael. *England is Mine: Pop Life in Albion from Wilde to Goldie* (Flamingo) 1998
Bradley, Lloyd. *Bass Culture* (Penguin) 2001
Butt, Gavin, Kodwo Eshun and Mark Fisher (eds). *Post Punk Then and Now* (Repeater) 2016
Doggett, Peter. *Electric Shock: From the Gramophone to the iPhone - 125 Years of Pop Music* (Vintage) 2016
Frith, Simon. *Music for Pleasure* (Polity Press) 1988
Frith, Simon. *Performing Rites. On the Value of Popular Music* (Oxford University Press) 1996
Glasper, Ian. *Burning Britain: The History of UK Punk 1980-1984* (Cherry Red Books) 2004
Glasper, Ian. *The Day the Country Died: A History of Anarcho Punk 1980-1984* (Cherry Red Books) 2014
Keenan, David. *England's Hidden Reverse* (SAF) 2003
De Koningh, Michael, and Marc Griffiths. *Tighten Up!: The History of Reggae in the UK* (Sanctuary) 2003
Kureishi, Hanif, and Jon Savage (eds). *The Faber Book of Pop* (Faber and Faber) 1995
Lambe, Stephen. *Citizens of Hope and Glory: The Story of Progressive Pop* (Amberley Publishing) 2013
Milner, Greg. *Perfecting Sound Forever: The Story of Recorded Music* (Granta) 2009
Murphy, Gareth. *Cowboys and Indies* (Serpent's Tail) 2015
Neal, Charles. *Tape Delay* (SAF) 1987
O'Brien, Lucy. *She Bop* (Penguin) 1995
Reynolds, Simon. *Rip It Up and Start Again: Post-Punk 1978-1984* (Faber and Faber) 2005
Reynolds, Simon. *Totally Wired: Post-Punk Interviews and Overviews* (Faber and Faber) 2009
Reynolds, Simon. *Retromania: Pop Culture's Addiction to its Own Past* (Faber and Faber) 2011
Rimmer, Dave. *Like Punk Never Happened: Culture Club and the New Pop* (Faber and Faber) 1985
Robb, John. *Death to Trad Rock* (Cherry Red Books) 2009
Robb, John. *The North Will Rise Again: Manchester Music City (1977-1996)* (Aurum) 2009
Roberts, Chris, and Hywel Livingstone and Emma Baxter-Wright. *Gothic: The Evolution Of A Dark Subculture* (Goodman) 2014
Savage, Jon. *Time Travel. From the Sex Pistols to Nirvana: Pop, Media and Sexuality, 1977-96* (Vintage) 1997
Schaefer, John. *New Sounds: The Virgin Guide to New Music* (Virgin Books) 1990
Shaar Murray, Charles. *Shots from the Hip* (Penguin) 1990
Shapiro, Harry. *Waiting for the Man: The Story of Drugs and Popular Music* (Quartet Books) 1988
Stanley, Bob. *Yeah Yeah Yeah: The Story of Modern Pop* (Faber and Faber) 2013
Stratton, John, and Nabeeel Zuberi (eds). *Black Popular Music in Britain Since 1945* (Ashgate) 2014
Thompson, Dave. *The Dark Reign of Gothic Rock* (Helter Skelter) 2002
Worley, Matthew. *No Future: Punk, Politics and British Youth Culture, 1976-1984* (Cambridge University Press) 2017
Young, Rob. *Electric Eden: Unearthing Britain's Visionary Music* (Faber and Faber) 2011

80s
Brech, Ronald. *Britain 1984: An Experiment in the Economic History of the Future* (Darton, Longman and Todd) 1963
Bromley, Tom. *Wired for Sound: Now That's What I Call an 80s Music Childhood* (Simon & Schuster) 2012

Jones, Dylan. *The Eighties: One Day, One Decade* (Windmill Books) 2014
Laurie, David. *Dare: How Bowie & Kraftwerk Inspired the Death of Rock'n'Roll & Invented Modern Pop Music* (Something In Construction) 2015
Majewski, Lori and Jonathan Bernstein. *Mad World* (Abrams) 2014
Simpson, David, and Richard Callaghan. *1984 / Nineteen Eighty Four* (My World) 2013
Stewart, Graham. *Bang! A History of Britain in the 1980s* (Atlantic Books) 2013
Taylor, Neil. *C86 And All That: The Birth of Indie, 1983-86* (Puncture Publications) 2017
Turner, Alwyn W. *Rejoice! Rejoice! Britain in the 1980s* (Aurum Press) 2010

Dance music
Brewster, Bill, and Frank Broughton. *Last Night a DJ Saved my Life: the History of the DJ* (Headline) 1999
Cotgrove, Mark. *From Jazz Funk & Fusion to Acid Jazz: The History of the UK Jazz Dance Scene* (Chaser Publications) 2009
Harding, Phil. *PWL from the Factory Floor* (Cherry Red Books) 2010)
Haslam, Dave. *Life After Dark: A History of British Nightclubs and Music Venues* (Simon & Schuster) 2015
Hook, Peter. *The Hacienda: How Not to Run a Club* (Pocket Books) 2010
Toop, David. *Rap Attack 2: African Rap to Global Hip Hop* (Serpent's Tail) 1991

Art, design, fashion and photography
Elms, Robert. *The Way We Wore* (Picador) 2005
Frith, Simon, and Howard Horne. *Art Into Pop* (Methuen) 1987
King, Emily (ed.). *Designed by Peter Saville* (Frieze) 2003
Knee, Sam. *A Space Between: Tripping Through the Fashions of UK Indie Music 1980-1988* (Cicada) 2013
Knee, Sam. *The Bag I'm In* (Cicada) 2017
McDermott, Catherine. *Street Style: British Design in the 80s* (Design Council) 1987
Pepper, Terence, and Philip Hoare. *Icons of Pop* (National Portrait Gallery / Booth Clibborn) 1999
Robertson, Matthew. *Factory Records: The Complete Graphic Album* (Thames & Hudson) 2006
Shaughnessy, Adrian, and Julian House. *Sampler: Contemporary Music Graphics* (Laurence King Publishing) 1999
Smith, Graham. *We Can Be Heroes: London Clubland 1976-1984* (Unbound) 2012
Williams, Val. *When We Were Young. Derek Ridgers: Club and Street Portraits 1978-1987* (Photowerks) 2004

Locations
Bailie, Stuart. *Trouble Songs: Music and Conflict in Northern Ireland* (Bloomfield) 2018
Bradley, Lloyd. *Sounds Like London: 100 Years of Black Music in the Capital* (Serpent's Tale) 2013
Chemam, Melissa. *Massive Attack: Out of the Comfort Zone* (Tangent Books / PC Press) 2019
Clayton-Lea, Tony, and Richie Taylor. *Irish Rock: Where It's Come From, Where It's At, Where It's Going To* (Sidgwick & Jackson) 2002
Cohen, Sara. *Rock Culture in Liverpool* (Oxford University Press) 1991
Flowers, Anna, and Vanessa Histon. *Sweet Dreams! 1980s Newcastle* (Tyne Bridge Publishing) 2013
Galloway, Vic. *Rip It Up: The Story of Scottish Pop* National Museums Scotland) 2018
Hill, Dr Susan. *Blerwytirhwng? The Place of Welsh Pop Music* (Ashgate Publishing) 2007
Hogg, Brian. *The History of Scottish Rock and Pop* (Guinness Publishing) 1993
Johnson, Phil. *Straight Outa Bristol* (Hodder and Stoughton) 1996
Keilty, Martin. *Big Noise: The Sound of Scotland* (Black & White Publishing) 2006
Lilleker, Martin. *Beats Working for a Living: Sheffield Popular Music 1973-1984* (Juma) 2005
Miles, Barry. *London Calling: A Countercultural History of London Since 1945* (Atlantic

Books) 2010
Noyer, Paul Du. *Liverpool: Wondrous Place* (Virgin Books) 2002
Prendergast, Mark J. *Irish Rock: Roots, Personalities, Directions* (O'Brien Press) 1987
Reeder, Mark. *B Book: Lust and Sound in West-Berlin 1979-1989* (Edel Books) 2015
Skillen, Paul. *Scouse Pop* (Equinox Publishing) 2018
Smyth, Gerry. *Noisy Island: A Short History of Irish Popular Music* (Cork University Press) 2005
Whitney, Karl. *A Journey Through the Industrial Cities of British Pop* (Weidenfeld and Nicolson) 2019

Music Press
Frith, Mark (ed). *The Best of Smash Hits: the '80s* (Sphere) 2006
Godfrey, John (ed). *A Decade of i-Deas – Compiled and Produced by i-D Magazine* (Penguin) 1990
Gorman, Paul. *In Their Own Write: Adventures in the Music Press* (Sanctuary) 2001
Long, Pat. *The History of the NME* (Portico Books) 2012
The author's collection of cuttings from NME, Sounds, Melody Maker, Record Mirror, Smash Hits, Number One, The Face, i-D, BLITZ, Zigzag, Debut, and numerous fanzines. (Strangely, presciently, although I'd never bought Smash Hits before 1984 or since, I bought every issue during that year and still have them in a couple of well-thumbed binders).

Novels
Amis, Martin. *Money* (Jonathan Cape) 1984
Burgess, Anthony. *1985* (Hutchinson) 1978
Orwell, George. *Nineteen Eighty-four* (Secker & Warburg) 1949
Peace, David. *GB84* (Faber and Faber) 2005

Politics
Aston, Martin. *Breaking Down the Walls of Heartache: How Music Came Out* (Constable) 2016
Beckett, Andy. *Promised You a Miracle – UK 80-82* (Allen Lane) 2015
Cloonan, Martin. *Banned! Censorship of Popular Music in Britain 1967-92* (Arena) 1996
Denselow, Robin. *When the Music's Over: The Story of Political Pop* (Faber and Faber) 1989
Lynskey, Dorian. *33 Revolutions Per Minute: A History of Protest Songs* (Faber and Faber) 2012
Rachel, Daniel. *Walls Come Tumbling Down: The Music and Politics of Rock Against Racism, 2 Tone and Red Wedge* (Picador) 2017

Radio, television and video
Barron, Steve. *Egg n Chips & Billie Jean: A Trip Through the Eighties* (CreateSpace Independent Publishing) 2014
Cavanagh, David. *Good Night and Good Riddance: How Thirty-five Years of John Peel Helped to Shape Modern Life* (Faber and Faber) 2015
Evans, Jeff. *The Story of Rock & Pop on British TV* (Omnibus) 2016
Garner, Ken. *The Peel Sessions* (BBC) 2007
Frith, Simon, Andrew Goodwin and Lawrence Grossberg. *Sound and Vision. The Music Video Reader* (Routledge) 1993
Gittins, Ian. *Top of the Pops: Mishaps, Miming and Music* (BBC) 2007
Hamilton, David. *The Golden Days of Radio One: Hotshots, Big Shots and Potshots* (Ashwater Press) 2017
Heatley, Michael. *John Peel: A Life in Music* (Michael O'Mara Books Limited) 2004
Hebditch, Stephen. *London's Pirate Pioneers: The Illegal Broadcasters who Changed British Radio* (TC Publications) 2015
Humphreys, Patrick, and Steve Blacknell. *Top of the Pops: 50th Anniversary* (BBC) 2014
Inglis, Ian (ed). *Popular Music and Television in Britain* (Routledge) 2010
Mark, Craig, and Rob Tannenbaum. *I Want My MTV* (Penguin) 2011

Simpson, Jeff. *Top of the Pops 1964-2002* (BBC) 2002
Stoller, Tony. *Sounds of Your Life: The History of Independent Radio in the UK* (John Libbey Publishing) 2010

Record labels and industry
Aston, Martin. *Facing the Other Way: The Story of 4AD* (The Friday Project) 2013
Balls, Richard. *Be Stiff: The Stiff Records Story* (Soundcheck Books) 2014
Cartwright, Garth. *Going for a Song: a Chronicle of the UK Record Shop* (Flood Gallery Publishing) 2018
Cavanagh, David. *The Creation Records Story: My Magpie Eyes are Hungry for the Prize* (Virgin Books) 2001
Garfield, Simon. *Expensive Habits: The Dark Side of the Music Industry* (Faber and Faber) 1986
Griffiths, John. *Nimbus. Technology Serving the Arts* (Nimbus / Andrew Deutsch) 1995
Gronow, Pekka, and Ilpo Saunio. *An International History of the Recording Industry* (Cassell) 1998
Heylin, Clinton. *Bootleg! The Rise & Fall of the Secret Recording Industry* (Omnibus) 2003
Jones, Graham. *Last Shop Standing* (Proper) 2009
King, Richard. *How Soon is Now? The Madmen and Mavericks Who Made Independent Music 1975-2005* (Faber and Faber) 2012
Middles, Mick. *Factory: The Story of the Record Label* (Virgin Books, 2009)
Napier-Bell, Simon. *Black Vinyl White Powder* (Ebury Press) 2002
Napier-Bell, Simon. *I'm Coming to Take You to Lunch* (Ebury Press) 2005
Nice, James. *Shadowplayers: The Rise and Fall of Factory Records* (Aurum Press) 2010
Ogg, Alex. *Independence Days: The Story of UK Independent Record Labels* (Cherry Red Books) 2009
Rogan, Johnny. *Starmakers & Svengalis: The History of British Pop Management* (Queen Anne Press) 1988
Salewicz, Chris (ed). *Keep On Running: The Story of Island Records* (Island) 2009
Southern, Terry. *Virgin: A History of Virgin Records* (Virgin Books) 1995
Watkins, Tom. *Let's Make Lots of Money* (Virgin Books) 2016
Young, Rob. *Rough Trade* (Black Dog Publishing) 2006

Reference books
Gambaccini, Paul and Tim Rice and Jonathan Rice. *British Hit Singles (10th Edition)* (Guinness) 1995
BPI Yearbook 1984 (British Phonographic Industry) 1984
BPI Yearbook 1985 (British Phonographic Industry) 1985
The Rock Yearbook 1984 (Virgin) 1983
The Rock Yearbook Volume V (Virgin) 1984
The Rock Yearbook Volume VI (Virgin) 1985

Index of Artists

375

Index of Artists